The Story of the
Great Prince Oribeau

FROM THE SAME AUTHOR

The Discovery of the Austral Continent by a Flying Man
ISBN 978-1-61227-512-3
Posthumous Correspondence (3 vols.) ISBNs 978-61227-513-0; 514-7 & 515-4.
The Four Beauties and the Four Beasts (Ouroucoucou – 2) ISBN 978-1-61227-602-1

The Story of the
Great Prince Oribeau
(The Fay Ouroucoucou – 1)

by
Nicolas Restif de la Bretonne

Translated, annotated and introduced by
Brian Stableford

A Black Coat Press Book

Introduction

Les Veillées du Marais, ou, Histoire du grand Prince Oribeau, Roi de Mommonie, au pays d'Evinland & de la vertueuse Princesse Oribelle, de Lagénie; tirée des anciennes annales Irlandaises, & recemment translatée en français par Nichols Donneraill, du comté de Korke, descendant de l'auteur [Evenings in the Marais; or, The Story of the Great Prince Oribeau, King of Mommonia, in the country of Evinland, and the Virtuous Princess Oribelle of Lagenia; extracted from the ancient annals of Ireland and recently translated into French by Nicholas Donneraill of the County of Cork, descendant of the author], here translated as *The Story of the Great Prince Oribeau*, was first published in four volumes 1785 with a title page advertising that it had been printed in Waterford, capital of Mommonie. It was actually printed in Paris by the Widow Duchesne, and was the work of Nicolas Restif de La Bretonne, who had initially intended to issue it in a series of "posthumous works of N****** [i.e., Nicolas]," which had earlier included *La Découverte australe par un homme volant, ou Le Dédale français* (1781; tr. as *The Discovery of the Austral Continent by a Flying Man; or, The French Dedalus*).

In fact, the full title, as rendered above, makes no sense, and the reference to Nichols Donneraill only appears on the title page of the first volume, being omitted from the other three. That is because, in the text as it is presented, the story is not taken from written annals at all, but narrated, in French, by an Irishman who is temporarily resident in France, having been exiled along with supporters of the descendants of the Stuart King James II, and who relates it to a Parisian bourgeois family. Within that frame, however, there is a second, the primary narrator ostensibly translating an earlier verbal rendering given by an Irish gentleman named Kerry in a tavern on the outskirts of Waterford at an indeterminate time in the past, some four or five generations after the events recorded in the main narrative. To add a further layer of complication, that main narrative has several subsidiary inclusions referring back to even earlier periods of history.

That unusual structural complication reflects and embodies a highly exceptional thesis regarding the nature of the entanglement of history and legend, and particularly with the way in which remembrance of the distant past is routinely "polluted" by elements of the marvelous, whose effect is to transfigure that remembrance into a particular kind of fantasy. The four "layers" of historical perspective featured in the work illustrate a process of evolution by which the imagine past undergoes a progressive transformation, this permitting an attempted analysis of the process by which that happens, and the logic of its occurrence, dissecting the peculiar connection between historical events and *"contes bleus"* [marvelous tales]. To that effect, the story of Prince Oribeau is simultaneously represented as a *conte bleu* in its own right, and as a desupernaturalized story that has been transformed into a *conte bleu* by legend-mongers.

In the quest to understand and explain how and why that transformation has happened, the numerous extraneous interpolations in the patchwork text include three additional *contes bleus*, which, together with the main narrative and two further examples contained in an earlier patchwork text, *Le Nouvel Abeilard* (4 vols., 1778-79), make up a set of six, all featuring the character of "la Fée Ouroucoucou," or, as the name is more often rendered in the present text, the Fay Wrwcwcw. (Following my usual practice I have translated *fée*, which means "enchantress," as "fay," rather than as "fairy," as it is often translated in English texts.) The two earlier stories—to which the present text explicitly directs its readers' attention—extracted from the long and cumbersome work in which they first appeared, are translated in a companion volume to the present one, entitled *The Four Beauties and the Four Beasts*.

The introduction to that companion volume explains that the sequence of the six stories, and the peculiar manner of their publication, illustrates a perceived problem that Restif had in producing *contes bleus* and offering them to an audience in what was supposed by the contemporary intelligentsia to be an Age of Enlightenment. The literature of past eras was, of course, replete with *contes bleus*, but they had always been regarded with some suspicion, as tales perhaps fit to amuse children but not suitable fare for intelligent adults, for whom belief in their fantastic apparatus was impossible. That had not stopped eighteenth-century writers from producing such tales in abundance, but in order to excuse their activity they had usually used the strategy of presenting their fantastic devices as satirical exaggerations requiring sophisticated decoding in order to perceive their intended meaning. Restif was not averse to that—indeed, he could not resist the temptation even in the course of stories that set out with a different agenda— but he felt that it distorted the element of the marvelous that made such stories attractive in the first place, in a fashion that robbed them of their naïve impact.

The other principal apologetic strategy adapted by eighteenth-century writers of *contes bleus* was most famously associated Charles Perrault, who had argued that what came to be known as *contes de fées* [tales of enchantment, but typically translated as "fairy tales"] recycling or modeled on traditional folktales had an important role to play in a supposedly skeptical society, because the marvelous could and ought to function as a "sugar coating" for moralistic apologues that were useful, and perhaps vital, in what he called the *"civilization"* [moral education] of children. The whole point of *Le Nouvel Abeilard* was to enable Restif to attack the educational theory proposed by Jean-Jacques Rousseau in *Émile* (1762), based on that philosopher's assertion that "civilization," in all the meanings of that word, is a bad thing and what education really ought to do is preserve and bring out a supposed innate goodness that the influences of corrupt adult society can only spoil. Vehemently opposed to that way of thinking, Restif's text argued, like Perrault, that the methodical "civilization" of children is, in fact, vitally necessary, and that if *contes bleus* are useful instruments to employ in that process, then their contemporary composition is not merely permissible but something that ought to be encouraged and esteemed.

Restif was, however all too well of the snag contained in that "if." There were plenty of skeptics around who suggested that telling children blatant untruths could only confuse them and promote superstition, and who were prepared to question not merely the moral effect of *contes bleus* but also their moral validity. For that reason, the rhetoric of Restif's *contes bleus* was, from the very outset, remarkably complicated, always battling with the assumed suspicion that they are not what they pretend to be and cannot have the effect that they aspire to have. In the present work, however, Restif not only set out to explain his own argument for the necessity of civilizing children by all possible means, and the roles that *contes bleus* could and ought to play in that process, but went further, in attempting to develop a new kind of *conte bleu* that might, in principal, replace the traditional kind based on the adaptation and imitation of traditional folktales.

In the course of that ambitious project, Restif produced a kind of ultimate version of the nature and narrative role of the fay Ouroucoucou in the main narrative of the present work. Some secondary sources allege that an earlier version of it had been published previously as a supplement to the second edition of Restif's novel *La Confidence nécessaire*, supposedly published in 1779, in which the central character had been called Prince O-Ribo. There is some doubt as to whether that book actually exists, but there is certainly no copy available for consultation; the Bibliothèque Nationale only has the first edition of 1769; no second edition is included in the bibliography of Restif's work compiled by "P. L. Jacob le bibliophile" [Paul Lacroix] in 1875, and the text is not included in the supposedly-definitive collected edition of Restif's works published by Slatkine in the late 1980s. References in other works by Restif, however, and some secondary sources, offer a few details as to the contents of the story of O-Ribo, although the final version contained in *Les Veillées du Marais* obviously underwent a very considerable rewriting, which changed its essential nature completely.

In one of Restif's quasi-autobiographical novels, *Le Paysan perverti* (1775), the central character claims that "I have written a story; it appears to me to be exquisite; there is imagination in it, and the most extraordinary events, indicated by the most fortunate title: *The Noble Deeds of the Very Valiant Prince O-Ribo and the Marvelous Adventures of the More-Than-Virtuous Princess Pucellomanay*." In the alleged second edition of *La Confidence nécessaire*—specifically, in pp. 108-194 of volume II, the pagination implying a length of approximately 15,000 words—Pierre Testud, in *Rétif de la Bretonne et la création littéraire* (1977), claims that the published title is *O-Ribo, or the Horrible Obstacles, Monstrous Adventures and Incredible Labors of the Charming O-Ribo, Prince of fifty villages in the beautiful land of Hibernia, for the amour of the beautiful Princess Pucellomany, etc.*

If the B section of the preface can be trusted, Restif wrote the first version of the story in 1774, but when he decided to transfigure it for use in *Les Veillées du Marais*, which he cannot possibly have done prior of 1784, for reasons made obvious in the text, he had clearly changed his mind, not only about the nature of the story and the label applied to its setting, but also about one of its key characters; although it does feature a Princess Pucellomaneh, she is no longer the object of Oribeau's amour, but plays a very different and much more complicated role.

The three separate *contes bleus* interpolated, among various other intrusions, into the convoluted text of *Les Veillées du Marais*, "Mellusine", "Sireneh" and an item untitled in the portmanteau but referred to elsewhere as "La Fée Ouroucoucou," were almost certainly written considerably earlier than 1785, but underwent some adaptive modifications before being inserted into the narrative of the novel. Among other things, those adaptations relate the genealogy of the fay

Ouroucoucou and her daughter Pucellomaneh to the imaginary history of the story, and to the known history of the world, in a fashion that is as ambitious as it ultimately become ambiguous. The adaptive material also provides, in passing, a detailed account of what Restif would have called the "physics," although everyone else would call it the metaphysics, of Faerie, explaining its location and its contiguity with the perceived world. "Mellusine" and "Sireneh" are both transfigurations of well-known legendary tales, while "La Fée Ouroucoucou" is an allegorical apologue similar to some of those contained in the dream stories written by Louis-Sébastien Mercier, with whom Restif had begun to form a fast and crucial friendship in 1783.

Mercier was clearly one of the principal influences on *Les Veillées du Marais*; one of the large-scale modifications made to the pre-existent story of Prince O-Ribo is the intrusion of a long section in which Oribeau takes an elaborate tour of the city of Waterford in order to see all the horrors that are in dire need of political repair: a tour highly reminiscent of the account of the horrors of contemporary Paris that are seen to have been amended in Mercier's classic visionary account of *L'An deux mille quatre cent quarante* (1771; revised 1786; tr. as *Memoirs of the Year 2500*) and which were currently being presented in the raw in the same author's *Le Tableau de Paris* (1781-88). In Restif's text, that educational tour is embedded in a broader exploration modeled on François Fénelon's *Les Aventures de Télémaque* (1699; revised 1717; tr. as *The Adventures of Telemachus*), one of Restif's favorite books, with Oribeau's tutor O'Barbo playing the role of Mentor.

The third major influence on the text, which facilitated its transformation, was not a book but an event, best detailed in the annotations to the text when the influence in question becomes manifest. The work also has to be seen in the context of the evolving pattern of Restif's published work, specifically with regard to the sequence of utopian tracts he published, beginning with *Le Pornographe* (1769), the content of which is summarized in *Les Veillées du Marais*. He had previously ventured into the realm of utopian fantasy in *La Découverte australe*, and *Les Veillées du Marais* is, among other things, an intermediate text between that novel and his subsequent venture into *roman scientifique*, *Les Posthumes* (first draft written 1887-89; revised 1896; published 1902; tr. as *Posthumous Correspondence*). Like the earlier novel, *Les Veillées du Marais* offers a detailed program for social reform featuring an odd combination of communism and monarchy, which has strong affinities with the similar juxtaposition employed by Mercier. It also has to be borne in mind that *Les Veillées du Marais* was one of a number of novels that Restif deliberately prepared for illicit publication, knowing that he had no chance of getting it past the censor to acquire the requisite royal license for legal publication and distribution (hence the blatant falsehood of the indicated place of publication).

The text has certain stylistic eccentricities that require some preparatory comment, the most obvious of which is its use of letters rather than numbers to differentiate its sections, and its initial attempts to organize the contents of the chapters alphabetically. That structure is not consistent even while it survives—the letter U is not always put in the same place in the sequence, and is sometimes omitted—but it has some odd effects on the compositional strategy, which often had the author searching dictionaries for esoteric terms, especially those beginning with the letter K and X. The keywords do not always translate easily, requiring some improvisation on my part to maintain the pattern without disrupting the meaning too much. The notional "translator" of the original text added a note to the end of the second preliminary section alleging that what he is doing is improvising in French a pattern reproducing one in his fictitious original, and suggests that the Bardic practice followed therein was initially devised by the Egyptians as a mnemonic aid and borrowed by the Hebrews in *Psalm 118* and the *Lamentations of Jeremiah*. He explained there, however, that it would have been impossible to continue it for long within the chapters of the main text, for the same reasons that he found it difficult to maintain, even in the alphabetization of the first words of the chapters, without the aid of some bizarre neologisms.

Because Restif, who worked as a typesetter for some years before embarking on his authorial career, did all his own typesetting, he was free to indulge various eccentricities in the design of his texts, which are more obvious in *Les Veillées du Marais* than any of his other texts. He was a propagandist for simplified spelling, so he frequently replaced double letters with single ones, the diphthong *ph* with *f*, the letter *y* with *i*, hard *c* with *k*, etc.—but he did not do so consistently, and often set the same word in different ways at different points in the text. This causes a particular problem with the transfiguration of Irish place names and the improvised names of characters, which are often rendered in different ways in different places. In keeping with the spirit of the exercise I have not attempted to introduce a perfect uniformity in my rendering of such names, although I have markedly reduced some of the author's more extravagant eccentricities and inconsistencies.

The most troublesome of all the author's typesetting idiosyncrasies is the fact that he uses an identical symbol for the lower case letter *f* and the long *s*. Although it is usually possible to work out from context whether, for instance, "Je fais" is supposed to mean "I do" or "I know," it is not always clear how the symbol is to be translated in words whose spelling he has deliberately altered or, even more awkwardly, in invented proper names. Thus, I really have no idea whether Oribeau spends his childhood in the Mountains of Stefenon or Stesenon, or whether the Fay Wrwcwcw's alleged arch-enemy is Perforimoth the Black or Persorimoth the Black. The difficulty becomes especially frustrating because of the author's enormous fondness for anagrams. The fact that he spells *philosophe* [philosopher] as *filosofe* is slightly disconcerting in itself, but it becomes doubly disconcerting when he renders it anagrammatically as *folifose* in order to suggest that the philosopher in question (himself, in one of several disguised cameo appearances he makes in the course of the text) is considered by his fellows to be something of a crackpot. Problems of this sort are probably not unconnected with the fact that neither *Le Nouvel Abeilard* nor *Les Veillées du Marais* has ever been reprinted in France, except in Slatkine's photographically-reproduced facsimile editions and recent scans of the original text.

I have coped with these problems as best I can, but certainly cannot guarantee that I have correctly discriminated between *f* and *s* in all the place names and anagrams. I would not, of course, have bothered to try had I not considered *Les Veillées du Marais* to be a particularly fascinating work, not only within Restif's oeuvre, but within the context of the evolution of imaginative fiction. Because it is such an awkward patchwork it is, from a purely literary point of view, a complete mess, but precisely because it is such an elaborate and complicated portmanteau text it attempts narrative maneuvers that no other text has every attempted, and although it certainly does not answer all the questions it raises with regard to the propriety and significance of *contes bleus*, it certainly serves to highlight the questions, and to provide abundant food for thought regarding their nature, significance and utility. Its many flaws are the result of overreaching ambition, and the ambition in question, meritorious in itself, was certainly not without its rewards.

This translation was made from the London Library's copy of the 1785 edition, with occasional assistance from the facsimile version of the same edition issued by Slatkine in 1988, reproduced on the Bibliothèque Nationale's *gallica* website. I have omitted some of the author's footnotes, which seemed irrelevant or unhelpful, giving preference to my own notes, which might seem a trifle overabundant to some readers. I have also omitted certain passages that are literally untranslatable, but have added footnotes in the relevant places explaining why that is the case.

Brian Stableford

THE STORY OF THE GREAT PRINCE ORIBEAU

PART ONE

Advice of the Translator. a.

Admitting the truth, the utility of publishing an Irish story is very little, but what has tempted me is that, without attempting, like so many other serious authors, to give lessons to those who bring up Princes, I thought I could see in this antique work one of the most useful ways of forming one who will one day command.

Banishing all pedantry, therefore, and only thinking of spreading a few verities, which people may pick up as they wish, I am publishing a tale, like all other tales, destined for the amusement of the human race.

Consider that telling tales is necessarily instructive. It is in accordance with that maxim that it is necessary to judge my intentions; if I can help to pass a few agreeable moments, if my work suspends, for a few unfortunate mortals, the weight of life's tribulations, I shall be content.

Do let us each give what we can: the orange-tree does not bear chestnuts, nor the walnut-tree grapes; the useful cultivator who enables the earth to produce by watering the carefully-drawn furrow with his sweat, gives another fruit than the billiard hustler, who spends his life devouring dupes with the masterpieces of his culpable industry.

Embedded between those two extremes there are a thousand other estates, which all offer useful productions: the artisan, the artist, the merchant, the physician, the moralist, the man of letters, the man of law, the warrior and the magistrate.

I have produced my fruit, my reader, in my youth, by manual labor; now, I shall do as old men do, who tell tales in order still to be useful, until the moment when I cease, by reason of death, to be among the number of your fellow citizens.

Fault-finding and criticism are easy; everyone has the right to do that; but one only ought to do it with the respect due to the governing powers; that is what the Irish author has done. He has seen that Authority always has excellent intentions, to which subalterns hardly ever correspond faithfully.

Groaning over abuses, but a respectful son of the fathers-of-the-people, he goes to lead a royal infant by the hand and show him the reforms to be made, in order that he might execute them one day.

Happy are people like those of Mommonia, governed by a good King, whose Minister is a Sage. Fortunate is the city of which the Magistrate whose estate is to maintain good order resembles the Great Judge of Waterford.

Inevitably, there are people who, having broken all the rules, fear the penetration and vigilance of magistrates; they want to slander the upholders of laws from a distance, and seek to dissolve the bonds of confidence and respect; and when they are punished, they cry barbarity.

Just citizens never spoil their plumage thus; they never seek to remove themselves from the laws that are made for the wellbeing of society.

Kynanchie,[1] all that. Those people, by virtue of a kind of rabies, bark like dogs and pull their tongue hideously, like them.

---

[1] The nearest English equivalent of *Kynanchie*, a French medical term deriving from the Latin *cynanche* [sore throat], and referring to a kind of laryngitis, is quinsy. That English term is however, nowadays applied specifically to a kind of abscess resulting from tonsillitis. I have explained the word here because it does not reoccur in the text; the exotic words that are employed in the text are sometimes explained there by the author, and I have added comments there where appropriate.

Lauding good Princes and good Magistrates is such a sweet pleasure; the soul expands delightfully, as when a pious son praises an excellent father.

Ministers of the best of Kings, who governs the most flourishing kingdom of Evinland; respectable magistrates, all of whose arrests are dictates by justice itself, you have suppressed the abuses that Oribeau the Wise saw; we no longer have anything to do but bless you.

Nemesis, the barbaric avenger, is banished from the land; sage magistrates now anticipate crimes, and Vananis, the goddess of hope, has replaced her forever

Oribeau has made justice reign; Oribelle has raised altars to the future; we shall call her the goddess of clemency.[2]

Pacifier of all Evinland, Oribeau the Sage seems to have made it into a single Empire. He extends his hand to the weak; he does not make war on the strong; he presents him with the laws of justice and reason.

Query: who could enumerate his good deeds? Still young, he has advanced the wellbeing of his people, who were less happy for centuries in less enlightened times.

Renouncing his own rights, he has been seen to liberate former serfs; he has sometimes risked his person to help individuals.

Savior of his people, in times of famine, he has gone without food himself in order to nourish them; His worthy spouse, no less generous, has merited the name of Mother of the People.

Touched by the fate of the poor, Oribelle bears them in her heart; she has often asked for clemency on their behalf when severe Justice alone would have made its terrible voice heard.

---

[2] The author adds a note to a subsequent section explaining the meaning of the names Oribeau and Oribelle as "as beautiful as gold" and suggests that the ancients would have written Auribeau and Auribelle.

Veritably virtuous, she is devoid of affectation; gaiety always marks a contented soul.

Uniquely occupied with her duties as wife, mother and sovereign, she fulfills the first chastely, the second with delight, and submits the exercise of the third to the will of her august husband, but she herself makes the happiness and joy of all those who surround her.

Waterford blesses its King and Queen; that happy capital adores them and only swears by them.

Xés—i.e., perfumed—both of them, by their virtues, Oribeau and Princess Oribelle, spread the odor of the good life and set the example of thrift and frugality.

Yes indeed, is there any country better governed than the realm of Mommonia?

Zahorie, with lynx-like eyes, would not find in the universe a King who surpasses Oribeau, a Queen who surpasses Oribelle or a Minister who equals Dondanuck and O'Barbo; and the Great Judge of Waterford in care, vigilance and paternal solicitude.

Babble. b.

Becalmed for ten years waiting for the tale of Oribeau, people no longer expected to see it emerge from the author's portfolio; there are so many insipid tales already that the world could easily have done without reading another.

Cited already in a famous work, however, the particular merit of this one raises the hope of a fortunate exception.

Dedicated to the idea of being useful to his century, the author has entirely reworked this ancient and very moral Irish story in its details.

Excising what he thought to be too marvelous, he has conserved the educational, which he has rendered plausible.

Fantasy and magic spells all have to disappear in a century like ours.

Giants, dwarfs and ridiculous personages can amuse a child or the idle, but if one does not put verities beneath that bark, history becomes nauseating for sensate people.

Habituated to virtue by a sage, Oribeau travels in his estates and gets to know his people before reigning; that idea is the Irish author's.

Initiated in all the secrets of the nature, politics, mores, customs virtues, vices and needs of his people, such a Prince ought to be a benefit of the Divinity.

Judiciously, he never disdains an item of knowledge, a detail or an individual, however paltry they seem.

Kern before becoming a general, he passes through all the military ranks after having seen all the orders of citizens.

Legislator of an enlightened as well as humane kind, he only enacts sage laws, like those that Louis the August is nowadays giving the French, Franz Josef II to the Empire, Frederick to Germany, Charles III to Spain, Catherine II to Russia and the Grand Duke to Tuscany.

Moderately occupied with the historic by comparison with the moral, the French imitator has substituted our mores for those of the Mommonians.

Naturally, our literature, our abuses and our laws comprise the tableau that sometimes replaces another absolutely foreign to it.

Oribeau has a multitude of adventures, which lead him to obtain Oribelle.

Princess of Lagenia, a neighboring country, that heiress is the party that politics gives the Prince of Mommonia.

Quantitatively speaking, four years of labor, virtue and combats are scarcely sufficient to merit her.

Rendered more virtuous by the vices he has seen, Oribeau, although he is susceptible to amorous weaknesses, nevertheless commands his appetite for them, and is nonetheless a hero.

Surmounting everything, he is seen to sacrifice the unknown Oribelle to Oribelle the Princess.

The tyrant of Lagenia, Ratchlin, who has revolted, appears to oppress the Queen and the Princesses, but is overcome solely by the virtue of Prince Oribeau.

Victors and vanquished, the two peoples are henceforth only one after the fortunate union of the King of Mommonia and Princess Oribelle.

Whigs and Tories are all united under a peaceful reign, whose tranquility is bought by the young King's valor and virtue.

Xistarch as well as monarch, Oribeau is the procurer on his people's behalf, as well as abundance, of fêtes, spectacles and pleasures of every kind.

Yapou is the name of the bird that always precedes Oribelle, and indicates the presence of a protective fay.

Zamolxis[3] and his worship are abolished; religion becomes mild and easy; he is loved; everyone is happy.

Conclusion. c.

Coping with winter evenings, especially, the bourgeois women of the Marais make their imagination shine, or the fidelity of their memory.

Disencumbered of daily labor, they only occupy themselves then with pleasant or facile things.

Embroidering, sewing or knitting while chatting, they fill their time

Fables, romances, tales of Faerie, all are good, provided that they are amusing.

Gaily, every Sunday, in winter as in summer, the good Monsieur Gaudet, a bourgeois of the Rue Courtaudvilain,

---

[3] Zamolxis was a god of the Getae, of whom a relatively elaborate account is given by Herodotus, leading to many further mentions, both ancient and modern.

takes his family to the Hautborne, to a pretty house that over-
looks one of those vast gardens known as *marais*.[4]

Honest neighbors, men and women alike, are invited to
come and share, in summer strawberries, cherries and raspber-
ries, and at all times, good wine and good stories.

Ignorant, without being stupid, partly-grown youth listens to them avidly.

Jabbering is a great pleasure, of which story-tellers of either sex never weary.

Kyrielle: a tedious litany, one might say, of fables and
insipid stories, frightening or ridiculous.

Linguistically pedantic, those tales are often full of wit,
as witness the one that I am going to set before your eyes.

Magic, spells and enchantment, all can be found their
without wounding verity.

Naïve and witty, the narrator will present therein the
most extraordinary events, while according them with reason.

Oribeau is a very old story, brought to France by two
volunteers who followed the exiled English King James II.

People were unaware of it, except for the two Irishmen,
until the evening in winter when they related it to Monsieur
Gaudet of the Rue Courtaudvilain in the Marais, after drinking.

Questioned about the tales of their homeland, Sir Patrick,
the wittier of the two, announced that he would tell a story
capable of astonishing everyone.

"Really, nothing would be more agreeable to us," said
those in attendance.

"Should you tolerate it if it lasted longer than a week?"

"Try to make it last thirty; it will only be more agreeable
to us," everyone shouted.

---

[4] The term *Marais*, as used to refer to the quarter of Paris
known by that name, refers to a market garden, and I have
used that translation henceforth where the term is used as a
trivial noun.

Vouchsafe that you'll be content, then," said Sir Patrick, "for my tale is so long that it will take up at least eight evenings.

Unanimously, he was thanked, and begged to commence.

"Writ, a writ!" he cried. "What writ do you need?" replied the worthy Gaudet.

"Xerosage,[5] for preference," replied Sir Patrick. "I can only see dry and thirst-producing aliments; I need a writ for the wine-waiter, in order that he should always have a tankard of old wine beside me, for the throat gets warm when talking.

"Yzquiepatli!" cried his comrade from Mayo, nicknamed Zoïle, "they did well to give you that nickname, for you're as wily as a fox—for you know, Messieurs et Mesdames, that Yzquiepatli is an American fox."[6]

"Zoïle, don't criticize me," replied Sir Patrick, "unless you can do better.

And he immediately started speaking, in order to give first of all, an abridged exposition of the story he was about to tell, by reciting the summaries of the chapters, which he did after reciting the following dedication:

---

[5] The prefix *xero-*, from the Greek, means "dry."

[6] The word yzquiepatli does exist in early Dutch descriptions of the West Indies, where it originally referred to a bird rather than a mammal, although the *Dictionnaire universel* of 1727, where Restif presumably found it, does indeed attribute it to a Guatemalan fox.

Dedication. D.

Donneraill, author, dedicates his work

to:

August and Great Prince of Mommonia
Bountiful and virtuous Princess Oribelle, his spouse;

to the:

Councilors, the sage and benevolent Minister,
Dondanuck, the most skillful of legislators;
Excellent and just Baltamore, overseer of Waterford;
Facile and humane Aymstay, supreme chief of tribunals;
Grave and zealous O'Brisk, President of the Senate;
Honorable, eloquent and persuasive Scribreen, orator;
Indefatigable and vigilant Theblack, great judge of Waterford;
Judicious and penetrating O'Skinner, prefect of merchants;
Killpoole the valiant, generalissimo
Laudable and indulgent Ostownoseye, prefect of Letters
Magnificent and far-sighed Clanekitty, prefect of Finances;
Noble and courageous Killemanna, Owny, Illeag, Ikerrin,
    troop-leaders
Obliging and enlightened O'Barbo, instructor of Princes;
Pacific and prudent Fermery, great civil judge;
Qualified, laborious and popular Uppethird, public censor;
Religious and respectable Decy, great druid;
Solicitous and beneficent Tallo, public man;
Tolerant and philanthropic Middlethird, public man;
Valiant and invincible Slevvarda, commandant of the navy;
Unique in happiness Beautifulwalker, celebrated businessman;
Wily and courageous Corromroe, commandant of the cavalry;
Xistarq Bunratty, charged with forming young nobility;
Yeoman Killnataloone, sacred bodyguard of the Prince;
Zetetic and savant Shellilogher, whose enlightenment illumi-
    nates the Nation;

Deign, worthy Prince and good Princess, and all of you, O great men, to accept a dedication made to your patriotic work and your sublime qualities,

> by the grateful
> Donneraill, Irishman of the County of Cork in the province of Munster, formerly the realm of Mommonia.[7]

---

[7] Mommonia is, indeed, given as an old name for Munster in various eighteenth century documents (written in Latin). Similarly, Lagenia and Langenia are both offered as originals of Leinster, and Ultonia as the original of Ulster.

Exposition of Chapters. e.

Volume I; Part I; Evening I

A. Advent in the establishment of an old innkeeper.
B. Birth of Prince Oribeau after adventures in a Palace and a Cavern.
C. Conchèse: The marvelous conception and birth of Oribelle.
D. Dondanuck becomes Minister, and what he wants to do.
E. Embarrassment in which Queen Conchèse finds herself.
F. Favor unworthy of Dondanuck, and how he has Oribeau instructed by a Sage in a cavern in the Mountains of Stefenon
G. Government and instruction of Oribeau in morality as well as science, by the sage O'Barbo.
H. Horrible story that Oribeau hears on leaving the cavern of Stefenon to return to Waterford.

Evening II

I. Itinerary of Oribeau; he returns to Waterford. Pomp of Thor: The Statues.
J. Jejune fare; what Oribeau sees in the temples and among the Druids.
K. Karmess, Kabacks and Public Gardens.
L. Luxury of Waterford; adornment of women, affection of men; foolish expense.
M. Misery seen by Oribeau in hospitals and prisons. He witnesses an execution. The Prince and his Guide are imprisoned.
N. New enlightenment. How Oribeau and the sage see justice rendered.
O. Oribeau continues to see judgment. How he heard pleas before the sovereign court.

Part II; Evening III

P. Proceedings, Patrons, Procurators, Public Pestilences.
Q. Question of the amusements of Waterford that young Prince Oribeau sees.
R. Recitation of what Prince Oribeau sees among the actors, at the estaminet and the dance-hall
S. Scenes of interest seen by Prince Oribeau in a café (not called such).
T. Tableau: How Oribeau sees the Bards and knows their merit.
V. Verities that the Bards pronounce while talking about their works.

Evening IV

U. Union of a monstrous kind in the great theaters of the city of Waterford.
W. Waterford seen as ugly by the young Prince.
X. Xistes (continuation of the preceding chapter).
Y. Yapou, Taverns, Drinking-dens, etc.
Z. Zeal of O'Barbo to educate Oribeau. The Prince lodges with a cultivator. He labors. His presents reveal his identity after his departure. The joy of the laborer and his family. Oribeau leaves his Estates after visiting them and goes to the realms of Meath and Lagenia.

Volume II; Part III; Evening V

2A. Alrunes. Admirable invocation made to them by old Ennisleague.
2B. Blunder of O'Brisombaum, husband of Conchèse. He is imprisoned. Oribeau's good sentiments. Horrible crime meditated by Ratchlin.
2C. Communication of how the Prince of Meath lived in his early years with the shepherd Debundeh his favorite. He sees Oribeau.

2D. Debundeh, after giving dinner to Prince Oribeau and the
Sage, tells tales in response to the plea of his pupil
Cahincaha. First tale: Mellusine.

Evening VI

2E. Exposition of the moral of the tale of Mellusine. Connection with the Second Tale: Sireneh.
2F. Feats and deeds of Prince Beaudame, hidden under the
name of Cahincaha.
2G. Generous and fine actions of Beaudame since his childhood.
2H. Histories and marvels that the shepherd has recounted to
his pupil.
2I. Interruption. Unexpected separation. Rosée. Princess
Belletête. What Oribeau finds in a castle.
2J. Jealousy of Oribeau against Beaudame. A meal with the
Dunvalanian. Julia.

Part IV; Evening VII

2K. Kanaster. Ahissa; her story and that of old Kilcullen. Six
good deeds ordered. Oribeau performs the first.
2L. Laudations to generosity. Daura. Oribeau's second good
deed.
2M. Magnification of Oribeau. Coronation. Fillira. The third
good dead.
2N. Nominations. Canora. The fourth good deed.
2O. Oribelle-Friga. Abduction. Fifth good deed.
2P. Preparation for war. Oribeau's disguise. O'Barbo ambassador to Lagenia. Assault on Killensay Castle.
2Q. Questions of an impertinent kind. The drawbridge captured and the castle taken. Supposed violent death of
O'Brisombaum.
2R. Regrets of Conchèse. She is besieged by Ratchlin.
Beaudame, deceived, comes to the aid of the traitor.
Oribeau is captured.

2S. Sarbacane. Oribelle understands that Oribeau is the prisoner. He escapes. Dinameh, going to Beaudâme's camp, is
surprised by Ratchlin, who has her arrested. Beaudame is
undeceived.

Evening VIII

2T. Treason of three officers. Beaudame taken prisoner by
Ratchlin. The indignant troops of Meath join Oribeau's.
Beaudame is condemned to death. Oribeau is captured by
treason while racing to his rescue.
2V. Victory without combat. Dinameh is liberated by Oribeau
and returned to her mother. Dondanuck's arrival.
2U. Unanimity. Conversation of Oribeau and Oribelle. How
the Princess is Canora, Ahissa, Daura, Fillira, Julia and
Rosée.
2W. Warrant in twenty-six articles.
2X. Xé. Xague. Choice of Xistarchs. The Little Wool-
Merchant
2Y. Ynchik. The courage of Yeomen. Quiripanga. Oribeau is
reported in his Estates.
2Z. Zahorie. The sixth good deed, a King's masterpiece. Marriages. Conclusion.
& Etc. Wrwcwcw endowing FitzOribeau, the fourth descendant of Oribeau the Wise.

"Friends," Sir Patrick added, "such is the order of the
events I am going to relate. Lend me serious attention. I shall
begin."

First Evening

Chapter A
Advent in the establishment of an old innkeeper.

In the name of Thor and Worden, bless the inventor of letters and writing!

Alphabet[8] of great deeds of the valiant Prince Oribeau.

Betimes the history of famous men is enveloped in fables that a severe critic might discount, but the people are not upset by that; they love things that appear extraordinary to them and which nourish their insatiable curiosity.

Clearly, as we shall see.

Duo: two inhabitants of Waterford, capital of the kingdom of Mommonia in the land of Evin[9] were once drinking beer in a tavern. One was named Younghall, the other Kilmactomas.

The old innkeeper Ennisleague, who had served them, was spinning at the door when she saw the young King of the land pass by, followed by his entire Court. "There goes our beloved Prince Oribeau," she said to the drinkers, "may Thor

---

[8] In the original the alphabetization of chapters A-F dictates the separation of the paragraphs, but in some instances this produces very long paragraphs extending over several pages, often containing entire dialogues. In the interests of contriving a more comfortable layout of the text, I have broken up those long paragraphs into a form that is nowadays more conventional, and have highlighted the alphabetization by putting the key words in boldface. After making a token attempt to continue the pattern in chapter G the author gives up, except with regard to the first letter of each chapter.

[9] Author's note: "A beautiful name, for Evinland signifies productive land)." In fact, Evin is presumably a corruption of Erin, whose etymology is uncertain but probably means "west," Ireland lying west of Great Britain.

and Friga bless him. Do you know the story of his sixth ancestor, the valiant Oribeau the Wise and that of his wife, the excellent Princes Oribelle? It's marvelous."

"What is it?" said one of the drinkers.

Immediately, the innkeeper, who loved to talk, replied:
"If I were sure of your discretion, I'd tell you some very
strange things."

The two drinkers assured her of their constraint, asked
for a new tankard and settled down to listen to the marvelous
story.

Ennisleague had hardly opened her mouth when a nobleman came in, a great hunter. He asked for service.

One of the plebeian drinkers said to his comrade: "These
noblemen spoil everything; there's our pleasure lost."

"Why is that?" asked the hunter.

"Because we wanted to hear the story of the sixth ancestor of our young king, which the innkeeper was about to tell
us."

"I can do it better than that old woman, who will only tell
you fables, whereas I'll tell you fables and the truth. I'm a
gentleman, it's true, but popular, and your friend."

"In that case, speak," said the two drinkers. "We're listening."

The hunter therefore commenced his story in these
terms:

"**Fabulous** or true, the story of the Princes of a country is
always interesting for the people they govern, but how much
more so ought to be a story stripped of fables, without nevertheless silencing them,[10] which tends to make virtue loved by

---

[10] Author's note: "The Irish narrator will, in fact, report everything, but he will have the art of not confusing folklore with
history. He has absolutely cast as folktales the episodes of a
marvelous genre. Let us give here the full title of the *Tale of
Oribeau* such as it is in the original: *The deeds of the valiant
Prince Auribeau, King of fifty villages in the country of
Hirland, and the authentic adventures of the excellent Prin-*

showing us a young Prince, scion of the august House that has governed us for so many centuries, brought up by a Sage; a great Minister calumniated, who does good solely for the love of the good; and finally, a young King, father to his people, all of whose needs he wants to know! I shall get to it.

Chapter B
Birth of Prince Oribeau after adventures in a Palace and a Cavern.

Behold a good son, King and husband: nothing was lacking in good King Oribeau, nicknamed O'Facfac,[11] except to be a father. He had reigned for twenty years over the flourishing kingdom of Mommonia in the famous country of Evinland in Karrikmakgriffin, his favorite castle in Waterford, his capital, but the beautiful Princess Dadameh, his wife, had not yet given him an heir.

Chasing foxes one day with the Queen—for the Prince was a great hunter—they each went astray. The Queen was carried away by her horse, which had been frightened by a

---

cess Auribelle; Abridged from the ancient annals of Airland, or Hirland." In the endnotes attached to the final volume the author expands further on this point, saying: "The singular names and certain bizarre features in the story will surprise some readers...but we have been obliged to conserve these features, which are the foundation of the Irish story, as well as names that are the inventions of the original author." He labors the point in other occasional notes, which I have not reproduced.

[11] There is more than one way that this strange name might have been derived, but it is probably adapted from Latin, and appears in more than one eighteenth-century French text in a quotation allegedly taken from St Augustine: *Fac fac vel timore poenae, si nondum potes amore justicia* [Act, act for fear of punishment, if you cannot yet do so out of love of justice].

loud clap of thunder. The charger stumbled in a pothole. For-tunately, Dadameh, young and vivacious, leapt lightly to the ground and drew away.

As for O'Facfac, surprised by night and the storm, and harassed by fatigue, after three hours he perceived a pale light; he spurred his horse and reached the gate of a castle that he did not recognize. While he has the gate opened to him, how-ever, so that he can recover his exhausted strength by means of a delicate supper, let us return to the Queen.

Dadameh, after having walked for some time through a dense wood, did not find a palace but a frightful lair, which the storm constrained her to enter, tremulously.

Scarcely was she there than she saw approaching, it is said, a man clad in a long black robe with a bonnet made from the skin of a large bat, whose attached wings formed its brim.

The Magician—for he was one of the most powerful of those—approached the Princess courteously. "Milady," he said, "are you not Queen Dadameh?"

The trembling Princess replied to him: "Milord, if you're the Devil, don't do me any harm!"

"No, I'm only a sorcerer."

"Mercy!" cried the Princess. "Oh, sir, don't put a spell on me."

"Far from it; I intend to remove the cruel spell by which you are obsessed."

But the poor Queen could no longer hear him; she had fainted.

Dondanuck—that was the necromancer's name—employed the secrets of his art to recall her to life. Afterwards, he said to the Princess: "Madame, by means of what carriage would it please you to rejoin the King, your worthy spouse? Would you like a chariot drawn by owls or by dragons? Would you like me to carry you myself, or would you be con-tent with a mule that I nourish in this lair?"

The Queen accepted the mule—which was none other than the fay Wrwcwcw,[12] the protectress of the House of Connacy, from which Dadameh descended—the Magician put her on it and assured her that he had just read in his grimoire that before the year was out, she would bring a Prince into the world.

Enjoined to enter as if under compulsion, King O'Facfac allowed himself to be led into the castle. He was served by domestics, without seeing the master or mistress.

As soon as he had supped, he was urged to go to bed, but scarcely had his weary limbs touched the eiderdown, than he felt a soft plump hand pass over his face.

The Prince was no coward, although he believed in ghosts, and he had the courage to exclaim: "Who's there? What do you want?"

A soft and silvery voice, which resembled that of Queen Dadameh, replied: "O King Facfac, I am a fay, and unfortunate, in spite of my power, for having always resisted amour. I refused to marry the genius Perforimoth the Black, and in order to avenge himself he made a talisman that forces me to fall in love with a mere mortal; fortunately, it's you! My name is Pucellomaneh,[13] protective fay of the House of Langenia, and perhaps you've heard of mention of me, although I'm presently almost forgotten by men and entirely unknown to women. Judge my difficulty—the cruel genius, who surpasses me in power, against all the laws of Faerie, has condemned me to

---

[12] The call of a trogon is sometimes rendered as *couroucourou*, but Restif is unlikely to have known that, and his term is almost certainly an onomatopoeic version of the call of an owl (or, strictly speaking, two owls), usually rendered in English as "too-wit-too-woo."

[13] *Pucelle* in French means virgin, often applied to Jeanne d'Arc; *maneh*, which Restif attaches as a suffix to the names of many of his fays would have been familiar to him as a Biblical term for the coin or unit of weight known in both French and English as a talent.

take the first step and offer you myself what once I would only have suffered to be asked of me. Have pity on my fate, and render me my first virtue, in making me lack it..."

That speech was followed by a kiss, which the fay imprinted on O'Facfac's lips.

"One moment, my love," said the Prince, who sensed Pucellomaneh becoming pressing, "Let's see first whether you're pretty."

"Can you doubt it?" replied the fay. "Do you remember how beautiful Dadameh was at sixteen?"

"As if I could still see her."

"Well, I resemble her feature for feature, and tomorrow you'll have the proof of it. Remember that everything you do with me will operate on the Queen, and that if you do as I wish, within a year you will have a son."

That promise made a marvelous impression on the great O'Facfac; he surpassed himself, and broke the talisman that submitted the fay to the harsh law of Perforimoth the Black. So, as soon as the Prince was asleep, the fay, who had recovered the right to modesty, climbed back into her chariot and disappeared.

Fatigued and tremulous on the Mage's mule, the Queen was carried by her mount to the fay's castle. She was received there with all the respect that she merited, and was taken to the room of her husband the King. What passed between them was not revealed, but the following day, having awakened at the same time, they were very surprised to find themselves in the same bed.

"Milady," said the Prince, "I've just had a beautiful dream."

"And I, Milord, have just had a frightful one."

And they told one another what I have just told you.

They had only just finished when they saw the lords that usually accompanied them on the hunt arriving.

"Tell me," O'Facfac said to them, "whether we were hunting yesterday and where we are at present, for this apartment resembles exactly the one in my palace at Karrickmacgriffin?"

The lords assured Their Majesties that they had not been hunting, that they had gone to bed together after having supped on roe-deer pâté and a brawn of wild boar.

"But that was the day before yesterday!" cried the Queen.

Her Majesty was assured that she was mistaken.

Great effect of the conjurations of Dondamuck! The day that the King and Queen had lost was forgotten by humans, and the King and Queen, who were the only ones who remembered it, took it for a dream! But what proves that it was a reality is that a few months later, Dadameh found that she was pregnant, and before the year was out, she gave birth to a son, as handsome as the day, who was named Prince Oribeau.

The fay Wrwcwcw, the wisest of his ancestors, endowed him with beauty, a fine stature, graces, intelligence and a desire for education.

The entire nation was drunk with joy. Couriers were sent to notify his maternal grandfather, Perforimoth the Severe, the King of Connacy, of the birth of the Prince, as well as old O'Empthor, King of Lagenia, the wise Dunnaghall, King of Ultonia and the feeble Baisitiding, King of Meath.[14]

"**Ha!**" interrupted the old innkeeper. "You'd like to make is believe that the magician's cavern and the fay's palace were dreams—but they were real!"

---

[14] The author inserts notes here to identify Connacy with Connaught; Lagenia with Leinster, the location of Dublin, formerly Balaclay, and the region of Kilkenny, famous for the beauty of its daughters; Ultonia with Ulster; and to identify Meath as a humble "dismembered" principality of Lagenia. He adds: "It is necessary to observe that the names of these Kings are the same as those of genii, because all peoples, in their tales, from the Greeks to the Irish, take pleasure in making their ancient Kings marvelous beings, gods, genii, fays or heroes."

"**If** you wish, my dear," said the gentleman, "but everyone has his fashion of telling tales, and that's mine.

"Speak! Speak!" said the two drinkers. "For you speak well, and if ever you stand for Parliament, we promise you our votes, as well as those of our friends. And you, good woman, listen."

Joy as keen as King O'Facfac felt on that happy occasion was previously unknown to him. He had been generous and good before, but he became even better. To everything that the Queen and his Ministers asked of him, he only responded with his favorite phrase: "So be it."

But he did not enjoy the happiness of being a father for long.

Kerry—that was the hunter's name—finished his tankard at that moment; he asked for another, which pleased old Ennisleague. Then he resumed speaking.

Chapter C
Conchèse: The marvelous conception and birth of Oribelle.

Consequently, five years went by after Oribeau saw the light of day; he was learning to ride a horse and hold a sword when the beautiful Conchèse, Queen of Lagenia, became pregnant in a most extraordinary manner.

Delicate, adored by the people, who trembled that they might lose that last offspring of Kings, the only daughter of the great O'Empthor had just succeeded him.

The young Princess, who was only sixteen, was dear to the fay Pucellomaneh; she fled from all men and only saw in a familiar fashion the daughter of Baron Kilkenny, the late King's Minister. Maidman, alias Knoctoser, slept with the Queen, and loved her as much as she was loved. She often said to her:

"**Excellent** Princess, if only I were of a sex different from yours!"

"I desire that as much as you do," replied Conchèse, "but it's an insensate wish."

"Not as much as that, Milady."

For it is necessary to say here that Maidman, in coming into the world, had had all the appearances of the female sex, but as she had grown older, the prerogatives of the other sex had become gradually manifest. At fourteen, Maidman was a little more male than female; people were already inverting her name and calling her Manmaid. Soon she was a perfect man, without anyone suspecting it except for her father, who had his reasons for not saying anything. It was in that fortunate epoch that Manmaid lay with Conchèse and formed the wish to be a different sex.

"**Great** is my desire," Manmaid said one evening to her sovereign, "that the gods grant my wish.

"I would like that too," said Conchèse, sighing, and sadly went to bed.

Manmaid, who shared it, as usual, emboldened by the Queen's response and favored by the fay Pucellomaneh, tried out her new faculties and brought the adventure to a conclusion without Conchèse imagining that it was anything but the caresses of a girl. In consequence, she mistook the inconveniences of pregnancy for the symptoms of a dangerous illness.

However, imagine her astonishment one day when, having found herself very indisposed, a violent colic concluded with her bringing a beautiful Princess into the world.

Conchèse could not believe three of her senses, which assured her of it, and nearly concluded that she was only imagining what they wanted to impose upon her. Finally, however, it was necessary to yield when she saw all the Orders of State coming to congratulate her on her fortunate fecundity, and begging her to name the fortunate mortal who had been able to please Her Royal Majesty.

Innocent as she was beautiful, Conchèse told the delegates that she knew nothing about it, and that no man had approached her. It was thought at first that Her Majesty was blushing at her choice and dared not admit it, but, the Queen's ingenuous responses having convinced the chiefs that she was telling the truth, it was published throughout the realm that the Sovereign had given birth to a Princess whose father was a genius. In order that that should be more credible he was named; the genius Baisitiding had the honor of that glorious paternity.

By order of the Queen, the young Princess was named Oribelle; she was given the prettiest woman in Kilkenny as a nurse, and all the public documents were issued in the name of Conchèse and the genius Baisitiding, her invisible spouse.

Kilkenny, Manmaid's father, who had governed the State for a long time, notified the barons of the realm and all the neighboring Courts that the Queen of Lagenia had given birth.

There was great rejoining in the Court of Meath, because the Sovereigns of Lagenia and Meath were originally from the same family, which meant that the Princes of the two countries always took their spouses from one another, those of Meath from the House of Lagenia, and the Princes of the latter country from the House of Meath, from which Conchèse emerged.

In the Court of Mommonia, however, there was surprise at the notification. For three of four centuries the Mommonians and the Lagenians had been sworn enemies. That is why they could not imagine why it had been decided in Balaclay—as Dublin as then named—to give the Princess a name similar to that of the young Prince of Mommonia. Some took it as an evil omen, others as a good one, but everyone talked about it as something that would have extraordinary consequences.

Learn that the secret reasons that had determined Conchèse to have the young Princess given a foreign name came from a dream that she had had two days before giving birth. She thought she had seen the fay Pucellomaneh, the protectress of her House, who pronounced the following words distinctly

"**My** daughter,

"**Name** your daughter,

"**Oribelle.**"

Chapter D
Dondanuck becomes Minister, and what he wants to do.

Dadameh, meanwhile, had become regent of Mommonia, for it is necessary to know, since I have not yet said it, that the good O'Facfac had fallen into infancy a week after the birth of his son, and Queen Dadameh, remembering the necromancer who had announced the birth of Oribeau to her, summoned him to be governor of the State.

As soon as Dondanuck had the reins of government in his hands, he was seen to dedicate himself to making the people happy. He wanted to publish a Law to which the inhabitants of Mommonia would owe all their felicity, but he was opposed. I shall report it as is it conserved in the Archives of the city of Waterford.

"**Exegesis** of the King and Milady the Regent

"**Fitz**-Oribeau, by the grace of Thor, King of the fifty villages of Mommonia, Counties of Clare, Limerick, Kerry, Cork, Tipperary and Waterford, Lord of Karrikmakgriffin, etc., and the very illustrious Princess Dadameh Knockfergus, heir presumptive to the Kingdom of Connacy, Counties of Sligo, Thomond and Roscommon, to all our faithful subjects, salutations.

"**Grieving** at the absence of our worthy spouse, the great O'Facfac, and forced by the unanimous cry of our people to take responsibility for the government of the Estates of the King, our dear son, during his minority, we have resolved to render the memory of our regency immortal forever by working for public felicity. Of all the means that have presented themselves to our mind and our excellent Council, we have not found any more efficacious and shorter means than to hinder a certain number of men who are avid to take possession of everything and reduce their fellow citizens to poverty. Moved by these causes and others, and our certain knowledge, omnipotence and royal power, we have decided, instituted by statute and ordered the following, that we:

Article A

"Adjudicates is that three months hence, all the particular customs of the different counties that compose our Kingdom of Mommonia will be extinguished and superannuated, and there will no longer be any but a single, simple and uniform law composed of all that is best in the aforementioned customs and abrogated laws, which we are presently drafting, for publication at the end of the aforesaid three months;

Article B

"Banished are all differences in weights and measures of all the said Counties, Lands and Lordships;

Article C

"Commanded from the day of publication of the present ordinance is that all the real estate of our subjects shall be equally shared between them and all debts cancelled, but in such a manner that if a debtor comes to be richer than the creditor one day, the said debtor will be constrained to restore equality with the said creditor, and until then the debtor will be subject to that obligation, but during the present century only, because at the beginning of each century, equality will be reestablished;

Article D

"Declared is that all furniture, money, livestock and other commodities will be similarly divided in proportion to the needs of the age, strength and number of persons, in order that all should be compensated in such a manner that all our subjects enjoy an equal wellbeing;

Article E

"Established is that all the contestations in which our said subjects might be involved, whether civil or criminal, will be judged gratis; the culpable individual will be punished personally, and none of that penalty will fall directly or indirectly upon their families; and with regard to civil amends imposed on litigants in bad faith, care will be taken that they do not prejudice their children in any way;

Article F

"Forbidden is any subject, who has merited distinction by his services to enjoy them other than personally, it not being just that the State should take responsibility for the onerous illustration of any bad lots that might emerge from a valiant man;

Article G

"Guaranteed is that in future, judges will be selected from the wisest old men of any town or village; they will number eighty in big cities, twelve in the smallest and six in boroughs and village; they will serve for a year; every court will judge in the last resort but the following year's court will review the judgment on the complaint of one party and in that event the case will be rejudged by two different and distant jurisdictions at the same time and on the same day, which will only be known to one another subsequently, and in the event of a difference of decision a third will pronounce definitively without having seen the decisions of the other two; all without expense, the honor of being a judge taking the place of spices;

Article H

"**Hasten** our Minister and our great officers to have the aforesaid Exegesis or clear Exposition of our will executed in the fifty villages of the Kingdom of Mommonia.

"**Inscribed** in our annals in the first year of our reign.

"**Judged** appropriate and just, Oribeau, King; Dadameh, Queen Regent; and (lower down) On the King's behalf, Dondanuck.

"**Karrikmakgriffin**, our abode."

Legally, the Minister would have had all of that executed in spite of the obstacles raised by the rich, for he was convinced that the disproportion of fortunes is the most dangerous reef of mores. Although his necromancy put him above cabals, and he consented to be charged with the execration of the blinded public, provided that the young King and the Queen Regent were blessed by the people, he believed that he had the right to render men happy in spite of themselves.

Moderation did not, however, preserve him from the hatred of the foremost in the State, who, having perceived that the Minister was amassing a great deal of money, resolved to make use of that opportunity to doom him by accusing him of embezzlement and violating his own laws.

One day, therefore, they came in a body to find the Regent and ask her to order Dondanuck's arrest and a search of his house. The Princess, surprised and troubled, did not know what to reply, when the Minister arrived. He said that the Mommonians' demand was just and he handed over all his keys; he even wanted his accusers carry out the search.

The astonishment of the latter was great, however, when nothing was found in Dondanuck's house but a few old clothes, books and instruments of chemistry, with the most frugal provisions of food. They searched everywhere. The Minister encouraged them, laughing.

Afterwards, taking pity on them he told them to follow him to the guard of the Royal Treasury. There, he showed them all the sums that he had amassed, divided into various labeled begs; he invited them to read, and they saw on the first of the bags:

Notwithstanding the law of equality, as the Mommonian lords reduced to equality by the law that we have proposed, are not accustomed to labor, they might fall into need, and below the very equality that we wanted to establish, which would not be just. In consequence, we have asked the Queen Regent to amass considerable sums, reserving it to ourselves to advise her on their distribution to the grandees of her realm incapable of maintaining themselves after the execution of the law, in proportion to their needs. I estimate that it will be necessary to commence with the proudest, because they will only complain in the last extremity; they are O'Furh, O'Droungth. etc., (the principal lords were named, who were precisely those who had accused him) *and hope that Her Majesty will continue to cast a paternal eye over their needs in future.*

One can easily imagine the confusion of Dondanuck's accusers; they withdrew, after having begged the Queen's pardon for their temerity.

Preserving himself from such inconveniences in future, Dondanuck postponed the execution of his law and occupied himself with the education of the young Prince Oribeau. I shall briefly summarize the manner in which he thought a good King should be formed.

"**Question!**" said one of the drinkers. "That law was not enacted?"

"**Reckless!**" said the other. "Nothing more dangerous; the idle and the indigent would find themselves as advanced as honest men, which would not be just."

"Would you care to refer that to this gentleman," replied the first, "Who has more interest than us in the non-existence of that law?"

"**So be it!**" said the second drinker. "What do you think, honest gentleman?"

"**Thus far**, all my expressions have proved that I lean toward the law. It's not that I don't sense its inconveniences, the most dangerous of all being that it might remove the most powerful fiber of the State, each individual no longer having the expectation of raising himself above others by his labor and his industry, of transmitting to his posterity the flattering elevation and distinction that have honored him; that one might see savage apathy taking possession of society and the most flourishing nations falling back in a few years into barbarity, or falling prey to active and vigilant enemies who had not adopted the same regime.

"You sense that one can envisage the matter from another angle and respond that those fears are commercial, that happy and free people would cherish their constitution, that they would be full of activity because, by means of equality they would enjoy all their labor, that pleasures, amusements and enjoyments of every species would always succeed occupation; that there are a thousand means of exciting and maintaining competition and activity; that in handing over power to the old, its execution to the mature, putting youth in subordination by labor in the time of strength and the necessity of learning in childhood, there would never be murmurs, because every moment would be carrying a man toward power and honor; that the example of republics, inferior to monarchies in vigor, is of no relevance here because those republic are imperfect regimes, etc. There are fors and againsts. Let us consult the decision of our aged hostess."

The innkeeper, flattered by that arbitrage, replied: "Equality would be excellent if the world were only composed of good people."

"**Vouchsafe** the sequel to the story," said Younghall.

The gentleman continued.

Chapter E
Embarrassment in which Queen Conchèse finds herself.

Evidently, in Lagenia, Queen Conchèse did not have the same good fortune as the Regent of Mommonia. The virility of Manmaid became more manifest with every passing day. A bushy beard came to shadow her chin and she was obliged to quit the clothing of the sex she no longer had.

People laughed at first at that metamorphosis of the Queen's friend; afterwards, they reflected that it was less natural to attribute the fecundity of Conchèse to Baisitiding than to

Maidman, as she was still called. Hence, it was concluded that it was necessary for the young lord to marry the Queen.

Conchèse would have liked nothing better and everything would soon have been concluded if Kilkenny's enemies had not conspired together to prevent the marriage of his son with the Sovereign. They claimed that it was debasing royal Majesty to clothe a dubious individual like a hermaphrodite therewith; that a Queen required a definite man; that Princess Oribelle really was the daughter of the genius Baisitiding—and the proof they brought was that MacChoukas, the priest of Thor, had thus decided.

Contradicting themselves thereafter, as often happens when one is blinded by hatred, they accused Kilkenny of the crime of *lèse-majesté*, saying that he knew that Maidman was a man, since he had initially given her the name of Knoctoser, but that ambition had determined his conduct and had suggested that infamy to him, knowing that there was then no Prince to marry in the House of Meath. They proposed the son of the Pontiff to marry the Queen, who refused him.

The rebels then chose MacChoukas and his son for their leaders, and the people, accustomed to respect the ministers of their religion, rallied to their side. Manmaid and his father were captured in battle and handed over to MacDonoght, the son of MacChoukas, who was himself a priest of Worden, the god of war.

Favored by strength of arms, as soon as MacDonoght had his enemies in his power, he took measures to doom them more surely. In order to succeed, he had an oracle rendered by Worden that demanded the sacrifice of the two most illustrious prisoners of war. Kilkenny and Knoctoser, or Manmaid, were taken to the altar crowned with laurel.

Guided by ambition and jealousy, MacDonoght had already raised his arm, ready to plunge a large knife into Knoctoser's breast, when a brilliant machine was perceived in the air borne, suspended by golden and azure chains, by four rocs and four condors and directed by a goddess.

The novelty of the spectacle astonished the priest and all the people. Meanwhile, the rocs and the condors lowered the chariot over the altar, and they saw, on a throne enriched by diamonds, a woman of superhuman beauty. It was Pucellomaneh.

"Feeble Lagenians," she said, "I have taken under my protection Queen Conchèse, her daughter Princes Oribelle, Knoctoser and Kilkenny. As for MacChoukas and MacDonoght, this is their fate..."

At the same time, she touched them with her wand, and instead of two men, nothing could any longer be seen but two moles, which immediately started digging in the earth and disappeared.

"**Happy** inhabitants of Lagenia," the fay continued, "your young Princess will one day be a phenomenon of nature. She will be a prudent, beautiful and modest woman, tender and reserved, affable and proud, facile and the most severe of daughters."

"**It**'s impossible to combine all those qualities!" cried Kilkenny.

"**Judiciously**, I shall build an inaccessible fort on the point of those two rocks," Pucellomaneh replied. "I shall enclose the Princess therein; it's the only means of giving a beauty all the qualities that I've just expressed. She will see no one except her governess and nurse Clomaneh; she will never be flattered, and all the natural penchants of women will be devoid of effect, unless a young Prince succeeds, by dint of virtue and good deeds, in destroying the talisman with which I will seal the doors."

The fay immediately removed the little Oribelle, aged three years three months and three days, from her mother's arms; but she softened Conchèse's dolor by giving her a talisman to enter her daughter's dwelling. Pucellomaneh sealed her in the castle of Makredin, situated between the county of Wicklow and the kingdom of Meath; it was there that Oribelle was brought up by Clomaneh, her nurse and governess.

Knoctoser found himself without a competitor; he asked for Conchèse in marriage, humbly, from the assembled Estates, who consented to raise him to the level of their Sovereign if the Queen agreed.

Left to her own devices, Conchèse, who had not yet known a more amiable man than her dear Knoctoser, gave her royal consent. Oribelle's father married the Queen and took the name of O'Brisombaüm.

Misfortunately, the marriage was not happy. O'Connor the Handsome, the castellan of Ratchlin in the county of Longford, appeared at Court; the Queen, charmed by his good looks, made him her Minister and rendered him omnipotent. O'Brisombaüm sulked and then complained bitterly; the Queen had bad moods and they quarreled.

Conchèse then had a second perfectly beautiful daughter, but the fay Pucellomaneh, irritated by the disharmony between the two spouses, endowed that younger daughter with as much stupidity and malevolence as Oribelle had intelligence and mildness.

The Queen heard the fatal gift that the fay had just made and was greatly afflicted by it. To increase her distress, Pucellomaneh told her that Mijoreh the Beautiful, Queen of Meath, Her Majesty's cousin, had just brought into the world a hunchbacked, lame one-eyed and bandy-legged son, who had been named Beaudâme and nicknamed Cahincaha, endowed with as much intelligence as he had ugliness; that the young Prince could not be embellished, nor the little Princess become more intelligent and good, but that the former might succeed, in spite of his ugliness, in making Dinameh love him—that was the name the fay had given to the second Princess of Lagenia—provided that no one revealed to them the secret on which their fates depended.

No less afflicted, the Queen of Meath deplored the deformity of her son Beaudâme, nicknamed Cahincaha. The fay, who was similarly present at her childbirth, assured her that there was a remedy for it, and that if the Prince was loved one day by little Dinameh, his cousin, in spite of his ugliness, he would become as handsome as he was intelligent.

"Never—he's too ugly!" said one of the Queen's ladies-in-waiting.

"Intelligence embellishes ugliness," retorted the fay.

On which the little Prince was given for a nurse a woman of Ballnalu named Nursimaneh; she was sent to Mullengar, between Lake Hoy and Lake Ennel, in west Meath, with orders not to return to court until Cahincaha was embellished.

Chapter F
Favor unworthy of Dondanuck, and how he has Oribeau instructed by a Sage in a cavern in the Mountains of Stefenon.

Fatigued by her childbirth and her husband's reproaches, Conchèse, under the pretext of seeing her elder daughter, went to shut herself away in Makredin, where Oribelle was being brought up, and who was profiting marvelously from everything that the vigilant Clomaneh was teaching her. Let us leave her there to amuse herself in her solitude, where only the Minister Ratchlin had the liberty to enter, and return to Waterford.

Gaining the love of her subjects increasingly, the illustrious Dadameh reigned peacefully and gloriously, with the aid of her Minister Dondanuck, who formed the virtue of Prince Oribeau's youth. He showed him by example and taught him what all Princes ought to know, but which they never do know unless they have been simple individuals: to know men and their different conditions.

High-minded and constant in his projects, in order to execute them, the Minister dared to engage the Queen to confide the Prince to a celebrated Mage named O'Barbo, who had retired to the Mountains of Stefenon, with whom Oribeau would visit all of Evinland and spend time in England in Scotland and as far afield as the Orcades, examining the mores of towns and villages, working with his hands and conversing with men of all estates.

The Queen, who was always receptive to the advice of her Minister, consented to what he wished. The young Prince disappeared secretly from the Court and Dondanuck, guided by the fay Wrwcwcw in the form of a bird—it is said—named the Yapou, took him to O'Barbo's lair.

It happened that they found the Sage in a garden that he had made by the power of his art, between almost inaccessible rocks, and that garden, by virtue of its beauty, formed a contrast that embellished even the horror of those vast solitudes. As soon as he perceived his old friend, Dondanuck ran toward him and kissed him three times, without saying a word.

"**Joy!**" said the hermit. "I haven't seen you for a long time."

"What can you expect? I'm a slave."

"What does it matter, if your soul is free?"

"You don't know my kind of slavery; it even enslaves the soul. I'm the Queen's Minister."

"O Heaven! You've been able to... My friend, the ordinary slave has only one master; if he serves him well and makes himself loved, he leads a mild and tranquil life, but the public slaves, to the number of whom you belong, having to bow down, cursing the fact, before a malevolent and jealous crowd, have nothing for which to hope. If they make themselves loved by the master, they are cursed by the people; if they are out of favor they are scorned—sad alternatives, horror and scorn."

"What would you say of a Sage, enough of a friend of humanity to devote his every moment to making the happiness of those from whom he can only hope for horror or scorn?"

"I would say that he is the greatest of men, and that man, I find in my friend."

With that, the two Sages embraced again; after which Dondanuck explained the purpose of his visit, declaring to his friend what he expected of his virtue.

"**Kaperguin!**" said O'Barbo, sighing and casting his gaze over his garden, to which he had given the name of his home town.[15] "Kaperguin, is it necessary to leave you?" Soon ashamed of that weakness, however, he took the hand of the young Prince and made him this oath:

"**Law** that consecrates humans to the homeland, I bless you

"**Myself**, I swear by Thor and by Worden to devote the rest of my life to this young Prince. O precious child, a man is not enough to form you; you and your peers require a god. If you are good, how happy you will make people; if you are wicked, you will become a scourge for the human race more dangerous than lightning, floods and volcanoes. I shall always strive to persuade you that you are only a man, who will command men, and that your authority will only be legitimate insofar as you use it or their advantage.

"**Never** say or think that you obtain your power from the gods; the gods give life and humans royalty; all men are equal in the eyes of the Supreme Being; the instant of death reminds Kings of that, if they have forgotten it."

O'Barbo the Sage thus dared to tell the truth to a young Prince who was beginning to be capable of hearing it, and Dondanuck, charmed to have succeeded in his project, sire of the man to whom he had confided, the hope of the State, resumed the road to Karrikmakgriffin alone.

Passing through the environs of Makredin, he wanted—it is said—to see the retreat of Princess Oribelle. He perceived the nurse Clomaneh, who told fanciful tales to cheer up the child during the frequent absences of the Queen, who was working with her Minister. Little Oribelle, already curious and sensible, listened to those tales with pleasure; her dainty mouth smiled, and sometimes her beautiful eyes became

---

[15] Eighteenth century geographical dictionaries published in France did list a town in Ireland called Caperguin; Restif, of course, routinely changes hard Cs to Ks.

moist. Clomaneh stopped then, in order to mingle the tales with heroic songs.

"Young Minvane was gazing at the sea from a rock. Modesty and sadness were mingled in her face. She perceived young warriors returning, covered by their arms. 'O my lover, O Reyno, are you coming back with them?'

"'Reyno, Reyno has fallen on the plains of Allui.' 'The arms that felled him must have been very powerful, then. O Reyno, will you never see Minvane again?

"'Ah, I am left alone! No, I shall not remain alone. Winds that agitate my hair, my sighs will not mingle with your whistling for long. O my love, O Reyno, I must find you again.

"'I do not see you today returning from the hunt, with the strength and grace of youth; eternal night surrounds your beloved Minvane. O my love, O Reyno, etc.

"'Where is your faithful dog? where is your sword as brilliant as the lightning that departs from the clouds? your spear always stained with blood? O my love, etc.

"'Alas, I see your arms heaped up in disorder in your ship! I see them soiled with blood…ah, it is Reyno's blood! O my love, etc.

"'The dawn will not tell you any more: get up, young warrior! Go away, beautiful dawn! Reyno is sleeping with the dead; the deer are bounding over his tomb. O my love, O Reyno, etc.

"'I shall get up silently, my King, I shall slide softly into your bed; my soul will lie down in silence beside my dear sleeping Reyno. O my love, O Reyno, etc.

"'My young companions are looking for me, but they will not find me; they are following the paths in the forest, tracking my footprints. Oh, I no longer hear your songs, my comrades; I am asleep with Reyno!'"[16]

---

[16] I cannot locate the original of this "song," but there is a description of it in the March 1777 issue of the *Journal encyclopédique*, which gives the name of the male character as

When the careful Clomaneh stopped singing, little Oribelle, softened, smiled tearfully, and the Graces smiled with her.

Dondanuck, seeing that the good nurse was about to begin again, knocked three times on the shutter. Clomaneh shuddered and pricked up her ears.

"That's a story that hooks me," said Kilmactomas, while Kerry drank.

"Me too," replied Younghall.

"And me even more," cried the old innkeeper.

"As, I was saying," the hunter went on, "Clomaneh shuddered and pricked up her ears..."

Chapter G
Government and instruction of Oribeau in morality as well as science, by the sage O'Barbo.

"**Gabrien!** Gabrien!" cried Dondanuck, when Clomaneh had finished her song.

"Brya! Brya!" she replied.[17]

The Minister, who recognized her as a demi-Fay, to whom Pucellomaneh had confided Oribelle, went on: "I see that you can hear me, and that you're an adept. How is the young Princess?"

Ryno and notes that it is an imitation of Ossian (Ryno is represented as the son of Fingal in *Fingal*) but not the work of that poet (whom we now know to have been an invention of James Macpherson, although Restif did not).

[17] These exclamations are enigmatic, but one eighteenth century French dictionary finds the terms "Gabrien" and "Beya" paired in alchemical jargon, the former referring to sulfur and the latter to a mercurial liquid. Given that the characters are supposedly a Mage and a demi-fay, they might well be accustomed to such language.

"You know that," replied Clomaneh. "However, I shall tell you out of politeness. She is growing more beautiful with every moment of her existence and will be a miracle of beauty one day; her soul is even more beautiful than her body, and if you want to make sure of that you have only to come closer"—for the Mage was talking to the nurse through a window, to which, it is said, he had raised himself up by the power of his art.

"No, said the Queen of Mommonia's Minister. "I don't want to violate the law of the fay Pucellomaneh, but be careful of the black genius Perforimoth!"

"I have no fear of him," said the nurse, "as long as I retain the virtue of the Living Ring."

"That's true," replied Dondanuck, "but you might lose it. Prince Oribeau, whom Heaven destines for your Princess, is an accomplished lover, as beautiful as her and as virtuous, or will become so. I am having him brought up by my old friend, the great O'Barbo of Kaperguin, the very same who, by his sublime science, rendered two armies about to do battle immobile and held them in that situation long enough for them to consume all their strength by hunger, thirst and impotence. Then he rendered them movement and knowledge; the generals, officers and soldiers were immediately seen to run to the food supplies and sate themselves gluttonously. Sleep surprised them thereafter.

"The two armies slept for three times twenty-four hours, an interval of which O'Barbo and other Sages like him took advantage to remove all the weapons from the soldiers on both sides. When they awoke the found themselves disposed to fight, but, no longer having any swords, spears or arrows, a panic terror took possession of them and they were seen to turn their backs on one another and flee more than sixty miles into the interior of their lands—with the result that on the second day, they were sixty or eighty leagues apart.

"One of the Sages was indiscreet, it became known who was responsible for that marvel; it was interpreted badly at O'Facfac's Court and O'Barbo was obliged to flee into the

Mountains of Stefenon, where I have just confided my Prince to him."

"May he be blessed," exclaimed the nurse, "and may my beautiful Princess be his spouse one day!"

As she finished those words, an invisible hand gave her a slap, and Dondanuck withdrew...

"Honorable O'Barbo," the gentleman continued, after a momentary interruption, "all Mommonians ought to bless you, for you have formed an excellent Prince!"

Now, know that the first concern of the Sage was to make himself loved by Oribeau, by always occupying him agreeably and mingling the exercises of the body with those of the mind, but while giving the latter the preference that they merit. He knew full well that it was not a matter of making a Prince a physically strong individual, but of giving him a just mind and a good heart. The exercises of the body, however moderate they are, sometimes harm the thinking faculties because they bring to the limbs they exercise the intelligence that ought to fortify the interior senses, which are memory, attention and judgment. Exercise the peasant and the artisan, but cause the man of study to repose, whose head alone ought to act; he will not live as long, but what does it matter? He will do what it is necessary for him to do.

Every morning O'Barbo made his pupil get up at seven o'clock. They sang together a hymn to Berda, or the Sun, conceived in these terms:

"Sun, eye of the world, source of life, spouse of the Earth our mother, I salute you! I salute you, O Sun, son of Thor, who makes fine days and nebulous days, whose divine presence vivifies everything, and whose absence plunges Nature back into the chaos from which you extracted it. Receive, O Sun, the homage of your children!"

After that prayer, the Sage made the Prince learn by heart fifty lines of the poems of the kaldes[18] for the morality, and a hundred of some poem for the victories of heroes.

"Here," said O'Barbo, "are a few of the moral maxims of the poems of the kaldes that remain to us; they were consigned to a Scythian book called *Havamal*,[19] or Sublime Discourse:

"'Has the guest who comes to you frayed knees? Give him fire. The man who travels the mountains needs nourishment and dry clothes.'

"'Fortunate is the man who attracts the praise and benevolence of men, for everything that depends on the will of others is hazardous and uncertain.'

"'There is no friend surer while traveling than great prudence, and no provision more agreeable. In an unknown place, prudence is worth more than treasure; that is what nourishes the poor.'

"'There is nothing more useless to the sin of the century than drinking too much beet; the more a man drinks, the more he loses his reason; the bird of forgetfulness sings before those who get drunk and steals their souls.'

"'The man deprived of sense believes that he will go on living if he avoids war, but if the spears spare him, old age will give him no quarter.'

"'The gluttonous man eats his own death, and the avidity of the insensate is the derision of the Sage,'

"'Love your friends and those of your friends; but do not favor the enemy of your friends.'

---

[18] I have retained this word as it is given in the original; it is an esoteric variant of "skald."

[19] "Hávámal" is an item found in the thirteenth-century *Codex Regius*, a collection of Old Norse poems; it includes a series of maxims attributed to Odin. Many of the maxims are rendered into French in Constant Dorville's *Histoire des différents peuples du monde* (1770-71), when Restif probably found them,

"'When I was young I was alone in the world; it seemed to me that I would become rich when I had found a companion; one man gives pleasure to another.'

"'Let a man be moderately wise, and have no more prudence than he needs; let him not seek to know his destiny if he wants to sleep tranquil.'

"'Get up early if you want to enrich yourself or vanquish an enemy; the wolf that is abed does not find prey, nor the man who is asleep victory.'

"'I am invited to feasts when I only need a breakfast; my faithful friend is the man who gives me a loaf of bread when he only has two.'

"'It is better to live well than to live for a long time; when a man lights his fire, death is in his home before he puts it out.'

"'It is better to have a son late than never; rarely does one see sepulchral stones elevated on the tombs of the dead by other hands than those of a son.'

"'Riches pass like the blink of an eye; they are the most inconstant of friends. Livestock perishes, parents die, friends are not immortal, you will die yourselves; I know of only one thing that does not die and that is the judgment that is brought to the dead,'

"'Praise the beauty of the day when it is over, a woman when you have known her, a sword when you have tried it, a daughter when she is married, ice when you have traversed it, beer when you have drunk it.'

"'Do not trust the words of a daughter or those of a wife, for their hearts are made like a wheel that turns; lightness has been put into their hearts. Do not trust either the ice of a day, or a sleeping serpent, or the caresses of the woman you are to marry, or a broken sword, or the son of a powerful man, or a newly-sown field.'

"'Making peace between malign women is like wanting make an unshod horse walk over ice, or like making use of a two year old horse, or being in a tempest without a tiller.'

"'There is no malady crueler than not to be content with one's lot.'

"'Never reveal your chagrins to the malevolent, for you will not receive any relief.'

"'If you have a friend, visit him often; the road fills with grass and the trees soon cover it if one does not pass over it incessantly.'

"'Never be the first to break with your friend; dolor corrodes the heart of the man who only has himself to consult.'

"'There is no virtuous man who does not have some vice, not a wicked one some virtue.'

"'Do not mock an old man, nor your decrepit ancestor; he often has wrinkled skin but words full of sense.'

"'Fire expels maladies, oak strangles them, straw destroys enchantments, runs destroy impressions, the earth absorbs floods and death extinguishes hatreds,'

"O Prince," added the Sage, nourish your heart in these ancient maxims, for it is in practicing them that your ancestors were raised up above other men.

"To give you an idea of true courage, sometimes sing beautiful songs composed on those of your ancestors who merited the throne, such as these:

"*Pronounce the name of Fear after the victory, but beforehand, let a sword pierce the tongue of the man who names Fear.*

"*When the brave chief of the Coriandys was captured by the Veliborys and he was condemned to death, he said to the soldier who was about to kill him: 'Stroke the face and see whether my eyes blink.'*

"*Fortunate is the man who dies like the great general of the Voldys, singing a hymn to Vananis on the battlefield where he lay wounded!*

"*Let us sing to the courage of brave Enniscorthy; he fought against the Ulternys; he was wounded, fell, laughed and died.*

"*If the slave runs ahead of the army in combat, let him be freed; if the free man runs ahead of the army in combat, let him be ennobled; if the nobleman runs ahead of the army in combat, let him be made a general.''*[20]

"But courage is not enough to be a great King. How does it serve a people that you defend against enemies from without if you devour them yourself from within, like the butcher who only preserves his flock from wolves in order to cut their throats? It is necessary to be a father to these people as well as a hero; the hero who is victorious but cruel is a thirsty tiger; the hero who is a good king is the best of beings; he is a benevolent god.

"The people believe that your mother's family is protected by the fay Wrwcwcw; that is a false idea that has been allowed to strengthen. I do not think it useful precisely because it is false; but that Wrwcwcw is one of your maternal ancestors, who was regent of Connacy and was renowned for her great wisdom; from that viewpoint she is infinitely respectable. She often had fine words in her mouth: 'I shall try to render my people happy, in order that my name, after my death, will be a blessing, and that it might be said of each of my descendants: 'He is as good as Wrwcwcw.'"

Such were the maxims with which the wise O'Barbo ornamented the mind of the young Prince confided to him. He added others still.

Chapter H
Horrible story that Oribeau hears on leaving the cavern of Stefenon to return to Waterford.

Honor, beneficence, justice, activity, prudence, courage, that is what makes the glory of a Prince.

---

[20] The author adds footnotes to this passage identifying the Veliborys, the Vodys and the Ulternys as ancient tribes of Ireland in the principality of Munster, identifying Vananis as the mother of amour and hope, and Enniscorthy as a name signifying the chief of an island in ancient Ireland. The first four names appear to be invented.

Those words were written on the wall of Oribeau's retreat. The first, above all, was incessantly on the Sage's lips. The second requires circumspection. The third is a sacred duty. The fourth enables a Prince to avoid all misfortunes. The fifth regulates his steps. The sixth defends his people and makes his neighbors respect him. All produce glory.

After two years of such instruction in the mountains of Stefenon. O'Barbo, seeing his young pupil almost formed, resolved to make him execute what had thus far only been shown to him in speculation. They departed one spring and came on the first day to Dunlavan, a small town eight miles from their solitude.

The Sage made the Prince observe how happy the people were in their Estates under the government of Dondanuck; agriculture was flourishing, commerce in vigor, and the peasants in abundance.

"Interrogate these fortunate inhabitants," the mage said to Oribeau.

They went into the house of one of the most well-to-do burgers of Dunlavan and requested hospitality. They were received with honor. The master led them to a big fire; he had a table laid, which was immediately charged with meat, game and fruits. When they had eaten, while drinking an excellent beer, the young Prince said to his host: "Under what government do you live in this canton where everyone appears so rich?"

"This town, young stranger," relied the Dunlavanian, "is in the realm of Mommonia, which is presently governed by Queen Dadameh, the widow of the great Prince O'Facfac; or rather, we have for a tyrant a certain Dondanuck, a sorcerer by profession and the greatest rascal in the world. The Queen is guided by his advice in all things; it is said that he has caused the young King to perish in order to take possession of power, and it is certain that he disappeared two years ago; people are sure that the sorcerer has enchanted Prince Oribeau by is conjurations, who gave us all the greatest hopes.

"O'Facfac had banished the magician for certain grave offences; Dondanuck swore to have his revenge. He went on his own to a cavern in the Mountains of Stefenon. He filled an urn of black marble with clear and limpid water, which pours from fissures in the rock; he lights a fire of resinous wood, arms himself with a dagger, plunged it into the throat of a nine-day old child and makes the first nine drops of his blood fall into the black urn; then he delivers his victim to the flames, which consume him in honor of the genius Perforimoth the Black.

"Suddenly, the cavern shakes; a dense cloud fills it; one sees blue flashes and flaming serpents flying; vampires, specters and the shades of executed criminals do battle; the cavern is heard to resound with the cries of owls of various species and filthy toads; a roaring of lions succeeds them and Perforimoth the Black appears. He has the head of a beautiful woman, the body of a billy-goat, the tail of a frightful dragon and the feet of a goose. 'What do you want?' he cries. A hundred thunderclaps accompany his voice.

"'The death of O'Facfac,' replies Dondanuck.

"The genius drinks three times from the bloody water in the black vessel, washes his face therein three times, vomits flaming monsters three times, spreads an odor of sulfur three times, and vanishes. Immediately, one hears in the depths of the cavern something like the stamping feet of a man choking; a plaintive voice cries three times: 'O'Facfac is dying! O'Facfac is dying! O'Facfac is dead!'

"That is the fashion in which the present Minister caused our good King to perish, under whom everyone could conserve his wealth, make his debtors pay, command his slaves and punish them when they did not acquit their duty. Instead of which, Dondamuck would like to render us all equal, in order not to have powerful lords who oppose his pernicious designs, while he would like to put the crown on his own head."

"And what has he done to enchant the young Prince?" Oribeau asked.

"That's something that will make the hair stand up on your head," said the Dunlavanian. "He took him to a cavern in the Mountains of Stefenon; he made him drink a certain beverage; he blew on him three times, and the poor young Prince became as yellow as wax, and so weak that a breath would make him fall down. Then he laid him down on the moss, and every day he has him given for nourishment two spoonfuls of brother of roads, vipers and bats. I know people who say they have seen the unfortunate Prince, in spite of the two frightful dragons that guard him."

"He has been seen!" said Oribeau, turning to O'Barbo, who was smiling.

"As I see you," replied his host.

Oribeau then asked for further details, which were all recounted with the same verity by the good Dunlavanian. Then the two travelers asked to go to bed.

Early the next morning, they set forth. After they had sung their hymn, O'Barbo said to his pupil: "Are you content with the news that you have learned? You doubtless didn't know that you were 'as yellow as wax', or that you were 'laid down on moss' in a cavern, that every day you were nourished with two spoonfuls of toad soup, and that two frightful dragons guard you, but so maladroitly that someone has been able to see you?"

"That's what men are like, then," replied the young Prince, "and the greatest Minister is the man about whim the most ridiculous and most frightful things are believed and published! How, then, will they treat me one day?"

"Well, if you are a good King; the same things that revolt them on the part of your Minister will make you admired; your rank will put you too far above them for them to be jealous of you. Instead of that, my friend being only their equal, they poison even the good that he does and publish atrocious things against him in order to render him odious to the multitude. It is a hundred times easier to be a good King than a good Minister; let that verity console you and your entourage.

"If you knew how they recount the story of your birth, that of a beautiful Princess destined for you, of her younger sister and a neighboring young Prince who is disgraced by nature, you would think that a subhuman being had invented all those puerilities. For example, it is said of the young Prince that he is as malevolent as he is ugly, that he indulges, with a herdsman who is raising him, in the most crapulous debauchery, which ensures that he dare not show himself at the Court of the Queen, his mother. You will know one day whether these accusations are as true as they are widespread.

"The elder Princess of Lagenia is the only one about whom evil is not spoken, but she is treated as a bastard. Her sister is reputed to be an imbecile. Men console themselves for their dependency by making up extraordinary stories about the royal family, but a good King forces them to be just. You have just heard what is said about you; as we continue our route you will hear and see many others."

The three listeners, the old innkeeper and the two drinkers, were scarcely breathing during the story. The gentleman smiled.

"It's late," he said. "I'm refreshed, goodbye."

"What! We aren't going to hear the rest of the story of the wise Oribeau!" said the two drinkers and the innkeeper.

"Yes, yes," replied the gentleman. "I'll come here every day to refresh myself, until I've finished. But can I trust your promises?"

"You can count on us," said the two drinkers. "When one recounts so well, one ought to speak even better in Parliament."[21]

The gentleman went away; the two drinkers got up and, when they had paid their bill, the old innkeeper said to them:

---

[21] Author's note: "One can see that this story has been retouched by some uneducated modern hand, since there is mention of Parliament, which did not exist under the petty kings of Ireland."

"He tells a tale well; he tells all, and I'm beginning to believe, like him, that the story is true, but that the fays and spells are perhaps false. Until tomorrow, good folk, and bring me some of your friends." (For the old lady was always thinking of her interest.)

The next day, the drinkers and several of their neighbors preceded the gentleman to the inn and drank while they waited. He finally appeared, and after refreshing himself, he resumed the story of Oribeau the Wise.

Second Evening

Chapter I
Itinerary of Oribeau; he returns to Waterford. Pomp of Thor: The Statues.

Indicating a village to the young Prince, O'Barbo said: "This is Timolinn, and further away is Castledermoot."

During the day he pointed out him Catherlagh, Laughlin Bridge and the river Barrow, which is crossed at Wells. In the evening, after having covered twenty-five miles, the two travelers stopped in Graignamanagh, fifteen miles from Waterford, capital of Mommonia, where they arrived the following day at two o'clock in the afternoon.

O'Barbo immediately informed Minister Dondanuck, who came to see the young Prince, and took him that evening, in disguise, to the Queen's apartment. The Princess was delighted to see her son again; they embraced tenderly, but her surprise and satisfaction were inexpressible when she had heard him speak with a consummate wisdom. She remarked on her joy to her Minister and gave a fulsome welcome to O'Barbo.

Then it was decided that the young Prince and his guide would be lodged in a distant part of the palace, where they would live incognito until Oribeau was perfectly informed of the mores of the capital and his subjects.

The day after their arrival, the young Prince and his tutor, dressed as mountain men, began exploring the city.

They had hardly taken a hundred paces when they were stopped by a moving crowd that filled the whole of a broad street.

"What's this?" asked Oribeau.

"It's a procession in honor of Thor; he's paraded this ceremonially, in order to ask for absolution for all the sins committed in the last hundred years."

"And is Thor influenced by that promenade?"

"They believe so."

"But you've told me that Thor was the ultimate in order; would he not prefer it if everyone kept to his occupations and fulfilled them, obliged his neighbors and attended to his own affairs?"

"You're right, but the druids would not have the opportunity to preside over that assembly, to lead that flock of women, to give themselves a kind of authority and receive offerings in the name of Thor, Worden, Friga, Vananis and Berda."

"I understand; it's for the druids that all this is done."

"Your Minister dares not touch that abuse; that will be your work."

After having waited for a long time, the Prince and his guide traversed a square, in the middle of which there was a pedestrian statue.

"That's a beautiful work!" said the young Prince.

"True," replied O'Barbo. "It's the image of the most famous of your ancestors, the redoubtable Oribeaumagne, who extended the Estates and whom his contemporaries accused of aspiring to the universal monarchy of Evinland."

"Did he, in fact, aspire to that?"

"To tell you the truth, I believe he did, but, the project having become ridiculous because of the obstacles, the adroit monarch pretended never to have had it."

"Why are those slaves chained at his feet?"

"They're nations, of which each of these statues has the attributes. There you see the proud Ultonian, vanquished but not submissive, who is in irons but is promising himself to break them soon. At that corner, the vulgar Connacian is imploring his destroyer with the design of deceiving him. In the other, the Lagenian betrayed by fortune is astonished that the redoubtable colossus of his strength has been felled. Finally, here, the county of Thomond, stolen by the Connacian, is regretfully resuming the yoke of his former master."

"Why eternalize the shame of his subjects and neighbors?"

"Flattering Ministers, to pay court to their monarch..."

"I understand," the Prince interrupted. "You'll approve if I remove that scandalous stone one day, in spite of its beauty."

O'Barbo made no reply.

"But what do I see?" added Oribeau. "*To the immortal man* is inscribed in runic language on the pedestal. Who is that immortal?"

"That's Oribeaumagne."

The Prince smiled. "People were persuaded that he was immortal?"

"No, but he was believed to be invincible, although that no-less-foolish error was destroyed before the end of his career."

The Sage and his disciple quit Immortal Square and continued their route. They found another square, more beautiful and more regular, in the middle of which there was a majestic equestrian statue.

"Who is that august monarch?" asked the young Prince.

"That's Oribeaumagne again."

"What pompous inscriptions!"

"You shouldn't be astonished; that Prince had produced a kind of enchantment; the heads of all his subjects were exalted, and as soon as it was a matter of praising their monarch, they thought they could never do so too highly; glamour always imposes itself on men, but it disappears with distance. Instead of which, solid qualities—justice, generosity, vigilance, paternal love for his people, make a King appear greater as the centuries go by; Time makes his apotheosis. On the day of his death everyone cries, while weeping: 'Our father is dead! He was a good King!' After a century, the grandchildren of the latter say: 'He was a hero!' A second century goes by, and Posterity makes a god of the good Prince, while forgetting the conqueror."

"You're inspiring me," said Oribeau. "It's better to be good than great, and benevolent than victorious."

As he finished those words, the young Prince and his guide emerged from the city. Superb edifices, recently finished, struck their sight, and in the middle of a vast space, absolutely bare, they perceived a statue that only appeared as a dot.

"Who is that Prince?" said Oribeau.

"That's your grandfather."

Immediately, the son of O'Facfac knelt down, and after having rendered his homage to his grandfather, he examined the vast enclosure in which the monument was erected. He was surprised by the expense that the futile and buried ornamentation decorating it must have cost. As no ensemble was presented to view, it was necessary to see everything in detail. Every part was small and pretty—which is to say that it was not made for a great work.

"It has no effect," said the young Prince.

"Pardon me," replied the Sage, "but that work, executed on a small scale, depicts the century in which it was made; if it subsists for a long time, which I don't believe, it will be a book for posterity."

While regretting the lost beauties of that square, the master and the disciple went up the Shure, which traversed Waterford, and reached a large bridge, massive and devoid of elegance. In the middle of that bridge, on the point of an island that divided it in two, a small enclosure had been fabricated in which a statue was visible, at which all the people looked with a profound veneration.

"Who is that hero, so respected?" asked the young Prince.

"That is a good King," replied the Sage. "Tested by misfortune and adversity, he knew the miseries of humankind before reigning and sympathized with them, so he governed paternally. Since the great MacErrick has ceased to live, his glory has always been augmented, and before long, you will see the Mommonians putting him in the rank of their gods. They already swear by him, and they make him intervene to cement the faith due to oaths.

Softened, Oribeau gazed at the august author of his dynasty. "O my father," he exclaimed, "I do not ask to be as great as Oribeaumagne, but as good as you." Addressing the Mage, he added: "Have our kaldes and bards celebrated that good Prince?"

"Yes; the most distinguished of them, the famous Iratlove, has made an epic poem in his honor;[22] it is an admirable work and universally admired for a long time, but envy, at first enchained by the sublime talents of the kalde, has preferred not to believe the venerable mortal, enfeebled by age; emerging from the somber dungeons of Tartarus sometimes in the form of MacWasp and sometimes that of Lalelubaelem; it has distilled its venom over the envelope of the work, not daring to attack the foundation, too respected by Mommonians. A universal indignation avenged the kalde and his hero."

"Have the perfidious MacWasp and the cowardly Lalelubaelem been punished?"

"No, the Republic of Letters must be free; the public is the sole judge of works of intelligence, and the scorn with which it heaps the malevolent and bad writers is such a tortuous shame that it is sufficient; the Authority ought never to interfere."

After having quit with regret the state of the good MacErrick, Oribeau and the Sage continued to go up the Shure. They reached a square devoid of symmetry that served as a drain for part of the city; they saw on one side a vast edifice in poor taste, on which was inscribed the runic name of Waterford. They then passed under an arcade, and after a very unpleasant street they found a superb one, which conducted them to a square whose presence Oribeau would never have guessed if O'Barbo had not pointed it out to him.

---

[22] The veiled reference is to Voltaire's *Henriade* (1723), the equestrian statue in question being a analogue of the one on the Pont Neuf.

That square was regular enough, but too enclosed. In the middle of the square was an equestrian stature of the King five generations removed from Oribeau, as the Sage told his pupil.

"A weak Prince," he continued, "but under whom great things were done."

"How is that?"

"It was because he had a Minister more powerful than him."

"What was his name?"

"MacCapcoupe."

"More powerful than his master!" said the young Prince.

"Yes, because he was able to take possession of his mind, and the Minister had more determination than a hundred men combined He was excessively ambitious, but it was through his master alone that he wanted to satisfy it; he rendered him absolute in order to be so through him; he caused him to make war, in order to vanquish through him; he rendered him inexorable, in order to avenge himself through him.

"Did he survive his master?"

"No, but his master scarcely survived him;[23] that monarch was crushed by the weight of his power as soon as he no longer had MacCapcoupe to exercise it.

"He could not find another Minister to command for him?"

"Yes, but he did not find in anyone the iron will of MacCapcoupe, which subjugated him and delivered him from his uncertainties. The Great Errick, who was able to reign by himself had had a minister of his bounty rather than his power named MacYllus. You will see one day what one of our bards[24] has said about him. The Queen Regent, who governed

---

[23] Louis XIII died in May 1643, six months after Cardinal Richelieu.

[24] Author's note: "Perhaps in the Eulogies of the Bard Homtas, of the great College of Bards of Evinland. One finds therein a magnificent eulogy to the Minister MacYllus." Maximilien de Béthune, Duc de Sully, was Henri IV's chief minister; the

previously, had had a husband and wife for Ministers; they were foreigners they were detested and both perished miserably, for having used their credit too much rather than having abused it.

"The reign of Oribeaumagne was also preceded by a Regency, but having become master, that great Prince had Ministers of his grandeur and magnificence, whom he always held subordinate to his will, which ought to be attributed to the troubles of his minority rather than to the kind of tutelage in which the Queen Regent's Minister, named O'Finsinelli,[25] had held him. That Minister was not as great as MacCapcoupe, but he was wilier and equally well able to serve his master—fortunate if he had been able to render his people content!

"The two Ministers that Oribeaumagne had in his maturity each had their department, O'Rhudhabord had war and everything dependent on it; MacArtlove protected the sciences, the arts, trades and commerce; he enabled the interior of the realm to flourish while O'Rhudhabord sought to make it respected outside the power of the monarch and the State.[26] I shall not talk to you about the Ministers who succeeded those two; let it suffice you to know that under their administration the glory of Oribeaumagne was almost entirely eclipsed.

"That Prince died and a child succeeded him, but he had a genius for a guide, who had borrowed the features of a Prince of the royal blood. I have seen him, and my admiration for him is undiminished by time; my respect for him has increased. O great MacOrlandoh, fortunate the nation that has a King possessing your enlightenment! The genius did not govern for long; he disappeared. An old man who scarcely resembled him succeeded him; O'Floring was disquieted by vain disputes that it was necessary to scorn, but he maintained

---

belated eulogy in question, by Antoine Léonard Thomas, was published in 1762.

[25] The analogue of Cardinal Mazarin, Queen Anne's Minister during the minority of Louis XIV.

[26] The references are to analogues of Le Tellier and Colbert.

Mommonia at peace, an inestimable benefit that redeemed all the faults of his administration.[27]

"I shall stop there; we live with the contemporaries of your father's Ministers and you cannot fail to be instructed regarding everything concerning them."

It was thus that the first excursion passed that the Sage and Oribeau made in the capital of Mommonia. The two travelers went to bed, and during the night, Oribeau dreamed that he had a Minister like MacCapcoupe, which made him very angry when he woke up.

Chapter J
Jejune fare; what Oribeau sees in the temples and among the Druids.

"Juvenile Prince," said the Sage to his pupil, as soon as day began to break, "today is a great day of fasting. The druids of all the Orders and the people themselves will not eat until after the eleventh hour of the day.

"Why?" asked Oribeau. "Does fasting honor God?"

"It's the doctrine of the druids, which appears to me to have for a foundation error and truth at the same time. Not eating, experiencing need, cannot honor God, but to accustom men to sobriety, to make them envisage an excess of food as a form of brutishness is a fine moral idea—and if one combines with it that of engaging the rich to give to the poor what they deny themselves, the idea becomes sublime."

"I can see that," said the Prince.

"Besides which, those sorts of abstinence temper the excessive effervescence of the passions, and consequently retain people who gorge themselves on everything in a kind of modesty.

---

[27] The references are to analogues of Louis XV's first two prime ministers Louis-Henri, Duc de Bourbon and Cardinal Fleury.

"Yesterday we visited the public monuments that interest you most directly; today, our attention will turn to the temples of the gods and their ministers. You will see those among the priests who make a particular profession of disinterest, fasting and mortifications of the senses. It's necessary to warn you that there will be things that will shock you, but suspend your judgment and consult me. You have been confided to my experience, it is for that to enlighten you."

They set forth immediately.

The first temple that struck them was that of Friga. As you know, she is the foremost of the goddesses, eternal Beauty being honored under the name, and her generative power is taken for that of the earth, our common mother.

It was a vast, obscure edifice devoid of elegance but majestic nevertheless. A High Priest, fifty druids, a dozen chosen children, kaldes and sacrificers filled the enclosure of the sanctuary, where the praises of Thor and Friga were being sung.

Oribeau, for whom that ostentation was new, examined with an attentive gaze the ceremonies of the worship rendered to the Immortals. After a long silence, which the Sage took care not to interrupt, the Prince said: "What is the point of this imposing display? The religion you have taught me is simpler and more worthy of Thor."

"It is thus that all straight hearts devoid of experience speak. You're right, and yet what you see is necessary. For two sane men who live in solitude, this apparatus is unnecessary, so the ancient contemplative druids were content with the hymn we sing and the homage of the heart; but my dear Prince, when it is a matter of an entire people, in which two in three people are vulgar and can only be moved by external splendor..."

"I understand," Oribeau interrupted, "but what does it matter whether those people have a religion, and ought the essence of worship to be destroyed in order to adapt it to their vulgarity?"

"Religion is one of the bonds of society,[28] Prince; it is therefore important that everyone has a religion. Look at it politically, and you are sufficiently enlightened to have no need of its brake, for you have been brought up in such a way that reciprocity alone can contain you; you sense the force of the eternal verity that it is necessary to do unto others as we would have them do unto us. That maxim, the basis of all morality and all association, is sufficient for a just mind; he senses that its violation is a violation toward himself and that everything is toppled; among human beings there ought to be but one law, to wit: 'In any subject of complaint, the Judge will examine whether the offender has done something other than what he would have wanted done to him, and will be obliged to repair the harm.'"

On quitting the temple of Friga, the Sage directed his pupil's steps toward an edifice built on the top of a hill, in honor of a celebrated druidess respected throughout the canton, named Vananis.[29] She had been a shepherdess and her virtues cause her to be honored today by Kings. Modern architecture shone on the frontispiece of that basilica; it was decorated with ornaments in the best taste. The young Prince could not weary of admiring it.

"Let's make a tour of it," said O'Barbo.

---

[28] Author's note: "Do not forget that it is pagans who are speaking; thus, one should not be surprised that they envisage religion as an exterior bond." He adds a supplementary observation: "*Religio*, in Latin, means *second bond, bond added to the law*; a religious man is a man re-bound, doubly submissive to the laws of morality, politics and nature."

[29] An analogue of Sainte Geneviève, the patron saint of Paris. The Panthéon, originally built as a church dedicated to her, was still incomplete when the author penned this passage, although it had been under construction for more than twenty years.

He observed his pupil when they were on its sides; he seemed disagreeably affected; then asked that was the body of which he had just seen the head.

"Yes, Prince, and what a simple glance can discover immediately, the Artist has not seen; without increasing his labor or the expense he could have made a superb basilica, but did not want to."

"So the same monument will cover him with shame instead of covering him with glory," said Oribeau.

"That is the just punishment of great artists, writers and even Kings: their mistakes are immortal."

It would take too long to render an account of all the other temples that the Mage and the Prince visited. They admired the beautiful frontispiece of a small temple dedicated to a devotee of the first ages; the majesty of another, built by a Druid who was its priest and whose tomb could be seen there, struck them with a respectful astonishment.

They penetrated then into a few abode in which druids lived in common. Oribeau found superb buildings everywhere, spacious courtyards, elegant gardens, immense orchards and vast kitchen gardens. He saw strong and vigorous men, hampered by ample and uncomfortable garments, who spent their days in absolute idleness. Some had liberty, others were entirely shut away, somewhat resembling livestock being fattened

"What!" said Oribeau. "Does inaction honor the Author of Everything?"

"No," replied the Sage.

"Why, then…?"

"My Prince," O'Barbo interrupted, "ancient abuses resemble tumors on the human body; in waning to excise them one might cause death."

"Is there no other means…?"

"Yes, but it requires a regime so exact, cares so particular..."

"Ha!" said Oribeau, in a low voice, as they came back. "I shall extirpate them..."

The Age heard him. "…That it awaits a celebrated monarch, the brother of a beautiful Princess, to commence the work of reform. The glory of the commencement is reserved for him; another no less great awaits you. One day, you will be the pacifier of all Evinland. Then, heaped with glory, you may dare anything you please, but with the wisdom appropriate to you, and which your youth announces.

They had forgotten to drink. Old Ennisleague had forgotten to urge them to do so while listening to the discourse, when the hunter interrupted himself.

"We've gained a great deal from your arrival," Younghall said to him.

"I said as much," exclaimed the innkeeper. "I'd never have said those beautiful things to you. I didn't know a word of them."

"Serve those who lack beer, my good woman," Kerry said to her. "I'll wait for you."

Ennisleague served, and when the aged innkeeper had resumed her place, the hunter resumed speaking.

Chapter K
Karmess, Kabacks and Public Gardens.

"Karmess! Karmess!" [30]
Such was the cry that the two travelers heard in the morning when they emerged from their dwelling. The young Prince asked the Sage what it was, and whence came the kind of fair that they saw in the square.

"Today is the feast of a temple," O'Barbo replied. "What you call a fair is a karmess, a rejoicing. Once you would have

---

[30] I have left this term as it is in the original, although it is an obvious adaptation of the same Dutch term that is adapted into French as *kermesse* and obsolete English as *kermis*, originally related o the celebrations associated with the founding of a church but broadened out to various other celebrations.

seen processions, masquerades and a thousand extravagances, but the Mommonians have abandoned all that and have left it to the Belgians, who still practice it. Here we no longer have anything but a small fair in the vicinity of the temple, where delicacies are sold and toys for children."

As the Sage stopped talking, carts carrying wine passed by, all of which traversed an arm of the Shure to go to an island decked with superb quays.

"Where are those carts going?" asked the young Prince.

"To acquit the duties that are part of the revenues of State. Once, in this State and almost throughout the North, all the inns were Kabacks—which is to say, places were beer and all liquors were sold to the profit of the Sovereign, who was that State's sole tavern-keeper, but for a long time your ancestors have no longer been tavern-keepers. They have left that title to their subjects and have contented themselves with levying a duty on all the goods sold in Kabacks.[31]

"Let's go along that little street; it will take us to an ancient and celebrated bridge where we saw that statue of the good MacErrick yesterday. We'll go across it and, by turning left, will immediately find ourselves before a superb palace,[32] for its necessary to examine the outside before going in, Prince. After the temples it's necessary to visit the palaces and their magnificent gardens. One day, you'll be too busy to see all that tranquilly."

On the banks of the Shure reigns a superb gallery terminated on one side by a palace, followed by vast gardens, and

---

[31] This word, defined as a shop selling spirits, can be found in Jean François' 1777 *Dictionnaire roman, wallon, celtique et tudesque*, where the author presumably found it while searching for words beginning with K.

[32] If one turned left after crossing the Pont Neuf to the right bank in the 1780s one found oneself confronted by the obsolete Louvre Palace, part of which was adapted into a museum after the Revolution. At that time the Grande Galerie still connected the Louvre Palace to the Palais des Tuileries.

on the other by a masterpiece of architecture. A majestic colonnade, the honor of the reign of Oribeaumagne decorates its façade; in the interior courtyard the richness of the ornamentation is astonishing; made to excite admiration, the traveler stops respectfully and recognizes the dwelling of Kings; but when he emerges from his enthusiasm, what astonishment strikes him on seeing the top of a part of that superb basilica destroyed by time, presenting in the bosom of its magnificence the image of ancient ruins!

Oribeau could not believe his eyes. He could clearly see the traces of recent work, but they had been abandoned. However, the ensemble of the palace, which the imagination easily completes, so simple is its design, inflamed his young heart with the desire to immortalize himself by putting the fishing touches to it

"How long would it take to erect a similar gallery?" he asked the Sage.

"Without trampling the people? Twenty years."

"That's a long time! All those buildings will be demolished; an immense courtyard embellished with suitable ornaments will form the most superb square in the capital; I'll destine it for the exercise of troops."

"That's a fine idea," said the Sage, "but only praiseworthy if carried out slowly."

They continued to advance, and through small dark passages they reached the palace garden. Two large pavilions overwhelmed the principal building, which ought to have dominated them. Given that great fault, the details were the greatest beauty. On entering the garden, the young Prince was delighted, but the rapid effect of the first glance was gradually effaced by the tedious monotony. The genius of the celebrated artist who was the author of the garden was too compartmentalized; the designs were charming in the plan but of small effect in reality.

There were pools, but the water in them was not beautiful, although the proximity of the river gave the greatest facility for making magnificent ones. The arbors were well-placed, and so vast, that one might have thought one was in the middle of a forest if the relative causes of good morals had no obliged their denaturation in order to enable clear views. There were superb terraces there; one was sheltered to the north, allowing it to profit from the feeblest rays of winter sunshine, the other, which overlooked the river, was appropriate to the freshness of a fine morning or a calm evening.

All these marvels, however, were nothing compared to the spectacle that had just struck the young Prince's gaze. It was spring and it was midday; a sky of the most beautiful azure heightened the dazzling glare of the sun; an innumerable crowd of both sexes was assembled on the winter terrace, and the brilliant and varied ornamentation of that undulating crowd was a match for the most beautiful flower-bed; the sparkle of diamonds as visible there, the vivid color of roses and the dazzling whiteness of lilies; the prism itself could not offer anything more brightly nuanced.

Oribeau stood there as if in ecstasy. His young heart, which nothing had yet moved, palpitated with pleasure at the sight of young beauties whose cheerful expressions, easy gait and graceful movements developed all charm. But one object effaced the other, and the Sage observed that these public places gave a great deal of pleasure to the sight almost without danger to the heart.

"These women are charming," said the young Prince. "Their adornment has an elegance that leaves nothing to be desired, but I think it too costly."

"You're right. Observe that husband; through the air of satisfaction that his tickled vanity gives him, you can glimpse a host of anxieties in his eyes; only his companion is enjoying the triumph of her charms, without thinking of tomorrow—but the husband is calculating and when they go home he will be in a bad mood. Look at that other; it's a young woman that he maintains that you see with him; she's showing him all the other women more richly dressed, and instead of the gratitude that she owes him for the enormous expense he made for her yesterday, he only receives reproaches; he's accused of stinginess, threatened with abandonment. That unfortunate, in ruining himself, has not even the sad satisfaction of momentarily contenting the brazen capricious individual to whom he is sacrificing everything."

"Do you think that a sumptuary law, without taking anything away from pleasure, would diminish the expense?"

"A sumptuary law in isolation would serve no purpose. Our Minister has a project, which he will communicate to you one day, for he will propose that you go to the source of the evil, by reforming mores.[33] We'll examine the question of luxury together, when you know the capital better."

"But tell me why the most distinguished women all have that vile rouge, which renders them almost ugly?"

"It's more to distinguish them from common women than to embellish themselves, for they know full well that the mask doesn't embellish them. When you're married, you'll be the master of putting an end to that ridiculous custom."

"How?"

"By engaging the Queen to banish rouge and face-powder from her toilette. All women glory in imitating their sovereign; fate will favor you, because the Princess that the gods have destined for you is so beautiful that whatever costume you ask her to put on, she will render it charming; she will create a horror of rouge, when it will be seen to disappear entirely without effort."

"That's the first time you've talked to me about that beautiful Princess since we've been together; when shall I see her?"

---

[33] Author's note: "A system of reform published in Waterford under the titles of *Gynographe* and *Anthropographe*; the editor has translated both into French." The references are to two of Restif's utopian tracts, *Les Gynographes* (1777) and the work actually published as *L'Andrograph* (1782), although Restif had originally planned to issue it with the title quoted here.

"The time has not yet come, Prince, and you'll have many obstacles to vanquish, but with courage and virtue, you'll overcome them."

As he finished those words, the Sage led the Prince away.

They crossed the Shure by boat and saw in passing the palace of a Prince of the royal blood, whose famous ancestors had obtained the nickname "the Great" without having worn a crown, and then the retreat of the old defenders of the Fatherland.[34] Oribeau scanned them hastily; he saw everything and was not content.

The Sage observed him, and remarked with pleasure that the young Prince sensed all the abuses, so honest and sane was his judgment. *What will he do*, he thought, *when he has experience?*

"We'll come back here," said Oribeau.

Then they went to see another establishment that had not lasted long; although in speculation it had offered the finest hopes its utility had been doubted subsequently.[35]

"This was a school for young noblemen," said O'Barbo. "It was desired by that means to give them a military education that would serve the nation."

"And that establishment was abandoned!" cried the young Prince.

"Yes, but not entirely. A fatal experiment had been made; the fact is that all of those young men, prepared at long

---

[34] In the eighteenth century the Bourbon Palace was still a country house, as originally constructed by the Princesse de Condé and the Invalides was still a hospital and retirement home for soldiers.

[35] The École des Cadets-gentilhommes, organized in 1777 by the Comte de Saint-Germain, did not last long under that title, but survived as the École militaire, which proved O'Barbo's observation when its star pupil turned out to be Napoléon Bonaparte, who joined in 1784, shortly before the present novel's publication.

range for an estate, were almost always less apt than those whom change and their inclinations had brought there."

"Why was that?"

The cause was natural. You make a duty of teaching youth exercises; they are, for them children's exercises and in consequence not much continued; they come to seem tedious, not by themselves but because they are prescribed at an age when one has no appetite for them; the métier is then followed mechanically and without enthusiasm; people become blasé and the taste never returns."

"I understand," said Oribeau, "but would it not be possible to remedy that inconvenience, for the establishment of a military school pleases me?"

"Your Minister will occupy himself with it one day," replied the Sage, "but I can tell you in advance that it will never succeed so long as proud children who think themselves above other men are admitted without examination, purely by reason of their birth; that pride is bad, always harming the service of the State. The State is made up of the people and the aristocracy in the proportion of a thousand to one, so the people are 999 times more of the state than the nobility. Now, one always serves that which one scorns poorly. But your Minister is wise, he possesses all the necessary knowledge to the highest degree. I advise you one day to give him a warrant to regulate everything in your Estates. You will profit from his school; you have in your family a fine example to follow. O'Finsinelli was far inferior to Dondanuck, and yet Oribeaumagne listened to him in regard to everything and obtained the benefit of his enlightenment. Your father, the good O'Facfac did the same with regard to O'Floring."

Oribeau promised to conduct himself in that regard as Oribeaumagne and O'Facfac had done.

They retraced their steps and, going along the Shure, they saw the public edifice destined for the Mint; the architecture seemed noble to them and appropriate to its destination and placement., but they cursed the Minister O'Finsinelli, who had wanted to build a public school, the two detached buildings of which spoiled the fine quay that they should have ornamented. A puerile motive had been suggested for that disposition but O'Barbo told the Prince that he did not believe it to be true, and that the poor taste of the artist, who resembled those frogs that puff themselves up, had determined the placement and its ostentation, as if a school ought to be a palace.

The Sage added that its ridiculousness made foreigners smile, especially the Angles, who were the nearest; that the same fault had recently been committed, with as much and more stupidity, for the schools of manual medicine.[36] By contrast, the National Theater, where all the riches of art could be deployed, had the modesty of a college of surgery or a school of jurisprudence. Oribeaumagne was not exempt from reproaches, for having put too much magnificence into his retreat for old soldiers, albeit for better reasons than those of O'Finsinelli and the architect of the school of manual medicine. It could be said that it was necessary to give a retreat for old soldiers the decoration of a superb palace in order to render their retirement more glorious. It was for that reason that he had deployed the greatest magnificence in the Temple of Worden he had built; he knew that old soldiers are devout and had the generosity to want to satisfy them in that.

After some detours the Sage and his pupil reached a palace of Italian architecture: a broad street, decorated with a few hotels, left the entire façade uncovered. They went into the garden, which was vast and rural; it would have seemed beautiful but for the one that the young Prince had just quit—but there was compensation in the pure air that was breathed there, and the solitude it procured in the middle of the capital for those who, weary of the tumult, wanted to enter into themselves. In that palace there were superb paintings made by a

---

[36] The now-obsolete French term *médecine manuelle* [manual medicine] covered disciplines that would nowadays be classified as osteopathy and orthopedics.

Belgian of the greatest merit.[37] Oribeau, who sensed by virtue of a natural instinct everything that was truly beautiful, was enchanted by them.

"May I have the pleasure of recompensing such an artist!" he exclaimed.

"You're right, Prince, but the man of letters who paints virtue is above him."

"That's true."

"And the philosopher who practices it and makes it loved…?"

"Is the benefactor of humankind; even Princes ought to honor him."

"Let each one be in his place, then, my Prince, and all will go well. If the pleasurable arts obtain all consideration, what will remain to encourage morality?"

"Is it unnecessary then, to honor artists?"

"Pardon me, but it's necessary not to imitate the King of the Angles who gave them more consideration than the sacred Ministers of the law and the most necessary men. When you recompense a man, first examine his merit in itself and classify him; then; then depending upon whether he excels, place him in the first or second rank of his class. But what should regulate all classes must always be the importance and the utility of the occupation rather that its difficulty; that does not mean that you will put a tailor or a shoemaker above a painter, because those useful men have no other merit than a facile routine, but when merit is equal in invention, the necessary and the useful should hold sway over the pleasurable."

On emerging from that palace, O'Barbo showed several others to his pupil, and they ended up in the one that the Minister MacCapcoupe had built. A part of it had just been restored, having been destroyed by fire. The architecture was very rich in regard to the gardens, but for the rest it was of a

---

[37] Marie de Medici, the wife of Henri IV, commissioned a series of 24 paintings from Peter Paul Rubens for the Luxembourg Palace.

taste below mediocre. The destiny of the palace was always great; MacCapcoupe had made it so firmly the center of his royal authority that the Regent, Oribeaumagne's mother, thought that she would render hers more respectable by going to live in it, but she soon recognized that it was the man who had rendered the place respectable. O'Finsinelli had mumbled whereas MacCapcoupe had made everything tremble. After the long and glorious reign of Oribeaumagne, the great MacOrlhandoh fixed sovereign power within that palace again, which has remained to posterity.

While the Sage explained what has just been said, he and his pupil had already traveled the length of the main pathway in the garden, shaded by ancient trees that formed a magnificent arbor. It was dusk.

The young Prince was surprised to see a crowd of young beauties waking, trotting and running, passing close to men, whispering into their ear, drawing them away or quitting them abruptly; everyone seemed busy, reminiscent of merchants at market. "Who are they and what are they doing?" he said to his guide.

"That which is bad, which you will criticize, but which you will be obliged to tolerate. In any case, I will show you a project of Dondanuck's which will diminish the evil. It will inform you of things about which I find it repugnant to talk to you."

They went out and as they were returning home they saw the most beautiful street in Waterford garnished with the same nymphs, who were talking to passers-by with the greatest familiarity. One of the prettiest came to assail Oribeau.

"Ha! How pretty he is! But he's a page. I can see that by his sly expression!"

The Prince, sensing his hands in those of the girl, was emotional, and nature was perhaps already...but a severe glance from O'Barbo made the siren let go.

"Go away, wretch, and let your impure breath not foul that which you ought to respect!"

The nymph did not understand that language and emitted a burst of laughter.

"What's wrong with the old rogue? He's jealous, I believe, because I didn't address myself to him!"

She pursued the Sage with a torrent of insults, whose effrontery inspired so much disgust in the Prince that they were the antidote to the dangerous disturbance that girl had just caused him to experience.

Chapter L
Luxury of Waterford; adornment of women, affection of men; foolish expense.

"Let us read the great book of public mores," said the Sage, as they went out in the morning of the first day of three festivals. "It's there that we'll find the truth. If you only saw your capital once, and that was today, you would think yourself the King of joyful sylphs who only breathe for pleasure. Sovereign as you are, you would regard yourself, on entering into yourself and examining your means, as the poorest and most unfortunate of men.

"That idea would be false and highly prejudicial to the people, by taking away commiseration; you would resemble one of those futile beings, raised in softness and abundance, who have a dangerous theory, which is that the habitude of distress takes away the sentiment. I would ask them whether the habitude of their cruel ennui diminishes for them the horrible torture that they experience everywhere and which forces them to make convulsive movements, to throw themselves into dissipation, prodigality and crime.

"When they see a poor man buckling under a burden; a vine-grower exhausted by labor and burned by the heat; a laborer tracing a furrow painfully, propping himself up on the plow that harassed horses are drawing; a poor artisan with a family to support contenting himself with a thin slice of bread for his meal, they say: 'That would be cruel for us, but those people are accustomed to it...' Accustomed, barbarians! Ha!

One does not become accustomed to suffering, to excessive pain; one feels it more, or more dolorously, after ten years than on the first day.

"Prince, we are going to see your capital at its best: the sky is pure; the sun, father of the day and the greatest of the gods, is going to provide a delightful daylight; all the citizens, enclosed for a long time, are going to emerge in a host from the gulf of mud and smoke in order to breathe freely. The moment of that emergence is the most beautiful; the whole world is fresh; the anticipation of pleasure renders all physiognomies cheerful; you're going to see the image of felicity. If you waited until this evening, the scene would have changed somewhat. Those alert and gay citizens will come back limping; those laughing men who are playing will return drunk, for the most part, or quarreling, or at least sad, for having expended for the pleasure of a single evening as much as they can, and having nothing or the rest of the week but the prospect of privation."

As the Sage finished these words, the young Prince saw a joyful group composed of a grandfather, grandmother, father, mother and children, numbering seven, three boys and four girls; it was an entire family who were going to amuse themselves in the wood of Lugobnoe. The young girls were dressed with the neatness of pretty individuals, the boys with simplicity, the father and mother in a serious manner, and the old couple in the antique style. The eldest daughter gave her arm to her grandfather, the second to her father, the third to her youngest brother, the fourth walked alone. The eldest son supported his grandmother, the second appeared transported with joy to be his mother's cavalier.

O'Barbo appeared to soften as he looked at the family. "I'm sure," he said to the Prince, "without having talked to these people, that they're virtuous."

"What tells you that?" asked Oribeau.

"The filial respect. A vicious father and mother are never respected by their children; that is the most beautiful and surest prerogative of virtue."

"Shall we accost them?" asked the young Prince.

The Sage approached the grandfather. "Honest old man," he said to him, "I congratulate you. You're about to savor the pleasure of a walk, breathe pure air and have a meal outdoors seasoned by appetite with your amiable family, who are not abandoning you to the solitude of old age."

"Abandon me!" exclaimed the old man. "That youth emerged from me would refuse themselves the pleasures of their age if I could not share them! Abandon me! It's me and my wife who season the amusements of our little children. The part that we take in them is the measure of their enjoyment; they consult our eyes, and when they see them moist with contentment and happiness, they deliver themselves without measure to the transports of their innocent joy.

"Afterwards, when they are well diverted, they ask my old wife and me to tell them about the amusements of our childhood, what we did at their age, how we acted with our brothers and sisters—and we tell them, and the shiver with pleasure on listening to us when we tell them how we venerated our good parents and how they contented us, how penetrated with respect and affection we were, and how they returned to us that mild and pure affection.

"Then they ask us how we made love, and I tell them how I have never loved anyone but my wife, how I sought her honestly and tenderly, how she listened to me modestly and with reserve and how she preferred me, without appearing to favor me; for she did not say much to me, almost fleeing. She did not speak at all to the other young men, but without pride; she fled timidly, and not disdainfully.

"And when I have told all, my aged wife unveils to them in her turn the virtuous and pure sentiments of her heart when she was young, and says to them: 'I can talk, now that I am old, about my first years, for I am the mother of several men, whose birth freed me from a part of the restraint necessary to girls and young women. With age, the sexes are, in a sense, annihilated; at a hundred years, there is no longer a man and a wife but two old people, or, if they are still spouses, it is for the children; relative to one another, they are no more than two old and intimate friends. O my daughters, a life without reproach is the salutary balm that softens old age; for it is a life without reproach that gives good children! Be good, dear children, to do honor to our good life.'

"And afterwards, when she has spoken, she cheers up our family, with the story of the little coquetries of girls of her age; then she tells us the stories of their marriages, and the influence that their mores and character have had on their happiness or unhappiness. And what charms all of the members of that dear family is that not one of those marriages has been as happy as ours."

"Old man," exclaimed the Sage, "how fortunate you are. I too have been a father, but cruel death has stolen my children; I would already be half dead in the tomb without this young pupil that the gods have given me: his fortunate dispositions, his high destinies...may Heaven conserve him and give him all the virtues! But wise old man, what means are employed in your family to render hereditary virtue and fecund nature therein?"

"Alas, I hardly dare tell you in this century, when a celebrated man has excited enthusiasm by means of a few verities and numerous paradoxes...for it is Ussuaero of whom I speak...that are contrary to nature. What does nature say? That is what our ancestors examined. A secret voice replied to them that nature brings everything to the individual, that it renders it personal, and moist; that it tells us to water everything, not to suffer any yoke, much less any insult; to repel violence by a double violence. Nature is not to be heeded at all in moral education; it only ought to be followed in physical education, with a few modifications. It is reason alone that ought to be heeded, directed by the social regime.

"And what does reason say? Everything contrary to nature. It teaches humans to make their wellbeing depend on public order, to put, by way of patrimony, their contingent into the mass of general wellbeing, in order to withdraw their share. The perfection of that conduct, to which parents ought to shape their children from the cradle, by the sacrifice of all their natural fantasies, is what is called virtue. The word *virtue* signifies strength; if virtue did not demand an effort, its name would be false. Against what ought that effort to be directed? Against nature and its disordered appetites.

"What is a scoundrel? He is a man delivered to nature, who cuts the throat of his fellow—which is to say that he takes away everything, life, in order to procure himself a slight advantage.

"What is a vicious person? He is a man who does not dare to be a scoundrel, because reason is sufficiently powerful in him to prevent him from so doing, but who yields to all the natural satisfactions that please him, however harmful they are to others and to his own health.

"What is an honest man? He is a man who forbids himself, by reciprocity, everything that might harm or wound other men, and who renders them the services that he should.

"What is a virtuous man? He is a man who goes even further than the honest man, in making the obligatory choices by inclination.

"What is a generous man? He is a man whose virtue bears him singularly to beneficence, and so fortunately organized that he enjoys the good that he does.

"What is a hero of any genre? He is a sublime man, honest, virtuous, generous to the extent of enthusiasm, who carries all the virtues to the highest degree.

"From the cradle, venerable stranger who is interrogating me, the passions of my children have been constrained, in order to make them human beings more appropriate to society, more submissive to the laws. When Ussuaero said that the law alone, with reason, ought to speak, and never the man, he spoke the most seductive of his paradoxes, but at the same time the most obvious. Who does he want to notify the law? An angel? Who has made the law if not men? It is, therefore, always the man who speaks, either through the mouth or through a book. I do not like the ticklish delicacy that does not want to see the mouth and the eye that command. The orders of my venerable father, intimated by himself, had a hundred times more unction than the dead and frayed letter of a book.

"I've lived for a long time," the old man continued, seeing that the two travelers were listening avidly, "and I've seen many things, so I can judge everything, a little. Would you like to come with us? We can chat, examining all the objects that strike our gaze; one will often omit an excellent observation in one's study, which does not escape outdoors because one encounters the objects there that nature makes?"

The Sage and the young Prince accepted the old man's proposition. They saluted the entire family. The young women, seeing a charming young man that their grandfather was welcoming, fluttered their eyelashes and blushed. Fredegonde, the eldest, was tall and rounded, ashen chestnut hair swept back from her forehead formed a chignon. Brunichilde, the second, was almost brunette, she had an animated coloration, bright eyes and her every gesture announced vivacity. Walpurge, the third, was the most beautiful; long blonde hair covered her head, without the aid of any coiffure; for ornamentation, it only had a few flowers. Canora, the last, was perhaps the most amiable; her frank and naïve gaiety announced the purity of her heart; she touched the Prince, who appeared to occupy himself with her pleasurably; as she was alone, he accompanied her, but while listening to the old man.

There had been a few moments when the conversation was general and everyone had something to say about the objects that struck their eyes, when two brilliant carriages, followed by several others—they were still in the city—came to cross paths. The crowd of people hastened to avoid them, but an old man and a child fell. They were about to be trampled under the horses' hooves or crushed beneath the wheels when an apprentice carpenter, strong and vigorous, with the aid of a boundary-marker, leapt on to the seat, knocked the coachman over and hauled back the horses.

All that happened in the blink of an eye. The master emerged from his carriage furious, sword in hand, to stab the carpenter, but the cries of the people and the firmness of the young man stopped him. Companions of various estates threw themselves on the coachman, thrashed him, cut the horses reins' and made it impossible for the carriage to advance.

Oribeau, quivering with indignation against the Mommonian lord, ascertained his name, wrote it on his tablets and promised himself to punish him one day.

Meanwhile, the other carriages passed by. Near the exit from the city there was a muddy area, where water had not drained away. Some distance away an elegant woman was walking, with her lover, a popinjay, between two boundary-markers, on the other side, several young maidens, as clean and white as lilies in flower, were bordering the road.

It appeared to amuse the valets who bore the name of coachmen to cover with a mask of mud the elegant woman, her popinjay and the young maidens clad in white; they moderated their sped, as if in concert, but at the instant when their horses set foot in the mire, they gave them a violent crack of the whip; the horses reared up; their front hooves fell back into the liquid mud at the same time, covering the elegant woman with black slime, blinding her and filling the open mouth of the fop, who swore, soiling the lilies covering the young maidens from head to toe and metamorphosing them into muddy canes.

The fop, who had spent three hours dressing himself, only saw with rage his discomfiture and that of his nymph. He had a sword and he ran through the knee-deep mud at the coachman, knocked him off his seat with a punch in the abdomen and ran off, favored by the people. Meanwhile, the nymph and the maidens excited the derision of the people surrounding them; everyone ignored the bloody scene that was happening fifty paces away.

O'Barbo, the young Prince, the old man and his family drew nearer. In the wounded coachman's carriage there were fainting women and furious men, who were talking of having someone hanged and calling for the Guard. The Sage recognized among them a lord that he knew; he approached him and said to him, quietly but in a severe tone: "You're the aggressors; besides which, it's a fine day, why don't you and your wives go on foot like us. I saw everything; if your coachman, and the one who has just been tipped off his seat a hundred paces further on were not dangerously wounded, I'd have them punished; they'd be condemned to public labor. Go away, and free the passage immediately."

The Mommonian lord withdrew, confused. He had one of his valets mount the seat, and all the carriages disappeared.

No one except the young Prince had perceived the effect that O'Barbo's speech had just produced. They were surprised to see the people who had been making so much noise before escaping, as if fleeing.

"That's not enough," said Oribeau. "I'm distressed that these young women, who were about to enjoy the pleasures of such a beautiful day, have been deprived by the malevolence of a wretch, and because it pleases the nobles of Waterford to nourish insolent individuals."

"We'd reveal ourselves in wanting to repair everything right away," said the Sage. "I only want to console them with a few presents that will be agreeable to them."

And the Sage, summoning a young street-hawker, gave various items of jewelry to all the maidens, who seemed transported with joy. He gave one a pearl necklace, another earrings, this one bracelets and that one headbands, a beautiful belt to another and finally, an artistically embroidered veil to the most beautiful. Everyone applauded, and, public malevolence no longer having any aliment, people ceased to mock the mud-splattered. To the elegant woman O'Barbo gave nothing; he knew that she was a prostitute, pretty enough to climb from vice to vice as far as aristocrats, who would give her a carriage in which she would be seen every day, returning with interest what had been lent to her.

That scene had interrupted the conversation of the old man and the Sage.

"There's a great deal of luxury in this capital," said O'Barbo.

"Yes, replied the old man, but is there too much? That's what it's necessary to know, and what we'll examine shortly, when we're in the country. Here we are at one of the most beautiful promenades of Waterford; let's see everything and make a provision of ideas."

As the old man finished speaking, a company of a dozen persons was seen arriving on the boulevard, five men and seven women. The latter were dressed with an elegance that caused them to be taken for women of quality. The Sage and his company studied them. The two older daughters of the old man's son appeared to be looking at the elegant women with the envious desire to resemble them, but Walpurge, and especially Canora, examined them indifferently. Their grandfather, whom nothing escaped, spoke to the younger two.

"Walpurge," he said, "and you, Canora, what do you think of those beautiful ladies?"

"They're well-dressed, Grandpapa," Walpurge replied, "but they don't seem to me to be any more pleasing for it. I observe that the confidence they have in the richness and magnificence of their adornment causes them to neglect giving themselves the agreeable, good, mild air without which beauty, as you've told us a hundred times, only inspires a cold admiration. Those women are not beautiful; their advantageous expression is ridiculous and almost insolent."

"And you, Canora, what do you think?" said the grandfather.

"I think, Grandpapa, "that my sister is a little too severe, even in speaking the truth; however, I agree that those ladies are going to a great deal of trouble in order not to be more likeable. They would be better with attire like ours, but that isn't their goal; their adornment, such as it is, says to the public what they want it to say: 'We're women above the ordinary; you can see that by our costume; we could wear things that were more becoming but they would not distinguish us from a pretty commoner; we do not want to please but to be envied.' I don't think that any of my sisters are curious for that pleasure."

Fredegonde and Brunichilde hastened to respond that they thought they looked a hundred times better in their simplicity than those women with their fine clothes.

"There's vanity in that thought, my daughters," their mother said to them. "I know that you're well enough dressed—which is to say, tastefully enough—not to envy anyone, but what gives value to a woman's attire, and doubles its grace, is modesty. Be modest, my dear daughters; the rarer that quality becomes in our day, the more you ought to conserve it in your hearts, in your speech and in your manners."

A man and a woman who passed by at that moment who, by the richness of their clothing, might have been taken for aristocrats, said to one another, pointing at the ladies that the Sage and the old man's family were considering: "My God, what elegance! That's Madame Pecuinies, wife of a lawyer and daughter of a procurator. That's her sister-in-law, the daughter of a bookseller and that one's the wife of a jeweler of Tanisnorohe Street. The others must be cut from the same cloth. Wouldn't one think that they were duchesses? They are, however, the wives of jewelers, procurators and other men of law."

The woman who said that was recognized at that moment by the old man. "And the one who's criticizing them is the wife of a bailiff."

"But her husband is wearing a sword," said O'Barbo.

"That's because he wants to distance further suspicions regarding his estate. A man with long hair is always regarded as practical, and that man wants to pass for a gentleman today."

Those people were lost in a brilliant crowd, which covered the most frequented area of the boulevard. The Sage, the Prince, the old man and his family went into it. They saw cafés—as they were not yet named—filled with beautiful women displayed like merchandise for sale, for they seemed to be there uniquely to be seen. A host of fops were moving through the ranks, looking down their noses at them, praising or criticizing, as if the beauties were statues or slaves for auction.

The pathways of the boulevard were even more brilliant; women of the finest quality were to be seen there, whose carriages had stopped on the main road in the middle. They were there to show themselves, like the commoners, and like them, they swallowed the dust with the praises given to their charms.

"If you judged Waterford by what you see here," the Sage said to the young Prince, "you might think that your people were the happiest and richest in the world. Not at all, and we shall see the truth elsewhere, but today, let us only examine their luxury; it is extreme and cannot rise any higher."

"But is it an evil?" said the old man, who heard that.

"That is what we shall examine when we've emerged from this swarm of handsome men and beautiful women, sylphs and sylphides. And let's not delay in getting out, for I fear this spectacle for your daughters."

"The older two are not as fortunately disposed as the younger," replied the old man. "That's because their mother, brought up in a foreign family, had not yet absorbed our principles when she brought them into the world; but I hope to cure them of their folly by the means that I employed to cure my daughter-in-law; I will tell you what they are. For the younger two, especially the last, my lovely Canora, there is no danger; she is so fortunately born that she only sees vices to abhor them more.

"However, let is quit this catascopic rendezvous where men and women show themselves off to one another and make mutual use of spectacle. One observation that I make in these assemblies is that self-esteem is not what is dominant; the men and women here are so modest, so just, that they willingly put themselves, for appearance and attire, beneath those who outshine them; one even sees women taking justice so far in that direction that, after having seen beauty that eclipses theirs, they quit the promenade and go home, enraged, and torment their husband until he has given them what charmed them in the object of their forced admiration.

"As soon as they have it they return, on another day, proud and glorious, to display their luxury and their graces—but that same day, if a coquette whose imagination is richer and more fortunate reappears in a new adornment, those modest women go home again even more discontented with themselves, desolate. They need that adornment, which made them disdain the one they had desired so keenly. They ruin their households thus with foolish expenditure, unaware that it is not what charms them in others that can embellish them, but what is becoming to their own figure, their stature and their stride.

"It is women devoid of taste and physiognomy who push luxury to excess; beautiful women, those whom everything suits, are will-o'-the-wisps for the ugly, which lead them astray; the latter follow them and, never finding what they're searching for, the graces, they fall into the abyss of ruin and poverty: a worthy punishment for their folly!"

As the old man finished, a great noise became audible in the direction of the city. Everyone ran that way. It was a wine-merchant—wine was rare and precious in Waterford—who had just, in a moment of excitement, laid out his wife, dead or dying, with a blow to the head with a stick. All the people of Waterford, very zealous on behalf of women, although they hold them in low esteem, were baying for the husband's blood. They were answered; he was taken to the house of the justice of the peace, but he was not there, so the guilty party was taken to a commissaire.

O'Barbo, the young Prince and the old man followed them, after the latter had told his family where he would rejoin them. The commissaire received the declarations of a host of witnesses; he was about to send the man to prison when the old man approached him.

"It's necessary to know, first," he said, "whether the man has killed his wife, for if he has not killed her, where is the law that condemns him to prison? You've listened to this blind and unprincipled populace, whose members depose what they think they know. Ask the man why he struck his wife; and in the meantime, send your clerk to find out how the woman is."

The commissaire listened impatiently to the old man, and he had opened his mouth to respond harshly when the respectable man said to him: "Measure your words for fear of preparing a repentance." Then he approached his ear and whispered something to him.

The commissaire blushed, showed the greatest deference to the old man and sent his clerk, who found the woman on her feet, lamenting and complaining about her husband. The people surrounding her served as an echo, and although she was neither dead nor wounded, they hoped to have the pleasure of seeing the wine-merchant hanged—for such is the mania of Waterfordians, that they will see a man hanged pitilessly, for inflicting a scratch on a woman, whom they scorn.

As soon as the woman was told that the commissaire's clerk was asking for her, she pretended to be very poorly—she did not know that he had been listening to her—and seemed to be unconscious. The clerk saw her malice. He summoned two porters, had her put on a stretcher and took her to the commissaire. All the people, seeing her pass by, even those— especially the women—to whom she had just been talking, sustained that she was dead. *Vox populi, vox dei!*

Meanwhile, the commissaire interrogated the husband with kindness and gravity; with a single word, the old man had made another man of him.

"Why did you strike your wife?"

"This is why, sir. I've heavily burdened this year. I said to my wife a few months ago: 'My love, we can't make any extraordinary expense in the next eighteen months without exposing ourselves to shortage. You have clothes, I don't need anything; we'll get by as we are; we'll work twice as hard, we'll economize, and this year, if it's fortunate, will decide our fate...'

"At the same time, I put before her eyes an account of my assets, which cheered her up, and my obligations, and, finally, the means of supporting them. She seemed quite content. I hoped that she would help me. However, there were new demands every day, trivial, in truth, but too multiplied. I made the observation to her; she didn't say anything at the time, but she sulked. Then she seemed to make it her task to increase all our small necessary expenses, to incur a few debts for which she engaged the creditors to demand immediate payment. She tormented me thus like a man suffering multiple pinpricks. My patience gave out; I cursed my wife's contradictory spirit.

"Finally, this morning I see her wearing a magnificent English dress beyond our means. I kept quiet, though; I say to myself: 'She's surely put something by from the daily augmentation of our expenditure; it wasn't the time to do it, but, after all, she's satisfied; I'll deprive myself of as much in order to repair the expense.' But that wasn't it! Scarcely had she tried, received and put on the dress than she sent the seamstress to me with the bill, not only for the making up but for the cloth and the fittings. It came to a hundred écus.

"It was impossible for me to pay it, but even if I had been able to do so, my wife's conduct would have been no less excessive. I declared that I wouldn't pay the bill, that she could take away the clothes. My wife came in, in a fury. I let her speak, but I was beside myself, and desolate to be bound to such an unreasonable individual. She came at me, heaped me with atrocious insults, and finally threw a wine bottle at my head. I didn't think that insolence ought to be tolerated; I struck her with the stick; she fell down and played dead. I'm sure that it's an effect of her malice, and I beg you to order that she be pricked in different places on her body, to force her to show that she can still feel."

The husband had finished his story when the clerk arrived with the stretcher-bearers and the woman. The husband went pale. "What if she's dead?" he said.

The clerk gave the commissaire a sign of intelligence, which he understood.

"Justice is prompt in this country," he said, loudly. "Here's a dead woman; it's necessary to inform the Great

Judge, and if she doesn't come round, that the husband be hanged in an hour."

The dead woman did not move. She was left in the room, surrounded by a few guards, and the husband was taken to another room.

After the clerk had explained to the commissaire, before the old man and the two strangers—O'Barbo and the Prince— what he had discovered, it was decided that they would take the proof to the end.

They went back into the room were the pretended dead woman was; the sentence was read to the husband, and it was added that as it was a holiday, he would be hanged in the courtyard. He was taken out. Everyone hid.

As soon as the dead woman could no longer hear anyone she opened her eyes slightly and then raised her head; seeing that she was quite alone, she went quietly to the window. She saw a gibbet in the courtyard and her husband, who was about to be attached to it. They expected that she would cry out, but she went quietly back to lie down on the stretcher again and continued to play dead.

"You see," said the old man, "that a woman frustrated in her taste for coquetry does not forgive, and would have her husband hanged if she dared. That is because, in fact, woman is made to please, it is her natural destination, and to thwart her in that matter is to take away the most precious portion of her existence, unless she has a great deal of virtue. Let us excuse this one, but let us correct her."

The husband was brought back into the room where his wife was; he was told that she was not dead, and that he could take her home.

"Get up, Madame," the commissaire said to her. "You've just been to the window, you can either sit up, or we'll carry out a little operation..."

She did not budge.

"Prick her with a pin."

Nothing; she did not give the slightest sign of sensibility.

"Cut off her hair."

At those words, she moved, extended her arms, uttered a sigh and opened her eyes slightly. Perceiving the clerk, scissors in hand, who had taken hold of a handful of hair, she pushed him away, leapt from the stretcher and fled to the other side of the room.

Everyone burst out laughing except the old man—for it is necessary to say that the old man was the Great Judge of Waterford. He adopted a severe expression.

"A woman can love adornment," he said, "she can have a liking for neatness, and a certain elegance, but that liking, taken too far, will ruin your husband...what am I saying?...has rendered you cruel enough to allow him to be executed in cold blood! It's a vice, in your hard and ferocious heart. How, with a face so pleasant, can you be so malevolent? It comes from a bad education; it's necessary to rectify it. By virtue of the authority vested in me, I dissolve your marriage, for your husband is dead for you, since you have consented to his death. You will be put in the hands of the wise widows consecrated to the worship of Berda, who will impose on you the punishment you deserve; you will stay with them until there is a sure amendment; afterwards, you will be permitted to marry again."

The Great Judge turned to the man. "You are free to take another wife."

"No, milord," replied the wine-merchant. "Return her to me; I love her, and if she wants to be good, I'll cherish her."

"She'll be returned to you—but at the first serious fault, you'll no longer be permitted to keep her."

The husband took the wife away, and the scene ended thus.

O'Barbo, the Prince and the old man went out by a back door because of the crowd and continued their walk.

Oribeau said to the Sage in a low voice: "It seems to me that the Great Judge is an excellent man.

"Yes, he's a friend of your Minister, and mine; if the opportunity to reveal himself hadn't presented itself, I would only have told you when we quit him. But we're going to make him talk about luxury; he's a learned man, a true philosopher. He's old; death might soon take him, and I'd be very glad if he gives you his ideas himself; they will be better engraved in your memory having emerged from his mouth; the memory of the man who has pleased you will fortify that of the truth that he will have told you."

"Does he know me?"

"Yes, but he doesn't know that you know that."

As he finished speaking, the Sage, who had kept the conversation private, approached the old man.

"It seems to me," he said, "that you're very indulgent to luxury."

"I ought to explain my principles to you," the old man replied. "You can see by my conduct that I don't like luxury for itself, or by inclination, but after long reflection, this is how I envisage it.

"The luxury of the capital presently extends over everything. People wear superb clothes, or at least very expensive ones; the lightness of fabrics renders them inexpensive, but they don't last and the multiplicity of fashions renders them dearer than cloths of gold. All the people who have a little fortune grant themselves a carriage, no one any longer goes on foot. The horse, that useful animal, the laborer's companion, consumes good forage here, while the laborers are poorly nourished; even the fertilizer is lost, the Shure carries it away.

"Tables are ten times as sumptuous as of old, served in profusion, with delicacy. Fires are multiplied in the houses; one alone consumes what was once sufficient for the heating of two or three. It is the same with candles and everything that serves for lighting; night has been made into day, and day into night; people sleep while the sun illuminates prayers, in order to work, enjoy themselves and eat—to live, in sum—by the artificial and costly light of candles.

"We pay for three elements—earth, water and fire—and only air remains to be paid for as we pay for light; that will doubtless come. The purest air in the world is in Evinland, but it will soon be corrupted in cities by some new invention, and those who want to breathe it pure, in their homes, in theaters and public places, will be obliged to pay in order to have a ventilator under the nose that preserves them from the poison exhaled by the perfumes that women, fops and young druids wear.

"The luxury of accommodation and furnishings has risen to the highest point possible. Go into the homes of our Mommonian lords, or the homes of our merchants, and you will find vast rooms, richly ornamented, which only serve as passages to reach the master's study. The rich burger does not fail to imitate that luxury in his fashion; he is expensively and expansively lodged. Without the number of its inhabitants having increased, Waterford has grown by a third in ten years; it has been necessary to invade the market gardens, whose soil is excellent because of fertilizer accumulated over generations, in order to make a new city and drive back the gardeners to the sterile and bushy hills that surround us; because of that, the prices of staple vegetables have increased.

"It is not that the city is full; there are empty quarters, but they are ignoble, and it is almost dishonorable to live in the southern part of Waterford, while the western and the northern are the fine quarters, those where all luxury and all the splendor of wealth shine. I think that it would be better, however, to fill those southern quarters rather invade our market gardens and fallow land. In truth, they're unhealthy, but the cause is easy to suppress by introducing a little more cleanliness and making another rivulet flow therein than the one that serves to tint it scarlet, by means of sluice-gates opened every evening that will purify it without rendering it less useful. But I'll return to our luxury.

"It is excessive, for I haven't yet talked about that of unnecessary servants, even more ruinous for the State than that of horses. The luxury of servants harms the population infinitely, because the majority of masters want domestics, concierges, and unmarried porters; it's regarded as dupery to take those who have children, because children are inconvenient and one imagines that one is being exploited by them.

No one blushes to put in the newspapers of Waterford an advertisement for the employment of 'a man and his wife without children who would like to have a place as porter and concierge.' I have followed these advertisements, to see who places them; I have seen, with a dolorous horror, that it is everyone. Then I have examined the mores of these enemies of children; they were harsh and lax, in a word, uncivilized. I have seen a rich physician, whom a concierge had served in his country house for seven years to his great satisfaction, discover at the end of that time that she was married with six children, become furious and throw her out.

"'But you were content with her!' someone said.

"'She has children, she must have stolen from me...'

"I could have strangled that monster; he did not belong to the human species. The eulogy of that physician was put in the *Necrology of Celebrated Men*!

"Another kind of luxury is that garments are no longer made of anything but silk, because that is out of reach of the people, and even the people wear silk. It follows that wool is neglected; it is less costly; the sheep is less precious and brings less; the peasant breeds fewer, and that is one fertilizer less. We draw our fine fabrics from abroad, etc.

"From that point of view, luxury is dangerous. Look at this promenade, at all the young people of both sexes. It is necessary to work relentlessly, and to live poorly, in order to dress like them; it requires very little for some to become swindlers or run up ruinous debts, or for the young women to go to the bad. Look at those two numerous families; that man is a merchant, how much must that wife and six children cost him, four of whom are daughters, dressed with that elegance? Perhaps he'll be unable to support that burden for long—for that is the situation of men today; they're too heavily burdened with everyday expenses, and the slightest cessation of earnings brings them down, hence so many bankruptcies.

"Luxury is a worm that eats them away secretly; they shine and they suffer. They prefer to shine and suffer because modesty in clothing is no longer supportable; it is a shame, unless one has transcendent merit or illustrious birth—then one is free to dress like the poor, if one wishes. The reason for that idea, in our century, is quite natural. People have a taste for luxury; the impotence to show it is the only thing that prevents it. That impotence is the mark of incapacity, of lack of talent. Now, you can understand that no one consent willingly to be deemed incapable and ineffectual. Luxury therefore renders almost all the inhabitants of the city unhappy and makes them suffer. Should it be annihilated?

"No, for these are its advantages in a mercantile country: it excites, it produces activity. The citizens of every class, delighted, in seeing the families that they have before their eyes adorned, likeable and admired, desire the same advantages for themselves. Those young women enchant a young man; he desires one for a wife, but he senses that it is necessary that she not be deprived of the adornment that embellishes her; he works, he applies himself, he bestirs himself, he becomes a useful citizen. Without luxury, he would vegetate. He looks further ahead; he knows that he will not always be young; the lot of the happy father of the beauty that pleases him then presents itself as a distant prospect; he hopes, he savors in advance the same homages that he will render, in order to obtain it. Luxury makes him desire marriage, to become a father; luxury renders his wife and children more lovable; he works hard, but he is able to take pleasure in working; a Sunday, when he puts on a performance, with his adorned family, compensates him for six days of difficulty, or cares; he finds himself rewarded.

"Let us go further still."

"Suppress the crushing luxury of brilliant carriages; forbid individuals the superb houses, manors, etc., that can only tempt common people, and you take away the enthusiasm of interest, the indefatigable activity that makes certain privileged individuals make efforts to enrich themselves that sometimes animate a province or an entire realm by stimulating competition.

"The ancient savages of Evinland fought, ate, drank and slept. They woke up hungry, hunted, ate and slept. The next day, bored with that life, they went to make an incursion; they massacred the old men, disemboweled the women, crushed the children, pillaged, ate drank and slept. Whatever harm our luxury does, it is one of the causes and one of the effects of urbanity; it is preferable to the savage life. I don't even know if it ought to be regulated. I don't think so; it cannot be regulated without inconvenience, for if regulation is successful, activity diminishes, and if it is unsuccessful, disobedience diminishes the sinews of authority; people become accustomed to putting themselves above the law in conventional matters and one soon sees them violating essential laws."

"So you're in favor of the luxury that you do not have," said O'Barbo.

"Yes, but I have a sort of luxury of propriety. I believe myself to be obliged to that, it is a duty toward the State; I ought, by my expenditure, to encourage manufacturers and tradesmen. Without luxury, there is no commerce, for luxury is its parent; commerce enriches and luxury makes use of riches. Take away the usage and there is no more desire to acquire; people will no longer brave the furious waves; they will remain poor without being any more virtuous.

"I spend in proportion to my fortune, and appropriately; I pity those who do otherwise, but the State does not suffer therefrom; the follies of the prodigal contribute to activity; they enable fortunes to pass from hand to hand. He who dissipates loses, he who works ardently finds; unfortunate is the man who loses, fortunate is the man who finds—but it is a general advantage for it to be possible to find.

"The ancient Egyptians, if they were, as we are told, locked forever into their estate, could only have been a very sad people, who would soon have lost their activity, their energy, becoming despicable, and finally enslaved—and their history, which I have read in a Roman book that made a good deal of noise on the continent, has made me see that my thinking was accurate."

"Do you approve of the folly of the young Mommonian lords who ruin themselves?"

"No, but if it amuses them, I no longer hold it against them."

"And the sons of financiers who dissipate millions?"

"They are making restitution."

"You approve of them?"

"No—how can I approve of debauchery?—but I admire eternal Providence."

At that moment the company—which is to say, the Prince, the Sage, the old man and his family—met up again beside a mud-patch.

A brilliant carriage was advancing at a trot; the young women, timid and neat, moved away, but the young men, including Oribeau, who were bolder, scarcely disturbed themselves. The twenty-four iron-shod hooves of the six quadrupeds fell into the mud simultaneously and threw it right and left. The old man's sons, the young Prince and O'Barbo himself were covered by it.

One of the young men, very excitable, marked his impatience by a word and a gesture. Oribeau made a slight grimace. Three of the young women smiled; the fourth came to wipe her brothers, and the others did likewise; their mother occupied herself with Oribeau. As for the Sage, he said to the old man, smiling: "Luxury is sometimes very inconvenient."

"Oh, if you had seen the beautiful woman who was in the carriage!" said one of the young men.

"I glimpsed her," said Oribeau. "She's as beautiful as Canora."

The young woman blushed, and became even more beautiful.

"She's a foreigner," said O'Barbo, "and if I'm not mistaken..." He stopped.

Who do you think she might be?" Oribeau asked him.

"I'm listening," the Sage replied. At the same time, the cry was heard of a beautiful bird, which had a yellow tail, blue eyes, a black body and three crests.

"Oh, what a beautiful bird!" cried the four young women.

O'Barbo seemed pensive, for the bird indicated to him—according to the fabulous history of the Prince—the presence of a young and beautiful Princess; but was it the person who had just passed by in that superb carriage, or was it someone else, hidden from all gazes under some disguise?

One might have thought that the Sage would have had recourse to his art, in order to find out—and he did, but he did not say anything.

They continued to walk with the old man and his family until evening, admiring the brilliant attire of the Waterfordians, and their gaiety, for as long as the day and the pleasures lasted; but when dusk fell, the cheerful people seemed to have changed their nature. With the exception of a few drunkards of the lower class, who were singing or quarreling, everyone else was limping home sadly. The women were saying: "How tired I am!" The men were scolding them and carrying the little children, who were weeping with the desire to go to sleep.

Meanwhile, O'Barbo, who had returned to the city with the old man and his family, dropped back momentarily with the Prince in order to let a carriage pass by. When he wanted, or appeared to want, to catch up with the Great Judge, however, they could no longer find them.

"Let's return to our lodgings," he said to the young Prince, "for we're alone now."

"That magistrate is an excellent man," said Oribeau, "and I thank you for acquainting me with him. He said things about luxury that appear to me to be wise and sensible; it has given me an enlightened sentiment on that matter."

Having arrived at their lodgings they had supper, and went to bed.

Chapter M
Misery seen by Oribeau in hospitals and prisons.
He witnesses an execution.
The Prince and his Guide are imprisoned.

Mortified that there were three feast-days in succession, the Sage O'Barbo and his pupil came out for the second holiday, in order to continue to see public pleasures. They doubtless made many new observations, but the annalist has not transmitted them to us.

After the feast-days they went to visit the abode of dolor. A six o'clock in the morning they were at the door of the house where all the sick poor people were received.

"Let's go in here," said the Sage, "it's the Evidletho."[38]

The young Prince was almost suffocated. "Where are you taking me?" he said.

"Into the temple of dolor; come and take therefrom a lesson most useful to a King."

They perceived in a vast hall moribund old men piled up four by four in the same bed.

"What have these unfortunates done," said Oribeau, "to suffer thus the torture that cruel Duntalmo of Scotland condemned his victims? Apparently this house is poor."

"No, Prince, it's rich, but those whom the government put in charge of it grow fat on the blood of the unfortunate. The Grand Druid, who is their primary leader, has an excellent heart, but instead of occupying himself with the most important function of his position, which he would prefer if he were not obsessed by bunglers—that of visiting and caring for the poor—he amuses himself persecuting Thorists who think that one cannot be agreeable to Thor without mistletoe; he gives all his attention to that puerility. O Prince, remember that abuse one day, which your Minister does not dare reform as yet, not to punish it but to correct it!"

---

[38] Restif often replaces the letter u with v in his anagrams, as here in the anagram of Hôtel-Dieu.

108

From the hall of old men they passed into others, where they found invalids lying on their own, and better treated. They saw some of whom great care was being taken, and learned that they were recommended. O'Barbo did not criticize what was being done for them, but he would have liked the same attentions to be general.

From that house the Sage led the Prince to another, where the greatest cleanliness reigned.

"The sick are better off here," said Oribeau.

"Look closely," said his guide.

Indeed, the young Prince saw on the faces of those who were caring for them an expression of harshness and impatience; remedies were administered there with a severity that had no regard for strength or temperament, with the consequence that in a matter of hours he saw ten men expire, who were killed by the regime rather than their illness. At the same time he saw semi-convalescents sent forth whom a gust of wind might have felled, so enfeebled were they by the violence of the remedies.

"I'm indignant at this harshness," said Oribeau.

"The druids who serve here are not the only guilty ones," the Sage replied. "It's also the physicians that it's necessary to blame; under the pretext that dieting is useful, as soon as the body experiences some disturbance they prescribe rigorous fasting; to destroy fever, which is an irregular movement, they seek to bring about the cessation of all movement. What happens? The humors are not refreshed by healthy and new aliments, an ordinary fever becomes putrid and proves mortal. Or if some other acute malady is combined with it, the impoverished mass of the blood and the exhausted strength give birth to a crisis, which conducts the moribund to the tomb a few months after his convalescence."

"Why are these cruel abuses not repressed?"

"By virtue of impotence. The government cannot know everything, nor enter into every detail. However, the particular conduct of physicians ought to be enlightened. Look at the majority among them—they are careful not to follow the regime they prescribe to prolong maladies! If they are indisposed, they take healthy aliments that are easy to digest, in small quantity but frequently; in health they nourish themselves succulently, as their plumpness makes manifest. Interest, the good of base souls, is their sole motive. But I advise you soon to introduce a regulation with regard to diet, in accordance with the mature examination of the wisest, most honest and most experienced of the body. Once those regulations are published in your Estates, the superstitious and the medical fanatics will be enlightened and they will be preserved, while avoiding the two extremes, according to the maxim of a kalde that it is the middle course that is safest."

The Prince and the Sage retraced their steps, and in an isolated quarter of the capital they found a house named the Aitipé, full of young boys grotesquely dressed, dirty and unhealthy, accumulated in rooms where they breathed foul air, occupied in things inappropriate to their sex, ill-educated and directed in everything with a pettiness and degrading attention to detail. They saw arrogant maids of a sort, egotistical and shrewish, of an incomparable stupidity, who arrogated a boundless authority over these unfortunates.

Oribeau was more sensible to the misery of these poor children because the majority were nearly his own age. His indignation was ignited; he scolded the maids, threatened the wretches who had the title of Masters, and it would not have taken much for him to reveal himself, in order to inspire a just terror in them, but the Sage restrained him, promising him that he would urge Dondanuck that same evening to remedy such a great evil.

In order to relieve Oribeau of the sad ideas that he had just acquired. O'Barbo proposed that he should come into a public garden that was not far away, and which they had not yet visited. They found botanical treasures there; one could see by the order that reigned there the wise intentions of the skillful director of the establishment, and that, if there were innumerable negligences, they came from the nonchalance of subalterns,

Afterwards they climbed via a labyrinth on to an eminence from which almost all the city was visible, and the neighboring countryside.

"You see this charming place?" said the Sage. "It's not long since the subalterns excluded the public from it and made its arbors serve for excursions of libertinage; but either because the wise O'Funfbo[39] was informed of it, or simply out of justice, it has been returned to the public, and disorder, which always seeks exclusive places in which to hide, has been banished from it."

After O'Barbo had allowed the young Prince to breathe the pure air of the location for a while they left and found two horses at the gate, which the Sage had ordered. They mounted them and emerged from Waterford by the eastern gate.

On a hill that received the beneficent rays of the midday sun, they discovered in the distance a vast isolated house whose appearance was entirely agreeable. The young Prince promised himself the pleasure of visiting it. It was named the castle of Citrêbe.

"Let's go see that castle," said the Prince to the Sage.

O'Barbo smiled. "That's the destination of our excursion."

They arrived at the door. Oribeau went ahead of his guide, cheerfully, but scarcely had he set foot in Citrêbe than he shuddered in horror. Three immense courtyards filled with dirty, unhealthy individuals viler and more hideous than animals were contained therein; their host was afflicting to sight, wearying the ears with plaintive cries and wounding the sense of smell even more."

"What is this abode, then?"

---

[39] Restif uses "Funfbo" elsewhere as an anagram of Buffon; it is not obvious why he has added the prefatory O to it on this occasion. Buffon transformed the Jardin des Plantes in the mid-eighteenth century from a small apothecary's garden into a research center, subsequently adding the zoo and the labyrinth.

"It's the resource of the poor and the last refuge of old age."

"I thought it was a prison."

"It's that too; these wretches can only go out twice a week; it's feared that they might spread into the surrounding area and might beg; it's easier to lock them up than to treat them well."

"Oh! Why hasn't the Regent's Minister commenced by remedying that cruel abuse?"

"Because there are great difficulties, which you might be able to relieve, one day. If all men were reasonable, the science of government would be child's play, but they abuse everything. Here, for example, it is feared that the artisans might make a pleasant retreat, to neglect work and plunge themselves into idleness and drunkenness. The Minister would be overwhelmed with reproaches if, in trying to do good, he produced another evil—instead of which, if you, Prince, were to carry out that reform, people would only see your generosity. I'm not advising you to follow the movement of your compassion blindly, merely to suppress such establishments as this in order to charge each parish with its poor, who, then being familiar, would be treated as they deserve to be.

"These general establishments are only useful to their administrators and the officers that are employed here; the state is overburdened by them and the poor find nothing here but dolor, malady and death. A mild, humane, compassionate man before being employed in a hospital becomes a tiger as soon as he performs any function there, and that is natural; he is suddenly bewildered by the number of the unfortunate and he dimensions of the evil; the impossibility of relieving everything leads him to close his eyes, his ears and his heart, in order not to be touched by anything and not to render himself as unhappy as they are.

"A few years ago there were in this house and others that resemble it modest druids of a sort applied to their duties; they served the poor and consecrated the revenue of their patrimony to them, and every morning they prostrated themselves before Thor, saying to him: 'Be blessed, Father of Men, because we have what is needed to soothe your children; be blessed, O Thor, because we soothe and are not soothed, for in that we resemble you, who give everything without receiving; we thank you, O Thor, for our happiness, but preserve us from pride, for it is you who makes us desire and do good, you in whom and by whom everything exists, and without whom we would be nothing.' And after that prayer they went to serve the poor, like their fathers, their brothers and their children; one saw their faces radiant with joy in the midst of the rudest and most disgusting labors. If you had seen the poor bless them...

"But those druids were among those who believed mistletoe to be necessary to please Thor; an Archdruid of a different party arrived, who expelled them all. They quit their work with regret and spread out into the country, where they hid from persecution."

"I swear by Thor and by the august soul of my father the great O'Facfac that the Archdruid merits death."

"Be less ardent, Prince. Anticipate the evil that our druids might do; repair that which they have caused; have the houses in which they are brought up supervised, in order that they are prevented from losing public spirit to take on that of an isolated body, but let their blood never redden the scaffolds because of religion—that would be the means of attracting the veneration of the people to them and making you abhorrent."

"What! Would the people not sense...?"

"The people never go back to causes; they only see the blow that strikes, the blood that flows and the suffering individual; they do not ask whether it is only punishment..."

The Sage then approached a small door, which he had opened. But let us turn away from the sight of that abode of horror. There were madmen. Not shall I report all that O'Barbo said about the causes of madness, the manner in which one ought to treat those in whom that frightful malady commences in order to bring them back to mildness by an adroit assent to their ideas, etc. That wise doctrine would serve

no purpose here, and would focus too long on sad images—
but there will be mention of it somewhere.

They passed from there into another courtyard closed by
an iron grille. Two guards introduced them. First they saw the
obscure ventilation shaft of four profound dungeons. It was
there that unfortunates were precipitated destined never to see
daylight again, or those that had revolted, and would only
emerge to perish by capital punishment.

To the left was the prison where all the wretches who
had become necessary evils of society, spies, were locked in
together. To the right were a multitude of cells where bad husbands and bad sons were moaning, and those scourges of society whom their frightened families had retained in the route of
crime and infamy when they were already ripe for the scaffold. Perhaps, in some of those sad dwellings, calumniated
innocents were also groaning, but the Minister sought the truth
and what escaped him was reserved for the young Prince, to
whom the Sage explained everything. They interrogated several prisoners together, after having imposed on the guards by
the authoritarian tone they adopted.

"But it is necessary to make so many miserable in order
to avoid a few crimes?"

"That question, which all good Princes ask themselves,
has not yet had a satisfactory response In any case, Lord, when
you govern, you will try your strength, and if you feel strong
enough to make the wicked tremble without imprisoning them,
you will be the master. A King who knew all his subjects
would have no need of prisons, but in all great States, where
an inevitable confusion reigns, crime hides in the crowd and
does evil with all the more boldness because it is more difficult to distinguish it. Take note, however, that your Minister
has already emptied half of these cells, which were once insufficient. Since you my Prince, love justice so much, may all of
them become unnecessary and those frightful dungeons no
longer hear the moans of the culpable!"

"Have I not heard mention of a Minister who sometimes
filled them with innocents?"

"Have no fear, Lord, that he did it ought of wickedness; he was deceived by people who paid dearly for involuntary crimes and the infamies that sold the soul, the honor and the humanity of their master."

"Ha! I would not have punished them any less. One does not sell Dondanuck's humanity!"

The Sage made no reply. It was easy to excite a just indignation in the soul of the young Prince, but he did not want him to become too severe, because of the excess to which virtuous youth is often given, having not yet had sufficient experience to be indulgent.

In order to give his pupil an accurate idea of the harm done by inconsiderate rigor, he took his to the place where incorrigible children and bad lots were imprisoned. In a vast dormitory, they saw camp beds accumulated next to one another on which that unfortunate youth slept, almost abandoned to itself. They took one of those who seemed most reasonable and questioned him about the manner of existence and life.

The Sage observed that the poor and primitive nourishment that the children were given contributed to giving them vitiated blood, which the kind of abandonment in which they were caused all vices and crimes to flourish among them, borne to an excess that gave rise to horror; and that that treatment, named Correction, would have been better named a School of Perversion, the seminary of Tyburn and La-Verèg (to make use of terms that are known to us).

"You see, Prince," said O'Barbo, how establishments that are apparently the most useful become a public pestilence by virtue of the bad administration of subalterns. This youth, so maltreated and so unfortunate, far from being corrected, ends up here being hardened to crime."

"That's nothing," said the child to whom they had addressed themselves. "Would you like to see how rebels are punished? Have that door opened, if you have the power."

The Sage approached it; at the same time he heard a few inarticulate groans uttered. He order the door opened in a tone that marked his authority to command. He went in, leading Oribeau by the hand.

What a spectacle! A young unfortunate of about fifteen years was attached to a foot of earth against a wall by two iron shackles, one for his feet and the other for his hands. A Corrector, armed with scourges with steel tips, was striking the patient with all his strength, who had just fainted and whose skin was coming off in shreds.

The Sage and the Prince only saw two blows delivered, which were the last two of the prescribed number; the unfortunate was taken down; his wounds were bathed with eau-de-vie and vinegar, which brought him round; he was wrapped in an old shroud and carried to his bed.

The inhuman Administrator who had ordered that execution was sitting in an armchair and no trace of emotion was visible on his face. He ordered that another be brought in. The Sage wanted to see the prison from which he was taken; it was a damp little cellar, in which one could neither stand up not sit down—what a torture for a wretch eaten away, as all his companions were, by the cruelest of skin diseases!

They were about to attach him and lacerate him.

"Whatever his fault was," Oribeau whispered to his guide, "I cannot suffer this. Expel that tiger, or I won't answer for myself."

"I'll do a part of what you ask, but know, my dear Prince, that a sovereign must, above all, command his passions, including compassion and especially indignation."

At the same time, O'Barbo took the Administrator aside, and the result of the brief conversation they had together was that the patient was detached. The Sage only gave him a strong remonstration, and he was sent back to his comrades.

When they were alone, Oribeau swore by Thor that he would annihilate all such establishments.

"Either annihilate them, or reform them; but it would be better to annihilate them, and work little by little for the reformation of universal mores."

On emerging from the Correction, the Sage wanted to show his pupil that place where victims exhausted by debauchery were treated.

"My Prince," he said, as they went in, "see how vice is punished! Thus, Thor and Worden—which is to say, Nature—have determined: repose, happiness, tranquility and surety are only found in an innocent life. What does Nature demand of blind Mortals? Is it to renounce all pleasures? No; on the contrary; those that she permits are the most delightful; she only puts one condition on them: nothing to excess. But men do not know how to use; they believe they are only enjoying when they are abusing. Honesty and virtue are the most delicious seasoning of amour, and yet the majority of men seem to disdain them, in order to deliver themselves to debauchery, which poisons the pleasure and soon changes it into torture.

"If there were a law that obliged them to deliver themselves to the prostitutes that you saw at the exit from MacCapcoupe's palace, to drink and eat to excess, they would regard that law as the most insupportable of tyrannies, and if it were possible that it emanated from Nature they would complain to Heaven and accuse it of having rendered them the most unfortunate of beings. Exactly the contrary exists; the law is full of wisdom; Nature only prescribes what tends to render us happy and to conserve our health and our morals, but we seem to enjoy our existence by going against both!"

After that fatiguing tour, O'Barbo emerged from Citrêbe and took the Prince back to his lodgings; they dined with appetite, and after resting for an hour or two they recommenced their excursions.

"What are we going to see after dinner?" the young Prince said, as they set out.

"If this morning's spectacle has not disgusted you, we'll continue..."

"Disgusted! Me! But I was…is not your goal to teach me to be a King?"

"Yes, Lord."

"Have you not told me a hundred times that I must observe particularly that which it will be most difficult for me to see when I reign?"

"Yes. Come, O good young Prince, come—what a happy future I glimpse for the Mommonians. But be careful of flattery. Merited praise encourages, but adulation will corrupt you."

They commenced their second tour with the women's hospital: an abominable abode of which Tartarus is perhaps but a feeble image. Here one sees the mad, there the wretches who, having abjured all modesty, have exceeded the bounds of public tolerance; elsewhere the old and the immoral, groaning too late over the past; elsewhere, youth bastardized by an evil regime...

The Sage explained everything to his pupil. Oribeau understood that a place was required to sequester unfortunate beings who have lost their reason, but those prostitutes locked up together, idle, within reach of the help of the accomplices of their debauchery—for the Sage did not hide anything from him; he told him how there were infamous men who subsisted on the disorder of prostitutes, and inflamed the Prince so much that Oribeau swore to exterminate entirely that execrable human waste by rendering every individual skillful in denouncing pimps and every local commissaire responsible for the slightest negligence in that regard. They discussed means of reforming the most revolting aspects.

"If all women were pleasant, and everyone was married when necessary," said the Sage, these unfortunates, of whom you see such a considerable number here, would be unnecessary; but there is a host of bachelors and an infinity of insupportable wives, and men would deliver themselves to the greatest excesses of depravity if they did not find the shadow of sensuality with these facile women, who provoke it. In large cities especially, horrible things happen, of which rape and abduction are the least."

"So I can't annihilate them?"

"Your Minister has imagined a means of rendering them less dangerous, which would be to cloister them and to give them a regulation, with governesses, but it is necessary that it be the monarch himself that executes such a plan, in order to shut the mouths of the pretended Puritans and the ill-intentioned, those eternal enemies of all good, who incessantly bay for virtue, which they do not like.[40]

"Have you observed," the Sage continued, "that in all houses of public utility, a strange, destructive abuse reigns? It is that the people who are forced to put their head in these establishments think and behave as if they were made for them and not for the poor. Hence, the poor administration that you have remarked, the enormous expenditures that swallow up the funds destined for another usage entirely."

"You're right. It's also necessary to reform that abuse."

"Yes, but it's the most tenacious of all."

Having returned to the city, the Sage took Oribeau to the malefactors' prison, where trials where examining magistrates carried out their investigations. They saw there a most of unfortunates accumulated, idle, devoid of control or regulation, abandoned to all the perversity of their corrupt hearts.

They saw one of them who was sick, expiring in a corner of need and filth. They saw devout women who brought a little insufficient help to those vile dregs of society; they followed them into the cells where a few murderers charged with chains were blaspheming while awaiting execution. A culpable was taken out of that noxious place; he was immediately put to the question.

The Prince turned his eyes away.

"Look," said the Age. "A legislator ought to know the effect of his laws. Look, even if you cannot bear the spectacle that is in preparation."

---

[40] The author includes a brief note here referring readers to *Le Pornographe* (1769), his tract on the reform of prostitution, of which he gives a more elaborate account in due course.

Then the young Prince saw the feet of the patient put between two planks, which were fitted as side-pieces; wedges were inserted into the gaps and the planks were tightened until the bones cracked, while a physician took the pulse of the patient in order to determine the point to which he could be made to suffer without killing him.

During that horrible torture, the scoundrel was interrogated, who charged himself with a hundred times as many crimes as he had committed. He disavowed three quarters of them when he was at rest, and agreed that he would have confessed to a thousand more if it had been demanded of him.

"You understand, Prince," said the Sage to Oribeau in a low voice. "Torture, as punishment, is a futile torment because it is secret; as a means of conviction it is even worse, it can be used against an innocent, which is a horrible inconvenience."

"I shall annihilate it," said Oribeau, whom compassion was causing to sweat copiously."

Afterwards, the scoundrel was taken away to be executed. The Sage engaged the Prince to watch the execution.

An immense crowd of common people lined the streets and filled the windows; the square where the scaffold had been erected was full. They slipped through to a position as close as possible.

The unfortunate, after being put in a public dock in order to make his last testament, was taken to the scaffold, where his bones were broken. He uttered horrible screams, and the Prince fainted. O'Barbo soon recalled him to life.

They were about to withdraw when they perceived some tumult in the square.. Thieves had taken advantage of the moment when people were attentive to the blows to steal money and jewels from the spectators. Someone, having perceived them, had called for help, and one of the thieves, dreading being unable to slip away with his stolen goods, had taken it into his head to slip several items of golden jewelry into Oribeau's pocket.

The Sage saw what was happening, but, content that he knew where to find the thief, let him do it. The chain of one of the items of jewelry was sticking out of the unsuspecting Prince's pocket; it did not take long for it to be noticed. People threw themselves upon him and found several stolen items on him. He was led away and taken before a justice of the peace or local commissaire.

"What is your name?" the demi-magistrate asked him.

The Prince did not say a word. O'Barbo spoke: "He's my pupil; he isn't guilty."

"Not guilty! You have the air of being so yourself, you old rogue, and I think I recognize you. Have you not been made to wear a carcan?"

"You're mistaken sir."

"Oh, that little rogue could carry out some bad coups with his mild appearance! No one would suspect him! Tell me, my friend, this isn't your trial run?"

"Why are you insulting us without knowing us?" said the Sage.

"You're going to prison, you old ape; for it's as well that I cut short your conduct. As for this little crook, he'll be hanged; his physiognomy condemns him; there's too much risk in letting him live."

"But sir," the Sage interrupted, "Would you care to listen to a word in justification?"

"Your pupil has been found with the effects; you're his master in crime. To prison."

"But to condemn someone for the crime that they might commit one day, and which he might equally well not commit...?"

"He's arguing! Rebellion! Write it down."

"Sir!"

"Drag that old rogue outside, and don't spare him."

"Sir!"

The Sage was struck rudely and dragged away.

"If one wanted to listen to that rogue," said the magistrate, "they'd all be innocent, and there'd be no water to drink in our squares."

While speaking in that fashion he examined the jewels and proposed to himself secretly to appropriate them.

The Prince and the Sage were thrown into a small and dark prison, different from the one where they had been that morning and much more unpleasant; it was only populated by pickpockets. They wanted to send the two prisoners down to the dungeon, but the Sage found a means of preventing that; they were taken to the common room.

When they went in, the young Prince would have been subjected to the most frightful extremities if the supernatural force of his guide had not preserved him from them. All crimes presented their hideous face to him, but a little money finally drove away that infamous troop.

"Well, Lord," said the Sage, "What do you think of the justice of the peace?"

"That he's a scoundrel. Do all the others resemble him?"

"Not all, but many of them."

"Well, how can the Minister…?"

"Unless one finds oneself in the predicament we're in, one can't imagine that things are as they are. You'll see the official account of our capture, which will be sent to the Minister tomorrow morning. It would be necessary to name ourselves for anyone to think us innocent, and you'll be surprised yourself not to be guilty."

"O Heaven! These poor people!"

"They're often the victims of laws made to ensure their tranquility."

In return for money, the Prince and the Sage had beds in a room for twelve; they lay down and slept peacefully.

The following day they examined the conduct of their new comrades. It is a sad reflection on humankind that the worst torture an honest man could suffer would be to live with those wretches. All received ideas are overturned there; crime is heroism, crapulous debauchery voluptuousness, and pleasure is there a deformed composite of everything one can imagine of the perverse and the frenetic.

While the Sage and the Prince observed, they saw a woman come in. The man she had come to visit put his hat on the foot of his bed, and immediately, all the prisoners went out.

Toward evening, the Sage wrote to Dondanuck. Immediately, two of the Queen's Guards came to set the prisoners at liberty. Everyone, including the jailers, trembled before those two men, who had not been noticed before, as soon as it was known that the Queen and her Minister were interested in them.

Having arrived at the palace they asked the Minister to send for the commissaire. Dondanuck summoned him and interrogated him with a severe expression.

"Great Minister, may Thor give you a long life," relied the iniquitous individual, "but who would accept our positions if it were necessary to examine everything and answer for everything?"

"Why don't you do it in your position, since the Great Judge of Waterford does it in his, and since I do it in mine?"

"You're the first, then, and if you're phenomenon, am I obliged to be one myself? Anyway, if you want me to speak frankly, you're reputed yourself to be something of a sorcerer, and your transcendent science gives you many facilities that I don't have."

"So you toy with the liberty and tranquility of citizens?"

"No, but I seek my repose."

"You're going to see those you have treated unworthily appear."

At the same time the Prince and the Sage came into the hall, superbly dressed. The frightened commissaire threw himself at their feet and begged for mercy.

"No," said Oribeau, "if you were to continue in your responsibility it would not be clemency but connivance. You're dismissed."

And he was sent away, but was allowed to keep his official report. It was conceived as follows:

Today, the fifteenth of the month of September, two scoundrels were arrested in the public square of this noble city of Waterford, who had committed theft during the execution of one of their comrades. The thief who was the younger appeared to me to have acted on the instigation of the older. By virtue of the sagacity, penetration, prudence and perfect knowledge that my long experience has given me, I immediately recognized that the old man was a scoundrel; the indubitable symptoms that I had of that were the wandering eye, looking askance and alert, like that of the wolf, the fox and other carnivorous animals; his mouth, his features and his hands all announced a man accustomed to evildoing. As for the young man, his hypocritical air nevertheless had something criminal about it, which was easy to see by his eyes, in which we and our clerk, who is a wily individual, perceived the form of a gallows; his laughter is that of the Evil Spirit, his attitude base and he expresses a continual machination of evil and damnable designs. After these remarks we had no doubt that both of them were guilty, in spite of their protestations of innocence. That is why we proceeded with their interrogation in the following manner.

"By all the rules of physiognomy, you seem to me to have the air of two scoundrels, isn't that the truth?"

Silence on their part, which is the equivalent of an admission.

To the younger: "Haven't you stolen these jewels, that are shown to you?"

"They were found in my pocket."

It was written down that it was agreed that the stolen effects were found on him.

"Didn't you take them in the public square during the execution?"

He was unable to reply; shame closed his mouth, but the old soldier, whose pupil he is, answered for him: "He's my pupil and he didn't steal those effects."

The Clerk, a penetrating man, said: "The old man commanded his pupil to commit the theft, or did it himself and put it in his companion's pocket, hoping that his hypocritical air would prevent anyone from suspecting him."

The conviction being quite sufficient, after the admissions of the guilty parties, we, justice of the peace, committed to public surety, by virtue of the authority confided to us by the superior magistrates, which comes from the august Price Oribeau, our legitimate sovereign and Queen Dadameh our Regent, his august mother, both sage, immortal, incapable of human weakness, seeing everything, knowing everything and two whom all the best possible of honor and glory in all centuries in perpetuity, which is as true as it is true that the two guilty parties are scoundrels, summoned the old man to tell us his name, which he refused to do.

We summoned his pupil to tell us his name, who similarly refused, in spite of a few threats that we intimidated to them, even to have them submitted to the full rigor of the law of Evinland against voluntary mutes, which consists of lying the guilty party on his stomach and loading him by gradation with an enormous weight until he confesses or expires.

The two thieves having persisted in their refusal to tell us their names and homeland, or to disclose their employment and profession—which, however, were sufficiently known to us—we have, by virtue of the aforesaid power, sent them to the royal prison with the order to the concierge of jailer to send them to the darkest, most profound, most silent and dampest dungeon in the said royal prison, to stay there in secret, without having any communication with any living person, except by order of the superior magistrate, the Great Judge of Waterford. Which has been executed immediately, as is apparent by the report of the undersigned Officer charged with the execution.

The Sage then spoke to the Minister about the frightful disorder that reigned in the prisons, and Dondanuck decided to commence applying a remedy.

"Prince," the Minister added, addressing Oribeau, "one day, no doubt, you will change the manner of detaining the guilty, but let it be done with prudence. For example, this is the plan that I advise you to follow:

"1. Condemn the criminals to public works, in proportion to their crimes, under the guard of a few troops, which will only have the commandment.

"2. For capital crimes, such as any kind of parricide, rape and assassination, two years of the hardest labor, not softened by any amelioration, at the end of which time hanged and burned without hope of mercy.

"3. For murder, robbery, forgery and all other crimes liable to the death penalty, twenty years of hard labor, at the end of which, if the conduct has been satisfactory, semi-liberty—which is to say, a choice of labor or payment; in the opposite case, hanged in accordance with the law.

"4. For theft, fraud and all the other crimes that merit infamous punishment, ten years of labor less hard than the preceding, better nourished, etc.; after which, complete liberty in the case of good conduct.

"5. For ordinary cases of prison etc., a fixed time of the least hard but continual labor, at the end of which time, liberty.

"By that means, there would be no useless person, and the moral corruption that reigns in prison would be avoided, as well as much expense. Interrogations would be carried out without interrupting the work for more than an hour or two."

Chapter N
New enlightenment. How Oribeau and the Sage see justice rendered.

"Now, we have learned many things in the last two days," Oribeau said, on waking up the following day. He then conversed with his Government about their imprisonment, as well as Minister Dondanuck's project for the punishment of the guilty. That conversation determined the employment of their day. They went to see justice administered in the various tribunals of the capital.

The Sage first took the heir to the throne to an ancient castle, where one saw on the one hand the horror of dungeons and heard on the other the incessant baying of quibblers besieging subaltern magistrates who, by a preliminary judgment, flattened out difficulties and prepared an easier decision for the supreme judges, even when their judgment had been based in error.

They entered a large hall where civil cases were judged. A whining advocate who was pleading for a bankrupt supported his bad case on a multitude of laws that necessity had attached to legislators. The creditors' advocate thundered against the bad faith of the fraudulent debtor, and accumulated evidence of dissipation and misconduct, but he could not prevail against the present text of the law, by which his adversary was authorized; he lost, with costs. A sentence authorized the bankrupt to govern funds that he had not been able to administer and to dissipate the remainder of the creditors' pledges, because the straw men forming three quarters of them favored the infidelity.

The astonished young Prince said to his guide: "Tell me, do the laws of Mommonia protect bad faith?"

"No, Prince," O'Barbo replied, "but in the time when they were made, fraud was rare; people still had honor—which is to say that they feared the judgment of their fellows; the legislator came to the aid of unfortunate citizens whom accidents had ruined, and it is by virtue of that humane law that those brought down by luxury, men devoid of principles, true scourges of the fatherland, abuse today, bringing frightful disorder to society, rendering even the practice of virtue incapable of assuring the repose of honest men. Thus, one could say that fraudulent bankruptcy is a crime against humanity for which no punishment is too severe; it will be for your prudence to remedy this odious situation one day; you can see the abuses; how many sovereigns would correct them if they had seen them?

They passed then into another hall, where criminal cases were being judged.

"We are going to see," said Oribeau, "whether or not the life and honor of men are jeopardized, and whether such important decisions receive all the attention they merit."

"You're mistaken," said the Sage, "If you think that it is major cases that are judged with a public audience; those are decided in secret, and only cases of little consequence are, which only result in condemnations to fines and compensation, are conducted with all the trappings. Great criminals have no advocates, the witnesses are their judges, their party is the Prince himself; with the proof is complete, the law pronounces."

"But who judges whether the proof is complete?"

"It's necessary to agree that injustices are rare in that matter. Thieves and assassins, caught *in flagrante delicto* for the most part, will escape punishment if they are unjustly condemned, but there are other cases where partisan spirit, fanaticism, and the hatred of a powerful Minister can tip the balance and take for crime what only has the appearances of it; those cases are easy to detect, and it is appropriate that there is a monitor in every tribunal who is responsible for informing the Prince directly of those rare cases and sounding the alarm in order to warn the nation to keep open eyes on the conduct of judges, whose verdicts can only be executed after a considerable delay, in order that the accused has time to furnish all the evidence for his acquittal, either on his own behalf or by the ministry of his advocate. In any case, I think that it would be better if all criminal cases were judged publicly, that the evidence is clearly exposed and the confrontation of witnesses is public, without anything ever being able to dispense with it."

After that brief digression, a case was pleaded between a peasant and his lord. The latter had, according to custom, exclusive rights of hunting and fishing. The peasant, still young and uneducated, could not conceive how he had been deprived of the natural right of all men over animals; he had hunted; he had killed game and had been caught by the Lord himself, who had treated him outrageously. The peasant had revolted; he had raised his arm against his Lord and had insulted him.

The latter, for reasons that he did not specify, had only charged his vassal with the insults, for which he demanded a reparation, and that a rigorous punishment should be inflicted on the peasant in order to intimidate his peers and, he said, retain then in subordination.

The peasant, for his part, defended himself on the basis of the outrage received, which had rendered his defense legitimate, excited his anger and had led him to proffer a few insults; he invoked the right natural to all men, and even animals, of repelling violence with violence; he argued that he had not exercised that right with as much vigor as he might have permitted himself to do. He also denied the crime of poaching, with which he had not been charged, by arguing that he had expelled from his cultivated field wild pigs that were devastating it, and that if he had killed one, it was because it had attacked him.

These arguments did not make any impression on the minds of the judges; the peasant was sentenced to make a public apology to his Lord, to pay compensation and legal costs, with a warning against recidivism, under the greatest penalties.

"Is that judgment just?" asked the Prince.

"No, according to the law of Nature," said the Sage, "but yes, according to those that regulate human society. Subordination is necessary to the latter, without which there would soon be anarchy and disorder. The peasant has therefore been justly sentenced, for having broken that law of subordination; but the Lord is not innocent, and it is here that an equitable monarch, after having received an account of such a case, might inflict a punishment on the man that the law has caused to triumph. But what prudence is necessary in such encounters! So I would advise the sovereign to establish, for such occasions, a particular tribunal, which would be called the Court of Redress, which would be charged with punishing anyone who abuses a real right."

They were about to emerge from the temple of chicanery when they saw a large crowd of people who were running toward the door of the first hall that they had entered.

"What are they going to see?" asked the young Prince.

"Today is the last Friday of the month, when the prostitutes picked up by the Guard are judged, as well as the pickpockets and other bad lots who are to be locked up in the prisons we have seen."

The Sage and his pupil went in with the crowd and saw a spectacle most capable of causing a philosopher to reflect. Fifty or sixty prostitutes were assembled in the court, laughing and playfully insulting the men and women that curiosity had gathered around them. One saw there that the naturally timid and modest sex, once beyond its bounds, pushes impudence of effrontery beyond anything imaginable. Only one or two were hiding their faces and weeping; they were young and pretty.

Oribeau was touched by their tears; he waited impatiently for the judge to arrive and to hear the reasons for their condemnation. He finally arrived; it was the old man, Canora's father.

Almost all the prostitutes were only accused of having been on the streets late and attracting men into their houses.

"But it seems to me," said the young Prince, "that you told me that the Government tolerated those unfortunates?"

"That's true; nevertheless, from time to time it gives signs of disapproval of that obligatory tolerance."

"But it seems to me that, in accordance with the principles that you have inculcated in me, that, the Prince being the father of a family who ought to work for the general and individual wellbeing of his children, that conduct is not entirely just. The misfortune of these women is being treated coldly; there is at least some cruelty therein."

"I am glad that you have made that observation, Prince. So, when you govern, your Minister promises to propose to carry out the project I have already mentioned to you, which will remedy all these inconveniences."

The two young women who had interested Oribeau were summoned then.

The first was a young woman who had been loved and maintained by the son of a rich man; the latter had found out and had forbidden his son to see her, at the same time as he had tried to have her for himself; the girl had refused, because she loved her lover, and the irritated father had punished, not the disorder, but the refusal to commit a greater crime; however, the condemnation did not relate to motive but to bad conduct and the disturbance of the son of a family; the surplus was discovered by O'Barbo, who took pity on the unfortunate woman and had her returned to her family, with a pension that he exacted from the old seducer in order that the girl might live honestly.

The second was a tapestry worker; a young kalde had made her acquaintance and, although married, had seduced her with a few presents, but as he was very ugly, the girl, once debauched, had abandoned him for others. The kalde, having perceived that, took back a beautiful dress that he had given her. The young woman regretted that which served for her adornment more than her honor; she became furious; she went one day to wait for the kalde at the door of a lady in whose home she knew that he was reciting his verses, and when he came out, she seized him vigorously and began to maltreat him.

The poet, a thin debauchee, and hence feeble, saw no other means of getting himself out of the hands of the Fury than to send someone to fetch his wife. The latter came running and scolded her husband's mistress like a fishwife; inhibitions flying away, the champions rolled in the mud with so much intensity that it was necessary to send for the public Guard, who took the kalde, his wife and his mistress before a Justice of the Peace.

The wife spoke first; she explained the situation clearly. The mistress complained of the theft of her dress by the kalde, while agreeing that she had received it from him. The poet impudently set out the motives for his gift. The judge listened and pronounced: "You, Sire kalde, are married and you have mistresses—to jail! You, Miss, listened to another woman's husband—to the jail of fallen women! As for you, Madam, who have surely committed faults against your husband, since you have been unable to satisfy him, your punishment will be the embarrassment and expense that the imprisonment of your unfaithful spouse will cost you."

That judgment was very just, and the Sage allowed the girl to suffer the three months in hospital to which the Great Judge had condemned her, the petty kalde imprisonment, and the latter's wife the embarrassment and expense that would inconvenience her greatly.

Chapter O
Oribeau continues to see judgment. How he hears pleas before the sovereign court.

O'Barbo had only had time the previous day to show the Prince the subaltern tribunals; today he would take him to the

superior courts, which judge in the last resort. There the ceremony was more majestic; it even seemed that the frightened
quibblers were hiding their effrontery and only showing themselves in the mask of the Law. Oribeau was content with that
spectacle and waited impatiently for the cases to be called.

The first was that of a nobleman; notes of confidence
that he had given to a broker to negotiate in order to procure a
considerable sum had been reclaimed. The broker claimed to
have furnished the sum and showed his entitlement in the
notes; the nobleman claimed that he had not received it, supporting himself with various arguments: the lack of fortune of
those who claimed to have furnished it; the natural honor of
the class of citizens of which he was a member; the employment of the loan that had not been made, etc.

The broker lost the case, but Oribeau would have liked
complete proofs of the veracity of the nobleman and the bad
faith of the broker; he asked the Sage to discover the truth, if
possible.

"Gladly," replied O'Barbo, and immediately, they approached the broker who had just been condemned.

"Watch him carefully without him perceiving it," said
the Sage.

Oribeau observed all the unfortunate man's movements;
consternation, shame and discouragement were depicted in his
slightest gestures. He put his hand to his forehead, he shivered,
and one of his daughters, very pretty, who appeared to be
about sixteen years old, having approached him in order to
console him, he said to her. "Oh, Kilkonway, it will be necessary to marry your sister and you to obscure individuals. I had
opened such a fine career, but I'm falling back into oblivion."

"My father, Mama told you not to trust that Lord."

"Ah, I had him, if..."

At that moment, he perceived that someone was listening
to him, and drew away.

"Come to see the Lord now," said the Sage.

The young Prince therefore observed the Lord in his
turn; he saw in all his physiognomy a concentrated terror, like

that of a man who has just escaped from the hands of robbers. People ran to congratulate him; he responded with groans.

The Prince communicated to the Sage his observations of both parties.

"Now pronounce," said O'Barbo.

After that case, in which the famous Limerick had deployed all his rapid and compact eloquence for the nobleman, the Sage took Oribeau into another hall, where criminal cases were being judged. They heard two or three petty cases pleaded, in which it was a matter of abused girls demanding compensation for their lost honor and aliments for its fruits. The Prince observed that evidence of paternity was admitted very lightly, and that the men were never condemned to marry the girls they had seduced. He asked his guide the reason for that.

"It's because in such cases," the latter replied, "one is forced to be content with presumptions, and that in any case, that manner tends to render men more circumspect in familiarity with a sex that it is dangerous to see at excessively close range. In the second place, marriage is not ordered for very good reasons; that indissoluble bond ought not to be formed after a temporary attachment; one ought to esteem the woman that one takes as an inseparable companion and who becomes, by marriage, half of oneself. Finally, if a girl is easily accorded damages, in order that she may conserve her fruit, on the other hand, one does not want the inconvenience and facility to give entitlements to a libertine to cause herself to the rank of the mother of a family."

"And when comes the alms of three livres to which both were condemned?" asked the young Prince.

"It's an honorable fine for having offended public decency."

A man who was listening to Oribeau and his tutor, seeing an old man and his child, said to them: "That fine is a stupidity and an injustice; stupidity because it is founded on a puerility, injustice because it denotes the weakness of infamy and often less than weakness. A girl who has a child is not committing a crime; it is a natural action that even demonstrates that she is not a libertine, for those do not have children. It's an injustice, it makes a good action shameful for girls, and punishes them with death if they destroy their fruit.

"I would like, on the contrary, instead of fining girls who have children, there to be a law that orders, not libertinage, nor even compulsory marriage, but that all young men and woman who prefer to remain unmarried can only be admitted to any public responsibility, not even the mastery of professions, not even to hospital in case of illness—in a word, to public charges and benefits of any kind—after the age of thirty for women and thirty-two for men on showing that they are married or that they have two living children. Those who are incapable of being fathers and mothers should nevertheless be free to take responsibility for a child of poor people, of whom there are many, and represent them as their own.

"That law would be rigorous, every bachelor and every spinster of the requisite age would each be obliged to present a child, for the same one could not serve the father and the mother. That is a useful law, and not the stupidities that I see authorized. A Germanic king has enacted a similar one and it has been found good."

"Who is that man?" Oribeau asked his guide.

"He's a bard, one of those known as cynic philosophers.[41] He's right, from a certain viewpoint, but to establish his law it would require everyone to be a mad philosopher, like him."

When the petty cases were settled, one was presented that was much more considerable, which filled the remainder of the session. A married woman had been accused of the highest degree of perversion and libertinage, of having prostituted herself in a public place, where she had been caught. The woman defended herself by recriminations; she alleged that,

---

[41] The original text has *Folisefos-ciniqs*, the anagram of "filosofes" emphasizing the supposed folly of the bard in question (obviously Restif). When the same anagram recurs I have translated as "mad philosophers."

her children being dead, avid collaterals, relatives of her husband, had formed the black project of making her lose her matrimonial conventions; that in order to succeed in that they had recruited one of their friends, who had taken her to a brothel as if to the house of an honest woman, and that she had then been found there.

The Judges decided in favor of the wife, although it appeared that she was really guilty, but they were fearful of dealing a deadly blow to public honesty if their judgment certified to the realm that a wife existed who was capable of such infamy. What made their intention manifest, as the Sage observed to his pupil, was the severity with which they punished the brothel-keeper, who would have been innocent if the woman had not been guilty.

It was by these observations that the Sage enlightened the Prince, confided in his vigilance, and gave him a high opinion of the sagacity of the supreme judges. But O'Barbo did not believe that he ought to dissimulate from the heir to the throne the enormous abuses that were found in that part of public administration. He explained to him what bailiffs, procurators, clerks and patrons,[42] etc., were.

"Bailiffs," said the Sage, "are worse than robbers and thieves, their gross malpractices leap to the eye; they are seen and punished without being corrected; they are a public plague. Procurators are ordinarily those who see the plaintiff, listen to his arguments and then go to the patron, after having digested them, in order that there should be greater facility in drawing up the memoirs and the pleas; for them they take responsibility for what they call the documents, a kind of verbiage, a contest of pens, means of signification in a diffuse style and terminology even more diffuse, because one pays for the

---

[42] I have left the word *patron* as Restif renders it, as it would be obviously anachronistic to substitute "barrister," that being the nearest English equivalent of the legal role that Restif's "*patrons*" seem to play.

role instead of having to pay for substance and good arguments.

"Those practitioners confuse cases, embellish injustice and disfigure the law, which they crush the enormous mass of their roles, with the result that after a few years of their manner of instruction, the case is much less clear that it was on the first day. Their infidelities do not stop there; they steal by means of exorbitant fees; they steal items of evidence and sell them to an adverse party, and operate a thousand other infamous practices.

"Clerks commit more veiled infidelities, but which are infinite in consequence, either by allowing what ought to be secret to be seen or recording unfaithfully, etc. The Patrons are the most estimable in all regards; they only render themselves culpable in making use of their talents for the triumph of injustice, but even in those cases, they're not as dangerous as the others; the sagacity of judges protects them from seduction.

"Finally, there are men who can abuse their positions even more surely, because it often happens that an overburdened magistrate finds himself forced to leave part of an examination to his secretary, and if the latter is corrupt, he can lead the judge astray, which doubtless happens quite frequently—but that abuse is becoming rarer since your Minister has been attentive to giving the people only good magistrates and simplifying the laws greatly. You will complete that great work, and my friend will put before your eyes the *Thesmographe*,[43] or a project for legal reform, which will produce infinite advantages for your people."

At that moment the cynic philosopher, who had appeared to be occupied with something else, addressed the Sage...

---

[43] *Le Thesmographe*, the last of Restif's utopian tracts to reach print, was not published until 1789, but had obviously been written long before.

"But it's time to part," said Kerry to the drinkers and the aged Ennisleague. "We'll meet again tomorrow and I'll tell you things that are no less curious."

"We'll be punctual, Kerry," exclaimed Kilmactomas. "We've never heard anything so well-turned."

"Nor so true," added Younghall. "Until tomorrow, worthy gentleman."

"Until tomorrow!" cried all the others.

At this point, Patrick, nicknamed Yzquiepatli, said to the company in the market harden: "That's two entire evenings that I've taken up. I don't know whether my story is amusing you, for you didn't say anything to me yesterday."

"We were waiting to see what turn it would take. We don't like the magic; that's why we remained silent for fear of judging too lightly; we've listened to you today with interest, and we thank you, while assuring you that we're waiting for the next evening impatiently."

Eager to hear the continuation, the entire company of Monsieur Gaudet of the Rue Courtaudvilain met up again in the market garden at Hauteborne, where the good bourgeois was already picking celery, chicory and lettuce with his family—with the exception of his two younger daughters, who were looking for early violets. The Irishman Yzquiepatli, otherwise Patrick, who was telling the story, did not take long to appear, with Zoïle, or Mayo, his comrade. They drank a few cups, ate a remoulade, lit two street lamps and, with the location sufficiently illuminated, the young Irishman resumed his story where he had left it the previous evening.

Chapter P
Proceedings, Patrons, Procurators, Public Pestilences.

"Pacific old man," said the cynic philosopher, addressing the Sage, "You have just spoken with too much moderation to this young man about the imperfections of our laws and the deadly manipulation of trials; of the sumptuous and perfidious eloquence of our patrons; the admitted and public rascality of procurators and the dishonesty of the public pestilences known s bailiffs. If it is true that a wise master always forbids his pupils foolish disputes simply because of the waste of time, that is all the more reason for the monarch to forbid a part of trials by diminishing by three-quarters the cases that it is permissible to plead.

"Consequently, it would be necessary to establish that all trivia, such as brawls, disputes, the alimentation of children, should only be taken before the initial judge, whoever he is, who would be monitored unexpectedly twice or three times a year in order to ascertain how he conducts his tribunal. So-called petty cases, because of the ignorance of peasants could go to the second level, which would always be a city, but one would not see the senate of the nation spending its time debat-

ing trifles, the expense of which ruins poor people and enriches that despicable vermin of patrons procurators and bailiffs.

"Those people not only live on but corrupt the spirit of
the nation; they sour it; they deprive our rural areas of young
cultivators who come here to be their pupils and who, having
learned all the trucks of chicanery, hardened their souls and
acquired hearts of stone, false and teasing minds, return to
their homelands to becomes bailiffs, tax-collectors, procurators, bailiffs, etc. As they are educated in the means of succeeding in the senate, by their accursed formality, they vex
and oppress the peasants with security. The unfortunate and
ignorant cultivator trembles before them, and he is right to
tremble, for they can crush him without him having any means
of self-defense. Thus, all those leeches that you see in wigs of
various sorts not only live in the city of abundance on the substance of the people but also form petty tyrants who are their
emissaries in all the provinces and who send them clients.

"Oh, old man, if you had seen all that I have seen you
would shiver. Come to hear ostentatious pleading one day; one
of the two pleas must be wrong, and perhaps both; you will
see grave magistrates sitting, before whom an impudent patron
is reciting impostures, stupidities and false arguments with as
much assurance as if he were talking to a child.

"If someone takes it into his head to say to him: 'How
can you employ such pitiful reasoning?' he responds childish-
ly: 'I'm the patron of the poor, the widow and the orphan; I'm
the refuge of the persecuted innocent; I'm the defender of my
client; I have to support him and not abandon him in a cowardly fashion.'

"'Then defend him with good reasons.'

"He will not tell you that he has no good ones to give,
but will brazenly sustain that one must defend wrong as well
as right, and that bad ideas are good and excellent defenses,

"The other will speak thereafter. If he is right, or a little
less wrong than the other, don't think that he will get to the
nub of the matter immediately and prove to you that he is
right. No, he will go astray in a labyrinth, he will drown him-

self in a deluge of unnecessary words. And when he had
proved, at least, what no one contested, he will come to the
only useful point: he will explain it to you, turn it around and
back again, make it and remake it, beat it over and over again
so many times that he will finally succeed, by a masterpiece of
his art, in rendering it doubtful for you; or if you cannot doubt
it, he will make you hate the truth by virtue of the impatience
it has caused you.

"But it is the procurators who are admirable! They steal
more brazenly than pickpockets who rob you while their comrade is being executed, for they steal in the Temple of Justice,
with the aid of the forms of justice! Impious profaners, they
render Justice their accomplice. I would make them submit to
the penalty of sacrilege if I were Minister even for twenty-four
hours...

"You see that fat man laughing over there and speaking
so loudly with so much irreverence in the sacred Temple?
That's a rich procurator; he possesses 500,000 francs, which
cost him nothing but chicanery. The child of an exceedingly
rich family had chosen him for their procurator, for rich people have their own patron, procurator and bailiff, just as they
have their own physician, valet de chambre and coachman.
Maître Gerfaud—that's the name of the hangable rogue—
darted a glance at the fortune of his client, or rather his master;
the most beautiful plot of land pleased him and he decided to
acquire it. In consequence, he took care that he extended the
proceedings greatly; he complicated them, nourished them,
alimented them, followed them heatedly and won two-thirds
of them.

"When he had run up immense expenses he finally submitted his account; until then he had asked almost nothing of
the rich young man, but he suddenly stood up arrogantly and
wanted to be paid. He held on to all the evidence, all the documents; he wrote accounts and wanted to be paid. The young
man, like all rich people of his age, had no money, he spent it
as he received it. Gerfaud knew that; he makes a claim, has it
assigned; sentence, appeal; verdict; seizure; execution.

"Then the young man consults his patron. 'Maître Gerfaud is well-founded,' replies the latter. 'His accounts are accurate and not subject to reduction. It's necessary to pay.'

"'But how?'

"'It's necessary to see him.'

"They go to see Maître Gerfaud. He softens his tone, mentions the land. 'I'm due seven hundred thousand livres; I'll lose a third; abandon the title of your land to me and I'll let the rest go.'

"The young man is happy to get out of it so cheaply; the patron is also well paid for his advice.

"That other man, thin and pale, that you see further away, has lately indulged in even more unworthy conduct. A poor gentleman is attacked by a powerful neighbor; the expenses become considerable; the rich procurator puts them forward, but he mingles other demands adroitly with the just conclusions of his part. After a long and expensive trial, the poor gentleman wins the principal but loses all the incidentals; he cannot pay the expenses; his procurator takes possession of his land, and instead of the noble family of Gualtirk, to whom the estate of that name has belonged since time immemorial, it is now MacLarronet the procurator who lives in the ancient castle that holds the family trophies; the Gualtirks are expatriated, because of the unjust quarrel of a rich neighbor and their defender."

At that moment the judges, who had been deliberating, took their places again and the crazy man fell silent.

"Is what he says true?" asked Oribeau.

"Yes, to the letter," replied the Sage.

"Ha! I shall punish them, the monsters!"

"With prudence!" said O'Barbo.

The judges pronounced.

"And if I talked to you about the bailiffs," the mad philosopher went on, after the verdict had been announced, "what infamies! What infamous prevarications those public pestilences commit. A copyist of one of my works owed me a small sum, which he did not want to pay me. I had the weakness to have recourse to a bailiff. He took my entitlement and went to see my debtor. He gave him a summons; he slapped him with a second, a third. He obtained a warrant of seizure. The frightened Copyist wanted to pay. 'No,' said the traitor, don't pay; give me four livres ten on the sly and I won't seize. Every month or every fortnight I'll do the same, and you'll never have to pay.' That's what happened, Chapimon—that's the rogue of a bailiff that you see in a robe over there—received more than my sum, and the man eventually died insolvent. Then Chapimon came to ask me to pay the expenses for obtaining the seizure order and he kept my entitlement, in order to collude in my stead with the other creditors over the bookkeeping."

Oribeau made an angry gesture.

The Sage whispered to him: "Don't forget that it's with a cool head that a Prince ought to punish..."

"As for the other rascalities of procurators and bailiffs," the mad philosopher went on, "their rapacity, their art of chicanery, and augmenting expenses, their frequent infidelities, which cause them to betray their clients, and the general conduct of the former when a case is lost, of entering into collusion to produce what they call signified documents from procurator to procurator, which they make their clerks scribble day and night, to augment their expenses, etc., etc, etc. etc., etc. a thousand and one times, isn't all that written in the books of the deeds of the plunderers and pillagers of Mommonia?"

O'Barbo smiled, and agreed that the matter was ample, but still too arbitrary for his pupil, to whom he proposed to show things of another genre after dinner.

Chapter Q
Question of the amusements of Waterford that young Prince Oribeau sees.

Quarter by quarter, there was still an infinite number of important things to observe in the capital, but the Sage feared wearying his young pupil with a series of serious objects like the last ones that had occupied them. He thought he ought to render him a spectator of various public and private entertainments. He knew how many things of that sort relate to mores, being an indication and source thereof, an effect and a cause; he wanted the young Prince, therefore, to see them naturally and not as they are presented to a King on the throne, for whom everything is artificially prepared.

They began with the pleasures of the people, such as the taverns, games, dance-halls and street performances. One feast day they went to what are known in France as "guinguettes." An immense crowd of both sexes, like those they had already seen on the day when they had met the Great Judge and his family, guided them to an outlying district; that crowd filled the halls, courtyards and gardens of various places of pleasure.

Everywhere, a noisy joy reigned. Here, there was an entire family, father, mother, sons and daughters; alongside them were prostitutes with louts and soldiers. There one saw laundresses, vulgar women and herb-sellers accompanied by men of the same sort, whose effrontery they were surpassing in coarse speech and an appetite for strong beer, disposing to strike with their fists anyone who dared to offer them a polite remark that they construed as an irony. Lower down, a Mother of Venus had three or four "tender shoots" at a little table waiting for customers, with half a bottle of small beer that they were not drinking and a small loaf of bread. The latter were for "fashionable" men who came less to amuse themselves as to conduct business.

In the destined round of the dance one remarked vain women who were only seeking to be noticed, dancing with a sort of lubricity and frequently darting glances at the circle surrounding them. A crowd of young dupes, newly arrived in the capital from the depths of their provinces were devouring with their eyes the artificial attractions of the lascivious dancers.

Although the latter were always in the ranks, there were not sufficient, there were not enough of them for all the partners that presented themselves, and the latter sometimes went to fetch a young woman from the middle of an assembled family to dance with them. The little one asked for nothing better, but the parents often did not care overmuch for that kind of amusement for their daughter, because of the consequences; they permitted it once or twice and then refused.

It was necessary to have a good memory, for forgetfulness exposed one to unfortunate accidents. The Prince and the Sage saw one example. A father had permitted his daughter to yield twice to the urgings of the flower of the fops; a third was refused and retired discontented. The father, mother and a few little brothers had an ample meal, which lasted a long time; more cheerful, they were watching the dancing with pleasure when a young man came to ask the young woman to dance. She was seething with desire; the indulgent father permitted it. They took their places; the dance commenced, but scarcely had they taken two steps when the fop cleaved through the crowd, approached the girl who had refused him, gave her a slap, and the dance stopped. The man who had asked the girl threw himself on the aggressor; the father came running; the friends of the man who had delivered the slap came to his aid; a furious combat began, and the girl's father had an eye put out. The young woman, who was defending him, was bruised and insulted in various ways before order could be restored.

Oribeau wanted the aggressor to be punished.

"Gently," said the Sage. "The young man's action was brutal, but the father and daughter behaved very inconsiderately. What would become of politeness and urbanity if it were permitted, in public places, to display scorn or insulting preferences? Those women who expose themselves there ought to regard themselves as prostitutes to the gaze and actions, indifferent in themselves, of the men who are there; they ought, as soon as they have come in, either to escape furtively or to lend themselves to whatever is demanded of them, or to refuse everyone absolutely. Neither a girl, nor those who accompany her, has any right here to object to her being the object of brazen stares, etc. That is why sage young women never frequent guinguettes. Look, in any case, at the scenes that a young woman has before her eyes: over there, prostitutes are committing the most indecent acts; here, others are holding conversations and accepting propositions of which an honest girl should know nothing. Can you hear the obscenely coarse speech of those low-class women? That of the drunken men replying to them? Notice those gestures, those liberties; could a woman of good morals, although plebeian, permit herself to come here?"

"But why are such places tolerated?"

"It's an old custom that the government dreads abolishing—but I advise you to be bolder and, above all, to reduce the multitude of feast-days, which are merely an opportunity for debauchery. One day of rest in the week relaxes and does not render people libertine; two exhaust the purse, become tedious and throw them into drunkenness or gambling out of idleness."

The Sage then pointed out to the Prince a place where different games were being played, similar to those we know as nine men's morris, Siam, skittles, tennis, etc. All those occupied in these games, where the losses always outweigh the winnings, since the expenses of the game are taken out in advance, were quarreling, whereas, in devoting themselves to work, which is no less amusing than ordinary games, those who are reasonable enough to learn to like it are sure to win, and always content.

"Is there any reason to tolerate these games?" asked the Prince.

"Strictly speaking, no. These amusements, harmless in themselves, have been invented by the rich, who get bored, and the people, aping the rich, amuse themselves with them on days of rest, but bad lots who abuse everything make a dangerous occupation of them, a kind of trap by which they try to win the money of laborious men who succumb to the temptation of the amusement.

As professional players can only live on dupes, and they don't always find them, they have to seek other means of subsistence and find them in crime. They live off the earnings of prostitutes, they prostitute their wives, their daughters, etc. They rob and steal; they're imprisoned in the sad dwellings you have seen, condemned to public works or executed. It would be better to seize the evil by the root and suppress all the causes of corruption. Cut back, as I say, on all the festivals, except for the weekly day of rest, and don't permit public games, whatever they may be, on that day."

As the Sage finished these words, they heard a noise in a large hall, which the young Prince had initially mistaken for a warehouse of funerary monuments, because it was painted black outside with white sticks crossed diagonally. They went in; it as filed by a crowd of men of every estate, but especially the valets of lords who lived in the vicinity. There was a large table in the middle that was covered with a cloth on which two little white balls were being propelled with sticks like the ones painted outside, sometimes at one another and sometimes at a third, which was red. There were six holes at equal distances alone the edges and at the corners of the table; the skill consisted of making the colored ball, or that of one's opponent, fall into them by means of the one that one was propelling oneself with the long white stick. It was what is known in France as the game of "billiards."

The cause of the dispute that had just erupted was one of the rascalities commonplace in such places. One player had come to an understanding with a crook who bet against him, with the result that, by always losing, he enabled him to win large bets, by means of which his associate compensated him for his losses by giving him a part of the profit. When it was agreed that the crooked player was to win, the other crook abstained from betting on some pretext; the dupes fattened by that advantage, glimpsing the apparent possibility of winning, bet large amounts and lost inevitably. An honest gambler had just perceived the deceit and was making a great noise. The City Guard arrived, and the crooks were taken away with the plaintiff, who proved the fraud so well to the Justice of the Peace that the former were sent to prison, to be subsequently judged with the prostitutes and similarly imprisoned.

"Are you going to persuade me again that these gambling dens are necessary?" asked Oribeau.

"No, but it would be easy for me to justify those who initially tolerated them. All the evil comes, as I've told you, from the rich on the one hand, and on the other, from the excessive number of feast-days. The rich have set the example of idleness; they have invented games—which is to say, the great art of doing nothing—and not only have they employed it for themselves, but they have led their various domestics to imitate them. Games relax and amuse after work; individuals whose minds are false—and there are many of that stripe— have imagined that they would live very happily by devoting all their time to what is only amusement and recreation. They are as greatly mistaken as a man who, seeing that salt and pepper season his dishes, takes it into his head to compose his meals entirely of salt and pepper.

"Games are a pleasure, as long as they follow serious occupations and relax after work. The first sovereigns who permitted gaming houses had no other intention, therefore, than to furnish citizens with a relaxation and honest pleasures—in brief, a greater benefit. It did not occur to them at first that there would be men foolish enough to occupy themselves with an amusement and thus devote their days to inutility. Today, however, that abuse has reached a peak, and I think it will be necessary to excise it surgically and get rid of all these schools of vice.

"I will say more; it will be necessary to enact a law like the one that was in vigor in Athens, by which every man and every woman was obliged to indicate their means of subsistence. I would like that indication to be made initially without any disagreeable consequence for the adults of the time in which it is enacted, but that scrupulous attention should be paid to youth entering into society, in order to force them to take up a useful vocation, etc."

On emerging from the Billiard Hall, the Prince and his guide went up to a higher floor, where they found a numerous company of men who seemed more honest. Their amusement—or, rather, their laborious game—was singular; they had little crudely-panted figures in their hands, and various others imprinted in red or black; they were throwing these figures, which, in accordance with their value, won or were defeated, and they were then mixed up; they began again, and according to whether the figures were strong or weak, one saw in the player's eyes transports of joy or despair.

Prodigious sums of money vanished beneath the hands of an unfortunate player, and yet the fury of the player possessed him to the point that he could not tear himself away, even after losing his money; if he had been permitted to do it, he would have wagered his honor and his person, his wife and his children. One might have thought that the imprints were magical characters that cast spells.

The crooks had different means of deceiving here; O'Barbo remarked several of them, but they were so subtle that the opposing player, even if he perceived them, could only complain by means of insulting invective. The cheating player also had an understanding with someone laying wagers; an inappropriately played figure caused him to lose the game, the cheat won his bet and shared the sum with his accomplice. The Sage pointed out to Oribeau that that kind of game, although monitored by the police, was even more dangerous than the one he had just seen, and the Prince promised himself to ban it absolutely

Chapter R
Recitation of what Prince Oribeau sees among the actors, at the estaminet and the dance-hall

Relative to the education of his pupil destined to reign, nothing was omitted by the Sage. Continuing the following day to dhow the young Prince the amusements of the people of Waterford, he took him to the city's boulevards.

"See," he said, "the fortunate fruits of peace; what was initially destined for our defense, which was to be a field watered with blood, is now employed for places of pleasure. Fortunate Mommonians if the tranquility they enjoy does not enervate them and prepare a facile victory for their enemies!"

At the same time he pointed out to his pupil the places of refreshment, those where strolling players put on their farces; others where rare animals were exhibited; and finally those where one could go to admire mechanical prodigies, conjuring tricks and secrets of every kind.

"It is thus," he said to him, "that society procures people a multitude of pleasures unknown to savage hordes; let us try to appreciate them a little."

The tricks amused the young Prince, but a smile from the Sage caused the enchantment to cease; the Prince was humiliated by it and soon sensed the emptiness of all that. As for the mechanical devices, he gave more time to them, and although they were only employed for futile things, Oribeau easily understood the useful applications that might be made of them.

After the Sage had moved away from the charlatans exhibiting animal monsters, the Prince took a great deal of pleasure in considering the admirable productions of nature foreign to our climes. Most of all, he admired how the sovereign being has proportioned everything, in order that should not be a single point on the earth's surface not destined for life, nor a single species of aliment not to be devoured, thus to return from the state of death into that of animation But his guide did not stop at that vague knowledge; he went further and made him understand that organic molecules were not all equal.

"Some, he told him, are coarse and common to plants as well as all animals; others, like spirits and nervous fluid, are volatile, and can only be fixed in animate bodies in proportion to the extent that each of them is susceptible by virtue of its nervous contexture; the primary molecules form the lymph, the blood, the bones, the grease, the fecund elements, everything that is an organ of sensibility, like the nerves, the fluid that imbues them, life, knowledge, etc."

As he finished that observation, the Prince took the Prince into the principal establishment of the strolling players.

He saw there some of the efforts employed by humans to divert their fellows. But one verity that the Sage presented to him at that moment saddened that reflection: "They prefer to devote themselves thus to spectacle than to work tranquilly at useful occupations; that is the source of all vices, idleness, which is that of the talents that astonish here; they have fled work and, by a just punishment, have found more difficult work that can only dishonor them."

There was a rope-dance, feats of strength and equilibrium, two bad farcical comedies and a kind of pantomime. The young Prince, for whom all that was new, was amused by it to begin with, but when it finished, he felt the preliminary symptoms of disgust.

After the spectacle, they went into the place of refreshment that appeared to them to be the most crowded. Nothing resembled a guinguette more. At the back there was an orchestral stage, garnished with musicians and singers, which sometime made a deafening racket, especially when discordant drinkers joined their hoarse voices with the shrill voices of the demoiselles.

It was in that den of inutility that the two observers remarked the scandalous assemblage of libertines and suspect girls; they saw imprudent young women who had escaped from their parents' homes in order to come here and play the adventuress with some young popinjay, who believed that they were more honest in proportion to the extent that the liberties they took with them attached them more. They saw indecency, dissolution and an appetite for rowdy behavior reigning everywhere, and a certain brutality of manners.

"I'm bored in this dishonest place," said Oribeau. "Let's get out..."

The Sage consented to that, making the observation to the young Prince that dissolute youth corrupted everything, rendering their own pleasures crapulous as soon as they abandoned themselves to them; that it was necessary to go to the source, to impart good mores by establishing the subordination of youth to the aged, etc. The Minister was working on that, but it was long and difficult work!

When they quit that kind of music hall, the Sage took his pupil back into the city. They had only gone along a few streets when they heard instruments playing dance music in various places. They selected one, which they saw a few coquettishly dressed women entering, escorted by young baubles who seemed more feminine than them. They went in and saw a great hall where several groups were simultaneously figuring the same dance.

As soon as O'Barbo appeared, all the young scatterbrains took him for a masque; they immediately ceased the dance that was occupying them intently and surrounded him. A few took impudence so far as to tug his long beard. The Sage smiled, but the impetuous Oribeau had difficulty tolerating that lack of consideration for his master. With the dignified attitude that was natural to him he pushed away one of the fops, who took it badly and proposed to him that they cross swords.

Oribeau was young and he was seething; he accepted without reflection. He was going out with his adversary when the Sage, attentive to everything, retained him. "Prince," he whispered into his ear, "what you are about to do is contrary to reason, which requires that the peril to which one exposes oneself by proportionate to the advantage that might result; but that's not all; there is a precise law in your realm that forbids dueling."

At those words, Oribeau stopped. He moderated his anger and, repressing his courage, went to sit down between two charming young women. He was scarcely there than they got up and moved away from him, with a sort of confusion.

The Sage approached the Prince to tell him the reason for that procedure. "In spite of the excessive corruption of morals," he told him, "our nation has a sort of honor, of which it is idolatrous; you appear to have lacked courage; that is enough for women, who esteem that quality in us by reason of their weakness, to disdain you and shun you."

"What is necessary," replied the Prince, "to change the poor opinion that they have of me, for I can't bear to be scorned by women?"

"At the first opportunity, demonstrate an unequivocal valor."

"Yes, but in the meantime…I can't think without shivering that anyone has scorn for me!"

It was midnight. Piercing screams were heard coming from the street.

Oribeau ran outside; the Sage followed him. They both ran to the rescue of a man and a young woman whom assassins had just attacked. Of the noisy crowd in the dance-hall, not one dared to go down; they stood at the windows like the women, who reproached them for their cowardice.

By the light of a thousand candles that had just appeared at the windows, however, Oribeau was seen, alone against four, driving them back in spite of his youth, and by his side an old man with white hair, almost bald, who was striving to parry with his body blows that were aimed at his pupil. The spectacle appeared so touching, especially to the two young women who had scorned Oribeau, that they excited their comrades to go down, in default of the cowardly men that surrounded them.

At that moment, however, the soldiers of the public Guard arrived, and the assassins fled, except one, whom Oribeau had wounded, and who was captured.

The man who had been attacked had received a few superficial wounds; the young woman had fainted but she was still the most beautiful person in the world. The man shook her, while thanking his young liberator, but wanted to remain unknown, which meant that the Guard only took away the guilty party.

"May I at least know the name of the young woman I have rescued?" said Oribeau. "The name of a woman still young does not reveal anything."

"Her name is Ahissa," the unknown man replied.

"Beautiful Ahissa," said the young hero, "I congratulate myself for having served you."

As he finished those words Oribeau went back into the dance hall; all the young women surrounded him, and rendered him the same homages as if they had known his birth.

"You reign at this moment by your own merit," the Sage said to him. "Savor its sweetness, in order to become avid for similar pleasure."

Meanwhile, the dances recommenced; the young Prince joined in and was the object of all enticements, but it did not take him long to become bored. Everyone that surrounded him was corrupt; the young women were either libertines or imprudent individuals escaped from their parents' houses, whom indelicate men had led astray, treating them like towns ripe for pillage. He wanted to leave.

"What are these balls?" he asked the Sage.

"You know that there are dancing-masters in the capital, and as that métier is not very lucrative, they are permitted in winter to give balls of this sort—but they are schools of corruption and it would be a hundred times better if the government maintained the masters at its own expense than grant them the right to host schools of prostitution and safe rendezvous for all the scatterbrained young women who want to deceive their parents or their husbands. Dancing is a legitimate diversion, even useful to health, but it would be better to compensate that pleasure with some other exercise than keep it at the expense of morals.

In order to return to their lodgings the Sage and the Prince were obliged to pass through the most brilliant quarter in the capital. They found it as animated as in broad daylight, although it was one o'clock in the morning. They saw shops filled with masque costumes, rapid carriages heading from all directions toward a large house in which the crowd seemed to be absorbed

"What is that palace, then?" asked Oribeau

"It's the Eropa; there's a ball there this evening."

"Another ball?"

"But very different from the one we've just seen. Would you like to go in?"

The young Prince advanced toward the door.

"Don't you want to wear a mask?"

"No."

"You'll observe better."

"Let's put on masks, then."

They went into one of the shops. Oribeau chose a satire and O'Barbo contented himself with putting on a false nose. In that new accoutrement, they went into the ball.

They found an undulating crowd of people there, all of whom appeared to be occupied in looking for someone. The things to which they were paying the least attention were the music and the dancing. They were talking, they were bumping into one another, and they were following one another and trying to divine one another.

The women, in particular, appeared to manifest an impudence and a curiosity that marked their true character very clearly. One attached herself to the young Prince and began to flirt with him. He did not pay any great heed to it, but as it was very hot he eventually took off his mask in order to breathe more freely. The Lady, surprised to see a young man with such a handsome face, who was unknown to her, became more ardent; she flattered herself that he had only uncovered himself because of her. She followed him obstinately, and having by hazard found a place where there were not the Prince, the Sage and herself, took off her mask and allowed the sight of a charming face.

Oribeau, who had disdained her, was dazzled by so many attractions; he ceased to be cruel and responded to her advances. The conversation became intimate as soon as she was sure that the old man could no longer hear.

"Where have you come from, handsome mask? I haven't seen you before."

"I've come from the Mountains of Stefenon, Milady."

"What! Those savage places have produced such a beautiful rose?"

"That's what I would have said if you had been born there, Milady."

"Who is that old man?"

"He's my father."

"Does he inconvenience you?"

"No."

"What will become of you when you leave here?"

"We'll go home."

"Have you a carriage?"

"We came on foot."

"Where is your house?"

"Coshmore Street."

"That's on my way; I live in Glanchery Street."

"I've only seen one palace in that street, Milady."

"I live in it."

"Do I, then, have the honor of speaking to the beautiful Princess of Thomond-Clare?"

"What if you did?"

"I would congratulate myself greatly."

"But what is your name?"

"It's a mystery, Milady, that I shall reveal to you one day."

"What a woman of my sort asks a question, one ought to reply accurately, sir."

"That depends on the person of whom she has asked it, Milady."

The young Princess, who was unmasked, reddened with anger, but the Sage, who was approaching, prevented her from making the Prince a harsh response. She put her mask on again and went away.

"Can you divine the objective of that conversation?" said the Sage to Oribeau.

"No."

"You pleased the Princess."

"So what?"

"In spite of her wisdom, the intoxication of the ball and the license that one is permitted here might have made her desire to embark upon an intrigue with you."

"What would have resulted from it?"

"The imagination of young people does not go as far as that, but gradually, vague desires acquire a focal point and one does as those do that one believes oneself far from wanting to imitate. You could have had ten adventures for one here, if you had wanted to lend yourself to it."

"What, then," asked Oribeau, "do mores gain from these nocturnal assemblies?"

"Prince, all these diversions, of which corrupt hearts preach the innocence, occasion a thousand disorders; girls lose their innocence here, wives their fidelity, men the taste for true pleasures and attachment to their family. It will be necessary, Prince, to proscribe all that one day, without regard to the complaints of corrupt courtiers. Believe that one can never be sure that a wife will emerge from these assemblies with her virtue intact. Everything that one can see here is a trap; is it prudent to risk the danger? Who seeks peril will perish, say our Sages..."

But I ought to say here that the Princess of the Eropa Ball was not the Princess of Thomond-Clare.

Chapter S
Scenes of interest seen by Prince Oribeau in a café (not called such).

"Setting forth this morning," said the Sage to his pupil, "we're going to partake of what are called the pleasures of honest people. The leave their dwelling without breakfast, as is their custom, and after having traversed a few streets they perceive a house on the door of which is written, in runic language: *Here bellicose virtue is refreshed.* Let's go see that public house."

They went into a hall and saw large marble tables at which several persons were taking separately, with rather sad expressions, a liquid mixture. In the middle of the hall there was a large fire devoid of flame, which surrounded thirty storytellers, all nobles. O'Barbo and the Prince placed themselves as close as possible to that group and were served breakfast.

They were talking politics, and as Dondanuck had left the field free for that subject-matter they were not sparing the administration. First of all there was the question of the law that would bring about equality between citizens. It had inconveniences, as one can imagine, and it was only after a fairly considerable time that its good effects could be felt without admixture. It was, therefore, attached with a kind of fury. One complained of the insolence of his former vassals, whom the mere project of the law had rendered audacious. Another moaned that it would extinguish all competition. This one shivered at rubbing shoulders with a manual laborer; that one swore never to have an heir, for fear that his family would remain confounded with the human species.

Oribeau did not miss a word of all that was said. He asked O'Barbo to reply to the malcontents.

"What can one say to prejudiced individuals?" replied the Sage. "Let's leave their complaints to fall of their own accord; to reply to them would only blow on the fire. Take note, Prince, of what the fundamental subject is. It's that of not being dominated; everything comes down to that. Blinded by their passion, ancient prejudice and personal interest, however, they're incapable of listening to reason. Ask them by what right they claim to be above others. They'll reply to you that it's because their ancestors were ennobled for fine deeds. Then ask that nobleman, of the family of MacRoss, why he isn't debased and the last of Mommonians because of the treason of his great grandfather. He will reply to you that faults are personal and that he is not a traitor.

"It will be easy for you to conclude from that that noble Mommonians want the price of good deeds to be eternal, but that the punishment of crime should be momentary—and that's quite natural. But a wise monarch easily sees that by eternalizing recompense he diminishes in himself the facility of recompensing. If the son isn't guilty of the father's crime, why should the fine actions of a distant ancestor influence a descendant devoid of merit?

"The fixed point is that all men are equal. Politics demands that, in order to encourage men to maintain the social regime, recompenses and privileges are given to those who serve it with distinction, but the further they're extended, the less energy they have and the more pernicious they are to the very social regime that the favored individual has maintained. Let us honor with a kind of worship the hero who has served the fatherland, but let his son imitate him if he wants to be similarly honored. A virtuous and noble son will be preferred to another virtuous but not noble; that alone is just."

"You are giving fine principles to that young man," said a nobleman who had listened to the Sage. "Apparently you're one of the Minister's partisans, and doubtless one of those unfortunate peasants that his ordinance would have rendered our equals. Instead of cultivating the soil you come here politicking."

"Do you think," replied the Sage, "that after having labored all my life I cannot rest, at my age?"

"You! You're made to labor until the last sigh."

"And you, sir?"

"To command."

"By virtue of what law?"

"The law of reason, which wants noble blood to command an inferior being."

"What rendered your blood noble?"

"The great deeds of my ancestors."

"And what debased mine?"

"The servile occupations of yours."

"Have you your genealogy, sir?"

"Yes, of course."

At this point, the whole assembly drew closer in order to listen.

"How many generations do you go back?"

"Ten generations."

"Tell us, if you please."

"Not for you, but for this honorable assembly, entirely composed of nobles."

"Who pass their time here, doing nothing."

"Insolent!" cried a hundred voices.

"Your genealogy, sir?" said the Sage, imperturbably.

"Here it is, sirs. I descend in a direct line from the great Clongibbons, who gave his name to the cantons where the reigned. Clongibbons engendered Baron Bantry; Bantry engendered Baron Barrets; Barrets engendered Muskerry; Muskerry engendered Meaky; Meaky engendered Barrimore; Barrimore engendered Barriroe; Barriroe engendered Beer; Beer engendered Kilmore; Kilmore engendered Kinal; Kinal engendered Imokilly, Baron Clongibbons, who is me."

"And is that all you know about your genealogy?" asked the Sage.

"Yes."

"In that case, I am better informed than you are. Clongibbons had for a father Condons, who was a pirate; he was captured by King Ferguard, who had him hanged and reduced his son, the stem of your race, to slavery. That young man subsequently gained the favor of the King by shameful means and the Prince gave him in marriage to one of his bastards, along with the canton of Clongibbons."

"Calumny!"

"I'm certain of what I'm saying, for I too descend from that Clongibbons via his eldest son, and my branch has conserved the proof of what I've just said."

The petrified Imokilly did not know what to reply, while the nobles, seeing the O'Barbo was noble too, ceased to scorn him, although he was descended from a pirate who had been hanged. They resumed their political conversations.

"Let's be patient," said one of them. "The evils that we suffer will not be eternal and as soon as we have a King you'll see that things will change."

"But when shall we have a King?"

"It's true that strange rumors are spreading."

"If young Prince Oribeau is not...you understand me...care will be taken to enfeeble his mind, in order that he cannot govern by himself."

"What have they done with him?"

"No one knows, but it's said that he has been seen at Iraghticonner in Kerry."

"You're mistaken, it was at Rathcomneck, in Cork, that he's been seen."

"Not at all, I know someone who has assured me that he has seen him in Pobleobrien in Limerick with three young gentlemen who kept him faithful company and a young woman from Kilkenny, who has been given to him to entertain him."

"All that is false! The young Prince is imprisoned in a fort at Killnelongurty in Tipperary, where he does not speak to anyone; he has six young gentlemen with him and as many beautiful girls from Kilkenny."

"I've been told, myself, that he's been sent to Balaclay, to the Queen of Lagenia, whose daughter Oribelle is destined for him."

"Yes, if anyone knew where she is. Ratchlin has made her disappear."

"Brr! If it isn't the fay Pucellomaneh."

"A propos of Oribelle, do you know whether it would be a great honor for the Mommonians to have her for Queen? She's the daughter of a genius."

"Of a genius?" interrupted the Sage.

"Yes, a genius; the Queen had never seen the face of a man when she brought her into the world."

"Do you believe that our Prince is the son of O'Facfac?"

"Everyone knows what to think about that."

"I fear," said Oribeau to his guide, "that they're also going to give me a genius for a father."

"We're going to hear just how far these storytellers take delirium," O'Barbo replied.

"So, we'll have Princes of an entirely divine race."

"Or entirely infernal, for you're not unaware of what's said about the cavern where Dondanuck received the Queen."

"Yes, but it's to Perforimoth the Black that the honor of the paternity is due."

"Marvelous!"

"That powerful genius will always oppose Dondanuck's ill will."

"If Perforimoth the Black is not submissive himself. Dondanuck has the power to evoke him by his conjurations; how do you think he can be opposed?"

"But what about the protective fay?"

"The fay is also in favor of Dondanuck, since she made him a present of the Living Ring, by the virtue of which he can transport himself invisibly anywhere he wishes."

"He no longer has it. He's given it to Clomaneh, Oribelle's nurse."

"He no longer has it! He has it so certainly that he might be in our midst right now..."

At these words, all the noble Mommonians paled.

"I'd like to verify their terrors," said the Sage to the Prince, "in order to render them more circumspect in future and to make them cease this itch to criticize everything, but a dread stops me, which is that I'd augment their superstition, and the superstitious are capable of all crimes."

"Do it, do it," said Oribeau. "They can be undeceived later, in a much more efficacious manner that will make them blush more at their credulity."

Vanquished by his pupil's desire, the Sage immediately sent a notification to the Minister to come to the house. Dondanuck did not fail to do so. He was introduced by a secret door, entered without being noticed, took a cup of the liquid mixture, and when the conversation was renewed, O'Barbo addressed a few words to him, as will soon be seen.

After the last Mommonian had spoken had frightened all his compatriots there was a long pause. The nobleman whose genealogy the Sage had completed approached the old man and demanded proof that he was of the family of the great

Clongibbons. O'Barbo satisfied him. Then the nobleman asked him whether the handsome young man he could see was his son.

"No."

"Is he a nobleman?"

"Yes."

"Of what family?"

"Ask Dondanuck, who is over there."

The entire assembly immediately turned to look at the Minister.

"Take careful note of what is about to happen," the Sage said to Oribeau. "My Lord," he continued, addressing her friend, "it's fortunate that you're here, in order to tranquilize these illustrious Mommonians. Their love for their legitimate Prince does not permit them to be indifferent to his fate. I beg Your Excellency, on their behalf and mine, to give us news of our young sovereign."

"Excellent Mommonians," the Minister replied, "your curiosity is praiseworthy, and I shall satisfy it with pleasure. Our young sovereign is enjoying perfect health. He is being brought up by a Sage, for whom I went to search personally in the Mountains of Stefenon. The cares of the worthy mortal to whom our Queen has confided her illustrious son and the fortunate dispositions of the Prince promise you the happiest days.

"He loves the nobility, and in spite of the law that I have proposed, which has not had your suffrage, I am having him raised in principles that will suit you. He will regard you as his companions; he will not give you the onerous privileges of the people, but he will recompense you in another manner. If any one of you distinguishes himself, he will heap him with glory, individually, in truth, but in a fashion encouraging for the entire order of nobles.

"He will purify that respectable body; he will establish good mores forever, and such will be his future conduct with you that after he has governed you for some time, you will be more of my sentiment than I am. All virtuous nobles will be doubly noble; all vicious nobles will be doubly dishonored, as bad citizens and dishonoring his illustrious ancestors.

"The Prince will sow among the nobles energy, competition, civility and disinterest—all the virtues; they will germinate there, to the honor of the nobility and the advantage of that State. That is what the heir to the throne will do. That august Prince Oribeau, sufficiently instructed in the science of the druids and the bards, quit his retreat a month ago; he is traveling though his Estates; he is living with men, learning to know them, conversing with them as their equal. He has seen abuses, in order to remedy them one day.

"Finally, to say everything, in brief, he has seen you; he has heard his Minister calumniated—who forgives you, because he knows that it is the effect of human weakness. Adieu, Mommonian Lords. Be more reserved in future, not because you have anything to fear from the Prince's vengeance or that of his Minister, but in order not to dishonor yourselves with ridiculous tales and despicable superstition."

With those words, seeing that all the nobles had lowered their eyes, Dondanuck suddenly withdrew.

It was only some time after his departure that the boldest dared to raise their eyes. Surprised no longer to see the Minister, they thought he had disappeared by an effect of magical art. They questioned O'Barbo, who replied to them that he had seen Dondanuck retire by opening the same door through which he had seen him enter. But he assured them of that verity in vain; they did not want to believe it. Trembling with fear, they all left and went to hide in their houses, convinced that the Minister was still in their midst invisibly.

Scarcely had they gone than that very simple adventure was miraculized in passing from mouth to mouth, to the point that when it was related to Oribeau and his guide that evening, they were scarcely able to recognize it. There were people who affirmed that they had seen Dondanuck flying through the air as he returned to the palace, with two great bat's wings and a dragon's tail. Others had seen him with a crown of fire, but the sagest were content to affirm that he had been transported from the palace to the house, and from the house to the palace, by two familiar demons. Furthermore, no one had suspected that the handsome young man who was with the old man was the King. Far from it; what the Minister had said was regarded as a fable, pronounced to tranquilize the people.

"Are all men made thus, then?" Oribeau asked his guide. "Is ignorance so profound in Mommonia?"

"No, Prince; I'll show you another house to which, instead of ignorant noblemen, only bards and a few druids go."

"Are the nobles all ignorant, then?"

"Not at all—on the contrary. Today they form the most enlightened class of the nation. They're well-educated, even those who wield the sword, and even more so those who exercise the priesthood and the magistracy; but those don't come here to waste their time; they're occupied, and neither suffer ennui nor complain."

They traversed the MacErrick Bridge, went along a beautiful street and reached another house, where they found only placid people who were conversing about physics, history and the progress of the arts.

*

"Aged hostess," said Younghall, "could you have told us all these things?"

"No, no," replied Ennisleague, "and the gentleman Kerry is a clever man."

"Listen to me, then," said the hunter. "The young Prince has arrived at the House of Savants..."

Chapter T

Tableau: How Oribeau sees the Bards and knows their merit.

The men you see here," said the Sage, sitting down with his pupil in an obscure corner, "are savants, intelligent and inventive—or believe themselves to be. To enable you to understand the conversation of bards, it's necessary that I tell you what the condition of the sciences is at present in your realm. Enlightenment is brought in this canton of Evinland to a very high degree, although a potion of the public still believes in sorcerers, and even in Waterford, a manufacturer of flutes has been seen to try to persuade the capital that a familiar spirit comes to his house to form a concert with all the instruments found there.

"Thus, one sees in Mommonia the two extremes: an absolute exemption from prejudices and the blindest superstition. The druids, although perhaps the least credulous of Mommonians, maintain superstition with all their power, and among men of letters, each of them makes use of it to some extent, according to his interest or the degree of his enlightenment. In general, the majority of kaldes are novices in physics, astronomy, geography and even history; some of them, who only have an inkling of them, are even ignorant of their language, for want of having studied ancient runic, from which it derives. The latter are the most vain, the most jealous and the most stubborn. There are also some of rare merit, and I shall show you all these different individuals; they are in the house at present.

"Do you see that stern old man whose gaze has so much fire? That is the great Iratlove. Examine that other, who has a somewhat misanthropic air; that's the immortal Ussuaero. That noble and open face id the illustrious Funfbo. There is the delicate Rammentlo; here the wiry Hastom; beside him, note the profound Toddire; then the savant M'Albreted; then the skillful astronomer Nalleade. Over there, to the side, is the sensible Dadarnu, who is making fun inappropriately of the caustic Nacor who is facing him.

"The one who is holding those two books is the mellow Rureletoun, who has embellished the productions of the Angles Nygo and Paskarshee in translating them.[44] The other,

---

[44] Pierre Letourneur, who began his twenty-volume translation of Shakespeare's work in 1776, had previous translated Young's *Night Thoughts* (the u is dropped from the anagram of his name, as the m had previously been dropped from

who is chatting with his mistress, is the elegant and light Trado. That drinker of punch is the picturesque Enidase. Nearer to us is the bold Rimerec. That druid is the harmonious and fluent Lesdeli. The man with the red eye is the expressive Mirre'ee. The one who is smiling maliciously is the thunderous Tuglein, whose rapid eloquence has pulverized feeble adversaries. There is the damsel Duribamac, beside the enlightened Ubraamid, and then the unfortunate Lidesel.

"In the other room you can see the penetrating Nalluobrey; the enchanter Dranreb; the gracious Tiniasso, the elegant and chaste Bocconiri, who always dresses as an amazon; the druid Tropves, celebrated for the fecundity of his imagination; the tragic Nollicreb and his ingenious son Ibrollenc; the frightening Siduc, who paints vice followed by remorse; Baintlinsederom, whose tragic Hungarian made the talent of the mime Rocavru shine; Ossiplat, who has laid bare the treacherous and dangerous man and the seductive Courtisane, a fatal reef for mores and fortune; Lièvrequibrasined, who has proved by means of a charming tableau that he knows how to write something other than puns: Ipis & Rebra, who have painted nature in vaudevilles; their master Vatsra, already old but who appears still to be playing with the Graces: Chaebvalrissea, whose pleasant talent and delicate touch has painted our mores after another without being a plagiarist...

"It would take too long to name all the others for you. There for example, is the young Sensaton, whose brilliant verses are worthy of the Angle Pope; the judicious and penetrating Crevaleh. Further away you can see thirty others; I shall only name the ingenious Sonpeddruvén.

"In that room neighboring the last, at an equal distance from the celebrated men that I have named and the scribblers

---

d'Alembert's, for no apparent reason.) Letourneur also translated Macpherson's Ossian poems into French, on which Restif draws extensively in the later chapters of the present book, so it might be reckoned ungrateful not to mention them here.

grouped by the door, whom I shall not name for you, you see those who cultivate a dangerous genre of literature abhorred by good minds but which makes the delight of the wicked, to whom it appears honorable and facile. At their head is Ernorf, his gaze ardent, his ear attentive, his expression mocking and discontented. By his side you discover a little old man; he is caustic but full of with and taste, and very knowledgeable; he has read all the works of the ancient bards, which he prefers to the moderns; he is holding an old book which he is scanning rapidly; he had two more under each arm, which he intends to devour after that one; his name is Redlenquo. Between those two men, can you not glimpse a paltry druidlet, who appears to be occupied in seizing on the wing the oracles that emerge from their mouths? That is because he is collecting them in order to compose a well written work full of excellent things, but is dishonored by a revolting partiality and a puerile affectation to give the sacred name of philosopher an odious signification. That work has been welcomed by evil hearts and those praised therein, almost all obscure writers beneath the mediocre. Its author, the druidlet, is a native of Donneraill in the county of Cork and calls himself Thi-Barbet-As.[45]

"In that obscure corner shadowed by those two vast spider-webs you perceive a thin little man; that is a starving critic. He is gazing with avidity at the great Iratlove and making grimaces at him a soon as he speaks; people sometimes laugh at his mischievous remarks but pity the fool who makes them. A few paces away from that critic, named Nitemlenc, the man you see is Lalelubaelem; he is using for a table an open copy of the divine poem in which Iratlove celebrates the great MacErrick. He is excising lines with a pen-knife; he collects them separately on a blank page, surrounds them with stupidi-

---

[45] The anti-Voltaireans referenced in this paragraph are Élie-Catherine Fréron, Anne-Gabriel Meusnier de Querlon and Abbé Antoine Sabatier de Castres—to whose anagram Restif adds two extra letters; it is not obvious why Restif links the last-named with Cork.

ties and then says to all those who approach him to examine his work: 'You see that old Iratlove? He's said all these stupid things...' Observe how people are folding their shoulders with indignation. But Lalelubaelem, who believes himself to be applauded or feared, swells with pride and sets to work with a new ardor, and devotes himself to correcting Ernorf, who will soon publish him.[46]

"Directly under that timepiece, whose running sand marks the hours, you will discover a pensive man with an ardent gaze who seems to be supporting with an equal impatience the critics, the flatterers and the plain writers. That is Ossiplat, whom I've already mentioned to you; he is holding in one hand a medallion of the Angle Epop and in the other the work of that kalde entitled the *Nudecadi*,[47] which he strives to imitate, spreading floods of bile over all his contemporaries; his judgments are ordinary founded, his style is found to be harmonious, and that work, malevolent as it is, does him honor, but a sad comedy in which he took it into his head to march

---

[46] One of the additional anti-Voltaireans mischievously cited is Laurent de La Beaumelle; Nitemlenc is probably Jean-Marie-Bernard Clément, whose name has been made into an anagram of "inclement" as a joke.

[47] Charles Palissot de Montenoy's satirical imitation of Pope's *Dunciad, La Dunciade, or La Guerre des sots* (hence the spelling of the anagram), was first published in 1764. Palissot subsequently had difficulty getting his plays produced, including the two cited in the previous reference to him, *Le Satirique, ou L'Homme dangereux* (1770) and *Les Courtisanes, ou L'École des moeurs* (1775). The comedy subsequently cited, *Les Philosophes* (1760), based on an idea by Voltaire's *bête noire* Fréron became notorious and caused Rousseau to write a letter of complaint to the publisher, Nicolas-Bonaventure Duchesne, whose widow published the present work—which might help to explain Restif's mixed feelings. Duchesne was one of the printers for whom Restif worked as a typesetter.

in the steps of the Greek Aristophanes, mocking the immortal Ussuaero, would have covered him with shame if he had not compensated for the vice of his intention by innumerable beauties; that critic is well above all the others! As he does not work in their genre, his is worthy of merit; it requires genius.

"There are also many other critics in this house; they are recognizable because they are almost always alone, like their models, the birds of prey Here are the names of some: the elegant and refined Rhadepelar, who pitilessly crushed the kalde Altebonerde not long ago; the ephemeral X****, who had always borrowed the pen of Redlenquo; the indomitable Eleleufderticomure; the druid Yxuoro; the judicious Timbre, who embellishes with ingenious tales the work entitled *The Hippogriff*,[48] etc.

"That genre of literature, astonishingly, is as cultivated as it is lucrative; journalists make perpetual war on bards and kaldes, and yet only fatten themselves on the purest substance of those veritable authors. So the ferocious tiger ravages, kills and massacred out of inclination, without thinking that its devastations will soon render the substance more difficult. Critics are only birds of prey who make continual war on nightingales, canaries, linnets and finches, and sometimes even poultry.

"However, Prince, not all of them are destructive genii; there are estimable men among those I have just shown you; and there are reasonable critics who analyze with impartiality, praise with pleasure and always declare their sentiment politely; those do not vegetate in ignorant solitude, and great men sometimes smile at them. Such are the judicious Lhaftonile, the diurnal Taureaus, the Angle Ellefanton, the medical

---

[48] The reference is to Ariosto's *Orlando Furioso*; the now-forgotten Barthelemy Imbert (1747-1790) produced several volumes of fables and tales.

Guloni; the estimable editors of the *Diary of Newcastle*,[49] the druids Tuatreb and Nontayef.

"One rather peculiar thing, however, Prince, is that, except for a few independent bards, a host of writers who do have merit, although detesting the birds of prey in the depths of their hearts, hasten to come here to pay court to them. Some send them presents in order to be praised, others incline before them and pretend to venerate them, for fear of being torn apart; for is one who is braver than the others dares to stand up to them, the scribblers crush him, and, malevolent as they are, they find others even more malevolent to laugh at their sarcasms.

"The writers who are distinguished today work in all genres: physics, history, economics, the arts, poetry, serious novels, free or tender morals; religion is discussed in writings for and against; all points of morality are treated. Medicine and surgery lend a hand and enlighten one another mutually. Jurisprudence abounds in savant commentators; the three theaters of Waterford each have a thousand plays to put on. The slightest event produces a flood of odes, mediocre, in truth, but sometimes a few songs full of compensatory wit.

In addition to the plays accepted by the theaters one sees every years a host of dramas destined simply for reading; they put all sorts of subjects into action; Rimerec is distinguished in that genre.[50] An obscure writer named Goutrane, seeing that

---

[49] The reference is to the *Newcastle Journal*, a weekly newspaper published between 1739 and 1788, founded by William Cuthbert and Isaac Thompson

[50] Although Restif's friend Louis-Sébastien Mercier is primarily remembered nowadays for his utopian writings, he was most renowned in his own day as an important pioneer of the theatrical genre of drama, championed by Denis Diderot and others as a means of breaking the traditional mold of the alternative genes of tragedy and comedy; many of his early plays were printed without ever being produced. I have translated Restif's *ramed* [i.e, *drame*] as "drama" as there does not seem

that author has treated certain trivial subjects successfully, imagined that by imitating him in triviality alone one cannot fail to succeed. In consequence he had made a drama entitled *Regnavudi-Elbisnes*, which, fortunately for him, no one read except me and the man who gave him the ridiculous idea, for this is how authentic memoirs report the origin of the *Regnavudi-Elbisnes*:

"'Goutrane is not the author of the R.-E. That author has not invented anything; his sage and reluated imagination never works alone for fear of going astray; it always follows a route traced by another. The true author of the celebrated drama of the R.-E, was an estimable Mommonian named Dhamcran, who was only making a humorous play on the words *Regnavudi* and *Elbisnes*. He scorned the piece after having written it and abandoned it, it is said, to Goutrane, otherwise Teraguon or Gronauet—for he has three names—who, like the mistletoe so revered by our forefathers only lives on the substance of those to whom he attaches himself. Goutrane read the play, and as he had exquisite taste, only entered into the spirit of his protector to the extent of devoting himself to a miserable play on words; he found the drama very correctable without understanding the author' idea. It resulted from that doubtless perfectly understandable mistake that he took old Dhamcran's jokes seriously and of a humorous piece designed to ridicule other dramas he made a disgusting *galima-heroi-bucochant* of it. The Memoirs add that Rimerec, imagining that Goutrane, whom he knew, wanted to avenge himself by

---

to be any point to that particular anagram; similarly, it is not obvious why Restif renders other generic descriptions (dictionaries, letters and anecdotes) in anagrammatical form, so I have substituted unscrambled English equivalents, as I have for painting, painters, sculptors and engravers. The imitator cited is Pierre Nougaret, author of *Le Vidangeur sensible* (1777), whom Restif came to detest after briefly befriending him; the scathing account of the play's origin is repeated, at similar length, in *Les Posthumes*.

reducing the caustic old man's play to a cacophony, offered him thanks that were not understood.'

"Drama is in honor in Waterford, but not all dramas are good; some of them have been the shame of the entire assembled nation; one, among others, for having profaned a subject that its author was incapable of treating. That reckless individual would have had the poor taste, in wanting to celebrate him, of debasing the great MacErrick, if that were possible.[51]

By virtue of an entirely opposed taste, on the same stage, plays are performed that are futility itself, in which laughter is only excited by mistakes and blunders—but we shall soon see plays...

"To the taste for dramas and stupidities, Mommonian bards join that of dictionaries and letters; they reproduce those works in all forms; the former are tolerable, often accommodating, but the latter are only a tedious repertoire of beauties destitute of life.

"Anecdotes are another kind of fashionable work. Xicrodale, the panurge Protalede, and the amiable Nirput are distinguished in that facile genre, and have been followed at a distance by Goutrane, who has published in that genre a book entitled *Canodetes-des-rats-xuabe*; that work is so full of mistakes and faults of ignorance that all veritable men of letters have blushed to see literature thus dishonored.[52] However, a few of the critics ardent in attacking works of true merit have shown indulgence for that one, apparently because they only want to deprecate veritable talent. The druid Homnalie is the only one who has listed the multiple incapacities of *Canodetes-des-rats-xuabe*.

"The reason for that conduct is that the critic in question is knowledgeable, unlike almost all his colleagues, who are, for the most part, crassly ignorant, incapable of discovering a

---

[51] The reference is to *Henri IV, drame* (1774) by Barnabé Durosoy, another writer that Restif detested.
[52] Nougaret's *Anecdotes des beaux-arts* was published in 1776.

plagiarism by themselves (it is necessary to except Redlenquo.) True savants, as I said, ashamed of such a monstrosity dishonoring their century, would have kept silent if they had not learned that to the two volumes of *Canodetes-des-rats-xuabe* that treat painting were to be succeeded by two others, of which they were themselves to be the subject, since they would be literary anecdotes. They joined forces to prevent Goutrane from travestying them as he had done the painters, the sculptors and the engravers. Dondanuck, impressed by their reasons, forbade the ignorant Goutrane to undertake a work beyond his strength and gave him the privilege of a calendar of the fair, in which he was permitted to report all the quips made by Pierrot, Gille, Arlequino and Jean Farine.

"Also cultivated, but less madly, are the genres of literature; the great men of the last century are celebrated, and one sees with satisfaction the humble and useful citizen alongside the Minister and even the Monarch. Patriotic writers sometimes undertake excellent project, from which the Minister might profit. Everyone cries against works of fiction, and no century has ever produced them in such large numbers, but the majority are only the cold narration of thin adventures or gigantic assemblages of bizarre and implausible events. One sees a few rising higher, however, such as the ingenious works of the bardess Bocconiri; those of Rimerec; Neragout's *Cetulet*;[53] the charming tales of Rammentlo; the recreations of

---

[53] Given Restif's hatred of Nougaret, it is perhaps generous of him to include an analogue of his *Lucette* (1765) in this list, albeit with a variant anagram of his name, following Madame Riccoboni and Mercier, of whom he was far fonder, and ahead of Marmontel, Voltaire, Prevost and Samuel Richardson. Modesty did not prevent him from including his own *Le Paysan perverti* (1776). The fact that the anagram of Madame de Genlis' *Adèle et Théodore* (1782) has an extra letter is presumably a mistake, although the H deleted from the anagram of Rousseau's *La Nouvelle Héloïse* is probably a result of phonetic simplification.

the great Iratlove, who has made so many masterpieces; the *Lonelvue Liosee* of the illustrious Ussuaero; the interesting novels of the druid Tropves; the *Yappansirrevet, Leeda et Rhodorete* of a celebrated bardess, and a few others. But all the Irish works of that genre with the exception of the *Lonelvue Liosee* are inferior to those of the Angle Nordaschir, an astonishing genius who surpasses, for the natural and plausible in fiction, everything that the ancients and moderns have produced.

"That it is what it is necessary to tell you, Lord, in order to enable you to understand the conversation of the principal bards of your kingdom, of whom hazard has assembled almost all today in this house, their usual rendezvous."

O'Barbo then had a few refreshments served to the Prince, paid for them in advance, contrary to custom, in order to be able to leave without being seen, and gave his attention to the bards' conversation.

Chapter V
Verities that the Bards pronounce while talking about their works.

"View, and especially hear, now that that preamble has informed you," the Sage went on.

The young Prince Oribeau, who wanted nothing more, did not reply, and lent an attentive ear. The subject-matter was interesting; the bards were talking about their works, but not as in our day, in France, an obscure and cowardly writer produces a false review in secret, dictated by malice and jealousy, which he then sends to a foreign journalist; they were discussing the merits and faults of productions whose authors were present; everyone listened to their responses, reasons and the explanations they gave of their expressions; the whole was weighed sagely and a plural pronunciation was then made. The next day, those judgments, pronounced before the authors, after they had been heard, were printed in the *Waterford Diurnal*, along with the author's best defense if the judgment was unfavorable. Among us, on the contrary, a journalist who has never read the work employs the tenebrous extract out of idleness, or indifference to the truth; he calumniates with impunity.

The first work that was examined in hat great session, to the great satisfaction of the young Prince, was the *Ellerutan teriosih* of the illustrious Funfbo, the Evinlandish Pliny, who has far surpassed the Latin Pliny. The critic Yxuoro reproached him for the elevation of his style, too poetic for history.

A man of about fifty, named Sfiertaledoneber,[54] undertook the defense of the illustrious Funfbo. "Young man," he said, "do not confuse the *Ellerutan teriosih*, which is the history of divine marvels, with the history of obscure and paltry facts of which human beings are the authors. On the former, the historian is almost always a poet; in the latter, a humble and modest author is required to speak modestly about the follies or stupidities that he is recounting; would he redeem the turpitudes by a brilliant style? He would render them even more turpid. But when the bard Funfbo describes the majestic elephant, he proportions his style to the grandeur of the living creature that he is describing; he is a poet. When he speaks about the horse, the useful animal that relieves humans in all their labors, he expresses himself as a poet, regarding its beauty, its utility and the amity we owe it. He speaks as a poet of the humble animal that follows the superb steed. He speaks as a poet about the courageous bull whose female is the nurse of humankind, but his style softens, like his subject, when he describes the placid animal whose fleece protects us from the rigors of winter."

"That isn't the only reproach that one has to make of him!" exclaimed the druid Yxuoro. "What is his theory of the

---

[54] It is not obvious why the anagram of Restif's pseudonym is two letters short.

interior construction of the Earth? I have pulverized his glass nucleus."[55]

"You have only made a cold antithesis," Sfiertaledoneber replied to him. "It's not that I share the sentiment of the great Funfbo on the reality of the nucleus of glass, which he only offers as a hypothesis himself, but I believe that it is permissible for a writer to make a supposition in order to establish a theory from which he draws hypothetical consequences. Neither Funfbo nor any other man has been able to penetrate far enough into the entrails of the Earth to know of what they are composed; we can only scratch its epidermis, the layer of dirt that covers it, which contains the vegetal earth, nurse and creator of plants and animals, and the mineral earth in which all minerals are concreted, such as calcareous stone, pebbles, diamonds, crystals, sulfurs, metals etc. We have not yet been able to go further.

"That bark is certainly not the living part of the Earth; it is its insensible part, proportionate to its size, as we have an insensible part of the epidermis proportionate to ours, in which animalcules lodge and live, which their smallness prevents us equally from seeing and feeling. Nature has made it impossible for us, by various means, to dig deeper than that and inconvenience our mother and nurse, the Earth, firstly by the waters, secondly by the lack of air and light, and finally by taking away the means of transporting the matter we displace. It is as impracticable for us to dig down to a league in depth as it is or us to build to a league in height in the atmosphere.

"It follows from that argument that there is every reason to presume that the Earth, the other Planets, the Comets, the Sun and all the fixed stars have their own central heat, a heat

---

[55] Thomas-Marie Royou—usually known as Abbé Royou, who was Élie Fréron's brother-in-law—published his supposed refutation of Buffon's theory of the Earth, *Le Monde de verre réduit en poudre* [The World of Glass reduced to Powder] in 1780. Restif adds a spurious x to the anagram of his name.

of life, and not only a communicated heat like that which fire gives to a cannonball."

"So the Earth is a living being?"

"That is the sentiment of Pythagoras."

"So be it," said Taureaus, "but I can't forgive the great Funfbo for having followed Tsarseced in his errors, in making animals into simple machines. If he is as enlightened as he appears, he has not said what he thinks. Animals machines! We have a hundred proofs of the contrary every day, and the philosophy of Tsarseced is, in that regard, odious, dangerous, false and despicable!"

"Gently, young man," exclaimed an old man, a druid even more venerable by his mores than by his white hair. "Tsarseced has as many arguments in his favor as you can allege to the contrary. It is to justify Providence against indiscreet complaints that he sage Tsarseced found that ingenious theory; if it is not true, at least it responds to everything."

"A poor manner of responding to everything!" exclaimed Thi-barbet-as. "Tsarseced is a romancer, the Angle Vevunot[56] audacious, Funfbo an atheist, Iratlove a dishonest man and a bad poet, and Ussuaero a madman. Goutrane, Nitemlenc, Lalelubaelem, Ernorf, Brtegil and I great men, whatever Ossiplat says, who treats us as rabble—but we give as good as we get, for..."

"You only know how to utter insults or platitudes," Ossiplat interrupted, "and you're losing sight of the question: are animals machines?"

"No!" cried the sensitive Dadarnu. "I know that my dog has a soul. He's attached to me; I love him, and I'd suffer too much from thinking him insensible..."

Sfiertaledoneber then took the floor. "I'm sorry," he said, "almost never to share the opinion of the illustrious Funfbo, whom I revere sincerely, but the evidence is there, not against

---

[56] i.e. Newton, another of Fréron's regular targets—he coined the term, "roman scientifique" to describe Newton's theory of gravity.

him but against the theory that he has stubbornly adopted, in spite of his own persuasion. Look at him demonstrating his veritable opinion in the history of the beaver; he belies, in two pages, everything he had said at length, albeit eloquently in his *Discourse on the Nature of Animals*. They are our younger brothers, although inferior beings; they are not us, they do not have our intelligence, but they have their own, which is less perfect but also much less troubled by the multiplicity of ideas. That is not, as the dreamer Almablerench dared to advance,[57] because Thor acts directly in the animals that they have a sure instinct, but because they have few ideas, that they do not intersect like ours, and they always, or almost always, go straight to the objective, while humans, by virtue of their excessive delicacy, their excessive facility of thought, the multiplicity of objects that can occupy them simultaneously, are always troubled—with the result that they do what they to less well, while animals, although natural, are capable of doing better."

"That's good," said Timbre. "I'm content with that reasoning."

"But let's talk about the great Iratlove," said Rimerec.

"I said all that could be said a few days after his death," said Thi-Barbet-as.

"You're a Xuta," Rhadepela said to him. "What did you say a few days after the death of the great Iratlove? A flat enumeration of all the sciences, in which you claimed to have proven that the great man only excelled in one. As if Iratlove's verses were not worth as much as Nilcronel's! As if they were not equal to those of the harmonious Enicra, without resembling them! As if the *Boucochants* [58] of that kalde were not

---

[57] Yet again, it is not obvious why the anagram of Malebranche's name has an extra letter.

[58] Author's note: "Xutas who are listening to me, know that this word signifies Tragedy." The word does not appear to exist in this precise form outside the present text, but is evidently derived from French terms signifying "goat song," the

equal to those of Nilcornel, Enicra and Nollicred, and did not surpass those of all others, including Sidu, including myself, who surpasses all the moderns! In what genre was the great Iratlove inferior? In one alone, in physics. What energy there is in his Boucichants, what fresh and bright colors in the imaginative debauches of the Ausonian. What charm and vivacity in his light poetry; in his novels he is inimitable, in history he seduces and enchants. What does it matter if he mistakes a few dates? In comedy he is not Rimolee, not Douchesset and not Haussacele, he is not the farceur Roncaud; he is himself, his *Anenin* and *Tenansigrdupe* will always be the charm of the spectacles that our mimes give us. The Xuta Thi-Barbet-as dares to dispute that he excelled in philosophy? That he enlightened Evinland? What has Thi-Barbet-as done, then, in his rhapsody, which I have heard a hundred times before he wrote it? That is what children and practical jokers do, who mock the merit they do not have. He repeats a platitude already done to death—and he says to us today, as if we were children or simpletons, 'I have made a masterpiece! I have appreciated Iratlove! Poor man, who repeats what has been said a hundred times out of envy, jealousy, during the life of the great man, but which no one but you has repeated after his death. It is as in his *Sot-riclissee*, where he sometimes appears to have taste and a sufficient intelligence to judge; it was not in him but in *Ane-attelle-ren'rir*, which he has consulted, in order to extract all that was good...."[59]

---

supposed etymological root of the Greek *tragodia*. Xuta, however, does exist in French; it means a screech-owl. The speaker, an analogue of Jean-François de La Harpe is exaggerating wildly in saying that his own plays surpass all the moderns; he cannot have thought so, and Restif is being malicious in making him say so. The comedies referenced are *Nanine* and *La Prude*, although the latter title, of a derivative work, is rendered as part of a portmanteau.

[59] The two scrambled titles are *Trois siècles*, meaning Sabatier's *Les Trois siècles de la littérature française* (1772-1775)

Rhadapela fell silent, and immediately, loud applause burst forth from the entire house, from the bards, Mommonian gentleman and even chess-players, who had been listening. Thi-Barbet-as tried to speak but a hundred voices shouted: "No Thi-Barbet-as! No Thi-Barbet-as!"

A little ugly and thickset man, whose eyes were sparkling with intelligence and malice, shouted: "Iratlove is a great man, but it's necessary to give me his works to correct, in order that honest men can read them..."

At these words, everyone turned to look at the speaker. His presence surprised all the fine minds of Waterford, who thought he was in Westminster among the Angles. "It's Vilgent! It's Vilgent!" cried fifty voices. "What is he doing here?"[60]

"And I'll correct Ussuaero, who is thought to be dead," responded Sfiertaledoneber. Vilgent looked at him, not knowing him.

"What!" a tall young man said to him. "Vilgent doesn't know the bard who made the *Yaponsirrevet*?"

"Ha!" said Vilgent. "He's that man? I thought he resembled the owls and never appeared in daylight. And you, comrade, what's your name?"

"I'm his friend; my name is found in all the letters in Yugnipat, and has that of Yranelerie, by which I'm known, has been added to it."

"I'll ask Sfiertaledoneber, how he'd correct Ussuaero," said Vilgent—and asked the question.

"Tell me first how you'd correct Iratlove?"

---

and *L'Année littéraire*, Fréron's periodical, to which Sabatier was a contributor

[60] "Vilgent" is an analogue of Simon-Nicholas Linguet, an advocate and journalist who had to flee Paris more than once in the year before the publication of the present text and spent two years in the Bastille; he is also cited in *La Découverte australe*.

"It would only be by cutting; sometimes, though, I'd change certain lines or thoughts."

"Infamous sacrilege!" cried a tall man who was behind him, in a loud voice. Everyone recognized him by his vivacity as Hairamuseh. "How dare you say that?"

"I was joking," said Vilgent, who feared that old nabob. "But permit me to interrogate Sfiertaledoneber."

"I'll answer for him," cried a stout pale man, a sworn enemy of the rich, and the unfortunate MacTadbras, "And I'll name myself; I'm O'Bebelel, I knew Ussuaero, as I knew MacTadbras. Bolder than you, I'll attack Ussuaero, who has just gone out, at the foundation of his moral doctrine; I'll call him the corrupter of our moral education. I'd say to him that since the publication of his *Liemé*, young Mommonians are no longer recognizable; and this is how I'd criticize him if he were present.

"'Ussuaero, whom I honored, whom I revered in my childhood, I would not have dared, once; the mob of your partisans would have overwhelmed me; I would have been doomed and the M****** would never have been finished. But I dare today, when one can see the sad effects of your education. I laugh at your impotent cabal. Oh, Citizen Allobroge, it is in the folly of my heart that I honor you. It is against you, against your dangerous theory of education that I shall speak before all these illustrious bards. Yes, I have seen that you have doomed the present generation, that the one that follows it, if it is not careful, will be even the more surely doomed. O cruelest enemy of my country, tell me, what have we done to you for you to employ your pernicious cleverness to mask your paradoxes with a few trivial truths that make us devour them?

"'You have said: Mothers, nurse your children! It was said a thousand times before you, but you said it forcefully, and people thought you were the inventor of an eternal verity! You have said, but in a touching and perfidious manner: Don't render your children unhappy in childhood! Alas, perhaps they will only live that age, and you might have to reproach yourself for making them unhappy throughout their life. Immediately, all the good wives of Evinland, all the fathers without firmness, and all the mothers blinded by an unreflective tenderness, uttered cries of joy and consolation. They blessed you...

"'It was, however, a dangerous sophism, invented by you alone, reproved and belied by all antiquity! Oh, if you let people approach you, I would have dared to come all the way to your retreat, carrying with me the books of Ossian,[61] those of the ancient and modern kaldes, and I would show you your foolish opinion belied on every page. Yes, you have invented the pernicious and damnable maxim that it is necessary not to contradict children. I know that you mitigate it adroitly in your book; it would not have seduced anyone without your sophistic and culpable eloquence! Oh, perfidious mountain-dweller, never has your hatred for my nation, which penetrates all your works, been so clearly manifest as in the publication of that maxim!

"'It was not on arriving in Waterford that you published it! You were crafty outside, but pusillanimous. In any case, you were devoid of credit. You waited prudently, until you had a name, and as soon as you believed that you were an important person you betrayed those you had admired, adulated and revered; you blackened, lacerated and calumniated the people who were worth less than you. I shall only cite Albreted; he is not my partisan; I have no interest in flattering him; I expect nothing from him, nor from the great Iratlove, the greatest and most virtuous of men, compared to you (I am devoid of interest, for he has no esteem for me, although what I have written does not merit it). Iratlove and Albreted hate you, because of your ingratitude, your perfidy in their regard...

---

[61] The entire corpus of James Macpherson's fake epics, attributed to the bard Ossian, had been translated into French by 1777 and were extremely popular there, admired by Diderot and parodied by Voltaire.

"'I was saying that as soon as you believed yourself a great man you became a malevolent man...I'm mistaken; you *revealed* yourself as a malevolent man; you had been one since childhood...and then you resolved to deal the Mommonians a deadly blow, worthy of your hatred, envenomed by the cutting sarcasms of Iratlove. *What harm can I do them*, you said, *that will be as durable and eternal as my hatred? I shall corrupt the future generation in the present; I shall punish the fathers who insult me by way of the children, who will spit in their faces.* Perhaps your expressions were more eloquent, but that was the meaning.

"'And you set about composing your *Liemé*, a crazy book that your admirers do not understand because it is incomprehensible. You laughed at every page and you said: *They'll admire it, for it's gibberish.* And when your impetuosity had made you write an entire volume of impracticable means of education, implausible in your manner, you sensed that patience would escape, and you sustained attention by the episode of your Allobroge druid, which you were also able to put in the middle of your *Liosée*, in the mouth of your Suerptinas, or in your own at the beginning of your *Sonisetones*. And you recommenced producing gibberish for two volumes, and more, forming in your *Liemé* a man that could only exist in your head.

"'And you said to yourself: *There's a good thing, but it's impracticable; they won't do it; here's a bad one, oh, they'll do that. Good! Good!* And you piled paradoxes on follies, antisocial maxims on paradoxes, and you shivered. And yet, as you had intelligence, you sensed that your malign pleasure had taken you too far; but you said: *Good! Scarcely a hundred Mommonians will read this hotchpotch in four volumes*—for your four volumes are very long, in spite of your eloquence; I'll confess that it took me two years to read it—*they won't read it in four volumes; a hundred Mommonians at the most, my blind admirers, will have that courage; they'll repeat it, abridging my maxims, diluted by a hundred thousand, and all my relaxed morality, which will strike them more, will be*

*propagated. Perhaps they'll only repeat the saying that it's
necessary not to contradict children.*

*"'Then the Mommonians, who are easily enthused, will
take that dangerous maxim from me and be doomed. Undisci-
plined children, anti-social non-citizens, will rebel against
magistrates and laws; they'll overturn the State. And who
knows—for after all, Rome isn't worth Vegène—whether
Vegène might not make the conquest of corrupted Mommonia?*
That idea is crazy, but it's worthy of you. And yet you sensed
that the hundred Mommonians, your blind admirers, couldn't
read a fourth volume like the previous two, and you invoked
Friga. And you found a situation of delightful romance. And
when you had created your Wisdom, you slapped your thigh
and you said: *I'm sure now of the success of my* Liemé. *A scene on a stage play is sufficient to make Mommonians applaud
wildly; it will be sufficient in my romance to conclude with one
Wisdom. Oh Friga, how much I owe you!*

"'You were not mistaken, unfortunately. All Waterford is
infatuated with your romance of education. I have seen from
my window a young and delicate mother nursing her son, diverted during the carnival, giving him hot milk and causing
him to die covered with a universal crust. One day I saw another who wanted to regulate her own and not feed him at
night, and he died; and a thousand others are dead. But that
was the fault of the mothers. This is yours.

"'It is no longer possible to go into houses in Waterford
where there are children to talk business, unless you choose an
hour when they are not awake or wait until they go to misbe-
have in public promenades under the guidance of their mother
or their maid; you're deafened; you can't hear two words in
succession. The father quits you to respond to a stupidity from
his fear son or daughter. One day I heard a man say to a merchant: *Monsieur, you have your son with you at every moment;
I only have this one, please give me preference.* Monsieur, the
great Ussuaero says that one ought not to contradict children.
Devil take your Ussuaero, said the man, angrily. He left immediately, and all along the road he cursed you. He went to a

vulgar merchant who did not know you, and who made his children shut up, who listened and who sold to him.

"'Yes, Ussuaero, it is against your doctrine that I stand up; I say that it is necessary to preach subordination to children, as to women. Yes, it is by rigor that ne trains the human animal, to make a human being of it. Go preach your paradoxes, not to the new inhabitants of the Orcades, Yell, Uist and Fara, but among the savage hordes, if your plan is practicable; but among us it is a social human, surrounded by relations, needs and equals that it is necessary to bring up! Equals, you understand, whose rights it is necessary to avoid wounding, not only in a material manner but by an arrogant manner capable of humiliating them.

"'That, Ussuaero, is the kind of man that it is necessary for a father to form in his son, the kind of woman that he ought to raise in his daughter. How, for example, can a daughter raised in accordance with your captious principles, always misunderstood, make a submissive wife, a complaisant spouse for her husband and patient for her children? (For, fortunately, your system is self-destructive and will not be able to subsist for three generations!) She has not been able obey her father or mother; everything has ceded to her will! When reason contradicts her, she will fly into a fury. I have actually seen with my own eyes a new bride raised in the Ussuaero manner; she beats her husband and whips an eighteen-month-old child who cannot see her without trembling.

"'O Ussuaero, you are the cruelest enemy of sane morality! Although you have not been the direct partisan of the insubordination of women, you have achieved your goal in a more adroit manner. You have preached the reform of nature, in order to corrupt us more completely. As for me, may I give some sage advice to my fellow citizens? May they profit from it and no longer believe in the perfidious foreigner who abuses them!

"'What a difference there is O Mommonians, between your compatriot Iratlove and the foreigner Ussuaero! The former, a pleasant philosopher, intelligent, humane toward all humans, except the wicked, diverts, astonishes, instructs and enlightens the nation. The latter sets traps for fathers, mothers, children and educators. He declaims, as a paradoxical fanatic, against the sciences that raise our century above other centuries, not out of conviction but by a detestable singularity. Judge those two men, O Mommonians!

"Iratlove has only done good.

"Ussuaero has only done evil."

"If that is the way you respond for me," said Sfiertaledoneber, "you have not expressed my veritable sentiments. I was only joking in wanting to say that I would correct the immortal productions of the genius of Ussuaero; because I have recently seen the numerous works of the druid Tropvés corrected for style, taste and thought by the young bardess O'Kraéli. In truth, I sense that what O'Bebelel has said, a trifle harshly, is only too well-founded; our education is doomed, not because *Liemé* has readers but because it has come at the wrong time; under the reign of Oribeaumagne it would have produced some good, and perhaps even more if it had only arrived under that of the young Prince Oribeau."

"How do you know what the young Prince will do?" said the caustic and bilious Vilgent, sharply.

"I presume it, by his education and his fortunate dispositions, and the virtues of the young princess who is destined for him. Oribelle has been brought up by the wisest of mothers; she is beautiful; she will be good. Education makes a god or a goddess of a handsome youth or a beauty, although it only makes a man or a woman out of an ugly person. The Sage who is educating the young Prince..."

At these words, Sfiertaledoneber was interrupted by the buzzing of several bards, of whose names it is necessary to be silent.

The indignant Rhadepela brought the conversation back to literature by naming, at hazard, the kalde Lesdeli..

Sfiertaledoneber exclaimed: "he's a charming poet.

"Him!" replied the kalde Béor, rolling his terrible eyes. "Him! Look how he has rendered this beautiful piece of an

ancient Roman kalde that he translated into the Evinlandish
language! You know Latin, or some of you do?"

"I don't know it," said Goutrane.

"What!" cried Béor. "You're no more than a puppet-
master—but I'm not speaking for you... A few savants, like
Rhadepela, Hatoms, Ramentlo, M'Abreted, Toddire, Nalleade,
Rureletonu, etc. say that they know the language of the Roman
kaldes."

Then the kalde Béor, raising his voice, recited some
beautiful lines.[62]

"But before you read Lesdeli's translation, I shall report
that of another of our bards, named Canfrelgnonpimaped. That
translation is weak and vague. A man generally scorned has
made a second in prose, less inexact and much colder. I have
corrected a few expressions of Sansdeofi in reporting this passage to you. Now here is Lesdeli's translation...

---

[62] The lines that Béor recites, given in full in the original, are
taken from Book II of Virgil's *Georgics*, lines 323 to 342, but
are slightly misrendered. As it would serve no purpose to attempt to compare the three French translations that the original
presents by translating them all into English, I have skipped
them, as well as the elaborate comparative commentary that
follows. The first translation is by Jean-Jacques Le Franc,
Marquis de Pompignan (1709-1784), perhaps better known
because it is quoted in part in a letter of comment sent to him
by Voltaire (among whose enemies he is generally counted)
than in the original. The second, credited to "Sansdeofi" [i.e.,
devoid of faith in God] is untraceable, and might be Restif's
own. The third is a 1769 translation by Jacques Delille, whose
name Restif appears to be misspelling, thus aiding a confusion
in his first list of bards where two different anagrams with the
same letters occur, the other probably referring to Jean-
Baptiste Delisle de Sales (1741-1816). Delille was sometimes
known as "Abbé Delille" although he was not a priest, thus
providing some license for other bards to refer to Lesdeli as a
"druid."

"O great men, who once composed these immortal works, what is your fate? Your language dies; it is only any longer understood by a few savants, who want, they say, to know your beauties; they translate you…what am I saying? They travesty you. When one has read the Roman Virgil in Lesdeli, it is not Virgil that one has read, it is Lesdeli."

"Young Senaston took the side of the druid Lesdeli and sustained that translations in verse could only be imitations.

"I agree," Béor said to him, "but then, title them *Imitation*, or *Feeble Imitation*, and don't say that you have translated."

"I don't believe," said Sfiertaledoneber, "that one can make more agreeable verses than those of the druid Lesdeli.

"Oh, you praise everybody, like the Periodist Quinard.

"That's because I'm good."

"It's because you fear them."

Fortunately, the subject was changed, for the conversation had ceased to be instructive for the young Prince.

The Sage stood up and having joined the circle he said: "It's envy that makes criticism, and on that topic I'll cite you a highly significant ancient tale."[63]

All the Bards looked at the Sage in surprise, and, seeing his venerable beard and his appearance, which seemed to announce at least a hundred years, some took him for and Adept who was speaking to them in the language of his youth, but the rest were content to honor his old age.

---

[63] The "tale" that the Sage quotes in full is a *fabliau* in Old French, credited to Jean Bodel (c1165-c1210) and is known in English as "The Fable of the Covetous Man and the Envious Man" or "Greed and Envy." It describes how a covetous man and an envious man encounter St. Martin of Tours, who offers to do them a favor: the first to make a wish will have it granted, the second will get twice as much. The covetous man refuses to go first, wanting double whatever his rival wishes for, and the envious man, out of spite, wishes that he will lose one of his eyes, in order that the other will lose both.

O'Barbo drew away gradually, and said to the Prince: "It's late; the bards are going to have supper. They'll no longer say anything interesting; let's go."

They left by the back door without being noticed, at the moment when two young women of the house returned from a walk, and who attracted the gazes of the whole assembly because they were charming. Even the Prince did not see one of them without pleasure, but she had a sad expression. The master of the house spoke to her in a manner that was even more respectful than tender. She crossed the room without raising her eyes and went up to a room with her sister. As the Sage and the Prince left they saw the beautiful bird with three crests, which perched on a window of the room of the young and beautiful Daura.

At this point the Irishman Yzquilpatli stopped talking and the evening finished. He went home, as did his comrade, promising to return the next day. And the next day, having returned, he resumed speaking.

Chapter U
*Union of a monstrous kind in the great theaters of the
city of Waterford.*

Usages, pleasures and amusements of every kind: the
young Prince had to see everything in the capital before going
to visit the country; it was only after having acquired a perfect
knowledge of the people he would soon command that
Oribeau could think about his marriage to the beautiful Princess of Lagenia.

The day after the long session in the house of bards, the
prince went to the National Theater—for there were three in
Waterford, one for music and dance named the Eropa, the second destined for the masterpieces of the Mommonian bards,
whose actors were the Fricasan, and the third, where frivolity
was sometimes seen to triumph and lugubrious plays were
sometimes performed, whose actors were known by the name
of Saléniti.[64]

The Fricasan was staging a beautiful play by Iratlove entitled *Thomame*, in which the great man attacked a celebrated
conqueror, who made religion serve his ambitious designs.[65]

---

[64] It was routine in late eighteenth-century Paris to compare
and contrast the Théâtre Français [Fricasan] and the Théâtre
des Italiens [Saléniti], tacitly recognizing that there was a kind
of popular French theater descended from the Italian *comme-
dia dell'arte*, employing the same stock characters, in contrast
to the classical French traditions of tragedy and comedy, although a wide range of works were staged at both the actual
theatres in question.

[65] Voltaire's tragedy *Le Fanaticisme, ou Mahomet le prophète*,
was premièred in Lille in 1741 and published with a title-page
claiming publication in Amsterdam, because it was too con-

The young Prince, greatly moved, experienced pity, terror and alarm.

When the play ended, the Sage asked him whether he had a judgment to make of the play.

"Yes," said Oribeau. "I believe that one sees therein a hero calumniated very cleverly by a man of genius. During the play I did not make that reflection; I was carried away; I felt all the sentiments that the kalde Iratlove and his mime Kanile wanted me to feel, but now I feel that things do not happen that way; it's an illusion that I've just seen and not reality."

O'Barbo shed two tears of joy on hearing his pupil, the young Prince, speak thus, and he approved with a nod of the head.

It had chanced that the Prince and the Sage were placed, at that Boucochant in front of Ussuaero and Ossiplat, who were side by side. They were chatting together without knowing one another by sight, and the Sage heard Ussuaero say to Ossiplat:

"That's a fine play. I once judged it defective, but today I see that I was mistaken. What do you think, neighbor?"

"Like you, I regard it as the most muscular of our Boucochants; Iratlove is a great man. I see only Ussuaero who equals him, without resembling him."

"Are you a friend of Ussuaero, then?"

"No, on the contrary, but I'm just."

"Ah," said the illustrious Ussuaero, weeping, "that's the most agreeable thing that that unfortunate man could hear. Since the rumor of his death has spread, I see that he no longer has a more ardent detractor in all the world than Ossuplat."

"It is Ossiplat who is speaking to you," said the author of *Folisefos*.

Ussuaero looked at him for a moment and said to him: "It's Ussuaero who is speaking to you."

---

troversial for Paris, though not for the reasons that it would probably attract violent reprisals if it were staged today.

Ossiplat threw himself on to Ussuaero's hand in order to kiss it, and the author of *Liosée* embraced him tenderly.

"I congratulate you both," O'Barbo said to them. "More often than not, it's for want of seeing and hearing one another that men are enemies.

"Who are you?" Ussuaero asked him.

"A man whom you would like if you knew him. I'm the tutor of this likeable young man."

"Might he be virtuous?" said Ussuaero.

"It hope so," said the Sage, "for he's handsome and he has excellent dispositions."

Meanwhile, the entr'acte finished and the curtain was raised again and the actors appeared, singularly dressed. The young Prince's surprise was extreme. He whispered to the Sage: "Why are these despicable farceurs dishonoring the National Theater thus?"

"This is a play by the father of the theater," O'Barbo replied. "It's entitled Canguaceroup;[66] the artful Rimolée composed it in a time of famine, in order to substitute for his masterpieces, too strong for his century, in the shadow of madness; today, when there is no longer a need for it, people are obstinate in conserving these despicable farces out of respect for their author, and there are even people who claim that they are masterpieces; it's the same as if I told you that the battles that Oribeaumagne lost at the end of his life were victories, because he had previously obtained such striking ones over his enemies."

"The comparison is just," said the young Prince, "and I sense it. I'll put order in that when I'm an adult, but after having taken care of more important things. I don't feel any repugnance for these mimes; on the contrary, I deem their art noble, but they're debasing it and debasing themselves."

---

[66] Molière's *Monsieur de Pourceaugnac* (1669) is a "comedy ballet" with music by Jean-Baptiste Lully

"That's a young man who reasons well," said Ussuaero, who had only been able to overhear the final words of Oribeau's speech.

"That's because, in nobly-born souls, valor doesn't wait for the passing of the years," replied the Sage.[67]

Oribeau was watching the play impatiently, except for one moment, when a pretty Languedocian girl, voluptuously clad, came running on stage. That object stirred the young Prince's senses, but he was discontented nevertheless with the rest.

The next day, O'Barbo took his pupil back to the Fricasan, where a single play was being performed, entitled *Orifag*, to which all Waterford had been running for three months. The young Prince had heard a good deal said about it, good and bad; some praised the pay, others tore it apart, but they rushed to see it, to the point that it was difficult to get a seat.[68]

"You can judge for yourself," the Sage said to his pupil, "for if you relied on what is being said you wouldn't have any sentiment; one opinion would cancel out the other. Listen..."

The play began. It made the Prince smile; then it gripped him; he gave it his full attention; he was interested, moved, drawn in, experiencing all the pleasures of the soul.

When the play ended, the Sage asked: "What's your opinion?"

---

[67] The Sage is quoting Pierre Corneille's *Le Cid* (1637)

[68] The controversy surrounding Beaumarchais' play nowadays knows as *Le Mariage de Figaro*, but originally entitled *La Folle journée*, written in 1778 but not premiered at the Comédie Française until April 1784, was raging when Restif wrote the present work; he subsequently became one of the author's most ardent supporters. The previous work featuring the same central character *Le Barbier de Séville* (written 1773; premiered 1775), had not stirred up such a fuss.

"This is it," replied Oribeau, after a momentary reflection. "It's was profitable to me as one of our excursions, and we haven't wasted our time."

"It's for that reason that your Minister has permitted it."

The following day, O'Barbo took his pupil to the Saléniti. Three plays were being performed: *Fiose, ou le Chamaricagé*; *Quarlin-age-sauve*; and the *Xiprerd*. They began with the last of the three.

"Ah!" said the Prince, seeing two clownish valets in love with a servant girl, "to what theater have you brought me?"

"One moment," said the Sage. "All mimes are strolling players; you'll see the proof of it, but it isn't at the Saléniti as it is at the Fricasan; the latter are reasonable at first and end up in folly; they only send away their audience after having taken away all the good things they've given them. Here it's the opposite, they begin with follies but they send you home serious. It's a pity that the best pieces are of no great merit, but the manner of their presentation is good.

After the *Xiprerd, Quarlin-age-sauve* was performed.[69] On seeing the same burlesque actor reappear, Oribeau made a gesture of disgust and impatience, but he soon changed his opinion; the same man who had displeased as a valet seemed natural to him as a savage. He was touched; he wept when he saw the naïve stranger duped by customs, which he did not understand. He shivered at the reproach, the best line in all the plays: "Wretch, you've made me quit my homeland and you've brought me to yours in order to teach me that I'm poor."

---

[69] I cannot trace *Les Perdrix*, assuming that that is the anagram in question, but the second play is *Arlequin sauvage* by Louis-François La Drévetière, first performed in 1721 but revived at the Italiens, not for the first time, in 1773. There is more than one play from the period entitled *Sophie*, but I cannot identify one that was performed at the Italiens or one that has an alternative title comparable to the one in the text.

The third and final play was *Fiose*, or the *Chamaricagé*. The interesting Fiose charmed the young Prince; he finally find nature, which he had not yet seen in the theater, for *Thomame* had nothing natural about it, *Canguaceroup* was nature degraded, *Origaf* offered an excellent depiction of human weakness and the mixture of life; there was nature in the *Xiprerd*, but base; and there was only savage and uncultured nature in *Quarlin-age-sauve*; but in *Fiose*, Oribeau recognized himself; he saw a likeable young woman and an amorous young man who said tender and sensate things to one another, a father like all fathers, far-sighted and economical—which, in the theater, is often called miserly—he saw a generous man who removes the obstacles opposed to the union of two lovers (a trivial but always pleasant denouement) and when the play finished, the Prince was content.

On Friday O'Barbo proposed to the young Prince that they go to the Waterford Eropa. A charming spectacle was being presented there in which all the arts concurred in causing three hours to pass in enchantment. They went there through the crowd. A celebrated kalde had accompanied his lines with a delightful music; the subject was interesting, that of a woman who gave her life to save that of her husband.

The curtain went up and the young Prince, placed on the floor very close to the orchestra, on two stools, did not miss anything, either for sight or hearing. The orchestra played in a superior manner, it was said, but he did not find its execution moving, either because at a play one expects everything one can hope for of the best, or because the auditorium spoiled it; one is, so to speak, in the orchestra and a certain distance is required or instrumental music as a viewpoint is for painting. By an opposite effect, however, one is always too far away for vocal music. That comes from a defect of proportion between the instruments and the vices; the instruments are too loud or the location and the voices often too weak or too shrill. Thus, the spectacle only appears to the majority of the spectators as a slow and sulky pantomime, because the sounds, no matter how pleasant they are, do not connect, if the intelligence of things expressed does not put heart and soul into the combination. The instruments always drown out the voices.

An interesting actress was playing the role of the good wife; it was the nymph Tubrasinleh; she delighted with the natural and pathetic quality of her acting, although one could hardly hear her, but all the other actors seemed like marionettes who opened their mouths without speaking. Afterwards there were dances and pantomimes. There the music, although still too loud, as in the overture, at least did not harm the expression, and that part of the spectacle was an enchantment.

As they left, Oribeau said to his guide: "What do you think of the Eropa?"

"But what about you, Prince? I ought not to give you my opinion first."

"I think," said the young pupil, "that the Mommonians understand a little better what relates to pleasures than all the rest, but they still lack it."

"How is that?"

"They fear, in their spectacle, too much illusion, so much does it remind them that it's artificial: the ridiculous applause, the distractions of the actors, especially the actresses, and that deafening orchestra…but whoever wants to reform those things will reform them. However, they help me to know the genius of my people."

Chapter W
Waterford seen in its ugliness by the young Prince.

"Waterford," said the Sage, "is ordinarily only seen by sovereigns at the Fricasan, the Saleniti and the Eropa, or during their entrances. They only perceive the brilliant, the cheerful, and the prepared. You've examined the beautiful places, you've been to its spectacles; as for its prisons, it's not be those horrible places that one can judge the particular situation of a people, but its hospitals have began to give you an idea of it; in order for a sick person to go in search of refuge there, things have to be very bad at home!

"You're going to see the people in the quarters that only they occupy, and even individual habitations, their sad diversions, without being known to them, and seeming to be one of their equals."

The Prince and the Sage emerged from their abode, and took a steep street that led to the Temple of Middlethird, which they entered to worship Thor. Then they continued their route through tortuous little streets which led them to Fourfardem Street—which is to say, the high street of poverty.

They could have believed that they were no longer in Waterford but in a vast hospital similar to Citrêbe, where men, women and children had been confounded.

"These people are very poor!" said the young Prince,

"I'll soon acquaint you with the reason," the Sage replied.

They traversed the entire quarter, going to the right and left into lateral streets; some were deserted, others dirty and noxious; a few ran alongside or were traversed by a river of filth, into which O'Barbo advised the young Prince to divert the waters of another, called the Veteti, one day, in order to clean it, but in the fashion, nevertheless, that the waters of the latter only mingled with it for that purpose, because of the precious quality of those of the Virèbe for scarlet dye.[70]

"Oh, what a quarter! What wretched people!" the Prince exclaimed incessantly. "Is there no means of changing its sad state and embellishing these afflicting dwellings?"

"Yes, and all that depends on the Prince, but it's necessary for him to know the evil that he has to remedy. Would you like us to go into one of these houses, in order to know the manner of these people's existence in depth, who seem to be a class apart?"

"Yes, let's go in," said Oribeau.

---

[70] The dyer Jean Gobelin established his factory by the Bièvre in the fifteenth century, and made scarlet dyes there that added a distinctive tint to the river for centuries.

They opened a door, and perceived an unpaved hovel in which there were two cam beds and about a dozen people—men, women and children—occupied in sorting rags and other things of similar value picked up in the street; the silk was being separate from the linen, the pieces of paper from the parchment, the bones, the wood, the coal from the ash, which was passed through a sieve and made a choking dust, the black glass from the white, etc.

At the sight of a venerable old man and a charming young man, all the work ceased. An old woman, dirty, hunchbacked and bandy-legged, approached the door.

"What do you want, sirs?"

"We're travelers," said the Sage, "and we're curious to know all the occupations of this great city. What are you doing there?"

"We're separating our pickings, of course."

"What is your profession, my good woman?"

At your age, you can't see what I am? I'm a rag-picker. My husband picks up ashes, my oldest son trades in broken bottles, my younger scrapes the gutter. My daughter, hunchbacked and bent-legged like me, washes the rags, my younger one sieves ashes, but it spoils her stomach, and as she isn't ugly she's quitting that to be like her sister, who isn't bandy-legged or hump-backed."

"Where is your second daughter?" asked the Sage.

"She's a whore in Tanisnorohé Street."

"Just heaven! Your daughter...and you don't blush! Your daughter is lost and..."

The old ash-collection burst out laughing and pointed at his wife, his hunchbacked daughter and the younger one. "They're the lost women, for they're poor, not the other, who's a whore and earns good money, but has the good heart, every time I pass, to feed me, and I'm only dressed in what she gives us."

"What a degree of corruption...and misery!" said the Sage to the Prince.

"Old man," said the wife, "at your age you're astonished at what ought not to astonish you. So that you know, I'll tell you something: it's that in every land where there are people poor enough for vice to make them a little better off than honor, the people will have vice, and not honor. I have none; I'm reckoned in the city of Waterford, where I live, as filth and excrement, less than the dogs; a daughter of ours, in becoming a whore, isn't falling, she's rising, and if that isn't true, it's the opinion of society. Such as you see me, I was of a good enough family, but my father was ruined by a procurator who reduced him to beggary. The procurator, seeing me nice enough, though hunchbacked, gave me a child and then married me to my man, who beat me for nearly fifteen years and half-crippled me. Seeing that, I let myself go, as you can see, to filth, and I said that, at any rate, my daughters would do better than me. As there are some gorging them on everything, while I live on shit, I've wanted a hundred times to advise my man and my son to murder."

"I'd be broken on the wheel."

"Well, what does it matter? You'd be avenged on the rich, and you'd die with less scorn, perhaps with less suffering, than in the poorhouse. Go on, old man, and you, young man, if things were a little more evenly divided, there'd be enough for everyone. The poor man kills and steals because he has no bread, no honor and no esteem, and the rich man is insolent, buying the maidenheads of girls, rendering them whores, keeping great idlers at his door, splashing us and crushing us with his carriage, because he has too much money and power. Bring the two extremes closer—that would be better than preaching and laws..."

"Good woman," said O'Barbo, "here's a gold coin; it's an Oribeau, and this is my dwelling. Come and find me tomorrow."

The old woman took the Oribeau and said to her husband: "Need to pay the rent; there'll be four sous left, with which you'll have a waistcoat, for one can see your skin."

"And me shoes," said the boy.

"Shoes! I haven't bought any of those for twenty years. I put on those people throw out on the rubbish-heap.

"Here, Mother," said the daughter, "here's some that a lady threw into the street in front of me; they'll do me?"

"What!" said the old woman. "No, it's a pity but they're good enough to sell."

"But I want to put them on," said the daughter.

"You can't."

"I'll put them on anyway, or I'll smash them up…sieve for your shoes if you want, but I've had enough and I'm going to join my sister."

The mother gave in, and the daughter picked up the sieve again."

O'Barbo gave her a second Oribeau, whose employment he specified, and he withdrew.

"Oh, what people," said the young Prince.

"They're yours. There's more philosophy in what you've just heard that unfortunate woman say than has ever penetrated into out colleges of druids. Don't forget it, you who are destined to reign. People declaim against the corruption of morals, some attribute it to one cause, some to another, some even dare to attribute it to philosophy, which purifies them. It has only one cause and that's the extreme opulence that always occasions extreme poverty. There's only a certain sum of wealth; if three men in a hundred have half of it, ten a quarter and twenty others half a quarter and forty the last half-quarter, that's the totality between seventy-three; twenty-seven remain who have nothing at all. What do they do? Baseness and crime: they one have that deadly resource. What do the foremost thirteen do? Indolence and seduction; they mock the laws above which they find themselves; they corrupt morals by buying the honor of the poor; and the top three often make use of the twenty-seven to overthrow the State, or bring corruption to it.

"The excess of wealth and means and the absolute lack of subsistence and means—that's what destroys all morality. *A hungry belly has no ears*, the proverb says; *nor virtue*, I add.

Now, the interest of the human race is that there should be virtue; the Prince is like the procurator of the human race; it's up to him to make virtue reign. To succeed in that, he ought to employ the most efficacious means…and I'm seeking to help to know them. A druid once wrote a very fine book entitled *Ameletque*, but it was only a book filled beautiful maxims.[71] A Prince only sees things that embellishes and denatures them. I hope, Prince of Waterford, that you'll see with me, in reality. It's sometimes repulsive, like the one we've just encountered, but only the truth is useful."

"I'll answer to you," said the Prince, "for bringing an efficacious and prompt remedy to everything I see. But how does it come about that this quarter is deserted, while market gardens extend the city in all directions?"

"There's another thing here that will demand your attention and that of your Minister. The city is extending too far. It isn't that it would be advantageous to pile up the habitations; on the contrary, that's unhealthy; but it's necessary to begin by filling the confines of the city appropriately—this quarter, for example. I'd even like Waterford to be interrupted by gardens at intervals, the vegetation of which would purify the air and I'd reserve that while building this. I'd place a few public establishments here, and one of three great spectacles, or only one of those of the boulevard, which I'd exempt from going to two great fairs. I'd prune the city absolutely; I'd immediately widen certain streets, and I'd immediately uncover the quays and bridges; by the means the air in the capital, pure enough in itself, would acquire a further measure of salubrity…"

While speaking thus, the Prince and the age advanced. A fetid odor made itself felt, and Oribeau held his nose.

"What's that?" he exclaimed. "Is there a refuse tip nearby?"

"No," said the Sage, "But look at that wall; it encloses a cemetery."

---

[71] The reference is to Fénelon's *Télémaque*, one of the principal models for this section of Restif's narrative.

"A cemetery!"

"Your Senate ordered that they be transported outside the city into the open air, but the druids opposed it."

"The Senate!"

"Yes."

"Isn't there a law that obliges them to obey the Senate?"

"Yes, but it's been bent."

"I'll see about that! How can such a salutary and simple law not be executed?"

As they went back toward the interior of the city, after a fairly short distance, the Prince heard a loud noise, like children talking.

"It seems to me that I recognize that building," he said.

"Yes, it's the hospital of the boys who have been nursed at the orphanage; those of poor parents who can't raise them are also received there."

The young Prince had already visited the orphanage opposite the botanical gardens. As they went forward they walked alongside a low wall, which extended on one side along almost the whole of Shure Street and on the other a part of Tanisvritoc street.

"Those are vast gardens," said Oribeau.

"They're those of the druids of Tanisemillethird, whose house is named after Tanisvritoc Street."[72]

"Are they very useful?"

"They have a public library."

The Prince and the Sage then turned left and went up a rather steep street which took them back almost to the entrance to Fourfardem Street. The entire quarter, although situ-

---

[72] The Abbaye Saint-Victor, which gave its name to the Rue Saint-Victor rather than vice-versa, was, of course, suppressed in the Revolution. In the following passage and one or two subsequent ones, there are sentences where Restif tracks the progress of his visitors through streets that no longer exist; the lists of anagrams become tiresome as well as pointless, and I have omitted them.

ated on a hill, although the houses were not tall and some were quite broad, us dirty and stinking; one breathes a fetid odor there caused by the dirtiness of the inhabitants and the lack of latrines.

"It would be useful," said the Sage, to oblige all owners to equip their houses with convenient latrines on every floor, and even down below, which passers-by might use. The streets wouldn't stink, the air wouldn't be corrupted, as it is by these depots of ordure and the urine thrown out, etc. I'd also like a system of fines to be established, against anyone who, having entered a public latrine, offends against the rules of propriety. That law would have equal advantages for hygiene, health, sight and pleasure, sojourns in the country being less necessary to busy citizens; they would neglect their business affairs less under the pretext of their health; one wouldn't go in vain to a broker or a banker, etc. twice or three times a week."

"I understand all that marvelously," said the young Prince. "I propose to govern my subjects like an attentive and affectionate father with the aid of your advice and those of my other's Minister."

Oribeau and the Sage then went down into a quarter where proud poverty appeared to have established its empire. The streets were dirty, the houses poor and badly-constructed, while one saw the feathers of hens and capons before all the doors, but discovered underneath the jawbones of cows and the skulls of sheep. O'Barbo made that observation by stirring the piles of feather with his staff.

"What are you doing?" asked the young Prince.

"I'm uncovering misery and frugality hidden under pride and the appearance of good cheer. You know that the inhabitants of this quarter are all clerks; that they're all poor because their work is badly paid, and yet, in the bosom of their poverty, they have a great deal of pride. Little sensible to the pleasure of good cheer, they live with the greatest frugality, only buying offal or the cheapest cuts of meat, such as sheep's heads; but as they want to appear opulent and would believe themselves dishonored if the inhabitants of other quarters saw the sad debris of their meals, they have the rule that, every evening, in the dark, five or six apprentices take turns to go to pick up the feathers of chickens and other birds killed during the day by rotisseurs, with which they cover the dishonorable jawbones and sheep's heads in order that the following day, all the passers-by, seeing the feathers, will exclaim: 'Ha ha! They eat well within those walls; there are no sheep's skulls there; it appears that one has bodily health and the profession is good.' When it's presumed that people are talking about them thus, they're content and eat cheerfully, at their meals, the vulgar nourishment that they can procure."

"Do you think," asked the young Prince, "that glory is a fault?"

"Yes, if it leads to idleness, for it's a kind of proud frugality that leads to it. I believe that it will be necessary one day to augment the salary of all the professions in which it is below reasonable necessity, and that the people in those professions will only be more hard-working for it. The despair of reaching their goal wearies their arms. I recognize in people who earn little that tailors are not discouraged, but that's because there's an opportunity to compensate themselves by nibbling at the cloth...

"Speaking of tailors, we've walked a long way. Would you like to take a poor meal with them in one of their inns?"

"Gladly," said Oribeau. "I only ask to see everything for myself; I'm hungry and I think I could eat their dishes. Are they not beings of my species?"

"You won't only see tailors, but locksmiths, carpenters, masons, shoemakers, and even water-carriers."

"So much the better. Let's go—I want to eat with those people; they're the most useful fraction of my people, locksmiths, masons, carpenters, tailors and shoemakers—one can't do without those artisans."

The Sage and the Prince quit the quarter where they were and went to another, in the middle of which the worthy Thorel, lived, the famous hostess of what was inappropriately named a "hash house."

"That's like me," put in old Ennisleague. "there are people who call my place a hash house, although one is properly served here, and you're witness to that, sirs—but people have to speak ill of everything.

"Orders of the day, good woman!" said one of the drinkers. "You're interrupting the gentleman's story in an untimely fashion, and that's unconstitutional!"

Miss Thor-el—for she was a spinster—was about forty-five years old; she had grown as fat as a hogshead, although she ate very little. It was said that the continual fumes of the dishes she cooked obstructed the pores of her skin, retaining the mucus therein and forcing it to change into fat; but she had for assistants a nephew, and an older and younger niece. As for the aunt, no longer being able to move, she remained sitting on a solid seat from which she was able to see everyone coming in and out; she was only occupied in ordering service and receiving the five sous that everyone gave her for dinner, for soup and broth, and in the evening for two dishes, roast, stew or salad. Like the other restaurateurs, she had once offered meals at four and a half sous, but her great fashionability had obliged her to put up her price, which had not diminished the crowd.

On seeing a venerable old man come in, with a charming young man, the good Thor-el was struck with respect and simultaneously felt the greatest pleasure.

"Frank," she said to her nephew, "serve these gentlemen well and make it tender for the grandfather."

For their part, her niece Julia and her cousin Mary hastened to rinse glasses; the former was pretty but a trifle serious, the latter alert, with her nose in the air. Julia placed a glass as clean as crystal before Oribeau, blushed and lowered her big blue eyes. Laughing, Mary said: "Here's your glass, Grandfather; would you like strong beer or small beer? We have excellent ones."

"Give us the best," replied O'Barbo.

Julia immediately ran to the cellar and brought back a jug of strong beer, which the aunt kept in reserve to regale her intimate friends. "You'll find it good," she said to Oribeau. "Taste it." And she poured it herself.

The young Prince admired the complaisance of the young woman. He drank, after which she served the Sage.

"That girl is charming, and above all good," he said to his guide, "but she seems to me to be too free with the men."

"Observe her!" said the Sage.

Oribeau observed all Julia's actions, and soon perceived that she was only obliging to him. She served everyone else with a cold modesty, without speaking and without raising her eyes, but at the slightest glance of the Sage or Oribeau she flew toward them in order to discover whether they wanted anything.

Meanwhile, the young Prince observed the customers. In spite of their large number, a profound silence reigned in the hall; everyone was doing what he was doing with ardor; Miss Thor-el stimulated the idlers herself, in order that they would make way for others, who arrived successively.

"I beg your pardon, Miss," the old man said to her, "but I'm a little slow in eating."

"I'm not talking for you," the hostess replied. "I know what one owes to your age. But you have a fine grandson there—for you must be his grandfather?"

"He's a good lad," the old man retorted, "and I hope that one day he'll be the joy and glory of his mother, who is a wor-thy woman."

Julia had remained immobile during that conversation, although she was carrying a plate laden with meat.

"Hey, Julia!" exclaimed the aunt, seeing her mouth open. "Have you swallowed your words?"

Ashamed, Julia completed her route.

A water-carrier, tightly laced-up, who was at the same table as the Prince and the old man, then said: "Youth likes youth and Miss Julia likes that handsome fellow better than me and all the others, but it's also that he's very polite and Miss Julia, who is very polite, likes it that he's polite as her.

"That's enough!" said Miss Thor-el. "Don't make our girls big-headed. In a house like this one I won't suffer compliments except to me."

A young tailor earning his soup whispered to one of his comrades: "If she wanted to give me money I'd do anything she wanted."

"Me, I'll marry her if she wants. I'd make myself a master and I'd work for my own account, and I wouldn't ask for any more to be happy."

"Me, I wouldn't do anything; I'd amuse myself."

"Me, I like my estate."

"I should think so! You have a crooked hand, and you're living while I'm dying of hunger, but you won't have her; she prefers the carpenter, that pretty fellow who always arrives last."

"Good! She wants to give him Mary."

"That's all sham, she'd like to fix him up with Julia, but Julia won't have any of it."

"She's a little difficult, Miss Julia," said a shoemaker. "If you touch her it's *get off, and go wash your hands*."

"She's a little hypocritical," said a locksmith, "but at least she doesn't have a preference for anyone."

"That's because she's good," said a stone-carver

"Yes, yes, she is," said one of his comrades, "and her aunt says she's sure of her."

All of that was murmured in low voices, in order that Miss Thor-el did not hear any of it; in any case, she was occupied in receiving payment from five or six shoemakers and a dozen tailors who had just drunk their soup and swallowed their meat without chewing.

The Sage and the Prince listened attentively. When all the men had stopped talking, Oribeau said to his teacher: "The attention that young woman has shown me flatters my heart, as when I saw the modest Canora prefer me, or the trembling

Ahissa thank me. What a pity that such a pretty girl has an estate so low."

"You need an alliance proportionate to your rank," said O'Barbo, "and which contributes to the security of your people by procuring you the amity of a neighboring state. I can only see one Princess in all Evinland who is suitable for you, and that's Oribelle, the elder daughter of the Queen of Lagenia. She's five years younger than you; she's Julia's age; she'll be a perfect match for you."

"I don't know," said Oribeau, "how it comes about that I'd like Julia to take Oribelle's place."

"It's the effect of a communicative sympathy. Julia, whom you've affected agreeably, has looked at you with pleasure, with a sentiment of amity and preference; and the emanations of those lovely eyes, mingling with the emanations of yours, have formed a secret liaison between the two of you."

"You think that happens naturally?"

"Nothing is more certain. Dondanuck, your Minister, is equally instructed in these great verities, but the people of Mommonia are still too coarse for us to be able to communicate them to them. One day, they'll be as vulgar as our neighbors the Angles, who will receive philosophers from a celebrated realm beyond the sea named France, under the regime of a young Prince who, at twenty-six, will have pacified two hemispheres, the one we know and another that we don't yet know. His name will be Loïsauguste; he will be the son of the most excellent of men, who only reigns in order that all of that powerful kingdom will be eternally regulated without the glorious and beneficent reign of his son...but let's pay and go...

"Miss Thor-el," the old man said, "Here's twelve sous for me and twelve for my pupil.

"I'll give you change," said the fat innkeeper.

"No, the beer that Julia gave us is the best, and I'll pay the price."

Julia blushed; her aunt looked at her, but she smiled, which reassured the pretty girl.

Immediately, the beautiful bird with three crests made its shrill cry heard.

O'Barbo made a sign of intelligence to the good Thor-el, and left.

As soon as the Sage and his pupil were in the street, the former resumed his speech: "That young king will have a wife as beautiful as Oribelle, the daughter of a Princess, whom mortals will take for virtue personified, and the best, I don't say of Princes but of men; she'll be the sister of the sovereign of Germany, a prince whose name will be forever immortal by virtue of the wisest laws, the most useful reforms and heroic acts of generosity, such as are expected of you; but the most beautiful of those virtues will be to have adored his mother, cherished his sister the Queen, the wife of Loïsauguste, and all his brothers and sisters.

"That good Loïs, who does not reign, will be the son of a King that had him at your age, but he had no mother. He succeeded the great Loïs XIV, whose reign will be the epoch for all future generations. The great Loïs XIV will be the grandson of the good Errick, head of the dynasty, but who will emerge nevertheless from the royal family, which commences in our day in that kingdom by the extinction of that of the powerful Karlomagne, whom I have sometimes mentioned to you...

"But I'm letting myself get carried away by the desire to talk to you about a celebrated people and kings, the only ones in the world who will be constantly fathers of their people. Here we are at the MacErrick Bridge; conversation shortens the route. I've shown you our poor capital; I want to show you the rich in another quarter, but debased by vice and scandalous debauchery.

"Don't be surprised that the abuses you know already are allowed to subsist; they're indestructible; but I once composed a project myself destined to operate a general reform."

While speaking thus, the two Observers arrived in the vicinity of Recel'Bras Street. O'Barbo proposed to go into a house celebrated for the famous players of draughts that assembled there.

"That's a strange kind of celebrity!" said the young Prince. "Are these people necessary to the State?"

"They're not professional gamblers," replied the Sage, "with the exception of three or four. The majority are merchants and artists who don't come to gamble but to unwind after work. The recreation is permitted. The master of the house is an expert in the game of draughts; he has written a book on the subject entitled *M'Orivan's Rules of Draughts, good moves, traps than one can set for one's opponent, with the indication of a facile means to rescue a seemingly lost game: a very useful work for people who have nothing to do. Published by the Author in Waterford, Cl'éole Square, near Recel'bras Street.*[73]

The Sage asked for a pot of tea and placed himself near to two players who were about to commence an interesting game—that is the name given to the famous games where the stake is twenty, thirty, forty or fifty gold pieces; the players do not say so aloud; often they only put a silver coin beside the checkerboard, but the gallery knows the true stake.

The game started; those placing bets became animated; after futile coups in which the players felt one another out, they exchanged a few pieces equally in order to open out the board and prepare for major coups. Two men were seen buried in profound reflection, planning all possible moves and their combinations, sometimes risky, whose ripostes required ex-

---

[73] Although the title is fictitious the reference is to an analogue of the first book on the game of draughts published in 1770 by "Manoury," the head waiter at a coffee-house called the Café d'École, whom Restif apparently knew quite well; he figures in Restif's *Nuits de Paris*, which began publication in 1788, as the proprietor of the fictitious "Café Robert," similarly located on the Place de l'École at the corner of the Rue de l'Arbre-Sec. *Nuits de Paris* also offers a more elaborate and revealing account of the maneuvers of *croqs* [crooks].

quisite judiciousness. After an ill-made choice, although apparently advantageous, one took on the assured air of a winner; the other continued to struggle by means of adroitly set traps, with balanced and delayed his adversary's triumph. Finally, the fatal coup was delivered. The loser blushed; half those laying bets went pale, and the fortunate, transported by joy, pocketed the money. Another game commenced.

"Is it possible," said the young Prince, who had been solidly brought up, "that men put such great importance on the displacement of little pieces of ivory and ebony? They seemed to me to be as occupied as the Minister ought to be when he is dealing with the most important affairs of State. Is that a game? Is that a relaxation?"

"No," replied the Sage. "One is sitting tranquilly, the humors stagnant, the attention fatigued, transpiration arrested or forced...but it's nothing. Let's pass on to the other room; you're going to see a crooks' game; they have a separate room; that's M'Orivan's politics, who can't close a public establishment to people but wants to preserve his ordinary customers from ambushes. These crooks bring in their dupes from outside; at first they hide their game in order to embolden them...."

"I see," said Oribeau, "all human perversity in summary..."

"You know what few of your peers have known. But let's leave this house. You're going to see a more instructive and more striking spectacle."

The two observers went back to the superb quay that borders the Shure, went past the MacErrick Bridge and found themselves on the quay popularly known as the Whore's Quay, where they went into a noble billiard hall. The room was full to bursting with men in rags.

"What!" said the young Prince. "These wretches have money to lose?"

"Yes; I'll explain that to you when we come out; let's watch the players for a moment."

A very petty game was being played; the most astonishing skill was employed by the actors, while the trembling gamblers only bet with the greatest circumspection; but when one of the players made a bad shot, the portion of the rabble that had bet on him heaped him with the most vulgar insults, and even threatened to beat him. When the game was over the losers forgot the player in order to quarrel with the winners; they hurled coins at their heads, which the winners received avidly, often knocking people over in order to pick up coins that fell to the ground. Meanwhile, the players recommenced another game, and the gamblers came to grips again with equal ardor.

"What is this inferno, then?" asked Oribeau.

"It's a billiard hall where crooks, the bad lots who swarm in the capital, come to wager between them what they have cleverly accumulated in all the other billiard halls. Those who win the most money here get dressed up and then go to shine in the more honest billiard halls, where they find dupes. You ask me why they come to play here? They have an excellent reason: the individuals against whom they exercise themselves throughout Waterford are not of their strength; they're obliged to hide their skill in order to take advantage; they begin to lose it if they don't come here from time to time to "sharpen it," as they put it.

"As for the government, which tolerates these bad lots, apart from the fact that it makes use of them for base but necessary work like arresting debtors and criminals, for discovering various malversations, it's not sorry to have a small number of wretches, lost in any case, whom it knows and keeps under surveillance, frightening fathers of families who might be tempted to abandon themselves to their passion for gambling.

"It's not that these wretches don't commit great disorders and cause great evils; they contribute for example, to the corruption of mores by sustaining prostitutes and rendering them more infamous. They do worse still, on the days when public carriages arrive, by water and by land, they lie in wait for young provincial girls who come to Waterford to go into service or to hide the consequences of a weakness, to escape from agricultural labor or dependence on their honest parents; they have duennas with them: brothel-keepers, who choose the prettiest, offering them their houses, as if for ordinary service, and who seduce them if the young women are credulous enough to follow them; but the present Great Judge of Waterford has made those abuses disappear. Often, the men take them away themselves, but those are provincial girls who are already half-corrupted, with whom there are fewer precautions to take."

"These wretches are needed?" said the young Prince, emotionally.

"Yes, until now; but it will be possible one day no longer to employ that dangerous means."

"I believe so, and I hope to do without it."

"It won't be impossible, but nor will it be as easy as you imagine today, since your Minister and the Great Judge of Waterford, both so well-intentioned, have not yet been able to do it."

The Prince and the Sage then went into another billiard hall, where they saw a few crooks exercising their skill in the most covert manner The crook who was playing lost all his games, but he gambled small amounts and was careful almost always to reach nineteen-all, appearing to lose only by accident. Wagers were laid. Two or three crooks, his comrades, dispersed in the hall, offered to bet against him. Honest connoisseurs who saw the unknown man play and found him reasoned, wagered against the honest player, who had less depth to his game.

A few lost games did not astonish them; they hoped to recover when the stakes were doubled; but they eventually perceived, too late, that he was a crook who did not want to win; they gradually withdrew; others newly-arrived took their place; the crooks made an ample harvest and disappeared when they heard murmurs, except for the players, who remained, continued to play and regained what he had lost, and more, by means of bets for him, in which he went halves with everyone else.

At the end of the session the crooks met up and the evening's profit was shared out equally; they only appeared in the honest billiard hall again after quite a long time, but others replaced them. The day after a good harvest, all the wretches went to the billiard hall on the Whore's Quay to settle between themselves who would carry off the spoils of crime.

"When it's absolutely exhausted," the Sage continued, "they go to beat up the prostitutes who are in their dependency in order to oblige them to furnish them with money with which to gable. Then they meet up with their comrades again and go to a billiard hall that the crooks have left in security for a while, extend their nets there and enjoy good fishing in untroubled water."

On emerging from that billiard hall the Sage and his pupil found themselves in Tanisnohoré Street, the most beautiful, most prosperous and busiest in Waterford. There was still an hour of daylight remaining; that is why O'Barbo took the young Prince to an Academy of Gaming.

Around twenty small oblong tables, at each of which two payers were sitting, a troop of men were gathered, who charged them with piles of gold or silver. "Only triomphe[74] and piquet are played here," O'Barbo said, "the other games being prohibited by the police in these public places, which have the sole privilege of playing host to card games, in order that they can be more easily monitored. It is in consequence of that plan that the owners of taverns and coffee-houses incur heavy fines if they permit card-games in their establishments; it would too difficult to maintain surveillance on all of them. In spite of the extreme attention given to it however, you will soon see that crooks are as numerous here as in billiard halls, that they employ the same ruses and similarly meet up with

---

[74] Triomphe [the French equivalent of the English word trump] was a primitive ancestor of the whist family of modern card games.

the crooked gamblers who surround them and affect the greatest honesty. Let us watch silently; you will see them more easily than me, of whom they will be suspicious as soon as they catch sight of me."

In fact, scarcely had O'Barbo placed himself behind a player's chair than the latter appeared ill-at-ease; he turned to look in all directions and became agitated, shifting incessantly. One of the gamblers asked him what was wrong.

"Call the manager," replied the player.

The manager arrived. "Mr. Smomoges," said the player, "there's a man behind me who's disconcerting me; make him go away."

The manager asked the old man to leave; O'Barbo then went to stand by another table, where he was tolerated without anything being said. Meanwhile, the young Prince had remained at the first and devoted al his attention to what was happening there. Intelligent as he was, he perceived easily enough that one of the players knew the cards, although they were shuffled frequently, and that he sometimes filched one of them. It was not the player who had had O'Barbo removed; that one was not yet a crook, he was a dupe and lost, but to his fury, Oribeau judged that he had a keen desire to be able to rectify his losses.

The Sage, for his part, made even more decisive observations because he had more experience. He saw two cattle merchants, three pork-merchants, six domestics and fourteen apprentice barbers cleaned out in very little time by facile means. Only one played and the others furnished the funds; the professional players played for small takes for a while, piqued their interest; they played double-or-nothing, and that concluded the affair; the stakes ran out and as pledges were forbidden, it was necessary for the players to withdraw for lack of funds.

Two crooks who had just despoiled all those unfortunates made signs to one another as to who would have the lot; they started to play. As soon as they were at grips, almost all the other tables were deserted; people wanted to see the duel between those two vigorous athletes. They expected one another's feats of skill, and pretended not to be protecting themselves from them, while hiding them from the eyes of the spectators, but they were countered by even more cunning ones, which rendered the spectacle interesting.

A profound silence reigned around them; they did not speak themselves; they understood one another by signs; their play had a rapidity that did not permit attention to relent; it was scarcely able to follow them. What a profound science of piquet! The penetrating eyes of the two men saw the undersides of the cards; they never made a false move. They played the cards with an art that would have defeated anyone less skillful than them.

The advantage was sometimes equal; after a few hands of varied success they went all in; it was at that point that attention was redoubled; the majority of the spectators were pale; the circulation of their blood seemed to be suspended, doubtless because, as associates of one or the other, they were interested in the outcome. The cards were dealt. One of the players had all the aces but it was the deal that gave them to him; it was crooked, but it did not have the fatal consequences that the other player feared; he had been able to procure the kings; he had a valuable quint, and an equal point. The other had the cards and the count had only two points of difference.

The second hand gave a considerable advantage to one of the players; at the third the game was decided. It was here that all the skill was employed; the one who was less advanced had recourse to all the finesse of the art, but with so much dexterity that no one could detect it; only his opponent could divine how he had been tricked. So, as soon as he had picked up his cards he was seen to go pale. "Play for five points," he said, with a convulsion, and lost. His adversary tranquilly arranged his hand. People spoke. The less advanced made ninety, picked up the money, got up and left, followed by half the audience. They other started working for new expenses.

As they emerged from the place, the Sage explained all the ruses to the young Prince, but as it would be dangerous, I shall not repeat them.

"Why?" said one of the drinkers. "Do you think we're capable of making evil use of them?"

"No," said the gentleman, "but they might be passed on, as I might have passed them on to you, and thus harm honest folk."

"I don't want to know them," said the other drinker. "I'm clumsy, they wouldn't be any use to me and might be useful to others; but I'm delighted by what you've said about swindles; I'll warn my children."

The gentleman resumed his story.

After O'Barbo had finished his discourse, he said to the young Prince: "Darkness has fallen completely; it's a favorable time to observe better than we have done a monstrous abuse that revolts nature and causes her to tremble, but which the government is forced to tolerate. We're in Tanisnohoré Street here; let's go in the direction of the Eropa.

The Prince and the Sage had hardly gone thirty paces when they perceived a pretty boutique with gauze curtains, which did not prevent them from seeing that it was garnished with a dozen very pretty girls.

"What is that boutique?" asked Oribeau.

"It's a fashion boutique."

At that moment a tall young woman emerged, passably beautiful, with a tray full of trinkets in front of her. Another, shorter one, who appeared to be a pupil, accompanied her. They went in the direction of the Eropa, with the consequence that the Sage and the Prince were following them. Opposite a house of highly esteemed druids, called the Ratonéoris, the young woman was assailed by six young soldiers. She cried out, trying to repel them, but they surrounded her and no one dared to help the young woman, whose little companion was desolate.

O'Barbo and the Prince drew closer.

"What are you doing there, Musketeers?" the Sage said to them. "You're committing an infamous action."

"She's a prostitute, old man," replied one of the musketeers.

"No, no, you're mistaken. Leave her alone." He tried to move them aside, but one of the libertines shoved him back.

O'Barbo then had recourse to the power of his art. He seized the young man and sent him tumbling in the distance. Oribeau, animated by a courage above his age and his strength, which gave him his moral zeal, moved the others aside successively. They came back at him, but, struck by the old man's majestic air and his pupil's noble pride, they went away.

"Oh, Fillira," said the younger woman. "Without this old man and his son, what have become of us?"

"Let's go," my dear Hasameh," replied the older one, "we're not amusing ourselves." And the young woman from the fashion shop continued her route, after having thanked the old man and, blushing, darted a keen glance at Oribeau, whom she called her liberator.

Immediately, the cry of the bird with three crests was heard.

"Really!" said O'Barbo, as if speaking to himself, "I suspected as much!" Then he addressed his pupil.

Chapter X
Xistes (continuation of the preceding chapter).

"Xacca[75] whom the Indians honor in the form of a white elephant, which is the last of his eight thousand metamorpho-

---

[75] Xacca could be found in late eighteenth-century France in the *Dictionnaire historique*, where he has a substantial entry identifying him as an Indian philosopher born a thousand years before Christ, allegedly highly regarded by the Japanese, to whom he taught the doctrine of metempsychosis, as their

ses, established places of public exercises where athletes tried their strength, and these places were subsequently named xistes by the Greeks. Later, Indian corruption consecrated these xistes, which were planted with trees, to the dances of strolling players; finally, a severe and sad morality gave them to a few contemplative Brahmins. It has been almost the same here; the ancient public exercises have been abandoned; the pleasure of the table, gambling and women have been substituted for them.

"You're about to see in the xiste of the palace a crowd of prostitutes; it's like a public market where all the beauties display themselves under the veil of darkness, which hides their indecency. But before then, let's cast an eye over those of a more common order who line the two sides of Tanisnohoré Street. That sight, so dangerous for another, will not yet be for you, Prince, in whom the age of vile passions has not arrived, since you have never been delivered to the idleness that awakens them."

After this little speech, the two observers approached a few groups of the prostitutes who were bordering the street, and who were particularly notable at the corners of lateral streets. The group at the end of Najetanisensid Street was only composed of unfortunates of the lowest class, sad victims devoted by their age and ugliness to the brutality of soldiers, manual laborers and street-porters.

"These don't render vice attractive," said O'Barbo. "They drive it away rather than giving a taste for it."

They passed by rapidly and came to the corner of Chantdure Street. Here the scene changed; the prostitutes were young, pretty and tastefully dressed; the majority appeared to be young women still in the first enthusiasm of debauchery; they were cheerful and enticing; they were gamboling like the lamb that, as it emerges from the meadow, will fall under the

---

legislator. Contemporary reference books also attributed to the Greek word xiste the meaning cited by O'Barbo.

butcher's knife. They excited the pity of the old man and the young Prince.

"Unfortunates!" said the old man. "Who has seduced you? Who has doomed you? Who has thrown you into this deadly estate, which only promises you a death as premature as it will be painful?"

One of them approached Oribeau; she was only fourteen years old. She tried to throw her arms around the Prince and kiss him; he pushed her away, and the Sage completed getting rid of her. She then spoke so freely and in such a revolting manner that O'Barbo took his pupil away before he was able to hear what she said.

The number of prostitutes they encountered thereafter was inconceivable. The young Prince shuddered with indignation, for the Sage made him observe from a distance the manner in which the unfortunates provoked the passers-by, young and old, and the way in which they were attacked by the rogues who roamed the streets by night, but they could not hear what they said.

"What! Women and girls with pretty faces debase and degrade themselves to this extent, by virtue of vile interest!" said the young Prince

"It's not only out of vile interest," the Sage replied. "It's an effect of poverty, of the debasement that you saw in the home of the old ash-collector. These young women, for the most part, are from the lowest class of citizens, and if they are of a higher order, they are vicious souls who love turpitude, or who have been corrupted by the rich before the sage law of your Minister, which will secure the happiness of Mommonians if it is executed."

"But is it not possible, then, for each man to restrict himself to a single woman? Are there not as many woman as men? And then, what can be the utility of these unfortunate women, who, according to what you have told me, are lost for the population of the State, and harm all the men who frequent them?"

"You're speaking in accordance with nature," said the Sage, "and from that viewpoint, you're right; in Evinland, as in almost all of Europe, there are scarcely any more individuals of one sex than the other; in consequence they ought naturally to be sufficient for one another and good mores should reign everywhere. That is not the case, however, and I'll explain the reasons to you...but let's go into this celebrated xiste, where, under the regency of the great MacOrlando, people only talked about political affairs and business."

The young Prince followed his guide into a beautiful xiste, where he saw many former captains, retired from service with honorable records, who were discussing political news under a bushy tree. The two observers passed by and reached the far end of the xiste, where a few men of sober appearance and intelligent physiognomy were surrounding a bard, under another tree.

At that moment the bard was saying: "My name is the Owl;[76] I have declared an immortal war on the Puritans, those infamous corrupters of all morality who hide beneath the bark of decency, annihilating decency by making it consist of nonsense. Bards, my colleagues, and all of you who are listening to me, mistrust the Puritans, those men devoid of virtue but not devoid of vices, who only have vile passions, interest, creeping ambition, the desire for a livid complexion, devouring jealousy, blind and unregulated fanaticism; those men who incessantly insult Wisdom and who have succeeded in making its name in insult, a crime; who, by an inversion of ideas will soon make the name of Fanatic honorable. One of them has already researched its etymology and proved that it was once a term of praise. But the name of Wisdom was also a term of praise once, except under the reigns of the Roman emperors

---

[76] This word is given in English in the original. While undertaking the nocturnal excursions that supplied the raw material for this part of the present text and the sprawling narrative of *Les Nuits de Paris*, Restif liked to style himself "le Hibou" [the Owl].

Nero and Domitian, those monsters whom nature abhors almost eight centuries after their death. My colleagues, love and honor wisdom, for it is the love of virtue.

"I have studied the human heart, as you know. I have gone back, by virtue of my reflections. To the source of virtue; I have analyzed it and I said to myself thereafter: 'What is virtue?' I fell silent, profoundly wrapped up within myself and I listened attentively to the response of my conscience, long occupied with the meditation of virtue. And my conscience replied: 'Virtue is nature, faithfully obeyed." What is that? 'Virtue is not eccentricity or singularity; it is nature.' What is that? 'Nature has given me the knowledge of reciprocity. Nature cries out, by way of compassion, *do not do harm*, and it adds, by way of compassion and reason, *for it will be returned to you*. She cries to me, by way of reciprocity, *do good, for it will be returned to you*; and way of wisdom, *for you will feel a delightful enjoyment after having done it*; and by way of religion, *for you are the brother of every living man and our beneficence will make you loved by the common Father*. And reason, which comes from nature, adds: *do not take pleasures to excess, for then they will kill you*. Wisdom adds: *for in excess, they become pain*; and religion: *For that is to weaken and denature the Work of God*. Employ your organs, use your passions, like veils, says Wisdom.'

"The Puritan tells us to destroy the passions, to live like stagnant water—which is to say, corrupt yourself. Governments only listen to puritans in regard to theory; in practice, they tolerate prostitutes: prostitutes, the degradation of the human species in the manner in which they exist today... Here, a puritan might stop me, and with a bitter smile, he might ask me whether a manner of prostitution exists that would prevent it from being the degradation of the human species. I reply to him by history, and I ask him in my turn whether he thinks there was any degradation in Babylon, where women prostituted themselves once in their lives, and whether there was any in the ancient Greek priestesses of Venus. No, no, entire nations do not consecrate themselves to degradation. It is not a degradation in Africa but an honor, and yet prostitutes are not in a situation very different from that of our prostitutes; they are necessary, in such a hot country, although marriage could be sufficient for a man's needs there. As here, though, young people are not always married as soon as they are nubile.

"Among the Babylonians, temporary prostitution was a religious duty; it was a form of alms, which the nation made to obligatory bachelors who had not yet been able to procure a spouse, and to foreigners long deprived of their wives; far from criticizing that institution, of which we are unaware of all the causes, let us respect it in silence. Perhaps, if some of the Sages of those times returned today, and if they could explain them to us, we would be forced to admire them. We inhabit a cold climate, and although Friga is the same as Astarte and Venus, she has not introduced the same worship here, solely because the climate is so different; but we have prostitutes. I groan, not because of that which is, but its manner. Before examining it, let us see whether prostitutes are necessary for us.

"In the great cities, we do not marry our young men until very late, after they have an estate; they ordinarily espouse the following generation; we have bachelors by vice, by taste and by estate. All those men are human; that word is understood, and offers to the mind of every thinking being, a vast and frightening idea, which enables a voice to cry in the depths of the heart that public women are necessary. It is not that nature is not revolted by the idea that public women present, such as they exist among us, but another idea immediately presents itself, more frightening still and the soul rises up in indignation and falls back into its own depths with the sad conviction that public women are necessary. At least they offer a shadow of the natural...but what horrible side-effects!

"Public women are necessary because of the abuses they cause to be avoided, but it is at least as necessary to regulate them, by reason of the abuses of which they are the organ or the occasion. I propose to establish a xiste—which is to say, a vast garden destined for men alone, from the age of puberty.

That garden will be planted with trees, surrounded by uniform buildings whose windows only overlook the garden. There will be a covered gallery around the perimeter, which will extend under all the buildings. At intervals there will be ticket-offices, one for each age of women from fourteen to thirty-nine.

"On the upper floor, above each office, will be women of the indicated age. There will be a notice in each window bearing two numbers, one indicating the age, the other the price. There will be two women at each window; if there is only one, or none, it is because they are occupied. The men, who will be walking alone in the xiste, will cast their eyes over the women at the windows, and according to the pleasure they will have, and the price, they will buy a ticket and then go up to the one consigned to them.

"People will come to that promenade with the design of seeing a woman, but in the streets and ordinary promenades there will be no unexpected encounters that impede business or morning resolutions. Young men and young women will not be scandalized, tempted or prematurely corrupted; young women, especially, will never have before their eyes the seductive spectacle of the elegance of whores and the luxury of kept women; neither will they any longer live in the houses of honest citizens, and the wives and daughters of honest citizens will no longer have to live opposite them. Pimps and pimping, which do even more harm than whoredom, will be annihilated.[77] A frightful malady will be prevented, of which several voyagers assure us that the populations of the torrid zone are afflicted, which commerce might bring to us and will be propagated by prostitutes left to themselves as they are today. That frightful malady, deadlier than smallpox, will inevitably ravage Europe if sage precautions are not taken.

---

[77] The terms "pimp" and "whoredom" are given in English in the original, followed by anagrams of the equivalent French terms in parentheses.

"O Mommonians, pay attention to what I am saying, for I have meditated a project, which I propose to set before the eyes of the great Minister Dondanuck, in order to regulate the deregulation."

When he stopped talking, the bard mingled with the circle of his listeners and disappeared. It was not that there was anything to fear in Waterford for those who exposed useful verities, but the bard in question had powerful enemies and he went away when he saw two of the most dangerous and most ardent approaching.

O'Barbo then took the Prince to one side. "I could not have spoken to you any better than that bard has just done, but you're still very young to understand such things. It's late; our day has been full; let's retire."

"I shall follow the plan of that honest man," said Oribeau. After a pause he added: "Sage, I wouldn't be sorry to go have supper at the good Thor-el's establishment; that woman pleased me.

"We should not," the Sage replied. "Julia considered you too much. Generosity, which is a duty in Princes, forbids you to risk that young woman's tranquility."

"I yield to that," Oribeau replied. "In any case, before commanding, it's necessary to know how to obey, and I'm taking my course in obedience."

"We can go to another inn at the same price, if you wish," said the Sage.

The young Prince agreed to that, and the two observers found an inn offering meals at the same price as that of the good Thor-el. But what a difference there was in cleanliness, the generosity of the aliments and the grace of the waitresses! Everything there was repulsive: tough meat, undercooked or burnt; a detestable stew that congealed grease rendered even more disgusting...

Hungry men, market traders, street porters, etc., were devouring those dishes which the Sage and his pupil ate philosophically.

"Where is the good Thor-el?" said Oribeau, with a smile of dolor. "Where are the good Frank, the lively Mary and the modest Julia?"

"This is how it's necessary to conclude the day," the teacher replied. "You know approximately the manner in which the lower orders of your people exist; you've tasted their food, you've eaten with them, you've heard them talk, you know them and you'll govern them as a good Prince when you've taken the reins of empire. Tomorrow, we'll finish exploring your capital and we'll then go on to the provinces and the regions inhabited by cultivators."

"In those days," said Younghall, "Princes were raised properly!"

"I've heard it said," replied a newcomer, whose name was Kinnagad, "that there was a land of black men where the heir to the throne, unknown to himself, was raised by a laborer, who did not know him either."

"Oh," exclaimed Ennisleague. "He must have been very vulgar."

"No, good woman," said Kinnagad, "a King becomes polished in a day."

"Silence, chatterers!" cried Kilmactomas.

Chapter Y
Yapou,[78] *Taverns, Drinking-dens, etc.*

"Yeoman! Yeoman!" said a waiter at the inn where the Prince and the Sage were lodging.

---

[78] The name yapou is attributed in a 1775 volume of Buffon's *Histoire naturelle* to the "cassique rouge" of Brazil, on the authority of Mathurin-Jacques Brisson's *Ornithologie* (1760), but the description given in the Queen's letter does not resemble any of the birds nowadays known as caciques. The Mexican cacique, which has the black body and yellow tail, does not have the Yapou's distinctive crests.

O'Barbo opened the door and the yeoman, one of thirty guards, seven feet tall immediately presented himself. He had brought a piece of paper in the Minister's envelope, a ukase of the sovereign conceived in these terms:

Dadameh, queen-regent of Mommonia, to our dear son King Oribeau and his Instructor.

You should know that we have just learned some bad news. The young and beautiful Princess Oribelle, the daughter of the Queen of Lagenia, the excellent Conchèse, has been expelled from the Estates that ought to belong to her one day, and her father, Prince O'Brisombaüm has been imprisoned by a faction whose prime mover is not yet known. That is why we are informing you, our very dear son, as well as our friend O'Barbo, your wise instructor, in order that by his superior enlightenment and the power of his art, he might try to discover the Princess who ought to be your wife one day. Dondanuck, our prudent Minister, assures us that the Princess of Lagenia is always preceded, when she is in the forest or the solitary mountains, or even in disguise, by a Yapou, a beautiful bird from Brazil, which has a black body, a yellow tail, blue eyes and three crests on its head in the form of horns. Neglect nothing, both to discover the beautiful and virtuous Princess and to help her. With that, we beg Thor, Berda, Worden, Vananis and Friga to keep you in their beneficent and omnipotent protection forever.

"Tell the Queen that we will obey her supreme orders," said O'Barbo, bowing, after having read that. The yeoman withdrew immediately, with that response.

"How can a princess of Evinland be preceded by a bird native to Brazil, an absolutely unknown country of which I have never heard mention?" asked Oribeau.

"That contains a mystery, which it's necessary to discover," replied the Sage. "The Yapou is a beautiful bird, but which smells very bad when it's irritated. There's an emblem in that bird, which your Minister apparently can't explain to you without inconvenience, but which you can try to discover."

"What concerns me more at the moment," said the young Prince, "is the fate of Oribelle. Expelled from her Estates, young, beautiful and alone, wandering..."

"If she overcomes this ordeal, without her virtue experiencing any affliction, she will be even more brilliant; a diamond only becomes dazzling after rude labor; that's the symbol of the ordeals of virtue. We'll only stay here one more day, in order to see what you haven't yet examined. Tomorrow we'll leave to seek the Princess, while visiting the country, the peasants, and the frontiers of your Estates—which it is very important that you know from experience, and in the greatest detail."

"But is this unfortunate Princess without aid, then?"

"I won't hide it from you that she's protected by a fay who loves you very much, the virtuous Pucellomaneh; but she is inferior in power to the genius Perforimoth the Black, the protector of the Castellan of Ratchlin, the perfidious O'Connor, the Princess's oppressor. He has only expelled her from her Estates because she refused to marry the dwarf Cahincaha, the son of the Queen of Meath. But we'll leave no stone unturned, and provided that we can discover Princess Oribelle, which will be easy for us because of our incognito and because she inspires a respectful tenderness in you, whatever her situation is, I'll answer for our success."

"That speech consoles me," said Oribeau.

At that very instant they heard a terrible voice that cried:

"Tremble, Oribeau! Every thought, every desire, every word and every action for anyone but Oribelle will distance you from her for a week, a month, six months, a year, or ten. If you commit an evil action, you will only obtain Oribelle after having repaired it; if it's a crime, you will never obtain her. Be careful, for your happiness depends on the possession of Oribelle, and the possession of Oribelle depends on your virtue. You will find the Princess of Lagenia one day, and your heart, if it is virtuous, will recognize her without the help of your eyes; but if it is not, your eyes will deceive you and your heart will betray you."

"Who is speaking to us?" said the Prince, smiling.

"What does it matter who is speaking to us?" replied the Sage, "if what is said expresses something useful?"

"I believe it," said the Prince, "In spite of the oracular air, which displeases me a little. However, I'm afraid of being distanced from Princess Oribelle for weeks. Canora pleased me; Ahissa touched me; Daura moved me; Julia interested me, not so much by her beauty as her modesty. Anyway, as I said, that advice is very good, and I sense that the manner in which it was given to me, first exciting my surprise, has disposed my attention never to forget it."

As the young Prince finished speaking, the cry of a bird was heard, and the Prince and the Sage looked up. They saw, over the trees nearby, a bird with three crests.

"What beautiful plumage!" said Oribeau.

"I believe," said the Sage examining it, "that it's a Yapou."

"Ah!" said Oribeau, excitedly. "So Princess Oribelle isn't far away!" Let's go look for her."

"We'll see whether we encounter her in the places we're visiting today," O'Barbo replied, thoughtfully, "but I doubt it. Your meeting won't be as easy as that. In any case, perhaps the Fay Pucellomaneh only wants to show it to you."

"You've mentioned the fay to me," said Oribeau. "Tell me sincerely what you mean by it. You've raised me above all superstitious prejudices."

O'Barbo smiled. "I'm talking to you as one does in ordinary education and as authors to come will write your story, but I'll tell you the truth in a little while. Let's go forward, in the direction the Yapou is taking."

The bird was, in fact, flying from tree to tree, always getting further away.

It stopped in the acacia of a tavern in the Tanismanireg district. The Sage and his pupil went on. They saw many people in the rooms and the booths and under the trees in the garden; they were amusing themselves, singing and dancing—for it was a holiday. That spectacle would have been joyful it had not been saddened by the coarse brutality of the drinkers. The majority only seemed to be amusing themselves in the manner of tigers and cats, all of whose pleasures are mingled with fury and bloody. They were quarreling over a word, and it was visible that the brutal pleasure they took in screeching at one another and hitting one another entered into their system of entertainment.

"What!" exclaimed Oribeau, "are these the mild Mommonians who are praised for their gaiety and good humor? They're ferocious!"

"Yes; the lower orders, men without education, are the same everywhere, in England, in Denmark, and even in the savage lands inhabited by the Scythians and the Tartars. There is the difference between a civilized nation and a savage horde that in the latter, the national character appears in all individuals, and one can say, in general, that Tartars have such and such a character; but in the former, two kinds of individuals no longer have the national character: the aristocrats and the people; they have volatilized their character to the point that they no longer have a territory. An aristocrat of Waterford is like an aristocrat of Balaclay, Tuam, Dunnaghall, Meath, London, Edinburgh or Paris, but the burger is different, he has the character of the locale, he only resembles himself. The miserable people, brutalized by difficulty, are brutish everywhere."

At that moment, Oribeau perceived Frank, the nephew of the good Thor-el, who came in with a pitcher. He was followed by Mary, who was carrying a jug. While he was considering them, Julia appeared. She was not carrying anything but she had the purse; he saw her pay the innkeeper's wife for the beet that Frank and Mary took.

The young Prince went to greet Julia, who blushed rose-pink.

Mary ran to him as soon as she saw him. "Are you coming back to eat at our establishment?" she asked.

"I don't know, my lovely girl," Oribeau replied. "We're leaving tomorrow on a voyage."

Julia, who was still red, went pale at that word.

"You won't forget us when you come back?" said Mary.

"No, no, I assure you," said Oribeau,

The young women and Frank left and the Prince, laughing, said to the Sage: "I'm sorry to have seen Julia again; in truth, now I'm even more distant from the Princess of Lagenia."

"Perhaps," said the Sage. "That depends on the kind of interest that Julia inspires in you."

"But I can no longer see the Yapou!" said Oribeau. "It's surely angry at the sentiment that Julia has inspired in me."

O'Barbo did not reply, but he let the tavern and proposed that they go to the drinking-dens where the people were amusing themselves.

They left the city and followed the boulevards for some time, which were covered with a prodigious crowd. They heard the sounds of musical instruments from all directions, and the cries of people having a good time. Elegance, coquetry and even opulence were shining everywhere.

They saw mountain women playing a very agreeable instrument; some were pretty, other ugly, but they were all dressed with a particular taste, and their clothing had a piquant grace. One among them was richly dressed; her clothing, which was admirably tailored, was garnished with gold fringes; her face was charming. Her name was Pelagie, Petite-Friga or Pearl—for she had been given three names. The Prince was looking at her with pleasure when the Sage said: "I fear that the Yapou might see us!"

Oribeau smiled. "Have no fear," he said, "that's not Julia, but if Julia were wearing that costume, I believe she'd be even more beautiful."

The Sage and Oribeau went into a house and were given very bad liquor, very bed beer and very bad ice cream; but the drinkers were made to swallow all of it by a new means, by tickling their ears with music. An orchestra with instrumentalists of both sexes was playing, and singing the most agreeable tunes of the Eropa or the Saleniti; that distracted attention, or fixed it; people drank without tasting what they were drinking.

"These places," said the Prince, offer the image of joy."

"Yes, and that's partly what attracts so many foreigners to Waterford; there's a continual fête here; the spectacle is ravishing and I fear that the human eye can't see a more agreeable sight; it's to take part in it, or merely to see it, that the artist, the merchant and the artisan of all classes work without a murmur, with pleasure, every week; the young women and men shiver at the promise that their parents or masters make them to come and walk here, to see the image of paradise, to imagine themselves there, either having a pleasant meal at one of those tables you see in the restaurant, or dancing, or simply looking as brilliant as the beauties from the public xiste by virtue of the elegance of their attire.

"After strolling for a while, well-to-do people go to relax at one of the Boulevard theaters; the traveling players whose games we've seen, although they only put on wretched pieces, for the most part, are not to be scorned by the Prince or the government. They procure pleasure, and 'pleasure is nought but virtue's gayer name,' as an Angle wisely said, whose works are very sad.[79] I regard pleasure as one of the constituent parts of happiness, and that, in my view, is how it ought to be envisaged: pleasure is a flash of lightning; it shines and instantly disappears; happiness is the soft and continuous light of the Sun; the difference between the two is that between pleasure and happiness."

"I understand that comparison perfectly," said Oribeau. "So, you approve of the pleasures of the people, whatever they are?"

"Yes, with a few slight exceptions, which we'll have the opportunity to see together. I'd like, for example, the boulevard spectacles of Waterford to be a little more directed to-

---

[79] Edward Young, in *The Complaint* (better known as *Night Thoughts*).

ward utility, and that the fidelity of spouses, in particular, shouldn't be turned to ridicule there. As for the other modifications that I'd like to make to the pleasures of the people, we shall see of what they consist. Let's leave this enchanted place, which only presents the image of happiness. Let's cross this open country; we'll find ourselves close to a guinguette called the Gentil-il-Pett, where the most miserable populace can forget its poverty and privation for an afternoon in crapulous pleasures, noisy and often ferocious drunkenness.

On the way the young Prince saw many hares and grouse; he expressed his surprise to the Sage that those timid animals were in such great quantity at the gates and almost in the outlying districts of the capital.

"They're the King's pleasures here," O'Barbo replied. "No one has the right to hunt here except you and a few individuals to whom permission is granted. A man would be severely punished if he killed a hare or a rabbit, or caught one in a snare; it would be a matter of nothing less than the loss of his civil status and condemnation to public labor in perpetuity."

"Do you believe that rigor is just?"

"Yes, it's just. The Prince ought to have prerogatives, and he alone can set the limits of them. I'll cite you an action of good King O'Facfac. Peasants had killed some pheasants that were being raised in the middle of one of his forests. The Minister, who was good, initially suspended the court proceedings that would have condemned the wretches, almost all fathers of families, and one day, when your father the King and your mother the Queen were passing through the forest he had the guilty parties put on their knees in their path with the pheasants sticking out of their pockets. The good O'Facfac arrived at the place where they were and seemed surprised by the singularity of their attitude; he asked what it signified.

"'Sire,' the Minister replied, 'they're men who killed some of the pheasants that were being raised for your pleasure,'

"The King liked pheasants a great deal, but he liked his people even more. 'Get up,' he said to the guilty men. 'I pardon you. Know, however, that I wouldn't kill a chicken that belongs to you, but you kill my pheasants, which give me pleasure and amuse the Queen my wife. That isn't honest.' He sent them away with a gesture as he finished. And since that moment, no one has killed your father good King O'Facfac's pheasants. Your mother the Queen took generosity even further, for, having learned that the wretches had been imprisoned for a week, she had the families compensated for the loss of their time."

"That action renders her even dearer to me," Oribeau replied, "for I want to be the father of my people and to be cherished by them forever. If there's a nickname that tempts me, it's that of 'the Debonair,' which was borne, it's said, by a King of the Franks, Emperor of Germany. I'd prefer such a nickname to that of 'the Great,' which was given to the Emperor Karles, that Prince's father."[80]

"You're right, but it's necessary that a King should be good without being weak."

That conversation led the two Observers to the Gentil-il-pett. In the first guinguette they went into, there were no violins to be heard, noisy songs of delight or joyful laughter, but a confused murmur of the voices of men, women, wailing children, drunkards swearing and wretches quarreling.

"This place isn't cheerful," said Oribeau.

"Let's see," the Sage replied, "Whether the view is more satisfying than what we can hear."

They went in. What a spectacle! A host of paupers in rags had large tankards before them, and cold food on paper or chipped plates, of the sort sold on street corners by women who collect the leftovers from inns and kitchens. One the same

---

[80] Charlemagne's son, more usually known as Louis the Pious than Louis le Debonair, succeeded his father as Holy Roman Emperor in 813; the Empire fell apart under his reign, but opinions vary as to how much he was to blame for that.

plate one could see fat and gristle, eggs, broth, fish, beans, lentils, spinach, potatoes, veal, mutton and salad; all of it was being gluttonously devoured by a troop of starvelings sitting on rickety benches, surrounding a half-broken table. Others were sitting on the ground; they were all growling at one another as they ate, like voracious dogs.

Oribeau shivered. "These are my people!"

"Yes, these are your people. Let's go on; I want you to know the profession of all these beings whose poverty revolts you."

The Prince advanced, not without some repugnance.

"Here," the Sage said to him, "is a shoemaker with his wife, his two daughters, his three sons and his four companions, two of whom are future sons-in-law. Look at them making love; their manners are coarse and ridiculous, but they please their intendeds, who know no better. At that table is a cobbler; he's almost naked but it's warm and he's not embarrassed; his wife and children are spending all that he has here in order that, no longer having any money during the week, he'll be forced to work; look at them eating while grunting and insulting one another; see with what avidity they drink! They're compensating themselves for six days of abstinence, but today's excesses will fatigue them more than fasting; look at their pallor, their thinness, their ill-health."

"Can't these excesses be remedied?"

"Yes, by having a law proposed by your Minister executed...here there's an old tailor with his family; she's dressed, and even clean, but long pauperized by her husband's misconduct, she conserves a taste for debauchery. You can't imagine how that man behaves! When he was young, he made his wife and children tremble, and beat them; having become old and feeble, his children, who are young and strong, now lay down the law to him, and have him beaten by their mother for the slightest fault; they keep him at work like a little child, and he's only permitted to get drunk on holidays, with them. When he's drunk, two of them carry him away, put him to bed, and don't wake him up until the next day in order to make him work for six days.

"Here's a paver, who needs, like dormice and marmots, to remain asleep for six months of the year, for he's only occupied in summer. He's working at present and no more thinking about the future than the animals deprived of our reasons, doubtless because they have no need of it and in their situation it would be harmful to them.

"On this side you can see a companion carpenter reduced to beggary because he undertook an enterprise without being a master; everything was taken away from him; he vegetates today and comes here to console himself with his fellows. Those two men that you see are his sons-in-law; the three women are his wife and daughters; the elder married a publisher's copyist, the elder the beadle of a small temple of Friga. Those two women are pretty but not good, which, far from enriching them, retains them in poverty because they neglect work and spend everything on amusements.

"Further away, that big table is occupied by wool-carders of both sexes; that métier, for which no one has deigned to search for an instrument,[81] attacks the lungs because of the quantity of dust particles one breathes, so see how pale the men and women are. Look at their children, who are even worse; it's one of the professions that impoverishes the human species. Dondanuck has already offered a prize for the invention of a mechanical carder sufficiently distant from the mouth of the operator not to inconvenience them by continually showering them with the mortal dust of long-enclosed wool.

"Over here, these jaundiced and pale men are poor shoemakers; their physiognomy is even worse than that of the

---

[81] If Restif were talking about contemporary Paris rather than an analogue thereof he would be slightly behind the times; mechanical carding machines were probably installed in some English and Welsh mills in the early 1780s, although Richard Arkwright's application for a patent for one in 1775 had been refused.

carders, because they have the bad habit of leaving beside them the buckets in which they steep their leather; that water is polluted and emits and odor to which they become accustomed, but which is no less dangerous for that; air charged with putrid particles passes through their lungs continually. But that isn't the only inconvenience of their profession, and the most irremediable is that they work bent over, continually supporting their work in the pit of the stomach; respiration and circulation are impeded and it's only the strongest men who aren't grievously inconvenienced by it.

"Notice their children, numbering more than a dozen, for there are four or five families there; by their complexion alone one can identify them in a hundred thousand as the children of shoemakers. I've also remarked, on the subject of comfortable masters of that profession, who cease to work themselves, that they recover a healthy appearance promptly, unless they've suffered too much, which only goes to prove how useful it would be if your colleges of bards were occupied in finding new, less awkward, ways of working for necessary professions.

"Look at that group of carpenters over there, how vigorous they are. Alongside them are butchers, whose appearance is quite bad, by virtue of the custom they have of working at night and remaining almost naked most of the time, whereas at other times they dress themselves like other men.

"Here are bailiff's assistants; they're drowning, in wine and crapulous drunkenness, the idea of their malodorous profession; those people earn enough good nights, but as it's debauchery and misconduct that leads them to embrace their estate, they remain poor, or the most part, and die young.

"We're now next to a table of boat-unloaders; you've seen them taking wood from the Shure to supply work-yards; that profession is even harder than that of bailiffs' laborers; they work every morning carrying wet wood from the river to work-places; you've seen them running to prevent them from getting cold. Instead of resting on days of liberty they come here to get drunk and see miserable scenes that they find amusing. I believe that it would be possible to employ animals for their work; one man could drive several; they would have solid horseshoes and could be relieved every half hour by the drivers.

"At that table you can see a troop of women who are making as much noise as the rest of the assembly combined; they're bleachers. Observe them; almost all of them have fine stockings and underwear and some have expensive clothes; that's not because these women posses everything; those who come here are heavy drinkers and gluttons; mostly they're naked, but on holidays they put on the products of their profession, which have that effect; they rebleach them every fortnight, for they don't spare themselves here. They wallow in the mud or on returning, or in the rye; they fight, throw ordure at one another, etc.

"Thus the vices of the low estates harm those who are more elevated, without the poor obtaining any profit from it, for all the debauchery you see here empties the purses of these unfortunates; they work poorly and precipitately in the following week. It's therefore important to care for the education of the people; but it can only be done by rendering them more comfortable and giving them some consideration, which will fall on all the professions, with the result that they call have an honorable title by reason of their utility. A man destined to be base and vile by his estate can never be educated: that's the real secret.

"Let the kaldes exalt chimeras in verse, the bards wrote superb things in political prose, the druids make long moral sermons—all that will be of no use for the reform and happiness of human beings; I've just told you the only, unique means of having happy, good people.

"Under that serpentine arbor you see a companion printer amusing himself with his family. He's been ill for about two months, but he belongs to a relief society at twelve sous a month, in which a sick man is given half an oribeau in the first week, if it's proven that he hasn't emerged from his bedroom; to have that sum, which he wouldn't have earned by working for four days, he's rested at home for an entire week, although he was cured on the third day, and he's come here to compensate himself with crapulous drunkenness for the tedium of six days.

In that corner, where they're eating better fare than elsewhere, are beggar-women from the Temple of Thor or Friga; they're treating their families or friends with the alms for which they've waited tranquilly at the door of the temple, where they spend every morning, sitting idly, when they might be spinning and producing something useful by means of their labor.

"Look in that other corner; that's a blind man with his wife and three children. He doesn't enjoy the sight of the scenes that are happening here, but they're described to him and he laughs at them as wholeheartedly as those who can see them. I hardly dare tell you one horror: one day he excited one of his children to become blind...

"It would be easy for me to list the professions of all these wretches that you see here taking sad pleasures, which are an evil, by virtue of the manner in which they are taken and their consequences, of which you're about to see the proof..."

In fact, Oribeau and the Sage having gone into another tavern, brighter because there was music and dancing there, they saw poverty capering in rags and gorging crapulously in the common garden, while they glimpsed the appearances of a fine party in a garden separated by railings. They wanted to flee the hideous spectacle of drunkenness combined with coarse brutality, malevolence and base rascality. Frightened, Oribeau asked his teacher more than once whether the beings they saw were human.

"Yes," said the Sage, "but humans far below the savages of the Orcadian isles or Schet, which are further to the north of Scotland and whose populations are the most brutish of men."

In one of the corners of the garden they saw friends who had just been eating and drinking together taking one another by the hair; the screams of women and children were heard over the stifled curses of the men confronting and striking one another. Further away, an affected libertine was giving a slap to a girl whom another man had just asked to dance; he accused her of lacking fidelity after having given him pledges. Immediately, the people at two tables rose to their feet, glasses and tankards flew, and the two armies engages in a hand-to-hand battle, some taking the side of the girl and others that of the young man, and the argument was settled with fists. Blood flowed; the girl was to one side, trembling, while the women of the adverse party heaped insults upon her.

The hard-hearted dancers smiled at the trouble they could see and, when their curiosity was satisfied, asked the rustic Orpheus to play a quadrille. Meanwhile, the beaters and the beaten wore themselves out; they finally got up, in a frightful condition. Each group went back to its table, grumbling, insulting one another after the blows, much as one sees a disastrous cloud, which commences with lightning and hail, end up in rain.

Another spectacle presented itself further away; prostitutes, with their dupes or their pimps, were giving the assembly a revolting scene of lust and impudence. The Sage drew the Prince away from that group and led him to the railings of the private garden.

Sergeants of the yeomanry were amusing themselves with their mistresses, for marriage was forbidden to them during the time of their service. The meal was finished; they were running around and frolicking in the pathways. Suddenly, however, the games ceased. One of the women perceived O'Barbo and the young Prince at the railings; they hid behind a hornbeam and one of the sergeants ran toward the grille.

"What are you doing there, old man, with that young man?" he said. "We're paying to be tranquil here. Go away."

"Why?" replied O'Barbo, smiling. "Why do you want to prevent us from seeing your games, if they're innocent?"

"You're arguing, I believe," said the yeoman. "Go away, or..."

"Soldier," said O'Barbo, "it isn't good for you to lack respect for old age."

The yeoman responded angrily with a barbaric word. Then the Sage said to him: "If you fear being seen so much, it's because your amusements are criminal, and I know what they are. Those women are married; they belong to rich individuals; they have become amorous of you and your comrades, and they come here to pay for your pleasures and theirs. Adieu. I know them; let them tremble, and you too, for I shall talk about it to someone powerful enough to put it in order..."

O'Barbo drew away as he finished speaking, while the furious yeoman called for the tavern-keeper to bring the key to the gate in order that he might avenge himself on the old man—but O'Barbo and his pupil left immediately in order to return to their dwelling.

That was the last day of their study of the mores of the city, and the following day they were to visit the inhabitants of the countryside, in order to know their usages, their needs and the abuses in need of correction.

"By Vananis!" said old Ennisleague, "the world then was exactly like the world today! People say, however, that the old days were better than ours."

"It's the same thing, good woman," Kilmactomas told her.

"Good," she replied. "I'll support the pains of life better, then, for I'd have regretted it if people had been happier in the past."

After having drained his glass, the gentleman resumed speaking.

I was telling you that the Sage withdrew. Meanwhile, the yeoman shouted, but wasn't heard—which made Oribeau and his guide smile.

Chapter Z
Zeal of O'Barbo to educate Oribeau. The Prince lodges
with a cultivator. He labors. His presents reveal his
identity after his departure. The joy of the laborer and
his family. Oribeau leaves his Estates after visiting them
and goes to the realms of Meath and Lagenia.

"Zest!"[82] said the Sage, as he went out. "You won't catch us, poor yeoman!" To the Prince, he said: You see how bored the soldiers become in the capital; I believe that it would be good to establish a severe discipline among them and to make them marry, but with precautions that would annihilate the inconveniences that the law requiring them to be celibate was intended to prevent."

"That's just what I was thinking," replied Oribeau.

Along the way, the two observers saw drunken men and women lying on both sides of the road, some of them quarreling with others. Some were asleep and others vomiting up the superfluity of their voracity.

As O'Barbo and his pupil had not eaten anything at the guinguette they went to have supper at the good Thor-el's establishment, and near the door they thought they heard the Yapou. Julia seemed to be delighted to see them again, but she hid it beneath the veil of modesty, and only her blush betrayed it.

"Amiable Julia," said the Sage, "We're leaving tomorrow, as you know, to travel in the provinces of Mommonia, but I've been charmed to see this house again, where one is so well treated at the lowest price; I regard your aunt as an estimable woman, and if I had any authority, I'd grant her a recompense. She's much more useful than many others who feed on pride, since she obliges necessary workers every day and eases the difficulties of their life. She's comparable, from the

---

[82] The obsolete French exclamation "zest!" was an approximate equivalent of the English "phew!"

point of view that I envisage her, to the greatest benefactors of the human species"

Julia retired modestly after that speech and the good Thor-el, who had heard it, gave the Sage a grateful smile. Then it seemed as if her head was surrounded by an aureole— a phenomenon that surprised Prince Oribeau extremely. He finished his supper hastily and when they were outside he said to the Sage: "Explain to me why. After you had finished speaking, I saw something like an aureole around the good Thor-el's head."

"I don't know what to tell you," said the Sage, "but if I can one day, be sure that I won't make a mystery of it. At present, it's impossible for me..."

The two travelers went to bed immediately and slept peacefully until five o'clock in the morning.

When he got up, O'Barbo woke his pupil. "Let's go," he said.

"Let's go," Oribeau replied. He dressed in a trice, and they went out.

"We're going to visit the peasants, who are the foot and support of the State," said O'Barbo, as they walked. "Although I descend from Clongibbons, I've been a laborer, and I'm more glorious in that quality than all the advantages of my nobility and the important positions I've occupied. Agricultural labor is the foremost of the arts; it gives the first nobility; all the others are beneath it, and aristocrats, except for the King, are only truly great when their origin dates from an agriculturalist; oppressive brigands can never transmit a true nobility."

"I think as you do," Oribeau replied, "but what about the glory of arms?"

"It ought to be united with agriculture. The laborious colonist, accustomed to hard labor, makes an excellent soldier; he is humane and compassionate in victory; he will not be a pillager, nor a marauder, nor a debauchee; only laborers ought to be admitted to the honorable métier of soldier, and it ought to be forbidden to all those who vegetate ignobly in cities. That would be the most efficacious means of having invincible armies. A soldier drawn from the indoor métiers of cities cannot support the fatigue or the coarseness of the nourishment, in addition to the fact that most of the time, he's enervated by a dangerous sensuality. I won't tell you, therefore, to leave laborious men to agriculture and take soldiers from the useless population of the big cities; I'll say to you: render the métier of soldier honorable, and let possible rather than real advantages be attached to it—which is to say that an honest, courageous, intelligent soldier should be capable of attaining certain lucrative and honorable positions; that the quality of soldier should be one itself, to a necessary degree.

"Associate with agriculturalists, for the capacity of service, hard-working men from the cities like masons, marketers, locksmiths, carpenters, sawyers, roofers, wheelwrights, porters, etc., and you'll see the good effect of that usage. Let there be no more militias; that means is ignoble and alarming; but let a son, in all the estates imposed on military service, not be capable either of marriage or personal establishment separate from that of his father; let him only serve in times of peace for three years and in time of war for the entire duration of the war if it commences in his third year—but nevertheless permitting marriage if the bond does not harm his service, giving him other prerogatives that his wife, his father, his brother or his nearest relative will enjoy during his time of service.

"There should only be dispensations of service for those absolutely incapable of it, but a height inferior to five feet should not be an incapacity. Let one of the privileges of a past, present or future soldier be that in case of rivalry and equality of merit, to set aside from any common pretention the competitor incapable of military service. Let citizens who are former soldiers have the advantage over all their equals who were not soldiers. Let a former soldier who takes any estate— magistrate, advocate, merchant, master artisan, etc.—be the senior, for honors and advancement, of all those, without exception, who are not five years ahead of him.

"What I say there is only a general sketch; but if you put it in vigor, I guarantee that you will be king of a redoubtable nation, which will be master of war and peace, the arbiter of its neighbors, etc. As for your nobility, let all be obliged to serve, and in the case that they have no employment, let them form regiments of volunteers from which officers can be taken as the need arises."

While holding these conversations, and similar ones, the two heroes, who had taken the road from Waterford to Cork, covered nine miles and found themselves in Kilmactomas, were they had a meal in the home of an honest druid who offered them hospitality, inviting them to stay with him for a day or two. That was what O'Barbo requested.

While they ate, the Sage asked about the work of the peasants, their wellbeing and their morals.

At that word, the druid sighed. "Sage old man," he said, "If you're looking for purity of morals, it's not in the country-side neighboring the capital. Debauchery, lust and bad faith reign here, as in the city; but in Waterford politeness and education take some of the ugliness away from vice among all those known as honest men, whereas in the village, people have all the vices of the city without having urbanity. People here love vice for its own sake; they think it gives them an air of distinction and grandeur by putting them above all the rules of decency and modesty, because they have glimpsed that those rules are violated in the city. My fellow citizens ape the people of the capital; they imitate all their ugliness, virtue alone being forgotten; its nuances are too delicate for them.

"You seem to me to be literate; I'll make you a comparison. When a skillful bard or a sublime kalde has made an excellent work, you immediately see creeping minds seek to imitate it; they avidly take up all its faults, exploit all the licenses that genius permits itself and redeems because it brings out the beauty thereof; they produce a flat imitation of a divine production. Such are my compatriots, and all country folk in general who can easily go to the capital in one day and return."

At that moment the druid was called to the aid of a sick person; he made his apologies to his guests, begging them to continue to refresh themselves, and hastened to his duty.

O'Barbo looked at the young Prince, smiling. "We've found a Sage in our druid," he said, "for those observations are equally fine and true. We won't stay here; we'll go as far as Dungarvan, and perhaps even Younghall and Middletown, where we'll get to know the veritable more and needs of country people better. Then we'll pass on to Cork, from Cork to Whitchurch and Fourmilewater, Malo, Karlestown, Kilmalllock, Bruff, Bridge and Limerick. Then well go to the other side of Waterford and see Rosbercon, Ross-on-the-Barrow, Mongarret, Polemon, Mullin, etc., for we'll visit the towns and villages that compose your powerful kingdom. Then we'll go as far as Tallagh, and finally Makredon, which are outside your Estates, but where you are to signal yourself by striking exploits..."

The honest druid came back after this speech and, the meal being over, the Sage thanked the druid humbly and bade him farewell.

Oribeau said to the minister of altars: "Your conversation and excellent meal will never be forgotten by the younger of your guests."

The druid, surprised by that language, looked attentively at the Prince, and, seeing the features of O'Facfac in him, exclaimed: "O Thor, have you granted me the greatest of favors?" However, seeing that his guests were drawing way, he did not ask them any questions, fearing to be indiscreet, and not wanting to delay them.

The Sage and his pupil covered eight miles in the afternoon, but they were not always following the road to Cork and made digressions into the fields to see the laborers and speak with them. So long as they were in the regions of Kilomactomas they remarked the verity of what the good druid had said. They heard nothing on the part of laborers, vinegrower, and especially gardeners, but licentious speech and empty words. They found low, servile sentiments, so much were their hearts corrupted.

Scarcely had they set foot in the territory of Dungarvan, however, than they perceived a change for the better. They dined in that village in the home of a druid, who did not seem to them to be as sage or as sensate as the one in Kilmactomas; he received them as kindly, but his discourse was frivolous. He was one of the druids known as regulars, with a congregation established in honor of Vananis.

The Sage interrogated him about the rumors circulating on the subject of Oribeau, the Regent, the Minister Dondanuck and the tutor that the latter had given the young Prince.

"I could tell you a long story about that," the druid replied, "because I'm perfectly acquainted with everything happening at Court, Karrickmacgriffn is only six miles from Clonmell, of which I'm a native. But as I like company, because of the solitude in which I continually find myself, I never recount the curious adventures that I have in great number the first time anyone sees me. If, however, you want to know them, come back to see me on your return to Waterford."

O'Barbo and the young Prince told him that they admired the politeness of his invitation and that they would not fail to see him again unless their affairs prevented it absolutely. They left immediately and followed the road to Younghall.

On the way, the Prince and the Sage, having perceived a peasant who was returning home from work, went toward him. He was a man of about forty-five, whose features had nobility.

"Tell me your name," O'Barbo said, "in order that I might salute you."

"My name is Bridge-Clonard, and I'm a laborer. The local people call me 'Honest Man,' because I merit it."

"Ah, said the Sage, "you're the celebrated laborer so generally esteemed. I bless Thor for this encounter. We'll talk together about things that it's good to know, especially for this amiable young man who's accompanying me, for he has a great desire to learn."

"That's a fine face," said Bridge-Clonard. "I haven't encountered one in my life that announced as much nobility, intelligence and generosity."

Oribeau blushed at that naïve praise.

"Nichols," said Bridge, to his son, who was mounted on a horse and who was preceding him a short distance away, "get down and come here, for it's good to listen to the speech of a respectable old man." To the old man, he said: "And you climb on to the horse, for you must be tired, and we can listen to you while walking around you."

"No," said O'Barbo, "the road is short and we'll walk slowly. We've come from Waterford and we've heard much talk of the Queen Regent and her Minister Dondanuck, as well as the young Prince, who's traveling, it's said, with an old man to visit his kingdom.

"Oh," said Bridge, "may I have the good fortune to encounter him and give him a meal, even without knowing him. In any case, if he passes through this neighborhood, that might happen, for I receive all travelers who want to enter my home; that's why I beg you to honor my house with your presence, you and this amiable and modest young man, who's blushing like a girl—in which alone he resembles my son Nichols, the eldest of my seven children, for he's modest too."

"We accept your offer with pleasure," replied O'Barbo, "in order to converse for longer with the Honest Man of Mommonia, whose conduct has caused him to be called the best of honest man. It's very praiseworthy of you to show such hospitality to travelers, who are often very embarrassed."

"Venerable old man," Bridge replied, do you know a story that is told in this canton of Evinland, which, if it isn't literally true, is nevertheless very useful and of good effect?

"There was once a good druid who received all the poor in his home. The more ragged and infirm they were, the more he welcomed them, for there were not then, as there are now, resources for the indigent, and if they're no longer in need, we owe it to the wisdom of the Minister as well as that of the Great Judge of Waterford. One day, a poor man covered in ulcers came to the good druid's house, who asked for the grace of a corner of the stable in which to rest for the night.

"The druid took his hand and led him to his fireside; there he dressed him in some of his clothes and threw the poor man's, which were dirty and full of vermin, into the fire. He had him sup with him and sleep in a bed that was warmed for him. The poor man said that he had never been so comfortable and went to sleep blessing the good druid, who, having retired to his room, heard him, and said: 'O Thor, bless you, for the contentment of that poor man has given me one even one than his own.' And the next day, he gave the poor man breakfast, and offered to let him stay in his house—but the poor man said that he was sufficiently fortified to continue his route.

"The next day, another poor man arrived, who was as dirty as the previous one, who presented himself swearing and cursing. The good druid received him in the same fashion as the good poor man, and treated him in the same way, but at a moment when he did not serve the bad poor man quickly enough the latter struck him. The good druid said to him: 'My brother, I excuse your vivacity, for it's the effect of your long suffering, but be careful lest it offend the great and god Thor.' But the poor man became even more insolent, and the next day he wanted to stay. The druid consented to that.

"Toward evening, another poor man arrived, in an equally bad way. The druid ran to him and received him with open arms, but the bad poor man, very angry, said: 'Tell him that another has been received in is stead, because he was in greater need.'

"'My brother,' the druid said to him, 'in anything else I would obey you, but not in this, which is unjust and inhumane.

"The bad poor man flew into a great fury, and wanted to bar the new poor man, but the latter pushed him away, showing him that he was the stronger, and the next day, the bad one went away, cursing the good druid and the new poor man.

"When he had gone, the poor man who remained said to the druid: 'I'll go too, for you've helped me sufficiently and it's necessary to make room for others; but I'll dare to give you some advice: don't receive everyone indifferently, and content yourself with giving alms to those who seem suspect.'

"'Oh," said the druid, 'how do you expect me to leave my brother at my door, with feeble assistance, exposed to the insults of the weather?'

"The second poor man went away, but as soon as he had gone, the druid perceived that he had robbed him.

"Toward evening, another poor man arrived. The druid ran to meet him. 'Come in, my brother,' he said to him, 'you won't be as comfortable as I would have liked, because I suffered a considerable loss this morning, but I'll share with you the little that I have. The poor man thanked him with a nod of the head, sat down by the fire and said to the druid: 'Since you have so much virtue I want to exploit it; I intend that you will be my slave and obey me in everything.'

"'A slave has no virtue,' replied the druid, "and as soon as you were my master I would no longer pity you, because you would be less unfortunate than me; however, I will serve you, as much as I can, by virtue of pure amity.'

"The poor man made no reply, but he seemed discontented. 'My brother,' the druid said, 'you're doing wrong to yourself, in what you've just said to me, and I'm sorry about that; that's why I'm begging you to change your sentiment, in order that other men will be willing to help you.'

"The poor man still remained silent. The druid served him supper and they ate together. Then he warmed the poor man's bed, undressed him and put him to bed.

"The next morning, he went to bring him a warm breakfast in his bed, but there was no one there. He was very surprised. He searched everywhere, and he found what had been stolen from him the day before, with the price of all that he had spent in his life in the poor, wrapped in a piece of paper, on which was written:

"*Thor, Worden and Berda, to whom nothing is unknown, having seen your conduct, resolved to test you; it was them whom you received in the last three poor men. Continue to give hospitality, for it is the virtue most agreeable to the gods, who will return to you one day what you have expended on your fellows throughout your life, but that is not the least reward that is reserved for you. We bless you.*

"That is the story that is told in these parts."

As Bridge-Clonard finished his story, they found themselves at the door of his house. The travelers were received immediately by the laborer's wife, still a beautiful woman, who seemed to be about forty, and who had three other younger sons as well as Nichols and five daughters, which made nine children instead of the seven that Bridge had announced. As she introduced them to the old man she named them.

"This," she said, "is Vananis, my eldest after my son Nichols; this one is named Rosée, my other daughter Oeillette; my second son Strabane: the third Gori; the sister who follows him Giroflée, the last Jasmine, and my fourth son Clamnis."

"While the laborer's wife had been speaking, Oribeau had kept his eyes fixed on the beautiful Rosée. He blushed immediately, fearing that he had been further distanced from Oribelle. In order to distract himself from the one who pleased him too much, he looked at Jasmine, the youngest. That pretty face was not unknown to him, but he could not recall where he had seen it before. His eyes sought out Rosée again, and they encountered those of the beautiful girl. They both blushed.

Meanwhile, the soup was served. Vananis, Oeillette and Giroflée had laid the table. Jasmine and Rosée were tired, having only arrived from Waterford that same day, and they were resting.

When they were at table, they spoke at first about public affairs, the Regent, the young Prince and the Minister.

"For myself," said Bridge-Clonard, "I can only bless the Queen and her Minister, who have made Agriculture and the Agriculturalist respected; we're considered today; consideration is the first amelioration of life; it makes the rudest labors bearable; it embellishes them and renders them more productive. Blessed be the Queen and her Minister; blessed be the young Prince, whose dispositions are excellent, I've been told—for people are sure that he is in Waterford, invisibly, under the guidance of a wise necromancer, who has the power to hide him from all eyes and to whom he's already given evidence of the greatest wisdom. It's a lady who has given us that good news, the same one with whom Jasmine and Rosée have come here."

"Ah!" said the Sage. "And may we know the name of that lady?"

"The one she gave to us was Mellusine, but she might have another. She said a great many good things about the Court and the young Prince. She also talked to us about a neighboring court, with which she isn't equally content, but she hopes that one day, with the protection of Heaven, all will be well—for she's a very pious lady."

"Have you not heard mention of the fables that are being related about the young Prince and the Minister?" asked the Sage.

"Oh, yes, but as soon as the Minister had shown what he is through his actions, we no longer believed anything bad about him—reasonable people, at least. For example, since it has transpired that the Prince is in Waterford, it's claimed that he has been imprisoned by an effect of the malevolence of the genius Perforimoth the Black, and that the Queen had already signed his death sentence when, by chance, she saw a beautiful unknown bird passing. She immediately gave the order that an attempt be made to catch it. The bird flew over the place where the two condemned men, the young Prince and his tutor, were. The Queen, who was at her window watching the bird, cast her eyes on the condemned, from whom all means of informing her of their misfortune had been taken away, and she recognized her son—with the consequence that she immediately sent a yeoman to get them and bring them to her. She has made them disappear in order to continue their journey, thanking Thor and Berda for the signal favor that they had just done in sending the beautiful bird. But wise people contradict that pretended miracle. What do you think?"

"I can tell you the truth," said O'Barbo. And he recounted what I have told you about the imprisonment of the Prince and his tutor.

"That isn't all," said the laborer. "It's alleged that the genius Perforimoth the Black, the great enemy of the good fay Pucellomaneh, disguised in the form of O'Connor Ratchlin, has had the two Princesses of Lagenia, the daughters of Queen Conchèse, abducted and that he's reduced them both to washing dishes in one of the inns of Waterford. It's added that he would have done even worse without the beautiful unknown bird, which has an odor mortal to evil genii, and that it's necessary for the young Prince to divine Oribelle beneath that disguise, and that he love her and crown her if he wants to be happy and to acquire the glory for which he is destined.

"It's also said, finally, that if the Prince makes the slightest step that doesn't have the Princess Oribelle for its object, she'll be lost to him forever and that the Prince will remain devoid of glory. But to tell you the truth, I don't believe a word of all these fatalities. Thor is good, and he doesn't set traps for children."

"You're right," said O'Barbo. "But what is true is that the interests of the State and the happiness and glory of the Prince require that he marry Princess Oribelle one day. That Princess is so beautiful, it's said, and has such fortunate dispositions, the misfortunes that she experiences render her so interesting, and give her a virtue so pure and knowledge so useful to a sovereign, that I can see no one but her in all Evinland suitable for our young King."

During that conversation one of the young women listened with her eyes lowered; that was Rosée. Jasmine raised hers from time to time, with a charming smile. Vananis, Oeillette and Giroflée, as well as their brothers, looked at the young stranger and the old man naively.

"This young man and I would be charmed," O'Barbo said to the laborer, "to participate in your rustic labors for a few days, and we offer you our arms, for it's necessary to have tried everything in life."

"I consent to that, since it gives you pleasure," Bridge-Clonard replied. "Our labor is rude, but as I've told you, honor lightens it. Once, we worked a great deal and were scorned and pillaged; a petty sovereign of Meath was even seen to impose such heavy taxes on laborers and bakers, under the pretext that the product of their labor as of primary necessity, that subsistence became impossible; the laborers all quit him; he had no bread in his palace and died of hunger with his principal courtiers. The same thing happened to one Chilperic, king of Soissons, in Gaul.[83]

"Before the reign of O'Facfac, the Queen's Regency and the Ministry of Dondanuck whose great merit got him accused of sorcery, we were insulted when we appeared in cities with the infamous term *villeins*. Today, when we go there, people welcome us; a mother says to her children, on seeing an old laborer: 'Children, that's a respectable cultivator, the man most useful to the State.' I won't tell you anything about our labors, since you want to share them for a few days; you'll experience them. That's better than seeing them.

"I like to read the productions of out bards and kaldes. I read something very wise the other day in a book, regarding the nobles, the lords of our villages: *Perhaps the greatest vice of modern empires is that of not giving enough occupation to noblemen and the rich, and not to inspire enough interest in them for public affairs. Strangers to all the parts of the Administration, they regard everything with an inattentive eye. If an edict is issued, they ignore it; if a tax is imposed, it is a matter of scant importance for them; if there is a change in the ministry, it is news that furnishes conversation for one supper. Overburdened by their leisure, in order to animate the repose that is overwhelming them, they seek movement, throwing*

---

[83] The reference is presumably to the Frankish Chilperic I, King of Soissons or Neustria from 561 until 584, who was treated very harshly by subsequent historians. It is unlikely to refer to Chilperic II, King of Neustria from 715 to 721, whom historians generally treated a little more generously.

themselves into dissipation, running after pleasures, living in futility, often in vice, and dying without having had the will to do a good and useful dead. That immorality of the rich is a necessary consequence of their idleness, and it is impossible that they do not communicate it, at least in part, to men attached to functions that demand labor and care.[84]

"And a little further on, the bard adds: *Almost everywhere the peasants are without wood, their pastures are devastated,. their common land devoid of value. What is delivered to all is delivered to depredation, and is not veritably profitable to anyone. However, by virtue of a police necessary to every village and very useful to the entire kingdom, immense mountains, only covered today by moss and heather, would be crowned with woods; fallow lands would produce grains; arid grasslands would become abundant meadows; and men, certain of being nourished on the soil that gave them birth, would not abandon it to go and overload the cities with the burden of their poverty, and perhaps soon trouble them with their vices and excesses. Those immense abuses have been seen, and the necessity of preventing them sensed, but no one will succeed in doing so, or will only succeed by means worse than the evil itself, if each community is not granted the administration of its own wealth and obliged to install administrators capable of extracting the greatest advantage from common land. I know all the objections that have been made against the project of putting those lands to use, and it is reason and examination that have taught me that there is only one that merits pause. I*

---

[84] This quotation and the next are taken from *Le Bonheur dans les campagnes*, by Claude-François de Lezay-Marnésia, whose title-page is dated 1785 but which has a foreword stating that it was actually printed in the provinces in December 1783. Restif presumably had access to an advance copy, perhaps sent to him by the author, whose utopian ideas had much in common with his. Lezay-Marnésia retains some notoriety for having supplied the article on Masturbation to Diderot's *Encyclopédie*.

shall destroy the most specious of all and will dispense myself with responding to those that are not even that.

" 'Livestock is one of the greatest riches of the country-side, without which the others would not exist, or would only exist feebly. It is, therefore, important to extend it, and to double it if possible. How is that possible if immense tracts are not conserved uniquely destined for the nourishment of animals?' Very easily. When woodland reaches the age of eight years, far from being removed from pasture, it offers one far more abundant. The grass, which their shade protects from being devoured by the ardor of the sun, grows better and with more vigor. Their foliage will also provide nourishment to livestock, which, far from harming the stems by browsing their inferior branches, force them to grow taller and more rapidly. In any case, it seems that where there is more there is more to harvest, and a cultivated field will certainly never produce as much as one that is left alone. While humans will harvest the grain for themselves they will amass for herds the straw that nourishes them through the winter; artificial grasslands will be established in damp places; herbage will be formed, and sterility will be succeeded by abundance almost everywhere. That method would be preferable by far to the custom of allowing unfortunate animals to wander in deserts, where they will find a few blades of grass, which do not so much let them live as prevent them from dying. When crops are harvested, the fields and meadows remain for pasture, and livestock only loses what could not nourish it, while gaining fecund means of subsistence.

"To succeed in putting the culture of communes in a flourishing state, it will be necessary to divide them between a large number of individuals, not by abandoning their woodlands, which the community ought, on the contrary, to conserve with the greatest care, and not by alienating funds, but by making rights of use and loans long term, which give tenants time and opportunity to make the most of the land and enjoy the fruits of their labor and intelligence. Those loans, of which it might be wise to demand the repayment partly in cash

and partly in produce, should be, as justice demands, made in the name and to the profit of the community, and the council should be charged with administering the revenues in accordance with the plan that we shall indicate.

"One of the most learned citizens, Monsieur Quesnay,[85] has proved that we lose four-fifths of the product of our cultivation annually. To that unforgivable depredation we also add the loss of a fifth of our land, under the pretext of nourishing herds that the terrain in question does not nourish. Let us hasten to conquer for ourselves that which our idleness, prejudice and ignorance steal from us."

The laborer, as he finished speaking, perceived that his sons' eyelids were becoming heavier. He stopped reading, took the two strangers to their room, lit a lamp that was therein and wished them good night.

The next day, Oribeau was woken up by the sound of plows departing, and cattle and sheep that were being taken to the fields. He leapt out of bed, and saw O'Barbo already prepared. They went out together and went to join the laborer's family. We had a fortifying breakfast served by Vananis, Oeillette and Giroflée, under the direction of their mother. As for Rosée, Jasmine and Frigameh, a fat woman who had arrived with them and whom the young women addressed as Aunt, they were still so tired that they were left to rest.

After breakfast, they departed. O'Barbo said to his pupil: "'The plowshare is ennobled under the hands of a good King.'[86] You are about to know the labor that is the veritable source of the wealth of a State. Commerce fails if the earth

---

[85] For some reason, Restif replaces this name, which I have restored to the form which is given in its source, with "*Dunmanawai*." The reference is to the physiocrat economist François Quesnay (1694-1774), who contributed the article on "Grains" to the *Encyclopédie*, from which this argument is taken.

[86] This quotation is attributed to Lezay-Marnésia in secondary sources, but does not appear to be from the book cited above.

does not furnish what is needed to sustain it. There might be a few exceptions, but they confirm the rule; the nutritive productions of the earth are the only real value; all other wealth is artificial and representation. Favor agriculture, therefore, and the multiplication of herds, the unique basis of all treasures. Commerce is born of abundance; one always seeks to sell that of which one has too much, to devote the superfluities to luxury, all the commodities of life; and it is by that means that commerce and luxury itself encourage agriculture; but be careful that those two gluttonous branches, commerce and luxury, do not attract all the vigor to themselves; the tree will perish!"

Having arrived at the field to be labored, Bridge set himself at one plow and gave the other to the Sage to guide; Oribeau took the water-sprinkler. The old man O'Barbo proved that he knew the first of the Arts; Bridge, seeing him labor, called to him: "You're a past master, honorable ancient, in the work I do every day!"

"How do you know how to labor so well?" Oribeau asked him.

"When I was obliged to leave the Court after my disgrace, not wanting to return to the bosom of my family, whom the sight of me would have saddened, I went to the province of Balaclay in the Kingdom of Lagenia and settled in Blessington, in the home of a laborer, who took me on as a plowman. I worked courageously; my body ached but I found that infinitely less than my mental distress. I was healthy; I ate with appetite. No one knew me; everybody told me the truth frankly.

"I sometimes heard talk of aristocrats at Balacay and I was surprised that everyone knew what those in government and in favor did not. I compared them to the blindfolded individual in blind-man's-buff, who cannot see anyone but all of whose movements are known to everyone else. That situation, new for me, was very agreeable to me; I felt pity for my peers, and I could sometimes have rendered them great services.

"After more than two years of that life, which I found happy, a lord from Mommonia passed through Blessington, who caught sight of me and recognized me. One of my fellow plowmen perceived him pointing at me and, thinking that I was a deserter, he came to warn me. I left him with that idea and fled into the mountains of Stefenon, where we have spent some time together. That's how I learned the art of laboring; you know that I cultivated my garden; you helped me in spite of your youth and that's what fortified you."

Oribeau, whom the Sage had not previously informed of those circumstances, wanted to guide the plow in his turn; he took the A, or fork, to which the plowshare was attached, and the old man led the horses, but the young Prince could not continue such arduous work for long and he handed the A back to the old man, saying: "What hard work it is obliging the earth to nourish us!"

"That's true, and people in cities don't suspect it. Observe our neighbors who are laboring in the same canton; they're almost all brutalized by the excess of distress; their limbs never obtain sufficient repose, and they grow heavy and stiff. Look at their gait: it's that of exhausted men. It's for that reason that it's necessary to honor this vital estate, in order that the difficulty doesn't deter those who exercise it. Let the certainty of being loved, cherished and considered by the sovereign and the aristocracy compensate them; they won't work any less; they'll remain in their estate more willingly, when they know that easier work is not as highly esteemed, and especially that domestic service in the city and the houses of lords is a shame. If you take soldiers from the countryside, as I advise, it's necessary to occupy them with difficult work after exercise, as the ancient Romans did."

After three hours work in rich terrain Oribeau could do no more, although he had only been leading horses and distributing water. He was looking forward to the time to return to the house, but it was necessary to wait for midday, The Sage's discourse no longer amused him; he was exhausted.

"I see," he said, "that the excess of labor weighs down the mind, as you told me once, but it's necessary to go through it, in order to know better."

Midday finally arrived; they unhitched the plow-animals and returned to the laborer's house. Oribeau was so tired that he had to mount a horse, while the old man, Bridge and his sons came back, if not lightly, at least with an appearance of strength.

They found a meal ready, but before going to table, Bridge's sons took care of the horses and have them all that they needed. Meanwhile, Oribeau rested. The laborer's five daughters surrounded him, along with Gemmeh, their mother and the good Frigameh, their aunt. They commiserated with his fatigue, as if they had known the reason for it, Rosée, most of all, sought to anticipate his desires, whether to refresh him or to give him a more comfortable seat.

"Oh," said the young Prince to his guide, "how likeable that girl is. I sense that I would rather she were Oribelle than Canora, Ahissa, Daura, Julia herself, or Fillira!"

"You can see by that," replied O'Barbo, "that great prudence is required in the choice of a spouse, and that the man who makes up his mind on his first impulse is preparing himself for long repentance. But what do you think of the mother?"

"She's very pleasant, but Jasmine and Rosée are far superior."

They ate.

The Prince and the Sage remained in the house, without being known there, for nearly four years, during which Oribeau, in order to fortify his body, hardened himself by labor. He learned to swim, the art of guiding a boat on the sea and military exercises, in a manner that I shall tell you.

O'Barbo received information from Dondanuck that there was no point seeking Princess Oribelle in Lagenia because she was safe, under a disguise that put her out of range of any attainment. In the same message, the Minister exhorted his friend to give the young King all the knowledge that he lacked in a manner proportionate to his strength. At first the Prince had seemed delicate; he had been spared, but his way of life had finally rendered him so robust that O'Barbo thought that he ought to accustom him to the rudest kind of labor and the fatigues of war. Agriculture prepares for that, in that it renders a man almost indefatigable; the Sage reckoned that the first element of the military art.

As Evinland is surrounded by seas and filled with lakes, swimming in all weathers, naked or dressed, seemed to him to be essential. To train his pupil in it, he gave him the sons of the laborer for competition, especially the eldest, Nichols. Then, in imitation of the ancient Coriandres,[87] the first known inhabitants of the land, he put various things agreeable to youth in a boat, which he took a certain distance from the shore—fairly close at first, and then further away as the swimmers became stronger. All of them dived into the sea or the lake simultaneously and the first to reach the boat chose the six most agreeable things from the pile. The next chose five, the third four, the fourth three, the fifth two and the sixth took the one that remained. The size of the pile was adjusted according to the number of swimmers. In the first attempts the Prince accepted the prize, like the others, but when he became the most skillful he became ashamed of always winning. He proposed to guide the boat that served as the target and come back swimming; then to go back to fetch it after the contest and bring it back towing it while he swam.

While Oribeau learned to swim, his instructor exercised him, mounted on a horse, in armed combat against another rider, or on foot, hand to hand. The young Prince, who sensed the importance of those exercises, gave himself entirely to them in the country, under the pretext of play. O'Barbo, who knew the art of war perfectly, organized simulated combats among the youth of Younghall. Oribeau normally commanded them, but sometimes it was O'Barbo himself, and then his pupil was in the ranks of the soldiers. He showed heroic courage, and no one was ever able to snatch victory away from him. When he commanded, O'Barbo observed him, and pointed out errors of encampment or attack, if he made any. He

---

[87] This allegation appears to be original to Restif.

praised him if the distribution if the disposition and the castrametation were equally fine and good. The pupil soon succeeded equally in those two important points; he vanquished O'Barbo himself, who sometimes commanded the opposing party. People came from miles around to watch those exercises, whose soldiers they called "the Volunteers of Evinland."

When O'Barbo saw that the young Prince was sufficiently exercised in what he needed to know of the military art, he said to him: "My King, you know the interior of your realm, the situation of your people, their work, their pleasures, you have seen what there is of the good and the bad; you are ready to reign. Speak: what do you want us to do?"

"I want to obey you for a little longer," the Prince replied. "Continue to be my guide in everything."

"I'll do that, but remember that henceforth, I'm commanding you on the orders of the King of Mommonia himself, and whatever he wants, I shall obey..."

Now, it is necessary to know that for the three and a half years that Oribeau had been living in the same house as Rosée, he had never had an intimate conversation with her. He respected her, esteemed her and loved her; that is why, three days after the conversation I have reported, O'Barbo said to the Prince: "It's necessary to depart."

"Oh!" said Oribeau. "It's so good here."

"It's necessary not to repose before work. Think of your destiny. You are to render your people happy but your acquired enlightenment. When you are on the throne, truth will flee from you, instead of which, today, it will show you as much as you wish. It's necessary to depart."

The laborer's entire household was saddened by the news of the departure of the two strangers. They loved them like a father and a brother. The old man had charmed by this mildness and is moral excellence, the young Prince by his beauty, his skill, his courage, the respect he had for his guide and his extreme politeness to his comrades, Bridge's sons. The day before, in the evening, it was agreed with Bridge that the old man and his pupil would leave early in the morning, un-known to the family, but that the laborer alone would accompany them for a few miles, as far as Middletown

That was what they did; all three left in the early morning, without making any noise. When they arrived in Middletown they ate breakfast sitting by the roadside, with what Bridge-Clonard had brought. Then they said adieu, but before parting, O'Barbo gave a box to the laborer, telling him that there were presents inside for his family. Clonard received it gratefully, and they separated.

When he arrived home, the laborer announced the departure of his guests and showed them the box he had received on quitting them. Rosée went pale and was ready to fall ill. Meanwhile, Bridge opened the box. He found presents, labeled: a magnificent one for Rosée, another almost as beautiful for Jasmine; others for Frigameh, Gemmeh, Nichols and all the other children.

In Rosée's there was a piece of paper on which was written: *Prince Oribeau, who is quitting you, makes a present to the beautiful Rosée of this diamond, this ring, this immortal bouquet, these ear-rings and this golden crown. May she take pleasure in them, and never forget the man who made them for her, by the hands of O'Barbo, his teacher.*

On reading that note, the family uttered a cry of joy, and Bridge-Clonard saw that he had been doubly honored.

But let us leave him in his admiration and follow the two illustrious travelers. From Middletown they went to Cork, following their plan, from Cork to Whitchurch, then Fourmilewater, then to Mullo, to Karletown, to Killmallock, to Bruss, to Limerick. Then they passed to the other side of Waterford and saw Rosbercon, Ross, Mongarret, Polemon and Mullin. Then, turning north, they reached the coast of the kingdom of Lagenia, which they entered through the county of Kilkenny from which they went, traversing Queens- & Kings-country, to Mullanger in West Meath, at the junction of the Lakes Hoy and Ennell, where I shall soon say what happened to them.

The hunter Kerry stopped there, promising to come back the day after next, because the following day he had business in Iraghticonner, He left his entire audience in admiration and in the desire to hear the continuation of the story of Prince Oribeau and Princess Oribelle.

And as for the Irishman Patrick, alias Yzquiepatli, he also stopped speaking, and the evening finished, to the great regret of Monsieur Gaudet of the Rue Courtaudvilain and his entire family. The narrator returned home with his friend Mayo, alias Zoïle, offering to return to the market garden soon—but he would not swear to anything.

Charmed by everything they had heard, Monsieur Gaudet of the Rue Courtaudvilain and his family were waiting impatiently in their market garden in the Hauteborne for Sir Patrick Mohill, alias Yzquiepatli and his comrade Sir John Mayo, alias Zoïle, when they received the bad news that the two Irishmen had just returned to their own country, where the government had returned the property confiscated from their ancestors who had followed King James to France, and not only their property but the plenitude of their rights as citizens. An assembly of volunteers had resolved that the right of Catholics to vote for the election of Members of Parliament would be restored.

Monsieur Gaudet was sorry about all that because he had lost the continuation of the story, but he was amply compensated. A maidservant from the two Irishmen's furnished hotel came the same day to bring the following manuscript, written by Sir Patrick's hand; it was the completion of the story of Oribeau, which was read in the evening, because Monsieur Gaudet and his family had their occupations during the day.

Chapter 2A
Alrunes. Admirable invocation made to them by old Ennisleague.

Alphabet Two, containing the adventures of the excellent Princess Oribelle and the continuation of the great deeds of the valiant Prince Oribeau.

"Alrunes,[88] divinities of the hearth and the pothook, I invoke you, in order that the worthy gentleman who is telling us

---

[88] Author's note: "Alrunes. Household gods, Penates or Lares among the ancient Germans, Saxons, English and Irish; fetishes of a sort, like those of Negroes." The word in question, an alternative spelling of *alraune*, does not seem ever to have

the admirable story of Prince Oribeau and the beautiful Princes of Lagenia will soon arrive, for since he has been telling his
tales in my tavern, it is always full of people! My little
Alrunes, I will ornament you every day with fine red, blue and
green garments and the coffer in which I keep you will be garnished with cotton and lined with aurora cloth; I make that
view and I shall keep it..."

The old innkeeper had no sooner finished that prayer to
her Penates than the first two drinkers arrived, followed by a
dozen more. The gentleman hunter only made them wait for
the time necessary for all those people to arrange themselves
on their seats and get ready to drink while listening to him. He
was received with transports of joy all the more enthusiastic
because they had gone a day without seeing him. They were,
in any case, very content with the druid of Dungarvan and the
laborer Bridge-Clonard; above all, they were anxious about
the young Prince, who was about to quit his Estates and go to
Mullanger, at the junction of Lakes Hoy and Ennell.

"My friends," said the hunter, on coming in, "yesterday's
absence has made me sense that I love you. I know where I
stopped, but today I shall leave the story of Prince Oribeau for
a while in order to start that of the excellent Princess Oribelle,
from whom our young King descends. May he vanquish the
Meathians, for it is said, in the predictions of the Fay
Mellusine, Pict Princess, that Evinland will one day be subjugated by the Angles on the occasion of the troubles that the
Kings of Lagenia and Meath will excite, unless they observe
religiously the last dispositions of Princess Dinameh, which
prescribe that the four sovereigns of Evinland should remain
united, under penalty of being dethroned and their children

---

referred to anything but the notorious mandrake root. There is,
however, a connection in German folklore between that root
and the household spirits of Teutonic mythology, kobolds,
mandrake roots often being used to carve representations of
them like those used in her invocation by Ennisleague—a
practice mentioned by Jakob Grimm, among others.

reduced to the status of ordinary individuals. Let us therefore invoke Thor, Berda, Worden, Erda, Vananis and Friga for our young Prince and the other Kings of the land..."

All the drinkers cried at once: "Long live our young King Fitz-Oribeau! And may he force the Kings of Meath and Linster to live in peace, in order that they will not, one day, by their quarrels, be the cause of the subjection of the beautiful land of Evinland to the yoke of our neighbors the Angles!"

Those cries were heard throughout the neighborhood, and attracted a great many people to the old woman's establishment, who blessed her little Alrunes for it.

When everyone was tranquil, the gentleman hunter spoke again:

"Adversity is often a favor of the gods, who prove mortals by that means, and lead them along the road to virtue with blows of the rod..."

"That's true!" said Younghall.

"I've seen it many a time," added Kilmactomas.

The hunter Kerry made them a sign, which demanded silence, and he went on.

Chapter 2B
Blunder of O'Brisombaüm, husband of Conchèse. He is imprisoned. Oribelle's good sentiments. Horrible crime meditated by Ratchlin.

Braved by the Minister Ratchlin, O'Brisombaüm only suffered with difficulty the insolence of that favorite. He resolved to rally to his party the principal Lords of Lagenia and to expel the Minister; for O'Brisombaüm was not cruel and the idea did not occur to him of exposing his enemy's life. Secretly, he assembled the Barons who had reason to complain of Ratchlin; they were Longford, Balaclay, Kildare, Greathill, Thenehinch, Wicklow, Katherlagh and Wexford, all his peers before he had married the Queen.

"Dear Barons, my former comrades," he said to them, "you know that it was not out of pride, nor to raise myself above you that I sought the hand of the Queen our sovereign. I loved her; I was loved by her. Deceived by my mother,[89] who doubtless had her views, my father was persuaded, and I was persuaded myself, that I was a girl, in order to place me next to the Queen. You know what happened. I do not think that anyone has reproached me for ambition; I have not yet known the sentiment. When the priests of Thor and Worden revolted, you were for me; you remembered the artfulness with which my mother, under the name of a fay, used the singular stratagem that saved our lives, for the Scot MacChoucas and his son would no more have spared you than me father and me.

"The people have made a great marvel out of my mother's finesse; it is necessary to let them believe it; it can still serve us. Four large canvas birds, gummed with borax, were filled with smoke; my mother caught the wind as the sacrilegious ceremony began, allowed herself to be lifted high into the air by the four large birds dilated by the hot smoke;[90] the wind carried her over the scene. She had two hundred pounds of lead in her chariot, which she threw to the ground at the moment when the faithful Patrick, our serf attached a rope to the trees that retained the chariot and the birds. My mother spoke. In the fear that the marvel caused, two men instructed by my mother seized the two Scotsman MacChoucas and MacDonoght; they dragged them out of the circle and went to throw them into the cavern of Lake Erg, where they still are.[91]

---

[89] Author's note: "Brisombaüm destroys here the marvels of chapters C-E. It will also be seen that the discovery of aerostats was made by the ancient Irish but had been lost since."

[90] The Montgolfier brothers made their first public demonstrations of hot air balloons in 1783. Restif might have seen the manned balloon that took off from a château near the Bois de Boulogne on 21 November and flew over Paris for nine kilometers, and presumably incorporated the present passage into his story within a matter of months.

[91] Author's note: "This cavern of Lake Erg or Irg is two leagues east of the town of Dunnaghall, in the county of

"We were all liberated, and my mother, wanting to thwart the designs of the King of Meath, our natural enemy, who was bound to ask for Princess Oribelle's hand in marriage for his son in order to give him new rights to the crown of Lagenia, took possession of the young princess immediately after her birth. She secured her in the Castle of Makredin and destined her for the young Prince of Mommonia, whose beauty, education by a Sage and marvelous dispositions were the admiration of all Evinland.

"Ratchlin, on the contrary, who is our inferior since he is one of O'Longford's vassals, with ambitious views in conformity with his baseness, wants to give Oribelle, the elder of the Queen's two daughters, to the Prince of Meath, the disgraced Cahincaha. He thinks that the Lagenians, on seeing that monster, will never be persuaded to recognize him as their sovereign; that they will expel him and that he, Ratchlin, will remain their master. Perhaps he has designs on Princess Dinameh himself.

"Lagenian lords, will you obey the vassal of one of you, who has no merit save for his perfidious cunning and an effeminate face?"

Tirconnell in the kingdom of Ulster or Ultonia; it has since become famous under the name of the Purgatory of Saint Patrick; Irish monks have made it into a kind of lair of Trophonius, which brought them considerable sums before English reform put an end to that superstition." The cave known as Saint Patrick's Purgatory, on an island in Lough Derg, became famous in France; Marie de France translated a Latin document giving an account of a pilgrimage there into the vernacular in the twelfth century; that account and other accounts of pilgrimages to the site were reproduced frequently during the next three centuries, and it is mentioned in *Froissart's Chronicle*. The cave was closed in 1632, but pilgrimages, and literary works based thereon, continued into the twentieth century.

"No, by Worden," cried Longford, Balaclay, Kildare, Greatshill, Thenehineh, Wicklow, Katherlagh and Wexford. "Perish Ratchlin! We devote our arms and our lives to the service of the brave O'Brisombaüm of Kilkenny, husband of the Queen our sovereign, against the traitor Ratchlin!"

That conspiracy thus made, O'Brisombaüm thought himself the master of events. He decided to enter the Council, resist Ratchlin directly, and have him arrested as he left the palace. But he did not know that Balaclay had married Radelinde, the favorite's sister and the most beautiful young woman in Evinland; that Kildare was madly in love with Oribelle, whom he might have seen when accompanying the Queen to Makredin, and that Katherlagh had designs on Dinameh.

Those three Barons betrayed him. Ratchlin, informed by them, warned the Queen of what her husband was planning. Conchèse was afraid for herself in fearing for her Minister; it was decided that O'Brisombaüm would be arrested at nightfall and that he would be imprisoned in Killencay on the island of Allen in the county of Kildare.

To execute that plan in a sure manner that would not cause any trouble, the three traitors went to find O'Brisombaüm under the pretext of giving him a facile means of taking Ratchlin by surprise. The Prince believed them and went out with them; horses were ready; they arrived that same night at Killencay, where they stayed. O'Brisombaüm got ready to surprise his enemy, whom he had come there to see; he leapt on to the drawbridge first and advanced precipitately, but the bridge was immediately raised, with the result that when he turned round he saw his three companions on the other side.

He thought himself unlucky but not betrayed; full of courage, he went into the castle, where Ratchlin received him with affected respect. He went out, after the Prince had been taken to an apartment, and left the castle. O'Brisombaüm saw him from the window returning with the three Barons. He wanted to pursue them, but was told that he was a prisoner. At the same time, he saw a scaffold erected at his window. He shivered, but it was only fear. Three masons walled up that opening and there was no more daylight except through a round hole overlooking the courtyard.

Am I seeing things? O'Brisombaüm thought. *Have I been betrayed by those Barons? Am I a prisoner? Have I made the blunder of coming to deliver myself, and does my life depend on my cruelest enemy?*

Conchèse was informed by her minister of what had happened, and approved—but the people thought differently; they threatened an uprising if the Prince was not set free. That is why the Queen gave an exegesis of her conduct in these terms:

Conchèse, daughter of O'Emptor. Queen of Lagenia by right of birth, to all her faithful subjects, know this: That, having married the Baron of Knocktoser, son of the Baron of Kilkenny, one of our foremost subjects, we soon perceived that that Prince, seduced by bad advice, wanted to arrogate over our person, which should have been sacred to him, an authority that did not belong to him. In consequence, we thought it our duty to oppose him and to maintain the sacred rights of our birth; which so displeased the Prince our spouse that he conspired against our person and tempted the fidelity of eight other peers of our realm, of which he is the first. That had already reached the point that he went to Killencay, in order to hold us prisoner there, as well as our Minister; an attempt that as so unsuccessful that he found himself a prisoner himself, thanks to the fidelity of three peers in whom he had confided particularly. We believe, therefore, that it is appropriate to leave him for some years in the fortress that he had chosen for our imprisonment, in order that he has time to reflect and open his eyes to his past conduct.

The present exegesis inscribed on the book of our royal edicts in the eleventh year of our reign.

Oisery is our abode. Conchèse, Queen. By order. Ratchlin.

That exegesis by the Queen tranquilized the people, who contented themselves with feeling sorry for O'Brisombaüm and doing nothing in his favor. The only person who was interested in him was the young Princess Oribelle.

"A great misfortune has just occurred," Nursimaneh said to her. "There is dissension in the royal family, for your father has been imprisoned by two traitors, who have delivered him to the Minister Ratchlin, and your deceived mother has approved that conduct."

Oribelle began to weep, for she had a sensible heart. "I shall beg my mother," she said, "not to do this wrong to his memory."

"Your father only has you who can take his side," replied Clomaneh.

The first time that the Queen came to see her older daughter at Makredin, with Dinameh her younger sister, whom she had kept at Court, Oribelle, as soon as she perceived her mother, ran to embrace her with a more urgent tenderness than ever; although Conchèse returned her caresses, however, tears flowed from the eyes of the young Princess. The Queen pretended not to notice them. Dinameh, who was then nine years old, said stupidly to her elder sister: "Fie! How ugly it is to weep, when one sees one's mother."

"I'm not weeping because I'm seeing the Queen," Oribelle replied. "Her presence will always be my most precious wealth. She is dearer to me than ever, since I now only have her, and my father is deprived or her tenderness and his liberty."

"Your father, my daughter," replied the Queen, "wanted to overthrow the State. You know that I am the legitimate sovereign; I have been forced, reluctantly, to thwart his designs."

"Oh, my mother," cried Oribelle, "He's your husband; he adores you, and I'll never be persuaded that my father has schemed against my mother. I judge his heart by my own..." Then, looking at Ratchlin, who was accompanying the Queen, she said to him, with dignity: "Be careful, Baronet, of what you make the Queen do. Her good heart will soon reconcile her with her husband and they will punish the bad councilor who made them quarrel."

That language, on the part of a young Princess of fifteen, surprised the Queen, frightened Ratchlin and encouraged the belief that there was a communication between her and her father. However, as Conchèse loved Oribelle dearly, that boldness did not displease her. That is what caused Ratchlin to conceive a horrible plan.

The Queen did not want to stay in Makredin, where she only came to see her elder daughter. After having dined there, she departed, leaving Dinameh in the castle, in order to examine what happened there and the means by which Oribelle maintained a correspondence with her father—for they had no suspicion of the good Nursimaneh.

As soon as the Queen had gone, Ratchlin sought the means of succeeding in his detestable project, by proposing to Conchèse that he remain alone in the vicinity of Makrein while the Princes returned to Oisery with her cortege. He waited for nightfall before going back into the castle, mulling over his evil designs.

I shall abduct the Princess, he thought. *The people are superstitious; I shall say that it is Perforimoth the Black, King of Connacy, of whom I shall make a dangerous genius. I shall suppose that Dondanuck, the wise minister of the Queen of Mommonia, is a magician, who has taken possession of the younger of the two princesses, and I shall pretend to have liberated them from his hands. I shall ask for Oribelle as recompense, and I shall give Dinameh to the dwarf; they will have no children and I shall reunite the two kingdoms one day in my family...*

While he was arranging his plan this, he jumped for joy, saying to himself: *I shall avenge myself on you, O'Brisombaüm, in the most terrible manner, and when I have everything, you will be informed of it, before drinking the cup of death.*

Thus the perfidious Rathlin spoke to himself.

When night fell, he approached the castle. He shouted to the porter to lower the drawbridge, on behalf of the Queen. The porter recognized the Minister's voice, obeyed, and lowered the bridge. Ratchlin went in.

The first thing he did after entering was to seize the porter with a vigorous arms and throw him into a ditch, saying to him: "Traitor, I only wanted to test you."

Meanwhile, Nursomaneh heard the noise that the Minister made and had a secret presentiment of some misfortune. She ran to Oribelle's bedroom; the Princess had just gone to bed...

But it is a long time since I have talked to you about the Prince of Meath, the disgraced Cahincaha.

Chapter 2C
Communication of how the Prince of Meath lived in his early years with the shepherd Debundeh his favorite. He sees Oribeau.

Confined far from the Court, the son of Mijoreh the Beautiful accomplished fifteen years, like Princess Dinameh of Lagenia. His only master, for reading, writing and the sciences, was a shepherd named Debundeh, whom the chronicles represent to us as a great sorcerer and to whom the chroniclers attribute many evil deeds. I will try to tell you the truth, without remaining silent about the fables.

As soon as Queen Mijoreh had give birth to Prince Cahincaha, he inspired so much horror in her that she ordered that he be sent with the good Nursimaneh of Ballnalu, his nurse, to the castle of Mullanger, situated between Lake Hoy and Lake Ennel in West Meath, forbidden to reappear at Court until summoned. Nursimaneh went to Mullanger the following day and nourished Cahincaha there, having no company in the castle except the concierge Kilbegan and the shepherd Debundeh, a very ugly dwarf.

Now Debundeh, apart from being a dwarf, like the Prince, far surpassed him in ugliness, with the result that

Cahincaha, in his early infancy, was afraid of him, but at length, he became accustomed to him, and when he grow older, in considering the shepherd, he thought him a handsome fellow, for the porter was an old curmudgeon who looked like a bear.

As soon as the prince was able to play in the fields, Debundeh did not fail to take him with him to guard the flock, telling him stories taken from ancient chronicles and teaching him all the histories that the kaldes of Evinland recounted in their heroic or gallant songs. Cahincaha took much pleasure in that that he followed the shepherd everywhere in order to hear another tale or a ballad, and the good Nursimaneh wept with joy on seeing her nursling profit so well.

While the Prince was young, the dwarf shepherd only told him tales of fays, gnomes and genii to amuse him and do him good, being careful to make him understand of each story that it was an instructive allegory. The most marvelous of those stories, and the ones that the young Prince liked best to hear, were those of the half-cock half-fay, the four beauties and the four beast-fays, which you know, for they run from mouth to mouth throughout Evinland;[92] that of the fay Mellusine, Queen of the Picts; the tale of the fay Sireneh, who changed into brutes all those who delivered themselves to the delights that she procured for them; that of Prince Beaudâme

---

[92] Author's note: "For several years the first two have been employed in the third model of the *Nouvel Abeilard*, entitled *L'Amour enfantin*. The reader is begged to see them in that useful work, which suggests to parents a means of conserving the pure morals of their children by honest love, cultivated by reading alone." The reference is to Restif's didactic epistolary novel *Le Nouvel Abeilard ou lettres de deux amants qui ne se sont jamais vu* [The New Abelard; or, The Letters of Two Lovers Who Have Never Seen One Another] (1877), a riposte to Rousseau; the two "*contes bleus*" [fantastic tales] cited here are translated in the companion volume to the present one, *The Four Beauties and The Four Beasts.*.

and of Princess Belletête; which are full of excellent morali-
ties—not to mention many shorter ones that he told him every
day. I shall only recite you three, when the time comes: that of
Mellusine, that of Sireneh and the story of Prince Beaudâme.
As for the story of Princess Belletête, that will be part of the
general narrative.

It is necessary to tell you that when the Prince was older,
the shepherd substituted for tales and ancient histories the
marvelous actions of Prince Oribeau, whose education by a
Sage he recounted, and the admirable conduct that that Prince
maintained at a tender age. These details were the same that I
have told you; that is why I shall not repeat them. When he
wanted to give the attention of Cahincaha a rest, he sang him
one of the ancient ballads of the kaldes.

"Listen," said Debundeh, one day, "to the sad end of an
ancient warrior who lived in this country. The melody is beautiful, the lines are touching; it's the work of the kalde
Fassadining, who was born in the beautiful country of Kilkenny, whose daughters are the most beautiful in the world and
the poets sweet and melodious."

The young Prince sat down, and appeared to be ready to
give his full attention. The dwarf climbed on to a high rock in
the middle of a partially-dried-up marsh through which the
flock was passing; he collected himself momentarily and then
sang, in a voice more harmonious than there would have been
any reason to expect in such an ugly man. [93]

"Whence departs the source of the years? Where is the
terminus toward which they flow incessantly? My gaze wants
to penetrate the obscurity of the centuries, but I can only see
an obscure and uncertain light, similar to that of moonbeams

---

[93] The following "song" is a somewhat elaborated paraphrase
of part of one of Pierre Le Tourneur's translations of James
Macpherson's alleged poems of Ossian, "The War of Caros." I
have translated Restif's French version back into English rather than going back to the text of the English original, which
Restif surely never read.

faintly reflected by a distant lake. Here, I perceive the frightful ravages of war; there I see a feeble and vile generation passing in silence without marking the years by any splendid action. Bring me my harp; that is what will revive the past and give substance and color to deceased heroes. I sense my genius exalted and warmed. I am impatient to sing. I want to sing the disastrous death of the unfortunate Hidallan.

"Finghal could no longer bear the sight of him since his imprudence had caused the death of his lover. He banished him from his presence, excluded him from the number of his warriors and ordered him to return to his father. Young Hidallan quits the battlefield as if quitting his fatherland. He draws away at a slow pace, in bleak silence. He wanders, sad and solitary, over the hills. His arms hang in disorder by his side. Hanks of hair protrude from his helm, floating at hazard over his shoulders. His eyes are swollen by tears and his breast with sighs; he groans in secret.

"He wandered for three entire days, delivered to his profound dolor. He finally recognizes the stream that passes by the foot of his father's dwelling and utters a sigh. His father is sitting alone in the shade of an ancient oak, his head resting on hi staff, listening to the water flow without seeing it. Old age had closed his eyes to the light of day. He reviewed his memories and murmured softly the events of his youth. He thought then about his son, whom he had sent to lead his people in Finghal's wars. He hears a noise and recognizes his son's footsteps.

"'Is that my son I hear,' he said, "or is it his shade that is passing before me? O my son, have you perished in combat and forsaken your old father? If it's you, if you're alive, why have you come alone? Where are my people? Have my people perished? You had the custom of bringing them back to me triumphant, to the shrill clash of shields.'

"'No,' replied the young man, with a sigh. 'Your warriors are full of life. At this moment they are covering themselves with glory. But my father, there is no more glory for your son. I am condemned to spend my days here in shameful leisure, rather than in combat.'

"'Ah!' replied Lamor. 'Your ancestors never rested, when there was fighting. Do you see the tomb of our grandfather? He never fled before the enemy. O my father, what has become of your glory and mine, since my son has fled?'

"'Why do you afflict my soul, my father,' said Hidallan. 'I have never known fear. It is Finghal who has robbed me of the honor of perishing in combat. I am the victim of the resentment that he has conceived against me, because of a woman. *Return,* he said to me, with an irritated eye, *go to your lands; go dry up over your roots, like a decrepit tree that the effort of the winds has curbed toward the earth, never to rise again.*

"'What!' said the old man. 'It will be necessary to see you languish in shameful repose, while thousands of heroes enrich their renown every day? Magnanimous shade of my father, guide Lamor to his final abode; my eyes are in darkness; my soul is overwhelmed by sadness and my son has lost his glory!'

"'In what places,' exclaimed the young man, shall I seek glory, to rejoice my father's soul? It is not in returning to the hunt that the sound of my arrows will charm his ears!'

"'It is necessary, then, said Lamor, 'that I perish like the oak that my hands are touching and which is deprived of its foliage. It raised its head into the clouds, but it had driven its roots upon a rock and the winds have toppled it easily. O clouds that cover my eyes, I thank you…you are hiding the sight of my son.' Addressing him, he went on: 'Go into my dwelling; the arms of our ancestors are suspended there; bring your grandfather's sword; he conquered it from an enemy whose vanquisher he remained,'

"Hidallan obeyed; he brought the sword and gave it to his father. The old man's wandering hand sought the point, felt it, and paused there. 'Take me to my father's tomb, my son. I need to repose there; it is noon and the sun is dominating our lands.'

"Hidallan led him there; they reached it. Lamor pierced his son's side. They reposed there together, and their deserted palace, which fell into ruin, covered the banks of the steam with its debris. At noon, phantoms wander in that place; silence reigns in the valley; men fear to approach that fatal place."

"Oh," exclaimed the young Meathan Prince, "how sorry I feel for Hidallan. How sorry I feel for Lamor. That song makes me sad. Happy is the man who can show his courage with weapons in hand."

The Prince had scarcely finished these words when he saw in the distance a venerable old man accompanied by a young man. They were alone and traveling on foot.

"There's an old man and his son," he said. "Perhaps they've gone astray in this solitary region; they're fatigued. Should we go to them, to save them the trouble of coming to us?"

"You're right," said the shepherd. "Travelers are ordinarily so exhausted that they don't turn willingly from their route unless they need help."

Immediately, Cahincaha and Debundeh drove their flock in the direction of the road from Athlone to Mullanger.

"Old man," shouted the shepherd, "and you, young man, have you not gone astray in these remote cantons full of bogs?"

"Honest shepherd," replied the old man, "We're going to the kingdom of Lagenia; we're travelers visiting the various countries of Evinland in order to know their mores, in order to adopt the good and avoid the bad, for I'm the guide of this young man and his parents have charged me with his instruction, in order that he will know everything useful."

"Old man," replied Debundeh, "poor and deformed as you see me, I too am charged with the instruction of this young man, six years younger, for yours is approaching his twentieth year; will you grant me the favor of staying here for a month, in order that you might rest and enable my pupil to profit from your wise conversation? Perhaps you won't be sorry, for he belongs to honest parents and ought ne day to have an establishment in the world, but it's necessary that he fulfill various conditions for that."

The old man consented to the shepherd's request, and to commence the acquaintance Debundeh took from his sack the provisions for his meal and Cahincaha's, which were more ample than usual just then. There was a wild boar's ears, a pig's brawn, a roasted hazel grouse and a few fruits. The dwarf set all that out on a piece of tarred cloth in which he wrapped himself on rainy days; they sat around it and, after having blessed Thor, Worden, Berda, Vananis and Friga, they started eating.

"Old man," said the shepherd, while serving, "from what country do you come?"

"From the flourishing kingdom of Mommonia," O'Barbo replied—for you can see that it was the Sage and Prince Oribeau.

"You come from a strange land there, about which many extraordinary things are recounted," said Debundeh. "It's said that the Minister wants to make himself King and that he has enchanted the Prince—but I don't believe any of it. Popular rumors are rarely true. In any case, what use would royalty be to an old man accustomed to living poorly?"

"You think justly," said the Sage. "The Minister has nothing in view but the advantage of the State and the young Prince, who is being educated in a manner appropriate to the rank he will hold one day."

"You fill me with joy," exclaimed the shepherd. "Crimes sadden me, even when I don't suffer from them. They make me scornful of human nature. Would you like to tell me the story of Prince Oribeau, if you know it? It will instruct my pupil better than any other discourse."

The Sage consented to that, and he told that which concerned Oribeau, until the moment when his young pupil, having quit the mountains of Stefenon, arrived in Waterford. He stopped there—not that he feared being recognized, but it was necessary that the two young princes did not know yet who they were. Oribeau knew himself, whereas Beaudâme was unaware that he was the Prince of Meath; one was being openly educated, but the other was like an ordinary individual, who would only find himself a sovereign Prince with the greatest astonishment one day.

When O'Barbo had finished his story, in which he detailed all the instruction that he had given his pupil without revealing his situation, and those that Oribeau had received during their long sojourn in Bridge-Clonard's house, Debundeh thanked him.

"I ought to return the favor," aid the shepherd, "and also tell you how I am forming this young man, who has been confided to me by a good woman, his mother or his nurse, who lives in the isolated castle whose rooftops you can see above the lakes to either side of it.

Debundeh went into all the details of what he had taught Cahincaha, and under the envelope of marvelous histories he exposed the Evinlandish traditions, as many of them fabulous as historic, on the origin of the royal houses of the island. The two travelers said that they would be charmed to hear some of the tales such as he had told them to his pupil; the dwarf promised to satisfy them after the meal.

As soon as they had finished eating, Cahincaha, who loved the tales passionately, reminded the shepherd that he had promised to regale his guests with an interesting story.

"I'd like that," replied Debundeh, laughing, "and I'm glad that you reminded me, for it proves that my tales give you pleasure." He gave a part of his leftovers to the dogs, replaced the best of what there was in his sack, took his guests on to a rock from which they could see the whole flock, and commenced the first tale.

Chapter 2D
*Debundeh, after giving dinner to Prince Oribeau and the
Sage, tells tales in response to the plea of his pupil
Cahincaha. The first tale: Mellusine.*

Distantly, in the land of the Picts[94] that once conquered
Scotland, there was once a protective fay named
Ouroucoucou, who was the mother of Pucellomaneh and several other daughters, including the celebrated Mellusine. The
latter remains hidden in her lair nowadays, surrounded by inaccessible rocks, but as soon as a great crime is committed, or
some conspiracy is woven against her descendants, the Princes
of the land, or public wellbeing is in danger, her piercing voice
is heard resounding, as forceful as the whistling of the wind
and the sound of the irritated waves. That is what has given
rise to the saying commonplace among the Gauls and Franks
"to scream like Mellusine."[95]

---

[94] It is by means of a play on words that Restif associates the
Picts, legendary one-time inhabitants of Scotland, with the
Poictevins, natives of the French province of Poitou, centered
on Poitiers. The Poictevin House of Lusignan distinguished
itself during the First Crusade, eventually supplying the royal
family of the Kingdom of Jerusalem as well as the Kings of
Cyprus and Cilicia in Armenia. The descendants of the House
subsequently invented a kind of creation myth for themselves,
centered on the figure of the fay Mélusine and Raimondin of
Lusignan, an elaboration of whose synthesized legend is here
transplanted by Restif into the context of his extraordinarily
elaborate account of the descendants of the fay Wrwcwcw.

[95] In the traditional version of the story of Mélusine, the earli-
est extant version of which dates from the end of the fourteenth century, the fay screams when surprised in the bath by
Raimondin, hence the popular phrase *"pousser des cris de
Mélusine"* [to scream like Melusine].

The fay Ouroucoucou, whose name we write Wrwcwcw, had had Pucellomaneh in legitimate marriage, of the genius Perforimoth the White, her husband. The young fay was as beautiful as Friga, which was to become fatal, for, having refused to marry a wicked and vile genius, her father's brother, known as Perforimoth the Black, became annoyed with her and imposed upon her the rule that she must offer herself, in spite of her own will, to the first ten men married to a faithful wife that she encountered, when she went out.

To avoid submitting to that punishment, the chaste fay stayed indoors for a long time, but she finally became bored and, considering that after ten men she would be her own mistress, she ventured forth. I shall not give you the details of her ten subjections; all that I can tell you is that it took her a thousand years to complete them. She only found one man per century whose wife met the required condition; the woman in question had to be faithful even in thought.

Of each of the first nine men the fay had a daughter who was only half-fay—which is to say, mortal, unless she followed certain rules that were imposed on her in order to become a complete fay.

The first of the daughters was known in the world under the name of Semiramis, the most powerful Queen that ever existed; she killed her husband, not wanting to be submissive to a man as she was half-fay, but she was punished for it by her own son, who stabbed her without knowing who she was.

The second was the wife of Orpheus and was named Eurydice; although mortal, her mother was able to return her to life once, on condition that her husband, present at the conjuration, did not look at his wife—something that he understood. She died young, for having committed a slight infidelity with a genius disguised as a serpent, and her mother, pressed by the husband, made the conjuration. Orpheus observed faithfully all that had been required of him until he heard Eurydice, who said to him: "My dear Orpheus!" He raised his eyes, and she disappeared immediately, like a light cloud.

The third was named Sappho; she made divine verses, but she preferred a debauched life to the wisdom that would have give her immortality; she fell madly in love with a young man who scorned her; she did not want to survive her shame and precipitated herself from the Leucadian rock into the irritated sea, which returned her body, broken on the reefs.

The fourth was Olimpias, the mother of the great King Alexander, of whom the Greek and Roman histories speak. She had commerce with the genius Perforimoth the Black, who, in the form of a serpent, was the father of Alexander, otherwise the Constrainer, for that is what his name means. She was cruel toward her son's widow, which, combined with her infidelity, excluded her from Faerie. She perished unfortunately, by the ambushes of, Alexander's successor Antipater.

The fifth was named Phryné; she chose the profession of courtesan; she was born in the same century as her sister Olimpias—although it was very corrupt, that century furnished too faithful wives! Her father was a certain Phrynis of Mytilene who came to settle in Attica. One day, Phryné was accused of atheism before the Aeropagus for having allowed herself to worship Friga. She only replied to her judges by uncovering her breasts, which she showed them, as if she were saying to them: "This fine work attests a god..."

Pucellomaneh then went a century and a half without encountering a man capable of emancipating her. Her sixth daughter is well-known; her name was Cleopatra. The name of her father is unknown. She gave herself to the most frenetic debauchery and perished from the bite of an asp that Perforimoth the Black brought her himself, disguised as a peasant.

The seventh, named Berenice, was loved by an Emperor of Rome named Titus.

The eighth reigned in approximately same region as Semiramis; her name was Zenobia; she had eight sons and eight daughters by her husband Odenat, whom she loved uniquely, but for one single infidelity; that is why she was vanquished by the Emperor Hadrian and taken to Rome, where she bore her misfortune courageously.

The ninth was named Sireneh; she was the daughter of a muleteer and I shall tell you her story.

Finally, the tenth, and the only immortal one, was Mellusine.

One night, when the Prince of the Picts, the handsome Raimondin, was passing close to the Soësve spring, fleeing after inadvertently killed King Aymery, his uncle, while out hunting, the moonlight showed him three ladies bathing in the basin of the spring. He was surprised to see women bathing alone in the middle of the night in a vast forest, but, fearing that he might be recognized, he turned his bridle without examining whether they were beautiful or ugly, and tried to go away.

Mellusine, the liveliest of the three ladies and the only one who did not have a lover perceived his intention. "I believe," she said to the other two, who were her cousins and descendants of Zenobia, "that that knight is in bad trouble. Otherwise, he wouldn't be so discourteous as to go away precipitately on perceiving ladies. I want to talk to him."

As she finished speaking she ran lightly and, cutting across Raimondin's path, stopped his horse.

"Knight," she said, "am I mistaken in giving you that name? Your education scarcely responds to the rank you appear to hold. To pass ladies without rendering the duty of the simplest politeness isn't knightly courtesy!"

Raimondin remained silent.

"What!" said Mellusine. "Have you never spoken, then, has your lady, if you have one, imposed a rule of silence on you?"

Raimondin continued to remain silent, for he was very surprised.

"Have no fear of being courteous to a lady," Mellusine added, "one never repents of it."

Raimondin admired her; he was unable to respond.

Astonished, Mellusine, beginning to get annoyed, took him by the hand, a trifle rudely. "Surely, Sire," she said, "you're asleep! What! You're insensible to the advances of a pretty woman—for I flatter myself that I'm beautiful."

At those words, Raimondin emerged from his lethargy, and shivered like a man who the murderous weapon of an assassin obliges to have recourse to his weapon; he feared that the King of the Picts' men wanted to seize him, and drew his sword.

Mellusine smiled. "Brave knight," she said to him, showing him the most beautiful person in the world, "where, then, is your enemy? Is he pressing you, that you put yourself on guard? But know that I'm on your side, for I've always been the friend of unfortunate virtue."

Raimondin looked at the young and beautiful Mellusine; he was amazed to have encountered such a charming person in the middle of a vast forest. He dismounted from his horse and saluted her, saying: "Forgive me, Milady, but I hadn't yet seen you, although you had taken my hand, for know that I am in great difficulty, from which I can see no issue. That is what was occupying me internally, and held me as if buried in a lethargic sleep. My honor is in danger, for my innocence might be suspected. May it please the gods to divert the storm that is rumbling over my head!"

"I like a hero to honor the gods, and invoke them in danger," said Mellusine. "I like the sentiment of honor that you have just shown, and I don't believe that it was by virtue of impoliteness that you didn't reply to me. But tell me, where are you going? If you're lost, I'll return you to your route, for I know all those in this canton."

"Milady," replied Raimondin, "I have been lost in the forest without being able to find my way since this morning."

"My dear Raimondin, why hide your difficulty from me? My heart wants to share it; know that this heart is yours."

When the knight heard himself named, he was so surprised—for he was sure that he had never spoken to the lady before—that he remained mute.

"Why hide an embarrassment from me," Mellusine continued, "in which I might be of service to you? I know that you have killed the King of the Picts, and that you did it unintentionally, since, seeing the enormous boar that you were hunting together charging him, the blow that you destined for the animal alone killed the Prince, after having pierced the monster. I know that you loved Aymery and that you're in despair, for he cherished you like his own son. It's not when one has done the good deed that I read in your eyes that one is capable of parricide; for know that, if the gods and the tutelary genii of men never leave a crime unpunished, much less do they leave a good deed without recompense.

"Do you remember the day when, in battle, you gave victory to the King of the Picts by your valor? You quit the trophy on which you were elevated to run to a house from which screams were coming. You arrived at the moment when one of your most valiant captains, your friend and relative Alain the Armorican, was about to do violence to a beautiful prisoner. She was disheveled, her eyes tearful, on her back beneath a menacing blade. An old man with white hair was hiding his face in his hands; a weeping lady, the daughter of the old man and the mother of the young woman, was pleading with the barbarian on her knees. Two young male children were in the hands of soldiers who were holding them up, ready to crash them against the wall if the young woman did not yield with good grace.

"You threw yourself on your friend, your relative, and you said to him: 'Before committing such a vile act, you'll take my life.' Alain gave in. You liberated the desolate family; you consoled the old man and the lady; you returned her two sons to the later and you went out, pure and modest, without having looked at the young woman..."

Raimondin's astonishment increased as the beautiful Mellusine read in his eyes—for she appeared to be reading everything she said therein. "Most honored lady," he said, "I cannot imagine how you learned my misfortune and my entire history so quickly, and I'm all the more disquieted by it."

"Don't fret, my friend; give me your faith and I'll put you out of peril. I'll do more; I'll render you the greatest lord in the country; no one will talk any longer about anyone but you, and you will have a glory of surpassing your ancestors, for people will gladly settle down under your laws."

The misfortune that seemed to be a cloud from which lightning was emerging rumbling over Raimondin's head and veiling the sun of joy from his eyes, was gradually brightened by that pleasant discourse. From the frightful obscurity of a host of terrible thoughts, the Pictish Prince finally passed to more cheerful ideas; he glimpsed hope—hope, the benevolent god that holds out a hand to beaten mortals and helps them to get up again. He envisaged, on the one hand, the danger of returning to his homeland, and on the other, the advantage that the beautiful lady was presenting to him; his heart opened with confidence.

"I pledge you my knightly faith," he said to her, "to do everything that depends on me to obey you—provided, however, that there are no spells, nor any magic, murder or perfidy."

"I like that promise," replied the fay. "Lying and knavery have never had charms for me, and my heart detests them."

The fire that shone in her beautiful eyes as she expressed herself thus made Raimondin understand how much she desired to reassure him with regard to his fears, by shoeing him a tender sentiment. He responded to it by the amour that he was beginning to feel; however, in order to have a greater assurance, he contented himself with saying; "Adorable Princess, why this constraint and these efforts, which distance you from my heart? It is tender, and does not stifle the flame that amour lights there. Speak clearly and render calm to your knight."

Thos words, long awaited, made such a strong impression on Mellusine that, no longer able to constrain the efforts of her tenderness—fays are not obliged to as much restraint as human beings—she replied: "I'm not making efforts to prevent myself from loving you; they would be futile; but before I render you service it's necessary to fulfill one condition, which is imposed on me, in order to love and be loved; I can only work for my husband. Swear to me, then, only to burn for me. But what am I saying? Are you not the husband that Destiny is sending me? I give you my faith; will you give me yours?"

"I swear to you," cried the knight, placing his hand on the breast of the goddess, only veiled by her blonde hair.

"That isn't all," the fay went on. "It's also necessary for you to promise me never to see me on a Saturday, nor ever to seek, out of curiosity, to know where I am or what I am doing on those days."

"Milady," Raimondin replied, raising his hand toward Heaven, "I swear, by honor, never to do anything voluntarily that might displease you; content to possess your charms and your heart, I shall only form desires for your felicity."

"We shall be married," said the fay—whom he did not know to be such—"and I shall love you without crime; you shall see how tender and zealous I am for my husband." And she presented him with her face to kiss.

"Now," said Mellusine, "I can give you the means of escaping the deadly consequences of your involuntary crime and meriting me; but don't forget a syllable of what I'm about to recommend to you. Return to the palace of the King of the Picts. When you arrive, all the hunters having returned, they will ask you for news of your uncle. You will reply that you lost sight of him at the beginning of the hunt, because as you advanced into the forest near the Soësve spring, you heard young women laughing who were taking a bath. Your curiosity piqued, you advanced to close range, in order to see what it was. One of them having perceived you, she emerged from the spring, veiled in her long blonde hair and stopped your horse in order to speak to you.

"While they're astonished by your adventure, the King's men will bring him on a stretcher made of two tree-branches and traverses of foliage, followed by the boar that has caused his death. People will run from all directions, and while everyone is in an astonishment of horror, a beautiful bird that has never been seen in these cantons will come to fly over the body crying 'Yapou! Yapou!' and will throw itself upon the dead boar. Immediately, everyone will say that it is your uncle's shade, which has come of its own accord to say that the boar has killed him—which is true, in a sense.

"People will admire the courage of the King, saying: 'The great and valiant Aymery is dead, but his enemy has not survived him; even in dying, and already sensing death, the valiant Aymery has given it to that monster, which no man alive today would have dared to attack.' He will be regretted, he will be praised; people will put on mourning, and, when the funeral is over, a day will be fixed to crown the young Prince, the son of the dead man, your cousin. He will be raised on the platform, in order that he succeeds, and all the lords will pay homage to him. You will signal yourself by appearing first everywhere, in homage, at the dead man's funeral and at the oath of allegiance. But on the eve of the homage to the new sovereign, you will return here, and I shall be waiting for you."

With those words, the lovely Mellusine made Raimondin the present of a ring in which a carbuncle was shining, wrested from the dragon of the Hesperides, saying to him: "Receive this first present, as a pledge of my faith."

Touched, softened, grateful, and above all amorous, Raimondin washed Mellusine's hand with tears, and kissed it a thousand times. He promised the lady an eternal fidelity, and Mellusine read in his eyes that he was sincere. That is why she said to him: "Go, dear lover. I see that you are the one that Destiny ought to give me. Oh, may I be more fortunate than my sisters! May I acquire *immortality*, and remain the eternal *protectress* of my descendants!"

After that wish, in which she pronounced the two words *immortality* and *protectress* in a very low voice, having difficulty pushing away the young Prince, whom she was almost clasping in her arms, she made him mount his horse again, and draw away. But he turned his head continually in order to see her, until the moment when the trees and the obscurity hid absolutely the sight of the most beautiful object there was in nature—for the fays are well above mortals for charms, the beauty of the features, and a certain enchantment, which holds the heart as if intoxicated, However, there are women who have that omnipotent charm; such are Oribelle and Dinameh, the two daughters of the beautiful Conchèse, Queen of Lagenia.

Now, there was still a law in the family of the fay Wrwcwcw, grandmother of Mellusine, which is that the daughters of that house who had remained virtuous could nevertheless only be immortal or fays after have brought into the world eight male children and eight daughters before the mortal who had married them had violated his promise not to see them on Saturdays. If he saw them before the sixteen childbirths, completed and perfect, the fay would become mortal, but would stay with him until the end of her days. If, on the contrary, the husband only violated it after the sixteen children, the fay would acquire immortality, but she would be forced to quit him, and the husband would perish of languor and ennui in very little time. Finally, he would not die and would remain string and vigorous, as long as he had not violated his oath not to see his wife on Saturdays.

Such courage is above humanity; no man has ever had it, and none every will have it. It is for that reason that Mellusine, wiser than nine of her elder sisters, had chosen the most virtuous and the most valiant man of his century, and, her good fortune having determined that he was also the most handsome, she would he happy for a long time. But no man is without some imperfection, and it seems that immortality is not made for him!

As soon as Raimondin had disappeared, Mellusine returned to her two companions, who were still bathing in the Soësve spring. One was named Circileneh, who was the Queen of Ultonia, the other Odolameh, who was the Queen of Connacy.

"Well, my sister," said the beautiful Circileneh, what have you been doing for such a long time alone with that knight?"

"I know before she says it," exclaimed Odolameh. "She gave him the living ring, by virtue of which he won't fall into any danger, for the ring will warn him.

"I also know," exclaimed a fourth fay who had come to find the three bathers on the part of Wrwcwcw, their grandmother, and who was named Agacalaneh. She was as beautiful as the dawn that rises every morning crowned with roses and azure; she was the cousin of all three, and was the Queen of Lagenia. Mellusine and the three cousins returned to their palace promptly, where the fay Wrwcwcw was waiting for them.

"My daughters," she said to them, on seeing them arrive, "I am content with you, and especially with Mellusine, whose prudence and penetration fill me with joy, for she has made the choice of a worthy husband today. Oh, my Raimondin never follows anything but the movements of his heart, without listening to the advice of others. But in the end, Fate has spoken... My daughter, marry Raimondin; Destiny wishes it and I wish it too."

Mellusine threw herself into her grandmother's arms, who hugged her to her bosom. The beautiful Mellusine only withdrew damp with tears, but they were of joy. The fay Wrccwcw immediately struck the pose of a goddess and said: "My daughters, let me predict your future.

"You, Mellusine, my very dear daughter, will be immortal, and the mother of sixteen children, eight boys and eight girls, who will reign gloriously in all the climes of the earth; for the eldest will succeed his father one day, who will be King of the Picts; the second will reign over the isle of Cyprus; the third in Armenia; the fourth in Flanders; the fifth will succeed among the Scythians of the icy lands, who will be Tsar; the sixth will reign in Pannonia; the seventh will pass over the sea and will civilize the peoples among whom gold is born; finally, the eighth will obtain the daughter of the Great Negus and govern the Ethiopians.

"As for your daughters, the eldest will marry the most powerful Prince in Europe, Lord of the Frankish Lords and will wear his crown with him; the second will marry the King of Bretagne, which will one day be named England; the third the Emperor of Germany; the fourth, the King of Spain; the fifth, the King of Denmark; the sixth, the King of Poland; the seventh, the Greek Emperor; the eighth the King of Scotland, from which will emerge one day, by the female line, the unfortunate Stuarts"—the fay uttered a profound sigh—"who will have merited their misfortune...

"As for you, Odolameh, you will marry the King of Connacy; one day, one of your descendants, the great Dadameh, Queen of Mommonia, will give birth to a hero, the famous Prince Oribeau, beloved by peoples, the honor of the human race; for he will reign as a man and not as an imperious master; he will have studied men under the guidance of a Sage; he will know that he is King for the people, and not for himself, and all his conduct will be directed by that verity; to the glory that he will acquire with give her the immortality of gods.

"At twenty-five years of age he will break the irons of an entire hemisphere; at twenty-six those of the former serfs remaining among his people; at twenty-seven he will give peace to the entire world, from the lands were the rising sun darts its first rays, on emerging from the waves to the climes where that star descends beneath the seas, in order to depart again at the same point and recommence its brilliant career; at twenty-eight he will show the purest and most disinterested virtue in returning to his allies what he has conserved for them by the force of his arms; at twenty-nine, he will be seen to welcome generously the heroes who have carried the glory of his name to distant climes and honor them as a father receiving his children, as a friend receiving his friends. The glory of that Prince will only be augmented thereafter, for he will have for a companion the most beautiful and most sensate of Princesses, and the greatest glory of a man is to have a good wife. O fortunate centuries, which will see such great things, I salute you!

"In your regard, Circileneh," Wrwcwcw said then, turning toward the second of her grand-daughters, "your glory will not be inferior to that of your cousins; you will love the Prince of Ultonia; I announce to you that one of your descendants, called Conchèse, will give birth to two daughters, who will do honor to their sex. Both beautiful, one will be beauty itself, united with virtue; I shall give her a beautiful bird, which will precede her everywhere, in order to protect her from the perils that will menace or days or her modesty; the other will not appear so fortunately born at first, but with time, and when her mind is enlightened by experience, it will guide her heart into the route of virtues; she will be blessed by the peoples of Lagenia and Meath, as Oribelle will be by the peoples of Mommonia and Connacy.

"And as for you, Agacalaneh, who are delicate and pretentious, you shall be Queen of Lagenia; a daughter will emerge from your loins who will one day be Queen of Meath, who will be subjected to a great proof imposed by my daughter Pucellomaneh; but if our descendant supports it courageously, there will be a remedy...

"Adieu, my daughters; I am returning to my aerial Empire, in which your semi-human nature prevents you from being able to dwell. For you know, by virtue of having come there sometimes with the aid of the great cloth bird filled with smoke, that just as the humans populate the surface of the earth and certain animals that of the waves, the surface of the atmospheric air is inhabited by light beings such as genii, of whom the fays are the wives; with the difference that, being lighter, it is the fays who have the principal authority there. The surface of the atmosphere is garnished with cities invisible to the gross eyes of humans, there is cultivation there; it produces diaphanous foodstuffs suitable for nourishing fays and genii, just as the surface of the earth produces vegetables and animals for the subsistence of material humans. Higher up, there exists in the ether, or subtle matter, of which the Sun is composed, sylphs and sylphides, which live there and which cultivate the surface of the Sun and the fixed stars from which they draw aliments.

"Finally, at the height of the atmosphere of Suns, are the beings that are like the fays of the sylphs, which are named, I believe, Urises. The beings whose importance places them immediately above those perfect beings are the planets, which are animate, like us; then the Suns, which are like he males of planets, comets and satellites. Finally, above the Suns we know nothing but God alone—which is to say, general Being, in which everything is, of which everything that exits is a mode: Being par excellence, in short, which unites by itself, in an infinite degree, all the existence of other Beings.

"Such is, my daughters, the religion of the fays, of which I have informed you; never forget it. Adieu."

As she finished this speech Wrwcwcw rose up naturally beyond the atmosphere—which is to say that she got rid of two quarter-pound weights that were holding her down—and in a few minutes, she reached the city of Paris, the capital of the realm of the fays, which corresponds to the land called France on the Earth. The four young demi-fays then withdrew into their palace, of which this is the disposition.

Between two rocks, on an esplanade of about four thousand square feet, built in precious marble, the middle of which rose to the clouds; for it was so high that, aqueous vapors incessantly surrounding it, as they surround the summit of high mountains, there is always a kind of lake there, perpetually filled with snow and ice, which accumulate there in cold and nebulous weather; the snows of that lake, gradually melting, at the slightest breath of a zephyr, furnish water to a spring that, falling in cascades, broke up and became very salubrious when they reach the kitchens of the palace; a single stream, guides by a stone channel, fell into a kind of reservoir, where beverages were put in summer to cool them.

The central building was destined to lodge Wrwcwcw and Pucellomaneh when they came to earth. The four lateral buildings only had the ordinary height of well- proportioned edifices; they were inhabited by the four young demi-fays, who each had only one, but the entire castle belonged to Mellusine. The pots and pans in the palace was magnificent, gold, silver and brass were seen shining there; the furniture was made of precious aromatic species of wood unknown in Europe, but which the fay Wrwcwcw had been able to find where they were, with the consequence that, in addition to the beauty of the hues, they exhaled an agreeable perfume, The beds, especially, were of a softness as yet unknown to humans. In brief, the palace contained all the commodities, the useful being combined there with the magnificent, the sumptuous and the voluptuous.

Mellusine, Odolameh, Circileneh and Agacalaneh put themselves to bed, because their mortal fraction, which they obtained from their fathers, had need of repose in the same way as us; but the only needed half as much; three hours of sleep was the equivalent of six, and to get up at nine o'clock was for them getting up at midday. In the same way, they only ate half of what the most delicate woman eats, but they combined it with the delicious nourishment of the fays, which Wrwcwcw furnished them. They were twice as penetrating as the most intelligent woman, lighter and hence more lively, more loving and hence more tender, etc.

But while they slept, and Mellusine had a pleasant dream about the handsome Raimondin, the young Pictish Prince arrived at Poitiers.

Everyone surrounded him in order to ask for news of the King, his uncle. He replied with what Mellusine had dictated to him, word for word. "I lost sight of my uncle while I was pursuing a frightful boar. The bird of death flew in front of me and seemed to frighten my horse with its cries." Raimondin added thereafter what Mellusine had advised him to say, and it was not without astonishment that he heard people reply to him the same things that she had announced to him.

He felt his confidence and his amour redoubling. The whole court was astonished that Aymery had dared to pursue the enormous boar, of which Raimondin gave a description; the great Prince's courage was admired.

"Oh, how he merits our praise!" said some.

"Let us run after him," cried others.

Even the Queen participated in the enthusiasm, and was eager to see the hero—but that was in vain; Aymery no longer existed.

Raimondin had just finished replying to the same question a hundred times repeated when it was perceived that the King's men, who had been searching for him in the forest, had found him dead. Eight were carrying him on a stretcher of foliage; sixteen others were dragging the monstrous boar on a hurdle of branches, but from a distance no one could yet make out what it was. A loud and groaning voice, which seemed to be emerging from the forest, then made plaintive tones heard. Meanwhile, the troop drew nearer. The dread redoubled; fear took possession of all hearts. The voice became louder—it was that of Mellusine, who, for the first time was warning the royal family into which her marriage was about to cause her to enter, of its misfortunes: "Weep, Picts! Weep for your Prince, who is no more! His courage, which had served him so well in war, was useless to him against the monster of the forests that has caused his death; but he has not withered his laurels; he has killed his enemy."

Immediately, all the inhabitants emerged from their houses. Some surrounded the Queen and consoled her; others ran to the body of the King and surrounded it, weeping. A few admired the enormous boar, fearfully, the menacing appearance of which was still terrifying.

But while everyone was desolate, a beautiful bird was perceived, which flew above the stretcher; it had three crests, a black body, a yellow tail and blue eyes. It uttered a shrill cry, which obliged the Queen to raise her tear-moistened eyes to Heaven, The beautiful bird struck her with admiration. Then, collecting herself momentarily, she cried: "It's the soul of my husband, who had come to bid me adieu! Dear Aymery, Destiny is separating us, but you shall see me eternal dolor!"

The bird uttered a further cry, so shrill that everyone trembled. No one doubted any longer that it was the response to the Queen's grief. Then the bird pecked the boar three times, and disappeared.

"It's a Yapou," said Raimondin, "which is native to the most distant countries."

The body of the King of the Picts was deposited in his palace; he was put on a bed, with his face uncovered, while everything was prepared for his funeral, which would take place on the eighth day, with pomp worthy of a King. The Queen had a great relief for her dolor at that lugubrious ceremony; she knew how much the King, her husband, had been cherished by the Picts. Each of them wept as if for a father.

When the Princess gave a great funeral meal, in which all her people were to take part, the enormous boar was served there; but its meat gave such horror to all the guests that a great fire was lit in front of the temple of Vananis, into which everyone threw the morsel of the boar that they had received—with the result that no one ate any of it, except for a celebrated glutton named Josselin; but he was observed and was seized by the young people, who coated him with molten pitch, rolled him on the ground where the funeral birds had been killed, and sent him home covered in feathers.

A few days after the funeral of Prince Aymery, while preparations were being made for the coronation of his only son, Bertrand, Raimondin stole away discreetly and took the road to the Soësve spring—the same one what originated from the waters of the central building of Mellusine's palace. After traveling for a few hours he perceived a mountain that he recognized. Having reached the summit he discovered the rock, the stream that formed the spring, the beautiful once-arid grassland that it watered and rendered verdant, and, at the end, Mellusine's palace.

He hastened to arrive there. He was received at the door by several damsels, who introduced him to their mistress' apartment. At the sight of her, Raimondin experienced such a keen joy that he could neither speak nor sustain himself. Everyone withdrew, in order to leave them at liberty.

"Calm yourself," said the Princess to her lover, "and remember that I love you."

"I need that precious assurance, for I cannot think that so much charm, above human nature, is reserved for a younger member of the sovereign branch of the Picts."

"It's your merit, not your birth that determines your fate," Mellusine replied. "Your future happiness depends entirely on you, and I have told you the condition. At that price I promise to enable you to succeed in all your enterprises..."

The beautiful lady was about to continue when a knight came in. He knelt before Mellusine and said to her: "The table is served, Milady."

"Let's go," said the Princess to Raimondin. "Come and refresh yourself."

She led him by the hand into a room where there were several tables, all sumptuously laid. She made him sit in the place of honor and sat down beside him. The carvers brought a large hollowed ox, the hide of which had been removed and which had been perfectly roasted. The ox contained an entire deer, filled with birds of every species, including pheasants, grouse, quail, woodcocks, herons, skylarks, thrushes and ortolans. What was most admirable of all was that all those animals were served by a waiter who released a living one of the same species while putting the roasted bird on the guests' plates.

When the pastries came, half were found to be full of wild ducks, grouse and skylarks, cooked and larded with young lampreys; the other half, of the same form, as soon as they were opened, released a living bird, which immediately flew away. At dessert, when the sugared items were served, it was as if there were little golden fishes swimming in the sweetened liqueurs. Finally, all those who were serving wore crepe over their faces, for fear that their breath might soil the dishes that they brought.

Raimondin, surprised by so much apparatus and magnificence, could not help asking Mellusine who all the gentlemen sitting at the inferior tables were.

"These lords are all at your service, my love," she replied.

After dinner, she took him to his apartment and made him lay down on a large bed, as soft as it was magnificent, in order to rest from the fatigue of his journey.

When the Pictish Prince was rested, he summoned a page, who informed Mellusine that he was awake. She came to find him immediately, and gave him advice, in order to obtain from the new King of Poitiers, in full sovereignty, the tract of land where the palace, the rock and the grassland watered by the stream of the Soësve spring were. You shall know shortly what means Mellusine suggested.

As soon as Raimondin was instructed, he departed again for Poitiers, in order to attend the coronation ceremony. All the Pictish lords knelt before King Bertrand and rendered him their homage. Raimondin's turn having come, he spoke to the young sovereign in these terms: "Would you be so kind, powerful monarch, and you, my lords, to listen to my request, and to grant it to me if it seems appropriate?"

Bertrand and the Lords replied that they would be charmed to oblige a Prince of the Blood who had always served the State so well.

"My Lords," Raimondin went on, "I shall ask you for a favor that might perhaps seem singular to you. It's neither a city nor a castle, but as much area, in full sovereignty, as I am able to cover with a deer-skin.

"I grant it to you," replied the King, "and I'll add that neither I nor my successors can ask anything of you there, nor claim any rights of justice there."

Raimondin thanked him and asked him for letters sealed with his own seal and that of the province. That was accorded to him, and the grandees of the kingdom sore to guarantee the gift grated to the Prince. That done, Raimondin went away.

As he left the King and the Court, Mellusine's lover encountered a man carrying a deer-skin, who asked him whether he wanted to by it.

"I would," replied the Pictish Prince. "What price do you put on it?"

"Thirty gold pieces."

"I will give them to you. Take it to my house quickly, for the bargain is concluded."

They went to Raimondin's house together.

He wanted to pay for the skin. "Wait," said the man. "It's necessary to carry out an operation." And he extended the skin over a table, and then cut it into thin strips, which he attached together at the ends. Afterwards, having bent down as if to pick something up, he disappeared without anyone seeing. Raimondin understood immediately that he was an envoy from Mellusine. He returned swiftly to the palace and said that the deer-skin was ready, if it pleased the king to name commissioners. King Bertrand named them without delay, and Raimondin left with two Lords, charged with delivering him the place he chose, in full sovereignty, in return for covering it with the deer-skin.

They arrived at the mountain that overlooked Mellusine's palace and Raimondin unrolled his strips The King's envoys, seeing such thin strips, were quite astonished; they did not know what to do. Then they saw two men dressed as peasants, who told them that they had been ordered to help them. They thought that they had come on behalf of the King, and, immediately deploying the skin, they extended it for two leagues around the wood and the mountain where Mellusine's palace was, which could not be seen because of the trees. As more of the skin remained, Raimondin employed it for the meadow, which was adjudged to him entirely, as well as the stream formed by the Soësve spring, which was capable of turning ten millwheels.

Raimondin and the two commissioners then returned to Poitiers, where they rendered an account to the King and the Queen Mother of what they had just done.

The Queen said: "There's something marvelous in all this, for Raimondin only made his request in order to have the mountain and the new spring, on the banks of which adventures often happen, and I'm convinced that one has happened to him. I beg you, Raimondin, to tell us about it."

"There's nothing more, my lady, than the commissioners have told you."

The King, who loved his cousin, did not want to interrogate him, for fear of mortifying him, and Raimondin withdrew.

As soon as he was free he hastened to return to Mellusine. He was advancing, pushing his horse hard and saying aloud: "Go, go, my friend. I cannot arrive too soon beside the-one-who-is-more-perfect-than-nature," when he perceived something moving in the bushes. He was convinced that it was a wild beast and, wishing to pay court to the Princes with it, he detached his spear in order to pierce it.

His arm was raised when a beautiful hind emerged from the bush and came straight toward him. Raimondin admired it, but as it came closer, his fascinated eyes cleared and he saw Mellusine herself. He leapt from his horse and ran to her. He kissed her, for his Lady extended her arms to him, and they remained there without speaking for a few moments, so emotional were they.

Finally, Mellusine spoke. "My dear love, you who are my happiness and whom my heart will cherish forever, listen to your mistress, who cannot live without you. Since you have done all that I told you to do, the secret obstacles are lifted; you will be my husband.

"This very day!" cried Raimondin.

"No, it's necessary to invite the King, the Queen, the Counts and the Lords to honor our marriage with their presence. That is an official condition; it's necessary that the King of the Picts, your cousin, and the Count of Forès, your uncle, consent to our marriage, without revealing my origin. Only tell them that you are not lowering yourself in allying yourself with me, and that the nymph of the Soësve spring, the source of which is in the clouds, counts great Kings among her ancestors. It's necessary that they don't demand to know any more;

it's up to you to determine that—if your love is true, it will render you sufficient eloquence."

"If love renders one persuasive, I shall succeed," Raimondin exclaimed.

He did not want to go as far as the palace, he was in so much haste. He kissed Mellusine's hand and remounted his fine horse.

"Bring all those you wish," Mellusine said to him, "and assure them that they will be well treated."

The two lovers separated then, without regret, because they would soon be reunited.

As soon as Raimondin had returned to Poitiers he went to the Court, in order to propose his marriage with the nymph of the Soësve spring whose source is in the clouds. The King, the Queen and the Count of Forès, who had come to Court to attend the coronation of the King, his nephew, showed the greatest surprise.

"My cousin," said Bertrand, "we are charmed to see you taking a wife, but it seems to me that you ought to have informed us of your design at the first moment."

"Don't be annoyed, my Lord," Raimondin replied. "Love has so much power over good hearts that it makes one forget everything; and in my case, I am so smitten that I could not speak."

"May we at least know with what family you are about to ally yourself?" said the King.

"I only know this, my Lord; she is the nymph of the new spring that has surprised everyone, and which is named the Soësve spring."

"Ah!" said the King, laughing. "The adventure is good. Raimondin is in love, Raimondin is marrying, and he does not know who his prospective bride is—perhaps not even her name?"

"My Lord," the Pictish Prince replied, "what I know is sufficient for me, and ought to be for you and milord my uncle, the Count of Forès—forgive me for speaking frankly. All that I know for sure is that I am marrying a Queen, who has three other Princesses in her palace, who are presently being sought by three great Princes. One is the sage Dunnaghall, Prince of Ultonia; the second is named Perforimoth the Severe, Prince of Connacy; the third is O'Connor, hereditary Prince of Lagenia in Evinland. They should soon return from their homeland, where they have gone to request the permission of their parents.

"That's very good," said the Count of Forès, "and if my Lord the King is content with what you say, I shall be content."

"I'm delighted that this marriage is turning to your advantage," said King Bertrand. "I pray that the gods protect you and grant you happy days. I promise you, in addition, that I, my mother, your uncle and mine, and all of our Court, will attend your wedding."

"My Lord," said Raimondin, "I hope that you will approve of my choice when you have seen the Princess, and that Milord my Uncle will give me his approval."

Having spoken thus, Raimondin bowed and left.

Then the King said: "This new and marvelous Soësve spring must be the effect of the power of a Fay who is protecting Raimondin." And from that moment on, King Bertrand seemed pensive and thoughtful. However, he sent word to all the Lords of his realm to come and receive his orders for attendance at Raimondin's marriage, in order that all should appear in their splendor.

For her part, Mellusine made preparations that would render the celebration the most pompous that had ever been seen in those cantons, worthy of the great King who was to honor it with his presence.

The Court of Poitiers spent a week in preparation, and on the Monday the King, the Queen Mother. Princess Gisèle, the monarch's sister, the Count of Forès and all the Lords of their retinue set out for the Soësve spring, guided by a dozen brisk gentlemen whom Mellusine had sent.

When they reached the foot of the mountain, they found Raimondin there. waiting for them. The King asked him for news of his future spouse. Mellusine's lover bowed without responding—which made the King anxious, as well as the Queen, Princess Gisèle and the Count of Forès; they feared that something unfortunate had happened. Meanwhile, all the Lords dispersed over the mountain, which belonged to Raimondin in full sovereignty, admiring the fact that a location that was previously a desert had become a place of delights in such a short time; for the spring of the central edifice had animated everything with its refreshing and salubrious waters, which irrigated the rich pastures.

At the end of the pleasant valley perfumed by the sweetest flowers, they saw the five buildings of the palace, the middle one of which was lost in the clouds. On one of the ridges of the mountain there was an artificial village destined to lodge the entire Court; it was built of wood painted in all colors and gilded, forming a dazzling visual effect. Over each door was inscribed the name of the Lord who was to inhabit the gilded house, which was surrounded by others devoid of decoration, painted in the colors of his livery, to lodge his servants, with stables for the horses. But the artificial palace destined for the King, the Queen and the Princess was superb, and as comfortable inside as it was brilliant outside, with the result that the monarch was amazed. The Queen Mother and the young Princess said to him that Raimondin's future wife must be a very great Lady to have had such beautiful work done in a week. Further away were the kitchens for the feast, garnished with an infinity of rare animals and delicate meats, with others coarser but succulent for the domestics. And that was not all.

Scarcely had the King and the Lords arrived than they perceived an elegant troop of nymphs and young men, who emerged from another artificial village further away. They came to mingle with the guests in order to do them the honors of such a beautiful abode and procure them all sorts of amusements.

It was in the midst of all that gallant apparatus that Mellusine appeared, accompanied by her three cousins, to whom three Princes were giving their hands—their lovers, who had just arrived from Evinland in order to marry them and attend Mellusine's wedding. The bride and her three relatives were wearing so many diamonds that they dazzled the eyes. King Bertrand, struck by their glitter asked Raimondin loudly whether the ladies were fays or mere mortals.

"My Lord," replied Mellusine's future husband, "all that I know for sure is that my Princess is worthy of being allied with your blood."

They immediately walked toward a temple built on a rock on honor of Vananis, in which the High Priest of Thor was waiting for the two lovers, to unite them in the presence of the gods.

"Milady," said the Queen to Mellusine, "I have never seen a Princess as richly adorned as you and the ladies accompanying you."

"They are my cousins, Milady," Mellusine replied, "daughters of the greatest Kings in the world. They are accompanied by three Princes destined for the throne, who will marry them on the same day; that is why you see them crowned with diamonds."

At the same moment, music was heard into the temple, to which a chorus of instruments deployed outside replied, with the consequence that before entering, the one inside appeared in the distance, and when they were in the temple, it was the one outside—which had an inexpressible charm that spread a mild languor in the soul.

The ceremony followed, with splendor. The pontiff joined the hands of Mellusine and Raimondin, blessed them in the name of Thor, Vananis and Friga, and the music responded to his benedictions with a charming concert. The other three couples were then united, separately.

Scarcely had the ceremony finished, however, than something like a cloud was perceived in the air; it was the fay Pucellomaneh with her chariot, borne by rocs and condors. She landed on the plain, where she took a few steps on the ground. Immediately, the four Princesses, her daughters, ran to salute her and embrace her. The fay commenced by receiving the caresses of Mellusine, whom she returned to her husband; then she had the other three nymphs climb into her chariot with their husbands, and as soon as all six were aboard, the rocs and condors, alerted by a golden thread that each was holding in its beak, rose up until they were lost to sight, leaving the King of the Picts, the Queen, his mother, the Princess, his sister, the Count of Forès and the entire Court in admiration. So today the elite of Parisian beauties see a Montgolfier or a Robertine[96] rise up; all eyes are fixed on the aerostatic balloon; gazes follow it until it is lost in the clouds; one believes that one can still see it when it has long disappeared...

While the fay Pucellomaneh took away three of her daughters and their husbands in her chariot, Mellusine, whom she had left behind, led the company to a superb pavilion erected in the middle of the meadow. A sumptuous dinner was served there, and everyone sat down at table, talking about the fay who had just risen up in her chariot. At each table there was a fountain of hippocras, so the cups could be refilled by turning a tap. No one could understand how the newlyweds had succeeded in procuring such a prodigious quantity. On the other hand, the valets served with an agility no less admirable than everything else; every gesture or movement was understood, and they often glimpsed the desire in the eyes and satisfied it before it had even been expressed. All the services were made on gold and silver trays, without the same ones ever appearing twice.

In those ancient times there were no feasts without tourneys. As soon as the dinner was finished, everyone got up from the tables and the knights got ready to joust. The bride,

---

[96] The Robert brothers built the first hydrogen balloon for Jacques Charles, which made its first manned flight on 1 December 1783 and made a flight of 186 kilometers in September 1784. Restif—his interest primed by having written *La Découverte australe par un homme-volant*—probably witnessed at least one of the ascents.

as well as the Queen, the Princess and all the ladies, was taken to a theater set up expressly, in order to be within range of seeing the knights who were to duel. The joust was opened by the King and the Count of Forès, who showed a great deal of skill. An unknown knight came forward then, but he did not want to fight either the King or his uncle; he contented himself with putting all the other Pictish nights out of the lists, who numbered more than thirty. While he inflicted such ravages throughout the nobility, at the moment when the irritated King was getting ready to fight him, another knight arrived clad in white, mounted on a superb charger, which did not appear to be of the local race. That was Raimondin, and the beautiful horse was a present from his wife.

Scarcely was he in the lists than the Count of Forès presented himself. Raimondin toppled his uncle at the first pass, but so cleverly that he unhorsed him without wounding him. Everyone was frightened, and people cried out from all directions: "Raimondin! Raimondin! Where is Raimondin? Let him fight the white knight!" But Raimondin could not fight himself.

The King was very curious to know who the white knight was. He put on his buckler and came to present himself with his lance lowered; but Raimondin, who recognized him, did not want to fight his King. Having perceived three or four newly-arrived knights, in order to show his strength, he charged in their direction and toppled them one after another. The entire arena of the tourney resounded with applause. Everyone shouted: "Long live the knight in white armor!"

As dusk was falling, everyone thought that the joust should end. The bride, the Queen Mother, the Princess and all the ladies were taken back to the artificial village in order to rest before supper and have the pleasure of bathing in the silvery stream of the Soësve spring. After they had washed their beautiful bodies they went to the great pavilion, where everything was ready for the first service.

It was then that Raimondin was recognized as the valorous white knight, because he came to lay the prize of his valor at Mellusine's feet. Immediately, the King, the Count of Forès and the entire Court gave him the compliments he merited so well.

The Count said to him: "I was ashamed of having been toppled, but since it was by the hand of my nephew, my fall turns to my glory, for it was by my blood."

"Was it not necessary," said the King, "that Raimondin vanquish everyone today, since love has rendered him the conqueror of the most perfect beauty there is in the world?"

Mellusine blushed, and had never been so beautiful.

"When supper had finished, she went out with all the ladies and the men started drinking, as was customary. It was then that the King said to Raimondin: "Another career awaits you, my cousin, for I perceive a knight who is asking for you."

It was the unknown knight who had fought first; the Queen and the other ladies had sent him to inform Raimondin that his spouse was in bed, in these terms: "Lords, bring Raimondin, I beg you; for his party is ready..."

That made all the Lords laugh, who retired, saying: "That generous combat needs no witnesses."

When the two spouses were finally together in their apartment, Mellusine opened her heart to Raimondin entirely. "My very dear husband," she said to him, "I thank you for the honor that your family has done me, and the secret that you have kept so well; above all, don't forget that by always keeping, it in the same way, you will become the most powerful of your family. On the contrary, if you divulge what you know, you will gradually decline and will die buried in forgetfulness. But let's turn away from such fatal presages and hope that the gods will protect us forever! I'll answer to you for a religious fidelity; you will never have the slightest cause for jealousy, and your happiness depends on you alone."

"Oh," said Raimondin, "those assurances complete it, and I can see very clearly that I haven't married an ordinary woman. Content with my glory and my felicity, I shall be as discreet as I am amorous."

His actions proved what he said, but the purple veil of amour ought to cover the chaste pleasures of spouses.

The next day, nevertheless, Mellusine got up early, as soon as dawn appeared, without waking her husband, and went, silently, to place magnificent presents at the feet of the beds of the Queen, the Princess and the ladies. Afterwards, she withdrew.

When the Queen woke up, having opened her curtains, she was struck by the gleam of superb vases in gold and silver, gems and jewels for her adornment, which she saw on a side-table. She sat up in order to consider them, and saw inscribed on a broad strip of vellum: *Presents from Mellusine, wife of Prince Raimondin, to the Queen of the Picts*. She made herself heard, and her women came in. The Queen did not say anything to them but got dressed promptly and went into the bedroom of her daughter the Princess, in order to make her party to what had surprised her so agreeably, but she had only taken one step forward when she perceived at the foot of Princess Gisèle's bed superb dresses, jewels and a hat ornamented with pearls, diamonds, rubies, sapphires and emeralds, so rich on its own that its value could not be estimated.

"Who is this Princess, then," said the Queen, "who can make such magnificent presents? Is she one of the fays about whom marvelous tales are told, or the daughter of some powerful Prince of Asia?"

She woke Princes Gisèle herself and went to find the King.

"My Lord," she said, "the presents that your sister and I have received announce in Mellusine a being above humanity."

"I shall discover who she is," Bertrand replied.

He went out immediately with the Count of Forès and encountered Raimondin, who was coming to pay his respects to him. He said: "My dear Cousin, tell me, I beg you, who your wife is? We can see that she is very highly-placed. Her grave manner, her noble bearing, and the distinguished grace of her attire all announce the daughter of a King, but we would like to be informed more clearly."

Seeing the Raimondin was not replying, the Count of Forès added: "My Lord, I am agitated by the same curiosity as you, and I was about to ask my nephew the same question; he has loved me too much until now to refuse me a clarification, which can only turn to his honor."

Raimondin was very afflicted by these questions, and was not able to hide it well enough for the King and the Count not to perceive it. On the one hand, he would have desired not to refuse anything to his Lord and his uncle; on the other, he was retained by the dread of displeasing an adored spouse, and even of losing her.

"My Lord, and you, my uncle, your request is just, and I sense all of its importance, and powerful motives oblige me to satisfy you. You have a right to know my wife's family. She is the daughter of a King who was very valiant and terrible to his enemies; she has permitted me to say that, but she does not want or intend any other title to prevail with regard to you but that of the nymph of the Soësve spring. I do not know any more than I am telling you, and I am content with it. I only seek happiness, not honors. I adore her; I am happy; all the rest is merely frivolity."

The King and the Count of Forès shook their heads, saying: "You'll tell us when it pleases you; let's not talk about it anymore and only think of enjoying ourselves."

The celebrations lasted for a fortnight, during which the noble guests were always served with the same magnificence; and such was the ascendancy of Mellusine that she won all hearts, to such an extent that neither the King not the Count of Forès asked any further questions of Raimondin until the departure.

The Princess and all the ladies left heaped with Mellusine's presents, while Raimondin gave ones as rich to the men, to the extent that the greatest Prince in the world could not have gone as far.

They escorted the King for some distance, after which the Queen and Mellusine separated.

Bertrand said then: "Don't you want to tell us the name of the King, your wife's father?"

"It's impossible for me," Raimondin replied.

"I won't ask you again," said the King. "Adieu, Cousin, and be happy, as I desire."

They—which is to say, the King, the Count of Forès and Raimondin—quit one another thus.

Raimondin return to Mellusine, who enquired curiously as to what the King and his uncle had said to him, and what he had replied. She was very satisfied with the Prince's sage restraint. "Every day," she said to him, "I congratulate myself more on my choice; it is as I had hoped; always be faithful to me and you'll see that you'll succeed."

When they had recovered from the fatigue of the celebration, Mellusine resolved to built a castle that would be memorable forever. She summoned a large number of masons and laborers, to dig trenches, fill in precipices and to make an esplanade at the summit of the rock, on which a fortress would be raised capable of sustaining a siege without being taken.

The work advanced rapidly; it seemed that the masons were up to the task. Towers were seen rising up everywhere, vaults forming as well as watchtowers, banks and gates. Everything was dominated by an inaccessible spur of rock. Raimondin's wife gave the castle a name formed from her own, Stai-Lusinan—which means "the dwelling, or palace, of Mellusine."

She gave birth to a first son, who was named Uriam, a week after the dedication of her new palace; it is from Uriam that the Princes of the Picts are descended. At the first visit that her husband rendered her, Mellusine, delighted to be a mother, took his hand and revealed to him that he had large properties in the kingdom of Bretagne.

"The traitor Josselin," she added, "has taken possessions of them; he is enjoying them with his son Olivier, after having excited against Errick de Leon, your father, the young Count

Galafre, the King's nephew, because of the confidence with which the monarch honored him and the good advice that Errick gave him. That is the usual crime of those who do their duty! The young Count was reprimanded by the King of Bretagne for a fault that he was made to commit by Josselin, who advised him to avenge himself in Errick. Galafre took his arms and lay in wait; when your father passed by the young Comte threw himself upon him, crying: 'Accursed instrument of my disgrace, pay for your cowardly treason!'

"Errick had only to turn around, and the young Count, devoid of experience, fell at the feet of the man he had attacked, by virtue of his momentum. Count de Leon, unaware of who he was, leapt upon him and snatched away his sword; disdaining to pierce him with it, contented himself with giving him a blow on the head with the pommel, which was sufficient to kill him. Such a prompt victory surprised your father; he wanted to see his enemy. Imagine his surprise and dolor on recognizing the nephew of the King of Bretagne. He ran home, took his money and, followed by one of his most faithful domestics, fled to the land of the Picts.

"There he found a Lady, whose name I cannot tell you, who helped him so well that in very little time he had a town whose fortresses put its inhabitants out of peril. He then obtained in marriage the daughter of the King of the Picts, the sister of your uncle Aymery, who killed the boar.

"That is what happened to your father. The traitor Josselin, who had animated the young Prince Galafre against him, denounced him as a murderer and obtained the confiscation of the de Leon lands; but it is necessary to go back there, and I would not esteem you any longer if you suffered his possession of them any longer. Go to Bretagne; you will find Count Alain there, your other uncle, to whom you must make yourself known. You must go together to see the King, of whom you will demand a trial by combat, in order to prove your father's innocence; and Thor who is just, will grant you victory."

Raimondin as so inflamed by this speech that he decided to leave immediately. The Princess, his wife, gave him more than five hundred knights, each having a varlet. Al Bretagne marveled at seeing richly-equipped gentlemen arrive, who paid for everything generously. Raimondin collected in passing his uncle Alain, who was in the King's disgrace since Errick's flight. They presented themselves before the monarch together, and Raimondin swore by Thor as to his father's innocence and demanded combat against his accusers.

The King said to Count Alain: "That's a noble and magnificent knight! If he is Errick's son and swears to his innocence, I ought to grant him combat against Josselin, who testified against his father by accusing him of my nephew's death and thus obtained the confiscation of his lands."

And the monarch summoned Josselin, who came immediately with his son Olivier, a tall and vigorous young man. Then Raimondin formulated the accusation against them, saying: "There are the traitors who accused my father falsely; I give them the lie and offer to fight to the death to prove them calumniators, for my father was only defending his life."

"You are a liar yourself," cried Olivier. "I am not guilty, for I was not born when your father committed his evil action, but I believe my father."

"You are a traitor," cried Raimondin, and you will bear the punishment for your father, the true guilty party, who will not be exempt for that, for I shall fight both of you and will purge the earth of monstrous flatterers who corrupt the soul of Kings."

"This is my pledge for my father and for me," cried Olivier, transported with anger; and he threw his gauntlet at Raimondin's feet, who picked it up, saying: "No respite; I'm ready; let's fight; the battle will decide the right of the matter, for Thor is just."

Immediately, the battle-horses were harnessed and the two combatants went to arm themselves. Raimondin came back with shield hung around his neck and his lance at his thigh, clad in a coat of arms embroidered with silver. He mounted his beautiful horse, entered the lists and came to make his submissions to the King and the Lords of the Court. Then he descended from is horse and went to the chair prepared for pronouncing the oath.

Olivier and his father Josselin appeared then; they saluted the King but they could not compare to Raimondin; their bad cause gave them a bad countenance. Olivier got down promptly and sat in the other chair to swear. The image of Thor was then presented to Raimondin, and he swore, on getting up, that Josselin was guilty of the crime of which he had accused him. Then he sat down. Josselin immediately got up, and swore, trembling and ill-assured, that he was not guilty. Olivier did as much, but with force and courage.

When the ceremony was over, a herald cried: "Let no one make any sign to the champions, under pain of being hanged." With that, everyone withdrew, and only those guarding the doors remained. Raimondin, Josselin and Olivier immediately picked up their arms and held them in arrest until the herald cried: "Let your horses go and do your duty."

Scarcely had the herald pronounced those words than Raimondin stuck his lance in the ground in order to secure himself in his stirrups. His enemy perceived that and spurred his own horse, lowering his lance, and came to strike Raimondin, who was not yet on guard. But the thrust, although rudely delivered, did not wound Raimondin and only knocked his lance to the ground.

"Traitor!" cried Mellusine's husband. "You make good use of the principles your parents taught you, but you can't escape me!" Immediately, he took the shield that was hanging from his saddle-bow, which was armed with three spikes seven inches long, and while Olivier was making a feint, he caught him by the visor and pulled it toward him forcefully, uncovering his face. Olivier lost countenance somewhat, but did not want to yield. He drew his sword, like a knight who has no fear of his enemy and made use of it courageously.

The combat lasted a long time without any marked advantage, but finally, Raimondin dismounted from his horse, picked up his lance and turned on his enemy, who from then on only sought to avoid death. He had a horse that served him well, he wanted to tire Raimondin out until nightfall; but Mellusine's spouse, seeing that the moments were becoming precious, took his horse's bridle in one hand and his lance in the other, and came to present himself before Olivier.

Josselin's son spurred his horse, believing that he could surprise his enemy once again, and struck at his breast; but Raimondin was able to parry the thrust. He threw himself on Olivier and struck the forehead of his enemy's horse so hard that the steel spike entered its head.

Josselin's son immediately let go of the bridle and spurred his horse, but without giving him any quarter, Raimondin fell upon him a second time and toppled Olivier with a thrust in the side at the same time as the horse collapsed.

Raimondin leapt to the ground and struck his enemy so rudely and so repeatedly that he robbed him of the strength to get up. He ripped away his helmet, put his knee in his stomach, gripped his throat with his left hand and took a knife from his belt with the right, saying to him: "Traitor, will you surrender or shall I plunge my knife into your throat?"

"I'd rather die under the hand of a valiant knight like you," the unfortunate Olivier replied, "than that of another."

Raimondin did not kill him, though, and asked him whether he knew anything of the treason.

Olivier replied that he knew nothing about it, not having been born then, but that he still sustained that his father was an honest man.

At those words, Raimondin took pity on a son who had merited a better father, and, knowing that he would be ignominiously hanged if he let him live, he struck him on the head with a gauntlet, which took away the little life that remained to him. He then dragged him by the feet, in accordance with custom, to the barrier of the lists and threw him over.

He turned to the King. "Sire, I have done my duty."

"Yes," said the monarch. Let Josselin and his son be hanged from an infamous gibbet."

"Mercy! Mercy! I'll tell everything!" cried old Josselin.

"If you tell me, I promise you mercy," said the King.

"Sire, since you no longer want anything to be hidden from you, the knight's story is true."

"I asked no more than that," said the monarch. "Let them be hanged, he and his son; the crime is too enormous to be pardoned."

"O King," exclaimed Raimondin, "don't assimilate the criminal treason of this old man to the noble courage and piety of the son. One has fought worthily and valiantly, out of duty to nature; he ought to be honorably buried, and I will render him the funeral honors. As for the other, he's an old man who can do no more harm; since my father is innocent and his glory and mine are untarnished, permit this old man, deprived of a worthy son and hence punished enough, to live on my land. I will redeem him from death."

Hearing Raimondin speak thus, the King, in his admiration, said to his courtiers: "That is a very disinterested man. But I am King to render justice in my Estates; let Josselin perish; let the de Leon lands be returned to Raimondin, and let all the calumniator's property be added to them."

That sentence was immediately carried out, but the generous Raimondin, to prove that he only had honor in his heart in making his claim, gave the de Leon lands to his uncle Alain, and Josselin's property to Errick, Alain's son, both of whom rendered homage to the King.

The Breton Lords, who had admired Raimondin until then, murmured between themselves, saying: "The knight must be very rich, if he only recovers such a rich heritage to give it to Count Alain and his son, who are already powerful."

A relative of Josselin, the Castellan of Orval, stoked up jealousy among the Breton nobility and indisposed them further; he formed a conspiracy against the valiant Raimondin, but it did not burst firth yet. There were celebrations and jousts, during which the Castellan of Orval tried to kill

Raimondin treacherously, but Mellusine's husband always emerged victorious, which made the King regret Olivier, for he said: "I had a valiant warrior, then, since he disputed victory for so long with this one, against whom no one can hold for an hour."

That speech by the King, misinterpreted, encouraged the conspiracy of all Josselin's relatives, who, believing themselves sure of a pardon, prepared secretly to kill Raimondin in the forest of Guerande when he returned home, as he had announced. They went to lie in wait for him there. But Raimondin, when he quit his uncle and his cousin Errick, saw the Yapou perch in a tree on the day of his departure, uttering shrill cries, and then fly toward the forest, as if to indicate an ambush.

"There's something in this," said Raimondin. "Let's arm ourselves and follow that bird, for it belongs to my wife."

That speech astonished everyone. Some six hundred men, comprising the knight's retinue, armed themselves. Four hundred went on ahead and the other two hundred followed, surrounding Raimondin. The bird was still flying, guiding them as far as the forest. It was then that Raimondin new the utility of the advice given by the bird and his wife, for eight hundred horsemen emerged from the wood and tried to surround him.

The Castellan of Orval, who only wanted Raimondin's life, said to three of his cousins, who were accompanying him: "Let us run at the murder of Olivier and Josselin!" At that moment, all four pushed their horses, lances lowered, and fell upon the Pictish Prince, who, struck by four blows at the same time, was knocked down with his horse. His horse got up, sharply pecked in the nostrils by the Yapou. Raimondin leapt up lightly, although armored; he struck the Castellan with such a rude thrust that he knocked him over and sent his sword flying away.

At that blow, the tumult increased; there was a pitched battle; the dead and the dying were trampled underfoot. The trumpet recalled the four hundred gentlemen preceding

Raimondin; they turned round and took the enemy from behind. The carnage became terrible.

Meanwhile, the Castellan had got up again. He was given a new horse; he reappeared at the head of his troop, reanimated it, and rallied those who were fleeing. But that new effort could do nothing against the valor of Raimondin and the knights that his wife had given him. The Castellan was captured and brought to Raimondin. Immediately, his troops disbanded and those who could took flight, the sole means of avoiding the death that the traitors suffered who fell into the hands of Raimondin's men; for Alain and his son Errick, naturally cruel, had all the prisoners hanged. That displeased Raimondin, who gave the Castellan of Orval a knight and four soldiers to guard him in order to send him to the King of Bretagne, along with all Josselin's relatives captured in the battle. The monarch, beside himself with wrath, disabused them in a deadly manner of the opinion they had had of him, for he had them all hanged without remission.

During Raimondin's absence, Mellusine had built the town of Lusinan, or Lusignan, as it is pronounced in Gaul; she had fortified it and flanked it with towers, one of which, higher than the mothers, was called the Trumpet Tower. On returning to it, Raimondin perceived the Trumpet Tower from afar and the high walls surrounding the new town. He thought then that he was not on the right road; but his surprise was soon greater when he heard the trumpets of the tower responding to the fanfares of its own, and he no longer doubted that he had gone astray.

He summoned one of the wife's principal knights and asked him: "Where are we, pray?"

"At the Castle of Lusinan."

"But what is that town and those trumpets I hear from the top of that tower?"

"My Lord," replied the knight, "that town has been built during your absence and those trumpets you can hear are announcing your return. All the inhabitants of the town will arrange themselves in two hedges to receive you."

While he was still speaking, Raimondin perceived Mellusine, who was coming to meet him, accompanied by all her ladies. The foremost, following the order they had received, cried: "Long live Raimondin, our Prince, husband of Mellusine!"

The Queen presented herself then, and embraced her husband tenderly. She said to him: "You augment my esteem and my tenderness every day; you have rendered honor to your father, but afterwards, you have proven nobly that you only wanted honor, by giving all our property to your uncle and your cousin. Do not grant them too much confidence, however, for they acted cruelly toward the prisoners. They do not have your generous and compassionate soul; perhaps one or other of them will be harmful to you one day."

"My dear wife," said Raimondin, "they are good relatives, but I will only give my entire confidence to you alone."

They entered the town, which was superb, and the two spouses went to the palace between two hedges of inhabitants, who all appeared to be rich and transported by joy.

Some time after Raimondin's return, Mellusine gave birth to a second son and a daughter. The son was named Odon, and later became King of Cyprus, having married Hermine, the daughter of the King of that island; and the first daughter, named Clotilde, is the same one who married a Frankish Lord, ancestor of Robert, who was the father of Hugues Capet.[97]

The third son, who was similarly born with a daughter, was named Gulon, and is twin sister Brunikilde; the son later reigned in Armenia, by means of his marriage with Princess Florie, the daughter of the King of that land, who was a relative of Mellusine; as for Brunikilde, she married the King of Albion, since named England.

---

[97] In one of the end-notes the author points out that the father of Hugues Capet was actually Hugues le Blanc; the latter was also known as Hugues le Grand, and his father had been named Robert.

The fourth son of Raimondin and Mellusine was named Antonin and the twin sister born with him Basine. The boy subsequently married Cristine, daughter of the King of Luxembourg, and his sister Cunegonde married the Emperor of Germany.

The fifth son was Renart, who married Aiglantine, the only daughter of the King of Bohemia, and Batilde, his twin sister, married the King of Spain.

The sixth son was named Godefroy Longtooth; he married Melide, the only daughter of the Duke of Austria, and his twin, named Audovaire, was given to the King of Denmark.

The seventh son was Frigimond, who applied himself to sacred things and was Grand Druid; his twin sister, the beautiful Minvanide, married the King of the Sarmates, later the Poles.

Finally, the eighth son, a very cruel man, was nicknamed Perforimoth the Severe, and he reigned in Evinland by right of conquest. He had four sons, between whom he divided the island, giving the eldest Lagenia, the second Mommonia, the third Ultonia and the fourth Connacy; and to ensure their rights he made each heir of a conquered kingdom marry four daughters of three of his mother's cousins, Odolameh, Circinleneh and Agacaleneh. As for his twin sister, who bore the lovely name of Pulquerie, her hand was sought by the Greek Emperor and became Empress of the Orient.

The eighth daughter came into the world alone and terminated Mellusine's fecundity; she was named Mary, and subsequently married the King of Scotland; her posterity frequently uttered piercing cries to Mellusine, for it was from Mary that the Stuarts emerged.

Mellusine did not only give her husband fine children of both sexes; the King of the Picts, the son of Aymery, having died of a fall from a horse while still childless, and the Count of Forès of old age, Raimondin succeeded them in their Estates, which he governed wisely, as much by virtue of the advice of Mellusine as the fortunate dispositions that he had naturally.

These are the towns that his wife built by means of her superhuman power: the castle and burg of Melle; that of Vouant; the burg and tower of Maxiant; the town and castle of Partenay; the town and towers of Larochelle; the town of Xaintes, which was then named Linge; the burg of Caumon, and that of Tamondois.

After all these labors, Raimondin and Mellusine were living happy and tranquil in their Castle of Lusinan when one day, the desire took them to go to Marmande to savor the pleasure of the country. They spent a few days of recreation there together, like a lover and a mistress, for Mellusine was still as beautiful as on the day of her marriage, except that she had more gravity, because she was the mother of a family.

Saturday having arrived, she withdrew alone and went to shut herself away as usual. Raymond was anticipating a whole day of boredom when he learned that his cousin Errick, the son of Alain—the one to whom he had ceded his property in Bretagne—had just arrived in Marmande. That news gave him pleasure, but he paid dearly for the amusement that the relative in question was to procure for him.

After having ordered great preparations to receive him well, he went to meet him, full of joy, and brought him to a superb hall where a splendid meal was served. They sat down at table, but Count Errick, not seeing Mellusine, about whom renown had published so many marvels, asked which a cha-grined expression whether the Queen find not judge him worthy of her company.

Raimondin was all the more struck by that complaint because it was the first one that anyone had addressed to him. Slightly troubled, he replied to the Count: "You'll see her tomorrow, Cousin; the Queen has never appeared on a Saturday in twenty-five years of marriage; but she'll prove to you tomorrow the pleasure she will have in seeing such a dear relative."

They drank and they ate. When their heads were slightly tipsy, Errick expressly pushing his cousin by often requesting more to drink, that curious relative insisted again on seeing the Queen.

"Tomorrow, tomorrow," said the King of the Picts.

"Not at all!" cried Errick. "I want to see her now; have her come."

"That cannot be," Raimondin replied.

"What!" said Errick, maliciously—because he wanted to know the truth about the rumors that he had heard. "Is there reason in what I've been told? I'm your relative; I have the right to speak to you frankly, and to open your eyes to things that would not be to your honor if they were true. Everyone say that she has intelligence with a druid, whom she only sees on Saturdays, but to whom she devotes all the day, even to your exclusion. Your prudence, Cousin, and you great courage belies it here; is it necessary for me, who comes from far away, to be the first to warn you what is happening in your own house?"

Raimondin, slightly drunk, lost his head at those words. He got up from the table, ran to his room, took his sword, turned is steps toward the apartment to which Mellusine had retired, and was stopped by an iron door that he had never perceived. He rotated the point of his sword, which as of fine steel, against the door, and succeeded in making a little hole therein.

It was through that hole that he saw a large marble basin fifteen feet in diameter, where there were steps down to the bottom, in which Mellusine was bathing tranquilly. Alongside her was a golden comb, with which she was combing her beautiful hair, and further away, everything she required for her toilette.

Raimondin immediately sensed his fault, and repented of having been too credulous. Sadness took possession of his heart, and, seeing that he had broken his word, he fell into a frightful despair and returned furiously to his cousin.

The latter, believing that the King had just been convinced and was punishing himself, cried: "You see, dear cousin, that I spoke the truth!"

"Flee, traitor, flee," cried Raimondin, "or this blade will cut short your days! Oh, gods, was it necessary that I should be too confident in this ingrate relative, to whom I have only done good? I'm losing an innocent wife, who loved me so much, and I'm losing her because of you alone."

"Without replying, Count Errick got up from the table, remounted his horse with all his retinue, and returned, in the sad thought that he had occasioned the death of the innocent Mellusine.

It was then that Raimondin, left alone, abandoned himself to the most cruel resentments, no longer against Count Errick but against himself; he accused himself alone of the fault he had committed, and spent in groans and tears the time until midnight, when Mellusine returned to her husband as she had quit him at midnight on Friday.

Raimondin heard her come in, fell silent and pretended to be asleep. Mellusine lay down as usual and placed her hand on her husband's heart, which she found beating rapidly—which caused her to anticipate some misfortune.

"What's the matter?" she said. "Has some accident occurred?"

Raimondin replied that he had a fever, but that he wanted to rest.

"Sleep, dear love," replied Mellusine. "You'll be better tomorrow."

Scarcely was it daylight when Mellusine got up. She opened the window to look at the weather. It seemed dark to her, but she soon realized that it was not a cloud but the fay Pucellomaneh, her mother, who was arriving in her aerial chariot.

"Ah!" she said to Raimondin. "Dear husband, have you violated our oath?"

The King of the Picts only replied with a profound sigh.

"Dear husband," the Queen cried, dolorously, "we're going to be separated! Oh, I'm culpable, for not having inspired sufficient confidence in you to prevent you perjuring yourself!"

"No, no!" cried Raimondin. "Only I am guilty!"

"A wife is never entirely innocent," said Mellusine "when her husband lacks confidence in her!"

Raimondin told her how the thing had happened.

"I'm immortal," replied the fay, "according to the rule that was imposed upon me, but that will only be for me to sense your loss eternally, dear husband! I shall flee into the caverns formed by the rock that is washed by the Soësve spring; I shall spend my days there watching over my descendants, and as soon as some misfortune threatens them, I shall warn them with my cries."

Meanwhile, the fay Pucellomaneh was descending slowly.

"Feeble Raimondin," she shouted, "I've come to take back my daughter."

"Take her, cruel woman!" cried the King. "But take my life at the same time."

"I shall let you live, to groan... Let's go, my daughter, come!"

But Pucellomaneh appealed in vain; Mellusine had fled through the wood and had retired to the cavern of the Soëvse spring. She only responded to her mother's voice with a piercing scream.

"Oh, my dear daughter," said Pucellomaneh, then. "I cannot oppose your resolution, since you still love an ingrate, but can I soften your fate!"

No, no!" replied Mellusine. "Rather soften that of my dear Raimondin!"

Immediately, Pucellomaneh had her rocs and condors depart, and she disappeared.

As for Raimondin, he died of grief in a short time.

Since that cruel separation, Mellusine watches over all the royal families emerged from her and Raimondin, either personally, among the Picts and the Franks, or throughout the world by means of her Yapou.

O'Barbo and the young Prince thanked Debundeh for the tale that he had just told and they got up to follow the flock, which was beginning to disperse. It was taken into a lush pasturage and, the four individuals having assembled afterwards to have a snack, Cahincaha reminded the shepherd of another tale that he had so far only told him once. They chose a comfortable spot, and the dwarf was getting ready to resume speaking when he was delayed momentarily by Oribeau.

"I didn't know that story," said the god Ennisleague. "Well, I bless Thor and Vananis for having allowed me to live this long..."

Meanwhile, Kerry drank a few gulps, and when he had moistened his palate, he resumed speaking.

"I was saying that the dwarf, ready to narrate, was stopped momentarily by Oribeau..."

Evening VI

Chapter 2E
Exposition of the moral of the tale of Mellusine. Connection with the Second Tale: The fay Sireneh.

Extremely astonished by what he had just heard, the young Prince of Mommonia asked the shepherd to tell him whether be believed in fays.

"No, but all that is allegorical. In any case, the marvelous is required to attach the attention of youth. Mellusine isn't my invention, of course; I'm conforming to the popular tradition. And the denouement presents a beautiful moral, which is that as soon as confidence is lost between two spouses, their happiness is destroyed forever. The tale I'm about to tell you is perhaps even more moral; the subject isn't new either; it's an allegory that has run around among all peoples, each of which has embellished it in its own manner, fundamentally and circumstantially."

There was once a fay was malevolent as she was beautiful, although those two qualities, beauty and malevolence, seem contradictory. Pucellomaneh had had her of Merovée,[98] initially a muleteer and then leader of one of the Frankish tribe that devastated and conquered the Gauls.

Now, such was the rule imposed by Perforimoth the Black that Pucellomaneh could not constrain the inclinations

---

[98] This name has obvious associations with that of Merovech, the legendary founder of the Merovingian dynasty of Frankish kinds, after whom they were supposedly named. History says nothing about him, but legend dropped vague hints about his being the descendant of a sea-god, which lends him a vague connection with Sireneh via her name, the mythical sirens being daughters of the river-god Achelous, and to the story of Circe, whose mother was supposedly an Oceanid.

of her daughters. Little Sireneh was therefore entirely willful, not listening to any of her governesses, for the reason that she was superior to mortals by virtue of her mother.

When she had grown up—which is to say, when she was fifteen, Pucellomaneh asked her, as she had done her eight older sisters, Semiramis, Eurydice, Sappho, Olimpias, Phryné, Cleopatra, Berenice and Zenobia, that she should choose, in order to be happy in future, between three things that she proposed to her: firstly, to marry a sylph, who would regard her as beneath him, because she was only a demi-fay; secondly, to consecrate herself to the worship of the great Ether, the source of all the fire that exists in the universe, and by that means, to elevate herself to the rank of perfect fay, either becoming the purifier of everything mortal there was within her; or thirdly, to spend her life in sensual pleasures, which would lose her that which she had of the fay in order to render her entirely a woman, but with the advantage that she would be able to take, and make others take, any form she wished, as soon as they had eaten something in her home or participated in her favors.

Sireneh reflected momentarily, and as she had a reason much more highly developed, although she used it badly, she settled on the third choice—which made the fay sigh, for she believed that her daughter had a bad character. But as I said before, such is the law among the Fays, Sylphs and Kings, that when they have reached the age of reason, each can choose their way of life; fortunate is the one who chooses well!

The fay could only employ exhortations, much as a Queen Regent does in handing back the reins of government to her son the King; he can do as he likes.

"Daughter," Pucellomaneh said to the young Princess, "the choice you have just made will not render you happy! On the contrary, you're preparing cruel punishments for yourself."

"I'll support them," replied the demi-fay. "but I want a life that has keen pleasures, or I prefer death."

"You can only die after having lived; that's the difference that your birth puts between you and mortals by both parents. The latter can die whenever they want; you, on the contrary, by conducting yourself sagely, might be immortal; by leading an excessive life you'll live for a hundred years at the most, and you'll have all the symptoms of old age at eighty."

"A hundred years!" exclaimed Sireneh. "That's more than I would have asked for. Come on, I want to exercise my rights right away."

"Oh, my daughter," cried the fay, "I'm being cruelly punished for the involuntary fault I committed on seeking out your father! Reflect again. I love you tenderly, and to prove it to you, I'll change this desert island made by the two branches of the Shannon into a superb palace." Ceasing to speak, the fay lifted her arms, and at a sign made by a long golden wand that she always carried, ten thousand genii appeared and as many common fays, who built a superb palace on Urilove Island, surrounded it with magnificent quays, planted trees of every species there, with the trunk, foliage and fruit, and thus formed delightful gardens in a trice, the trees of which would not suffer transplantation.

The palace was furnished voluptuously and the fay instructed an old peasant fay to keep the grain-lofts, pantries and cellars of the palace perpetually full of provisions, and to fill two cabinets, one with gold and silver and the other with diamonds and pearls. All of that was completed in three days, during which Pucellomaneh left Sireneh to her own devices.

On the third day the mother-fay reappeared. "You can see how much I love you, my dear daughter," she said to Sireneh, "by all that I've done for you. Change your plan of life while you still can; I have experience and I assure you that the first two proposals I made you will render you as happy as one another, while the third will be fatal for you."

"I've chosen," replied Sireneh, rather harshly, "and I won't change my mind."

The mother-fay sighed and went away; Destiny did not permit her to insist any further. Pucellomaneh was even forced to leave two very ugly dwarfs and two hideous female dwarfs with her daughter, in order to follow her orders.

As soon as Sireneh found herself free, she was only embarrassed by the choice of pleasures; she was ignorant of them all. In order to instruct herself, she consulted her two female dwarfs.

Luxuriette,[99] the uglier one, replied: "Milady, we'll teach you, my sister Friandine and I, one for one thing and one for another, and when you want to have your orders carried out outside, my brother Debauchin will go anywhere; if you want to amuse yourself in the interior of the palace, with things that require the arm of a man, my other brother Crapulophile in devoted to your will. Speak—or order me to suggest ideas for your amusement to you."

Sireneh smiled. At first she had only considered the two female dwarfs Luxuriette and Friandine, with repugnance, and the two male dwarfs Debauchin and Crapulophile with horror, but that speech reconciled her perfectly with the four monsters. She even saw them with pleasure assembling around her and presided over the council they held regarding the best means of amusement.

Luxuriette opened the session.

"You're young, you're beautiful, you inspire desires, but it's necessary that everything relates to you. You're too wise to think about having children, who will torment you one day and make you grow old. If you have any nevertheless, it's necessary to expose them, to let anyone who wants them take responsibility for them. You must obtain the submission of the men who have pleased you, and if the servile instrument of your pleasures displeases you, you must annihilate him, in order to savor the pleasure of change incessantly. You must avoid amour but if, by chance, that passion enters into your heart, it will be necessary temporarily to give me a fraction of your power, which consists of metamorphosing men into animals."

"I'll give it to you," said Sireneh.

---

[99] *Luxure,* in French, means "lust." *Friandise* means "gluttony."

"Do you swear on your faerie?"

"I swear on my faerie that I will cede to Luxuriette half of my power of metamorphosing men into brutes, to use as she wishes."

"That's sufficient. As soon as I see you smitten, I'll immediately turn your lover into an animal so hideous that you'll soon be free. I also have, by myself, the power to show nakedly the most secret thoughts of every human being, and I'll take advantage of that for your profit. What pleasures you're going to savor!

"And when Milady is weary of them," said Friandine, "she'll hand her over to me. I'll prepare her the most delicate dishes; I'll assemble in her cellars the most exquisite wines in the world and the finest liqueurs; she'll savor the pleasure of good cheer, then that of drunkenness; then…I'll hand her back to my sister, who will put her back in the arms of voluptuousness."

"You speak as if you can do everything!" exclaimed Debauchin. "Who will bring you the handsome men? Who has been assembling those wines, liqueurs and delicate dishes here for a long time?"

"Me, it's me," Crapulophile put in, "who will give them seasoning; it's via me that you'll enjoy, without wearying, lust and gluttony, drunkenness and debauchery, delightful crapulousness! It's me who served Sardanapalus, Chilperic, Mustapha and many others; it's me who rendered them happy. They've been criticized, but they enjoyed themselves. All the other advantages of mortals are mere smoke."

"I abandon myself to your zeal," Sireneh replied. "Don't leave me the time to desire, for desire makes me impatient."

The four monsters smiled, and went to their posts—but Luxuriette's was beside Sireneh.

Her first concern was to give the demi-fay adornment, something so provocative and at the same time so well-adapted to her genre of beauty that no one would be able to see her without feeling the keenest desires. She set her at the window of her palace, which overlooked the highway from the famous city of Rome to the famous city of Dublin, in order that she would be seen by all the Princes, all the knights and all the handsome men traveling from either of those two great cities to the other.

A handsome cavalier was just passing, with his bow in his hand and his arrows in his quiver, gracefully attached behind his back. Sireneh looked at him very attentively.

"Shall I invite him in to refresh himself, Milady," said Luxuriette.

"No, no," said Sireneh, sighing slightly. "I dare not."

"What! You're timid with regard to a man! You, Fay! Think, then, how far you are above him."

Those words reassured Sireneh; she made a sign to the cavalier, whom the monster's *psst* had caused to raise his eyes. He stopped, surprised, and as if in ecstasy, for the trees that surrounded Urilove Island had hidden they fay's palace from him until that moment, and he was seeing it for the first time. As the arm of the Shannon by the side of the road was very narrow, the cavalier saw all of Sireneh's beauty; she alone existed; without her he would have admired the palace greatly, but he scarcely paid any attention to it.

"Princess, or Fay," he shouted, "tell me how it is that this island, previously deserted, has been changed into a delightful garden and covered with a palace worthy of Worden? How, above all, does it contain such a touching beauty?"

Luxuriette, who had retired behind the Princess, showed herself immediately and replied to him: "Young cavalier, turn the bridle of your horse and go to the west of the isle; there you'll find a superb drawbridge made of cedar, ebony and campeachy; a dwarf who guards it will lower it as soon as you have pronounced the two words *Foudre-Love*.[100] Go, and don't forget them."

---

[100] The "magic words" are given thus in the original, deliberately adjoining the French word for "thunderbolt" or "lightning" with the English term, and leaving no further doubt as to the intended significance of the island's name.

The cavalier could see all that there was of the marvel-ous, but he was too valiant to be frightened; he was unaware that when one has to combat sensuality, it is in the manner of the Parthians and the Massagetae, while fleeing. He went back to the west of the isle, and as he turned he perceived the dwarf guarding the bridge, who was amusing himself playing with a donkey and a pig, his two favorite animals.

"As soon as Debauchin saw the cavalier, he put on a gra-cious expression in spite of his ugliness and shouted to him: "Young stranger, what renders you so bold as to approach this bridge confided to my guard? For know that I am the guardian of this delightful isle, named Urilove Island, inhabited by the Miracle of Beauty, young Princess Sireneh, whom her mother, Queen Pucellomaneh, has imprisoned here in order to guaran-tee the virtue of the young virgin from the attacks of man."

The cavalier, angry at the dwarf's audacity, shouted to him: "Lower the potences,[101] in order that I can enter the is-land and the palace."

"No!" said the dwarf, laughing. "There are two powerful words, which alone can open the passage to you. Pronounce them, and these beams will fall on to their supports."

Then the cavalier recalled the two words the Luxuriette had spoken. "Foudre-Love!" he cried.

At those powerful words, the donkey stated braying and the pig squealed, to which their females replied, and the draw-bridge descended gravely, offering the cavalier a comfortable, solid and spacious passage. He entered the isle feverishly; immediately, the two bridges were raised again and their chains were lodged in iron crampons.

The cavalier dismounted. The dwarf showed him a sta-ble, equipped with everything necessary. Debauchin unsad-dled the charger himself and his brother Crapulophile, who

---

[101] In French this word can mean "crosspieces," but it can also mean "gallows." Its English meaning, the quality of being potent, adds a further layer of sexual symbolism that might or might not have been intended by Restif.

had arrived, took responsibility for guiding the cavalier into the palace.

Finghall—that was the cavalier's name—followed the second dwarf, who first took him to the kitchen, where the dwarf Friandine was.

"It's necessary to refresh yourself," the male and female dwarfs said to him. "You'll appear more advantageously before the Princess."

"No, no," said Finghall, "I'm in too much haste to see her."

"You can only talk to her after you've taken your boots off, put on new underwear and a superb coat that we're going to give you."

"I want to appear as I am!" cried Finghall, swearing.

Crapulophile and Friandine smiled and said: "It's necessary to oblige you, but at least take a glass of this fine wine, whose gleam surpasses rubies; she how it shines! It comes from France, and the King of the land doesn't drink a better one."

"I only want a glass of beer or honeyed liquor," replied the cavalier.

He was served honeyed liquor in a goblet made of a single ruby, which had the same appearance as the wine. Finghall put it to his lips in order to taste it; he found it too delicious and rejected it without swallowing it. He got up immediately and told the dwarf to take him to the young Princess.

"We'll summon the one who ought to introduce you," said the two dwarfs. Immediately, they whistled, but with so much accord that their whistles rendered the most harmonious sounds.

Luxuriette appeared. "Ah, it's you," she said, recognizing the cavalier. "Is he refreshed?"

"No, he didn't want to taste anything."

"You can appear before the Princess nevertheless," said Luxuriette. "Come." And to her two comrades, she said: "You prepare a delightful snack; I believe the gentleman is too courteous to refuse to take part in it with the Princess."

She took Finghall to Sireneh, who received him blushing.

The cavalier was amazed by the charms of the ravishing Beauty, but an idea occurred to him: *Perhaps she's an ugly old woman who has only put on a deceptive appearance...* And that idea cooled him down.

He remembered that he had from the fay Wrwcwcw, the protectress of his family, a secret to destroy charms. He made use of it immediately.

"Pardon me, Milady," he said to the Princess, "but would you come on to this terrace?"

Luxuriette, who had read his thought, made a sign to her mistress to go out into the daylight. Then the cavalier took a magic glass from his pocket, which had the power of reassembling the sun's rays and dissolving the charm surrounding a decrepit old lady—but Sireneh only appeared even younger.

"Oh, Milady," cried Finghall, "how beautiful you are!"

Sireneh smiled, blushing, which embellished her further. She had had such tender sentiments for the cavalier at first that she had said to Luxuriette: "If this one wants to love me, I sense that my heart will be fixed on him; I'll ask my mother for him as a husband and bring joy to his heart"; Finghall's conduct however, the motives of which she had penetrated, indisposed her toward him and made her want to avenge herself.

As she was unaccustomed to it, she was not able to disguise the movement of her eyes well enough for the cavalier not to see something harsh there. He was suspicious, and remembered another admirable secret, which he had from his mother, who had it from the fay Wrwcwcw; it consisted of an operation that resembled somewhat the art of drawing. One took a pencil; one looked at a young and pretty woman; one sketched all the lines without filling them in, without shading them, and one had her face stripped of flesh, as it would be at eighty or a hundred years of age.

Finghall asked for a pencil and vellum. Luxuriette, who needed to see him operate in order to read his thoughts, gave him what he requested. He drew the beautiful fay; the attention he gave to that work cooled his heart again, which became tranquil, and when he had finished he kept his eyes fixed upon it.

Luxuriette, surprised by all that she saw, said to her mistress, in the language of the fays, which mortals cannot hear: "*Sacamadeh; tolosebeh; souramih; sosquédémah!*"—which is to say: "This man is protected by some powerful fay; in order to subjugate him, a powerful amour is necessary, such as you felt at first." In the language of the fays, as you can see, each word expresses an entire idea.

In staring at the sketch that he had just made, Finghall really saw Sireneh as she would be at a hundred years of age; the talisman that operated by the power of the fay Wrwcwcw, showed her aquiline nose entering her mouth; her vivid eyes extinct and red; her rosy cheeks taking on the color of a lizard's belly; her reed-like waist encircled; her square back rounded; her slim legs bent; her supple and delicate feet covered in calluses and wrinkled.

The knight made a gesture of disgust. "Adieu," he said, without looking at Sireneh. "I have urgent business, which doesn't permit me to give my time to *girls*. My friend Rathemor is waiting for me help against his enemies, and I'm reproaching myself for the time lost."[102]

He went out immediately, without Sireneh having had any power over him, and he went to get his horse. He heard whinnying on an esplanade of grass that was on that was at the western tip of the island. He called: "Come, my dear Northailade" Come to your master." The horse was accustomed to obeying his voice, but it did not come.

Annoyed, Finghal advanced in the direction from which he had heard his horse's whinnying. He saw a beautiful mare, which was delivering itself to the pleasures for which Friga inspires the desire. He ran to his charger, cracking his whip so

---

[102] Like Finghall (Fingal), Rathemor (Rathmore) is an adaptation of a name taken from Ossian.

loudly that the entire island echoed it, but what was his astonishment and dolor when, approaching, he only found a donkey! The mare kicked twice and drew away.

Finghall tried to dissipate the charm that was disguising his horse, but his efforts were futile. Northailade started braying and fled into a clump of trees, farting.

The desolate Prince looked for the dwarf, in order to chastise him for his negligence in guarding his horse, but he searched everywhere without finding him.

The drawbridge was lowered; Finghall passed over it, and as soon as he had set foot on the ground the two chains were raised. Then he saw the dwarf Crapulophile descending from the tall tree in which he had been hiding, who shouted to him: "If you'd eaten and drank before presenting yourself to the Princess, none of that would have happened to you. Adieu, handsome gentleman; you'll never enter this isle again."

Finghall went away on foot, therefore, very annoyed by his adventure. When he was opposite the window at which he had first perceived Sireneh, he only saw Luxuriette, to whom he complained about the loss of his horse.

She burst out laughing and replied to him: "Come and take him back. It's a trick of the dwarf; I'll return your horse to you, on condition that you taste the snack that has been prepared for you..."

At the same time, she opened a window, whose panels extended from one bank to the other, and showed him the meal, set out. Finghall was tempted, but a secret voice told him that it was better to lose his horse and continue his route to the next village, where he could obtain another, such as he might find it. He therefore walked for about two hours and finally arrived at a village called Rocelib, where he asked about the palace on Urilove Island, the Princess who lived there, etc. No one appeared to know anything about it.

Was it an illusion? he wondered. *But it's only too real that I've lost my beautiful horse Northailade!*

He sent two peasants, who were joined by twenty others, to ascertain the truth, while he looked for a horse, which he could have saddled while he ate dinner.

The Rocelibans ran with all their might; they soon arrived at Urilove Island and were strangely surprised to see the delightful gardens, a superb palace, a drawbridge and, at the windows, a beautiful Princess, two female dwarfs and two male dwarfs. There was also a mare with a donkey, which she was leading by the halter and which she was kicking, a pig, and another donkey, which appeared at the portal of the drawbridge. After examining everything, they went to make their report, which caused such great astonishment throughout the canton that people never ceased to come to see those marvels, rumor of which reached the ears of the Prince of the land, named Dermid.

As for the brave Finghall, seeing that he had not been mistaken, he chose a good horse and continued his route until he had arrived in the Estates of his friend Rathemor.

As soon as Prince Dermid was informed of the existence of the marvelous palace of Urilove Island and the beauty of the Princess, he formed the resolution of going there in disguise, to see everything for himself.

He soon arrived as he at Urilove Island; his surprise was extreme on seeing the superb palace and the magnificent gardens, but it increased even further when, having arrived opposite Sireneh's windows, he perceived the beautiful princess, who smiled at him. He was alone at that moment; on his orders, his retinue had remained behind a clump of trees that hid it from sight.

He responded to the Beauty's smile with an obliging salute. Immediately, Luxuriette called to him: "Handsome cavalier, go down a little further, following the course of the river; at the western tip of the isle you'll find a drawbridge guarded by a dwarf. Pronounce the word *Foudre-Love* and the two beams will be instantly lowered on to their supports, and you can come and refresh yourself in this delightful abode."

Dermid spurred his horse and arrived at the drawbridge in a trice.

"Open up!" he shouted to the dwarf, who was playing with his donkey and his pig.

Debauchin did not seem to hear him.

"*Foudre-Love!* Open up, then!" shouted the Prince.

Immediately, the drawbridge came down of its own accord and the Prince entered the island—but the two beams rose up again and close the passage to the Prince's retinue.

Without being astonished, he said to the dwarf: "Take me to the Princess that I saw at her window, for I can only perceive tortuous paths through the bushes and I don't know which route to follow.

"Lord," the dwarf replied, "I'll hand you over to my brother, who will take you to my elder sister, who will take introduce you without delay to my younger sister, who will take you to the Princess. But you seem to me to be very weary; I have an excellent French wine here—would you like to taste it?"

At the same time he poured the Beaune into a ruby cup.[103]

The Prince was thirsty; he drank it in one draught. The dwarf sniggered joyfully and conducted Dermid to Crapulophile. On the way, a sweet odor was exhaled by a flowery bouquet garnished with violets, lilies-of-the-valley, lilies, tuberoses and red, white, yellow and mottled roses.

"That odor is delicious," the Prince said to his guide.

"That's nothing, Lord; you're going to smell one a hundred times more agreeable when you approach Princess Sireneh, my mistress."

The dwarf had scarcely finished speaking when Dermid's sense of smell was agreeably struck by the perfume of the delicious dishes that Friandine was preparing.

---

[103] Beaune is a well-known *appellation*, but it is probable that Restif has a *double entendre* in mind; *beau-âne* would mean "fine donkey."

"Come closer, handsome cavalier," said the female dwarf, "and taste the sauces I'm making. See these delicious dishes! They'll be served to you as soon as you've saluted the beautiful Sireneh, my mistress."

As she finished, she presented the Prince with a mouthful of what she was preparing, with poultry, game and fish. Dermid took a few mouthfuls and found the taste of the dishes exquisite.

Meanwhile, Luxuriette came forward. She took the cavalier by the hand, and as soon as she had touched him, he felt a devouring fire flowing through his veins. He pressed her to take him to the young beauty that he had seen at the window. The female dwarf introduced him into a voluptuous and magnificent room, at the back of which he perceived Sireneh, sprawling limply on a big bed. Full of ardor, Dermid ran to her, and knelt down.

"I adore you, Celestial Beauty," he said to her, "And I shall grant all your wishes. Speak, dispose of my fate!"

"Handsome cavalier," the perfidious Sireneh replied, "I am young and naïve; I do not understand the language of gallantry; however...what you say...flatters my ears agreeably..."

At these words, insidious and true at the same time, Dermid stood up, transported; he pressed the fatal Beauty in his arms; he could not command his desires...

But it was too late. Sireneh could not succumb with a mortal until he had resisted other attacks. She looked at the Prince with a disdainful smile. "Moderate that audacious haste. May I know who my vanquisher is, and if he is worthy of me?"

"Beautiful Princess, or rather, young Fay," replied the feeble Dermid, "You do not have to blush at your lover. I am the King of Ultonia and I descend in a direct line, at the sixth generation, from the great O'Boruma, of whom an Oracle predicted that his posterity would one day unite all Evinland under his laws.

"I know from my mother," Sireneh replied, "that the Boruma family, sons of Kemiredi, which will one day be named the O'Brinne or O'Brien family, will be covered with glory and honors; but, King as you are, and whatever your nobility, you have fallen into my nets and I can dispose of your fate."

In the meantime, she picked up a Japanese porcelain cup full of water, which she threw in his face.

Dermid immediately fell on to all fours, and started to bray when he tried to speak.

Such was the first trial of Sireneh's power. The two female dwarfs and the two male dwarfs burst out laughing. Sireneh was delighted herself with the power to do evil. Debauchin put a bridle on the new donkey and Luxuriette climbed on top of it, made it run, trot, walk and perform all kinds of maneuvers—which amused the Princess greatly.

Afterwards, they took the donkey to the stable, where Debauchin's was lodged, along with his pig, as well as Finghall's horse, now a donkey—and the metamorphoses of those two new colleagues were so similar that it was necessary to put a mark on the newcomer in order to be able to recognize it. Luxuriette thought that mark ought to be a *salière*,[104] and gave the unfortunate Dermid the name of Insiposubolaneh, which, in the language of the fays, means "he has lost the salt of his wisdom."

Meanwhile, the men following the Prince asked to enter the island. Sireneh, still timid, was reluctant to receive fifty

---

[104] This is a complex play on words; *salière* normally means salt-cellar, but it can also mean a kind of groove or hollow— modern dictionaries offer the example of a groove above a horse's eye, but one eighteenth-century dictionary cites "the hollow that thin women have at the height of the breast." Presumably in illustration of the latter meaning, the original text puts a long s in brackets after the word, while the translation offered of the name in the language of the fays attributed to the new donkey echoes the connection with "salt," perhaps bearing in mind "Attic salt," or wit.

men, as many guards as pikemen, but Luxuriette made her understand that she had nothing to fear.

Debauchin lowered the drawbridge and the entire troop entered, asking for their master. The dwarf porter put them in the hands of Crapulophile, who offered them wine and liqueurs. They threw themselves upon them, for they were thirsty, and drank until they were completely drunk.

In that state, there was no need for Sireneh to metamorphose the drunkards herself; it was the work of the inebriation alone. They went to sleep as men and woke up as pigs.

Sireneh and the four dwarfs wanted to give themselves the pleasure of witnessing the awakening of the new herd of pigs. It was delightful! While they were asleep, Crapulophile had stripped them absolutely naked. When they woke up, believing themselves to be still human, they tried to rub their eyes and looked for their clothes. Not finding any, they tried to speak, and grunted. Then, looking at one another and seeing themselves surrounded by pigs, each of them tried to pick up a stick in order to chase away the sordid animals—but they no longer had fingers; one of two pointed horny growths enveloped the thumb and index-finger, and the other the remaining three fingers. Surprised, they looked at one another, the hair on their backs bristling with horror; they all started grunting in unison, so horribly that the entire island resounded with it and the frightened birds flew away.

After Sireneh, Luxuriette, Friandine, Debauchin and Crapulophile had laughed at the scene, holding their sides, Sireneh ordered that Insiposubolaneh be brought to her. On seeing him, all the new pigs formed a circle around him. Large tears fell from the donkey's eyes; he tried to speak, but it was an explosive braying, to which all the pigs replied with deafening grunts.

Sireneh, disgusted to have such guests, had the drawbridge lowered, and Debauchin, aided by his brother Crapulophile, both armed with whips, chased the entire herd off the island, as well as all their horses, metamorphosed into hares.

Scarcely had the band touched the land where Sireneh no longer reigned than all of them stood up on their feet and became human again, but they were all so fatigued by their position—especially the Prince, whom Luxuriette had made to gallop—that they could not move. They looked at one another with a sort of imbecility. Finally, they recovered a little reason. Dermid was put back on his horse; his guards climbed on to theirs as best they could, and they returned to Killnackrenan Castle, where they recovered from their fatigue—but their memories never came back entirely.

Meanwhile, Sireneh, who had become more malevolent by the exercise of malevolence, renewed her cruel amusements every day. Sometimes they were simple travelers that she drew into her abode and then metamorphosed into various animals, according to her caprice. Sometimes she attracted to her island common men and women; she left the former to Luxuriette and Friandine, and delivered the latter to Debauchin and Crapulophile—after which, she metamorphosed them, sometimes into billy-goats and nanny-goats, sometimes into boars and sows, and sometimes into dogs and bitches. In that new situation she kept them for a few weeks in order to amuse herself with their antics, especially with their manner of making love; when she wearied of them she had the drawbridge lowered, expelled them from the island, and had the cruel pleasure of seeing their stupid astonishment at their change of state.

Several more years went by, during which Sireneh delivered herself unreservedly to the cruel deportments. Meanwhile, Dermid had a son, a young man of the greatest promise, as courageous as Finghall and as virtuous, but a lover of peace and all modest virtues. He had attained the age of twenty when his father said to him one day:

"It seems to me—although the idea is like a dream—that I once had the most extraordinary adventure on an island formed by a river similar to the Shannon. At the window of a palace I saw an accomplished Beauty. A female dwarf, it seems to me, made a sign to me; a drawbridge came down and

I entered the island. I was served delicious dishes; I tasted all the delights of Friga. It seems to me that I walked thereafter on all fours…but I only have a confused memory of all that; perhaps it was only a dream. All that I can recall is that the island must be outside my Estates; it's either on a river on the continent or, at least, in the kingdom of Lagenia, Mommonia or Connacy.

"That day, I had come out of Dunnaghall by the Fermanagh gate; I marched or a long time and went astray. Take the same road, my son, march straight but at hazard; perhaps you'll come upon it, as I did; then we'll know the truth about a matter that has troubled me for a long time.

Fitz-Dermid, excited by his father's discourse, only delayed his departure for the time necessary to make preparations for is journey. He took with him the elite of the youth of Ultonia, and on the appointed day, he emerged from Dunnaghall by the Fermanagh gate.

The Prince and his troop marched for a long time, and reached the Shannon. They went along it and passed through Limerick. Finally, in the fourth day, they went astray without being able to recognize where they were. The countryside appeared to them to be uncultivated, offering nothing but the image of a frightful desert. While they were very anxious, they heard a cock crowing at midday. They directed their steps in that direction.

Shortly thereafter, they heard a peacock screeching to the north. They did not know what to think, and stopped. A horse whinnied in the east; a moment later, an ox bellowed to the west.

While the Prince and his troop were astonished to find themselves surrounded by habitations that they had not seen, the cock crowed, the peacock screeched, the horse whinnied and the ox bellowed all at the same time, without discontinuity. The Prince took his troop southwards, and soon they saw a great river through the trees, which they mistook at first for the sea. On emerging from the wood, however, they saw both its banks; in the middle there was a large island, at the eastern tip of which stood a superb palace; all the rest seemed to be an enchanted garden.

"That's the abode of the dangerous fay!" exclaimed the young Prince. "Remember, all of you, that Finghall escaped from her hands, and mastered her by refusing everything that was offered to him on the island, but that his horse, having taken something, was metamorphosed into a donkey. Arm yourselves with courage, not for combat—one is only attacked here by gluttony and lust—but to overcome our appetites. Let those who think that they will not have the strength to refuse a good meal, an agreeable liqueur or the caresses of a pretty woman not enter that island!"

The young Prince added: "Look at that host of animals of all species with which it is populated! They were once men and women, whom the cruel fay has plunged into brutality. Dread such a cruel fate and constrain yourselves; for if you drink a single glass of beer in that place, eat a single mouthful or take a single kiss, you will be in the power of the cruel Sireneh, all of whose pleasure consists of doing evil."

After that speech, the young Prince spurred his horse in the direction of the palace. As soon as she had perceived him in the distance, Sireneh had posted herself at the window, and when she was within the range of sight she smiled at him and made obliging signs. The young Prince responded, saluting her courteously.

Then Luxuriette spoke. "Young and handsome cavalier," she said, "you and your brilliant troop must be tired; this isle abounds in refreshments of every sort. Go down to the western tip; you'll find a drawbridge there, which will be lowered to let you pass as soon as you have pronounced the words *Foudre-Love*." As she finished speaking, she withdrew, and drew Sireneh away, in order that the cavalier would not reply.

Fitz-Dermid descended along the river and reached the drawbridge. He perceived Debauchin, who was amusing himself with some newly-metamorphosed leverets, who were licking his hands and face while caressing him.

"Dwarf, lower the drawbridge," the Prince called to him.

Debauchin did not seem to hear him, and continued playing with his leverets, uttering bursts of laughter so loud and so piercing that the Prince was deafened by them.

Fitz-Dermid was reluctant to pronounce the words that the female dwarf had given him, and the idea occurred to him to take the island by storm. He assembled his troop; faggots were cut from the nearby hedges and they tried to fill in the ditch.

Debauchin smiled. "Insensates," he shouted, "who believe that they can take pleasure by force! You're mistaken. It's by means of laughter and games that one attacks the beautiful Sireneh; her lance only inflicts gentle wounds; her quiver is only full of arrows that tickle as they wound, and instead of blood they cause sensual tears to be shed."

At those words, although pronounced y a deformed dwarf, the entire troop stopped working; but as they had already thrown a great many faggots, the courageous Prince wanted to see whether he might be able to cross the ditch. He looked at it, but to his surprise, each of the faggots had been changed into an iron spike, the sharp and menacing points of which offered nothing to the reckless but pain and death.

Fitz-Dermid understood that he could not combat a supernatural power with human arms. Encouraged by the example of Finghall, he pronounced the two talismanic words that would give him passage into the isle. Immediately, the beams lowered and Debauchin hastened to come and offer his services to the Prince as well all his retinue. With one hand he presented him with a delicate cloth to wipe away the sweat that was covering his face, and with the other a glass of ruby liquid that had an odor of ambrosia.

Fitz-Dermid rejected the fine cloth, pushed away the fatal cup with his other hand and told the dwarf to conduct him to Sireneh.

"My brother will introduce you into the palace," relied the dwarf, smiling. He hastened to hand Fitz-Dermid over to Crapulophile, who made every effort to engage him to take some refreshment. The young Prince refused, and, turning to his retinue, he exhorted all of them not to accept anything. The majority, however, burned by thirst, had already succumbed; Debauchin was moving among them in order to engage them to drink or eat.

Crapulophile handed Fitz-Dermid over to Friandine, who tempted the young Prince's sense of smell with the perfume of the most delicate dishes. Instructed by his father's misfortune, however, and by the courageous resistance of Finghall, he overcame the fire of the lust-of-taste. He was the only one who had that empire over himself; Friandine finished seducing all those whom Debauchin and Crapulophile had tempted unsuccessfully.

Meanwhile, Luxuriette had come running, and, seeing her sister occupied with the Ultonians who had followed the Prince, she took Fitz-Dermid to Sireneh.

The fay, who had secretly witnessed the Prince's courage and the attack, previously unseen, that he had just mounted on the drawbridge, employed all the skill of her seductive art. She took a few steps toward him when he appeared at the entrance to the room.

"Young hero," she said to him, "you have overcome me. No one, before you, had dared to seek to take this isle by right of conquest; it was a glory reserved for you. I recognize that I am vanquished and surrender to you, the master; command here as sovereign; my power will cease throughout the time that you dwell here. Such is the law to which I am submitted by my destiny that I owe conquest of the hero who, braving my charms, has attempted to reach me weapon in hand."

As she finished speaking she looked at the Prince languidly, and swooned into his arms, her upper body half-naked.

Fitz-Dermid shivered involuntarily; the beauty of Sireneh, and her soft and suppliant expression, stirred a tender compassion in his entrails. But great hearts have resources unknown to the vulgar; what ought to have diminished his courage reanimated it.

It's virtue that raises me above her and will defeat me, he thought. *Let's follow virtue, which preserves from enslavement.*

He pushed Sireneh away gently, looked at her without emotion, and went out to call to his companions—but how great was his pain when, having reached the middle of the palace courtyard, ne no longer saw anything but pigs, dogs, donkeys, rams and deer. He called the Ultonian Lords by name. Immediately, two pigs, six donkeys, four large dogs, three rams and two deer approached, shedding tears.

"Oh, my comrades, my friends!" exclaimed the young Prince. "Is it like this that I shall take you back to your homeland? Rid yourselves of the monsters you're dreaming that you are! You're men, and it's only a deceptive bark that covers you!"

Sireneh followed the Prince. "Their cure depends on you," she told him.

"Yes, it depends on me," said Fitz-Dermid—and, seizing the fay by the hand, he said to her: "I'm taking you with me to the King, my father, and you'll remain imprisoned until you have returned my companions to their natural form."

Sireneh smiled; then, raising her wand, she struck the air three times.

Immediately, a violent wind rose up, which uprooted trees and caused rivers to flow back toward their source. All the animals, seized by panic, sought to flee; Fitz-Dermid feared that they might throw themselves in the river and drown there. He seized Sireneh by her beautiful hair and threatened to run her through with his sword if she did not stop the storm. The fay fell to her knees, her breasts uncovered, and gazed at the Prince with an expression capable of disarming the strongest courage. However, Fitz-Dermid was still threatening her, his sword raised, when he felt its tip seized. All the animals uttered a shrill cry and lay down on their bellies.

Fitz-Dermid turned his head and saw a tall woman, still beautiful, in a chariot suspended in mid-air by four flying dragons.

"Prince," said Pucellomaneh—for it was her—"you have overcome my daughter, she is yours; she is losing her power as a fay at this moment; she is becoming a mere mortal; but she will have this palace, this island and the kingdom of Connacy for a dowry. Marry her; I will answer for her affection. She will love you tenderly and will give you handsome Princes who will bear your name gloriously. I shall remain the protectress of your family and I shall watch over its wellbeing; if any Princess thereof is sterile, I shall remedy it with my power."

"Milady," replied the young Prince, "I have a father, who is my King. Let us go to find him, and if he consents, I'll marry your daughter."

Immediately, the fay Pucellomaneh touched the animals with her wand, and they all resumed human form. They left the island then with Fitz-Dermid, who returned to his father, the King.

The old King of Ultonia consented to the marriage of his son with the fay's daughter. The marriage took place on Urilove Island, but the celebrations were held at Tuam, the capital of Connacy, and then at Dunnaghall. It is since that time that the fay Pucellomaneh protects the house of Connacy, of which Queen Dadameh of Mommonia is the issue, and she watches in particular over its perpetual conservation, the greatest Princes of Evinland having emerged from that house.

Tomorrow, I'll tell you a story that I haven't yet old the young man that you see; he's my pupil and he was confided to me by his nurse, the good Nursimaneh of Ballnalu, who lives in that castle, where I offer you hospitality for as long as it pleases you to stay there.

O'Barbo and the young Prince thanked the shepherd for his story, which announced such fine destinies for the Prince of Mommonia, and they accepted his offer. They chatted while returning to the castle.

Oribeau considered the dwarf without affectation and said to himself: *What have these deformed beings done to the gods to be so wretched? For all the moments of life are poisoned for a man whose sight can only inspire repugnance or pity?*

Those ideas, which were passing through the head of young Oribeau, only rendered him more affectionate and more attentive to Cahincaha, who conceived a strong amity for him.

When they arrived at the castle, Nursimaneh showed the greatest joy on seeing the two strangers that the dwarf Debundeh was bringing, and she made them very welcome, for the good nurse did not see anyone in Mullanger, and it was a fête for her when hazard brought her someone. She prepared an excellent supper, which she served to her guests; and when they had slaked their thirst and eaten, they gathered around a great fire, which engendered the itch to tell stories while they warmed themselves.

Chapter 2F
Feats and deeds of Prince Beaudame, hidden under the name of Cahincaha.

"Famine and lassitude are two great evils," said the shepherd. "Now that one has passed and the other is passing, I have the desire to tell you the story that I promised you, of Prince Beaudâme and Princess Belletête, otherwise Dinameh. One is the son of Mijoreh the Beautiful, the other the daughter of the beautiful Conchèse.

"Speak," said O'Barbo. "We're listening to you with pleasure; for we can't stay here for long."

Debundeh immediately began speaking as follows.

This is the genealogy of the children of Mellusine's three cousins: Agacalaneh had of O'Connor, King of Lagenia, Provokameh, who married O'Donnall, King of Meath. From that marriage came Dadameh the First, who married MacErrick, King of Mommonia, Prince of Scotland, but the issue via his mother of the ancient Kings of Waterford, which gave him the right to that crown. From Dadameh the First issued Oribelle the Blonde, who married Slego, Prince of Connacy, from whom emerged Bellotine, wife of Thollin, King of Ultonia, mother of Mijoreh the Beautiful. The last-named was Queen of Meath and wife of Baistiding, and she gave birth to Prince Beaudâme.

There is no need to give the other three genealogies in detail; let it suffice to say that Dadameh the Second, the wife of King O'Facfac, mother of Prince Oribeau, takes her origin from Odolameh, Queen of Connacy, whose descendants, after having married the Kings of the five realms of Evinland, all find themselves united in Dadameh, Princess of Knockfergus and daughter of the sovereign of the same country of which Odolameh had been Queen.

Conchèse emerged from Circileneh, who wore the crown of Ultonia with Dunnaghall. After a cycle of vicissitudes, the daughter of King O'Emptor found herself the sole heir of the first kingdom of Evinland; she married Knocktoser, son of Baron Kilkenny, as being her first subject, in spite of the intrigues of the Scotsmen MacChoucas and MacDonogh, who exercised the priesthood in Lagenia.

Evinland, at the birth of Prince Beaudâme, was in a flourishing state. All its Princes loved justice and made themselves famous by their good government. There are centuries that seemed destined to wellbeing, as there are others in which superstition and the fury of wars desolate humankind and it seems that cruelty is an epidemic scourge, communicated to minds as the plague is contagious for bodies. But let us get back to the origin of Prince Beaudâme and the manner in which his ancestor, O'Connor, had the good fortune of obtaining for a spouse a Princess above him by birth.

One day, when Agacalaneh was walking in the forest near the Soësve spring, she perceived three knights passing by, who appeared to be lost, for they were looking hither and yon.

She amused herself in their embarrassment, instead of showing them the way, by responding to their voices like a deceptive echo, and immediately running away. They laughed at
their error themselves, saying to one another: "It's an echo!
It's an echo!"

In the end, however, one of them, the tallest, stopped to
listen. "My friends," he said, "I think that I heard someone in
those trees. Let's form a circle, in order that no one can escape
us, for they seem to be hiding, and we'll oblige that person to
inform us as to our route.

Immediately, they surrounded the clump of trees and
started shouting: "You who are hiding, come and point out the
road of Poitiers to three knights who have gone astray."

Agacalaneh immediately showed herself. The three
Princes, surprised by her beauty, were nonplussed.

"You," she said to the one who had spoken, "are the
Sage Dunnaghall of Ultonia, a powerful Prince and relative of
the Kings of Lagenia." To the second she said: Your name is
Perforimoth the White, or the Severe, of Connacy. And you
are O'Connor, King of Lagenia."

The surprise of the three Princes was even greater when
they heard themselves named and the found themselves divined by a young person who did not appear to be fifteen
years old.

"Beautiful lady," they said to her, "By what good fortune
are we known to you?"

"I can't tell you that," she relied, looking at them disdainfully. "I never lower myself to giving explanations to
men." At the same time, she drew away.

The three Princes followed her, presuming that she must
be going to an inhabited place.

The demi-fay climbed lightly on to a rock, from which
she appeared to plunge into a precipice. Dunninghall,
Perforimoth the White and O'Connor arrived there in their
turn and, on looking in all directions, they perceived a castle
on an esplanade, built in the form of an ancient temple with
four equal edifices. They went there and were received by

Mellusine, who had not yet met Raimondin, by Odolameh, Circileneh, her two cousins, by the fay Pucellomaneh, their aunt, and three other older fays, the oldest of whom was the fay Wrwcwcw herself.

Two of the marriageable young fays were delighted to see such accomplished cavaliers as Dunnaghall and Performioth the White. Odolameh welcomed the latter while Circileneh appeared to prefer the former, and both responded to their advances.

As for Agacalaneh, she disdained all three equally; that is why Pucellomaneh, not wanting to have anything for which to reproach herself, said to her: "My daughter, here are three Princes; my science tells me that one of the three is suited to you, and that they have been sent here by your good Destiny.

"I don't want any of them," replied Agacalaneh, proudly. Pucellomaneh, not being able to constrain the inclination of her daughters, fell silent, but Wrwcwcw became very angry.

"You'll have one of them," she said to her descendant, "who will be the ones your cousins have left. She immediately gave her O'Connor, who was short and hunchbacked; and as soon as Wrwcwcw had invoked Friga, the disdainful Agacalaneh fell in love with the Prince of Lagenia.

In short, the three marriages were made, as Raimondin's was made, and on the same condition, imposed by Pucellomaneh: that the husbands must never see their wives on Saturdays and that they should never have any suspicion or jealousy on that subject.

None of the four Princes observed the imposed rule, however. O'Connor was the first to violate it, as soon as the third year; he was jealous of his Minister Balrudery, whom he believed to be in love with his wife. In order to punish him doubly, the two fays condemned him to dementia, until his sons-in-law cured him, and they determined that the son to whom Mijoreh, her great grand-daughter, would give birth one day, would be the ugliest of men, except for his tutor; but they consented that he would have a soul as beautiful as his body was hideous. It was from that that the name of Prince Beaudâme came, whose story I am about to tell you.

As for Dunnaghall, he was only indiscreet on the occasion of a dream, in which he seemed to see his wife, having gone astray, enter the cave of a magician. The Prince had his suspicions and he was punished by a malady of languor of which he died. Finally, Perforimoth the Severe only dared to infringe the imposed law in the sixth year of his marriage, but it was in a manner so revolting that the fays inflicted the cruelest of punishments on him, that of being odious to his subjects...

Let us get back to the Prince of Meath.

The same day that Beaudâme was born, Conchèse, Queen of Lagenia, Mijoreh's cousin, gave birth to a second princess as beautiful as the dawn, but as limited, it was said, as she was charming. And it was ordered, by the law of the fays, that Prince Beaudâme would have to be beloved by her in order to lose his ugliness, as it was necessary that the Princess would have to be adored by him in order to become intelligent. It was necessary, in addition, that neither the Prince not the Princess should know themselves for what they were. Thus, it was necessary to send the Prince away with his nurse and his tutor, not to see his parents again until after the fortunate revolution.

The nurse was a demi-fay, like her mother, but, having married for love a man beneath Princes, she had lost the rank that she would have held naturally; she was submissive to the demi-fay Princesses. She took Beaudâme and went to confine herself in a castle situated, like the one we inhabit, between two lakes, where she nourished him with her milk.

In the early years the little Prince was mild and easygoing, for the nurse and the tutor did not speak to him as the heir to the throne, but as a young man destined to be virtuous by mediocrity; at the same time, they paid the greatest attention to his seeing nothing that would bear upon virtue before he was in a state to discern what he saw. When he was in a state to understand and they talked in front of him, their discourse was honest, sage and measured, as if they were speaking in front of a young man of eighteen or twenty; for the fay Wrwcwcw often said: "What you pronounce and what you do before nurslings does not fall upon their organs in vain, but causes a disturbance there although they do not understand it, and when they become adolescent, without remembering you, they will remember the thing, and those who see them act will say: 'Oh, that child has bad inclinations...' That is not what it is necessary to say, but: 'Oh, that child has heard or seen bad things!' So, do not say anything but what is sage before the infant in the cradle. For he is molded to be intelligent and everything that is intellectual has an influence on him, even though he does not understand it yet." That is what the Fay-Queen Wrwcwcw said.

When he had learned to read, the tutor began to render him serious, saying to him: "It is necessary not to play any longer, but to collect yourself, for the occupation that you are about to have is that of men. First he taught him the five vowels, of which he traced the figures for him, expressing their sounds, which he identified with the figures; and when the Prince could say *a,e,i,o,u*, and designate them in writing, he paused there, recommending him to come every day to request further sounds.

The child did not fail in that; in speaking, hearing his nurse speak, or the tutor himself, or the laborers in the neighborhood he discovered new sounds every day and came to say to his master: "I have heard *ai, ou, eu, n, ain*." The master then wrote them, and made him write them. Afterwards, the child said: "But I hear *ca, da, ba, fe* or *fa, go* or *gi*, and all the other combinations that form the consonants. The master wrote them, and in order to render them more intelligible he classified them, writing all the words as they are pronounced, without unnecessary letters. It was not until afterwards, when the Prince could read well, that he wrote the words for him according to custom, giving the reasons for the caprice and the etymology.

Thus, about a year after the Prince had begun to read, not only did he know how to read perfectly, but also the fundamentals of grammar and orthography, having learned nothing by routine, nor by enjoyment, but with the natural order and seriousness that renders men attentive, for it is necessary to say to them in their infancy: "You will one day have duties; accustom yourself early to supporting them, for you are no longer a savage human being but a social human being, who will be subject to a thousand obligations, which are nevertheless preferable to the life of savages. For it is necessary never to scorn social life, as certain imprudent authors want to do; on the contrary, it is necessary to cherish it, and government with it."

At the same time as the tutor taught the young Prince to read, he instructed him in morality. Although he was very religious, the master did not think that he ought to found it, in the first instance, on fear of the gods, but on reciprocity, on fraternity. He excited compassion in his pupil and directed him by means of that noble passion—with the result that for everything the Prince did, he immediately showed him, on the part of others, a reaction that was always inevitable, good for good and evil for evil.

When the pupil was recompensed, or when he suffered, the tutor said to him: "The blackthorn does not bear cherries or apricots, and the peach-tree does not bear sorb-apples; you have the fruit of your action; if it is good you must have done well; if it is bad you must have done poorly. Observe that it cannot be otherwise; a pleasure excites good will; an insult a malicious act or a violent one excites vengeance. With animals as with humans, good produces good intelligence and harmony.

"What do you want subsequently for yourself? Are you content when someone strikes you? Enter into your heart and seek there the movement that excited the blow—in an insult, a humiliating malice—and you will find vengeance there and ill-will. Do good, then, in order that good will be done to you. And do not stop there, if you want to be solidly happy. Have the virtue—which is to say, the strength—that consists, when someone has treated you badly, in forgiving the evil and returning good; then the malefactor, astonished, will be confused at first and ashamed before you, and you will be avenged by that; afterwards he will like you in spite of himself, and you will no longer have an enemy but a friend. Re-enter into your heart then, and you will find there all that the man ought to experience who returns good for evil; for if you always followed nature, like the savage man, hatreds would be eternal.

"The good man, the virtuous man, is not the one who follows nature. The ordinary man, who does what is done to him, is only following a mechanical duty; he is not a monster, that is all; whereas the good man is the who finished, who interrupts the natural sequence of returning the evil for an act of violence done to him; the good re the benefactors of humankind; they are the creators of wellbeing; they raise humans above themselves and draw them nearer to the nature of gods."

That was the first thing the teacher said to the Prince regarding the Divinity, whom he presented to his mind first under the image of the Good; but he only spoke, in order to support the moral, at the age when young people are ordinarily beginning no longer to believe, because they have been surrounded by a religion of fables that is repugnant to reason, and, sooner or later, reason, in its force, will prevail over what has been suggested. No matter how hard one tries to glue it by means of superstition, it will always be more or less unglued in the age of strength; one can only dominate by superstition during the initial weakness and the concluding weakness; there are few people who are always feeble.

Thus, the prince's tutor presented the Divinity to him disengaged from all superstition, in the age when reason is perfectly developed. He said to him: "God is the motive force and the complement of the universe." Thus, the Prince is really religious; not once does he see Berda rise without singing a hymn to him, and asking him to take his homage personally to Thor, the foremost and sovereign of Gods—which is to say, the universal principle of all things. When the Earth our mother gives the harvest of grains, fruits and pasturage for flocks, the Prince prostrates himself and salutes her, saying: "O Earth my mother, daughter of Thor, who nourishes me through you, receive my homage and deign to carry to our common father my respectful and filial adoration." Not a single day passes when he does not say those ardent and forceful prayers, which come from the heart, because he believes in and loves the Divinity.

Since he has grown up, his morality has two bases: that of reciprocity, which can never weaken, and that of religion. So he is good and beautiful of soul, and it is hoped that one day he will be a great Prince...

I shall stop there for this evening, for it is getting late; I perceive Orion, followed by Sirius, which have risen. All of nature is in repose; let us go and rest too.

It was thus that the shepherd Debundeh spoke before Beaudâme himself, without the Prince understanding that it was his own story that was being told, for he did not know yet that he was a prince; neither the shepherd nor his nurse had said anything to him about that, in order that he might live with them in solitude without impatience.

The next day, Debundeh got up at dawn and woke Cahincaha, saying to him: "You know that in the heat of the day, the sheep don't eat; let us therefore take advantage of the freshness, or those animals nourish us and clothe us. It is thus, and even more naturally, that a Prince must think of his people, for they are not made for him, as the sheep are made for us; on the contrary, he is made for them."

O'Barbo heard the shepherd speaking, got up himself and got the Prince of Mommonia out of bed. They accompanied Cahincaha and Debundeh, who gave them an idea of the pastoral life, less arduous than that of the laborer, but which has its fatigues. After the flock was sated, the Sun having become hot, he gathered himself and hid his head between his legs in order to protect himself from sunstroke.

Then Debundeh took the livestock into the field destined to be sown in three months' time and left them there to pen them.[105] Afterwards, the shepherd chose a tree in an elevated place, from which he could see his entire flock and placed himself in its shade, in order to dine on the provisions that he loaded every morning on to a large ram. They sat down. Appetite is keenly excited by the open air and moderate exercise, so they ate tranquilly, with appetite.

When they had finished the frugal meal, O'Barbo said to the shepherd: "You commenced the story of Prince Beaudâme yesterday, but you only spoke about his education and you only cited one feature of the beautiful soul that gave him his name. I have heard it said, however, that he had more, and I would be glad if you would tell us about them, for it would give great pleasure to the young man who is accompanying me."

"There are several," relied the shepherd, "and since we are at rest here, I could tell you about them, but I would not like to take away from the good woman who cares for us the pleasure of hearing them; for it is a great pleasure for those who live in solitude to tell tales that interest them or hear them told. If you wish, however, I will tell you something about the studies in physics that my pupil and I have made—for we have never wasted a moment of our time.

"Ah!" said Oribeau, "I shall profit with pleasure from what you have learned or discovered by your reflections in

---

[105] The word I have translated as "pen" is *mariénner*, which is not found in French dictionaries but is thus defined in some nineteenth century accounts of pastoral jargon as a matter of sheltering the sheep from midday heat. Restif footnotes it himself, suggesting that it sometimes means penning the sheep and sometimes leaving them loose, but in either case with the ultimate purpose of fertilizing the terrain. He had doubtless encountered the word when tending sheep on his father's farm.

this solitude. Perhaps it will relate to what my father has told me about the system of the universe and all of physics."

"I'm delighted that you have that curiosity," said the dwarf Debundeh, "but as I have instructed my pupil carefully, it's him who will expose to you the system of the Sages such as it has been transmitted to us by the bards, and such as I have tried to purify it by my reflections, of which I will make the venerable old man, your father, the judge."

Invited to speak, Cahincaha sat on an elevated stone in the middle of his listeners and commenced, in these terms, the exposition of the principles of the physics and philosophy of the ancient Sages of Evin.

"Everything that there is, always was, but not in the same form, for forms change incessantly and substance alone remains. Thor is the soul of the world, and everything that exists is part of him; for he is everything and nothing can be outside him. Although we admit several gods, under the names of Worden, Friga, Vananis and Berda, the truth is that there is only one God, the universal principle, of which Worden and the other divinities are attributes; for it is Thor who gives courage to war via Worden; beauty, the generative power, via Friga; hope via Vananis; and the daylight that illuminates us via Berda; who aliments us via the fecundity of Erda, the Earth, our mother, etc. God is everything.

"Humans have always rendered homage to the divinity, since all have appealed to the aid of their laws the ineffable sight of the Supreme Being; almost all have established, to frighten the wicked and encourage the good, future punishments and recompenses. The homage rendered to the divinity is a duty; the established priest is the delegate of the people; that quality of the people's delegate, to offer the homage of the people, appeared so fine that the first sovereigns all attributed it to themselves. It was only afterwards, when drawn far away by wars, that they gave it to lieutenants, but they resumed the sacred functions in their old age. The first priest-kings were elected elders; that is why the union of royalty with priesthood was natural.

"People subsequently wearied of elections because of the troubles they occasioned; they established, not for the advantage of Kings but for their own tranquility, filial succession. And it was then that, having young Kings, they did not appear serious enough to be the delegates of the people to the Divinity; an old man was nominated as pontiff. But the priest should always remember that he is only the lieutenant of the Prince and the delegate of the people; let him not attribute any authority to himself; he is only the channel by which homages are combined and are offered to God be a single voice.

"But ought we to offer our homages to the Great Being, the source of everything, directly? It appears that ancient people held a different opinion, and thought that it was appropriate to address themselves to intermediate beings, such as Berda and Erda, who are the Sun and the Earth. Thus, instead of speaking directly to Thor, they presented their homage to the Sun, saying: 'Father of the day, of light and heat, we bless you; bless Thor, your father, for us, in blessing him for yourself.' They were convinced that the Sun, in presenting his homage to the Great Being, would also carry ours.

"In the same way, when they addressed the Earth, saying to her: 'O Earth, mother and nurse of animals, plants and all minerals, we honor you!' They thought that the Earth, in rendering her personal homages, would also present those of all the creatures she nourishes. That idea is so natural and so true that a new religion, already spread among the Angles and almost generally recognized on the continent, has put between the Great Being and men, a Son, or the most perfect production of the Supreme Being, to whom those people, who call themselves Christians, address their prayers, in order that he can present them to God the Father; and they finish them all with a common formula which charges that excellent production, which they call the Word of God, to give them value by his merits. That religion is said to be very beautiful, that it preaches disinterest, fraternity and absolute equality to humans, and that everything should be in common between those who profess it.

"The stories that my tutor, who is very learned, has told me about it, have transported me with joy. Oh, when all men embrace one religion, which renders them brothers, which not only prescribes for them not to be ingrate, but to return good for evil…! If I have done anything worthy of praise, it is since the knowledge that Debundeh has give me of that holy and sublime philosophy, which fraternizes all humans. Oh, why is it that we inhabit a land that the sea surrounds, of which one can only get out with difficulty, and which is almost unknown to other men?

"I said that a reasonable being can, and perhaps ought to bear his homage to the Sovereign Principle via the intermediate visible gods. We have before our eyes a fact that seems to prove that: it is that animals, plants etc., certainly praise the Author-of-All, but they only do so in a general manner, with the Earth our common mother, whereas humans can do it with the Sun and the other gods, in a virtual and particular manner.

"My master has spoken to me about what becomes of us after our death. It is claimed that the new religion of the continent teaches that, but he has not had and has not been able to communicate to me appropriate enlightenments. We are still in the ancient belief of our forefathers, which is that humans do not perish, but that they merely dissolve, with the result that since the world has been the world, the people of Evinland have been composed of previous Evinlanders, and will be, similarly, for as long as the human species lasts. One can say as much for plants and animals; there is a river of life that flows, which is always the same, and which, however, always appears.

"Beings are, in succession, one and others, and what prevents them from being eternal is that every existence of a human, a beast or a plant is a whole; death makes them lose continuity, along with sentiment. Now, if sentiment were not lost with death, dissolution would be a long and dolorous torture, during which humans would incessantly demand annihilation, Nature only toys with the life of humans, animals and plants for the reason that death is only a passage from the present state to the future state; everything is ever-present for her. That is why humans are sage and not mad, as some bilious moralists say, in occupying themselves with present things, in building cities, accumulating, cultivating, learning; they are working for themselves in working for posterity.

"It is a consoling doctrine, that of the immortality of humans, which ought to encourage us to be good; for if humans are wicked, by reason of their power, it might come about and will come about that the new combination in which they will one day re-exist will be oppressed. Let us therefore be good to one another; for it is the sole means of being happy in all our existences.

"When we die, we cease to form a center of life that had the consistency and intelligence necessary to its conservation; dolor is the door between life and death. The door is opened of its own accord by old age; it is forcibly opened and broken in war by an arrow or a sword-thrust.

"A suicide breaks it dolorously himself and throws himself outside life, which he finds an evil, but he is impatient and insensate. What engages him to cease to be? Either he expects that his dolor will cease or that it will kill him less cruelly. The worst evil, whatever one says about it, being death, the person who kills himself gives himself more in order to avoid less. I know that those sorts of death are praised as being courageous, but those who praise them can only be heirs, the jealous or those who feared the suicide, who is obliging them by disappearing from the world.

"To encourage suicide is to open the door to all crimes, since the person who no longer fears death might commit them all if he feels the inclination. Who will stop him? Society's most terrible weapon no longer frightens him. I conclude from that, that to give humans good morals, it is necessary to render them happy, to procure them pleasures and enjoyments that attach them to life, their homeland and the government; it is necessary to demonstrate to them that life is not a passing moment, but that after having existed we shall exist eternally in all the other humans with whom the materials of existence are common to us. It is those same materials that are common to all animals and plants, but humans and every species of animal have some that are exclusive."[106]

"That doctrine is that of the ancient druids," said O'Barbo then, "but the new religion that is nowadays establishing itself in the world gives virtue more solid supports. It shows people a God who punishes and recompenses. I want to be instructed in it and I don't doubt that I'll find powerful motives for adopting it. The principles that it teaches of fraternity, humility, mildness, generosity, tolerance and community delight me and I would very much like to have some of its sacred books, which could instruct me fully."

It was with those conversations and similar ones that the day went by. In the evening they came back to Mullanger Castle; they had supper, and after the meal, the god Nursimaneh proposed to the shepherd that he continued the previous evening's story.

Debundeh spoke in the following terms.

Chapter 2G
Generous and fine actions of Beaudâme since his childhood.

Glorifying virtue encourages it, but it is necessary not to praise it so much that it is denatured by pride.

Prince Beaudâme profited marvelously from his tutor's maxims, lessons and examples. He regarded all men as his brothers and was charmed when he found an opportunity to oblige those he encountered in the remote place in which he lived.

---

[106] Author's note: "It is necessary to observe here, Reader, that I am exposing the sentiment of ancient Irish pagans; Ireland is very savage, and Abbé Prévost assures us that there are still idolaters there." In fact, Christianity seems to have been firmly established in Ireland in the sixth century, long before the notional time of the narrative.

One day, when Beaudâme was alone outside the door of the castle he passed a poor man who asked him for a morsel of bread. The child gave him his breakfast, although the door was closed and he would have nothing to eat until his nurse and tutor returned.

Another time, having perceived a poor carter stuck in the mud with his vehicle, which he could not free, he went all the way to the next village in search of assistance, and did not quit the people he knew there until they came with horses to help the poor man.

A little boy had a malevolent stepmother who beat him without reason, although he was very mild; Beaudâme, touched by compassion, went to her one day as she was beating her stepson and exposed himself in trying to defend him, so that he received hard blows. The bad mother, frightened, came to beg his pardon. "I'll forgive you," he said, in a low voice, "if you never beat your stepson again; but the first time that happens, I shall know, and I'll complain."

A young girl from Mullanger was going to the market at Athlone; she was amusing herself on the way with some of her companions, who were playing in a meadow. A thief stole the goods that the girl was taking to market and ran off; it was a great dolor for the poor child, who was desolate. Having found her there, and seeing all the young girls saddened, Beaudâme asked what had happened. As soon as he knew the reason for her distress he took the girl to his tutor, and asked him to give her the money for the merchandise she had lost.

The master needed to be persuaded, but Beaudâme employed supplications and tears, telling him that the poor girl would be mistreated by her father and mother, who were poor.

"She'll be more careful another time."

"Oh, she'll be even more so if you oblige her," said Beaudâme, for she'll take more care, out of gratitude to you, than out of fear of punishment."

The tutor eventually gave in, and Beaudâme said to him: "Demand of me whatever you want, for the pleasure you're giving me; I'll do it."

"No," said the master, "you'd think yourself acquitted. For anything else, yes, but for a good dead you've given me the opportunity to perform, I can never acquit myself."

Beaudâme was already growing up when one day, in passing before a peasant's door, he heard sighing. He went in. There was a poor sick woman lying on her bed.

"Don't you have anyone?" he asked.

"Alas, no; it's harvest time, and if my husband and children stayed here to care for me, our crop would perish and we'd die of starvation in the winter."

Beaudâme immediately set about caring for her; he made her a fire, prepared a light meal, made her eat it, and went away; but he came back after two hours, and throughout the harvest, without telling anyone, he visited the poor peasant-woman four times a day, who got better. She did not know him, but one day, having encountered him with his nurse, she came to threw herself at his feet, saying: "Good young man, I owe you my life. May Thor and Friga bless you, for in the forced abandonment in which I was, the conduits of nourishment were beginning to be blocked, and I would inevitably have died of need."

That was how it became known what he had done, for she told the nurse, the good Nursimaneh, at length.

He did another good deed when he was fully grown. One day, as he was going past a cottage, he saw tax-collectors coming out, who were taking away a poor family's utensils and furniture. He went to them. "I have nothing," he said to them, "but if you come with me, I'll get you your sum. How much is it?"

"Six shillings."

"Do you think that all I have on me is worth that?"

"Just about."

"Well, I'll give it to you." And he stripped almost naked. Then he went home, numb with cold.

One day, he was passing through a deserted canton on his own, which he had gone to explore for pasturage. From a distance, he perceived a celebrated cannibal thief, who devastated the locale, taking away a woman, whom he was forcing to walk in front of him by holding the point of his dagger at her throat. Beaudâme was alone; he was delicate and of weak constitution; nevertheless, he ran to rescue the unfortunate woman.

As soon as the thief saw him, he quit the woman, whom he ordered to sit down, and ran at Beaudâme; but the latter, although feeble, was an agile runner. He pretended to run weakly; the thief, thinking that he was about to catch up with him, pursued him. By that means he took him far away from the woman, who then gathered her courage and fled. Soon seeing that, the thief left Beaudâme and ran after his prey, but the Prince then started pursuing him in is turn, shouting and throwing stones at him, so that the irritated thief turned round in order to catch him and get rid of him.

Beaudâme pretended to have injured his foot and allowed himself to be almost caught, in order to save the woman, who was still fleeing; then he saved himself, in order that he did not become the victim of his generosity, for the thief was ready to seize him. He escaped as lightly as a young deer. The thief, however, accustomed to fatigue, did not tire; he pursued Beaudâme relentlessly, seeing that the woman had got away. The delicate young man began to run out of breath.

Fortunately, he came to a steep slope covered in bushes and junipers. Beaudâme launched himself into them. The thief followed him, but while the latter ran into the valley, the Prince, hidden by the junipers, stopped, went back up and fled by a known route. The thief searched the bushes for a long time, and when he finally came back up he saw that he was too far ahead to dare to pursue him.

A week later, the woman came to thank her liberator. As she was pretty and the thief was lying in wait for her to capture her, the young Prince decided to employ her to catch the thief, for whom he set an ambush. The woman went along the path, but armed men were hidden close by, in a ditch dug during the night on Beaudâme's advice. The brigand did not fail to run after his prey, and as soon as he went past the ditch Beaudâme showed himself, shouting.

The thief came back toward him, saying: "I always run into that accursed hunchback!"

The Prince fled toward the ditch, from which the armed men emerged unexpectedly, and seized the brigand. They delivered him to the Law, and the region was thus freed of him.

Not long ago—for Prince Beaudâme is not old—two young women passed by who were fleeing the tyranny of a stepfather, unless they were two Princesses expelled by a usurper. They were wandering on the shore of Lake Selling, supporting a woman who seemed to be their mother. The young Prince saw them from a distance and ran toward them, but a malevolent local man got there before him, who offered to take the three fugitives to a nearby island, which was nothing but a sterile rock.

Deceived by that wretch, who was doubtless an emissary of their persecutor, the old woman and the two young women got into the boat, and the man took them to the rock, where he disembarked them. Then, with a thrust of the oar, as soon as they set foot on land, she started to laugh maliciously, saying to them: "I hope you find it pleasant on that island, Beauties!" And he drew away.

Meanwhile, Beaudâme arrived on the shore. He heard the cries of the young women, begging the evil man to return them to the land. But he mocked them, still drawing away. Beaudâme would have tried to reach the rock by swimming, but the waves were too strong; they would have broken him against the reefs. A beautiful bird then appeared in the air, which seemed to be inviting Beaudâme by its flight and its cries to follow the evil man, to see where the cruel individual disembarked.

Having seen him landing on the coast of Finay, he ran at top speed to catch up with him. He arrived at the scoundrel disembarked. "Why," he said to him," have you left three women on a rock in the middle of the lake?"

"Because I wanted to do it, and because it's necessary that they perish there."

"They won't perish there," said Beaudâme, "For I'll follow you, crying for justice against you, to the town of Finay. I'll pursue you, if necessary, as far as Polard, Delvin, Kinagard and Kilbegan."

Meanwhile, the evil man was mooring his boat. When he had finished, his anger was manifested by insults, and, throwing himself at Beaudâme, he tried to seize him—but the Prince, although fatigued, began running like a deer, drawing the man after him into the country. When he had taken him half a mile from his boat, he circled back and came back to the shore, with a long lead. He threw himself into the boat, detached it and drew way from the shore, heading for the rock.

In the meantime, the evil man threatened him, and looked for another boat in order to pursue him. He could not see one, but he perceived a fisherman in the distance. He made him a sign to come toward him. The fisherman came, and the evil man climbed into his boat in order to chase Beaudâme and sink him. Nevertheless, the latter had reached the rock.

He took the three fugitives into the boat and hid behind the rock in a little cove, where he moored it, intending to drive the enemy away by throwing stones. He put a heap next to each of the three women, which they were to throw with all their might.

The evil man did not take long to appear, with the fisherman, but he could not see Beaudâme, who was hidden by bushes. He approached the cove and prepared to go into it in order to take possession of the boat, mooring the fisherman's, which was too heavy to enter it. As soon as he had quit it, however Beaudâme descended with the three women, placed them in the fisherman's boat, whom he paid well, and charged him with taking them to safety while he kept the evil man busy.

The fisherman, who knew him, agreed to help, promising to come and pick him up that evening. Beaudâme climbed back up on to the inaccessible rock, from which he threw stones at the evil man—merely to irritate him, for he avoided killing him. The latter, wanting to avenge himself, scaled the rock like a chamois; Beaudâme, even lighter, started fleeing over the precipitous slopes. While he did that, the fisherman took the three women away, putting them ashore in Finay; they were already continuing their route toward Waterford, where they said they were going.

Meanwhile, the weary Beaudâme perceived that he was dealing with a strong and vigorous man. There was a precipice between the rocks into which, with a little skill, one could let oneself down, holding on to the bushes, and which would cut short the route back to the boat. He did not slip, and reached the bottom without being injured. His pursuer tried to imitate him, but being less nimble, he lost his footing and fell heavily, breaking his leg as he tumbled down the slope.

Beaudâme was touched by compassion then; he dragged him gently to the boat, placed him in it as best he could and rowed to the shore, where he handed him over to the fisherman, asking him to care for him, with a promise to reimburse his expenses if the man had no money. In fact, the evil man having gone away without saying anything as soon as he could, Beaudâme compensated the fisherman for everything he had spent during his recovery.

*

"I don't know," said O'Barbo, whether one ought to do good to evil men like that."

"Oh, why not do it for them?" exclaimed Cahincaha. "They're human, and might be touched by their enemy's generosity, to the point of becoming good."

"You're catching fire," said the Sage. "Do you have an interest in justifying the beneficence of Beaudâme toward an evil man?"

Cahincaha blushed and lowered his eyes. That was because he had recognized, because they had happened to him, the various events that Debundeh had just recounted, but he did not know yet that he was the Prince of Meath.

O'Barbo, who was perfectly well aware of that, took the floor. "Why is generosity a virtue?" he asked. "It's because humans, who have compassion, which renders them sensible to the pain of others, also have another natural, but horrible, sentiment: they secretly desire one another's destruction, in order to obtain sole possession. It's an obscure blind sentiment, related to the desire for self-preservation; it resembles that of predatory animals; they kill a fellow that wants to share their prey.

"Fortunately, another sentiment exists, as well as compassion, which is the need that beings of the same species have for one another, in order to have security; that need corrects natural egotism and civilizes to some extent. The cause of all the disorder that exists in society, however, is the other, anthropophagous, sentiment which wants everything for itself: a physical sentiment necessary to individual conservation but which, poorly regulated, produces all crimes.

"What admiration ought we not to have for those excellent beings who only appear to be born to love and oblige others, who overcome the blind instinct of nature and are benevolent in spite of her. King O'Facfac was thus, and the present Queen of Mommonia, Dadameh, still is, as well as her Minister Dondanuck; the Chief of the Tribunal, the sage O'Aymstay; the Great Judge of Waterford, O'Theblack; the respectable leader of merchants O'Skinner; the leader and members of the Senate and all those who occupy the foremost employments...

"I conclude, from what Debundeh has just recounted to us, that Prince Beaudâme is well-named!"

After that little speech, pronounced enthusiastically, which made the modest Cahincaha blush, they all went to bed.

Chapter 2H
*Histories and marvels that the shepherd recounted to his
pupil.*

Humiliated by having done less than Beaudâme, Oribeau
said to the Sage the next morning, when he got up: "I'm far
from having distinguished myself with such generous deeds."

"Don't complain of fate," O'Barbo replied. "You've
done all the good that was presented to you; if the opportuni-
ties have been scarce, they've augmented the desire to see
them born. But what do you think of this shepherd and his
pupil?"

"I revere the one and am touched by amity for the other."

"So much the better," replied the Sage, for I think that
you will be linked one day by interest and propriety."

As the old man was speaking they heard Debundeh taking out his flocks. His two guests hasted to go down to accompany him to the fields.

When they arrived there, the four shepherds were initially occupied with their ewes. Eventually, the heat of day made
itself felt and they assembled them in order to pen them. After
that, they gathered together in order to eat and to amuse themselves with instructive conversation.

When the meal was over, Debundeh spoke.

Not only have I told my pupil tales and spoken to him
about physics, but I have tried to ensure that he is not astonished by any of the things that are claimed to be extraordinary,
which only frighten ignorant people because of their rarity.
For that reason, we have read together a book on charlatanry
composed by superstitious druids, in order that my pupil, by
studying it with me, might be preserved from the lies that it
contains and that, if there are a few truths within it, he might
be able to disentangle them.

There were once druids who, having been unable to conceive why evil and pain exist in the world, took it into their

heads to imagine two principles, one of Good and the other of Evil: a monstrous ideas repugnant to common sense; for as soon as pleasure exists, pain exists, both being effects of the sensibility of living beings. Imaginary evil is similarly the effect of the faculty of thought and effect that humans have, and moral evil that of their liberty of action.

The druids departing from a false premise called the Evil principle Deümo; they sat him in a cotton chair, with a triple crown on his head, four horns, four teeth, a large open mouth, a similar nose and eyes, the hands of an ape, and feet like a cock. They built him a temple at Calicut in India, in the middle of a pond, with two rows of columns, with a huge stone altar; his festival lasted twenty-five days at the winter solstice, and it was established that all murderers, thieves and exiles could go there in all security, the laws being abolished during that festival.

Kings, however great they are, ought to remember that they are only human, and that their death is sometimes as unfortunate as that of the least of slaves.

Croesus, King of Lydia, claimed to be the richest and happiest of men; Cyrus of Persia vanquished him, ruined him and had him burned alive.

Polycrates, king of the Samians, had never felt the sting of misfortune; he was vanquished by Darius and crucified on the summit of a mountain.

Valerian, Emperor of the Romans, taken prisoner by Sapor, King of the modern Persians, was reduced so low that he served as a footstep when his vanquisher mounted his horse. He was eventually skinned alive and salted.

Zeum, the twelfth Emperor of Constantinople, was condemned by his wife to be buried alive.[107]

------

[107] Legend claimed that Zeno the Isaurian, who ruled the Eastern Empire between 474 and 491 A.D., was buried alive after falling into catalepsy, but his consort Ariadne would not allow his sarcophagus to be opened when he was heard calling for help.

Mempricius, King of the Angles, did not die in his bed, but was devoured by wolves.[108]

Popiel, King of the Polans, was devoured by rats, along with his wife, in a tower where they were imprisoned, only their bones being left.[109]

It was the same with Halo, the Grand Druid of the Gauls, who assembled al the poor in barns during a famine, on the pretext of giving them food, and set fire to the buildings in order to be rid of them at a stroke. The people, revolted by his barbarity, imprisoned him and he was devoured by rats in his cell.

The monsters to whom women sometimes give birth are sometimes a physical product and sometimes the effect of a disordered imagination. The two girls who lived until the age of ten joined together at the head but separated throughout the rest of their bodies; the boy and girl born among the Angles, separated as far as the navel but only having a single trunk and sex organ beneath; etc., are a natural junction of two individuals that ought merely to have been twins, made in the mother's womb. But the little Sarmatian with a kind of trunk, like an elephant, a nose like an ox's muzzle, a tooth to the side like a boar's tusk and a hairy back like a dog's, was produced by the mother's astonishment on seeing an elephant in the street, which doubtless frightened her. Half-human monsters are sometimes also the effect of an abominable commerce, such as the goat-man found in the Apennine mountains in Italy.

One thing of which parents ought to beware is not to leave their children, boys or girls, too much alone with their maidservants or domestics. There was a nurse in Rome who raised a boy left with her until the age of nine who became pregnant by the child, who died soon afterwards. A maidser-

---

[108] The story of Mempricius was briefly recounted by Geoffrey of Monmouth in his fictitious history of kings of Britain.

[109] Popiel II, a legendary ninth-century ruler of the Slavic tribe of the Polans, was indeed said by several chroniclers to have been devoured by mice and rats, along with his wife.

vant in a great house became so amorous or one of her master's children, aged ten, that she often provoked him, and eventually had a daughter by him.

The most precious of all stones is the magnet, which attracts iron; other precious stones, so raised for their qualities, which pharmacists always have in what they call their herbarium, only have the property of ornamenting those who wear them.

A Queen of the Angles called Emnia, the mother of Edward, was accused of misconduct before her son, who imprisoned her. To prove her innocence to him, she threw herself into an ardent fire, from which she emerged without the slightest burn, and her son the King believed her innocent. This is the truth: the young Prince, who loved his mother, fearing the Queen's accusers, suggested that means of justifying herself, and the fire was disposed in such a fashion that it could not burn her.[110]

"There has been much talk of mermen and sirens, but no one has ever seen one except by dint of illusion or optical error, or by the knavery of men or women who were skillful swimmers.

Comets, the hair and beard of which are so terrifying, are merely heavenly bodies like the others, but their course is eccentric. Ignorance alone makes them frightening. An ancient bard wrote that in the year that a cruel king named Mithridates was born there was a comet so brilliant that or eighty days it threw off a splendor that surpassed the light and heat of the Sun; if the fact is true, it is because the comet, as it approached the luminous Star, was prodigiously warmed, and by virtue of its proximity to the Earth it communicated its heat and light

---

[110] The reference is to Emma of Normandy, the mother of Edward the Confessor (Emnia is probably a misprint), whom legend credited with having walked over red hot plowshares in Winchester Cathedral in order to prove her innocence of a charge of adultery—but the "truth" cited by Debundeh is Restif's own interpretation.

thereto. There are also astronomers who claim that comets cause terrible revolutions on the Earth at times, to the extent of destroying a great number of humans and animals, which cause the frightened nations to lose all the sciences and arts and fall back into barbarity. That happens at certain intervals, it is said, sometimes distant and sometimes close together.

As for the reveries of astrology, they are merely falsehoods.

One day, Roman soldiers who were fighting in Spain lost a battle and two Scipios, their generals, were killed. They had fallen into discouragement when Lucius Martius, a knight, started to harangue them in order to revive their courage. He spoke with so much vehemence that a kind of flame was seen around his head, which did not burn him. That gave such great courage to the soldiers that they beat the enemy and avenged their generals. The reason for that phenomenon is that Lucius was on the edge of a marsh; it as evening; a fire follet came to attach itself around his head and was augmented by the emanations that his great emotion was causing to evaporate from his body.[111]

There were once among the Greeks, the most civilized people on Earth, gallant women known as courtesans, A philosopher whose name has come down to us, Aristotle, became so passionate for one of these women, named Hermia, or the beautiful talker, that not only did he languish from amour but he made sacrifices to her as to a divinity, which led to him being accused by a certain Demophile and obliged to flee Athens.[112]

---

[111] This legend seems to originate from *Histoires prodigieuses* (1560) by Pierre Boaistuau, Sire de Launay, from which Restif probably derived some of Debundeh's other examples; again the "explanation" is his.

[112] Author's note: "I warn that this is a calumny against the ancient philosopher; vice avenging itself on Virtue by attacking its morals." After the death in childbirth of his wife Pythia—the daughter of the tyrant of Artaneus, Hermias, in

Another courtesan named Archeanasse was cherished by Plato when she was already old. "Has Amour taken refuge in her wrinkles, then?" said the astonished philosopher.[113] Socrates spent as much time as he could with Aspasia, another courtesan, and appeared to want to insinuate that he owed part of his philosophy to her.

The famous courtesan Laïs of Thebes heard the wisdom of the Athenian philosophers praised in her presence one day and flew into a fit of rage. "I don't know," she said, "what they know, nor in what science they excel, and I know even less about the books of these philosophers you exalt, but what I do know for sure is that I often see them at my feet."[114]

Mentor recounts a singular story about two of those famous Greek courtesans, one of whom, who was Milesian, was named Plango and the other, a Samian, was named Bacchide. The former was passionately in love with young Colossian man, and was cherished by him, but Plango, having heard that the young Colossian had been loved by the courtesan Bacchide, who was not inferior to her in beauty, was gripped

---

some accounts, but a former courtesan according to others—Aristotle, who had fled to Lesbos following Hermias' defeat and death, lived thereafter with a courtesan named Phyllis or Herpyllis, who bore him a son, but the scabrous account of their amour given in Diogenes Laertius' extremely unreliable *Lives of the Philosophers* is markedly different from Debundeh's account.

[113] This anecdote is cited in a dialogue by Jean-François Sarrazin (1611-1654), which Restif probably read.

[114] Restif might have taken this anecdote from the anonymous *Histoire de Laïs, courtisane grecque* (1756), a scabrous volume adding voluminous detail to the alleged claim; there is, however, an extraordinarily detailed account of stories concerning Laïs (there identified as Laïs of Hyccara , although many Classical sources confused her with Laïs of Corinth) in Pierre Bayle's *Dictionnaire historique et critique* (1702), which conscientiously rejects most of them as fanciful.

by such jealousy that she resolved to break with her lover. The Colossian would have preferred death a hundred times over to Plango's indifference. What dolor he felt when he ran to her house, found her angry and heard her say: "You'll never find out where I am." In despair, the Colossian prostrated himself before her, imploring her to tell him what he had done wrong, adding that he could not bear to live if he were deprived of her tenderness and would kill himself.

"Go," said Plango, "And you want me to see you again, bring me the famous golden chain that hangs round Bacchide's neck." Without replying, the young man left immediately for the isle of Samos. He found Bacchide there and explained what had brought him there.

"At the price of my most precious treasure," said the courtesan, "since this chain is formed from everything that I have received from my lovers in my life, I want to show Plango that I surpass her in generosity. Take her the ornament that she desires and tell her that I know love better than she does."

Transported by joy, the young Colossian returned to Miletus and presented the chain of Plango, without keeping silent about what Bacchide had said. The Milesian courtesan was alarmed by that excessive grandeur of soul, and resolved to surpass it in her turn. She sent the chain back to Bacchide, cherished the young Colossian more than ever, and, in order that her magnanimity would be entire wanted him to spend six months with her and six months with Bacchide.[115]

Those courtesans were very different from those of our day, who are nothing but infamy and baseness. I even think that the ancient courtesans are the origin of our fays, particularly the three that I shall talk about, Lamia, Flora and Laïs.

The greatest charm of Lamia was in her eyes; no man at whom she looked could resist her. Flora seduced by the ame-

---

[115] This oft-quoted story originates from a poem by Callimachus, dating from the third century B.C., in which the Samian courtesan is named Philaenis.

nability of her conversation and the charm of her speech, sweeter than honey, Laïs by her tenderness and the harmony of her singing. All three had a perfect figure, a noble countenance and enchanting features. None of the three had any fault, from head to toe, the slightest part of them prevailed in beauty over all other women.

What made courtesans adored by certain men was, first of all, that they were the marvel of their century by virtue of their beauty; secondly, there was the seductive idea that being loved by women who were sought by the all most attractive men put their lovers, by virtue of a flattering preference, above humankind.

King Demetrius was the idolater of Lamia. The city of Thebes, her homeland, thought it appropriate to honor her as the most perfect image of Venus and raised a temple to her.

Pyrrhus, King of Ephesus, loved Laïs passionately but could not fix her. She established herself in Corinth and sold her favors so dear that she ruined several Kings. It was said of her that she had never loved any man, but that no man had ever seen her without loving her. She was the daughter of the high priest of the temple of Apollo, and he is said to have predicted his daughter's way of life on the day of her birth.

Flore was the daughter of a very rich Roman knight—all the financiers of ancient Rome were taken from the Order of Knights—and was orphaned at the age of fifteen, with a fortune with an immense fortune and an unparalleled beauty. She followed the consul Manilius to the first Punic war and spent a great deal of money n him. On returning to Rome she declared herself a courtesan and put a notice over her door saying: *Kings, Princes, Dictators, Consuls, Pontiffs and Quaestors may knock and enter*. Unlike Laïs, she never asked for anything, but she received more than if she had asked. Her wealth became so considerable that her house as an object of curiosity for all ambassadors and distinguished foreigners. When she went out to ride on horseback the entire city was activated, people formed two hedges, followed her, and praised her charms and her magnificence. She died at the age of sixty and left the Roman people her heritage. The value of her furniture alone was sufficient to reconstruct the walls of Rome.[116]

"It follows from these ancient stories and those of our time, which I could cite in large number but about which I shall abstain from talking, that it is necessary to avoid libertine beauties, who have never been anything but veritable Sirenehs. Their extravagance, their magnificence and the quests for their favors made by important men were bound to deal a deadly blow to morality, and did.

It is no less necessary to put young men on guard against false confidence in the virtues of herbs and simples. For example, all the ancients believed that the plant called *agnus castus*, whose leaves resemble those of the olive-tree had the virtue of rendering chaste, by means of its juice, or merely by carrying it on one's person. The first point is a superstition; as for the second, if the virtue of the plant were proven, it would be a true poison.[117]

The satyrion, whose effect is the contrary, would be an opposite poison.[118] It is the same with the orchid, of which the configuration of its root has given it an underserved reputation.

It was once said that the vegetable basil rendered insensible or lethargic. This has some foundation; people who garnish their bedroom with that plant in pots and close the win-

---

[116] This account, identifying the goddess Flora with a courtesan, originated in the fourth century from the writings of Lactantius, who invented it as a fanciful explanation for the origin of the Roman spring festival of Floralia, of which, as a Christian, he disapproved.

[117] The supposed anaphrodisiac properties of *Vitex agnuscastus* remain controversial, but it is still very popular as a herbal medicine.

[118] The name "satyrion" has been applied over the ages to various supposedly aphrodisiac plants, including orchids, but the original reference might have been to ragwort, which contains several toxic alkaloids.

dows tightly can be inconvenienced, but one can say as much of all odorous flowers. It is folly to say that by crushing basil and putting it under a stone one can engender a scorpion.

It is claimed that mint, thrown into boiling water, refreshes it; if that is true, I would believe that in ordeals by boiling water, the priest employed that means to save those who had paid him well.

The carline thistle,[119] or chameleon albus, is used as an antidote against poisons and venoms. I don't believe it.

Squill, suspended from the vault of a house, prevents the entry of charms and enchantments. One might as well say that it prevents phoenixes and hippogriffs from entering.

It is said that parsley is dangerous for epileptics and nurses; it is an old wives' tale.

Comfrey, or *Consolida majoris*, really does have the virtue of reuniting cut flesh, but to say, like Pliny and Dioscorides, that if it is put in a stew-pot with pieces of meat it will reunite them into a single piece is puerile.

The ancients believed that verbena dispelled melancholy; Pliny and Dioscorides go so far as to say that one is necessarily joyful in a room sprinkled with water infused with verbena. Those two authors did not believe it themselves but they wanted to prove that it was true by the fact that verbena was used in all sacred ceremonies.

The same virtues are attributed to Nymphea or the nenuphar lily as to agnus castus; it would be an equally dangerous plant if its pretended virtues were not imaginary.

Ivy, taken in an infusion, troubles the mind; that is why it was the symbol of Bacchus. We would do well never to take that useless infusion. Its berries, taken in a beverage, render men impotent, but fatten blackbirds and thrushes. It is also affirmed that those berries or clusters, taken in a beverage, protect against intoxication. Finally, it is said that melancholic individuals can be cured if they drank wine from ivy-wood cups—but might it not be the wine alone that cheers them up?

---

[119] *Carlina acaulis*, still popular as a diuretic,

As for poppy, who does not know that it is a very pernicious plant? The opium extracted from it is abundantly used in
Persia and throughout Asia, but would be deadly in our cold
climate.

The Italian mandrake, which comes from Apulia and
which is given to people about to have a limb amputated to
drink, in order to render them insensible, subsequently causes
by the sensory depression it procures, a disorder in the animal
economy difficult to repair. It is claimed that its root, boiled
for six hours with ivory, softens it and makes it easy to turn.

The leaves of the laurier rose kill quadrupeds that eat
them, whereas, taken in wine, they serve humans and a coun-
ter-poison—doubtless because they are a real poison.

Lentil gives frightful dreams because it is heavy.

Hemlock is a cold poison, especially in hot countries.
Yew, when mashed, kills like hemlock.

The bitter herb of Sardinia produces sardonic laughter by
contraction of the muscles, and kills.

Henbane intoxicates and renders insensate; wild pigs that
eat it dies poisoned, if they do not find water into which to
hurl themselves.

Aconite is the most violent of vegetal poisons, with the
exception of certain mushrooms that are even more dangerous.
Monkshood, a species of aconite that has leaves like a wild
cucumber, kills leopards; another species, wolfbane, kills
wolves when those animals browse it instead of dogtooth.
Such species are used for poisoning daggers and other blades
steeped in their juice

The celebrated plant named balsam comes from hot, dry
countries like Arabia; it is an excellent remedy for consump-
tives if breathed in.

Lion's-foot in a vulnerary, but it is a false to say that if
girls and women use it, it will render them the appearances of
virginity. [120]

---

[120] The term "lion's foot" is now more commonly applied to
an American herb, but Debundeh is referring to *Alchemilla*

It is claimed that rose hip protects from rabies by drinking the juice expressed in its milk

In Scythia a herb exists called licorice, the leaves of which, chewed and retained in the mouth, protect against thirst for ten to twelve days. That might be so, but the hoopoe of which Celian speaks, which gives information about hidden treasures, surely only has an imaginary virtue.[121] It is even worse if one makes mention, according to a mendacious Jewish author, of the baara root, which has the form and renders the light of flame; if someone tries to touch it in order to pick it, without having first sprinkled himself with a woman's urine or blood, it will strike him dead. Even that does not guarantee safety, for it always kills the person who touches it, with the consequence that people take the precaution of attaching a dog to its stem in order that it will pull it up as it follows its master.[122]

But let's change the subject.

Human gluttony and the excess of aliments that the ancients took must have enfeebled the species, for two reasons, which you will glimpse. Herodotus recounts that the Persians offered prizes to anyone who discovered new stews, or new delights of any kind; that in their meals, they ate and drank until they were obliged to relieve their overloaded stomachs; that as soon as hunger returned they recommenced, while poor people languished in need and misery when a King of Persia

---

xanthochlora, also known as Lady's Mantle because of the imaginary property indicated here.

[121] The hoopoe is a bird, not a plant, although it did have the legendary reputation of indicating the location of buried treasure.

[122] The baara root is mentioned cryptically in the Old Testament, perhaps by virtue of a mistranslation—the word means "flame" in Hebrew—but the fanciful account given here is due to Josephus, who might not have been entirely serious in advocating its use as an antidote to demonic possession.

had passed through a province-the presence of that monarch was a scourge, while that of our kings is a benefit.

A Roman Emperor named Geta gave a feast one day; he wanted there to be eighteen courses—which is to say, as many letters as there were in the Roman alphabet, which were A, B, C, D, E, F, G, H, I, L, M, N, O, P, Q, R, S, T and V. The first was composed of all the birds and fish whose names begin with A; the second of those whose initial letter was a B, and so on, all the way to V. At dessert, the fruits were served in the same way, as many preserved as natural, in alphabetical order.[123]

Heliogabalus went even further; he served dishes for ten or twenty persons of the crests and kidneys of cocks, tongues of peacocks and nightingales, eggs of grouse and tiny birds, etc.

It is said of a certain Audebout, King of the Angles, who wagered one day that he could eat until he choked; his competitors could only win, either the bet or by the glutton's death.

I have sometimes spoken to my pupil about the visions of phantoms that people believe they see, but I do not recall them; I shall content myself with one rather pleasant story.

---

[123] This curious anecdote seems to have first appeared in French in *Premières conceptions théologiques sur le Caresme* (1605) by Pierre de Besse, allegedly based on Aelius Spartianus' *Historia Augusta*. The feast is attributed there not to the emperor Geta but to a Roman consul named Antonius Geta. It crops up in several other books thereafter, with the attribution first switched to the emperor Geta in a 1662 book by Jean Dourban. Restif probably got it from *Le Conservateur, ou collection de morceaux rares et d'ouvrages anciens & modernes* (38 parts, 1756-58 & 1761; subsequently reprinted in volume form) signed by the Chevalier de Bruix, where it is immediately followed by the anecdote about Heliogabalus that follows it here.

A Mommonian went astray by night, traveling on horseback along the bank of a river, which he dared not cross. Desolate, he began to cry out: "Ho! Ho!" The echo from a nearby rock returned his plaint. The Mommonian, delighted to hear a man on the other side of the river, shouted: "Where can I cross?"

"Cross."

"Here?"

"Here."

"Ought I to cross here?" he added, in order to receive further assurance.

"Cross here."

The man, believing that there was definitely a ford, put his horse in the water, but soon perceived that it had lost its footing. Fortunately, it was a vigorous animal, which pulled its master out of danger. The following day, the man, having arrived home, went to complain to one of his friends that evil gods had induced him to error. His friend had the place described to him and, knowing that there was an excellent echo there, he took the superstitious man there and made him understand that the gods take no pleasure in deceiving mortals.

Nature sometimes produces monstrous human beings, but they are not, as the vulgar believe, prognostications of public misfortunes; it signifies nothing; it is an anomaly produced by natural causes. In Balaclay I have seen a girl double at the shoulder; she had two heads, two necks, but only one trunk, a breast under each head and two legs, the whole a little stronger than usual. The two heads slept together, spoke at the same time and had only one will—which seems to prove that the will comes from the diaphragm, or what the vulgar name the heart. That monster lived for about three years; but I saw a second one, less perfect, whose two heads did not look at one another. That monster was then twenty-six years old; it was expelled from the region because it frightened pregnant women.

More anciently, a child was born in Rome in whom all the viscera were visible. Such a being, had it been conserved, would have been a continual and living anatomy. It is said that the ancient Greek and Roman physicians requested, and the Arab physicians of today request, living criminals for dissection—a great cruelty! They can be excused, however, at least with regard to great criminals, because they are thus forced, it seems to me, to be useful to humankind, which they have offended. But that permission to dissect the living requires great circumspection.

Since we are on the subject of monsters, it is certain that all animals proportionate in size can engender together, a donkey with a mare, wolf with a bitch, a bull with a female buffalo, bison or hind, etc. I have seen a dog that had been engendered by a bear with a local mastiff. It is affirmed that it is customary, among the Angles, to procure these couplings. It is said, in addition, that an escaped bear, after having been imprisoned for a long time, retreated into the woods, abducted and violated a woman—the same thing happened among the Sarmatians—and that a hideous monster came from it, which was killed when already grown.

Monstrosities of every species come from three causes; ether a poorly-disposed female—for the female is like the mold of every species; or a simultaneous superfetation; or a monstrous coupling. In the first case, the forms are bizarre, but always tend to the human. In the second there is a junction of two individuals linked together, having two souls if they have two heads, two diaphragms and two hearts. In the third, there is a monstrous conjunction punished by the laws of every country, in that it tends to plunge nature into the confusion of which good mores have made it emerge.

The ancients did not punish the authors of monsters; they were content to stifle or drown them. It is claimed that the Janus of the ancient Romans was a monster with horse's hooves. It is affirmed that in Tartary, where men always live with their horses or mares, people with the feet and legs of horses are often found, which the ancients named hippopodes; that in India that there are amphibious androhippopotami whose upper bodies are human and whose lower part resembles a horse; that in the mountains of that country there are androcynes, or dog-men, who have human heads but bark and hunt like dogs.

It is affirmed that in Tongres in Flanders a sow gave birth to a piglet with a human head; that in Switzerland a woman gave birth to a child whose body, save for the head, was that of a lion; that a girl gave birth to a semi-dog from the navel down, all the rest being human; that among the Hyperboreans there are men with dog's heads, which bark instead of talking; they cover themselves with skins, live on rapine, eat humans and animals that they can trap. In Italy, near Montalto, in the vicinity of Verona, a mare gave birth to a foal with a human head; that monster had a voice so powerful that it frightened the peasant guarding the stud, who killed it with a knife—but that appears to be a fable.

As for marine monsters there are too many to linger upon them.

Naturalists affirm that a woman cannot put into the world more than five children at a time; a maidservant of the Roman Emperor Augustus had five; she died of it, as did the children. However, and author reports than in the time of Algemont I, the King of the Lombards, a prostitute gave birth to seven male children.[124]

The serpent is the most extraordinary and most frightful of animals. We who live in a cold climate, where they are rarely seen, and small, have little interest in knowing it, but one exists in Africa and other hot countries a hundred and

---

[124] This anecdote is found in *Traictés des histoires prodigieuses* (1561), signed "Boerhaave"—but not the noted humanist of that name—before being picked up in Laurent Joubert's *Erreurs populaires au fait de la medecine* (1578) and various subsequent texts, although Boerhaave's text refers to Algemont, the first King of the Lombards, not Algemont I, and gives an elaborate account of the future of the children, omitted by Joubert and subsequent citations. There is no historical trace of any such monarch.

twenty-five feet long; they are the color of old tree-trunks, which they resemble so closely that when they coil up, travelers have been seen to sit on them. They stifle deer, buffalo, and humans by surrounding their body while their tails wind around a stout tree, giving them a point of support.

For the basilisk, or king of serpents, however, one fears that its existence is a fable. What might have given rise to the tale that the animal in question can kill with its gaze is that, in fact, all hunting animals, such as the dog, the wolf, the lion, the tiger and even humans, can arrest with a fixed stare the animal they surprise and render it immobile with fear. The serpent paralyzes in the same way, by the dread that it creates and the fear that it causes.

One day, it was decided to clear out a cesspit in Waterford. The first workman who went down was suffocated, as was the second, and so on, until the fifteenth. It was presumed in consequence that there was a basilisk in the cesspit, but it was the mephitic vapor, as was ascertained, and it was vanquished by throwing in quicklime.

I read somewhere a fable that made me laugh: Hector Boece writes that in the Hebrides, islands near Scotland, the bird clakis is born of wood that is thrown into the sea and rots there.[125] Since then I have encountered people who affirm that they have seen it at Butkquanir or Lewis, one of those islands, from the castle of Pertalige, now Stechawn. Others go further, affirming that a vessel arrived at Edinburgh in Midlothian, which that had dropped anchor three times in the Hebrides,

---

[125] The Scottish philosopher Hector Boece, who signed his writings in Latin Boethius (1465-1536). In *Historia Gentis Scotorum* [History of the Scottish People], where the "clakis" is identified as a species of goose. Buffon and other eighteenth-century naturalists identify it with the barnacle goose. The place names cited in association with the bird are obviously mangled, as are many others in the text, but it is difficult to work out what the intended references might be or where the data might have come from.

found on its return, its rotting timbers full of those birds ready to be born. That is how these fables are accredited!

Finally, one thing even more marvelous, which is that trees are seen in Scotland whose leaves roll up, fall into the sea and change into birds. This is the truth: when large pieces of wood are thrown into the sea, or entire uprooted trees fall into it, the clakis build their nests on that floating wood. As for the leaves that change into birds, that is because little birds make their nests in the trees, attaching them to the leaves; the chicks become strong, agitate, detach the leaves, so that they fall into the water, whish unsticks them, and the little bird is disengaged.

One thing that I have heard that seems fabulous, and with is true, is that a wheat-tree exists. They have been seen in Italy in the year 553 in Rome, the same in which Hannibal was beaten.[126] The Spanish have recent discovered similar ones, which they are cultivating.

I have spoken to my pupil about volcanoes and earth-quakes, revealing their natural causes. Both are occasioned by combustible materials contained in the bosom of the Earth; those peats are heated up by fermentation and catch fire; then, the heated water and air expand, lifting up the earth, opening it up, and launching stones and molten minerals.

As for eclipses, that is a very simple thing; my pupil understood immediately how the Earth, coming between the Sun and the Moon, causes an eclipse of the Moon, and how the Moon being between the Sun and the Earth causes an eclipse of the Sun.

In the midst of all this knowledge that I gave him, a pretended marvel occurred in this very region. It is said that in the vicinity of Cork, in the village of Clon, a tree laden with fruits suddenly appeared in the middle of a plain where no tree had

---

[126] Hannibal's retreat from Rome was actually in 204 B.C. Reports of breadfruit trees found in the Philippines had reached France some time before Restif wrote the present book, and attempts to cultivate them were already being made.

ever been seen. We sought information about that pretended marvel; it turned out that it was knavery on the part of a few druids, who wanted to prove to their enemies that they were superior to them in merit and sanctity. The tree had been removed, rot and branch, and had been transported by night with the aid of a machine, and placed in the plan, where it continued to vegetate...

Chapter 21
Interruption. Unexpected separation.[127] Princess
Belletête. What Oribeau finds in a castle.

Internally, Oribeau was admiring the almost infinite extent of the knowledge of a simple shepherd, when piercing screams were heard from behind a nearby clump of trees. O'Barbo, his pupil, Cahincaha and Debundeh all rose to their feet at the same instant.

"What's that?" said the young Prince of Mommonia. "Let's run to the rescue of whoever is calling for help, for it's the voice of a young woman."

So saying, Oribeau ran toward the trees. In spite of his great age, old O'Barbo did not abandon him, and almost reached the place from which the screams were coming ahead of him.

A troop of armed men, at the head of which was a man with a handsome face but which seemed to be made ugly by malevolence in spite of nature, were taking away a young peasant girl who had just been abducted from Mommonian territory. As he drew closer, Oribeau recognized the beautiful Rosée.

He could not control his anger, and, approaching the leader he said: "Traitor! By what right are you abducting that young woman from the Kingdom of Mommonia, where she

---

[127] The insertion "Rosée," present in the original list of contents, is omitted from the chapter-heading as given here.

lived with her father, to take her by force into that of Lagenia?"

"Lord," said O'Barbo, addressing the commander, "Excuse the imprudent ardor of a young man who has seen that girl in the home of a laborer whom he aided for some time."

"He will be punished," said Ratchlin—for it was him. "Soldiers, tie him up!"

Oribeau quivered with wrath and threw himself at an armed soldier, who looked at him in astonishment and was preparing to defend himself when loud cries were heard.

It was Bridge-Clonard, followed by all of Younghall and the inhabitants of neighboring villages, who were running after the abductors of Rosée and Jasmine.

Immediately, a part of Ratchlin's troop was detached, dragging away the younger of the two sisters. The Prince of Mommonia, seeing that he was supported, pushed away the soldiers who were holding him, leapt on a horse that Bridge-Clonard presented to him and put himself at the head of the peasants in order to follow Ratchlin—but the traitor, who dared not fight an equal party, had such an excellent horse that he took Rosée away, without Oribeau or the Sage being able to prevent him.

Seething and full of courage, the Prince of Mommonia wanted to pursue him, but O'Barbo represented to him that that would be to engage recklessly in enemy territory, since the Kings of Meath and Lagenia were allied at all times; that it was necessary to go back into Mommonia, and send a herald to Queen Conchèse to demand the return of the young woman abducted from a neighboring State and, if the response was not satisfactory, to declare war on her. Then, they would march at the head of a disciplined army, and courage would be accompanied by prudence. Oribeau was obliged to yield to those arguments.

As they passed Mullanger, the young Prince and his teacher wanted to bid their hosts adieu, but they only found the good Nursimaneh, who said to them: "The man who received you here is the dwarf Debundeh, celebrated for his prudence as for his virtues, and his pupil is Prince Beaudâme himself, heir to the throne of Meath. They have joined Princess Belletête of Lagenia, whom Ratchlin is taking away, after having abducted her from the house of a laborer of Younghall in Mommonia named Bridge-Clonard, and he will try to please her in order to marry her."

At these words the young King of Mommonia felt a sharp pain, for he believed that it was Rosée—but he dissimulated it, at a sign from O'Barbo. They took their leave of the nurse, who told them that she was going to join Beaudâme, and they followed their companions, who were returning to Younghall.

It was almost dark, and they were all marching in silence, those who were on horseback forming a rearguard, when, on passing before an ancient castle, they heard a melodious voice singing:

A WOMAN'S VOICE.
How cruel it is to have to punish a lover,
When, ingrate as he is, one loves him tenderly!
My heart is suffering a frightful pain;
It ought to hate, but is forced to love.
The transports of love; the furies of hate,
Come to animate me by turns;
Is there're a ruder ordeal?
My heart is suffering a frightful torment!
How cruel it is to have to punish a lover,
When, ingrate as he is, one loves him tenderly!

A MAN'S VOICE.
Your rigor drives me to despair,
Adorable Oribelle, appease this wrath.
Inhumane, what is it necessary to do,
To obtain a fate more tender?

THE WOMAN'S VOICE.
You scarcely deserve to please me;

You merit my anger too much;
Odious prince, go away;
Leave me alone with my anger!

"It's the voice of Prince Beaudame that is responding to that beauty," said Oribeau, emotionally, "and she's rejecting him!"

"Do you think," said O'Barbo, "that she needs help against such a virtuous Prince?"

"But he mentioned Oribelle, and I ought not to neglect an opportunity to see her."

"It would not be appropriate to attack a Prince who has given us hospitality, but if you deem it appropriate, you and I could go alone."

Oribeau could ask for nothing better. He preceded the old man, and called for the drawbridge to be lowered for two travelers. That was granted.

Introduced into the castle, they found Beaudâme seated at the feet of a beautiful girl who resembled Jasmine, with an expression of naïve imbecility, whose eyes were blank. In the courtyard there were two tents set up for the men-at-arms who formed two separate corps. The first were Lagenians, under Ratchlin's orders; the second were from Meath, sent by Queen Mijoreh to bring her son back to the Court. The shepherd, as well as the good Nursimaneh, was accompanying the young Prince.

"Milady," said the shepherd to the Princess whom Beaudâme, while singing, had just named Oribelle, "You see the Prince of Meath, so you ought not to be surprised by his courage. If anyone had done you violence, he would deliver you."

"What!" cried Beaudâme. "I was the son of the Princess celebrated for her beauty, whom I adored, without knowing it? I'm destined for the throne?"

"Yes, Prince," the shepherd replied, "you were brought up in the country, leaving you ignorant of your condition and subjecting you to the work of the people in order to fortify your health, which appeared too delicate; it was by virtue of an excess of tenderness that the King, your father, and the Queen, your mother, sent you away from them. You have lost that good father, and your mother is recalling you in order to console her. The young beauty whom you see is the daughter of a powerful Queen; it is necessary to try to win her heart."

"Ah!" cried Beaudâme. "She already possesses mine, but can I flatter myself that I might please her—me, who is devoid of art, devoid of usage, deprived of the precious advantages with which Friga has endowed her in such profusion? No, I shall never have the joy of winning her affection."

"But you're not so very ugly," said Nursimaneh, "and I'm sure that if Milady deigns to look at you with some attention, she'll find you very likeable."

"But…yes…," said the Princess. "Prince Beaudâme is…good, and that…a great deal."

After these few words, pronounced indolently, Oribeau found that, in fact, Beaudâme was not as ugly as before.

"Is that Princess, whom the nurse has called Belletête, Oribelle?" said the young King of Mommonia to his tutor.

"I cannot answer that question for you. It's your heart that must instruct you."

"Let's talk to them," said Oribeau—for they had not yet been perceived in the crowd that surrounded them.

O'Barbo advanced and said to Beaudâme: "Prince, here are your guests at Mullanger, whom hazard has brought to this castle."

As soon as he perceived Oribeau, Beaudâme ran to him. "Prince," he said to him, "congratulate me. I've just met this beautiful Princess, whom the Queen of Lagenia, her mother, has recalled to her Court, at the same time that the Queen of Meath has told me that I am her son. I felt, at the first glance, before knowing what she is and what I am, that I adored her. I have dared to tell her so, but she has not yet relied to me as I would desire."

Oribeau cast his gaze upon the Princess and recognized her for the beautiful Hasameh, who had accompanied Fillira when they had saved her from the soldiers. He blushed in thinking: *What! That was Oribelle! I felt nothing for her but cold admiration. Again, at this moment, I don't feel anything!*

"Milady," he said to the Princess of Lagenia, your beauty is celebrated throughout Evinland."

"I know," said the Princess.

"Renown does not overstate the case."

"I'm more beautiful than my sister, am I not?"

"I cannot make the comparison," said Oribeau, "having never seen her."

"Say yes."

"I always speak according to my thought. Milady; how can one speak without ideas?"

"That's odd!" said the Princess. "I speak well like that myself."

Surprised by these responses, Oribeau looked at his guide, who seemed to be buried in profound meditation.

"I'm called Belletête," said the Princess, "but I have many other names. Ask my nurse, here..."

Oribeau darted a glance at a kind of governess, whose piercing gaze made him lower his eyes.

"It is for you to see," the woman said, "whether you can prevail in amour over Prince Beaudâme; the most affectionate of the two will obtain my ward, the Princess, for a spouse."

"Milady is beautiful, and I admire her beauty," Oribeau replied.

"Oh!" cried Beaudâme, dolorously, casting a passionate glance at Belletête. "If you're my rival, you'll prevail! In the name of the gods, leave me a young Princess, whose adorable innocence renders her even dearer to my heart! May I develop that fortunate character!"

"It's said that I'm stupid," said Belletête, with a kind of tenderness. "Am I? Tell me, you, for there is only you with whom I don't blush at anything, because if I'm stupid, you're ugly."

"I only see in you one thing, which is that you're charming; as for intelligence, you doubt that you have any; that very doubt indicates in you much more than there is in certain bards whose productions I read in my solitude."

"Ah, you see, my good woman!" said the Princess to the woman who was accompanying her.

Prince Beaudâme was becoming visibly embellished, and Prince Belletête's eyes were beginning to express something.

Oribeau remained immobilized by astonishment.

"Can that be the Princess of Lagenia that is destined for me?" he said to the Sage. "It's true that she's beautiful, but what does that familiarity with Prince Beaudâme mean? When she spoke to me at the ball, after taking off her mask, under the name of the Princess of Thomond-Clare, I found her intelligent, or at least like anyone else. Whence comes this idiotic naivety today? Is it a proof. I'm lost…is that the happiness that you have promised me so much? Oh, Canora, Ahissa, Daura, Julia, Fillira, Rosée, why couldn't one of you be Oribelle?"

As soon as the young King of Mommonia had formulated that wish, the Yapou's cry was heard.

"Let's go," he said to the Sage. "Something seems to be telling me that Oribelle isn't here, and that if the Princess we see is the Princess of Lagenia, it's because there are two of them."

O'Barbo followed the Prince, without making any response.

Chapter 2J
Jealousy of Oribeau against Beaudame. A meal with the Dunvalanian. Julia.

Jetsam of fate and amour, Oribeau advanced sadly. He had not taken ten paces when he heard the songs recommence.

The chagrins of amour have charms,
For a heart much inflamed;
My angry shepherdess has made my shed tears;
Her anger being disarmed,

The greatest joy succeeds my alarms;
I have savored more the pleasure of being loved.

DUET.
Tenderness
Is the mistress
Of all hearts;
In vain spite presses us
To treat a lover with invincible rigor;
When we see him dissolve in tears
The spite dies...
Etc., etc.

"They're in accord!" exclaimed the Prince of Mommonia. What powerful charm does the Prince of Meath have, then, that Oribelle—if that really is the Princess of Lagenia that we've just seen—affects a stupid imbecility before me to drive me away, while she shows him graces of intelligence and harmony as soon as he is alone with her? Is this one of the ordeals I must undergo? It was predicted to me that if my heart were virtuous, I would recognize Oribelle without the aid of my eyes; have I committed some crime? Tell me, wise O'Barbo—don't flatter me."

"I haven't seen you do anything criminal—on the contrary—but look into yourself."

"Oh, who can flatter himself with having nothing for which to reproach himself?"

"Do you feel that your heart recognizes Oribelle?"

"No, but if that's her, it's necessary that I must have rendered myself culpable...how fortunate Beaudâme is! It's the good deeds that were recounted to us that have won him preference! Oh, I sense that I'm jealous."

"Be jealous—but in order to surpass him."

While speaking thus, the Prince and his guide were still advancing, for they had to march day and night in order to arrive sooner. They had reached the high road that goes from Waterford to Balaclay.

They traversed the Mountains of Stefenon, where the Sage saw his garden again, with delight. Oribeau was charmed himself to find himself back in that happy solitude where he had spent the best years of his adolescence.

They had a morning meal in More-Eustace, from which they went to dine in Dunlavan in the home of their host of old, whom they found full of life and false news.

"Do you recognize us?" the Sage said to him.

After a moment's silence, employed in examining the old man and his pupil, the Dunlavanian exclaimed: "Ah! You're my guests from the Mountains of Stefenon! Oh, fine things have happened since I last saw you. But how the handsome young man has grown! How he's filled out; how strong, healthy and vigorous he looks!" He lowered his voice. "Do you know that our poor young Prince has been brought back to Waterford under an unknown name, and that by the cleverness of Dondanuck, who set a trap for him, he's been hanged in the public square as a thief? It's an insupportable abomination!"

"How do you know that?" O'Barbo asked him.

"From one of my friends who saw it, and who recognized the young Prince—but he dared not say anything."

Although a poor source of news, the Dunvalanian had a good heart; he had an excellent dinner served.

They were sitting down at table when the Yapou uttered a shrill cry. Oribeau shuddered, and ran to the door. It was Julia and Clomaneh, who had just come into the courtyard. They were each descending from a horse, on which they were mounted side-saddle.

Oribeau ran toward them. Julia, nimble and brisk, was on the ground, but he helped the stout Clomaneh, alias Madame Thor-el.

"Ah!" said the Dunvalaian, on seeing them. "Be welcome, my old acquaintances. Well, has the case been judged?"

"Not yet," replied Clomaneh, "but the crisis is approaching."

"Come on," said the gentleman, "sit down at the table." Then, looking alternately at Oribeau and Julia, he said: "How this handsome and vigorous young man would suit that lovely girl! If the case is won, we shall have to see! Is he a gentleman?"

"Of the finest nobility of Evinland," replied O'Barbo, "for he combines an illustrious ancestry with a taste for virtue."

"And your ward, my old acquaintance?" said the Dunlavanian.

"She combines an illustrious ancestry with a virtue as stainless as her beauty."

"Ha—it's a marriage to be made!"

"My ward has relatives," said Clomaneh. "There are obstacles; for they have conflicting views. One would like to give her to the son of a powerful neighbor, the other to the son of anther neighbor."

"And what does Julia think?" asked O'Barbo.

Julia blushed and lowered her beautiful eyes.

"I believe," said Clomaneh, "that she isn't far away from sharing the opinion of our host; unfortunately, it isn't him who will regulate her fate."

Oribeau was in a cruel embarrassment. If he abandoned his heart to Julia, he would lose Oribelle. However, he felt an insurmountable penchant for the good Thor-el's niece.

"Since Julia hasn't replied to me," O'Barbo went on, addressing his pupil, "will you tell me your sentiment regarding that marriage?"

"You know," Oribeau replied, "that my happiness depends on *Princess Oribelle*"—he pronounced the last words in a whisper. "All I can tell you is that if Julia were her, I'd be the happiest of men; but as she isn't; I'll overcome my penchant, not because of myself but for the wellbeing of *my people*, whose interest demands that the one I named should be my wife. Let's go—I sense that it's necessary—and continue our route."

He got up from the table immediately and went to fetch his horse.

O'Barbo smiled, as the young man left the courtyard he said to the Dunlavanian: "Don't believe false rumors, my dear Host. The man you have just see here at your table, whom you found so strong and in such flourishing health, is your young King, who is returning to Waterford to be crowned there. I'm his teacher from the Mountains of Stefenon, and I invite you to come and see the coronation and lodge in the palace. Ask for me; I'm the so-called magician O'Barbo. As for that beautiful person and her governess, have all the attentions for her that you would have for the intended bride of your young Sovereign. Adieu—don't forget what I've said."

The gentleman of Dunlavan could not get over his surprise, and O'Barbo had mounted his horse and was far away before his host had recovered the power of speech.

"Milady," he said, finally, to Clonameh, "if you too are a Princess, tell me, in order that I might honor you as you merit, and as I ought, for although I know you, for having received you here with that lovely young woman, I'm no longer sure of anything. I would never have thought that that old man and his pupil were our young King and his guardian, the friend of the omnipotent Minister."

"I'm this young woman's aunt," replied the demi-fay. "If she's only a simple individual, respect her age and her sex; if she's a Princess, respect her secrets."

The Dunlavanian bowed, and made no other reply.

"Ah!" said Ennisleague. That reconciles me with him.

"Peace, old woman," said a brutal drinker.

The hunter Kerry was refreshing himself, however, and catching his breath. After which, he resumed speaking...

They were at that point in the reading in the market garden of Monsieur Gaudet of the Rue Courtaudvilain when the poorly attached lamp fell on the reader's hands and trousers. Fortunately, the trousers were leather and slightly greasy; the damage was minor, but, the lamp having broken, the evening came to an end, and everyone groped their way to bed.

Distracted by the accident that had just occurred, the people sitting up late in the market garden of Monsieur Gaudet of the Rue Courtaudvilain had postponed the end of the story to the following day.

At the hour when the chandeliers were being lit in the houses of the nobles and the financiers, the candelabras in the homes of the bourgeois and the lamps in the homes of the artisans, the company was found to be complete and the eldest son of the good bourgeois resumed the reading as follows. May Thor and Vananis determine that he can finish it in merriment and tranquility!

Chapter 2K
Kanaster. Ahissa; her story and that of old Killcullen. Six good deeds ordered. Oribeau performs the first.

"*Kerns*[128] *govern themselves easily; and all is well, Hamir responds.* That's an old proverb," O'Barbo said, as he caught up with the young King, "for the infantryman is only carried by his feet, regulated by his will alone, whereas the cavalier, in addition to his will, also directs that of his horse, which is sometimes not in accord with that of its rider. Such is the situation of a man who masters a violent passion; reason

---

[128] Author's note: "A kern had for weapons a sword and a javelin, or dart, attached to a cord, in order to draw it back after being thrown. 'Hamir' was the response that a sentinel made to a Kern, or infantryman; it is formed from *Hhay hamier*, 'I am here.'" The assertion that infantrymen in Scottish companies serving various French Kings made that reply to sentinels—not the other way round—and the explanation of its meaning, are found in the *Dictionnaire militaire* (1745) compiled by François Aubert de la Chenaye des Bois

may tell him what to do, but it is if he were carried away by an impetuous horse that goes astray."

"I shall try to govern mine," the young King replied, "and I guarantee that I won't do anything unworthy of a Head of State. I sense that the further I'm raised above other men, the more I owe to society. An individual can follow his tastes; a Prince can almost never follow his, either in the choice of a spouse or that of his Ministers; it is reason and public interest alone that ought to guide him. You've inculcated those maxims in me too well for me to forget them."

"I know that you'll be a great King," O'Barbo replied. "When Dondanuck, my friend and yours, Lord, brought you to me instead of making me go to you, I sensed a pang of anxiety at his proposition, but that was before having seen you; your physiognomy alone, before you had spoken, told me that you would be. Today, however, the crisis has arrived. It's necessary to overcome your passions, and if Oribelle presents herself to you unknowingly, with all her charms, refuse her, in order to remain faithful to her."

"But she's with Prince Beaudâme."

"If that's the case, you know that she's virtuous."

"But what if she loves him?"

"You couldn't hold it against her, for it would only be because of his excellent qualities."

"I'll come back to Julia."

"Have you forgotten Rosée, to whom you paid so much attention during our life as laborers in the home of Bridge-Clonard

"To tell you the truth," Oribeau replied, "I feel that there has never been any difference between the sentiments inspired in me by Julia, Canora, Daura, Rosée, Fillira and Ahissa; those six beautiful girls have an equal power over my heart. That's what desolates me! I'd like a preference; it seems to me that a multiple taste is a vice, as if it were an announcement of libertinage."

"I don't think so," replied O'Barbo. "Since they please you equally, Oribelle, as soon as she appears..."

"Oh, Oribelle doesn't inspire me, I confess, with half of what I felt for Julia. But be sure that, if I marry the Princess of Lagenia without loving her, I shall nevertheless be a good husband; I shall see in her the benefit of my people, and I shall ensure the wellbeing and benefit of my people by all the means that depend on me."

As the young Prince finished speaking, the Yapou made its shrill cry heard in such a forceful manner that the horses reared up and all of the Prince's retinue were frightened.

They were approaching Katherlagh. Two strong mules arrived by way of a side-road, bearing a kanaster that contained a young woman.[129] An old man on a horse was guiding the kanaster. Oribeau looked at him, and recognized him, joyfully, as the man he had defended against assassins on the day when he had been insulted by fops in the dance-hall. He greeted him and asked him for news of his daughter.

"She's in that kanaster," replied the old man. "I need to take her to Balaclay. It appears that you're going to Waterford, so we won't be traveling together, but if you think it appropriate, I'll have the honor of entertaining in this village my dear liberator, and that of Ahissa, for whom she and I have both retained the most heartfelt gratitude."

"We're in a hurry to return," Oribeau replied, "but I wouldn't like to refuse."

"Let's accept," said the Sage. "Your followers need rest and this man merits consideration."

They went into an inn and the unknown man, after having taken Ahissa out of her kanaster, had refreshments served, not only to the Prince but to all his retinue.

---

[129] Author's note: "A kanaster is a large basket like those in which Persian ladies travel; the word in used on the Baltic Sea." Kanaster is in fact defined in this fashion in the *Manuel lexique* of 1770, although previous and succeeding dictionaries make no mention of the Baltic Sea and assert instead that the term is employed in several French provinces.

When they had begun eating, O'Barbo, noticing the admiration with which the young King of Mommonia was considering the beautiful Ahissa, said to the old man, who seemed to be her father or grandfather: "That young woman interests my pupil so much, that I think you'd oblige us by telling us how it comes about that you're traveling the world together and, above all, why you were both on the point of being murdered in the streets of Waterford."

"I'd like nothing better," the unknown man replied. "You should know, honorable old man, and you, our amiable young savior, that I am neither the grandfather nor the father of this lovely girl, but a former domestic in her father's house. My name is Killcullen. My master is very rich, but built edifices provoke thunderbolts if they have no peer. A division occurred in the family of my master and his wife, who was richer than him, proving the old maxim that it is useful for a man to have a chaste and poor wife. A Roman kalde expressed it in a verse: *Praestabat castas humilis fortuna Latinas Quondam.*[130]

"A handsome young man pleased the wife; she did not violate conjugal faith; the principles in which she had been brought up did not permit that, but she made him her favorite and her dotal domestic, as the ancient Romans would have put it, who administered her dowry independently of her husband. My master could not suffer that intruder and resolved to get rid of him. But he was betrayed by some of those in whom he had confidence, and as he was not the more powerful, he was oppressed. From that moment on, the favorite's insolence increased; he wanted to marry the heiress and to give Ahissa's younger sister to a rich neighbor, whom she hated, and of whom she would not have had children, in order that he might invade everything one day.

"You should know that Ahissa was brought up by an excellent woman, her nurse, who was well-born and only lent

---

[130] The author inserts a reference to Juvenal's *Satire VI*, in which the poet laments that "in the old days it was their low status that kept Roman women poor."

her breast out of amity. To thwart the designs of the favorite, she took her ward away and had her don various disguises, which changed her so much, by means of her costume, that she was unrecognizable. She wanted her to pass through various estates in order that one day, when she would be rich, she would feel compassion for the poor and soothe their distress.

"In spite of her precautions however, Ahissa was recognized by one of the favorite's emissaries, who assembled wretches in order to attack me and take possession of the heiress—but this pleasant young man came to our aid. Since then, Ahissa, hidden under different disguises, remained safe, until the day before yesterday, when she was recognized and abducted, with her sister. As you see, however, we found a means of escaping again. I'm taking her to her nurse, who won't leave her again, if possible, until the man that she loves out of gratitude has obtained her for his wife and will serve as her protector."

Such was the old man's story.

"I swear to you," said Oribeau, standing up fervently, "that if that man lives in the kingdom of Mommonia, justice will be done. As for the man the young woman loves"—he sighed—"I'd like to know who he is; I'll try to render her happy."

"It's you," said Killcullen, leaning close to the Prince's ear.

Oribeau blushed, and did not know what to say, but his heart was flattered. However, he replied: "This is my situation, old man: that I cannot dispose of myself, for, although the young Ahissa inspires tender sentiments in me, I could never abandon myself to them unless they were in accord with my duty. It is prescribed for me that I must overcome all my tastes and all my passions, and it is only at that price that I can become…what it is necessary for me to be."

As the Prince finished speaking, a soft and pleasant voice was heard, distinctly pronouncing these words, which seemed to emerge from a cloud: *Prince Oribeau has nothing for which to reproach himself, but before obtaining Oribelle and happi-*

ness, it is necessary that the perform six splendid deeds; he will then be submitted to a proof, which he will overcome if his actions are valid.

"What!" exclaimed Killcullen. "I have the honor of speaking to Prince Oribeau! Forgive me, Lord, for explaining myself with so much familiarity"

"Sovereigns are human," the young Prince replied, "as well as their subjects; and I believe that Kings are more constrained than anyone to the duties of humankind."

They got up from the table. The Prince, O'Barbo and their retinue mounted their horses, not without great regret on Oribeau's part, at going away thus from Ahissa, by whom he was loved.

They had hardly taken ten paces when they perceived a large troop of armed cavaliers who were galloping full tilt. Oribeau called his own troop to a halt, and arranged them in battle order, showing as much courage as if he already had experience of command. O'Barbo was by his side.

The leader of the troop having arrived within voice range, he shouted to the young Prince: "Do you intend to dispute the passage?"

"Yes, if you have evil intentions," replied Oribeau.

"I intend to take possession of a young woman named Ahissa, whom I can see drawing away on the road to Balaclay."

"If she is content to put herself in your hands," said the Prince, "you shall have her; but if she refuses, after you have named yourself, no human power will give her to you."

At these words, the cavalier advanced impetuously, but Oribeau, fortified by labor in the fields, met him half way, parried his adversary's blow, and landed his own with so much vigor that the cavalier tottered. Oribeau did not give him to recover, he swerved around him, striking incessantly, and unhorsed him.

Immediately, the cavalier's troop advanced to help him, but the Prince of Mommonia's followers, although fewer in number, ran to support their King, who performed prodigies of valor.

The enemies were defeated.

As soon as Oribeau saw that he had the advantage, he cried: "Spare bloodshed!! A victory soiled by blood, when one can dispense with spilling it, is an atrocity. Let us show our enemies and example of humanity, in order that they might profit from it one day in our regard."

As he finished, he raised Ratchlin up himself, without knowing him, rendered him his horse and his weapons, and permitted him to retire freely.

"Go," he said to him, "and know that the Prince of Mommonia is humane."

Chapter 2L
Laudations to generosity. Daura. Oribeau's second good deed.

"Laxity!" cried the vanquished leader, on rejoining his troop. "You allowed yourselves to be beaten and disarmed by a handful of men!"

"It isn't numbers," replied an old man, "but courage and a good cause that deliver victory."

Ratchlin wanted to strike the old soldier who had just replied to him so freely, but Oribeau prevented him from doing so.

Immediately, the two troops, the victorious and the vanquished, shouted: "Long live the glorious Prince of Mommonia, humane in combat, generous after victory! Fortunate are those who follow his traces in war, for they will have a tender father and a courageous leader, who will never turn his back on the enemy!"

All the voices fell silent at the same time, at the sight of a luminous chariot sailing through the air.

"What do I see?" said Oribeau to his tutor. "What is that prodigy? Genii and fays are fables, but I'm surrounded by marvels!"

As the young King stopped talking, a loud but very agreeable voice came from the chariot; it intoned a warrior song famous throughout Evinland, and even in neighboring lands:[131]

"'The wind and rain have ceased. The middle of the day is calm. The clouds are flying away through the air. The inconstant light of the Sun is fleeing over the green hills. The seething mountain torrent is spilling its reddened waters through the rocky valley. Its murmur pleases me. But what is that melodious voice that charms my ears? It that you, king of concerts, Alpin? Why are you moaning alone on the hill? The tones of your voice are lugubrious.'

"'My tears, O Ryno, are for the dead; my voice for the inhabitants of the tomb. You are upright, young man, in young majestic arrogance; you are the most handsome of the hamlet's children. But you will fall as Morar has fallen, and the sensible stranger will sit on your tomb to lament an unknown.

"'Brave Morar, whose sword shone in battle like lightning on the plain, how narrow and somber your dwelling is! In three strides I measure the space that contains you, you who were so tall! Four moss-covered stones are all that remain of your memory. O young Morar, it is true that you are no more? Have you not left a lover to weep for you?

"'But who is that old man coming toward us, leaning on his staff? Age has whitened his hair; he totters at every step.

---

[131] What follows is a variant of the Ossianic "Alpin's Lament of Morar" and its aftermath, from *The Songs of Selma*. Again, I have back-translated from the (abridged) French rather than reverting to the original, as Restif has obviously based his version on Pierre Le Tourneur's. It is by no means the only time that the piece has been appropriated to another literary work; the first part had been featured, without the extension featuring Armin's story, in J. W. Goethe's Romantic classic *Die Lieden des jungen werthers* (1774; tr. as *The Sorrows of Young Werther*), which was first translated into French in 1776.

His eyes are still red with tears they have shed. Oh, it is Morar's father! Weep, unfortunate father, weep! But your son cannot hear you. The pillow on which his head rests is far below the earth.

"'Adieu forever, bravest of men; the battlefield shall see you no more. The shadow of the forests will no longer be brightened by the glam of your armor. You have not left a son whose name and exploits will recall your memory, but my songs will save you from forgetfulness. Future centuries will learn your glory; they will hear mention of Morar.'

"At the songs of Alpin, dolor awoke in the hearts of all the shepherds who were listening; but the deepest sigh came from the heart of Armin The image of his children, who perished in the flower of their youth, returned to present themselves to his memory. 'Armin,' Alpin said to him, 'why is your sigh so profound? Do my songs sadden you so exceedingly? I only make them to soften and charm your soul. Why this somber sadness?

"'Yes, I am sad,' replied Armin, 'and the cause of my regrets is not light. Alpin, you have not lost your son, you have not lost your daughter. They live, they flourish before your eyes. But I am the last of my race. Will you listen to the story of my woes?

"'O cruel night! Rise, autumn winds! Blow over the black heather! Resound, mountain torrents, and you, tempests, bellow in the crowns of the oaks. Moon, rise over the broken clouds, show your melancholy face intermittently and recall to me soul the night full of horror in which I lost my children, when Arindal my son fell, when Daura my daughter died.

"'Armar, famous warrior, came to my dwelling and sought the love of Daura; he was not long refused. They were to be wed. The friends of the happy couple conceived brilliant hopes of their union.

"'The frightful Erath came to trouble the happiness of the lovers and their father. Furious at the death of his brother, whom Armar had killed, the coward, to avenge himself, had recourse to artifice. First he disguised himself on our shores;

he left his boat afloat and came travestied as an old man. His hair white, his eyes serious and calm, his stride weighed down by age, we were deceived. "Fair Daura," he said to my daughter, "a rock not far out to sea has a tree on its slope charged with the most beautiful fruits. It's there that Armar is waiting for you; I've come on his behalf and I'll take you to your lover."

"'She follows him. Perfidiously, he disembarks her on a rock surrounded by the waves and flees toward the bank, laughing. The poor girl, trembling with fear, calls for Armar; only the echo of the rock responds. She suspects her misfortune; she raises her voice, she calls for her brother, her father: "Arindal! Armin! Is there no one to help your dear Daura?"

"'Her cries passed over the waves and reached the shore. My son heard her first. He went down to the coast, bow in hand, followed by his faithful dogs, bristling with the spoils of the hunt. He perceives the traitor fleeing along the shore. He runs at him, reaches him, seizes him, ties him to an oak, winding strong bonds round his flanks and leaves him to charge the wind with his howls.

"'Then Arindal runs to his boat and races over the waves to aid his sister. O fatal error! Armar arrives. He perceives my son on the waves about to land on the rock. He does not recognize him in the darkness, and mistakes him for the abductor. Full of rage, he fires his arrow. It flies, plunges into your heart, my son; you die instead of the perfidious Erath. Immediately, the oar remains immobile, the boat breaks; Arindal has thrown himself on to the rock; he expires. What was your dolor, my daughter, on seeing your brother's blood running at your feet?

"'I finally arrived, succumbing to old age and fear. Triumphant, Armar had started swimming, determined to save his lover or die, but Destiny was pursuing us. Suddenly, a frightful cloud descends from the hilltop over the waves; the irritated sea swells. Armar struggles in vain against the foaming waves; his strength is exhausted; he sinks, and does not come up again.

"'Meanwhile, the cries of my daughter, left alone on the rock, mingle with the sound of the waves. In vain mine respond. Her father could not save her. All night I stayed on the shore. I glimpsed my daughter by the faint light of the Moon's rays. All night long I heard her cries. The wind was still blowing furiously and the rain beat the flanks of the mountain. Before the dawn appeared, her voice weakened, and was extinguished by degrees like the breath of a zephyr dying in the foliage. Finally, consumed by dolor and exhaustion, she expired. She left you alone, unfortunate Armin! Alas, I have lost the son who was my strength in battles; I have lost my daughter who was my pride among the shepherdesses.

"'Since that frightful night, every time the tempest descends from the mountain; every time that the north wind swells the waves, I come to sit down on the shore, and my gaze attaches itself to the fatal rock. Often, when the Moon shines before setting, I think I see the shades of my children pass by, conversing together sadly. In my delirium I call out to them, but they do not respond to their father. Yes, I am sad, and the cause of my dolor is not light. Roll over me, sad years, and since you bring me neither joy nor pleasure, open the tomb for me.'"

When the warrior song was finished, the chariot drew away.

"Fortunate," said Oribeau, looking at his weapons, "is the man who can help the oppressed stranger! I too know a Daura. May I serve her and defend her!"

They approached Waterford, and had already passed Rossbercon, which is only nine miles away, when the young King and his retinue encountered a poor man, the father of eight young children. He was being taken, for debt, into an isolated prison on the bank of the Shure. His wife was following him with three of the older children, who were carrying three of the smaller ones, the mother having the one she was nursing in her arms and giving her hand to the eighth. All the members of the family were shedding tears and lamenting.

Before Oribeau could be fully informed of what was happening, a young woman arrived, tastefully dressed, in the costume of girls who are known nowadays as waitresses. She was walking very rapidly, while her mother, who was very fat followed her, with difficulty, at a distance. The young woman went to the prisoner's wife and gave her a purse, saying. "This is for you, and I'll liberate you husband with this other sum."

The poor woman threw herself at her benefactress' feet "O Fay, rather than mortal, it's Vananis who has sent you to my rescue! May Thor and Friga bless you! May they give you the mortal you desire!" And she kissed her hands, while retaining her by her dress.

"You're preventing me from going to liberate your husband by retaining me," the beautiful young woman said to her.

The woman immediately let go, and followed her, heaping her with blessings. Then, addressing her children, she cried: "My children, my poor children, see this goddess that is going to free your father! See how beautiful she is! Look at her divine features! She's not a mortal, no, she's a goddess! Render her your homage, for she's the daughter of Vananis, goddess of hope!"

Immediately, the older children raised their voices, blessing the young woman in their childish language; they raised the hands of the smaller ones toward Heaven and made them babble benedictions.

Prince Oribeau suspended his march at that spectacle, and his excellent heart was so intensely moved that he shed tears of tenderness.

"Who, then, is that young divinity who has just exercised her bounty for my people?" he said to O'Barbo.

"Look, and recognize her, said the wise old man.

"It's Daura!" exclaimed the young Prince, approaching the beautiful girl. "Your father is rich, as a coffee-seller, but you're making a worthy employment of his fortune."

As the Prince said that, Daura's mother caught up with her daughter. The Prince was surprised to find that she bore an almost perfect resemblance to the good Thor-el, but as she did not give any sign of recognition, he thought he was mistaken. However, he addressed the most obliging things to her.

O'Barbo, seeing that the woman was not responding, said to her: "My good woman, it's the King who is speaking to you."

Immediately, the fat woman knelt down, but she did not say a word.

"Beautiful Daura," said Oribeau, "I shall never forget what you have just done."

Daura bowed without replying and blushed like a rose whose bud is just beginning to open.

The young King ordered the men of his retinue to take the poor family to Waterford and to give Daura, as well as her mother, the finest horses—but they declined.

"In truth," said the Prince to the Sage, "if the mother resembles the good Thor-el, Daura resembles Julia, Rosée and even the beautiful Ahissa. It's always the same genre of beauty."

Nevertheless, he drew away, albeit regretfully, for he wanted to master himself.

He was some distance away, close to the gates of Waterford, when he heard the Yapou behind him, uttering piercing cries. At the same instant, however, he perceived a great tumult on the banks of the Shure.

He ran toward it, fearing that something bad had happened that he could not repair. It was the wall of a house that had just collapsed, from decrepitude. The floor had fallen into the river, swollen by the rain, and on a bed that was still afloat were a mother, her sick husband and three children. No one dared go to their aid because of the danger.

Oribeau, who knew how to swim like the fish of Lake Ennel, took off his robe and threw himself into the irritated waves. Without knowing him, everyone was interested in him because of his youth and his good looks.

"Where are you going, young man!" they cried. "It's seeking certain death!" But Oribeau was already beside the bed; he seized one corner of a coverlet, told the castaways to hang on to the other, and headed for the bank. He had just reached it when the water got the upper hand and the bed sank. Cries of joy, and general applause, resounded along the banks of the Shure.

Then O'Barbo, weeping with joy, and surrounded by Mommonians, who were congratulating him s the father of the young man, shouted in a loud voice: "Fortunate inhabitants of Waterford! This young man you are proclaiming as the most virtuous in the world is…your King! It is the Prince who will reign!"

As soon as he pronounced the words "your King" a profound silence fell. Astonishment and joy suspended all faculties. But when O'Barbo added: "It is the Prince who will reign!" a universal hurrah resounded in the distance; transports of delight burst forth; there was an intoxication.

The Prince was surrounded, and as he did not appear to want to quit the old man, O'Barbo, the people carried them both all the way to the Queen's palace. The cries of the multitude preceded them, and the fine action of the heir to the throne crossed the threshold of the august Dadameh's palace before he did.

*

"The Prince who reigns over us today would do as much!" cried the good Ennisleague.

"Bless him!" said Kilmactomas.

"Accursed be the man who does not bless the descendant of Oribeau the Sage!" cried all the drinkers.

"Our ancestors thought the same way," Kerry went on, "but I left the young Prince at the Palace gates…"

Chapter 2M
Magnification of Oribeau. Coronation. Fillira. The third good deed.

"Mother even more fortunate than glorious Queen," cried the people, "we announce a son worthy of you! He is being carried by your people, whom he has delighted with admiration before being known to them! It is not only by the blood of our Kings that he merits reigning over us! He has just risked his life generously to save us! Long live young Prince Oribeau, Father of the People!"

Such were the cries that reached the ears of the Queen and the Sage Dondanuck, who was with her. The Minister sent a page to find out what was happening. The young man was informed by the first Mommonian he encountered, and came back promptly to make his report to the Queen.

Dadameh stood up and raised her eyes to Heaven, blessing the gods. Then she said to Dondanuck: "I shall be putting supreme power in good hands."

"I know, Milady. Apart from the fact that the Prince was born with such an excellent character that it would have been very difficult to corrupt him, even by leaving him at Court, my friend, who has formed him in retreat, was the most capable man in all Evinland of seconding nature. I confess, however, the Prince Oribeau is surpassing my hopes. What a triumph! He is being carried aloft by his people after an action that would merit four civic crowns for a simple individual! I'm not a vile and base courtier, but I want to kneel before him; the most perfect image of divinity is a compassionate sovereign."

Thus spoke the virtuous Dondanuck, the greatest and wisest of Ministers—and he knelt before the young King, who was coming into the palace.

"My friend, my father!" the Prince called to him. "One moment, and I'll be in your arms!"

Oribeau ran to those of the Queen, who washed her dear and august son with tears of joy. "Oh, my Mother," he said to her, "I owe you more than life, and I would not be acquitted toward you, if a son ever can be, with double what other children ought to do!"

After finishing those words, the Prince ran to Dondanuck. "Venerable old man," he said to him, "what a joy it is for peoples and for sovereigns when they have a Minister like you!"

Oribeau then put Dondanuck's and O'Barbo's hands together, adding: "I honor both of you equally; give me your wise advice, as good fathers to a cherished son."

The young King then went to rest, and his coronation was postponed until the following day.

At daybreak, all the inhabitants of Waterford were up and about. The streets were carpeted and strewn with flowers. The temple of Thor was ornamented with branches and ancient trophies of the Kings of Mommonia. The instruments of agriculture were brought, and those of all arts and métiers, and while awaiting the Prince, the druids and the people sang a hymn, which the bard Sfiertaledoneber had composed:

"O Thor, we bless you! You are the father of men and the great animator; it is to you that our ancient kings owe their trophies and their victories.

"It is you who have given us art and agriculture, in order to procure us an abundant subsistence and the commodities of life, with our superfluity.

"It is you who has given humans inventive genius, to find the arts, the instruments of which facilitate the exercise.

"You have given us métiers, to clothe us, to build, to ornament our houses, our gardens and our persons.

"Receive the solemn tribute of our gratitude.

"O Thor, you have given us a young King who will ensure the wellbeing of his people, for he has already shown the most heroic virtue!

"Bless the Sage who has formed him, the Minister who chose the Sage, and the Queen who chose the Minister!

"Thor, who has given us a good Queen, here is the King coming to the temple, to render his homage to the father of the gods. He is accompanied by the Queen, his mother; he is followed by the Minister and the Sage who have raised him; he is surrounded by his guards, who admire him, and who are unarmed. Why should they be armed?

"A choir of boys precedes him, singing his praises; a choir of young women follows him, celebrating his courage. Who is that young beauty who shines in their midst? It is

Fillira the beautiful, whom he saved one day from the hands of libertines, and her sister Hasameh. How modest she is! A pleasant redness is coloring her cheeks; a marvelous bird is flying above her head, and by its cries announces the Queen of Beauties.

"The young Prince is looking at her! He is surprised to see so many attractions! His magnanimous heart is moved, but he masters its impetuous impulse; the King is reserving his hand and his faith for the Princess Oribelle.

"He is entering the temple. Druids, prostrate yourselves, adore the gods!"

Such was the hymn that was sung when the young Prince, followed by his cortege, came to render his first homage, as King, to Thor.

As soon as he was at the foot of the altar, the Grand Druid addressed this prayer to the immortals:

"O Thor, and you, Worden, you, powerful and luminous Berda, mother Erda, who is the Earth, Vananis, goddess of hope, bless our King on this day of his coronation; give him justice, in order that he will not attribute too much of anything to himself, and that he will remember that he is made for his people."

After that prayer, the Prince emerged from the temple and went to the town hall, where the municipal magistrates of Waterford placed the crown on his head, saying:

"All your people and your city of Waterford gladly give you his crown, which falls to you by order of succession, recognizing that your person is only as worthy of it as you. Will you swear our rights?"

Oribeau extended his hand toward the Sun and said: "I swear by father Berda and mother Berda that I will reign for my people and not for myself, for I am a man commanding men, my equals, and I am only above them by their will. I swear to maintain royal authority in all its splendor, without ever suffering that it should bear the slightest stain, in order that it shall be the refuge of the good and the terror of the wicked. Thus I shall keep my oath, with the aid of Thor, father of the gods, Worden his son, mother Erda and father Berda.

All the people replied to the Prince's oath with a cry of joy, and everyone set forth to return to the palace of the Sovereigns of Mommonia, built on the northern bank of the Shure.

Meanwhile, the choir of young women sang one of the ancient poems composed by the kaldes two centuries before; it was a sad story, but Sages have said that it is always necessary to mingle a grain of sadness with the inebriation of joy in the celebrations that transport the human heart. It was the beautiful Fillira who set the tone; her harmonious voice resembled the sounds of the harp and the lyre when the strings, forcefully plucked, resonate dolor

"'Beautiful Oithona,[132] you promised me to wait in your palace for the return of your lover. I have seen your beautiful cheeks mist with tears at my departure and your beautiful bosom swollen with sighs. I am coming back to your arms the vanquisher of my enemies, and I do not see you coming toward me to congratulate me on my victory.'

"Such were the plaints of Morni on approaching the towers of Lathmon. Obscurity surrounds their walls; the night-star fears to advance, and seems to anticipate the sadness that will reign in this place. Morni is in the plain and hastening with rapid strides, but he does not hear any sound coming from the palace where he has left his lover. He does not see any light piercing the thick darkness.

"He goes in; he finds the doors open, and no sign of any living being. He sees he threshold strewn with leaves. The winds are whistling inside the apartments; he hears nothing outside but the murmur of the night. Sad and thoughtful, he sits down on a nearby rock. His soul shivers in the uncertainty of his lover's fate. He does not know which way to turn. Gaul, who has accompanied him, has stopped some distance away. He soon understands the unhappiness of his friend, but, seeing

---

[132] The eponymous heroine of yet another Ossianic poem, paraphrased once again from Le Tourneur.

him plunged in profound sadness, dares not raise his voice to speak to him.

"Slumber descends upon the two warriors. The dreams of the night awaken. Oithona appears to Morni. Her black hair is floating in disorder. Her charming eyes are flooded with tears. Blood is running over her alabaster arm. Her robe partly hides the wound in her beautiful breast. 'You are asleep, Morni, and your lover is buried underground. A vast sea surrounds the isle of Tromaton; it is there that I am sitting in tears in the depths of my somber cavern; and I am not alone, Morni! The frightful Duromath is with me; he is here with all the furies of amour; what can the unfortunate Oithona do?'

"A gust of wind shakes the bushy crowns of the trees more violently, and Morni wakes up. He seizes his spear and stands up, furious. He turns his eyes incessantly eastwards and curses the slowness of the daylight. Finally, the dawn appears. He deploys his sails and his vessel bounds over the waves of the abyss. On the third day, the isle of Tromaton emerges from the bosom of the sea before his eyes.

"The sad Oithona was sitting on the shore. She kept her gaze fixed on the rolling waves of the abyss. Tears ran from her eyes. But when she perceived Morni covered with his armor, she shivered with horror and turned away. Her beautiful cheeks are hollow and red with shame. Her tremulous arms hang by her sides. Three times she makes an effort to get up and flee his presence; three times her trembling knees give way beneath her.

"'Oithona!' cries Morni, from the bosom of the waves, 'why do you want to flee me? Is it death that you see in my eyes, and do you think that here is hatred in my heart? Are you not for me a ray of the dawn that comes to illuminate me in an unknown land? But your beautiful face is buried in sadness! Is your enemy nearby? I burn to encounter him. My sword is quivering by my side. Reply to me; can you not see my tears?'

"'Ah, Morni,' she replies, sighing, 'why have you come to seek the unfortunate Oithona over so many seas? Can I not die in secret, and pass like the flower that is born and dies unknown in a rocky desert? Oh, Morni, come to hear my last sigh! I am perishing in my youth, my name will only ever be pronounced with dolor. Why land on this fatal island where I have lost my virginity? Dear lover, I have never loved anyone but you.'

"'Oh my darling, I have come to fight your enemy; I see him already dead, or Morni will perish. If I succumb, build my tomb on this rock, in the place where you are sitting, and if you see some vessel passing, call with loud cries, give this sword to the navigators, that they might take it to my father, in order that the old man can finally detach his gaze from the deserted seas, waiting in vain for the return of his son.'

"'And you think,' said Oithona, 'that I can live on this odious island after you are dead? My heart is not formed of that rock and my heart is not as indifferent as that sea, which raises its waves with every wind. The same blow that fells you will lay me in the tomb, Morni; we shall die together. Yes, death is dear to me; the tomb has charms for me. For I shall never quit your rocks, fatal isle!

"'My brother departed for battle. Night fell. I was sitting alone in my dwelling by the light of my hearth. I heard arms clashing. I shivered with joy. I thought that it was you, returning to your lover. I saw the wild Duromath coming in. His eyes were sparkling. I saw blood on his sword. It was the blood of friends who had tried to defend me. What could I do? My weak arm was incapable of lifting a spear. Duromath seized me in my distress. Insensible to my tears, he dragged me weeping to his ship. But here you are, cleaving the waves, surrounded by your warriors. How numerous they are! Morni, what will you do?'

"'Fight. Retire to your grotto.'

"She draws away. A somber joy penetrates her soul. She is fixed in her resolution, and there are no longer tears in her grim eyes.

"Duromath advances slowly at the sight of Morni. Scorn contracts his frightful visage. An insulting smile is on his lips. His reddened eyes are half-hidden by the thickness of his black eyebrows. 'Whence come these strangers?' he said. 'Is it the winds that have pushed them to these shores, or have they come to take away the beautiful Oithona? Those whom my arm encounters were born on an unlucky day! It does not spare the weak. It loves to shed the blood of strangers. Oithona is a solitary star for me. I alone enjoy her beauty in secret. You can come to trouble my happiness, but will you return to your homeland?'

"'Do you not recognize me, coward?' said Morni. 'Have you forgotten, then, the day you fled before my blade, which pursued you?' With those words, Morni charged. Duromath fled and plunged behind his warriors, but Morni's spear reached him and pierced him.

"Morni ran and cut off his head as he bled to death. Gaul seized the bloody head by the hair and waved it in his hands.

"Duromath's frightened warriors fled. Arrows pursued them. Ten fell, lying at unequal intervals. The rest embarked in disorder and drew away from the shore in terror. Morni immediately ran to Oithona's grotto.

"He perceived a young man leaning against a rock; an arrow pierced his side; his eyes were extinct and languishing beneath his helm. Morni's soul was struck by sadness. 'Unfortunate young man,' he said to him. My hand might yet heal you. I know mountain herbs. I have often close the wounds of brave warriors. Who is your father? Were your ancestors brave? What mourning in your homeland! I see you perishing in the flower of your years.'

"'My brother,' the unknown man replied, 'is renowned in battles, Give him this helm.' The helm fell from Morni's hands, at the sight of Oithona dying. She had armed herself in the grotto and had come there to seek death. Her heavy eyes were already half-closed. Blood was still running from her breast.

"'Morni,' she said, 'prepare my tomb. The shadows of death are surrounding me. My eyes are troubled. Oh, why could I not remain in my homeland with my virginity? My years would have passed in innocence and joy. But I am perishing in the flower of age, and my father will blush for me in his dwelling.'"

The tragic story had scarcely finished than the Yapou flew over Fillira's head, uttering a terrible cry. People looked up, and saw a column of smoke rising in the direction of the wind. Arsonists had set fire to Waterford.

Immediately, the young King placed his crown in Fillira's hands, saying to her: "Young woman protected by the gods, of whom your beauty is the image, look after the crown. As for me, I shall fly to the aid of my people." As he spoke he pushed his horse, rid of its dragging cloth, and raced to where the danger was.

He arrived, leapt to the ground and ran into the flames. He was seen armed with a pitcher, seconded by his guards, less brave than him, turning the dwelling upside-down and concentrating the flames on one floor.

It was then that they heard screams from above. It was a group of young seamstresses shut up there by their mistress during the ceremony, with their children. The unfortunates, whom the smoke was about to stifle, were extending their hands through the broken window-panes. No one dared go to their aid; but Oribeau, brought up sternly, demanded a ladder. He leaned it against the smoking beams, climbed up, and broke the window-frames with blows of a hatchet. He received the children and took two of them down; another ladder was set up, and saved the young women, who, frightened, abandoned two other younger children. Oribeau went into the gulf of smoke and fetched out those innocent creatures. The floor collapsed, vomiting flame like a volcano.

All the people cried: "Long live the great Oribeau, savior of his people and the capital! Long live Oribeau, the greatest and most courageous of men!"

The danger was past in a matter of hours. The people, drunk with joy, made a crown of roses, and had it placed on the young King's head by the beautiful Fillira.

Chapter 2N
Nominations. Canora. The fourth good deed.

"Noble Mommonians, and you, citizens of communes," said the Queen to the assembly that filled the palace square, "my son has been crowned; I put supreme power in his hands, and I shall live in repose, as soon as I have given him the only spouse that is worthy of him by her virtue and her beauty. When that glorious marriage is celebrated, I shall retire to the palace of the Fay Wrwcwcw, in order to find the fate there that my actions will have merited."

As she finished speaking, the Queen handed the young King the seal of O'Facfac, descended from the throne, where she placed Oribeau, and sat down beside him, but a little below.

The young King immediately had the captain of his guard summon all the officers of his troops, whom the coronation ceremony had drawn to Waterford.

"Brave captains," he said to them, "I fear that after a long peace, we shall be obliged to sustain war against our neighbors. The Minister of Lagenia has, it is said, imprisoned the Queen's husband, and although that Prince was not the King, given that the illustrious Conchèse is Queen by hereditary right, the Minister's action is nevertheless a crime against royal Majesty. He has not stopped there; it is affirmed that Princess Oribelle, the legitimate heiress, and Princess Dinameh, her younger sister, have been obliged to flee his violence.

"It is in the interest of the State that the King of Mommonia makes an alliance with the Queen of Lagenia, in order to reconcile two kingdoms that have been enemies for a long time, although they were friends six or seven generations ago. Often, to obtain a solid peace, one is forced to make war! That is why I have resolved, on the advice of the excellent Minister Dondanuck, that of O'Barbo, my instructor, a former warrior, and that of the noble Barons of Cork, Kerry, Limerick, Tipperary and Thomond, the foremost great vassals of my crown, to make a general promotion in my troops."

After that speech, Oribeau took the advice of the Minister, O'Barbo and the Barons. Then he made the following nominations:

"Each of the five Barons will be a Millenarian, or chief of a thousand men. The Barony of Waterford, which belongs to us, will have two Millenarians, Dondanuck and O'Barbo.

"Under Millenarian Dondanuck will be two Quincenturians, Dungarvan and Tallo, brave officers. Under O'Barbo will be Lismore and Kaperguin. Those four Quincenturians will each have five centurions under them.

"Cork will have under him the two Quincenturians Killnatoloone and Klongibbons, with ten centurions, Imokill, Barrimore, Courcies, Barriroe, Ibaune, Carbury, Bantry, Muskery, Duhallow and Farmory. Kerry will have…, etc."

And the Prince made all the other nominations, which gave for the six baronies, Waterford counting double, seven Milenarians, fourteen Quincenturians, seventy centurions and even thousand subofficers and soldiers—which formed a formidable army, compared to any that neighboring states could muster.

As soon as the nominations were finished, the heralds sounded the trumpets to announce them to the people, and each of the Barons returned to his barony in order to make the conscriptions and get ready to march.

On the evening of that great day there were illuminations throughout the city and a ball at the Queen's palace. When dusk fell, the young Prince, after having shown himself to the people on the palace balcony, went back into the apartment where the Queen Mother was, with the two old men Dondanuck and O'Barbo.

"Milady," said the young Prince, indicating the latter, "Without the practical instructions that this sage mortal has given me, I would believe that all my people were happy, because the square is resounding with cries of joy, but I know, and cannot doubt, that there are individuals groaning in the midst of the public delight. That is why, as soon as I have opened the ball, with the most beautiful young woman in Waterford, I shall disappear with O'Barbo, to visit the prisons personally, to grant mercy to the prisoners who are not dangerous, and set the debtors free by paying their debts. Then I shall go to the hospitals and show myself to the invalids who could not come out to see me, for they are all the more dear to me for being unfortunate."

The Queen only replied with a nod of the head, but her heart was dilated with joy. Dondanuck asked the young King whether he might be permitted to accompany him.

"As long as we have the good fortune to possess you," Oribeau replied, "you shall give me young good advice, and I will follow it."

The ball soon commenced. Oribeau hoped to see Fillira there, but it was Canora, the young beauty that he had once seen with the family of the Great Judge of Waterford, who appeared the most brilliant at the fête. The young King opened the ball with her; then, after having put on an appropriate costume, he slipped away.

First he went to a prison where debtors were detained. He found them transported with joy and showering the young monarch with blessings.

"I did not expect to find delight here," said Oribeau.

"Lord," replied a debtor, who thought that he was only one of the nobles of the Court, "it is not astonishing that you see us joyful. A young woman as beautiful as Friga has just broken our bonds by paying our debts. 'Be free,' she said to us, 'on this day of the coronation of the best of Princes; I am paying your debts, in order that you might bless him, like all the other citizens.'"

"O Thor," exclaimed Oribeau, "I bless you! But who, then, has stolen this good deed from me?"

Immediately, the shrill cry of the Yapou was heard.

"What!" said the young King. "Can it be Princess Oribelle? Is she also in Waterford, then, with the Prince of Meath?"

As he finished speaking, he saw Canora, who was coming out of a more distant room and already ready to go out. The door was opened for her, and all the prisoners ran after her, blessing her, with the consequence that Oribeau was obliged to wait until they were all outside.

"O beautiful Canora," he shouted, "are you not the Princess of Lagenia? Or at least, since Oribelle resembles you...."

He went out with the last prisoner, to whom Dondanuck said: "That is the King, who came to liberate you; but a young goddess has anticipated him. Bless the King; bless her..."

At those words the prisoner uttered a cry of joy, calling all his comrades, to whom he recounted what he had just heard. The Prince of the Mommonians passed through their midst triumphantly, heaped with their benedictions.

Chapter 20
Oribelle-Friga. Abduction. Fifth good deed.

Oribeau had just arrived at the gate of the malefactors' prison when the Yapou made its piercing cry heard again.

"I don't understand at all," said the young King. "That bird ought, it seems to me, to be preceding Princess Oribelle, but I find it everywhere."

"I believe," said O'Barbo, "that it does indeed always accompany her, but she is apparently hidden from us."

They went into the prison immediately.

In the first courtyard, convicts were chained six by six, about to be sent to public labor; they were scoundrels, for the most part, but there were unfortunates among them who had only had a weakness.

"Oh," exclaimed Oribeau, "if I could only change your hearts! I would give you all mercy and liberty."

As he finished those words, a beautiful young woman who was veiled came to embrace his knees.

"Great Prince," she said to him, "Today is a day of clemency; only deign to listen, that justice might fall silent, but not prudence. Grant mercy to all these unfortunates who have not committed murder and send them home, charging each burg to occupy itself with them, to nourish them and answer to you for them. If they abuse that liberty, your justice will fall upon them without mercy. I will furnish what they need in order to travel."

"I cannot refuse you anything," Oribeau replied, "but who are you?"

The Beauty immediately uncovered her face. It was Friga herself, or Oribelle, but she resembled Rosée so perfectly that Oribeau uttered a cry of joy, saying: "I finally see you again, lovely daughter of Bridge-Clonard! I beg you, go to the palace and present yourself to my mother, the Queen, on my behalf. I would be delighted to find you again there."

Rosée went out, but again the Prince could not exercise his generosity in that prison; Rosée had provided for everything. Oribeau was content to name himself and to grant mercy or commute punishments for the greatest crimes, in order that there would not be anyone in Waterford who was not rejoicing.

Afterwards, he went to the house of the infirm.

The Yapou made itself heard again. The Prince entered, preceded by a herald who said: "Invalids who are suffering, the new King is not insensible to your woes; he is coming to visit you, to enable you to enjoy his agreeable presence; may he be for you a renascent Sun!"

Scarcely had Oribeau gone in than he perceived before him the beautiful Canora, who was consoling and tidying up the invalids who were getting up to see the Prince.

"O Thor," said Oribeau, "why have you given me a sensible heart and a limited power? If I had your divine power, I would cure all my subjects who are suffering."

Whether because of the joy of seeing the Prince and hearing him brought about a fortunate revolution, because the beautiful Canora had given them a sovereign liquid, because her touch had a virtue similar to that of the divine Mesmer,[133] or because Thor wanted to grant the wish of the virtuous young King whose heart was so pure, all the invalids appeared to get better, and only needed to be fortified. Oribeau left the asylum transported by joy.

Meanwhile, following his orders, a hundred criers went through the illuminated streets of Waterford saying: "Who is in pain? Whoever has chagrins or infirmities, let him know, let his friends and neighbors inform him, in order that he might be relieved, by the munificence of our good King and the Queen Mother."

As soon as that proclamation was known, all the afflicted were seen emerging, to form a hedge before Oribeau's passage, who relieved them all by his largesse, words of consolation and promises for the future. He caused the cessation of all the pains to which human effort could put an end, and made all the graces that a sovereign can accord.

While his beautiful soul floated in the joy, he was troubled by the cries of a few afflicted who could not emerge from their houses, and to whom all of Oribeau's good will and all of his power could not give relief.

"Oh," cried the young Prince, "will there be unfortunates, then, whose hearts will not expand today? Why, being King, am I only one man?"

As Oribeau finished speaking, the Yapou made itself heard more loudly than ever before, and Rosée was seen, in a pretty peasant costume, emerging from a house of afflicted individuals, who came to the window to bless her. She went into another.

"Thor has granted your wish," said O'Barbo to his pupil. "He has determined that you should be seconded by that beautiful young woman, who has taken responsibility for interior

---

[133] Restif's endnotes at the conclusion of the final volume offer the observation that this blatantly anachronistic judgment is "purely poetic" and adds that: "The Translator makes no judgment."

details. She is preceding you like a benevolent fay, and doing all that you could only order."

"What human power is great enough to recompense Canora and Rosée?" said Oribeau, sighing.

"Add Daura, Fillira, Ahissa and Julia; all six are seconding you at the same time."

"O Thor," exclaimed the young King, "I have blasphemed you in complaining that I am not a god. You are, and that is sufficient for the world; I adore you humbly and bless your divine providence!"

As soon as the Prince had pronounced those religious words, all the people of Waterford, transported, uttered a cry of joy, saying: "The Golden Age has returned, fellow citizens; we have a Prince who reveres the gods. He will be their living image. Let us bless Thor and Vananis; let us bless young King Oribeau the Wise!"

It was in the midst of those acclamations that, having traveled all the streets of Waterford, the Prince returned to the palace. He had only just arrived when he heard a loud noise. The Yapou uttered piercing cries and appeared to draw away from the city.

It was learned an hour afterwards that a party of Lagenians commanded by Ratchlin in person had come to abduct Princess Oribelle, who had been hiding in the city for three days.

Oribeau was very surprised. He had thought that she was with Prince Beaudâme; but he was told that he had been deceived, as the Prince of Meath himself had been; that it was Prince Belletête, otherwise Dinameh, the younger Princes of Lagenia, whom he had seen with Beaudâme, and that the Prince had succeeded...

Oribeau did not hear the rest; he had the kidnappers pursued.

He assembled his Council immediately. It was decided that before declaring war on Lagenia, for the violation of territory, an ambassador would be sent to the Queen to request and amicable reparation and to propose the marriage of Princess

Oribelle with Oribeau. In the case of refusal, the promise was made to make war vigorously, in order to obtain a solid and permanently durable peace.

Chapter 2P
Preparation for war. Oribeau's disguise. O'Barbo ambassador to Lagenia. Assault on Killensay Castle.

Persistently, during the night, Oribeau reflected on everything that had happened. He had enjoyed his good deeds, but his joy was tempered by the regret of not having known that Oribelle was in Waterford. With what joy he would have brought her to the Queen's palace!

"Milady," he would have said to his mother, I put this beautiful Princess under your protection; all the forces of the State will be employed to defend her, until I have gained the heart of the Queen her mother..."

Futile ideas! Oribelle had been abducted from the heart of Waterford, without him being able to defend her. He had not understood the cries of the bird, which had doubtless been sent by the gods...

"By the gods!" the Prince repeated. "Do the gods employ those means? No, they speak through the eternal order of nature and not by means of exceptions contrary to that eternal order established by themselves. The Yapou is an artificial bird, brought into play by humans. But are they friends or enemies?"

Such were Oribeau's reflections, during the intervals of sleep.

As soon as first light, he got up. The Court was not accustomed to seeing the Prince appear so early. He found himself alone. Having perceived a light in Dondanuck's study however, he went there.

The Minister had been working all night on O'Barbo's dispatches. The latter had come to join him, so the King found them together.

"I'm ready to depart," said the Sage. "I've been preceded by a hundred cavaliers who have been riding all night in order to try to take Ratchlin by surprise. They have wrapped their horses' hooves in sheepskin in order not to make any sound; perhaps they will have caught up with the abductor and the Princess."

"Ah!" said Oribeau. "I ought to have gone with them, but a King can't do everything he wishes. I'll do what I can."

He went out immediately in order to disguise himself as a yeoman; he came back thereafter and proposed that he go with his ambassador.

Dondanuck hesitated momentarily, but as O'Barbo seemed to approve of the young Prince's plan, the Minister gave in and took responsibility for going to inform the Queen. The dispatches were sealed, and, as everything was ready, O'Barbo left Waterford at sunrise accompanied by three hundred horsemen, in addition to the hundred who had preceded him. Oribeau, unknown even to the troop, appeared to be a young yeoman accompanying the Ambassador by distinction.

O'Barbo fooled the coast, going via Rosbercon, Ross, Montgaret, Polemon, Mulin, Graignamanah, where he passed the Barrow, Wells, Laughlin, Cloghna, Katherlag, Castle Dermoot, Timolinn, Dunlavan, More-Eustace, the Mountains of Stefenon, Blessington and Tallag, from where they arrived, on the evening of the third day, in Balaclay, the capital of Lagenia. The first troop had stopped at the place where the Shure separates the two kingdoms, so the Ambassador presented himself at the gate of Balaclay—now Dublin— accompanied by four hundred horsemen.

The sentinels sounded the alarm. The Queen of Lagenia assembled her Council and it was decided that a herald would be sent to the leader of the troop to discover what he wanted.

The herald, having reached O'Barbo, said to him: "I have come on behalf our Sovereign, the Queen to discover whether you are friends or enemies."

"We are friends," replied the Sage. "I bring honorable propositions to the Queen on behalf of the young King of

Mommonia and his mother, the Queen, who has just returned sovereign power to him. He was crowned four days ago."

The herald returned to convey that response to the Queen and her Council.

Ratchlin had returned Oribelle to Queen Conchèse; he did not want her to receive the Mommonian, and was supported by the Barons, against the opinion of the Queen herself, who desired that the Ambassador be admitted to her presence. Seeing himself supported, however, Ratchlin made her see that she was not the mistress. That discontented Conchèse so much that she left the palace, taking her two daughters with her, and, protected by the people, who adored her, she went to enclose herself in the Castle of Makredin.

Meanwhile, O'Barbo, who did not know that, received the response of the Council via the herald, who declared to him that he had to withdraw from the territory of Lagenia at a trot if he did not want to be treated as an enemy.

At that response, Oribeau quivered with anger, and made himself known to his troop.

"Sustain the honor of your King," he said. "I want to speak to the Queen and the two Princesses, and I want, with your help alone, to free O'Brisombaüm."

"Lord," O'Barbo said to him, "it is said in an ancient book that a King named Ulysses could only overcome all the obstacles that opposed his return to his Estates with the aid of Minerva. Now, Minerva is the goddess of wisdom."

"I shall follow, in everything, two guides," Oribeau replied, "your wisdom and my courage; grant it; I shall execute it."

"Well," said the Sage, "let us decamp from this place, but instead of returning to your Estates, let us go to the isle of Allen in the county of Kildare; before anyone can be informed of our design, we'll attack Killensaye Castle and liberate O'Brisombaüm. When we have him with us, if an opportunity presents itself to free Princess Oribelle, we'll return her to her father, from whose hand you'll receive her."

"That advice is full of wisdom," Oribeau replied, "and I abandon myself to it." To the four centurions who were accompanying him, he said: "Lift camp, and let's depart."

The Sage knew the route. He took the lead while Oribeau commanded the rearguard. They arrived at Killensay the following day.

They had only just arrived at the castle, which was summoned to surrender, when they perceived a courier riding full tilt. His passage was barred and he was taken to the Prince. He was carrying orders from Queen Conchèse to release O'Brisombaüm, which gave the Sage O'Barbo great pleasure. The courier gave him an account of the manner in which the Queen had quit the capital in order to go to Makredin with the two Princesses. He added that he was being pursued by a courier from Ratchlin, well-escorted.

Oribeau was delighted to learn that Oribelle was with her mother. He immediately had his troop hide in the trees and sent men on foot to set an ambush some distance away, in order to cut off the courier's retreat if he discovered the horsemen and tried to turn back.

At that moment, he was seen in the distance. He traversed the narrowest part of the lake that led to the island, but as soon as he disembarked he discovered the horsemen. He tried to leap back into the boat then, but the ambushers prevented him, jumped into it themselves and drew away from the shore. The courier and his escort were immediately surrounded. Their dispatches were captured and they were taken prisoner.

Then Oribeau approached the castle and had the trumpet sounded. The governor appeared on the rampart. A herald communicated the Queen's order to him. The governor asked whether they were accompanied by Ratchlin's.

"What!" said Oribeau, indignantly. "The Sovereign's orders are not sufficient?"

Instead of responding, the governor withdrew, and did not show himself again, although the trumpet summoned him.

"I shall enter the castle this evening, if you second my courage," the young Prince said to his men.

While they waited for nightfall, he examined the surroundings, but they were equally fortified everywhere; the ditches were deep and filled with water; surprise seemed impossible. However, they attempted to take possession of the drawbridge.

The governor reappeared then.

Chapter 2Q
Questions of an impertinent kind. The drawbridge captured and the castle taken. Supposed violent death of O'Brisombaüm.

"Quartermaster!" he said, addressing Oribeau in a mocking tone, "how do you think you can take the castle, by the tail or by the head? Who sent you, the helm or the wimple? What will you do to us if you take us, die laughing or of indigestion? What does a young girl do when she is in her wardrobe? Which do you like better, the rope or the strappado, to be hanged or drowned? When you get drunk, are you cheerful or sad, good or brutal? When you dream, do you do good deeds or evil ones? Just tell me those two things, and I'll know the depths of your soul."

The governor would have uttered many other platitudes, but an arrow unleashed by Oribeau hit him in the mouth and emerged through the back of his head. He vomited his stupid and malevolent soul, with floods of blood.

Immediately, they saw a man thrown from the battlements, but instead of falling he remained suspended by the neck. It was O'Brisombaüm, or so it appeared. The governor had orders to kill him as soon as there was no more hope of keeping him, and, as that officer had just perished himself, his lieutenant, a hard and ferocious man, had had the prisoner strangled. He hid in a subterrain with food supplies, and gave the garrison orders to defend itself.

Meanwhile, Oribeau employed everything that his imagination suggested to fill in the ditch. O'Barbo, who had experience, seconded the Prince. They succeeded, not without difficulty, in making a kind of raft with felled trees; the darkness hid it from the sight of the besieged, who remained tranquil. As soon as they were able to reach the foot of the beams of the drawbridge, they set fire to them, which was only perceived in the castle when the fire had made considerable progress. The drawbridge burned with a horrible sound and the flames drove the garrison back.

At daybreak, Oribeau was the first to cross the burning timbers; his troop followed him, and the castle was taken by storm. The soldiers of the garrison laid down their arms, and the Prince ordered that they be granted mercy. He asked for O'Brisombaüm. An officer showed the body to the Prince and told him how he had perished after the death of the governor. Oribeau had a search made for the lieutenant in order to punish him, but it proved impossible to find him.

Funeral honors were given to the father of Oribelle and Dinameh; the cadaver of the governor was abandoned to the crows; a monument was erected to the glory of the one, as to the shame of the other.

It was thus that the unfortunate O'Brisombaüm perished, who had employed trickery, in concert with his father, in order to raise himself up as far as the Queen. He was never happy, and it would have been better for him if he had married one of his beautiful subjects in the Barony of Kilkenny than to have obtained the hand of his sovereign.

O'Barbo then suggested to his pupil that, no longer having the support of the legitimate Prince, it would be imprudent to go to Makredin to deliver the Queen with a troop as lacking in number as theirs.

"I wouldn't go," Oribeau replied, "if it were a matter of waging war, but in order to deliver her, I'll fly there."

The Sage was obliged to yield. They departed without delay, after having locked Ratchlin's courier and his escort in the citadel of the castle. It is said that, thus secured, they began to run short of food, and searched so assiduously that they found the lieutenant's subterrain, took him out, appropriated his food supplies and hanged him from the same battlement to which he had had O'Brisombaüm attached.

Chapter 2R
Regrets of Conchèse. She is besieged by Ratchlin.
Beaudâme, deceived, comes to the aid of the traitor.
Oribeau is captured.

Retrenched in Makredin, the Queen of Lagenia was waiting for her husband, freed on her orders, to come to her aid with her faithful subjects, whom he would assemble, showing them the letters recalling him to the Court. Thus, she refused to hear anything that Ratchlin had to say to her. It was then that the favorite showed what he had in his soul, by hoisting the flag of rebellion.

He gathered all his partisans under the pretext that the Queen wanted to marry Princess Oribelle to the new King of Mommonia and reduce the kingdom of Lagenia to a simple province, of which Waterford would be the metropolis. The proof he gave was that Clonameh, as the Queen admitted, had even taken Oribelle into the Mommonian Empire in order to have her preferred by him, with the result that he, as Minister, had been obliged to go to abduct the Princess from Waterford, where she was seeking to make herself beloved by means of good deeds. He proposed to them that they force the Queen to return to Balaclay, in order that they could see all her moves, and constrain her to marry the two Princesses.

"Would it not be appropriate," he had added, "to give Dinameh to the Prince of Meath, in order to obtain an ally, instead of giving him Oribelle, to whom the throne ought to belong? We should reserve that one for a Prince of the land who is still young; we should unite them now, but retaining all authority. I did not hold that view at first, but circumstances have made me change my mind."

The nobles of Ratchlin's party, especially the Baron of Balaclay, his brother-in-laws, the husband of the beautiful Radelinde, had applauded that arrangement, in the hope of profiting from the troubles. But Ratchlin was deceiving them; instead of giving Oribelle to his son, he was determined, as soon as he had her in his power, to marry her himself. That is why he had assembled a few troops, with whom he laid siege to Makredin Castle.

As the capital of Meath was only a day's ride from Balaclay, he sent a courier to Prince Beaudâme and Queen Mijoreh, telling them that the Queen had been forced to take refuge in Makredin for fear of an army of Mommonians that had just entered the Estates; that was why he asked the King and Queen of Meath to assemble troops and come to his aid, promising them that as soon as the Mommonians were expelled, Beaudâme would be given as a spouse the Princess he loved, and by whom he was loved.

It was in consequence of that ruse that Prince Beaudâme put himself at the head of an army assembled in haste and came to camp next to Ratchlin, having Debundeh with him to guide him. But Ratchlin, it is said, had very sinister intentions. He was turning over in his head the plan of tearing Beaudâme's army apart as soon as it had got rid of the Mommonians, killing him and taking possession of his Estates. He would then, it is said, have taken possession of the Queen and imprisoned her along with Dinameh.

From the height of the towers of Makredin, Conchèse saw all the troops that were surrounding her. She thought at first, seeing those of Meath arrive, that it was Oribeau coming to her aid, but she was dolorously undeceived on seeing the two armies camp peacefully side by side.

"Oh!" cried the unfortunate Princess. "I am cruelly punished for my injustice toward O'Brisombaüm! Great gods, forgive me that fault, that I might repair it by means of everything that is henceforth in my power!" And she wept, for the two armies were drawing gradually closer to the walls and tightening their ranks in such a way that it was no longer possible for anything to get in.

Oribelle consoled her mother by means of her words, her caresses and her virtues. As for Dinameh, she was afflicted by the absence of Prince Beaudâme, whom she loved uniquely, and by whom she was adored; which determined that she was still intelligent and that the Prince was handsome. She could not imagine how he had united his troops with Ratchlin's.

Meanwhile, Oribeau, having left the isle of Allen, was advancing rapidly. At sunset, his scouts discovered the double enemy camp. They fell back to the principal corps in order not to be seen, and the entire troop halted. They took a few hours' rest; the horses were put out to pasture, and the Prince himself, with a handful of volunteers chosen from the most alert, went to observe the enemy. Everything was tranquil.

In the middle of the night, the troop descended the hill at a walk, crossing the fields in order not to make any noise. Having arrived at Ratchlin's camp, the Mommonians caught the sentinels asleep, forced the gate of the camp and, uttering cries in unison, commenced the battle.

The frightened Lagenians fled before the enemy, of whose numbers they were unaware; the disorder was general and the Mommonians remained the maters of a camp ten times too large for them. They could not set forth in pursuit of the enemy for fear of going astray and scattered. They waited for daylight

Then they saw the Lagenians united with Prince Beaudâme's troops, who were besieging them. Oribeau's party was soon trapped. He ordered that the gates of the camp be opened in order to launch himself into the midst of the enemy and try to reach the Meathans and talk to Prince Beaudâme; but although a part of that plan succeeded, the other could not be achieved. Beaudâme, full of courage, fought with a valor worthy of a better cause. Oribeau's troop cut thought the enemy host, scattering them with pikes, but could not make themselves heard. The Meathans would have regarded it as a laxity to lend an ear to their allies' enemy; they fell upon the rear-guard.

The Mommonians sustained the pursuit of the two armies courageously, as far as a wood in which they retrenched themselves, where they could not be taken by force, but they were surrounded.

From the top of the highest tower of Makredin, Conchèse, Oribelle and Dinameh watched the battle. They did not know its motives, and who those were who were fighting in their favor.

Oribeau, enclosed in the wood, defended its entrances, but was bound to be starved out soon. He decided not to let his troop be weakened by hunger. He observed everything himself, and, perceiving that a steep rock nearby was almost unguarded, he proposed to emerge in that direction. He brought his troop toward it as soon as the horses had been fed.

Darkness was beginning to lower its veil over the land. The troop emerged silently. Oribeau then perceived that all the issues beyond the rock were guarded, and the only path that was free was the one leading to the Meathan camp. He took it, and surprised it with so much fortune and skill that the two armies had no suspicion of it, took the guards prisoner, attached pickets to its tents, the ropes of which they cut, and emerged from the camp after having appropriated all its provisions. He left a letter in Beaudâme's tent informing him of the death of O'Brisombaüm and Ratchlin's true sentiments.

While Oribeau was making that expedition, the two armies continued to surround the wood. The Mommonian cavaliers, emboldened by the success of their first escapade, also surprised Ratchlin's camp and pillaged it. They would have set fire to it but for the fear of revealing themselves thereby.

Seeing that the two armies were still in their positions, Oribeau formed the project of getting into Makredin, in order to liberate the Queen and the Princesses. He therefore presented himself at the drawbridge and asked, but without the aid of the trumpet, which would have been overheard, to speak to the Queen.

Conchèse, suspecting a treason, refused.

The Prince, rendered desperate by that difficulty, dived into the ditch and traversed it swimming, reached a postern and demanded to be taken Queen Conchèse, alone. His hands were bound and his eyes blindfolded, and he was taken to the tower from which Conchèse had the custom of watching what was happening.

"He was taken to the tower!" said Ennisleague, alarmed, "with his eyes blindfolded and his hands bound1 A King! Oh, if I had been there I would soon have told them that it was not appropriate! But let's see what will happen..."

Kerry drew breath. Everyone made his comment until the hunter resumed speaking.

Chapter 2S
Sarbacane. Oribelle understands that Oribeau is the prisoner. He escapes. Dinameh, going to Beaudâme's camp, is surprised by Ratchlin, who has her arrested. Beaudame is undeceived.

Suspicious to excess since Ratchlin's perfidy, Conchèse could not resolve to allow the stranger who had just put himself in her hands to appear before her. She did not listen to anything he said to her. It is true that he did not name himself; the King of Mommonia would have thought it debasing his royal Majesty in the situation in which he found himself. He was left in a kind of dungeon, with his hands bound and his eyes blindfolded.

Meanwhile, O'Barbo was extremely anxious. He had not seen any movement inside the castle since Oribeau had gone into it. He did not know what that inaction signified. Eventually, he made the decision, at the risk of being discovered, to send a trumpeter to the edge of the ditch. Immediately, another appeared on the Queen's behalf, who refused any communication.

Oribeau heard the two trumpets and was encouraged. He tried to free his hands, and succeeded in doing so. Immediately, he removed the blindfold from his eyes, and, having perceived a small window twenty feet above him, he climbed up to it. It overlooked a garden, in which there were beautiful elder trees.

The Prince let himself slide down a sloping wall, looked for a sickle, cut the best shoots, removed the pith from them, made a sarbacane[134] and went to place himself under the Queen's windows. He called out: "Why, O Queen, do you not want to hear me? I've come to rescue you; there's still time. Trust the faith of a Prince, whose word is sacred!"

Those words reached the ears of Queen Conchèse, but instead of reassuring her they frightened her. She ordered that the prisoner be locked up again. Oribeau heard those new orders; he did not wait for their execution but dived into the water-filled ditch that surrounded Makredon. He only traversed it after swimming a long away at the foot of the wall, in order to avoid being seen. He finally succeeded in reaching a covered place. He emerged from the water and went to rejoin his troop.

O'Barbo was frightened by the peril the Prince had run; he urged him to run to his Estates in order to muster the complete army of seven thousand men and come back to dictate the law to the Lagenian rebels.

"But in the meantime," said the Prince, the two allies might force the Queen to surrender."

O'Barbo was persuaded, and, wise as he was, was very embarrassed. He wrote to Dondanuck.

On the other hand, Oribelle, who was with her mother, having recognized Oribeau's voice, said to Conchèse: "I as-

---

[134] A sarbacane is a blowpipe. I have preserved the term because is used in the chapter-heading to provide the key letter. The author obviously penned this chapter in a tearing hurry, and forgot to mention what Oribeau actually did with the sarbacane he made, but the reader can work it out easily enough.

sure you, Milady, that that is the voice of the young King of Mommonia."

The Queen was still suspicious, but she was soon convinced, for, having descended into the garden to see the prisoner, who could no longer be found there, her guards found written in the sand: *Oribeau, King of Mommonia.*

Conchèse was desolate not to have admitted him to her presence as he had asked. Oribelle, no less afflicted than her mother, was trying nevertheless to console her when a false report plunged her into dolor as well. A sentinel said that he had seen the prisoner dive into the ditch, but that he had not seen him emerge again.

The Queen and the two Princesses were convinced that Oribeau had perished. They were so distressed that the beautiful Dinameh left the castle, with no one but Clonameh, and ran to the camp of the King of Meath in order to inform him of that misfortune and detach him from Ratchlin's party.

They did not waste time, but at the moment when the Princess left the castle, the two armies having learned that the prisoners had broken out and that they had been duped by the young King of Mommonia, they had ceased surrounding the wood where no enemies remained and were returning to blockade Makredin. As they approached, the King of Mommonia's little troop withdrew in order to take up an advantageous position. They found one on a hill crowned with inaccessible rocks. Ratchlin was transported with rage when he found his camp pillaged and those left to guard it tied up, incapable of making the slightest movement.

It was at that instant of fury that Princess Dinameh appeared at the gate of the camp mounted in her palfrey and asking for the Prince of Meath. Surprised by that move, Ratchlin ordered that the Princess be bought to him. An officer presented himself, who begged Dinameh to come to the General.

"And you dare," said Clomaneh, "to intimate the orders of a rebel to your sovereign! Go away, or be sure that you will be severely punished one day."

At the same time, the Princess and her governess put their horses to the gallop, heading for Prince Beaudâme's camp. But Ratchlin had them pursued and severely punished the officer who had not arrested them. They were brought back to his camp and held prisoner there.

That caused a great rumor in the army, because only Ratchlin and the three Barons who were his accomplices were rebels; all the rest thought they were serving the Queen and the State, without knowing exactly how. The soldiers, seeing that Dinameh was being held by force, conceived suspicions in consequence. One of those most zealous for the Queen left the camp secretly and went to take the news of what had happened to Prince Beaudâme's. He was about to go in when he was stopped by a patrol from Oribeau's army, who were observing the enemy's moves. They took him to their general.

Oribeau, informed by the Lagenian soldier of the captivity of the Princess and the dispositions of Ratchlin's army, resolved to take advantage of it, not only to detach Beaudâme from the alliance of a rebel but to bring about a revolution in minds and save the kingdom of Lagenia from civil war. After having treated the soldier well he sent him to Prince Beaudâme with a letter in which he mentioned the one that he had already written and made him protestations of amity. The soldier was escorted by the Mommonians to the entrance to the Meathan came, and he was offered a refuge when he left it if he did not want to, or could not, return to his compatriots' camp.

Beaudâme was holding a Council of War and reading Prince Oribeau's letter when the Lagenian soldier arrived. Debundeh was following it with his eyes, and they both seemed indecisive. At the sight of the Lagenian that the camp guard brought them, they thought that there was an attack, but the soldier reassured them; he told them what had happened in Ratchlin's camp, and that he was retaining Princess Dinameh, who had come out of Makredin in order to come to speak to the King of Meath. The Prince and the shepherd were very surprised by that conduct. The Lagenian took advantage of that disposition to give them Oribeau's letters.

All the officers of the Council were of the opinion that it was a trap set by the Mommonians, that everything was false and that the soldier was a traitor to his country who had sold himself to the Mommonians, but Beaudâme and Debundeh, who knew Prince Oribeau, had confidence in his letters after being assured that they were in his handwriting. After that, they wanted to know whether the Princess and Clomaneh were really prisoners, and they only had to speak to the first Lagenian guard.

Then Prince Beaudâme resolved to go to Oribeau's camp with Debundeh to confer with him. Unfortunately, he did not hide that resolution.

At that point in the reading, cries of "Fire! Fire!" were heard. Monsieur Gaudet of the Rue Courtaudvilain and the entire company rose to their feet and ran to the aid of their unfortunate neighbors. That meant that it required yet another evening to finish reading *The Adventures of the good Prince Oribeau*.

Chapter 2T
Treason of three officers. Beaudâme taken prisoner by Ratchlin. The indignant troops of Meath join Oribeau's. Beaudâme is condemned to death. Oribeau is captured by treason while coming to his rescue.

Too much delay is fatal. If Beaudâme had carried out his resolution immediately after having formed it, it would not have been thwarted, but it was late and he put it off until the next day. Three traitors on his council took advantage of that to inform Ratchlin of their King's intentions.

A man who lacks fidelity to his sovereign does not hesitate at another crime. He asked Beaudâme for a moment's conversation at the entrance of his camp. The Prince of Meath was not suspicious; he did not think he ought to refuse. Scarcely had he arrived at the rendezvous, however, than Ratchlin's partisans surrounded him and took him to their leader. The rebel heaped Beaudâme with reproaches, had him put in chains, declared that he would use him as a hostage, and that the only thing he could do was to give orders in writing to his troops as if he were at liberty. He swore to him that at the slightest move the Meathans made to join Oribeau would cost their King his life. Then he had him lowered down between two rocks, where there was only just enough space to take ten steps, and as wide as his body. A few hours passed without knowing what had become of the Prince, but Debundeh, not seeing him return, had no doubt that there had been treason. He sent the Lagenian to Oribeau to tell him what had happened and asked him to combine his Troop with his own in order to attack Ratchlin and liberate Princess Dinameh and her nurse Clomaneh, as well as Prince Beaudâme.

Oribeau shuddered at the excess of Ratchlin's audacity; he wanted to run immediately to deliver the Prince of Meath and the Princess of Lagenia, but O'Barbo moderated him. A council was held; O'Barbo was interrogated as to the trust that they could put in Debundeh. All that the Sage said was: "He's my old friend." There was then only one voice in favor of joining him.

Oribeau's troop descended the hill, preceded by warrior trumpets. The Meathans were astonished at first, and ran to their arms; Debundeh appeared in the ranks and informed them of the union with the Mommonians—which did not generate as much pleasure as he expected; the Meathans were sensible of the pillage of their camp. As soon as the Minister had informed them of the detention of Beaudâme by Ratchlin, however, they quivered with rage and demanded vengeance.

It was then that the Mommonian troops arrived. On the orders of their leader, the soldiers began by returning everything that they had stolen from the Meathans, which reconciled two nations. Afterwards, Oribeau, his ambassador and Debundeh met and assembled a council of war.

It was decided that before attacking an army that was still stronger than the two united allied forces, they would attempt to enlighten the Lagenians as to the rebel's designs, and that sentiment prevailed as the wisest. It was not easy to put it into execution, however. Ratchlin was a skillful general, who neglected nothing. He came to harangue his troops, representing to them that the King of Mommonia could not escape them, that they were going to capture him and take entire possession of his Estates; that he was holding the King of Meath, that it was necessary to massacre his army and reunite all of Meath with the kingdom of Lagenia.

These grand plans seduced the army, with the result that when the soldier who had informed Oribeau and Beaudâme presented himself to speak to his comrades, he was arrested, taken to the leader and put in irons. He was unbound and lowered down to the same location as the King of Meath, who as still in chains, with the horrible condition that he would only be brought out again after having killed Beaudâme.

When Oribeau saw that his attempts to corrupt Ratchlin's army were futile, he felt a kind of joy; his seething courage did not want anything that was not due to him. O'Barbo and Debundeh, however, appeared very embarrassed. It was necessary to liberate the King of Meath, the Queen of Lagenia and the Princesses; it would be unfortunate if that could only be done by massacring their subjects—and if they were beaten, that would make their fate worse.

While the two Sages weighed all these arguments, Oribeau encouraged the troops; he had only to show himself to be loved by the Meathans, as he was by the Mommonian; all were prepared for battle.

As O'Barbo neglected nothing in order to be informed as to what was happening among the enemy, it was learned that they were going to be attacked.

"If they intend to attack," said Oribeau, "it's necessary to forestall them; the role of those who are defending is always disadvantageous."

The two Sages agreed that that maxim was true. However, O'Barbo begged him to wait a little, assuring him that Dondanuck could not fail to arrive within twelve hours.

"I'm not a diviner," he said, "but I've calculated the necessary moments since Dondanuck was informed, and I'm sure that he hasn't wasted any of them. Thus, according to my calculations, we'll see his advance guard within twelve hours.

Debundeh agreed with O'Barbo.

It was at that moment that a Lagenian soldier, whom Ratchlin had not seduced like the others, came to warn them that within two hours, Beaudâme would be dead. Ratchlin did not want to leave him alive before delivering battle.

"There's no longer time to listen to prudence," said Oribeau. "It's becoming cowardice."

The two Sages kept silent.

Immediately, the King of Mommonia cried: "To arms! Who wants glory, follow me! Let's go deliver Prince Beaudâme, condemned to death by the traitor Ratchlin!"

As he spoke thus, the Prince mounted his horse and had the gates of the camp opened. Guided by the Lagenian soldier, he directed the cavalry toward the rock, while the infantry, commanded by O'Barbo and Debundeh, advanced slowly into the plain, pikes lowered, in profound silence.

Trees hid the cavalry; they only saw the infantry coming from Ratchlin's camp, which was advancing in the open. Everything was in tumult. Ratchlin cried "To Arms!" and said, mockingly: "They're coming to surrender."

But he was mistaken. When O'Barbo had found a battlefield advantageous to his inferior forces he stopped and took his precautions, in order not to be forced, at the same time as he maintained a line of retreat in the direction from which he expected Dondanuck to come with the entire Mommonian army.

Meanwhile, Oribeau was advancing toward the rock, obliged to circle around it, it would be a long time before he would be able to arrive. They were seen, but the confusion was then so great in Ratchlin's camp that orders were only given belatedly to oppose the cavalry to him. Oribeau arrived at the summit of the mountain before it was possible to prevent him; he perceived the abyss, descended from his horse and looked into it himself.

The Lagenian soldier who was with the King of Meath, believing that someone had come to punish him for having delayed killing the King of Meath, raised his arm to strike.

"Stop, wretch!" shouted Oribeau. "I've come to free the Prince, and you with him."

Transported by joy, the soldier untied Beaudâme' hands, who could not have escaped his bonds otherwise; ropes were thrown down to him and he climbed up, along with the Lagenian soldier.

Oribeau and Beaudâme embraced. The two Princes mounted horses in order to return to their camp, but they perceived one of the numerous squadrons that had just attacked them barring their passage. Oribeau consulted the two

Lagenians; they showed him a narrow path by which they could descend one by one.

The Princes sent their guides on ahead and the entire troop embarked on the path, with the consequence that when the first Lagenian cavalier arrived, the last Mommonian was fifty paces along the path. While the first Lagenians awaited the orders of their commander, the Mommonians emerged on to the plain and ran to join the infantry.

At the sight of their young King, the Meathans made the air resound with cries of joy and demanded to fight. Oribeau and Beaudâme supported them, but the two Sages moderated that impetuosity, with the promise of charging the enemy as soon as they dared to quit their camp.

In order to accelerate the desired moment, Oribeau, at the head of his best horsemen, went to insult them at their palisades. The Lagenian cavalry had not yet retired, so the King of Mommonia could not be surrounded. Ratchlin quivered with rage, especially when he learned that Prince Beaudâme had been freed. He sent a herald to the King of Mommonia to propose that the difference between them be settled by single combat.

The two young Princes were alone with their cavaliers, O'Barbo and Debundeh having not quit the camp. Oribeau accepted.

Ratchlin was in all his strength, scarcely thirty-six years old. He emerged from the camp full of joy, saying to his initiates: "I'll terminate the war with a single blow!"

He advanced proudly on a fresh horse, whereas Oribeau's was fatigued. The two combatants took the field; the trumpet sounded; they launched themselves at one another. The King of Mommonia's horse could not withstand the effort of Ratchlin's; it was knocked down; but the young Prince leapt lightly to the ground and put himself on the defensive. The rebel had the cowardice to charge him with his lance lowered in order to pierce him. Oribeau avoided his enemy by his skill and agility.

He tired him, and at a moment when he found himself behind Ratchlin he cut the hamstring of his horse with a sword-thrust. The charger reared up and fell, Ratchlin fed himself and, arming himself with his terrible spear, he charged the Prince, who evaded him. The rebel was quivering with fury. Oribeau circled around him, made him use up his strength, and found himself within range to launch a blow at his head.

He fell—but the perfidious Ratchlin had given his orders; two of his soldiers immediately launched themselves at Oribeau, seized his sword, disarmed him and bound him. He was dragged to the enemy camp.

The Mommonians and the Meathans quivered with horror, and cried perfidy. They wanted to hurl themselves on Ratchlin, but he was surrounded by his satellites. He returned to his camp.

Chapter 2V
Victory without combat. Dinameh is liberated by
Oribeau and returned to her mother.
Dondanuck's arrival.

"Valiant Lagenians," said Oribeau, addressing the soldiers who were leading him, "is it possible that you have dishonored yourselves by seconding the cowardice of a rebel against his sovereign? I sent an ambassador to the Queen to ask for the hand of Princess Oribelle in marriage in order to form an eternal bond between the two kingdoms that would fortify them against the enterprises of our neighbors the Angles; but Ratchlin did not want my ambassador to be received, whom I accompanied in disguise in order to see the Princess and discover whether me proposition would be accepted. The traitor Ratchlin wants to seize the throne and annihilate the royal family, which originates, like all those in Evinland, from the great Queen Wrwcwcw, regarded as a fay by the people. O Langenians, will you second a traitor, who is keeping here as a prisoner one of the Princesses, daughters of your sovereign?"

That speech, made in a loud voice, but with the natural grace of the young Prince, interested the hearts of all the Lagenians, already discontented with Ratchlin's cowardly procedure, in his favor. Oribeau was surrounded; the satellites were shoved aside. The King of Mommonia was untied.

"To arms!" he cried, immediately. "Let us free the Princess, present your homages to the Queen and, O valiant Lagenians, renew your oath of fidelity to her! Ratchlin is a traitor, whom it is necessary to tie up, in order to put him in your sovereign's hands!"

Immediately—doubtless by an effect of the protection of the gods—the entire army proclaimed Oribeau the defender of Queen Conchèse and husband of Princess Oribelle. He was given a superb horse; they swore to obey him. Ratchlin was arrested, along with Balaclay, Kildare and Katerlagh, all three perfidious traitors.

They were brought before the Prince, who had them unbound. "It's not for me to punish you," he said. "I am not your sovereign. As for the personal insult you have just done to me, I pardon you, but you will be taken before the Queen, who will dispose of your fate."

"No one disposes of that but me," said Ratchlin. At the same time he seized the sword that had been left to him, and threatened the soldiers who were holding him with the terrible expression that they were accustomed to respect. He drew away.

It is said that he was seen to strike himself with that sword, and to cry with rage, as he pulled it out: "Would that I could plunge it bloodily into your heart, King of Mommonia." It is added that he expired after pronouncing those words.

At the same moment, piercing screams were heard. Oribeau ran toward them. Two of Ratchlin's satellites had daggers raised over Dinameh's breast and Clomaneh's heart. Oribeau cut off the arm of the first, while a Lagenian severed the head of the other with a single stroke.

"Oh, Prince!" said the beautiful Dinameh, whom Oribeau recognized as Jasmine. "It's to you that I owe my life!"

"And a spouse worthy of your charms."

"Alas, Prince Beaudâme is dead; I have just been told, and I know..."

"He's alive, and I have had the good fortune to rescue him."

"Great God" cried Clomaneh, "bless this generous Prince forever!"

For Dinameh, the two words *he's alive* had caused so much joy that she could not speak. Oribeau asked Clonameh to take the Princess to the Queen and to inform her of the fortunate revolution that had just occurred. Dinameh, in traversing the camp, wanted to confirm with her beautiful mouth the truth that Oribeau had told her. The delighted soldiers made the air resound with cries of joy.

Meanwhile, Prince Beaudâme had borne to his own camp the sad news of the treason carried out against the King of Mommonia. O'Barbo was penetrated with dolor, but in generous hearts, dolor is changed into courage. He was about to sound the charge, in order to go and attack Ratchlin, vanquish him or perish when he perceived Dondanuck arriving, six hours before the time he had calculated. The Sage then conceived hope, but feared despair equally, due to the perfidy of Ratchlin. He showed his troops the help that was arriving and told them that it was necessary to take the enemy camp by storm.

A cry of simultaneous joy and fury was the response to that desired order.

They march; they run; they arrive.

The songs of delight in the Langenian camp were regarded as the signal of Oribeau's death; the Mommonians and the Meathans launched themselves forward and tore down the palisade of the ill-defended camp. O'Barbo, Beaudâme and Debundeh encouraged them...

But Oribeau, lifted up on trophies, appeared in the breach. "No more enemies!" he cried. The Lagenians are our allies; come and share their joy instead of fighting them."

As he concluded those words, the Prince extended his hand to Beaudâme and made him climb up beside him. Then he embraced O'Barbo and Debundeh.

An envoy from O'Barbo had hastened Dondanuck's march. The Minister of Mommonia, on learning of the danger to the King, had raced ahead with five hundred horsemen to support the attack on the camp. He arrived at the moment when Oribeau was embracing the Sage, his teacher.

"What!" he said. "The victory is already won!"

"Yes, and the most signal of victories," replied Prince Beaudâme, "but it is your King who has won it, alone, enchained in the middle of the Lagenians' camp. Ratchlin is dead."

"Have you killed him or condemned him?" Dondanuck asked Oribeau.

"Neither."

"Ah! I bless the protective God. May his bounty preserve you from ever shedding blood! O Thor, deign to pour down your favors on a young Sovereign, your image! Inspire in him all the virtues, clemency and justice, give him discernment and wisdom, in order that in all his enterprises, he will be guided by reason, not by reckless courage, which is only a virtue in a soldier. Give him the virtuous companion that you have destined for him for so long, in order that he shall be happy with her, and give the throne an heir formed of the finest, noblest and most virtuous blood in the world!"

When Dondanuck had finished that prayer, the Yapou made its voice heard, flying over the camp—which filled the three armies with admiration. The bird directed its flight toward Makredin, as if to invite Oribeau to go there. The troops noticed that, and a thousand confused voices were heard exciting the Price to follow his celestial guide. Ratchlin's former soldiers were not those who exhibited the least zeal!

Chapter 2U
Unanimity. Conversation of Oribeau and Oribelle.
Clonameh tells the story of the Princess and that of her
sister Dinameh: Canora-Ahissa-Daura-Fillira-Julia-
Rosée-Oribelle. Oribeau is returned to his Estates.[135]

"Usurper of sovereign authority, you are no more," cried the Lagenian soldiers, "and we see in our midst a Prince favored by the gods, who seeks the hand of our Princess. May he one day reign over us!"

The nobles of Lagenia also approached Oribeau and warned him that if he married Princess Oribelle, of which they had no doubt, they would demand that the seat of the two Empires would be in Balaclay. Dondanuck and O'Barbo, after having been consulted, replied that they would consent to that, in the name of Queen Dadameh, the army of Mommonia and the people. Beaudâme and his troops also promised to acquiesce to that, with the consequence that it was unanimously agreed.

They took the road to Makredin Castle, the drawbridge of which had been lowered, on the order of Queen Conchèse, since she had been informed of what had happened in the camp by her daughter Dinameh.

Oribeau advanced with Prince Beaudâme at his side; Dondanuck, O'Barbo and Debundeh followed them. The beauty of the young King of Mommonia, his martial air, his youth and the kindness that his physiognomy radiated, united with his majesty, excited the admiration of the three armies. The Queen and the two Princesses, followed by Pucellomaneh, Clomaneh and the entire Court advanced to the perron in order to receive them.

Oribeau saluted the Queen, and said to her: "Milady, I honor you as my mother."

---

[135] This chapter heading differs somewhat from the one contained in the original contents list.

"Milord," replied the Queen, "I receive you as my son."

Oribeau then raised his eyes and saw in Princess Oribelle the Julia whom he had loved tenderly in spite of himself.

"Oh, beautiful Princess," he exclaimed, "how is it that I rediscover in you..."

He did not finish. Clomaneh presented herself, saying: "Recognize also Aunt Thor-el."

Oribeau's surprise was redoubled.

"And here is Mary," said Dinameh, then. "I have hardly ever quit my sister."

"It's necessary that I recount that marvelous story," Clomaneh said, "including several circumstances of which even the Queen my niece is unaware. Pour me a glass of escubac."[136]

Utility of the Marvels of Faerie, Oribelle's disguises and those of her sister Dinameh

Usquebaugh, a sweet red liqueur which our Evinlandish forefathers have made since time immemorial from saffron, fills my goblet in order to give me the fire and vivacity required by the story that I have to tell.

"Tell," said Pucellomaneh, getting to her feet. "I shall act."

Untroubled, Clomaneh continued:

---

[136] Numerous recipes for this whisky liqueur, also known as usquebaugh—thus adapting it to the alphabetization of the chapter, although the latter term as also used as a synonym for whisky itself—can be found in eighteenth-century reference books, when it was usually concocted with saffron, but it faded from the historical record somewhat until its recent reinvention as a sweet liqueur flavored with various aromatic herbs.

I am the younger sister of Queen Canora, mother of Conchèse, who reigns gloriously today in Lagenia, as well as Princess Pucellomaneh, who has remained a spinster because a Pictish pirate violated her in her youth. My name is Princess Rosée of Ultonia, and I am the cousin of Queen Dadameh the Wise, mother of Prince Oribeau, who listens to me, Queen Mijoreh, mother of Prince Beaudâme and Princess Nurismaneh, his nurse. King O'Emptor, my brother-in-law, married me to young Balaclay when he was still a child because he was the foremost of his Barons.

My husband grew up and soon marked his evil dispositions, but he constrained himself as long as the King lived. When O'Emptor was dead, as well as Queen Canora, the kingdom was governed by Baron Kilkenny. Balaclay, who was then only twenty-five—I was thirty-five—thought me too old; he resolved to repudiate me, but encountered difficulties in doing so, and he thought it simpler to kill me. I was pregnant when he formed that deadly resolution, although it's necessary to admit that he didn't know it, because I scarcely suspected it myself.

He asked me one day to visit the new apartments that he had added to his manor. As I descended a hidden staircase I noticed that three steps seemed odd but I continued unsuspectingly; when I put my foot on the first step, however, the three steps sank downwards and I fell into a well. I floated, sustained by my clothing; I perceived that the well had an issue through which sea-water entered, but the tide was low at that moment. I dragged myself into the conduit, and reached the shore.

It was only than that I sensed the full horror of my fate. I realized that my barbaric husband had wanted to end my life. Anarchy reigned in the State; Kilkenny had to be careful of everyone, especially in Balaclay; there was no hope of protection.

While I was making those sad reflections, a fisherman came toward me, who, seeing a lady of the Court soaking wet, thought that I had fallen into the sea. He offered to take me to his house to change and dry my clothes. When we reached his dwelling his wife and daughter gave me clean clothes belonging to the latter, which fit me very well, and set about drying those I had taken off.

I felt that I was not safe; I took advantage of the first moment that I was left alone to go back to the town costumed as a fisherman's daughter and I went to the young Queen's palace. I told her about my misfortunes but I asked her to dissimulate them. She consented to that. I was put in the ranks of women who served in the most obscure employments.

After eight months I brought a child into the world, who did not live. At the same time the Queen had Princess Oribelle; I asked to nurse her, and in order to hide me she sent me to Makredin Castle, in accordance with a pretended oracle of the fay Pucellomaneh, one of our ancestors, a role that Baron Kilkenny's wife played for me. For it's necessary to know that Sireneh, Baroness Kilkenny, had previously received a Mommonian scholar obliged to flee the persecution of his enemies. For the moment, I'll only tell you his supposed name; he called himself Sacripandi, a name that seems Roman and means something like "Opener of Sacred Things."

That Sage, apart from the moral philosophy that rendered his doctrine and conduct excellent, possessed several items of fine knowledge that he had acquired by the constant study of nature—among others, that of rising up into the air, which had earned him the reputation among the people of being a great magician. He taught my two sisters and me that fine secret; we sometimes made productive use of it, as you shall see, for we were taken for fays and the people, who were convinced of it, made up extraordinary stories about us.

"The principal secret that the Sage gave us was being able to rise into the air in a chariot sustained by large birds made of light tarred fabric, filled with subtle air that forced it to rise up; those birds had artistically- made wings, which beat and caused them to advance, to descend and rise up at will, by means of brass wires held by the person steering the chariot. Sacripandi carried out several experiments before us and we made several ourselves. My sister Pucellomaneh, who was the boldest, was the first to go up in the chariot and rose into the air until she was lost to sight; Nursimaneh, Sireneh and I took turns to go up with her.

Queen Conchèse had too many obligations to the Baron and Baroness of Kilkenny not to prefer their son O'Brisombaüm to all her other subjects in the choice of a husband, which the law obliged her to make among them for lack of a male heir. It was to avoid any argument and a civil war that young Knoctoser, later O'Brisombaüm, had been brought up as a girl with the young Princess; everyone was in accord regarding that disguise, of which my sisters and I were informed, and what resulted from it was what we desired.

In spite of our precautions, however, the Barons of the kingdom were no sooner aware of it than they formed a conspiracy and activated two foreigners, priests of Thor and Worden, who stirred up the people. It was then that my sister Pucellomaneh constructed a chariot and birds; she placed Baroness Sireneh in it, whom a long illness had rendered unrecognizable, hid herself under its drapery and enabled her to play the role of the fay Pucellomaneh.

The Baroness rescued her husband and son from the hands of MacChoucas, collected me and Princess Oribelle before flying away, and transported us out of sight, to descend again at the gates of Makredin, where my sister, the little princess and I, imprudently, all got down at the same time—so that a great misfortune happened to Sireneh. Relieved of such a considerable weight, the machine immediately rose up precipitately. Sireneh could not control it; one of the bird's mechanisms broke, and the machine, losing its equilibrium, fell into the sea, where she was swallowed up before our eyes.

That accident was concealed. My sister constructed another machine, which was kept ready in case of need. It was often employed to rise up out of sight and to cause to appear before Princess Oribeau her famous Yapou, which has often been seen flying in the air; it was Pucellomaneh, who uttered the bird's cries with a pierced funnel that she placed between her lips and teeth. But I'm anticipating...

The Sage Sacripandi had left us some time before Oribelle's birth, because of threats made to him by my husband, Balaclay. Retired to a cavern in the vicinity of Karrickmacgriffin , he had the good fortune of receiving Queen Dadameh during a storm. He did not announce to her that she would have a son—she was already pregnant with Prince Oribeau—but that service having put him in favor, malevolence published the rumors that ran around; for the people love the marvelous; bizarre facts please and amuse them. Sacripandi resumed his name, Dondanuck, and became Minister even while O'Facfac was still alive; after the King's death he aided the Regent of Mommonia and the good that he did is known throughout the world.

While the neighboring kingdom prospered, however, there were a few troubles in this one. Queen Conchèse was sage and prudent, but her husband went astray; he feared that the sovereign was turning against him and became involved in a conspiracy. It was then that Ratchlin appeared at the Court; he was virtuous when he arrived and if he ceased to be, it was because flatterers corrupted him. The nobles, jealous of Knoctoser's good fortune, demanded that the Queen appoint him as Minister and render omnipotent a noble who was beneath them, in order to mortify one of their peers whose children would reign. Conchèse, already irritated, lent herself to it for the sake of peace.

Castellan O'Connor of Ratchlin initially served the Queen with disinterest and fidelity. Her husband the Prince conceived a hated for him and wanted to have him killed; Ratchlin found out about it, provided evidence the plot to the Queen, and had her consent to depriving O'Brisonbaüm of his liberty. That was the epoch of Ratchlin's corruption. That action, for which the Queen has always reproached herself, appeared to him to be a complaisance on the part of the Queen rather than an act of justice. He was a widower; he formed bold designs, but, the Queen's marriage and the birth of two heirs rendering them impossible, he dared to think of marrying one or other of the young Princesses.

It was to my sister Pucellomaneh that he confided that. She was extremely annoyed, because she had formed the sage project of an alliance between the two neighboring Courts that had Princes, and it was she who, by means of the flying chariot, played the role of fay to destine Oribelle for Prince Oribeau and Dinameh for Prince Beaudâme. As for the rumor that the younger Princess was young and stupid, although Dinameh has always been beautiful and intelligent, as the King of Mommonia knows, my sister had her reasons for spreading it. She knew that ignorant people are easily led by the marvelous and wanted to profit from the beautiful invention of the Sage Sacripandi-Dondanuck to effectuate advantageous marriages that amour would one day render happy.

Ratchlin had too much intelligence, however, to be duped by the means employed by my sister. Seeing himself omnipotent in the State by virtue of the confidence of the honorable Conchèse, and without a rival since the imprisonment of O'Brisombaüm, he wanted to fortify it further by the alliance with Balaclay, whom everyone believed to be a widower, giving him his sister, the beautiful Radelinde. After that marriage he believed himself to be sure of obtaining Princess Oribelle, and he was about to employ very criminal means to take possession of her person when my sister made use of her machine to remove the two Princesses from Makredin Castle and take them to Waterford, where she left them under my guidance.

She informed Queen Dadameh of our arrival, asking her to allow us to maintain a necessary incognito. The Queen of Mommonia thought the two Princesses had been expelled by Ratchlin; it was the opposite; he would have liked to retain them, and my sister had brought Princess Dinameh along with her elder sister because Ratchlin, only guided by ambition, would have married one in default of the other. Before talking about what became of us in Waterford, however, it's appropriate to give Prince Oribeau and Prince Beaudâme a few details about the education of the two Princesses.

I have said that Oribelle was confided to me immediately after her birth; it was me who nursed her. From the cradle she showed a marked tenderness of character and a penchant for love that made her cherished. The advantage that I had of being in a castle far from the Court gave me the facility of preserving the young Princess from indiscreet speech that is dangerous before the usage of reason and the flatteries of courtiers. I only held pure discourse with her; I only put honest images before her innocent eyes.

Oribelle was five years old when her sister Dinameh was born. At my sister's solicitation, the Queen gave her milk in Makredin Castle, where she came to live; the little Princess received from me alone all the other cares of a nurse. My sister Pucellomaneh took charge of Oribelle from then on, and gave her the principles of virtue that will one day by the happiness and glory of her husband the King.

At about the same time we had a very disagreeable visit—that of a Sage who came one day to see another, to whom he had brought an illustrious pupil. My sister, informed of the place of the young King's retreat, took an important step. Prince Oribeau was twelve years old; Pucellomaneh rose up into the air with Oribelle and showed her Oribeau in the mountains of Stefenon, saying: "My daughter, isn't that young King likeable."

"Oh, he's charming."

"He will be your husband."

After that visit, she repeated every day to her young pupil: "It's necessary to render yourself worthy, by all the virtues of our sex, of the handsome Prince that I've shown to you."

These are my sister's maxims:

1. A young woman ought to be modest and fearful; boldness and courage are a fault in her; she can only give herself those virile qualities when she becomes a mother and when she is a widow, or deprived of her husband.

2. A woman ought to be chaste all her life; chastity consists of flight from all men, at whom you ought not even look; for a maiden must think that one day, her husband must find her eyes, her ears, her mouth and all the parts of her body pure, and above all her thoughts. When you are married, chastity will consist of an active tenderness for your husband, of seeking everything that will not only please him but give him a good opinion of you. Never forget that a woman must always be, in marriage, a modest maiden for her husband, and never a passionate lover; she must never anticipate his caresses; she must have, in that regard, the reserve of a maiden. As for the care of her person, she is all the more obliged to them because she only has that legitimate means of showing him her tenderness. Never allow your husband to see what modesty obliges you to hide; never allow your mouth to pronounce a word that expresses the liberty of marriage, not even: "I sleep with my husband." It is necessary to take purity to excess; a married woman who conducts herself thus might be called a prude, but she will surely retain her power over the heart and senses of her husband, which is essential for a wife.

3. If a husband ever commits faults of infidelity, be mute; you could not say a word about that subject that would not be a breach of honesty.

4. If a husband is brutal and angry, contrast it all the more with your mildness; meekness is the prerogative of the female sex, the clothing of the female soul, as the skirt, the corset and the cover of the bosom are the indication of the sex of her body.

5. Never stare at a man, not even your husband; a woman whose gaze can linger over an individual of the other sex does not have a chaste, meek, timid soul; she does not have a woman's soul; she is not what she ought to be—for if a firm and courageous man is a perfect man, a modest, meek, fearful,

timid woman is a perfect woman. The reason is that a bold woman can only please a cowardly man who does not have the soul of a man; now, what kind of woman destines herself internally to please a cowardly man?

The virtues of the two sexes are not the same in everything; they differ, like their bodies; some are common, like truth, justice, goodness and generosity, just as, in the body, both sexes have a head, eyes a mouth, arms and legs. Even so, there is a sexual nuance in the common virtues; the justice of a woman is more generous, her generosity more affectionate, her goodness more obliging; the man with the same qualities is not effeminate; they have something masculine in him; they are admirable. A woman is not manly in manifesting those same sentiments; she is a more consoling individual; her virtues are more tender. A woman is as necessary to the world as a man, but she has her lot, and it is so beautiful that she ought not to envy that of the other sex.

6. Having become a mother you will only be charged with rendering your children good; your husband will render them courageous. I repeat; only think of goodness; they will lose enough of it, with other men; and if you neglect it in order to give male virtues, you will be omitting a female duty that no one but you can fulfill.

7. You are a Princess; be indulgent, and never forget that you are destined for the throne, to create the wellbeing of an entire people. You are not being brought up like your peers; your worthy mother has wanted to profit from the example of the Queen of Mommonia, who is having her son the Prince brought up as a man; you will be brought up as a woman; you shall know what few of your equals know.

That is a benefit for which you ought to thank the gods; for you will be pious without bigotry; your devotion ought to be frank, and tolerant; it ought to make religion loved, whereas certain intolerant devotees make it feared and hated. Divine worship is an affair of sentiment; to command it is to close hearts to it, which would open to it naturally: a sublime verity that, astonishingly, many great men have not known, or have scorned.

Such were, in abridged form, the moral instructions that my sister gave when she was charged with the education of Princess Oribelle.

"How beautiful they are!" exclaimed the young King of Mommonia.

"An instructress who forms the spouses of sovereigns thus," said Prince Beaudâme, "merits men establishing altars to her."

Clomaneh resumed:

Several years had gone by when O'Brisombaüm, excited by traitors, had unjust suspicions that made him a conspirator. You know what resulted from it; those sad events are still before our eyes. Oribelle, my sister and I often wept for the fate of O'Brisombaüm, but it would not have been safe for him to set him at liberty because of the great power that Ratchlin had overtly acquired.

Oribelle reached the age of fourteen; my sister, as I have said, had the first indications of the intentions of the ambitious Minister. She resolved to oppose him by upsetting all his plans.

One evening, we saw O'Connor of Ratchlin arrive with a great deal of noise. I had a presentiment of his designs and communicated them to my sister. I was not mistaken; he had come to take possession of the person of the two Princesses. Pucellomaneh, with the consent of the Queen, disposed her machine; the Princesses and I climbed into it with two men of confidence, Killcullen and his son Frank; and, having observed the direction of the wind, she took it aloft.

We passed between Wicklow and Kildare, over all of Kilkenny and a part of Tipperary and descended half a mile from Waterford, where my sister left us under the guard of

Killcullen and Frank. She climbed back into her aerial chariot and returned to the Queen at Makredin.

As for us, when the gates of Waterford were opened, we went into the city and went to show our letters of recommendation to the Great Judge, a respectable old man who took us into his home. I stayed there as long as was necessary to accustom the two Princesses to our new abode. My sister had told me that Prince Oribeau and his tutor were in Waterford incognito, and that it was necessary to take advantage of that fortunate circumstance to let him see the Princess, in various disguises, which would be those of the conditions through which Oribelle needed to pass; for my sister wanted a Princess destined to be Queen to know her people, in order to be useful to them beside her husband, in an enlightened manner.

The first time that Princess Oribelle saw the King of Mommonia she and I were still in the home of the Great Judge, but Princess Dinameh was at the Court with a Princess of the royal blood who was showing her high society. Oribelle was using the name Canora and in the Prince's eyes she passed for the youngest of the Great Judge's daughters. You will recall, Milord, the wisdom with which she spoke when she was interrogated; the veritable Canora was with Dinameh, to keep her company in the home of the Princess of Thomond-Clare.

In the home of the Great Judge we saw a great many things useful for the instruction of the Princess; we heard, indirectly, all the complaints that were brought to him and almost all the secrets that were confided to him. I said to my pupil: "Listen attentively to what is happening in Waterford, for you will be the Queen and protectress of this people."

One day, when I had gone to the house of the Princess of Thomond-Clare to see Dinameh, I was retained for a ball, to which that Lady was to take the younger of my pupils. I immediately sent Killcullen to look for Oribelle, in order that she might participate in that diversion. It was while coming to meet me that she was attacked by secret emissaries of Ratchlin, who recognized Killcullen.

He owes you his life, Milord; you showed, at an age still tender, the courage of a man. It is true that my sister was watching over Princess Oribelle, but she was delighted that the Princess owed her deliverance to you. She was named to you as the beautiful Ahissa, and your modest restraint, which prevented you from examining her too closely, meant that you did not recognized in her the Canora who had already interested you.

Killcullen brought Oribelle to me as soon as you had gone back into the bourgeois dance-hall, and came with us to the Eropa ball. You appeared there, and as I knew you, I pointed you out to the Princess of Thomond-Clare, who, having changed clothes with Dinameh, got her to talk to you in her name, as you know. You surely took her for a frank coquette—but that was a proof we were making, for Oribelle, the Princess and I were all listening to you, all three of us disguised.

After you had gone, the lady said to us: "I could have divined all his responses, especially the last, When Dinameh said to him that one ought to reply accurately to a woman like her, he did well to reply: 'That depends on the person of whom she has asked it, Milady.' A Sovereign may disguise himself, but nevertheless, he always speaks as a master within a matter of seconds."

We stayed with the Princess of Thomond-Clare for a month, in order to see the Ladies of Waterford and familiarize ourselves with their mores, the intrigues of the Court, etc. There is no need to talk about the discoveries we made; Oribelle will profit from them.

"My sister came to make us change residence, for I found myself so comfortable in the Princess's home and Dinameh, especially, was so happy there, that I did not think of quitting that agreeable abode. The severe Pucellomaneh reprimanded me harshly for my negligence. Excited by her reproaches, I took my leave of our beautiful hostess and went to lodge with my two pupils in a house that was visited by a great many people, for it played host to bards and kaldes. The sister of the master of the house was an acquaintance; she received me as an old friend and represented my two pupils as nieces.

We led a very agreeable life in that house, where we only stayed until the time when the young King of Waterford came to it. In the meantime, we profited from the varied scenes that we had before our eyes on a daily basis, but we were not seen; we saw everything from a wooden cupboard placed beside the staircase that led to our hostess's bedroom. It was from there that we saw the Prince and his tutor. When they were ready to leave we went out by a door that opened into the courtyard and were perceived as we went back in.

The following day, on descending into the hall where no one was usually to be seen I recognized one of Ratchlin's emissaries. I went back up to my two pupils immediately and decided to follow an extraordinary piece of advice that my sister had given me, to establish myself as an innkeeper. Killcullen had rented the shop and gave me Frank for a waiter. I dressed my two pupils as waitress and took on an extra girl to wash the dishes. Dinameh, under the name of Mary, found it very repugnant at first to see herself in such an estate, but she played her part and became more cheerful. As for Oribelle, she never showed anything but enthusiasm for everything that served to enlighten her.

I can even add that after a fortnight of the busy and noisy life of my inn, the two sisters found great pleasure in it. They were sickened by the remarks of the workmen, and then amused when they repeated them to me. I often explained to them what they did not understand.

"What a difference there is between this society," said Julia, "and the one we're quitting! There, everything is disguised; no one ever says what they think; it's necessary to judge by contraries. Here, people display their thoughts all too crudely, and always speak the truth, no matter how harsh it is..."

I interrupted her. "That's precisely the reason why your mother the Queen wanted you to sample this condition, like

Prince Oribeau, in order to be his companion; your enlightenment will second his, instead of your ignorance being able to impede him, in the good that he intends to do."

"Just Heaven!" cried the good Ennisleague. "Princess Oribelle, from whom King Fitz-Oribeau descends, was once an innkeeper! Ha! I shall be proud of my profession! If anyone scorns me..."

"Good woman," Kerry said to her, laughing, "no useful profession is shameful; vice alone dishonors, However, although everyone knows that verity, I have just heard a few people behind me saying in low voices: 'A Princess a waitress! What a necessity! What's the point of lowering oneself to that?' First of all, I respond: such is the story. Secondly, I say that it is not a necessity, but that if a Queen knew all conditions and she had a good heart, she would bring back the Golden Age on earth. Finally, I add that it was necessary that Oribelle and Dinameh hide in such an estate because, Ratchlin having discovered the two Princesses in the home of the Princess of Thomond-Clare, it was necessary that they cut the thread of any pursuit by taking an obscure estate in which no one would look for them. That's what I was about to say when the exclamation of our worthy hostess interrupted me."

You have not forgotten that that the nurse Clomaneh has just referred to Oribelle by the name of Julia. It was the following day the O'Barbo brought the Prince of Mommonia to the inn to dine there. Mary seemed drunk with joy on seeing the Prince among our customers. Even Julia, although always very reserved, could not dissimulate her contentment; you know, Prince, how she testified it to you. That day was one of the most agreeable of her life...

I have only spoken briefly about the Yapou, which you heard so frequently. It only ever appeared when my sister flew over Waterford in her aerial chariot to keep watch on the steps taken by O'Connor of Ratchlin and defend the Princesses. I will add that in addition to her birds of tarred fabric filled with hot air, which she kept heated by means of an ardent lamp connected to as many pipes, she really had domesticated a few eagles or condors of the largest species, taken as chicks from the mountains, that with the help of a kind of halter she moderated them and had them direct her chariot where she wished when the wind was not too strong.

After your visit, Julia and Mary did not stay at my inn as regularly. To distract them, and to acquaint them with workers of their estate, I placed them with a fashion merchant in Yanisnorohé Street, but my sister and I kept watch on them with the greatest attention. However, their sojourn in that great street was so dangerous that one evening they were insulted; my sister was ready to punish those who were attacking her disguised as soldiers, but you and your tutor imposed yourselves upon them, and delivered the two Princesses, under the names and in the costumes of Fillira and Hasameh.

You saw Julia again, as well as Mary and Frank, in the tavern where the three of them went to obtain my provision of beer. You saw them at supper that evening, the eve of your departure. Her heart was attached to you without her suspecting it; it was a keen, tender, natural penchant, as honest as her thought. You interested her like a tenderly cherished brother. The news of your departure from Waterford made her go pale; she did not know that we were to go to reside, as well as you, in the home of Bridge-Clonard of Younghall. I did not delay giving her that information after your departure, on seeing her naïve dolor.

The next day, we made all our arrangements to leave Waterford; we set forth that evening in my sister's chariot, which set us down a few paces from Bridge-Clonard's house.

I knew his wife. "My dear Gemmeh," I said to her, "the two Princesses of Lagenia and I are fleeing the persecutions of O'Connor of Ratchlin; it's necessary to receive me as your sister and my two pupils as your daughters whom you put in apprenticeship in Cork and have recalled to your home."

Gemmeh received me with the greatest respect and served me zealously. You know the conduct that the two Prin-

cesses maintained in that house, Oribelle under the name of
Rosée and Dinameh under that of Jasmine; there is no need to
repeat the details to you.

You finally left for Mullanger and you sent presents via
Bridge that discovered you to all his family; those for Rosée,
especially, were worthy of a King. It was then that Oribelle
enjoyed, in your regard, all the sentiments of admiration, esteem and amour that you had inspired in her; for those obliging sentiments when it was known that you were the King, and
that the old man was a Sage of the highest condition, a friend
of the Minister and the Queen herself. Your slightest actions
were recalled, your slightest thoughts cited:

"Do you remember, brother, when he said that it was
necessary to be good to everyone?"

"And when he said that it was necessary not to be imperious?"

"And when he recommended us to love our mother?"

"To cherish our sisters and be their support?"

"To regard our father as the image of Thor?"

"To do good to everyone, because men are our brothers?"

"To treat foreigners well, in order that they will praise
and the nation would be loved and cherished?"

"And how he was helpful to everyone?"

"How he threw himself waist-deep into the mud one day
to help a poor carter who was bogged down!"

"If a poor old woman dropped the slightest thing he
picked it up and presented it to her politely, as if she were
young and pretty!"

"And when she was young and pretty, he lowered his
eyes, and even though speaking to her politely, didn't look at
her."

"He would have taken the food out of his mouth to give
it to someone who was hungry."

"He did everything better than anyone else."

"Especially military exercises."

"Oh, he was a past master at those—and he was compassionate."

"Do you remember how honestly and respectfully he spoke to my sisters?"

"Oh, yes, and that was what made me like him more."

"And how friendly and polite he was to us?"

"Oh, I remember, I remember, to such an extent that he always called me, who was the youngest, Master Clamnis...."

"And yet he was a King!"

"Oh, he'll be a good King!"

Then the daughters, who hadn't yet said anything, spoke in their turn, but with more restraint, with more tenderness than admiration.

"As for me," said Vananis, "I didn't know that the old man was a Minister and a former general, but it occurred to me more than once that he might be Thor, who had come to take a holiday in our midst in human form, and that the young one, whom I didn't know was a King, was Worden."

"Oh," exclaimed Oeillette, "I said more than once that it seemed to me that the old man spoke with respect to the young man, that the young man might be a good genius who had fallen in love with Rosée, for he sometimes looked at her for a long time—a long time!—and his eyes, his mouth and all his face seemed delighted!"

"And I," said Giroflée, "sometimes thought secretly that he was the son of Baron Cork, our liege lord, who had disguised himself in order to love Rosée, but when I saw afterwards how wise the old man was and how the young man obeyed him, I no longer knew what to think. What about you, Rosée, what did you think?"

"I thought," Oribelle replied, "that he was the King of Mommonia, who didn't want to be known."

"Oh, she had divined him, she had divined him!" cried the whole family.

"What about you, Jasmine?" said Oeillette.

"Me, I thought...like my sister."

Kilmactomas interrupted the hunter. "You told us that that Princess was an idiot who would only have intelligence one day if she loved Prince Beaudâme, otherwise known as Cahincaha, and yet, with the exception of a few responses to Oribeau before Beaudâme, I see her acting as sagely as anyone else."

"Your remark is just," Kerry replied, "but Clonameh has just told us that Princess Dinameh's imbecility was a popular tale, with no other foundation than the infinite superiority that Oribelle, her elder sister, had, and an illness that Dinameh had under the name of Jasmine. Now, as the younger Princess became Queen of Meath, and the Meathans and the Lagenians are enemies today, they make up tales about Dinameh, whose descendants they don't like. I promised to tell you the fables as well as the truth, but not to represent the former as the latter; listen to the rest of my story."

"We understand, we understand!" shouted all the drinkers.

Bridge and his wife Gemmeh only talked about Oribeau, after his departure, with tears in their eyes: "Oh, the worthy Prince! How good he is! How nice he is!"

"My wife, my children," Bridge added, "you have seen the most perfect image of God there is on earth: a young and good King."

And he raised his eyes and hands skywards, to bless the young Prince.

My intention was not to stay long at Younghall after our departure, Milord. I was waiting for my sister Pucellomaneh to come to collect us, in order to transport us to Mullanger, where we were going to spend a few days with Nursimaneh, but Jasmine's sudden illness kept us at Bridge-Clonard's longer than I had intended.

You'll recall that toward the end of your sojourn, the younger of the two Princesses suddenly changed, and from being lively and cheerful she became sad. After your departure she seemed more cheerful, but instead of her normal fine repartee she said stupid and ridiculous things. Her sister was greatly afflicted by that change and wept over it.

For myself, I seemed so tranquil that Oribelle sometimes reproached me. "It's necessary that everything takes its time," I replied, untroubled. She went to her sister continually to ask her amicable questions, to see how she responded to them, but either Dinameh received them badly or said naïve things. That conduct on Jasmine's part engendered scorn for her among all the local people. She served them as a victim when young people assembled, and they would have given her no respite but for her sister's remonstrations.

As she appeared so simple, there was one bad lot among the boys of Younghall who tried to take advantage of it. He persuaded Dinameh to go with him into a barn, and here he tried to violate her—but I was always on hand to rescue her. I appeared to his eyes in the form of a huge crayfish and took his arm in my claw; I caused him both a terrible fright and a terrible pain. Afterwards I had him lifted up by the rocs and condors, who took him to Makredin Castle, where my sister set him down. She employed him for the rudest labor for several years and it was only recently that she let him go.

That adventure and the talk it caused kept all the ill-intentioned at bay; Jasmine was regarded as protected by a divinity; people began to suspect that she wasn't Bridge's daughter; they made enquiries about the two sisters and soon discovered that Bridge's veritable daughters were dressmakers in Cork. Apparently, that rumor reached Ratchlin's ears, or those of one of his emissaries. Not long after our departure we saw a suspicious stranger arrive in Younghall who let it be known obscurely that he was Prince Cahincaha. Bridge made him welcome.

The stranger tried to talk to Jasmine and show her tenderness, but she rejected him and didn't want him to come anywhere near her. She was right; I had never been duped by the knave, who had come to make sure of where we were. As soon as he had recognized the Princesses he redoubled his efforts to try to make himself welcome to Jasmine. We were amused by his attempts, and having drawn him to a solitary spot, I had him taken away by my sister like the young peasant from Younghall—but he soon found a means to escape from Makredin and inform his master.

A few days after his removal, we saw the house surrounded by men-at-arms. Bridge and the boys were in the fields; we only had Gemmeh and her two younger daughters, Oeillette and Giroflée, with us—Vananis had gone to Cork to see her sisters. Frightened, I cursed my sister, who didn't come to our rescue.

They forced their way into the house very easily, and in spite of Gemmeh's cries they took the two Princesses and me away. Ratchlin told us that he was acting on the orders of the Queen, whom we demanded to see. I pretended to obey voluntarily, in order to win his confidence and to be less inconvenienced, but the wily O'Connor watched me so carefully that I couldn't liberate my two pupils.

Ratchlin had us march in short stages; his design was to take advantage of the journey to win Oribelle's or Dinameh's heart—it didn't matter which, amour being far from his heart; he only wanted to reign. He intended to give whichever of the Princesses would not be his to the Prince of Meath. As for you, Milord, you had always been an object of fear in Ratchlin's eyes, and it was because he knew that the Queen, as well as my sisters and I, wanted your alliance that he had long taken precautions to make that project fail.

Your youth, and the obscurity in which you lived, didn't reassure him. He knew how you were being raised; it was your education that frightened him. He said a hundred time to his confidants:

"In the neighboring kingdom, a lion in sheep's clothing is being raised for us. Beware of the young King of Mommonia. His mother's Minister is all the more dangerous for Evinland for being incorruptible; a certain O'Barbo, who is bringing up the Prince, is a man of iron smeared with honey. He'll give the Prince his hardness and pretended mildness.

Let's keep our eyes on that Prince and those who govern in his name during his childhood; they're too wise to undertake anything during his minority, but see them amassing treasures by economy; see them exercising youth in simulated combats! They've established schools of natation, archery and combat on horseback with the bow, the saber, etc. They're bringing out a nationalistic spirit by means of a dangerous philosophy; they've diminished superstition and the credit of druids; they're making the fatherland loved by rendering life their easy, although laborious; they've also contrived to make labor so honored and recompensed that it becomes a pleasure.

"If we allow Prince Oribeau to marry one of our Princesses, it'll be a master we'll be giving ourselves. Adieu, the glory of Leinster, as they're already naming our country; it will soon be no more than a province of Mommonia. Remember, however, brave Lagenians, that the gods have promised the city of Balaclay the empire of all Evinland under the name of Dublin, for that is the one that our oracles give it. Shall we allow our homeland to be debased on spite of the oracles? Shall we suffer the sovereign of Waterford to come and command us, and that the Head of State shall be of another nation than ours? That is a shame that I do not believe you disposed to suffer.

"Look at the Gauls of the continent; for a long time now the Franks of the Rhine have subjugated them, but the later have finally associated the vanquished with the rights of citizenship; the Frankish Kings are born Gallic and it is a maxim now received among peoples that the least of the inhabitants of a nation should have the right to the crown before a foreign Prince. So we see that these Frankish Kings are cherished by their subjects, that the succession occurs without the slightest trouble; that the person of the monarch is so sacred there that the faults of their Ministers are never attributed to them. If, by chance, it happened that those good people were oppressed, they would not be seen running to their arms and revolting; they would console themselves with the simple phrase: "Oh, if the King knew!" Admirable and filial confidence! Fortunate are the Princes who have inspired it! That, my friends, is the model to follow. Let us swear that no foreigner will rule over us."

All have sworn it—but Prince, you are Evinlandian and not a foreigner; you descend from the wives of ancient Kings of Lagenia, and it will be proved to your antagonists one day that your marriage with Princess Oribelle is not your only right to the crown. But I'll return to our abduction.

Ratchlin did not succeed with Oribelle any more than with her younger sister. You encountered us, and your courage made you undertake our defense, although without arms. You seized those of a solder and were going to fight, alone with an old man, against the kidnapper's entire troop when the cries of Bridge-Clonard and his men obliged O'Connor to seek salvation in flight, taking Rosée with him, whom I did not abandon. I was thus obliged to leave Jasmine with Prince Beaudâme— but the sage Debundeh was accompanying him, and I had no anxiety. I only recommended that the Princess should continue to feign the necessary naivety, in order to touch the Prince of Meath.

My sister finally came to our rescue. We were nearing Makredin when she appeared like a cloud above our heads. She frightened Ratchlin by throwing a bushel of sand that had served as ballast over his head. While he was trying to collect himself, she took Rosée and me into her chariot. You saw us again at Dunlavan under the names of Julia and Thor-el.

We resumed all our disguises successively, in following your tracks. After you had left the house of the Dunlavanian, Killcullen brought us a kanaster, into which the Princess climbed in the costume of Ahissa. She then became Daura, solely by the exterior arrangement of her person; for such is the effect of a woman's adornment, that it changes them absolutely, without the pretty ceasing to be so, or the ugly being able to become pretty. Oribelle appeared to flee your gaze under the identity of Fillira.

Meanwhile, O'Connor was furious. In truth, his anger was foolish, and anyone could have told him that he was only making plans and carrying out abductions to see the former fail and the second turn against him—but that is still a mystery of his conduct.

We saw all your good deeds, and several times the Princess shared the glory of them under the different names she had borne. She was interested in you by then; judge how touched she was by your amour and your virtue! For I remarked to her after every travesty how much you loved her and how much effort you were having to make, in order that she did not render you unfaithful to herself…!

Clonameh was at that point in her discourse when Princess Pucellomaneh's chariot was seen in the air.

"Prince!" she shouted to the King of Mommonia. "You know enough, and I would not have told you so much about Oribelle's dispositions. You are out of your Estates; everything here is pacified. Your virtue and your courage are known; you are worthy to command the Lagenians as well as the Mommonians. You are going to marry Princess Oribelle—which is to say, a wife endowed with all the charms, virtues and qualities that make a worthy spouse, a good mother and a prudent and sage sovereign.

"Come with me; I will take you in less than an hour to your palace, to your mother the Queen. The promptitude of your return will be the emblem of a great verity, that Kings, perfect symbols of divinity, must be everywhere at the same time. And know that one good deed still remains for you to do, which ought to surpass all the others and earn you all suffrages in the two kingdoms before marrying the heiress of Langenia.

"Are you coming?"

As she finished speaking she took the hand of the young King and obliged him to climb in beside her. "You," she said to Dondanuck and O'Barbo, "take the Mommonian soldiers back to their homeland."

Immediately, she tugged the brass wires; with wings of the birds flapped, and the chariot rose up.

When it reached an immense height, she showed Evinland to Oribeau, like a huge cake in the middle of the sea. The States could scarcely be distinguished.

"Prince," she said to him, "elevate your soul; see what Empires are…and conceive the grandeur of the gods. There is only one solid glory: that of doing good. All the rest, and ambition above all, ought to appear to you to be quite ridiculous. Be happy by way of your wife, your children and your subjects."

As she finished she descended over the palace of Karrickmagriffin. She lowered the Prince on to the terrace, saluted the Queen, and made the return journey to Makredin before Dondanuck and O'Barbo had emerged from it.

They did not take long, however, to return to Mommonia, and on the day of their arrival Oribeau held a council, in which Dondanuck informed the Mommonian lords that the law of equality that he had pretended to want to enact was only to make them look into themselves and render them humane.

"An aristocracy is necessary in a government," he added, "in order to graduate all the estates all the way to the supreme rank; it is, in addition, respectable in its origin, which is always either for signal services or virtue…"

"I think," said the young King, "that a good law, made with the consent of the nation, is a good deed above all others; that is why I am asking my Council for the plan of a Warrant, to which I shall only give the force of law after having it agreed by my people."

All the members of the Senate applauded. They worked for a week, at the end of which they presented the following Warrant to the King, who approved it, sent it to all the provinces, and eventually gave it the royal sanction.

Chapter 2W
Warrant in twenty-six articles.

Wall elevated by the King of Mommonia to separate his loyal subjects from all abuses:

Oribeau, by the protection of Thor, King, to all our faithful subjects in the great counties of Waterford, Cork, Kerry, Limerick, Tipperary and Thomond-Clare, greetings!

Having recently taken the reins of government, and proposing shortly to marry, to the satisfaction of our people, the august elder Princess of Lagenia, the chaste Oribelle, we believe before everything on the advice of our excellent mother the Queen Regent, our prudent Minister Dondanuck, our sage instructor O'Barbo, and our dear and grand vassals the Counts of Cork, Kerry, Limerick, Tipperary and Thomond-Clare, peers of our realm, that we ought to give our dear and loyal people of Mommonia an idea of our dispositions for its felicity, as much by the reform of abuses to which we have been witness during our education, as to encourage all useful occupation of whatever kind it might be, in view of the fact that one cannot do any good before the leaven of corruption has been destroyed; for we are persuaded that the double duty of a sovereign is to put a brake on vice and to encourage virtue. For these reasons, using our royal power, we order the following:

Article A

Abuses, whatever they may be, will be destroyed by the present warrant:

Amnesty, from the date of promulgation of the present law, for all faults committed beforehand, except murder, desiring that the day on which we take the reins of government should be a day of delight for all our subjects, expect those who, by the most horrible of crimes, have taken the lives of their fellow citizens. Let us say that those culpable of murder, for this one occasion only, will be put beyond the frontiers of our Estates and the fortunate island of Evinland, to be abandoned on a desert island in the Orcades; those who have violated the most essential of the laws of society do not merit being assisted by it. As for all the other guilty parties, we render them to the estate of citizens, with the charge to indemnify those they have injured, if it is within their means; we take responsibility for doing that for those who cannot; on condition, nevertheless, that if the guilty parties fall for a second time into faults subject to the animadversion of the government, they will be sold as slaves outside Evinland. With regard to murderers, if there are any in future, they will be forced to be useful to outraged society; they will be sold to the medical corps to be dissected dead or alive in accordance with the crime, and the price will be returned to the relatives of the victim.

Annihilation of all insolvable debt, which will be paid from public funds, on condition that those who have contracted the debts take up occupations and a way of life that can enable them to subsist in future; which will be provided by our Senate, our Great Judge of Waterford, our Police Officers established in the towns and villages of Mommonia, and the Censors.

Abolition of the exegesis published by our Minister Dondanuck, insofar as it might be unfavorable to the nobility, and confirmed for all the rest; admitting that it is just and useful that the illustration of great men should be perpetuated in their descendants in order to maintain harmony and subordination; people submit more willingly to a great name and the descendant of illustrious men than to new men, which operates an obedience useful to the State.

Announced, that in future, any man distinguished by heroism will be thus ennobled, as well as his posterity, people owing an eternal homage to their benefactors.

Annual renewal—which is to say, the first day of the new year—is fixed at the winter solstice.

Amour will be respected to the point that no one may take the mistress of another, or the lover of a maiden, except with the consent of the first lover or mistress.

Amity will be the knot that will unite youth formed by companies; the friends of a company will be chosen by inclination and never abandoned throughout their life, not even by death.

Article B

Bring wellbeing to the people will be our motto. We declare that we are only king in order to effect that, and these will be the means that we shall employ: 1. Only imposing necessary taxes, and administering them sagely; 2. Rendering justice precisely and promptly, without exception of anyone; 3. Ensuring that necessary food supplies are never lacking, and fixing the prices in such a fashion that the cultivator, the artisan, the merchant, the man of law, the physician and the druid can live without discomfort of the product of their occupations; 4. Conserving religiously the liberty, property, honor and reputation of all our subjects; neither permitting nor suffering the slightest injury to be done to them, and to repair it by our royal power if it is; 5. Procuring public diversions capable of soothing the vicissitudes of life, such as spectacles, dances, amusements, honest games, agreeable and instructive reading, joyful or heartfelt songs; while forbidding games of chance, prostitution, duels and other harmful things; 6. Prescribing to all the members of the Estate an occupation that protects them from need and idleness, said occupation always being proportionate to their situation, their tastes, their strength and their fortune; 7. Rendering my nation and my people respectable to their neighbors by the glory of arms as by wellbeing and interior dignity, so that it shall he said, not only throughout Evinland but in Albion, Scotland and as far afield as Gaul, Spain and Italy, that Mommonians are the most magnanimous, polite, free, comfortable and virtuous people in Europe and the entire world.

Benefit will never be wasted; all benefactors will be honored by society in general, and a certain number of benefits, remarkable by their importance and the purity of their motivation ennobling a person. If a culpable individual has performed actions that are sufficient to ennoble him, he will be pardoned for a serious crime, and the fine will be returned to someone who has only incurred a fine.

Article C

Culture and commerce are the two sources of wealth; by culture it is created; by commerce its value is augmented; culture only produces nourishment; but commerce, in ridding the State advantageously of the superabundance of nourishment, produces two immense advantages; it encourages labor and occupation, and it gives to those who have nothing but bread and meat all the other good things that delight our existence, such as wine, spices, gold, silver, copper, iron, pearls, diamonds and fine fabrics; it brings to a well-cultivated country, arts, sciences, philosophy and virtues. It renders a people celebrated, making it known throughout the world.

Culture only gives the necessary, but commerce gives all the pleasures, a desirable object that doubles or multiplies a hundredfold the price of life; it is therefore necessary to encourage and protect commerce; it is the hand of the State. It is necessary to welcome all the arts that embellish life, because the sole aim of a sage government is the wellbeing of the people.

Cats, dogs, birds, squirrels and other animals of amusement will be proscribed throughout our estates as requiring useless care and consuming that which might serve human individuals. Agreeable birds will be allowed to wander at liberty; only one dog will be allowed per village, for the utility judged by the local magistrate; cats will be proportionate to necessity alone; all zoolaters, or animal lovers who are in contravention will pay, to the profit of the poor, a fine capable of nourishing a man for five days.

Article D

Donations and presents on the part of the sovereign require great discretion; we have also heard it said that a miserly Prince is a good King for the people; however, a base vice such as avarice cannot produce a good; the proverb only signifies that, compared with prodigality, the avarice of a King is almost a virtue. In fact, to what does the unfortunate dissipation of finances not expose an Empire? It cannot defend itself if it is attached; it becomes the fable and object of scorn of its neighbors; it might be overturned by internal fermentation. But in addition to these general inconveniences there are particular ones. The Prince who dissipates can only give to his favorites or his mistresses; in the former case he exhausts his treasures and his people's to render as powerful as himself lords who might betray him; in the second, in addition to the scorn to which he delivers himself, he runs the risk of exiting public indignation for attracting everything to him without rendering anything, and thus inhibiting circulation. Thus, in truth, an avaricious Prince is a thousand times better than a prodigal one. We shall avoid those two extremes, thanks to the good advice of our Ministers and will administer the finances of the Empire so that money circulates swiftly and vivifies both agriculture and commerce.

Differences and quarrels between citizens will be judged summarily, conserving that the aggressor always be condemned, save for punishing the offender in proportion to his malice.

Article E

Elevation of children without giving them a good education is burdening the state rather than sustaining it. That is why we propose to indicate the means of forming virtuous young couples, who will one day become human beings useful to others and content with themselves—which is to say, happy: 1. The children of peasants will be adapted quickly to moderate labor, in order not to prevent them from fortifying themselves, while simultaneously preserving them from idleness; their day will be divided into three parts: the first after a breakfast composed of solid aliments, will be devoted to labor from seven o'clock in the morning until noon; the second, after lunch, to reading and writing, which will give them repose, until three o'clock in winter, or six in summer; the third will be devoted, after a frugal snack, to exercises in gymnastics, which will be and diversion as well as the closure of the natural day. In the winter there will be a vigil during which the young will be occupied by light and facile tasks such as dressing hemp or flax, or shelling hazelnuts or chestnuts, etc., while the master of the gymnasium, the head of the family or one of the most knowledgeable children under their direction, will read the laws of the country, both criminal and civil for an hour; and then religious morality for half an hour; after supper, young people will have an hour of conversation, instructive tales and stories told by old people, and then go to bed. In summer, however, the gymnastics and games will continue throughout the reading of the laws, etc., in order to fortify the body, with the consequence that the readings will only take place in winter.

Education of the children of artisans will be similar—which is to say that they will be occupied in the labors of their profession from six o'clock until noon, while the rest of the day will have the same destination as for young peasants. As for the children of aristocrats, their education will be directed in the morning in consequence of the employments they will exercise one day, and they will have the same occupations as the other classes thereafter, except that in the hour of evening recreation they will see society with their parents, as all the other classes will do on feast days and days of rest.

Excreta will be carefully conserved as fertilizer, not burned or thrown in the Shure.

Article F
"Family" comes from an ancient word that is also the origin of "femme," "faim" (hunger) and "fame." That ancient

word signifies "talk."[137] The family—which is to say—everyone in a house who talks—must be submissive to the father or head; and as the State is a great family, in which all the others are contained, and of which the individual fathers are only the children, everyone ought to be religiously submissive to the Head of State; as, for his part, the King ought to govern wisely and mildly desirous of efficaciously protecting the wellbeing of his political children. The respect of children toward fathers is a sacred duty, but the benevolence of fathers toward children is no less so. No son will ever be able to bring a lawsuit again his father, but there will be public monitors, who, in the case of oppression on the father's part, will interpose the authority of the general father or Head of State to put a stop to it; and in the case where a son has lacked respect for his father, the latter may complain directly—which the son may not do—and on his complaint the monitors will assemble; the father will place himself under an awning in the presidential seat and will judge his son himself in the presence of the monitors; but after the father's sentence is pronounced, if it is too severe, there will be a year and a day's delay before its execution, if no one has interceded on the son's behalf, the monitors will intercede themselves; and if the father persists, they will declare to him that he sentence against his son—with the exception of death—will be carried out, but that, as he has been devoid of mercy, he will have no hope of any from the general father if he commits a fault. But if the father has allowed himself to be touched and has pardoned his son, the pardon will be immediately sealed, with the extension of the father's right that if the son becomes guilty again he will be able to pronounce a banishment that will be executed immediately.

---

[137] This is completely fictitious; all four words, in spite of their similarity, have different etymological roots, none of which signify *parler* [talk] and the other derivations that the warrant tries to assimilate to the argument are similarly specious, eventually becoming frankly ludicrous.

Furthermore, the wife being part of that which talks in the family, she will be subordinate to her husband, as is appropriate to good mores, but all the rest will be subordinate to her; she will have the same rights over the children as the father, and in case of personal insult, it is the father who will judge, given that all condemnations made for having lacked respect for a mother will be infamous and will demand, in order to be repaired, two good deeds, whereas an insult made to the father will only require one, one made to a magistrate three, to a minister six and to the King or the entire State twelve; after which the offender will be rehabilitated in his rights; observing that as soon as he has begun to repair his fault by a good deed, his person will be secure for a year, and is penalty reduced, if he stops there by a twelfth, a sixth, a third or a half.

Filiation comes from the same source as family; a son, in our states, in addition to the respect owed to his mother and father, is obliged to protect his sisters; but daughters must also respect their brothers, as fathers younger than the veritable one, and will be submissive to them, after the latter's death, in all due and reasonable things until their marriage, which will be as specified hereafter. "Son" signifies literally, "other issue of the father"; "daughter" is the feminine equivalent; "brother" signifies "other son" and "sister" signifies "separate"—i.e., destined to quit the family to pass into another. That is why sisters, throughout our estates, will not have any part of immovable property; and if a daughter finds herself a sole heir, the man who marries her will be obliged to annihilate himself by taking his wife's name.

"Father" comes from "Ab," whence "Ba" or "Pa," as children more easily pronounce it in the occident. Ab signifies "first". "Mother" comes from an ancient word signifying "sheath" or "vagina" and was initially pronounced *Meater*, then *Meter* and finally *Mater*.

Furthermore, there will be, as there once were among the Angles, Magistrates known as *morigeneurs*,[138] who will monitor public mores with mildness and moderation; they will appoint beneath them ten men in big towns and two or villages, who will monitor the mores of youth.

Favor will have no place in Mommonia; the charges of State will be equally supported by everyone, in order that they might be lighter for everyone.

Article G

Governing people with wisdom, justice and bounty will be our aim, the goal and terminus of the law, the Warrant of which we are publishing today. A Prince's government ought to be sage; it ought to be founded on justice and the utility of his subjects; to give our government all the appropriate sagacity we have composed our Council if the most refined and most mature minds: former Ministers, former Ambassadors and men experienced in jurisprudence and the art of war; that is all that we can do and all that is within human capacity. As for justice, it depends on us, because it is an effect of the rectitude of the heart. In everything that we do, and in everything that we demand of our people, we shall examine carefully with our Senate, and only then, if it is just—which is to say, if the interest of our people, their glory, their security and benefit are in accord with our demand or our ordinances—will we employ our executive power. We will do so if, on the one hand, we are persuaded that the liberty of opposing the emanations of our sovereign power has been lost, or, on the other, we are fully convinced of the obligation we have to found our supreme will on reason and justice.

Given that the just is sufficient for the omnipotent Supreme Being, because he is the master of events, however, it is not the same for the sovereign; he must sometimes be more than just, and be generous. The reason for that is simple; it is

---

[138] This word has never existed in English, and barely exists in French; it means someone who scolds or remonstrates.

that the Supreme Being is never wrong; in him, justice is the supreme generosity, which rends to every action the salary that it merits; the sovereign, on the contrary, who is only human, sometimes wounds justice, and in order to compensate when he has put too much in one or other of the scales, he is obliged to put more than the just in the other. A sovereign who was sure of never being wrong would be more estimable in being just than generous, for he could not have generosity without a little indulgence for vice; if, however, what is called generosity were only indulgence for human weakness, it would then be justice. That is what it is necessary to distinguish, for Princes have often been called good who were, at the most, just. The good Prince is not the one who renders his people happy by a sage government in which everything is done prudently—such a Prince is only just—it is the monarch who goes beyond his duty by his attentions, a labor that could not be imposed on him. As the King then gives more than the society over which he presides has the right to expect, he is good. Let us be good—that is our ambition!

Graces will never be accorded unless they are not onerous to anyone; then the sovereign may show his munificence, observing in addition that they are of such a nature that people bless their author, who is softening the law usefully without violating it.

Article H

Human being: that title alone ought to open access to the throne to anyone who has a grievance. The poorest of our subjects, in presenting themselves before us, will be sure of being heard and of obtaining justice. Our uninterrupted attention will be to augment the number of people in our Estates and render them happy. Every man will be obliged to have a profession in order to live and will only be able to enjoy his wealth in repose after having earned or merited them, if he is rich, either by manual labor or by public employments, as much in the army as in the magistracy or finance. A man who has the pretension of living on the labor of others since youth will be expelled from our estates and deprived of his property, which will pass to his closest relatives.

Henceforth, every man will be obliged to reproduce himself by marriage in the manner detailed in article M. As for women, they will be brought up as girls on the same footing as men—which is to say that they will have an occupation, in which the labor should be appropriate to their sex, such as sewing, or the lighter tasks of dressmaking; they will only learn music in hours of recreation. There will be no law against these who do not want to do anything, because girls are incapable of that resistance, but those who only occupy themselves with futilities, who only like dancing and singing and also appear given to lasciviousness, will, after several warnings issued by the public censors of female mores, be condemned to take the estate of actresses, in order at least to amuse their fellow citizens, since they have not wanted to be useful by their labor. The censors of women, female themselves, will be established in the same was as has been specified in article F for the censors of men. The two general censors of a city will have one or several subcensors per quarter, who will inspect the mores of the youth of their own sex and make their report to the senior censors.

Honors: this word expresses a precious sentiment, which renders people just and magnanimous; honor will be the principal source of nobility.

Article I

Inebriation, debauchery and gluttony are dishonoring vices and anyone subject to those excesses will lose public consideration proportionately. Habitual and scandalous drunkenness shown in the streets will be punished, after several warnings, by exile from our Estates. Debauchery, easier to repress, will be, by effective punishments; but at the same time, a debauchee will be permitted to have a concubine, in order to take away any excuse, provided that he is in a condition to maintain her by means of his labor or his talents. As for the vice of gluttony, it will be a title for exclusion from honorific positions, but as it is not very scandalous, there will be no other punishment.

Insults that are grave in their effects or their motives will be severely repressed; our judges will examine them attentively and force the insulter to repair all the harm that his insult has caused.

Article J

Justice exacted will always be rendered, either by us or by our tribunals. The greatest of criminals, in our eyes, will be the iniquitous magistrate, and his crime will be punished like that of lèse-majesté, for we shall consider it as such. Long-delayed justice becomes a veritable injustice; that is why all cases will be judged in a single day; judges will have alongside the tribunal the two parties, civil or criminal; they will listen to them and see their titles; they will object and the parties will respond; that is the only means of discovering the truth briefly. No one will present himself for judgment without having prepared all his titles and all his evidence. No criminal can be judged unless all the witnesses are there, who, once summoned, will be constrained to appear at the court. The criminal will be discharged the same day if he is acquitted, but except in the case of *flagrante delicto* he will never be condemned on the same day; if he denies the charge, he will be heard again, and he witnesses testifying against him severely examined, unless the accused is a highway robber or a recognized scoundrel.

Judgment having been pronounced on a man who has not confessed, he will be left for a week with a man who will draw out a confession of all his faults and what led him to commit them, in order to render an account to the tribunal and clarify the remedy to be brought to mores. When the fatal day arrives the criminal sentence will be executed, or sagely committed, according to his confessions. If a man is sometimes executed on the same day of his judgment, that will be for an atrocious and well-proven crime for which outraged society demands a prompt vengeance. Only actions harmful to society or an individual will be regarded as crimes and punished with afflictive penalties; all other so-called crimes will only by regarded as actions subject to criticism, which the judge will criticize, with the threat of punishment of the scandal if the delinquent has caused any. Professional quibblers, once recognized, will be mulcted of a fine toward the State and the fatherland when they have succumbed.

Article K

Kantekas,[139] whether green or white, and other cheeses, salted or rotten fish, bitter beverages, etc., will be forbidden in our Estates as dangerous aliments, which contribute to giving the human species various maladies. It will nevertheless be permissible to continue to salt pork, especially in rural areas, but we exhort our subjects to mix fresh meat or vegetables in their pot when cooking that necessary aliment. We inform them that it would be beneficial to the human species only to use fresh and succulent nourishment.

Article L

Legislator by right, a Monarch who gives laws to his people would be wise to imitate the German King who had projected laws pinned to the doors of public buildings before promulgating them, in order that those whom the laws would regulate would be able to examine them and could their observations without compromising public authority. So we declare that the present warrant is only a project of law and a kind of consultation that we are having with our people, in order to establish that laws that will be agreeable and useful to them. The law, in order to be good, ought to be so advantageous to good people that they cherish it as their protectress and mother, and such as to intimidate and frighten the wicked without

---

[139] I can find no prior trace of this word, nor of any meaning of canteca—given that the term has presumably been transformed by one of Restif's typical phonetic amendments—that makes sense in context.

revolting them; on the contrary, it ought to convince them and defeat them by the force of verity.

Laws ought to be carefully weighed and well-examined, without obscurity and without objection; that is why we are submitting this project to our people, in order that all obscurities can be clarified and all objections resolved when the supreme authority promulgates them; they will then be a luminous sun devoid of any spots.

Law: the word will have the most powerful virtue, for everything will cede to it.

Literature is as important as the law; if the magistrate is the priest of the law, as the druid is of religion, the author is the priest of morality, science or amusement, three things equally useful to mortals. The moralistic author is a veritable persuasive legislator, whereas the Prince is the imperative legislator. The law of the Prince, if it is bad, is dangerous, whereas the morality of the persuasive legislator, if it lacks wit, falls into scorn; if, however, the author is so eloquent that he has his paradoxes devoured, then he becomes dangerous. The scientific author pushes back the bounds of human intelligence; he can be mistaken and draw others astray, but that is without consequence for morals; more accurate minds will soon follow who will rectify him, without public authority being obliged to meddle—for we are persuaded that it is a great evil for the Authority, which ought only to occupy itself with real things, to mingle in the disputes of scholars; it consumes precious attention therein, that it ceases to give to war, financial economy and the execution of laws.

Let it be said that the amusing author is sometimes the most useful and always the least dangerous of all; by his labor he amasses for others the honey of intelligence, in giving them for their hours of recreation agreeable tales, which suspend by the power of the imagination the real troubles of the mind. If he is a writer of fiction—the most useful genre, because it has a general application—he mingles a dose of good morality with his stories, which renders that light nourishment solid. If he is a dramatist, he gives the assemble nation lively pleasures, which he does with morality like the writer of fiction. If he is simply an amusing poet, he amuses by means of his sallies and moves by touching images; he polishes the language by the pleasure of his poetic elegance; he often encloses, in a brief fable, a striking moral lesson easy to retain. It is after these considerations that we recommend our people to honor magistrates, soldiers, druids and men of letters.

Article M

Marriage, including the procreation of children, is both a natural and a civic duty. Marriage will henceforth be favored in every possible manner, but any marriage without children will be declared null, even against the wishes of the parties, for the reason that no one is in the world for themselves alone, but for themselves and for the republic. Every well-conformed maiden ought to be married before the age of twenty-three. It will be permitted to the defective to remain celibate and fill certain houses destined for a tranquil life. Every healthy and well-made man who reaches the age of twenty-five without being married will pay a tax called "the infamy of bachelors" until the age of thirty; at that age the tax will be doubled, tripled at thirty-two and quadrupled at thirty-four, unless the aged bachelor has valid reasons to allege; at forty he will be declared infamous, erased from the number of citizens and obliged to wear ignominious clothing until the end of his days.

Marriage is intrinsic to private and public mores; a wife is as necessary to a man as air and nourishment; that is why soldiers will not be deprived of it. A man who has no wife is necessarily soiled by voluntary or involuntary actions that outrage nature. If a man refuses to marry in these climes, in which the number of the two sexes is very nearly equal, it is necessary that there is a spinster without a husband, abandoned to the ignominy of celibacy. The unmarried will be pursued extraordinarily and may even be deprived of their patrimonial fortune, but not their personal earnings. By means of great deeds of virtue or sublime works of the mind or body, a man will obtain exemption for the penalties of celibacy, but he will be deprived of the honors awarded to great married men and fathers of families, of which there will be mention under Article T.

Men who have the title of "husband" will each be the respected master of his wife, as well as her support and defender; he may not mistreat her but his complaints of misconduct or insubordination, well-proven, will always oblige the magistrate to grant him his reasonable demands.

Article N

Nobility and bravery ought to be inseparable. We have annulled the projected ordinance of our wise Minister Dondanuck, which appeared to deprive nobility of its rights, as capable of causing a dangerous upheaval in the State, but we believe it necessary to bring an efficacious remedy to the nullity of descendants of nobles in the following manner: the most noble member of a family will always be ennobled by his merit and good deeds; the son will be less noble than his father if he is futile, but if he performs an action as meritorious as his father his nobility will be increased by one degree; if his merit is transcendent he will acquire two or three degrees; however, his son will be less noble then him by one degree, in such a fashion that by ceasing to perform fine actions, a noble family were gradually fall back into the mediocrity from which its first author extracted it. We shall conserve the privileges of nobility religiously, provided that its possessors renew their right to those privileges by actions that render them useful and make them respected by the people. Every fine action will be appropriate to renew or reinforce nobility: an invention capable of relieving laborers; a good work of literature; a service rendered to unfortunates exposed to peril or in poverty; reconciliations brought about and good examples given; impartiality in the exercise of magistracy, etc, etc.

Natural children of any father whose origin is well-proven will have the second rank after the children of marriage; they will half a half-share of paternal property and a full

share of the mother's if she has remained unmarried; we renounce, in that regard, any right of bastardy.

Article O

Oppression of the people is, for Kings, what the crime of
lèse-majesté is for their subjects. We will give our full attention to avoiding the horrible crime of lèse-societé; we shall
examine carefully, and by sure means, whether any of the public men that we employ are rendering themselves culpable of it
in our name, and we assure our people that if that misfortune
occurs, we shall act with extreme urgency when it comes to
our attention. Anyone oppressed will have the right of complaint without exposing himself to any disagreeable consequences, unless he is an evident calumniator; but is, instead of
accusing a particular public man he is content to say "This
wrong has been done to me," he will always be admitted to the
proving of the wrong and the public man will only be impli-
cated as a result of proofs. At the first complaint, the public
man will be mildly warned that he is slipping into abuses in
his administration and he will be given duplicates of the
proofs; it is only with regard to recidivists, and proof of negligence or connivance, that the supreme chief of justice or the
Prince himself will make injunctions to him; it will be necessary for a man to be very hardened if he has not corrected
himself by then.

Obey before commanding will be a general principle for
all estates and conditions.

Article P

Punishment and recompense are the sinews of any government; but the sovereign ought to put a great difference in
the facility of recompense and punishment, on the principle
that, being the Prince for the wellbeing of people, punishment
would be an inconsequence if unmotivated by the maintenance
of general wellbeing. It ought therefore to be posited in principle that one ought never to punish unless the punishment is a
great benefit to society, for it is that benefit alone that can le-

gitimate the right to punish one's fellow. The magistrate who punishes an evil action out of passion or vengeance is as guilty, and perhaps guiltier, than an individual who does evil; the public utility of the punishment ceasing, the Prince ought to pardon, because punishment is not a law of nature but an exception to that law and exceptions ought never to be extended.

Public society, even as a body, does not really have the right to kill; it is by a sad necessity that it has attributed it to itself. It is therefore necessary to go back to nature as soon as a lack of injury to public interest permits. As for recompenses, the Prince ought to be economical with them in order not to debase them, but he ought to create ones that are flattering without being onerous to the state—which is to say, not accompanied by money, except toward those who are dying of hunger with their glory; and then the mark of honor should be lessened in proportion to the extent that the recompense is pecuniary.

Population is a oft-repeated word, but one whose full importance is perhaps not sensed. Whether a hundred men are unfortunate and poor or a hundred thousand are fortunate and rich, one cannot augment the number of people without augmenting their wellbeing. Erda, the Earth, always furnishes what is necessary to nourish them; luxury is contrary to population, in that it employs too many arms in things that are not of primary necessity; but if the soil were so fertile that the half of the nation occupied in cultivating it produced triple what was necessary to their subsistence, luxury would augment the wellbeing and opulence of a nation so as to render it the foremost in the world. However, it always ends up corrupting it and eventually rendering it unfortunate and poor; that is a sad verity that we announce to our people in order that they are not surprised by our future operations in the course of our reign.

People is a sacred name for the Kings of Mommonia; it reminds them, in two syllables, of what is more dear to them in the world, and of all the duties of sovereignty.

Article Q

Questioning under torture and imprisonment for life, or for too long a period, will be abolished under our reign, in order that there shall be the fewest possible unfortunates. We are the father of all the members of the State and we shall avoid particular evils with as much care as general evil. If, however, a man has violated the laws of society outrageously and if he is a member of a company of evildoers, he will be put to the question if he does not reveal them. If he does not admit anything under torture and there is no doubt of his crime, the refusal to name his accomplices will require him to be kept in rigorous imprisonment until he confesses.

Article R

Religion, piety, public worship and ministers of altars are established to fortify morality and to contribute to human wellbeing; Thor is the principle of all things; it is a natural idea to employ our reason to honor him; that establishes a glorious relation between the divine essence and humanity; the apparatus of worship is not vain apparel but solemnity. Let the druids never forget, however, that they are only human beings like others, delegated by them; that they ought only to occupy themselves with linking citizens together, far from disuniting them. As for us, considering that the supreme power ought to be one, we have resolved, after the example of several monarchs, to combine royalty with the sovereign pontificate. Two motives have determined that; we would be honored by the greatest and most holy of ministries, and we would honor the priesthood in confounding its leader with the Head of State. But we shall only exercise the high functions that render a human the minister of the divinity once a year, at its renewal; for the rest of the time we will have a delegate who will accomplish them for us, who will obtain his power from us and will only be able to act under our orders. That secondary Grand Druid will be changed every year, with the result that he will be unable to serve for two years in succession, and there will at least be an interval.

Religious professions will no longer exist in Mommonia, but everyone will be religious.

Article S

Sergeants, procurators, advocates and court clerks will no longer be, as at present, men of a separate profession, but capable individuals appointed by the judge to perform one of other of those functions once or twice. Thus, an individual who would like to be assigned one will go and ask a judge or a sergeant; the magistrate will appoint an honest individual to perform that function gratis, who will not be able to refuse; the assignation will be drawn up by the judge. If a legal dispute is engaged, the magistrate will appoint as gratuitous procurators two individuals recommended by their enlightenment, and then two advocates; as for the clerk, he will always be the immediate successor of the first counselor who dies during his exercise.

Such will be the procedure that, in order to be a judge, one will be obliged to have exercised successively the functions of sergeant, procurator, and advocate; from the function of advocate one will finally pass to that of counselor; the oldest of the counselors will always become the Great Judge, and will, in consequence, be honored with prerogatives all the more considerable because he will have no spices. Thus, before the judge can give the humblest of men the functions of justice, that of sergeant, it will be necessary for that individual to be prosperous and stainless, for that function is the first step that leads to mounting the tribunal.

Article T

Troops—soldiers, officers, commanders and generals— are the defense of the State. As magistrates obtain peace within between citizens, troops maintain it externally with foreigners. Every man will be a born soldier; only infirmities or public employments will dispense with paying with one's person.

However, the title of active soldier will be necessary for any public employment—which is to say that it will be necessary to have been enrolled for at least three years before being able to be a professional master or to obtain municipal or judiciary responsibilities, etc.

Those individuals whose estate demands long application, such as physicians, surgeons, botanists, bards and painters, will nevertheless be dispensed from all service. The first and second, however, will be required to exercise their arts in the company of armies or in hospitals for ten years before being able to settle in towns or villages. Any soldier who abandons the flag will be deprived of the title of citizen and reduced to the infamous title of convict labor; he will have to perform six notable actions to redeem himself.

Therewith, any soldier distinguished by his valor will be added to the general staff—which is to say, in the body of those who might attain the rank of general; merit alone will confer the right to the baton of command. If a soldier is a noble he will renew and augment his nobility by his feats of arms; if he is a commoner who effaces everyone by his merit and have saved the nation, he will be ennobled, at first for himself alone, but subsequently for one, two or three generations, in accordance with the grandeur of his actions. If a nobleman and a commoner are in concurrence, the advancement of the nobleman will be double, because the admission of the commoner the nobility is already a great recompense. If a nobleman commits a cowardly action he will lose one, two or three generations of future nobility—which is to say that his children will revert to the status of common citizens either immediately or after one of two generations, according to the number merited. If he is a commoner he will reenter oblivion—which is to say that his former services will be annihilated, wholly or in part, according to the ignobility of his action; but the noble and the commoner will be able to regain what they have lost by means of fine actions.

Troops will be treated with mildness and consideration by their officers, but obedience will be strict and the slightest failure will be severely punished; the soldier, in making the military oath, abnegates his will in everything that concerns his estate. Suppliers of equipment or food who prevaricate, either by supplying materials of poor quality or starving the army, will be examined rigorously and punished as criminals guilty of lèse-societé. A soldier will be clean and not boastful, an officer grave and not affected. All men admitted to the troops will be married, for the reason that the greatest misfortune that can happen to a man is to die without children.

This is how marriages will be made in our Estates in future: at the age of eighteen all well-made young men will be married, but will not establish households; the boy will remain in his father's house the girl in her father's; the husband will only go to lie with her in alternate nights. They will remain thus for a year, at the end of which all the newlyweds will be soldiers by law for three years. As they will have learned military exercises in childhood, they will serve immediately in time of war. In the intervals, they will return to their wives. After three years of service, or four if the same war endures, all soldiers of the same year will become citizens at the same time; they will quit he service if peace has been made and return to their families with their discharge payment, which will serve to establish a household.

The State will make sure that no citizen is indebted by poverty, and that everyone has a sufficient quantity of land to nourish them and pay the taxes necessary for the maintenance of the State. By that means the population will not suffer overmuch from the effects of war and thousands of men will not be debilitated by libertinage or harvested by swords before having reproduced.

Tributes, impositions and finances are things without which a State cannot maintain troops, make war, built useful establishments and carry out works necessary to the community. In consequence, every citizen will be subject by law to the payment of the tribute, but that payment will be an honor, for one of the greatest stigmata of infamy will be to be declared unworthy of paying the tribute or of serving as a soldier. That is because the payment of the tribute will be the first thing that will prove a candidate for responsibilities and honorable employment, for the military conscription of his children, for the nobility, etc. The reason is that, the tribute being the strength of the State, whoever does not furnish it will be regarded at least as an infirm limb of no value to the State. In consequence, financiers and receivers of tributes will be considered and respected as precious members of the State; their person will be sacred, like those of the tribunes of Rome; but their probity and disinterest will also be models to cite.

The worthiest financiers will always rise to the ministry; they will comprise the Council of Finances and furnish royal treasurers, etc. The Sovereign will regard the finances as a sacred treasure, accumulated by the labor and sweat of his people, and he will only dispose of them for the utility of the nation, but he will be the supreme judge of that utility; his councilors will only have the liberty of respectful representations, given that the authority of the monarch, in order really to be useful to the people, must be entirely sovereign.

Article V

Victuals and everything that serves for the nourishment of necessity, will attract our foremost attention and that of magistrates, in order to maintain both sufficiency and quality. Monopolists are duly warned by this warrant that their crime will be punished, like that of prevaricating food-suppliers—which is to say, as a crime of lèse-societé. The price of staple foodstuffs will always be the same for artisans, manufacturers, artists and shopkeepers; any augmentation that they would suffer would necessitate that of their prices, which would also affect the public, inconveniencing many workers, etc. Merchants of wheat, bread, beverages, etc., who have spoiled or adulterated these primary foodstuffs will be condemned to public labor for life, save for a redemption, which will be no less than fifty gold evinlands.[140] Anyone who finds a better means of cultivation will be recompensed by the nobility in proportion to the bounty of his invention.

Article U

Usages and customs will only be changed after a severe examination; however, time might bring about the necessity of changing ancient usages, and then it will be permitted to the bards to attack them; it will be them who awaken the Minister, so to speak. The people, in reading the work of bards, will examine the usages assaulted, and the public voice will either approve them or denounce them to the Minister, who will appoint wise individuals from all classes of citizens to examine them in committee and give their opinion in writing. No bard will be troubled for having attacked a Usage; he is only one voice and he might be giving good advice. In the same way, after the authorization of a usage, the bard may continue to attack it with arguments; we leave entire liberty to our bards in that regard. It will also be permitted for another bard to defend the usage attacked, whatever it might be, until both of them weary of it. We believe that imposing silence on human reason is violating the most fundamental of the rights of humanity.

Article W

Waterways, especially canals, locks and the dredging of river-beds, in order to operate prompt and easy communications within our Estates will never fail to attract our royal attention, with the aim of stimulating agriculture by the facility of irrigation.

---

[140] The author inserts a note to the effect that sum in question would be equivalent to about twenty thousand francs, but corrects that figure in a supplementary note, saying that he really meant two thousand.,

Article X

Xalane,[141] senna, rhubarb and other purgative remedies, poisons, antidotes etc., will only be sold by apothecaries, who will be answerable for their endeavors, for they are ordered only to sell drugs with the greatest circumspection.

Article Y

Yachts, warships or merchant ships will be commanded by noblemen in order to honor the navy. Sailors and marine soldiers will have double the pay of land soldiers; their service will be fifteen months less. They will all be married, and will live with their wives during the intervals between voyages.

Article Z

Zanies, strolling players, actors, acrobats, non-poetic singers, etc., will be regarded as beneath other citizens, whom they lower themselves to entertain, but actors in dramas retracing the actions of the nation's heroes will be honored as the equals of druids.

Thus given and proposed by us to all our loyal subjects, inviting them to communicate their reflections on the present warrant, in order to have regard thereto in the promulgation of the law; for we declare that we want to resemble the good King Oribeau XII, who permitted the bards and kaldes to criticize the failures of all the persons in is kingdom without exception, "in order," said that good King, "that mine should also be criticized." Wellbeing to all Mommonians.

---

[141] Author's note: "Quintessence or syrup of a purgative root from America particularly appropriate to evacuating humors." I can find no trace of any such word, and any such compound is unlikely to have been available in Ireland centuries before the discovery of the New World, even from licensed apothecaries.

Carrickmacgriffin is our abode. Dictated by the King himself; Dondanuck. In the first year of the reign of Oribeau the Wise.

Such is the warrant that King Oribeau published on the advice of his Minister and his tutor.

"That law is admirable in all its points," said Younghall, "and I'm sure that our young king will reestablish what time might have eroded."

"Have no doubt of it," said Kerry, and I promise to recite it in full Parliament, if I'm elected as a member of that august assembly.

"You will be, you will be!" cried all the drinkers, while the good Ennisleague knelt down and invoked the Alrunes for the gentleman's imminent election.

Chapter 2X
Xé. Xague. Choice of Xistarchs.
The Little Wool-Merchant.

Xochicopal was an Indian monarch who, like the tree of Mechoacan, whose trunk and branches emit an agreeable liquid, spread wellbeing himself and via his Ministers, which he names Xés, for the Xé is an animal that expands a delightful odor around it, which voluptuous Orientals hold in very high esteem.[142] The leader of a people, like the Xague, ought to

---

[142] Xochicopal is actually the Amerindian name of a Mexican tree, also known as the linaloe, belonging to the genus *Bursera*. Mechoacan is a species of convolvulus, similarly native to Mexico. The animal Xe is described by Athanasius Kircher's seventeenth-century account of China, where he gives the alternative name of muschus—obviously the musk-deer, which retains the generic name *Moschus*. The subsequently-mentioned xague tree is more elusive, but the accessible mentions suggest that it is native to India. Restif offers his

bear fruit appropriate to nourish, for that tree produces an acorn or nut in the form of a veal kidney, the flesh of which is an excellent nutriment.

Now you know that Oribeau the Wise, before obtaining his own individual wellbeing by the possession of Oribelle, occupied himself carefully with the good of his people. First he examined public sentiment regarding his warrant, and after having taken account of it, he gave it the force of law. In order to have it executed he appointed xistarchs not only in Waterford but in all the towns and villages of his Estates.[143] Those officers were charged with supervising the execution of all the articles, which there is no need to detail.

Among the xistarchs or Ministers appointed to maintain public wellbeing there was one named Baron Baltamore, who was admirably distinguished by his zeal and enlightenment. He was appointed in the capital. Oribeau noticed him and applauded the choice he had made. One day, he mentioned him to Dondanuck, who replied:

"Lord, a single action often reveals a man. Your Minister Baltamore performed one that was revealed to me recently which has caused me to place him in the highest esteem. It will doubtless have the same effect on you. It's a rather long story—expedite your affairs and I tell it to you afterwards."

"In that case," Oribeau replied, "let's postpone it until I go to the Queen's apartments to salute Princess Oribelle, who is arriving today—for the Queen my mother and Queen Conchèse have decided that the Princess should come here before the marriage in order to take secret account of the mores of the Court in which she must reign. The reason for that conduct is that, after the marriage, the disturbance is too great for a Princess who often commences to become a mother; it might fatigue her and harm the heir to the throne. I hope that

---

own explanations of the terms in a footnote; they are similar but abbreviated.

[143] Restif adds a note explaining that a xistarch is the chief of a xiste.

our story will please her. Have someone tell O'Barbo to be there."

The Prince and the Minister occupied them with business then, and at the appointed hour they went to the Queen's apartments. Oribelle had not arrived, which gave rise to some anxiety. However, Dondanuck began his story.

In Fermery in the county of Cork there was a farmer who had several children. Nichols, the third, considering that the elder two would have the farm and that he could not hope to form any other establishment than one that he made for himself, was alarmed by the sad future that awaited him.

One day, he heard his father talking about the beauty of the wool of Connacy and the profit one could make from commerce therein. That speech made a vivid impression on the child; he sensed within himself a talent for trade, before having the means; nothing had been said about it in his father's house. Nichols made his petty preparations in secret to go into commerce in wool; they were a few coarse garments appropriate to protect him from the rain, an excellent pair of clogs, such as are worn in Evinland, a small barrel in which to put water and an iron-tipped staff to defend himself from wolves if he were attacked by them. However, he had no money or anything to exchange.

He arrived in the county of Galway and asked for hospitality, sometimes only living on wild fruits. He did indeed see beautiful wool, which tempted him, but he understood then that in order to be a merchant it is necessary to have the wherewithal to give before receiving. That verity afflicted him without discouraging him.

During his sojourn in Galway he had learned that there was a Mommonian nobleman in the town whose reputation as an obliging man was known to everyone. That encouraged the little businessman. He went to introduce himself as a Mommonian who had come to Galway to buy wool and who lacked money.

Baron Baltamore was from the County of Cork himself. The sight of a child who had himself announced as a wool-merchant astonished the Baron. He interrogated Nichols, who gave him a naïve explanation of his plans and his future conduct. Struck by that singularity, Baltamore also noticed a good deal of intelligence in the boy, and being assured that he was not a fugitive libertine, lent him a sum of money.

He was convinced that it was a gift, that the child's ignorance of commerce could not fail to expose him to being duped at the beginning. To those who made him that observation, however, he said: "But I'll have the satisfaction of having paid for his apprenticeship."

Nichols, the possessor of a more considerable sum than he had dared to hope, ran to make his purchases, and, either because he had a good deal of intelligence or because the Connacians have scruples abut cheating the young, they were advantageous. He went into the counties where sheep were rare but where there was commerce, like Kings County, Kildare and Balaclay, and he disposed of his wool there at a fairly considerable profit.

It happened that Baron Baltamore had come to Balaclay; Nichols discovered that and before returning to Galway he went to present himself.

"Milord," he said, "what you have lent me had fructified; here is the principal, with a humble recognition. The product will henceforth be for my commerce; may Thor bless you for having pity on me."

The Baron was as charmed by the success as by the probity of the little wool-merchant; he wanted to leave him the initial loan.

"No, Milord," said Nichols. "I've taken a step forward, and to keep your sum would be to step back; but permit me, in whatever place that I find you, to come and render you an account of my little enterprise, the product of your generosity."

The Baron was even more content with the spirit of the grateful child than the first time, and promised to take a life-long interest in him. Nichols withdrew and departed immediately, in clogs, clad in the same peasant clothes, in order to go and buy wool from Connacy.

His return created confidence in him, and the rich tenant farmers confided more to him than he had cash to buy, on the promise that he would pay them on his return. He took away a considerable quantity of wool, of the finest quality, with the result that he sold it easily and lucratively in the kingdom of Lagenia, especially in Balaclay, where the Baron still was. Nichols did not fail to render him an account of his success and renew his thanks.

"You're grateful," said the Baron. "You'll prosper. Go, young man, and remember that I'm interested in your little fortune." Nichols left, heaping his benefactor with blessings.

He returned to Connacy, paid what he owed, bought everything he could afford, because he did not want any expense beyond the necessary, and doubled his credit. He then took the road to Mommonia and came to Waterford, which, being a beautiful and rich city, furnished him with a quick sale.

As he was about to return he learned that Baron Baltamore was in the capital of Mommonia. Nichols ran to render his homage to him. "I'm prospering, Milord Baron," he said to him. "I have money and credit."

"Sustain the latter exactly by the former," his protector replied.

"That I shall," said Nichols.

He returned to Galway the following day and paid cash for all his purchases without borrowing any more, on condition of a slight lowering of the price. He traveled around the fields and the farms and bought a part of his stock first-hand. Then he went to Ultonia, where he made a quick sale, especially in Karrickfergus and Belfast. It was in the latter town that he found his benefactor again. Nichols ran to his lodgings to salute him. He was still wearing the same garments and clogs.

"You're not making a fortune, are you, Nichols?" the domestics said to him.

"I'm content," replied the young wool merchant.

He went in to see the Baron, whom he informed of his success.

"I congratulate you, Nichols, but why don't you dress better?"

"I'm covered, Milord. Do you want me, by means of fine clothes, to tempt thieves, or at least to have myself over-charged by innkeepers? A well-dressed man has to eat, drink and sleep in consequence; with my coarse clothes I'm content with a slice of bacon and a measure of small beer; I sleep in the stable beside my beasts of burden and I make sure they don't want for anything during the night."

"Good, good, Nichols!" exclaimed the Baron. "You have more intelligence than those who criticize you. You'll prosper, especially if you double your profit with returns, but in case of misfortune, count on me."

Nichols thanked the Baron warmly and, all his wool being sold, he returned to the county of Galway, where he was awaited impatiently by those who had been unable to sell their wool to him on his preceding voyage.

Now Nichols had paid attention to what his generous benefactor had said about doubling his profit with returns. He had remembered what was sought after in Galway and had equipped himself with it in Belfast. He arrived in the former town with merchandise, which he quickly put on sale, and on which he made a considerable profit.

Oh, what good advice the Baron gave me, he thought. *I've just doubled my profit and made myself known more than ever. Everyone in the area is bringing me wool and coming to buy my merchandise, and I'll only take half the time to make my purchases.*

In fact, he only stayed in Galway for a little while, leaving after six days for Balaclay. The quality of his wool, which had been proven, allowed him to raise the price, and the sale was made more rapidly. On that voyage, however, Nichols did not have the satisfaction of seeing the Baron, who had, so to speak, always been on hand. He made purchases in Balaclay, as in Belfast, and sold them even more advantageously.

On the following voyage he went to Waterford, and then to Cork, the capital of his county, but he did not want to go and see his parents yet. He made his purchases and enquired after Baron Baltamore, but he was told that he had gone to the country of the Angles, to the town of Chester.

Nichols was very sorry not to see his benefactor and resolved to go and look for him. On his return to Galway, where he sold the merchandise from Mommonia, he made his purchases of wool, traversed Tipperary and Kilkenny, and came to Wexford. There he embarked his wool, departed from Carnsore Point and disembarked the same evening in Chester.

First he enquired about the Baron, and having heard that he was in the town at the castle, be began by selling his wool, which he sold cheaper than local produce although it was of better quality; that is because, money being scarcer in Evinland, products are comparatively much less expensive there. He went to see the Baron before making purchases for the return trip.

It seemed to him that in a country where industry was dearer, they ought not to be advantageous. He therefore took his entire fortune to the Baron's lodgings in cash and this showed him the reality of it.

"My friend," Baron Baltamore said to him, after having listened to him, "you'll be a great businessman and it's a man that I've given to Evinland! I share your sentiment about returns from here. Nevertheless, there are objects that are rare in Evinland and common in Chester; buy excellent woolen cloth and fine fabrics from Batavia."

Nichols followed that advice. He bought the best and finest for half his money and common woolen cloth and fabric with the other half. He left immediately, blessing the Baron.

On his return to Evinland he sold the common fabrics to the people, but he took the finest ones to Balaclay, Waterford, Dunnaghall and Tuam to sell them to the Kings, Queens and the nobles of their Court. He made such a considerable profit that he finally found himself in a state to go and see his parents in Fermery.

Nichols still had on the coat in which he had left his parents' house and worn during his labors. He arrived at the door of the parental house in that outfit one evening during supper, having left a domestic that he had had for some time with his beasts of burden in an inn.

He knocked. One of his older brothers came to the doorstep to ask: "Who is it?"

"It's me, Nichols."

"Ha! It's my poor brother!" said the elder bother.

Immediately, the mother and sisters came running.

The mother said: "Oh, it's my poor child!" and the sisters: "Oh, poor Nichols!"

They opened the door to the yard. Nichols embraced his mother, who said, as if congratulating herself: "The poor child! He still has the same coat!"

"Yes, Mother," Nicholas replied. "I've kept it. It reminded me of you."

The good farmer's wife took her son by the hand. "Well, my husband," she said to the father, "it's too long since we've seen him to scold him!"

"It's you, you bad lot!" said the farmer. "Here you are again!"

"Father," said Nichols, modestly, "deign to hear me out, after I've given a few little presents to my brothers and sisters."

At the word *presents* the farmer blushed. He looked at his son, who presented him with a purse of gold coins, in which there were a hundred, and then gave one of fifty to his mother, and then twenty-five each to his two brothers and three sisters.

""Wretch that I am!" cried the farmer. "What have I done to Heaven, for my son is surely a thief!"

"No, Father, may the gods remove that idea from your mind. Listen to my story."

And Nichols recounted how he had first gone to Galway; how he had found Baron Baltamore there; how that Lord had made him a loan; how he had repaid him; how he had prospered by economy, remaining poorly-dressed in order to avoid thieves; how the Baron had given him the excellent idea of returns; and how he had just seen him in Chester, among the Angles."

To that explanation, the farmer replied: "What? You're the little wool-merchant of whom I've heard so much talk, who buys it in Galway, in the kingdom of Connacy?"

"Yes, Father, and I give you as proof my domestic, who is nearby, my merchant's baggage, and everyone in these cantons, who all know me."

Immediately, the family uttered a cry of delight; they went to the inn to fetch everything that belonged to Nichols, who had kept presents in woolen cloth and cotton fabrics for his father, his mother, his brother and his sisters, and the entire household was joyful.

Nichols stayed in Fermery for a week; then he left to continue his commerce.

He went ten full years without seeing his benefactor again. At that time, having come to Waterford, he learned that young King Oribeau the Wise had appointed Baron Baltamore as one of his ministers. Nichols, still in his coarse coat and sabots, ran to his protector's lodgings, where he was very well received.

"Milord," he said, "fortune, by its favors, has surpassed my desires. I possess twenty-one thousand gold oribeaus."

"I congratulate you, Nichols, "but since you're rich, it's necessary to profit from it. There's no longer any fear of thieves under the reign of our monarch, and you can live more decently without danger."

"So I shall, Milord, but before then, I pray that you might grant me a favor. It's to permit me to make you a gift."

"Me, Nichols?"

"Yes, Milord."

"You can't think so, and if I didn't know you so well, I'd think that you were forgetting yourself."

"Milord, I'd be in despair of forgetting myself, but far from it. The gift will give you pleasure—at least, I flatter myself that it will, after the welcome that I've always received from Your Excellency!"

"We'll see what it is..."

The Baron, wanting to mark the consideration that he had for a distinguished merchant, had Nichols taken back home in his carriage.

"It's better this way than on foot," said the wool-merchant, "and Milord is right, it's necessary to enjoy the comforts of life a little when one has merited them by long labor."

Having arrived home, Nichols dressed properly. The next day, he honored his protector; he only appeared at his home emerging from a proper and modest carriage, which announced the ease that he enjoyed; his garments, without finery, were of a good soft cloth and an agreeable color; the most exact neatness was the basis of his new adornment.

The Baron was pleased to see him in that decent costume.

Nichols was carrying a box under his arm. "Milord," he said, "this is the gift I dare to present to you."

"Be careful, Nichols! You've assured me that it won't shock me."

"I believe it, Milord."

While speaking, Nichols broke the box, which was only sealed with nails. He took out a painted cloth, rolled up, with a dismantled frame. "Milord," he said to the Minister. "There are very fine paintings in your drawing room. Will you permit this one to mingle with them?"

"Let's see?"

Nicholls unrolled it. It as a portrait of him with his coarse coat, with clogs on his feet—in sum, such as he had been on the day when he obtained his first loan from the Baron. "Milord," Nichols added, "on seeing the portrait of a poor little peasant in the midst of your masterpieces, people will ask you: 'Why is that peasant there?' Deign then, Milord, to recount why he is there. Say, I beg you, that it's Nichols, who borrowed his first funds from you, which he increased so well that he travels by carriage today—for that's mine in your courtyard—that Nichols and his fortune are your work, and that all the good things he enjoys are as many of your benefits."

The Minister, whose soul was good and sensible, accepted Nichols' present, and placed it in a modest ungilded frame of aromatic wood. It is now the finest ornament in his study, and every time anyone is admitted there, the sight of the peasant Nichols augments the veneration they have for Baron Baltamore. One could even put for an inscription at the base of the painting: *The Virtue of Baltamore*."

That good deed increased the confidence that the monarch had his minister infinitely. "Baltamore is generous and humane," Oribeau sometimes said. "I could not place my confidence better, for the care that my government demands in my capital."

"And we have a Minister today who does as much!" exclaimed the good Ennisleague.

"That's true," said Younghall. "Let us bless good Kings, who always have good ministers."

"Silence!" said Kilmactomas. "The man who is tearful and says nothing is more touched than you."

Kerry resumed speaking, saying: "It's today that I'll finish the story of Prince Oribeau. Lend me your attention."

O'Barbo, who wanted to distract the young King, started citing a few fine actions of Oribeau's ancestors, especially MacErrick, who, having been born in Scotland, was summoned to the throne by the right of blood. Afterwards, quitting the islands nowadays called British, he passed on to the continent, cited the best Princes and Princesses of Gaul, and even those of India, continuing in these terms:

Chapter 2Y
Ynchike. Combat of Yeomen.[144] *Quiripanga. Oribeau*
reported in his Estates.

"Yukarande was the wife of Xochicopal; her name is that
of an excellent Oriental fruit, the exquisite flesh of which resembles that of the plum for taste, but is so large that a single
Yukarande can sate a man's hunger. In the same way, a sovereign ought to be sufficient for each of her subjects.

"Another symbol of a good Queen is the Ynchike; it does
not appear outside; it grows underground like the truffle; it has
the taste of an almond and furnishes a soothing oil that tem-
pers all inflammations. It is thus that the Queen, withdrawn to
her apartment, must incessantly excite the King to clemency,
reminding him of the interest of his people and procuring them
the amelioration of the woes of wife. Oribelle has taken
Yukarande for a model..."[145]

But alas, at that moment, the fate of the Princess of
Lagenia was unfortunate! Oribeau, who adored her, was very
anxious because she had not arrived, although he had sent a
troop of yeomen to meet her at the frontier.

After having listened to the story of Nichols, which had
suspended his anxieties, his attention was distracted. He inter-

---

[144] This heading differs slightly from the one indicated in the
original contents list, which referred to the courage of the
yeomen; the next chapter heading also differs trivially from its
initial version.
[145] I cannot trace the term Yukarande, but the size of the fruit
is suggestive of a kind of durian, perhaps the kura-kura durian.
There appears to be a mention of the Ynchik (as the name is
rendered on the original contents page) in one of Thomas-
Simon Guellette's Galland pastiches, *Les mille et une heures;
contes péruviens* (1733)—which would fit with fugitive mentions of the term in one or two botanical reference books as a
reference to a South American plant.

rupted O'Barbo. "But the Princess of Lagenia hasn't arrived,"
he said. Has some misfortune overtaken her? I'm going to set
forth with the rest of my guards to discover the cause of the
delay."

Oribeau's action was approved by his mother and his
ministers.

Scarcely had he left Waterford, however, than he heard
the cry, not of the Yapou, but of the Quiripanga, a small white
bird whose voice resembles a little bell. He looked everywhere
but could not see the bird, because the Quiripanga enjoys the
facility of being heard more than half a league away.[146]

Oribeau advanced nevertheless toward Kilkenny, where
he arrived the following day with his troop. He found the entire town in consternation. Three Barons had revolted in order
to prevent the marriage of Oribelle with the King of
Mommonia and that of Dinameh with the King of Meath. The
two princesses had been stopped by the rebels, who were
keeping them imprisoned in Kildare Castle. Balaclay and
Katerlagh, the latter of whom was in love with Dinameh, had
assembled their vassals to help Kildare, for in addition to the
fact that the two Counts Kildare and Katerlagh were in love
with the two princesses, and Balaclay had married Radelinde,
Ratchlin's sister, they had betrayed O'Brisombaüm and feared
the vengeance of his daughters when they were married to
powerful Kings. That is why they had resolved to overturn the
State rather than suffer two marriages that exposed their safety
and thwarted their ambition.

At this sad news, Oribeau was surprised, but he did not
lose courage; he learned that an attempt had been made to take
his yeomen prisoner, and that they were still defending them-

---

[146] The name that Restif gives does not seem to exist anywhere
else, but the description strongly suggests that the bird he has
in mind is the white bell-bird, *Procnias albus*; such birds are
sometimes known, along with other related species, as
arapongas.

selves, entrenched on a mountain. He raced to their rescue, aided by a few of Baron Kilkenny's troops.

As soon as the besieged yeomen heard their comrades' cries, they launched themselves out of their camp, drove through the besiegers and joined their Prince, the sight of whom inspired them with heroic courage; six hundred men defeated an army of three thousand.

After that victory, Oribeau went to Kildare Castle. The three rebels saw him approaching, and, discovering on the other side the King of Meath, who was advancing with an army, they had it declared by a herald that they were ready to perish rather than surrender.

In consequence, all three of them were seen to appear on the platform of a tower, holding daggers to the breasts of the two disheveled Princesses. A herald cried on their behalf: "If the Kings of Mommonia and Meath do not withdraw immediately, the two Princesses will be stabbed and thrown into the flames, for we have resolved to set fire to the place and perish here."

At that moment Oribeau had just joined Beaudâme. The two frightened Princes did not know what to do. Meanwhile, the herald cried: "We will only give you an hour. In an hour, the two Princesses will be killed."

Oribeau shivered. Beaudâme was in despair. Then they saw the Yapou and the Quiripanga appear above the camp; the two birds appeared to want to fight, but the Yapou put the Quiripanga to flight.

Oribeau said to Beaudâme: "That combat of birds signifies something; let's examine it closely."

Beaudâme, weak and timid, took up a position in an obscure place in order to try and find out what the two birds were announcing; the King of Mommonia, seething with courage, examined the fort. He perceived a poorly guarded place that a sheer rock rendered inaccessible—but trees had grown in the fissures.

Oribeau launched himself forward; he attached himself to it and climbed up, lacerating his hands, and soon appeared to Beaudâme's gaze at the summit of the rock. He threw himself into the fort.

Everyone fled before the young hero. He arrived at the foot of the tower; he forced his way through the guards and went up rapidly. He arrived at the instant that Kildare and Katerlagh, seeing the hour expired, were about to strike.

"Stop!" he cried. And with a vigorous thrust he disarmed Kildare. The rebel escaped, but Katerlagh was about to deliver the fatal bow. Oribeau caused the latter to drop his sword. Katerlagh fled with Kildare. Oribeau pursued him, but a door closed and hid them from his justice. He was about to go back up to rejoin the Princesses when an iron portcullis fell of its own accord and separated him from them.

Chapter 2Z
Zahorie. The sixth good deed, or the masterpiece. Marriages. Conclusion.

Zealous as he was amorous, Prince Beaudâme gave all his attention to what was happening in the air, forming prayers for the two Princesses and the King of Mommonia, enclosed between two doors in the stairway of the tower.

"O Thor!" cried Oribeau. "What can courage do against stone and iron?"

He had scarcely finished that prayer than he perceived that he was zahorie,[147] and that his sight was so piercing that it penetrated through the walls. Then, raising his gaze skywards, he discovered two birds flying at an immense height and Pucellomaneh in her chariot. He could even read the words written on a strip of paper:

---

[147] Zahorie is nowadays a region in Slovakia, but the 1772 *Dictionnaire universel, historique et critique* gives the definition: "People whose sight penetrates stones and the entrails of the earth, if one believes the Spanish and Portuguese." Several subsequent French dictionaries paraphrase that definition.

Princes, time is precious. Go behind the camp, out of sight of the fort, where the height of the white poplars will protect you. I shall descend there; climb into my chariot and rescue the Princesses. That glory is reserved for Oribeau.

"Ha!" he cried. "How can I rescue them? I'm a prisoner myself."

At the same time as Oribeau had read the written words silently, Beaudâme had heard them. That was because, if one of the Princes was zahorie, the other had the keenest hearing in the world. Beaudâme ran toward the white poplars that formed a fine shade behind Kildare Castle, and he found Pucellomaneh there, who landed. She got down from her chariot in order not to render it too heavy. The Prince of Meath threw himself into it, caused the wings of the great canvas birds to move with the brass wires and rose up above the fort.

Meanwhile, Oribeau, animated by what he had just seen, shook the iron portcullis, trying to rejoin the Princesses. He ripped up one of the stone steps, struck the bars with it, broke two of them, ran up to the platform and found the three rebels once again holding daggers at the breast of Oribelle and Dinameh. He uttered a cry that suspended the blows. He drove the assassins back, pressing them; they were ready to hurl themselves from the tower in order to avoid the terrible sword when Beaudâme, who was hovering, threw down a kind of net, adroitly, and enveloped the two Princesses. Having thrown away several sacks of ballast at the same time, he flapped the wrings of his birds, which rose a thousand feet above the platform in the blink of an eye, leaving the three rebels paralyzed by astonishment.

No longer having anything to fear for such precious lives, Oribeau recovered his natural generosity.

"Surrender," he said to the rebels, "and I promise you pardon."

The Barons replied: "If you are Worden, whose courage and beauty you have, speak; shall we fall at your knees?"

"I am Oribeau, King of Mommonia, lover of Princess Oribelle."

"In that case, you're man; we'll fight."

While Oribeau was attacked by three vigorous men, Beaudâme descended toward Pucellomaneh, to whom he handed over the two Princesses. The pretended fay led them into the midst of the two armies, while Beaudâme rose up into the air again and went to descend on to the platform where the three rebels were attacking the King of Mommonia

"I only want to use my courage against you," the latter said to them, "and not the protection of the gods, which is coming to my aid."

The three Barons attacked with no less fury, but Oribeau, similar to Worden, disarmed all three of them, tied them up himself, threw them into the chariot, rose up thereafter, albeit with difficulty, and deposited the three prisoners in his camp.

All the troops uttered a cry of joy, praising the valor of Prince Oribeau. Even the Lagenians named him the Son of Worden. Those cries were echoed by the troops of the Queen Mother of Mommonia, who was hastening to her son's aid with his Ministers and all his Barons.

The Mommonians met up amicably with the army of the Queen of Lagenia, which that Princess was leading in person in order to liberate her daughters.

The two Queens, when they met, learned how Oribeau had just freed the two Princesses and captured the three rebels. The young King handed them over to Conchèse.

Dadameh embraced her son tenderly; then, showing him Oribelle, she said to him: "She has suffered for you, but she has no other liberator."

The Queen of Lagenia also embraced Oribeau and presented him with the hand of Oribelle, saying: "I'm giving her a hero for a husband. After the preparatory celebrations for the marriage of my two daughters I had handed them over to your ambassador, but these rebels had raised troops to prevent the two alliances that frustrated their ambitions. They are my subjects; they will also be charged with another crime. I shall have them punished. But before then, since we are all gathered here, let the marriages be celebrated immediately, in order that I can put my dear daughters in the hands of their husbands."

That proposition of Queen Conchèse seemed appropriate. O'Barbo, appointed Grand Druid some time before, put on his pontifical garments and got ready to celebrate the two marriage, while the three relatives, Pucellomaneh, Clomaneh and Nursimaneh seemed to be conversing in whispers.

The two Queens, seeing them, were very intrigued and asked them: "What's the matter?"

"Prince Oribeau lacks something," they replied.

"That true!" exclaimed the young King.

"But what can you lack?" Queen Conchèse asked him.

"Milady, my marriage cannot be made without the thing that I lack."

"But what is it?"

"Six good deeds were imposed upon him," said Pucellomaneh. "He has performed five; he lacks the sixth—which, however, has already commenced."

"What! Isn't it sufficiently fine to have delivered my two daughters and captured my three enemies?"

"That might suffice for another, but for the Prince of Mommonia, it's not all," said Pucellomaneh. "It's for him to consult his noble heart."

"I'm thinking," said Oribeau. "It's not that nothing presents itself to my imagination; on the contrary, I'm embarrassed by the choice of things to do for my people, for I sense that this one ought to be of general utility, embracing all the orders of citizens, and making the day forever blessed when Princess Oribelle will become Queen of Mommonia."

"That's right!" cried Pucellomaneh, Clonameh and Nursimaneh, simultaneously.

Then Oribeau seemed to be animated by Thor himself. He mounted the throne that his Ministers had just set up in the middle of his camp, and pronounced these words:

"Every man and woman can tell me the truth without fear; not only will it not importune me, but it will please me and I shall recompense it. I swear it by Thor, the Father of Humans, and by Friga, who provides the delights of amour."

The entire camp uttered a cry of joy. And as the Prince remained on his throne, silently, a soldier with a noble face whose eyes were sparkling with courage quit the ranks in order to approach the King.

"Milord," he said, "I'm one of the least of your soldiers, but I want to see if I can use the privilege that you have just given your people."

"Speak freely," Oribeau replied.

"You reign," the soldier said. "You are elevated above all of us; but you are not a god, you are only a man. You promise us to be just—good; but if you become unjust, who will redress you?"

"The Law. The Prince ought never to command as an individual man but as a public man, by means of the Law. When I speak as a man, in my private affairs, I shall only have the rights of an ordinary man; but I shall only ever recompense or punish as a public man. The man and the King are two; the second, always sacred, will be omnipotent via the Law; the first can only do what is just for everyone."

"I understand," said the soldier. "Do you like making conquests?"

"Nothing is more appropriate to seduce a good King," said Oribeau, "especially if he has courage; or this is how I envisage conquests. Our neighbors are always our enemies; now, if a Prince can push back the boundaries of the community he governs all the way to the sea, or inaccessible mountains, he will have assured the repose of his people, their security and their wellbeing. That is not ambition, for a Province is not a patrimony; it is prudence, and protection for his people."

"With that principle," said the soldier, "you legitimate all wars, like the ancient Romans."

"That's true; but I declare that I will never be the aggressor."

"Now," said the soldier, "I have two sorts of things to ask, one of the man and the other of the King. Of the man I ask compassion, generosity and mildness; of the King, I only ask justice."

"Ah!" said Oribeau, moved. "I promise my people that!"

"Prince," said the soldier, "know that you owe me your life, and the Princess you are about to marry. But for me, a saber thrust would have cut short your days when you went to the aid of Ahissa, ready to perish:

> *What lessons for you, superb potentates!*
> *Watch over your subjects, in the lowest ranks;*
> *One, expiring far away under an oppressor*
> *Has perhaps saved your empire one day.*"[148]

Oribeau looked at the soldier, and said to him: "Since I owe my life to one of my subjects, let my people know that I am glorious in that debt, but I shall acquit it by devoting my every instant to their wellbeing.

"Prince," said the soldier, "you will be a great king, but you are not that yet, and your marriage cannot be accomplished."

"Is not the finest action of a Prince," said the Sage O'Barbo, "to give good laws to his people? Is not the utility of that general? Now, that is what the Prince of Mommonia has just done."

The soldier smiled, and replied: "Fine laws are all well and good; they're necessary; but if a law is the finest action of Sovereignty, it is not the finest action of a sovereign."

Oribeau, surprised by the soldier's reply, that the most excellent law, although a fine action on the part of a Prince, was nevertheless not the masterpiece that was demanded of him to obtain the hand of Oribeau, remained pensive and thoughtful.

---

[148] The frequently-reproduced quotation is from the patriotic play *Le Siège de Calais* (1765) by the actor Pierre-Laurent de Belloy, a pugnacious response to France's defeat in the Seven Years' War.

"I'll try to put you on the right path," said the soldier, "since you like the truth, and permit people to tell it to you. Know that it's necessary not to esteem the exaggerations of philosophers and moralists too highly; the physical takes priority over the moral. It is necessary to have children before raising them well; it is necessary to nourish people before pleasing them, to dress a daughter before ornamenting her, to give the necessary before the superfluous. Reflect in accordance with those principles as to what you ought to do."

"I have it," Oribeau replied. "But what you're asking of me isn't a single action, it's a sequence of daily actions. I can only make abundance reign in my Estates by a series of procedures, so contrived that labor will be in honor there, and idleness regarded as the most dangerous of vices; by inculcating in my nation that all occupations should have a productive and real goal, not only like that of commerce, which only transports products and wealth, but like agriculture, which creates them, extracting them from the bosom of the land, without exhausting it, since it returns its fecundity by fertilization. It is necessary, in order to promote good, to make virtue loved, and I can only do that by practicing it myself in a manner agreeable to my people."

"Unite all that in an instant, lord," said Pucellomaneh, "in order that your marriage can be accomplished, for it is ardently desired by the two nations; but it is up to you to discover how you are going to do that good deed, which will cap all the others."

"I'll think about it for a moment," replied the young King of Mommonia.

Oribeau went away as he finished speaking, having already made his decision in the depths of his heart.

The two Queens, the Princesses and the entire Court having learned that the Prince had left the camp, followed him secretly, in order to see what he would do.

He did not go far.

In the middle of a field was a laborer, who, in spite of the troubles that surrounded him, was placidly tracing numerous furrows, to which he was confiding the hope of his harvest.

"Father," Oribeau said to him, "according to you, what is the most useful action that a sovereign can perform?"

"I'm only a rude peasant," the laborer replied, "and I'm not clever enough to know that the masterpiece of Kings might be, but one thing is notorious, which is that the culture of fields nourishes everyone: Kings, ministers, magistrates, gentlemen, bards, druids—in a word, everyone. Now, it seems to me, solely by the light of human understanding, that the finest action a King can perform is to honor and encourage the productive labor of the fields, so that it would be more honorable to exercise it than all the less useful métiers; for this is what would come of it: there would be more arms in the fields, which would produce nourishment and render life easier by its abundance. And when culture has too many arms, which would be a necessary effect of the abundance of nourishment, those arms would go to exercise the métiers and arts, but they wouldn't blush to send their children back to culture, more honored.

"However, in my humble opinion, it seems to me that the light of the mind, which bring humans closer to the Divinity ought to be even more honored than agriculture. Thus, the man who, by the force of his mind, can find useful inventions or enlighten minds, so that by their light one can enjoy the beautiful organization of this vast universe, would be more honored than the laborer. The gentleman who defends the State that neighbors might invade would also be more honored than the laborer; the magistrate who devotes his life to common utility and the execution of the laws would be more honored than the laborer—but those glorious estates have no need to be exalted by the sovereign, whereas that of agriculture needs to be honored.

"From which I conclude that the finest action a monarch could perform is to take the plow and trace a furrow, and to publish it throughout his estates that he is the first of laborers, as he is the first of generals and the first of magistrates."

Immediately, the young King of Mommonia traced a furrow, and said to the laborer, surprised by his skill: "I've already labored for three or four years at Younghall, on the farm of Bridge-Clonard."

Meanwhile, several peasants had approached, following Pucellomaneh's chariot, which appeared in the air.

The young King said to them: "Laborers, I honor your profession, and I have come to exercise it, in order to become the first among you, for I am Oribeau, King of Mommonia, who is going to marry your Princess."

All the laborers uttered a cry of joy. They blessed the Prince, and having formed a crown of new ears of wheat, they gave it to the laborer Donneraill, in order that he could put it on the head of the Chief of Laborers...

At that moment, however, the tinkling of the Quiripanga was heard, a bird that Pucellomaneh affected to the service of Oribeau, just as the Yapou was destined for Oribelle. The Prince raised his eyes, and heard, to his chagrin, the four words: "That is not all."

Meanwhile, the laborers ornamented a superb bull with flowers; they placed the Prince on the back of that animal, so necessary to culture, and took him thus in triumph to the middle of his camp.

Pucellomaneh had already landed there.

"The Angles are threatening Evinland with a descent," she said. "I've just perceived their preparations from the heights of the air with my long-view. Ultonia and Connacy only have old sovereigns and their troops are in a poor state. The common hope is in you alone, and the King of Meath. It's necessary to appoint new officers to command, and promote those who already are. I propose to go with my aerial chariot to sound the alarm everywhere and have you named Generalissimo of Evinland; you will be King of Kings."

"For myself," said Beaudâme, "I consent to that."

"You will naturally have the command of my troops," said Queen Conchèse."

The Ultonian ambassador declared in the name of his master that the Ultonian army would be submitted to the supreme orders off the King of Mommonia. The ambassador of Connacy went even further, and said that even the officers would be chosen by Oribeau.

Everything was thus agreed. Everyone hastened to present his friends and his creatures, in order to have them appointed, not only to military employments but to civil charges, before the long absence of the King of Kings. Dadameh, Conchèse, Oribelle, Dinaeh, Clonameh and all the grandees of the Court spoke in favor of meritorious subjects.

Oribeau turned to the two Sages Dondanuck and O'Barbo, and said to them: "Name worthy people to me, and tell me their capabilities."

The two Ministers consulted one another.

Then the Prince looked at the Queens and Princess Oribelle, whose hand he kissed "Forgive me, but I shall not appoint any of your protégés; merit alone must prevail here, and these two Sages know it better than us.

A sound of confused applause rose from the assembly; Pucellomaneh advanced, radiant with joy, and said to the King of Mommonia: "You have just completed a King's masterpiece; your marriage can take place."

"That's also my opinion," said the Langenian soldier who had already spoken to the King, taking away the pellicle that covered his face and showing Ratchlin to the gaze of the astonished Prince.

"Milord, do you recognize me?"

"You're Ratchlin, I believe."

"O King, the gods wanted me to test you. I have always been faithful. O'Brisombaüm is not dead; I have kept him alive; here he is."

Immediately, Oribelle's father approached and was recognized by the Queen and her children.

"Ratchlin and I have always been in accord," he said. "Our simulated divisions were merely to prevent the nobles from stirring up trouble and the Angles from taking advantage of it."

Conchèse extended her hand to her husband and said to him, smiling: "I bless the gods."

The marriage of the Princesses with the two young Kings was celebrated the same day.

"Ah!" exclaimed the good Ennisleague. "There he is, the young Prince, married! By Erda, how your story has pleased me! But worthy gentleman, aren't you going to tell us anything about what happened to him when he was married?

"I'll respond to all your questions with an etc."

"Oh, I beg you to do that, kind gentleman!"

"Well, Oribeau took Oribelle to Mommonia; Beaudâme took Dinameh to the kingdom of Meath; Conchèse ruled in Lagenia with O'Brisombaüm, recognizing that Ratchlin, Kildare, Katerlagh and Balaclay had served him in pretending to betray her.

"As for the war against the Angles, those dangerous neighbors, frightened by Oribeau's sixth fine action, dared not make the projected descent; they returned to their ports and remained tranquil.

"And the conduct of Oribeau the Wise was that of an excellent Prince. He was the friend of peace, even though he could have excused conquests, for, in a little difficulty that he had with Prince Beaudâme, he made all the advances for accommodation and calmed the soul of his ally, who was very irritated.

"Princess Oribelle gave him a daughter, and then two sons, and then a second daughter. They lived happily for a long time, marking all their days with benefits. During a famine, the King and Queen deprived themselves of everything that they had of their own in order to relieve their people. They made sure that no one suffered from hunger and cold in their Estates, and defended from oppressors not only their subjects but those who were not. Oribeau was of such good faith that when he took back what had been taken from his allies, he returned it to them in affectionate haste. And everyone blessed him and his Ministers, who seconded their excellent master with all their might.

"The eldest son of Oribeau the Wise succeeded him and was also a good King. Four generations have gone by since then, until the father of the present King, Fitz-Oribeau, who is protected by the gods like Oribeau the Wise. And that is what I shall prove to you tomorrow by telling you a story about the protection of the gods over the father, for the instruction of the son. I can't guarantee its marvelous aspects, but what is certain is that our Prince shows great prudence in the choice of his favorites and the distribution of graces. And it's tomorrow that my stories will conclude. Remember the promise you made me, to give me your votes."

"You can be sure of it," cried all the drinkers, simultaneously.

"And I promise you to continue coming here, to give you an account of what's happening, and ask your advice."

"Bless you," said the good Ennisleague, "for thinking of me like that; may Friga render your daughters as beautiful as Oribelle, and your sons as courageous as Oribeau."

And the following day, Kerry came back to Ennisleague's tavern in order to conclude.

Chapter &
Wrwcwcw endowing Oribeau, the fourth descendant of Oribeau the Wise.

& in the fullness of time, the young Prince that we saw passing by when I commenced the story you have just heard having inherited the crown, he too was cherished by the gods, because he desired the wellbeing of his people. He obtained from them a portion of prudence similar to that of Oribeau the Wise, which makes people suppose that he is protected by the fay Wrwcwcw. That is why a bard, who is reputed to be ahead of his time, made in his regard an allegorical piece that I shall read to you:

To Fitz-Oribeau, the most glorious of the descendants of Oribeau the Wise, his great-great-great-grandfather.

Juvenale nocturne (Fifteenth.)[149]

Midnight chimes; Berda reposes; all men have retired; I no longer have anything to observe; let us dream...

O King, Oribeau your father was protected by the gods because he sincerely wanted the wellbeing of his people. He worked for it relentlessly, but success did not always crown his efforts.

"How does it come about," he wondered aloud, one night, "that my people are unhappy, in spite of everything I do

---

[149] The term "Juvenales" has a particular meaning in the context of Restif's works, which is linked to Juvenal's Satires rather than the *Ludi Juvenale* or Juvenalia founded by the Emperor Nero. It occurs in a projected second subtitle of *Le Hibou, ou Le Spectateur nocturne, ou Les Juvenales*, a work whose first subtitle was eventually adopted by *Les Nuits de Paris*. In the omnibus edition of *Le Paysan et paysanne perverti* (1784) Restif included a detailed list of the projected contents of *Le Hibou*, which includes the present item, entitled "La Fée Ouroucoucou" as no. 15, the first five having been included the volume to which the list is appended, the sixth in *La Malédiction paternelle* (1780), the seventh to the tenth in *La Découverte australe* and the eleventh to the fourteenth in "Une Séance chez une amatrice," which was one of the appendices to that novel. A further twenty-one were listed, which eventually appeared scattered throughout various works, and ten more were subsequently added, under the title of "Immoralités," which appeared in volumes XIV-XVI of *Monsieur Nicolas* (1797). I have left the French phrase untranslated because of its special reference.

for their felicity? I would give anything in the world to anyone who could reveal to me the secret obstacle that opposes my god will...."

He had no sooner pronounced these words that he scented the delightful odor of perfumes. He opened his curtains. A soft light that was becoming brighter by the second illuminated his room, and without seeing anyone, he heard a harmonious voice, which proffered these words:

"I am the fay Wrwcwcw, one of your ancestors, a friend of verity, protectress of the good and declared enemy of the wicked, loving especially to encourage the fortunate dispositions of my descendants. Prince, I want to aid your youth and guide it in the difficult art of reigning, by enabling you know those who surround you. Every man to whom you have given a position, from this moment on, will have a heart open before you; by my supreme power. I shall personify his principal virtue or his favorite vice; one or the other will always accompany him, and the stature that each of them has will be the measure of that which the vice or the virtue has in his heart. Adieu, Prince; continue to desire wellbeing and the gods will help you to create it."

The young King was very surprised by that apparition, and in the disturbance that it caused him, he could not quite make out whether it was a dream or a reality. He tried to go to sleep, and succeeded.

The next day, when he got up, he remembered his vision but, believing it to be a dream, only laughed at it. Having dressed, he went into the Queen's apartment; she was still in bed. Imagine his surprise, however, to see a handsome young man lying next to the Princess, who was still asleep. Transported by fury, he advanced to seize him, but the young man rose up, laughing, and by his wings, the King recognized him as Amour. Then, casting his eyes over his spouse, he saw her in the arms of a lovely young woman who had a pretty little dog on her shoulder. He tried to touch the goddess and her symbol, but he only made contact with a light shadow.

That's a fortunate trial! the young monarch said to himself. *It appears that it wasn't a dream and that the fay Ouroucoucou really spoke to me. I need to examine my courtiers today, and everyone that surrounds me...*

As the King concluded that thought, a kindly old man appeared, the Count of Cork. He had a cheerful expression, and one might have taken him for the happiest man in the realm. He approached the Prince respectfully and spoke to him very pleasantly, albeit with a hint of malice.

Surprised to smell a disagreeable odor, the Prince examined the Count more closely and saw beneath the little hat that the Lord was carrying under his arm the large heads of two serpents, which were emerging from his heart; they were agitating with a kind of fury, hiding and reappearing continually. The King noticed that when they drew back into the heart the Count's face as serene, but when they emerged, a sensible alteration as visible in spite of the laughter that strove to form.

That's singular, thought the Prince. *I would have thought him the most humane and well-meaning of my subjects.*

At the same moment, a celebrated warrior appeared. He had a hard and proud appearance. He darted a glance at the Count that was not one of esteem, and spoke to the King very sensibly. As the monarch listened to him attentively he neglected to observe the courtier, but he remembered him eventually and saw, to his astonishment, that the Count's two serpents had launched half their body-length out of his heart in order to pour their venom over the general, whom they were biting with all their might, although they could not dig their teeth into him.

The warrior had an eagle on his shoulder, which was distributing terrible pecks with its beak on the heads of the two serpents, to the point that they often seemed stunned; but at the slightest sign of esteem that the Prince showed the general they were reanimated, and darted themselves at him with a new fury. Finally, seeing that they could not penetrate his skin, they had recourse to another means; they quit the courtier's heart and came into his mouth; and every time the warrior spoke they spread over his discourse a penetrating and subtle poison that the courtier seasoned with a few winks and ambiguous responses.

The King was tempted to find the warrior importunate, too proud and too truthful; fortunately, he had the cause of the dispositions before his eyes. In addition, at the peak of his impatience, he suddenly saw a beautiful young woman appear beside the general, stark naked, who was weighing all the words that emerged from his mouth in a golden balance. The monarch had no doubt that it was Verity herself, and his noble heart quivered with joy.

While the King was listening to those two men, a third arrived, with a mild face and humble manner. The monarch was curious to know the vices or virtues of that man, who had filled an important position for a long time, but he saw nothing; the man was devoid of faults and also of qualities.

That's singular! thought the Prince. *I have, however, heard loud complaints about that man.*

As he finished that thought he saw beside him a telescope, directed at the capital. The prince put his eye to it, and saw in the house of a nobody, a kind of ********.[150]

"Ah!" the King exclaimed. "That will desolate my kingdom!"

The three courtiers were very surprised by those words.

The King, who realized that he had just committed a sight indiscretion, looked at the warrior, smiling, and told him that it was a distraction caused by a dream that he had had during the night. The general was tranquilized by those words, but when the King looked at the courtier with the serpents and the man devoid of virtues and qualities he saw a worm emerge from their heads that agitated with an extreme vivacity,

---

[150] At this point in the original text the author—who was, of course, also the typesetter—inserts seven lines of dots, implying that a considerable chunk of text has been removed, presumably intending to imply that its revelations would be too shocking to print.

launching itself in all directions, but especially toward the King's eyes, which it tried several times to pierce—which caused he King to raise his hand involuntarily in order to deflect it. They thought that some dirt had got into His Majesty's eye.

A fourth courtier arrived just in time to provide a diversion. The King held him in high esteem, and he had rendered services—well-paid, it is true, but even so, he had rendered them. How many people there are who are well paid but do nothing! He approached his sovereign with the attitude of a favorite.

The King touched him on the shoulder, but what surprised the monarch greatly was that he sensed, on patting him complaisantly, a sight pain like a pinprick. The Prince withdrew his had swiftly and searched with his eyes for what had wounded him, but saw nothing.

Let's see, he said to himself, *whether I can make this honest man's vice appear—for he has one; virtue doesn't do harm.*

The King began to speak affectionately to the general. Immediately, he saw a fox emerge from the collar of the fourth courtier, who seemed extremely wily, which launched itself in little bounds toward the warrior and nipped with little teeth the laurels with which his head as crowned, in order to put them on the sugary individual. While the fox was agitating thus, the fourth courtier complimented the general on his precision, good fortune, fidelity and bravery, and the intrepidity with which he had carried out the orders of the Cabinet. The warrior, a frank man, did not sense the cunning, and received the compliments in good faith, without nevertheless becoming vain. He said that one was only too glad when circumstances permitted a man of courage to do his duty without upsetting ministers.

The four men withdrew when they had paid their court. The monarch then received the visits of his family and the respects of the Princes of the Royal Blood. He had several brothers and sisters, with whom he lived in the happiest union.

They came in laughing and the King found himself in an amiable and mild familiarity that nothing troubled. The fay Ouroucoucou's gift only served to augment his joy in that instance.

As the monarch was amusing himself with his family, the Minister appeared. He came to remind the King that it was the time he had designated for an audience with the Ambassador of a neighboring power. The Queen, the Princes and all the Princesses were charmed to witness the ceremony. The monarch assembled his Council, composed of particular ministers for each department and the most enlightened men of the Court. When they were all gathered, the King consulted them as to what it was expedient to reply to the Ambassadors who were requesting an audience.

Each adopted a modest and disinterested expression, but the King, by means of the fay's gift, saw the motives that were making each of them speak. The Prime Minister was of the opinion that the neighboring sovereigns ought to be satisfied and that peace should be maintained. That was the sentiment of the monarch himself, who then addressed a great lord, the Minister's enemy.

"I'm for peace," he said. "War is a scourge." The King, who knew him for a friend of trouble, wanted to know the secret motive for that opinion; he had recourse to the fay's gift, by means of which he saw a strip of writing on the grandee's head, which said: *I fear war, because it's an opportunity for making Thomond-Clare's talents shine.*

Another minister advised quarreling with the Ambassadors and making war. He represented the good condition of the troops, the necessity of exercising them, the advantages of an opportunity to make Mommonia respected forever. At first the King listened to him without raising his head, but having finally sought his strip, he found written there: *I'm in the business of supplying food to the army; two women I like have relatives they want to advance in the service; and then, I want to oppose the Prime Minister.*

A third counseled peace, but by shameful means. The King sought his legend; it read: *I've received presents from the neighboring monarch, but so secretly that I have nothing to fear.*

The monarch then took the advice of other councilors, but as they were subalterns their motives were of scant interest. Afterwards, he declared that he had decided in favor of peace. The Ambassadors were brought in, who spoke at length and exaggerated their demands. On raising his eyes the King saw their true intentions, their ruses and their secret motives floating above their heads.

He showed an admirable penetration; he revealed their secret views to them, assuring them that he was well-informed; he threatened them with his assembled forces and saw the impression that such threats made. It was not what he had expected, given their dispositions, but he read that base traitors would starve the army, that obscure officers had been bribed not to support the general. He was frightened by the excess of corruption that he saw reigning in certain classes of men, while others, who showed little urgency, were cloudless in their fidelity. However, he made an advantageous peace, thanks to the fay Wrwcwcw, He perceived a thousand times hat without her, even his prudence might have gone astray.

After the peace was concluded, the monarch having received the ordinary ambassadors of all the Courts, he did not fail to see them all and to read their souls. He soon perceived that they all detested his nation, precisely because it was superior to the others. He wanted to dismiss his unfaithful servants, but before doing so he examined those who might replace them; they were even worse. Then the King decided to correct those he had. He summoned them individually, revealed their most secret thoughts to them, recommended them to mend their ways, and then examined them, reproached them for their hypocrisy and convinced them so thoroughly that he read in their thoughts that they would strive to be honest men. He encouraged those who were honest of their own accord, but, perceiving that they were borne to intolerance, tempered them.

It was then that the monarch was truly happy.

However, the fay Wrwcwcw had put a condition on the perpetuity of her favor, which was that the Prince ought never to need to hide his most secret thoughts—which meant that he had to be just, temperate, chaste, etc. If he came to be ambitious with injustice, one of two things would happen: either he would have to renounce the fay's gift, or other people would be able to read his thoughts as he could read theirs.

One day, therefore, when he was in Council, he perceived that one of his ministers could penetrate all his designs, in spite of the envelopes with which he covered them. He was surprised by that, but on observing him, he saw that the man, before replying to him, looked up in the air. The monarch approached him, put his hand on his shoulder and prevented him from being able Io look. Then the councilor no longer knew where he was. But at that moment, another councilor raised his eyes.

Immediately, the monarch, fearing to lay bare a project for aggrandizement, a nascent passion for a young woman and a new penchant for the table and liqueurs, renounced the fay's gift, in these terms, pronounced internally:

I return to the fay Ouroucoucou a precious gift, of which I am not worthy.

Scarcely had he formulated those words, than, raising his eyes to look over his councilors' heads, he no longer saw anything.

He was very sorry to have lost that advantage, but what could he do? It was only useful as long as it was exclusive.

The King strove to overcome his penchants; first of all he suppressed that of ambition. He had more difficulty forbidding himself the charms of the pretty girl but he married her off and immediately sent her with her husband to a distant country under the pretext of an embassy. He regulated his table frugally and forbade entry thereto to foreign liqueurs.

He wanted to have his gift returned, but the fay responded to him that the favor in question was only granted once—however, he could ask for another. The King asked for that of being immune to seduction by flattery, in such a way that every flatterer would produce on him the opposite effect to what was being attempted. That gift was granted, with the condition that the instant when, in spite of his wish, he desired to be flattered, he would lose the gift without perceiving it and would become the dupe of all flatterers. The King accepted.

He went a long time without the slightest desire to be flattered infiltrating his heart. Finally, though, the same cause that had made him lose he first gift, vice, made him lose the second. The Prince had tastes that he satisfied; he gradually drew away from his customary regularity; he neglected his duties; the people suffered in consequence, and complaints were made. Then, the weary Prince needed to be flattered, and desired it.

Immediately, flatterers surrounded him. He no longer heard anything but agreeable things; he no longer heard, instead of complaints, anything but cries of joy. People were paid to utter them as he passed by and to wish him a thousand blessings.

Several years went by. All the kingdom's affairs were in a deplorable dilapidation, but the King had no suspicion of it; he was even unaware of the alteration of his gift.

One day, when he was out hunting, he went astray on his own. After galloping for a long time, his exhausted horse stopped. The King dismounted in order to let it rest and take some nourishment. He sat down himself, devoured by hunger and thirst. An old woman appeared. The Prince, delighted to see her, stood up to call her, but instead of coming she fled. He ran after her and caught up with her.

"Why are you running away, my good woman? Did you take me for a thief?"

"No, Milord, I took you for a man of the Court."

"And you fled from me?"

"Yes; since flatterers have surrounded the King, it is the men of the Court that we fear the most. They pillage us or have us pillaged; they take our daughters if they're pretty to make whores out of them; if they're in between their valets take them; they only leave us the ugly. So we only dare make use of them and old women like me."

"You astonish me. And what does the King say?"

"Oh, the King! He doesn't know. People tell him that we're all happy and contented and that he's the best King in the world—which he might be, but a great deal of evil is done in his name."

"I'm very hungry and thirsty, my good woman; give me something to drink, I beg you."

"I will, but outside."

"What! I can't come in?"

"I've been caught like that, and I don't know where my eldest is."

"I'll return her to you, I guarantee it. I'll have her returned to you; let me come in."

"I can see that you're not as insolent as the others, so come in, but think of not making me repent of it."

The King went in to the fireside, and found two pretty girls there, who immediately went to hide. The Prince asked their mother to call them back. He drank, ate and warmed himself; someone went to fetch his horse and put it in the stable.

"I can't believe what you've told me, my good woman," he said to the old woman. "What! The courtiers do everything you've told me!"

"And a hundred times worse, but Milord, if you're one of them, grant me your protection."

"I grant it to you. Have you a husband?"

"He'll be back shortly, Milord, with my two sons."

"Give me some of their clothes; I want to see for myself, in that disguise, the conduct of the courtiers, for I can't believe it."

"Well, you'll see."

The old woman gave the Prince an outfit of her husband's, in which he dressed from head to toe. The three peasants arrived, and after they had rested, the King asked the father to send one of his to seek a courtier at the hunt's meeting-place, whom he named. The old man, refused, speaking a great deal of evil of that Lord. The King named ten others, and a similar refusal on the old man's part obliged him to name a twelfth, whom the peasant agreed to inform.

As the King had foreseen, that courtier did not come alone. Those whom the good people feared came in first and, only seeing peasants, threw themselves on the two young women. They were repelled by their brothers and by the King himself. The courtiers drew their swords; the girls fled to the grain-loft, pulled up the ladder and shut the trap-door.

The Lord requested then came in. "What are you doing?" he said to his friends.

They replied to him that they were going to chastise the manual laborers.

"No! Leave these unfortunate folk tranquil."

"But there are two charming girls up there!"

"My sisters!" cried the elder son.

"Oh, I have nothing more to say," said the appeasing Lord. "If they had been your wives I'd have undertaken their defense, but your sisters…you only have mediocre rights over them."

"What!" cried the King, making himself known by his tone and by his clothes, which he displayed. "The most virtuous of my courtiers is corrupt to that extent!"

The confounded Lords wanted to joke, but the King, without looking at them, cried dolorously: "O fay Wrwcwcw, I have lost a precious gift! I did not suspect it until just now, thanks to the plaints of this good woman. Unfortunate Prince! I thought my people were happy, and they are oppressed! Perhaps they are cursing me, and will put my reign in the rank of scourges! Begone, vile flatterers, let me never see you again!"

The King's tears were a salutary crisis of nature. The courtiers, confused at first, annihilated by shame, were gripped by dolor. They threw themselves to their knees before the King begging for pardon.

"It's true," he said, "that I am as guilty as you."

He put his clothes on again, mounted his horse and went back to the capital.

The next day he recalled a former Minister disgraced because of his rudeness.

"Be gentle," the King said to him, "without being less truthful. Can one not tell the truth without ill-humor?"

The Minister, instructed by misfortune, promised to be truthful without bitterness. He spoke; he obtained her monarch's confidence, and did not disguise anything. All the evil that the flatterers had caused was repaired; serene days followed, the pure light of which allowed thing to be seen as they were.

One day, when the monarch was sitting on his terrace in the evening taking the air, and reflecting on all the means he had of knowing the truth in order to render is people happy, he bitterly regretted the fay Wrwcwcw's first gift. The Queen, his wife, was behind his chair, but, hearing him thinking aloud like that, she did not want to interrupt his reflections.

"Oh, Fay!" he cried, "render me the faculty of reading all hearts!"

The Queen, doubtless carried away by an inspired impulse, replied to him: "Prince, you have the real means of knowing the truth without inspiring dread. The one you regret, if it had been divined—as it could not have failed to be, eventually—would only have surrounded you with tremulous slaves. It's necessary to be a man to live with men, and especially to govern them. If they were governed by a fay, a genius or a god, the excess of confidence would render them pusillanimous and irresolute; they would resemble children, who would not dare to take a step without their mothers; they would become less than animals. Be only a man, in order to command men, that they will honor you as their fellow, who does not surpass them in supernatural gifts, but in generosity, in humanity, in vigilance, in zeal for their happiness, in efficacious means of action, and in virtue."

The King was convinced that it was the fay who had just spoken to him; he did not turn round, and the Queen withdrew.

From that moment on, the King no longer thought of anything but being solidly virtuous in the manner of humans, and his reign was the finest and most glorious of all reigns.

It was thus that the stories the hunter Kerry told in Ennisleague's house, on the outskirts of Waterford, concluded. All the drinkers were content with the apologue of Fitz-Oribeau's father and the fay Ouroucoucou. The entire story of Oribelle and Oribeau was learned by heart, and since then, it has been told in Evinland on long winter evenings.

Here ended the manuscript of Sir Patrick, alias Yzquiepatli, which Antoine Gaudet, the eldest son of Monsieur Gaudet of the Rue Courtaudvilain, read in their market garden on the Hauteborne.

THE END

The author adds a brief concluding series of "observations" which are mostly trivial, some of which are corrections that I have made in the text, or integrated into the footnotes accompanying it. His final comment reads:

"The story of Oribeau, seen generally, is one of those works dictated by love of humanity; the Irish, its original inventors have mingled lessons with the fables. We have detached them slightly in the translation; however, there still exists in the tissue I know not what singular and bizarre complexion, which shows that true literature was little known when it was first composed."

www.ingramcontent.com/pod-product-compliance
Lightning Source LLC
Chambersburg PA
CBHW031925110726

47902CB00001B/46